INDIGO DARES

Get glowing - the world
needs your magic!

You never know who you
might inspire while on your
own journey!

x

Published by Somerset Press

Somerset Press Limited
3 Church End
Radford Semele
Leamington Spa
CV31 1TA

Paperback ISBN 978-1-9161480-8-6
Hardrback ISBN 978-1-9161480-9-3
.epub eBook ISBN 978-1-8383504-0-6
.mobi eBook ISBN 978-1-8383504-1-3
Cover design and layout by www.spiffingcovers.com

Printed by TJ Books Limited, Padstow, Cornwall

BOOK THREE OF THE INFINITY SQUARED SERIES

INDIGO DARES

S R SUMMERS

Book three, Indigo Dares, was worked on and created during the unusual year of 2020, which became much more about human contact and goodwill than anything else. My godmother, Hilary, was kind enough to proof read the book, and it was lovely to bring her into our small team.

Also, as always, my unstinting gratitude to my parents who have been amazing this year, and whose strength and kindness continually inspire, and are expressed in some of Mysty's most noble moments.

THE PIZZA AND swim and the sleep, they'd been so needed; but being in Vegas, remembering just how angry she was with Donny for never being there when she needed him…well, now she just wanted some way of expressing that. Her patience had been worn through, and Donny had been one disappointment too many.

"OG. Diversion. Next left, next right, next left. Then stop the car." OG wanted to argue, she could see that, and knew he was taking a chance trusting her. But he gave the order anyway, aware that her mood had been low and serious since dawn, and even food hadn't improved her temper. "I'll be five minutes, max, I promise. Unlock the door."

"You want us to drop you at the front door, rather than walk?"

"I'll go around the back. It's more discreet."

She gave him a tight smile, and he opened the door.

He sighed and rubbed a hand over his face. Had it been a good idea to let her go? This was not somewhere he could follow. He looked at his watch and knew these five minutes were going to feel like half an hour.

She marched down the dark corridor she would never forget, picturing the gruesome discovery that Friday night, so many years ago. But she wasn't afraid. She strode past the surveillance room, hearing familiar voices, but there was only one man she was there to see and she was on a time limit.

"Mysty?" Paulo appeared, stunned to see her.

"Paulo. Is he in his rooms?"

"Yes, but–"

"Save it."

Her face had no expression. Up the stairs, two at a time, she strode towards the door she used to love seeing; now it made her choke on the emotion it evoked, all that longing and love, and yet… Her eyes were scanned and fingerprints taken, and then she yanked open the door.

He was leaning on the desk, where he had been that very first conversation they'd had, arms crossed casually across his chest, body at ease. When he looked up, he saw trouble, and she saw his eyes widen.

"Sweetheart…"

"Don't 'sweetheart' me!" The door slammed behind her. "How could you? One night in the whole goddamn month and you said no? Too dangerous? Too fucking *dangerous*! Like I haven't lived with danger all my life? Like I haven't faced enough of it, even for you? What right do you have to tell me I can't bear a little of it for my sake as well?" She could see him struggling; he wasn't used to be confronted like this. "I can't keep doing this, Donny! I'm a person, not a pet! I need to see you more than just once every six months. When is it going to end? This 'keeping me safe' crap? You want us to be together. When is it going to happen? When? Because I know I've already made my choice, and accepted the risks – have you?" She pulled in an angry breath, recharging. "Seeing you was the only thing I wanted last night! You didn't even ring me yourself to tell me. You got *him* to tell me! I've asked so little of you! So why? *Why*?" Finally the tirade ceased and she breathed fast. Donny had in turn looked angry, then sad. Now he looked defeated.

"Sweetheart, please calm down–"

It was the wrong thing to say, in the wrong tone of voice. She let out a growl of frustration and her hand came up to slap him hard around the face, the sound so loud in the room. Now he looked astonished. She'd hit him! She'd actually hit him, and she meant it. But he didn't have a chance to say anything, because she then stepped forward, reached for the hair at the back of his head, and pulled it towards her and kissed him, soft demanding lips pressed against his. He reached for her, wanting to hold her, but a foot came up and pinned one hand to the desk, grasping his other wrist and holding it away from her. Here was pure passion, just as he'd felt for her so many times, and her tongue teased, driving his senses wild. He wanted more, he fought her grip, but it was hard to fight when he was so physically weakened by this kiss of hers. She had surprised and disarmed him completely, so much had he underestimated her.

Then abruptly, she let him go.

She stepped back from him, eyes bright with anger and passion.

"Next time, when you ask to see me, I might just say no."

She turned on her heel and the door opened and then slammed behind her in quick succession.

Donny breathed out.

"Holy shit," a voice from the other room said slowly, and Sebastian Merino, Lord of New York, stepped out of the shadow of the doorway. "Was that who I think it was?"

"Yes," Donny managed.

"Did she just do what I think she did?"

Donny glanced at Sebastian's incredulous expression, his forty-year-old face usually so impassive.

"Yelled at me, slapped me, and then kissed me? Yeah, spot on."

Donny turned away and leant his knuckles on the desk. He wished he could be alone so he could think more clearly, but that was not to be.

"Donny, the girl has a point." Franny's voice was not a welcome one either. He didn't need this audience to work out what had just happened.

"Donny, my friend, what are you doing? She is no average girl. You cannot wait forever," Don Salvadore spoke, with the patient chiding of a father to a son, wise words that fell on already abused ears.

"Thank you, everyone, for your amazing insights. As if I don't know her well enough," he snapped, her words echoing in his mind. "God knows I only want her safe."

"No one is ever safe in our world, Donny. I know better than most." Franny's grim voice was no consolation to his pain. "But she is willing to take the risk, so why won't you let her?"

"Because she has already been bathed in blood once! I will not have it happen again!"

Silence hovered for long seconds.

"Why don't you go after her?" Sebastian suggested gently, seeing the tension in Donny's body, like that of someone being tortured – and he'd seen enough torture to know.

"She'll be gone by now. Moves quicker than greased lightning when she wants to."

Goddamn it! He would have hit something had he been alone. He wasn't bothered his brothers had heard the exchange, as they all knew her well – except Sebastian who was a friend, and already an admirer after what he had seen of her – and were tolerant of her passion and fearlessness.

"I'll wait until she's calmed down. She has a temper to match her beauty, as you know, and she's in no mood to listen."

"She must love you very much to get so angry," Sebastian observed.

"She does. Very much. But I love her more, which is why I will not risk her if I can avoid it. I will not put anything before that."

There was nothing more to say. The silence ended after a few more seconds and they were back to business, one of their number paying less attention than he had been, a lump in his throat and a sting in his cheek he knew he deserved to feel.

OG SAW HER emerge from the alley with angry strides. He opened the door and pulled it closed after she got in.

"You alright, kiddo?"

"Just peachy, thanks."

He had two teenaged daughters and a volatile ex-wife. He knew she wasn't okay; he recognised the signs. He allowed himself an eye roll as he got in himself and prepared to tangle with his upset tiger.

"You still had ten seconds. You sure you're done?"

The tilt of her head relayed the message loud and clear: Don't try and make me laugh.

"Okay, you want to talk, you just say. I'm paid to be a shrink as well as your bodyguard." Lazarus moved over her to, nuzzling her, trying to get her to look at him. "Give him a hug; he's been worried about you."

She pulled the cat against her, and he went willingly.

"I think I'm going to declare myself forever single. Lazarus is the only one I can rely on."

He knew she didn't deserve to feel such hurt, not when she gave so much, when she was so loyal to those she cared about … the man she cared about. She hadn't done anything wrong, she'd just fallen in love with the wrong man…

"Most men are varying degrees of asshole, I'll give you that, but don't let's give up on all of them, hey, not just yet."

The journey was spent in silence and at Soleil she threw herself into her work, taking the headset, computer panel and handheld, going over everything from top to bottom, the people who would be helping her with the set, lighting and backstage, all there to answer any questions and start going through her requirements. OG watched her command, the consummate professional, mind on the job, no detail left out. But he could tell she was hurting, and resolved to get her home as soon as he could so she'd have some time to herself.

DARYL SAW HER get out of the car through the window of his jet, but she was not the happy girl he'd envisaged after a day spent doing what she loved. He'd been working hard, too, but was comforted by the report from OG that she'd been at Soleil most of the day. She was nothing if not committed; he couldn't fault her there.

He thought she might come and say hello, but there were no smiles tonight, only a tangible sense of distress. He flicked the camera on in the room and saw her drop her bag and lie down on the sofa, Lazarus jumping up next to her at the back of the sofa. She curled around him and turned to face the cushions. Oh dear.

"You want anything. kiddo?" OG paused in the doorway, but he knew there was little he could do.

"Bullet through my head?"

"That's a no then." Pausing, because he wanted to do something before he went to make her feel some comfort, he tried again. "You want the lights down?"

"Please."

With the lights off and shutters lowered, she would have peaceful darkness. He closed the door and he pressed the lock button, just in case.

"O'Grady."

"Sir."

"What has upset her so much?"

O'Grady looked round at his boss with a weary sadness etched on his face.

"She was deeply upset by Donny saying no last night. She went to see him for five minutes, and came out looking angry enough to set a few trees alight, worked all day at Soleil, and now … well, you can see for yourself."

"Five minutes?"

"It was all she asked for. Went in a back entrance. Came out and wouldn't talk about it. Apparently, she's going to be 'single forever'."

Daryl didn't know what to say for a second – this was just too good.

"I see. Well, time for you to relax for a little, O'Grady."

OG knew when he was being dismissed and left, nodding at Mac on the way.

A call came through.

"Daryl." It was a terse tone, as Daryl could have predicted.

"Donny."

"She's not picking up. Is she alright?"

"She's asleep or nearly so, but if she's not answering I'd say it's because she doesn't want to."

"I know."

Daryl sympathised with the weary voice: he was usually on the receiving end of her temper.

"I did tell her as gently as I could, I assure you, and I said nothing to provoke her."

"No, I know that as well. If you had she'd have come over last night, despite me avoiding seeing her – for her own sake."

"What happened today?" Daryl asked. "She's very upset."

"In a nutshell? She came in, raged at me quite impressively, slapped me, and then kissed me."

She slapped *Donny*? She was brave! Then again, considering the way Donny loved her, she wouldn't fear him in that way. And from the way he spoke, Donny seemed to have accepted his punishment.

"I'm sorry to hear all that." Especially the bit about the kiss.

"It's been on the cards for a while. Only so many hands of hearts you can play before the Queen of Spades makes her presence felt."

"What a very poetic way of looking at it."

"I'm a gambler. What can I say?" Donny sighed. "Look, if she wakes up soon or, I don't know … just tell her I called, to try to talk to her."

"I don't think words are what she's after," Daryl remarked slowly, wondering why he was giving advice to the man he wished to see fail. But, somehow, he knew it had to be an honest fight. If she and Donny ended, it had to be completely, and for real. Their love was too strong for mere disagreements to break them apart.

"No. Well noticed. You took her back last night…and grabbed a pizza on the way. Very good of you to pay such close attention to your new asset."

Daryl wasn't surprised Donny knew, and controlled the irritation in his voice. He had been conscious of the likelihood of invisible eyes keeping watch on them.

"Being on her own was the last thing she needed. At least I provide her with something to ridicule and argue with."

"True." Now he sounded vaguely amused. "Well, I'll go. I'm sure you're busy."

"I'm always busy, but rarely busy doing the things I want to do."

"I know that one. Safe trip," Donny concurred.

"Will do. Hope things calm down."

"They will. I've already seen to it."

Disconnect.

Daryl had never wanted to leave for Europe less.

IT WAS MONDAY night, the week after flying out of LA for London, and now, as planned, he was in Moscow meeting delegates about a trade agreement and a new pipeline, as well as exchanging new technology for greener, cleaner energy. But he was tired and, if he were honest, wishing very much he could walk away from some of the mammoth responsibilities that lay on his shoulders. Not least because he missed her. Had done from the moment he arrived in the UK. It was like going back six months and not knowing where she was, despite knowing exactly where she was. It was just she was so far away. Seeing her spend the last eight days at the dance studio, over fourteen hours a day, as well as doing more when she got home…well, she wasn't letting her unhappiness slow her down; if anything, she was using it as a distraction. Which Daryl could understand. All too well.

He was still wide awake, aware of the fact he would have to get ready soon for the new day, and all its somewhat dubious joys. He pressed the screen on, to see her at home. She was amazing when she was performing, and he loved her on stage, but he found her simple domesticity adorable, the way she padded around in jogging bottoms, the way she played with Lazarus. He could hear her humming when she was in the kitchen, fixing some food, and when she was finally done for the day, she would just flop on the sofa, totally inelegantly and relax in silence.

But what was she doing standing on the coffee table in pink running shorts – pink? – toothbrush in one hand, the other on her hip, and looking down at the floor? Lazarus was on the back of the sofa, looking at the same place.

"It's huge," she muttered. "So huge." Intrigued, he peered closer. "Why do spiders have to get so big?"

She was afraid of spiders? Daryl smiled at the thought.

"I'm not getting it. I think you should." She looked at Lazarus, who looked back at her with a tilted head that said, *Surely not*? She laughed, and then jumped from the coffee table onto the sofa. "Big scaredy-cat! It's a good job you've got me to look after you!"

Then the doorbell rang, and they both went completely still.

"Toby, who is it?"

"Database says it's your nearest and dearest."

Daryl grimaced. Why did Donny have to turn up? That had just ruined his morning.

"Do I have one of those?" she muttered.

She went to the door. Daryl switched camera. Yep, Donny was there, hands in his pockets, looking rather apologetic.

"What are you doing here?" Not much of a welcome.

"Can I come in?"

"I suppose it would be rude to leave you outside."

With that far-from-friendly answer she walked back to the lounge, stood to one side of the sofa, leaving him to close the door. Daryl watched intently; this was going to be interesting.

Donny followed her, slowly, obviously needing time, Daryl suspected, to organise what he was going to say.

"In answer to your question, I came to see you."

"Took you a week to fit me in, did it?"

Donny took the hit with a resigned expression on his face, refusing to get angry, and instead looking at her with quiet affection.

"Just so you know, I'm not going to make this easy for you," she added.

"No, I know that, but I'm not here to argue." She raised her eyebrows as if to say *You think I'm impressed by your 'not here to argue*? "I know you're angry, and I don't blame you. You were right in what you said, about a number of things." Donny looked away for a second and then half smiled, a little bashfully, and then back at her. "You didn't know it, but we had an audience to that conversation." Her face registered shock. "And Franny, Salvadore and Sebastian all came out on your side. I felt very out-numbered." It was an admission he didn't have to make, but he was clearly okay with it. "But the worst thing you said, was that you were disappointed, because you're the last person on this earth I would want to disappoint, in any way." Slow steps carried him closer to her, but she backed off, trying to keep the distance, despite the calmness of his words and the sincerity in his eyes. "And I know I don't deserve your patience, or your loyalty considering how little I see you and get to show you what you mean to me." Her back hit the wall, eyes still on Donny, who placed a hand either side of her head, against the wall, not touching her. She could easily have ducked under, but she stayed still. "And I think I owe you something from Saturday morning."

"We both know I'm quicker."

"No, not that. I deserved that too."

He smiled, took her hands in his and pressed them against the wall. And then he kissed her, not giving her a chance to move away. It was a deep, passionate kiss, and she didn't fight it, trusted him as he held her captive. There was no panic, just pure surrender.

Daryl went to switch it off, nausea roiling in his stomach, his day now ruined; but part of him wanted to see, see what she was like in defeat, having been won over at least most of the way. Hands released, she wrapped her arms around his back, holding on to his black jacket as his hand ran up her leg and over her hip. She lifted the leg, encircled him with it, pulling him tighter into her body. Daryl felt himself harden, wanting her. With her it would be so different. The passion would be real, not fake; it would not be a diversion, as with every other woman he'd known, but a completion, a joining. He looked away for a moment, aware he was intruding.

"I need you!" he heard her say, and his eyes returned to the screen. "I need you with me! I can't do all this on my own! I don't want to be alone anymore." A hand crept up and rested against his cheek, stroking the smooth skin she knew so well. "I don't like being away from you, not knowing what's happening. I live every day wondering if you'll need me there, like before. If anything happened to you, I'd never forgive myself." She looked so vulnerable, but still so full of passion, and Daryl was not surprised Donny had all the patience in the world for her.

"Oh kitten, you mustn't carry that burden, it's not fair on you. You have a life, a career – I want good things for you. I've always thought you deserved more than hiding all that talent. I know you love me, but I don't expect you to save me from every bullet." He stroked her hair.

"But I would, and I will, if you just let me come home." It was a whisper, a plea, a promise.

"I don't want you hurt. You know that is the one thing I would never allow."

"But I want to be with you, more than ever."

"And you will. You'll be in Vegas two times a week now, and Paulo will just have to get used to me coming to LA every so often. I promise things will be better. You were right. You've asked very little, and I have abused the trust you put in me. I apologise."

A small nod.

"Now tonight, if you can bear a little more of my company…" She buried her head in his shoulder, and he whispered, "I'm taking you out for dinner. I'm not flying back till tomorrow, and seeing as it'll be Tuesday night, you're coming to the mansion with me. I've already cleared it with O'Grady, and there's nowhere safer in LA, with three lots of security teams guarding you. A full twenty-four hours together. How does that sound?"

"You make me sound like the holy grail!"

Donny chuckled, and Daryl groaned. Why did Donny have to visit? Why couldn't he just let her go? He could never give her the life or support she needed.

"What is this 'candyfloss' doing on you?" Donny then asked, chuckling again as he regarded the pink shorts.

"I asked for new ones and they got me pink – the only colour I said not to get! I've already ordered some more; I just couldn't be bothered to worry about it today. Anyway, where are we going? I hope it's not posh because I won't know what to wear."

"Sorry, beautiful, but it is posh, because you deserve nothing but the best."

"You know I'd be happy with just us and dinner and a sofa."

"I know, but I want to spoil you, so I will. And don't you worry about what to wear…I bought a dress for you."

Donny's wide smile made her laugh with amazement. "You went dress shopping? For me?"

"Well, I'm hardly going to go dress shopping for myself, am I?"

"I'm not all that good at all that dressing up stuff, so you'll have to help me."

"I think you do just fine, you just need a little more faith in yourself." He lifted her chin up. "Why don't you go hop in the shower, and I'll have it brought in. We can leave whenever you're ready, so no rushing, alright?"

"You joining me in the shower?"

An impish smile, and Daryl felt the muscle in his jaw tighten. How could Donny not agree? How it made him ache to know she'd asked another to go with her, so willing and teasing.

"I'm very tempted, but no…"

She didn't argue, but she didn't like it. She was released from the wall, and with a dark look and a, "What's a girl to do?", her gait teenager-ish for a few seconds, until she reached the last doorway and dangled off it by her fingers as she peeked back at him. "You know how you can make me love you a little more?"

"How?"

"Please get rid of the spider!"

Laughing at his expression, she disappeared and left him to negotiate with the arachnid, which had obviously been ear-wigging so much it had failed to move far.

Minutes later, Donny sat down on the sofa, Lazarus coming to sit next to him, accepting a stroke as Donny made a call and asked for the dress to be brought up. Daryl recognised the brand on the box: this was not a cheap dress. He couldn't bear to see any more. He set the timer to record the next hour and went to get showered and dressed, hoping that the frustration, and lust, would abate. Why did he have to feel like this about her? Why couldn't he just ignore her, like he ignored pretty much everyone else? How had she got so under his skin? Anger, irrational and unstoppable, gripped him and he forced the emotion down, demanding control of himself again as he stepped into the cool cascade of water, determined to lose the desire for her that pulsed in his blood, and groin.

But it wasn't just desire; that was what worried him. He didn't just envy Donny the kisses, but the trust, and her honest words. He'd spent eight days enjoying the thought that she and Donny might split, but now? They looked closer than ever. He could order O'Grady to not let her go, but she would refuse and go with him anyway. He had to let her go. At least O'Grady would be near her.

He shouldn't watch the rest of the footage. But he knew he would, even if it depressed him further. He had to know what he was up against, or he would never win. And Daryl Blackmoor never gave up and never lost.

DARYL FINALLY RETURNED to his Moscow mansion, having not enjoyed a single moment of his day. No one had argued when he had declined dinner out; it was more of a social dinner, anyway, rather than business, and he had every right. He poured himself a generous measure of brandy, and forwarded through the footage to when she reappeared. When she did, he was stunned.

He hit Pause. With a shy smile on her lips, she was standing in the doorway, hair coiled on her head, with one curl trailing over her shoulder. She was wearing a pale gold version of the white dress she'd so loved on their shopping trip, and she looked a billion dollars. The style suited her perfectly, hugging every line of her body, the deep split at the side showing one shapely leg, to the thigh. Damn, Donny had excellent taste in clothes. She wore gold heels, and no jewellery other than the bracelet and necklace that Donny had given her. She looked demure yet regal; sexy yet innocent.

The press would be all over her; her picture would be on every newspaper and headline tomorrow for certain. With the wrong man. He hit Play.

"Wow…" Donny breathed when he saw her, and held his hand out. She came to him, letting him admire her, clearly pleased with his choice. "You like it?" he asked.

"It's wonderful, thank you…it's just what I would have picked myself."

"I saw it and I knew it was made for you. Just one more thing before we go." He reached around and started to take off the necklace.

"Why are you taking it off? I want to wear it."

"I know, but tonight you're going to wear a different necklace." Daryl watched as Donny pulled something from his breast pocket. Whatever it was, it would be fabulously expensive.

"Donny, you don't have to do this, really, you know…"

"Would you just shush?" Stern eyes silenced her and she bit her lip. He then opened the box and removed a stunning diamond pendant, the central white diamond surrounded by black diamonds. "You can't refuse, because I had it made for you." She gasped at its beauty, and then he fastened it round her neck, laying it against the flawless, creamy skin. "That's you, in the middle, so beautiful and so precious," he said. "And these…" He ran his thumb over the black diamonds. "You shine so brightly in all the darkness of the world. You always have, you always will. You are all I want. Don't ever forget that. No matter what."

He kissed her, gently this time.

"You still haven't given me any answers," she whispered softly when he pulled away, eyes huge and searching, begging him.

"I know. I don't have an answer right now. I wish I did but I don't. But I know you need one, you've made that clear, and I respect that. As soon as I have one I'll tell you, alright? I hope you will always be mine." Donny hung his head, his emotions rendering him naked despite the sharp-cut suit.

"You stupid man." The girl-Venus stepped up to him then, and put her arms around him, comforting one of the most feared men in America. Daryl was captivated by the intensity of their bond. "I'll always be yours. No matter what."

Long minutes passed as they held each other, and then they left the apartment, hand in hand, Lazarus trotting happily with them.

Daryl pressed the Off button. God in heaven, he felt ill. Like someone had punched him in the gut, and then mashed his kidneys for good measure. *Patience*, he told himself, *patience.*

As he stepped out of his suit he thought about Donny's words: 'You are all I want. Don't ever forget that.' Even in his experience, men did not say that to a girl they were confident about having by their side one day as their wife. Not when he knew that all she really wanted was to hear promises of wedding bells. Why hadn't Donny got her an engagement ring if he wanted to convince her of his commitment?

She, on the other hand, had made it very clear she wanted not just to keep Donny safe – which was natural, he guessed – but there was more to it than that. Donny was her family now, had been a saviour to her as much as she had saved his life. It didn't mean she didn't love him fully, as a woman could, but there was a degree of devotion there that wasn't about marriage alone; it was about security of a more psychological kind. Was that good? He didn't know exactly.

He stood looking out at the manicured gardens and marble figurines in their various poses, and had a sudden thought: he wanted some statues made of her. He could pick out his favourites from Celeste and have them made into marble statues of his goddess, one day to be replaced with her in the flesh.

He wondered if they ever would split. If they did, she would be utterly devastated, in need of someone to be there, someone to comfort her. He would definitely make himself available when that happened.

He sat down at the grand table, a computer panel already put there for him should he wish to peruse the latest data whilst eating. The room was quiet, and an old-fashioned clock ticked away on the ornate fireplace. He could echo her words himself, could understand every tiny bit of despair in her voice: I don't want to be alone anymore; he didn't want to be alone anymore.

In the meantime, however, he had brought two of his Cherries with him, with newly dyed and curled hair. With their shades on, he was sure his imagination could do the rest.

AFTER THREE LONG weeks across the Pond, Daryl was relieved to be back in the States, to be home. Even more, wanted to see her. He'd missed her new performance at Celeste, only seeing it on his big screen. It hadn't been the same as being there. Still, he would be flying to LA later that day, and he had just one more meeting in his New York office, a few other loose ends to tie up.

Stepping out of the elevator and entering his main office, he found the whole room perched on desks or standing around, no one doing any work whatsoever, not even answering the phones, and staring at the large screen on the wall. Had a bomb gone off?

He was not far wrong.

"So here we have a sneak preview inside the newly finished Cirque de Soleil in Vegas, with clips from the show everyone is talking about, and kindly given to us by the lady herself, who I have with me right now. Mysty…I can't believe I'm actually standing talking to you, you're rather hard to get hold of." The young perky-looking interviewer turned to the blonde goddess beside her, who was noticeably taller.

"I hope you'll forgive me being so busy over the last two months when you see the show," Mysty replied. "A lot of work has gone into it, so I hope it pays off."

Daryl stopped, his entrance completely unnoticed. He was annoyed to see his staff doing absolutely nothing at all, but decided to let it go –

considering who was on the screen – and watch too. It was so good to see her close up, and she was coping admirably with the forest of people around her, shades in her hair, white Pirate Queen t-shirt on. If he didn't know differently, he'd say she'd been doing this for years.

"The show is apparently very long, over five hours?"

"Yes, it's longer than most concert performances, I admit, but I don't think anyone will get bored." She offered a small smile of promise.

"And is that all show or breaks or intervals? Are you performing the whole night, or are there pieces that are just MJ videos?"

"There are two intervals of twenty minutes each, but I am performing in every piece except one. It'll be demanding, but not impossible. The concert dates do not run directly after the other, so I'll have time to have a rest and get ready for the next one."

"You have a pretty big dance troupe with you, don't you? Over a hundred people?"

"Different people have different skills, and not everyone can keep dancing all night, so I've used extra people so they can rest too in between performances."

"Every ticket sold out weeks ago, for thirty-five venues, so you'll have a packed house every time. How does that feel, knowing you have such big audiences waiting for you? Much bigger than the Ritz, for example?"

"Exciting, definitely. And there's nowhere I'm not looking forward to going to. Vegas for the first night will be amazing, but I've had so many emails and messages from fans all over the world, so it'll be really good to take something to them and give them a great night."

"And the size of the audiences? This is your first concert tour, are you ready for that many people?"

"We had 500,000 people at the Party in the Park, so, as far as I'm concerned, the more the merrier."

"Any chance of some extra dates being added?"

"I think that's a question for when we know people like the show."

"What's your message for any MJ fans out there who are a little dubious about a female, not even fully recognised artist in her own right, using his material?"

She took the question without a waver, almost expecting it. "I would say to them, I'm not walking out on those stages thinking I wrote the songs, or the music. It's a tribute to one of the greatest artists of the twentieth and twenty-first century, and I'm honoured to be given the chance to be the one to finish something he started and, sadly, never finished in 2009. I do not underestimate how important his music is to many, many people, even all these years after his death, and once people have seen the show I think the cynics will have something other than criticism for what we have put together. Every effort has been made to make it as authentic as possible, with a little extra. I've done it pretending he's looking over my shoulder, and hoping he approves."

Daryl could have clapped it was such a good answer. He'd heard some of the criticisms, and they were being slowly but successfully being squashed, and he had no doubt once the show was seen and reviewed they would be forgotten completely.

"And your Celeste performances are still going ahead?"

"It's a lot of travelling, and no doubt I will be utterly sick of flying by the time the tour is over, but yes, at the moment they are. Worst-case scenario, if I really don't think I'll manage when the distances are so great, any cancellations will be done weeks in advance and bookings moved for when I'm back in the US. Celeste is far too demanding on me physically to take any chances, and I won't risk a bad performance for as long as I live. I would never disappoint like that."

"Well, thank you so much for your time, Mysty, I know it's very much in demand. We all wish you the best of luck and can't wait to see what's in the show!"

"Thank you."

OG and two suits appeared immediately as she smiled and turned to leave. Impressive interview indeed. Clearly, she had needed no help dealing with the press.

Daryl gestured at Mac, who was waiting at the back of the room to pull the feed on the screen. At his nod, every screen went blank.

Everyone reacted, looking around…and then realised who was standing in their midst.

"Could someone please tell me why I have returned to find everyone engrossed in a news item? Is that what I pay you all for?" No one would look him in the eye, as they were all far too afraid of him when he was angry. "Would *anyone* like to take the chance that they won't get fired and tell me?"

A phone rang, and went unanswered, underlining the point, and proving just how reluctant anyone was to move beneath his gaze. Daryl began walking down the aisle between the desks to his office, glowering, letting them remain collectively condemned. Quickly they moved back to their desks and started pressing buttons again, or typing, trying their best to look very industrious to compensate for the momentary lapse in their efforts.

"My office. Now."

They were words that made Paul jump, and he grimaced as he followed his boss into his office, Mac giving him a dark look as he took up position outside the Blackmoor office.

"Paul."

"Sir, I'm sorry you saw that, it's–"

"I trust it won't happen again? Because I would have no hesitation in firing everyone, including you, despite it being a huge inconvenience to me. It that clear?"

"Yes, sir."

"Good. Anything else I should know?"

"Nothing bad. The Hugh-Perry contract has been signed."

"Excellent."

A third voice buzzed in the room: "Mr Blackmoor, your twelve o'clock appointment is here."

"Send him in, Marlene." Daryl prepared himself for putting on a reasonably friendly face for Mr Groves. He was a long-standing client, and being frosty wouldn't be right. "You know I'm off to LA later, but I'll speak to you this evening for a full catch up. I've seen all the emails so it won't take long."

"Of course, sir."

Paul ducked his head and backed away, trying to be as respectful as possible, hoping to dispel some of the displeasure by stepping aside for Mr Frank Groves, who appeared as portly and jovial as ever. He had a smile that hid a clever and calculating mind, with a brilliant business acumen acquired over his sixty-year life. He was obviously still hungry for more.

"Frank." Daryl stood and offered his hand.

Groves nodded to Paul, who left, leaving the two to settle themselves in their chairs.

"Mr Blackmoor, nice to see you. Been busy in Moscow, I hear?"

"Very. Glad to be back, though."

"And heading back to LA later, I understand? Not that I blame you. I would too if I had the Butterfly waiting for me." Frank's smile was wide and knowing, the kind of smile that only meant one thing: he had, quite rightly, guessed that Daryl's interest was more than that of mere business.

But Daryl was rattled. What was this?

"Frank, I'm her manager."

"Oh, come on, what's the story behind her handcuffing you to your bed? She can handcuff me to mine any time she likes, but, really, what is the deal between you two?"

Daryl sat for a full ten seconds in absolute silence. The bad mood that had not shifted, like a heavy monsoon, had just had some thunder added, and the lightning wasn't far away. What the…? She'd agreed not to tell anyone? Starting a rumour like this, at the expense of his pride and dignity, was unforgivable!

By some Herculean effort Daryl kept temper in check, his words polite.

"As I said, I'm her manager, and this is the first I've heard of this story."

The tight-lipped answer and sharp eyes warned Groves his words had not had the humorous result he had intended.

"Not surprised, not surprised," he said quickly. "You must have been busy, of course. The news people naturally went way over the top about such a little thing. You know how they are about anything like that."

"Naturally," Daryl snapped. "So, I understand you're looking at expansion and some upgrades?"

"Yes. We've got a whole new site underway, so we need a full security assessment, top surveillance capacity, and checks on all new staff – nothing new for you, I'm sure, but I obviously want the job done as best it can. I know you understand."

Daryl nodded, and pulled a tablet towards him, making a few notes, forcing his mind to concentrate on the new project that would be worth millions. He would be seeing her later, and it would be a most interesting chat. She'd better have some *very* good answers, or she was going to find out just how far she'd pushed him.

SEVENTEEN HOURS AFTER he was meant to have seen her, she still hadn't turned up. He'd rung OG to demand where she was, and was told she was asleep. He was furious. He'd barely slept he'd been so wound up, refusing to go to her apartment, glaring at it from his own. It was such wanton disobedience, and highly disrespectful.

He was not going to be gentle with her. He was not in the mood. What he was in the mood for was venting the huge amount of frustration that had welled up inside him. He'd had Melissa at his apartment last night, and she'd been something...but nothing. The release had been strong, satisfying, but it had lasted only seconds, and then he was back to wanting Mysty again. He must be mad. And it was not a madness he remembered agreeing to!

He heard the door, and glanced down at the newspaper headline that made his blood boil afresh: 'Lion of Manhattan Cuffed to his Own Throne'. He'd seen the picture of himself, looking distinguished and successful, next to the picture of her looking gorgeous in the golden dress. He'd even read a few sentences from the piece...What the fuck had she been thinking? She knew how to handle the press, so why had she chosen to be so damned irresponsible? Their own private ongoing dispute was somewhat different to public humiliation! And why the hell hadn't she shown up to the meeting he had called?

And then she was in front of him.

"Sit."

He saw her face register surprise at his biting tone, but she sat down in the nearest chair, slowly. She must know why he was ready to skin her alive. She had only just looked up before his first vehement volley of words launched at her, full of savage accusation.

"Is it your one goal in life to disrespect and humiliate me?"

"Excuse me?" She looked confused, and surprised.

"Why weren't you here at 6pm last night? As arranged? Do I have to staple your handheld to a part of you that pays attention to appointments?"

"I…I must have been asleep."

"Do you think my life, my *time* is a joke? That you have a right to waste it?" She still looked stunned, and tried to answer, but no words came out. "Do you have any idea just who I am? There are people around the world who would pay a great deal of money for an hour of my time, and yet you – you decide you're too good for a simple meeting, arranged for your benefit."

"I didn't mean to–"

"For God's sake, don't lie. You don't do it well and it won't work. You and I both know you absolutely love doing anything you can to irritate and mock me, and what better way than to have a ball with the American press." He picked up the newspaper with its offensive headline and threw it into her lap. Her crestfallen expression was enough to make him want to shake her. "Don't start playing the sweet and innocent card now, because of all the people in the world who would delight in exposing that to the press, it would be you."

"I didn't…I didn't say anything to the press, I swear to you! I didn't know anything about this!"

Why was she was lying to him! Lying was the one thing she'd never done, and he'd always respected her honesty, as infuriating as it was. Lying tainted her; made her no different to his adulterous, pathetic fiancée. It was a straw too many for the camel's back.

"*I said don't lie to me*!"

The blast of anger shocked her and she leaned back in the chair, away from him, no trace of temper, just confusion.

"I think I should go," she said slowly and stood up, not meeting his hateful eyes, putting the newspaper back on the table in front of her.

"Don't you dare walk away from me before I've finished with you."

His voice was so harsh and low it chilled her.

"Finished with me? What is wrong with you? I've not seen you for three weeks and somehow you're furious with me? I don't understand." She suddenly felt week, dizzy, and knew she shouldn't have come. What was wrong?

"Are you really so stupid that you don't understand? I am not someone you can toy with without there being consequences! You think I will stand for your behaviour forever? Your not arriving for a meeting, and disrespect for me in the press!"

She looked at him with alarm, and as if he were mad; but he wanted to see contrition and fear.

"Sit down before I shove you up against that wall and fuck you hard enough to teach you some respect."

She felt like she'd been punched. He'd said many things, but never threatened her like that before. And it was so crude, so beneath him. He might wear a pristine suit every day, and have world business at his fingertips, even have the looks of a god, but he was also just a man, as base as any other, and she understood the lustful violence that threatened her now. A shiver ran through her at the intensity in his eyes as they fixed on her. Not even Donny's rages could make her scared like he could. She felt her stomach turn over.

"Try it," she said.

"What?"

"Try it. See what happens."

"You don't want that."

"Try it or take back your empty threat."

She braced herself, forcing her tired muscles to obey. Eyes dared him, challenged him as he advanced on her. She moved away, step for step, not changing her expression.

"Don't do this. This is anger. Don't do it," she warned him, and he was reminded that she was horribly proficient in most, if not all forms of fighting. There was no way he could call for Mac, and only hoped, if he could hear the conflict, that he would stay on the other side of the wall.

"You brought us here."

"No. No, I didn't. Please don't do this."

"Now you're asking me for mercy?"

"No, I'm asking you to stop this and calm down."

Their eyes were locked in a battle of wills as her final step put her against the wall. He could hardly stand being so close to her, could feel the heat from her body, hear her breath in her chest. He reached a hand out, not sure what he was actually going to do with it, but it didn't matter, as she grabbed his wrist and twisted, and in two seconds he was forced down to one knee with his arm bent up between his shoulder blades, facing the wall. He strained against it, but it was a simple and very effective hold, his other hand useless as it couldn't reach her.

"Tell me you'll stop this and I'll let you go."

"Let me go."

"I don't like the anger in your voice. Try again."

The condescension only made him angrier. "Let me go. You're only making this worse."

"Ah shit." With a sad sigh she exhaled. She shoved his face hard against the wall, and pain registered in his forehead and nose, and then a split second later, she let him go. He stood, one hand bracing against the wall, fingers going to his nose. He drew them away, saw the blood. He was too dazed to do anything, and had a horrible feeling that there was more pain to come, especially when he was pulled backwards.

But he was wrong. This time she threw him onto the sofa, and with a soft frown on her lovely face brought a glass of water and some tissues. What was this?

"I always thought you were a little mad, but I didn't think you were totally insane." Crouching beside him she wiped the blood away from his hand and nose. "It's not broken, so don't worry, you'll still be as handsome as ever." She sighed, her eyes unreadable but not angry. "I didn't want to… but you…you wouldn't listen. Pinch the top of your nose." She closed her eyes, opened them. "I didn't come here yesterday, or go anywhere else, because I was in bed, because I've been ill for the past three days." She pressed her hand against her stomach and stepped back unsteadily to sit down in her chair again. "OG sent you a message…haven't you looked at your mail?"

Ill? She was never ill?

He looked at her with softer eyes than she had ever seen before.

"No, I haven't seen anything, I've been so busy." *Too goddamned busy, like I always am. Now look at what I've done.*

"The good doctor, in his eternal wisdom, decided I needed some vaccines or vitamins, or something, and stuck a load of God-knows-what in me on Thursday afternoon." The facts came flooding back to him: the vaccines he'd approved the week before; he'd been so busy he'd completely forgotten about them. "I didn't feel too great Friday. Somehow, I managed the Celeste performance, but the first thing I did was throw up as soon as I was off the arena floor. Saturday and Sunday…I don't really remember. I was asleep most of the time. I would have come if I'd felt able, but I couldn't. And contrary to your belief, I don't take every opportunity to ridicule or disrespect you, and I don't underestimate how important your time is. Despite what you think, I don't go causing trouble just to hurt people."

She picked up the newspaper he had tossed in her lap earlier, before dropping it from her fingertips with distaste.

"As to this, as I said, I didn't say anything to the press. I'm not stupid. I know how something like this reflects on you. It was a private matter, between us, and no one else needed to know. I got asked about it in an interview, which surprised me. I don't know how they got hold of it, but no one outside of that room, even the security boys, could ever have known."

Daryl felt suddenly guilty. Of course it hadn't been her.

"I don't know if Harvey or someone said something when they got a little drunk, and somehow the wrong people found out. What I do know, is that I lied through my teeth to discredit the story, making it clear I didn't even think the topic worth discussing."

She reached across and pulled out another paper from the stack on the table. There was another headline: 'The Product of a Very Bored

Mind.'

Daryl's guilt deepened.

"I've never lied in my life, but I wasn't going to let this create such a mockery of you when it was none of their goddamn business."

He didn't know what to say in response. All of his anger had long since dissipated, except the anger he felt with himself. He hadn't looked through all the papers, hadn't seen the article written in his defence.

"I'm going to be sick. Where's the bathroom?" She looked at him for help, her eyes panicked.

"Just through there." He pointed at the heavy mahogany door. "The light will come on automatically."

She pushed herself up and walked unsteadily to the door. Oh God, how weak she looked. He ran a hand over his face. Checked his nose: no blood. He gathered the bloodied tissues and took them to the waste bin.

He heard a small, choked cough and a gasp for air. He didn't think; he just went. He was tired of standing on the sidelines as she suffered, particularly as he was the one generally responsible for her distress.

She was sagged against the wall, and started violently when he touched her forehead. Very hot. He saw how pale she was. He should have noticed when she first arrived. Should have been paying attention to more than just his anger and his offended ego.

He picked up a flannel and soaked it with cold water, the same silent gentle care she had used on him repaid as he put it against her forehead and raised her hand to it. She didn't have the energy to speak, to fight him, when he bent and gathered her into his arms. It felt so good. He wanted to smell her hair, rest his cheek against those silky curls, but now was not the time. He could feel tension in her, despite her lack of a fight, and little wonder. He berated himself for having been so hasty in his attack.

"Here we are." He set her down as gently as possible and fetched her a glass of water, which she took and sipped slowly. She didn't protest when he sat down next to her, lifted her wrist to check her pulse. "Have you been throwing up every day?" he asked quietly.

"Yes. But there's nothing to throw up as it's so long since I've eaten anything. It's just water or energy drinks. OG keeps trying to get me to eat, but I can't." She pulled the cloth away from her head, and he took it. It was very warm. "I'm so weak and I hate it…I don't know what's wrong with me."

Daryl pressed through on the intercom. He wanted longer with her, but he also wanted her to rest; anything, in fact, if it would make her better.

"O'Grady."

"Yes, sir?"

"I need you to take her home. She needs to be in bed."

"Has she been sick again?"

"Yes." His favourite pair of eyes looked at him, as if it were her fault. He would have held her, except he doubted she'd let him. "Her temperature is high, and her heart rate is fast."

"I'm on my way."

Disconnect.

"I should have checked my messages again."

It was the closest thing to an apology, and she knew it, and she smiled sadly.

"You're too busy. You need a twin brother."

Even after all he'd just said she still wasn't nasty to him. And she hadn't lied, not to him. But she had to the press, for him, which was the biggest compliment she could give him. She'd tried to preserve his dignity during his absence, without being asked; she'd done everything she could to undo the damage.

"I wish." He took the glass from her and put it aside, seeing her shiver. "Would you like my jacket? You're cold."

"I'm hot then cold, then hot then cold. You keep it on, it looks better on you."

"I don't know, I think you'd look quite cute." She almost smiled. "Would you like me to cancel tomorrow night, at Celeste?"

"No. My temperature has dropped, and I've not been sick as much so far today. I'm getting better. I have another day to improve."

"But you're weak…you won't have the strength?"

"I'll be fine, really. Enough gel packs and bowls of cereal. Wednesday I will spend sitting on the sofa eating crisps if it makes you happy."

He wasn't convinced. "I don't mind pulling one show…you've got a busy week."

It was true, what with the last Ritz performance, Celeste, and then the first MJ concert on Sunday night.

"I won't let everyone down, and I don't want the media running the story I'm too ill. That's not the headline I want preceding the concert." She looked at him sternly. When had she become such a publicity expert? Then again, a lot of it was common sense and understanding people, and she had plenty of both. "I know what I'm doing, please just trust me."

"Promise me you'll only do it if you're one hundred per cent. I know you like that number – so do I."

"I promise. You think I'd go and fall off my perch and let you off putting up with me for the next eight years?"

He almost laughed with relief to hear that; but his concern far outweighed everything else he was feeling.

The door opened, and Mac and OG both came straight over, OG putting a hand on her forehead.

"Can't leave you alone for five minutes," he chided gently. She looked up at her trusted bodyguard, who seemed to fulfil every role that came along. "Sleep is what you need; I knew I shouldn't have let you get up."

"What can I say? I had a summons from God himself," she replied, making Daryl smile.

"Shouldn't she see Baden?" he asked.

"She doesn't want to, understandably, considering. I did ring him when the symptoms became apparent, and he gave me some advice, but there's not much he can do. The concoction he gave her means there are a number of things it could be, and more drugs aren't going to help. Her body has a strong dislike of anything that is put in it."

"I am here, you know," she said, and OG laughed.

"Are you alright, sir? There's blood on your shirt?" Mac said suddenly.

Daryl looked, not sure how to explain it, not wanting to say she'd hurt him and it was his fault.

"Nosebleed. Don't worry, I patched him up just fine. I've been an experienced first-aider since the age of four. Probably too much time on private jets flying around checking too many computer screens, and enjoying late-night parties, loose women and martinis."

Daryl looked at her with warm affection, wished she'd look at him to see it. Trust her to find a way to avoid any complicated explanations… and to have a dig at him for his lifestyle.

Mac and OG were looking at him with unashamed amusement, and then OG gently pulled her up from the sofa and, with his arm around her waist, led her slowly to the lift.

"You need to get better. I only take criticism from people who look me in the eye and aren't falling asleep."

"First time for everything."

"You've got eight years to reform me, but you can't do it like this. O'Grady will get you home."

"You're just worried I might puke over your very expensive suit."

"I get free dry cleaning, and free suits."

"How come I don't get free suits?"

"You look better in hot pants," Daryl replied.

"You don't like me wearing hot pants."

"How do you know?"

"Because you always scowl at me, or say something rude when I do!"

If only you knew, Daryl thought, enjoying the banter, as he always did. "I don't like your suits, but I don't scowl at you for wearing them!"

"What would you rather I wore?"

"Hot pants. Or how about one of those costumes – you know, the big furry ones that people wear as mascots for football teams. I'd love to see you in one of those. Have a 'come to work in costume day'."

"Well, good job I get to choose my own clothes, else I really would be on the front of the newspapers, and probably lose business clients as well."

The doors opened and O'Grady stepped in, three suits with him. Daryl was sad to see her go. "Let me know how she goes, O'Grady."

"Will do, sir."

"She might ring you up and tell you herself!" she said, and an indignant, albeit weak, fist attempted to thump OG's shoulder.

"I hope she does."

"A NOSEBLEED," MAC said.

"Yes, nothing to worry about."

Daryl had never lied to Mac about anything, but what had happened between him and Mysty stayed between them.

"I'll be leaving at 6pm tonight, Mac," he added, and strolled back to his office, wanting a few moments to himself. All the anger since seeing Groves earlier, and the newspaper headline – it had all been wrong. His faith in her was fully restored. Of course she wouldn't have gone to the press. But God, why had he made such a mess of it? She'd not deserved that fight, and he winced remembering what he'd said. How crude it had been, how unjustified. He could still hear her voice: 'Don't do this, please don't…'God knows she'd witnessed enough violence.

He brought up the picture of his newest surprise for her, that he had spent two weeks arranging for her and still wanted to give her, despite feeling a bit of a fool for organising it. He wanted to be there when she first saw it.

He was wracked with guilt, still. She might have forgiven him his anger today, but he wondered if she would forgive him if she knew it was his fault she was ill from the vaccines. Baden had warned him that giving her five different concoctions might have been detrimental in the short term, but Daryl's belief in her strength had made him choose the simple one-time option. He wouldn't have done it if he'd known it would make her so sick.

Stupid thing was, he wanted her to know it was his fault; wanted to be honest with her so she blamed him, not Baden. He would tell her, and take the chance that his honesty would work. After all he'd done to her, he owed her that, or else she would never respect him or trust him. And that, he concluded, as he leaned back in his chair, was the only way he was ever going to get close to her.

He'd been so angry. So close to ending what he'd started, parts of which she knew nothing about. But now? The same creature that faced him down across the room with more backbone than anyone he'd ever met, slammed his head into the wall, was the same one that had wiped away the blood afterwards. He didn't want to end anything.

Was he willing to give her up? Absolutely not.

"SIR?"

"O'Grady? I hope you have some good news for me." Daryl put down the computer panel. Having been too restless to sleep or relax with a book, he'd started on tomorrow's long list of jobs.

"Very. She woke up at 5pm. Her temperature has dropped, she's just drunk a pint of milk and polished off five slices of buttered toast, and fallen asleep again, but no sickness. I think, sir, she's on the mend."

"Excellent. Try and get her to have something else to eat tonight. She's got some catching up to do."

"Yes, sir. I've already got a few of her favourites stocked up in the fridge. I'll keep you posted, of course."

"Thank you. I trust you're satisfied with the security on her new conveyance?" Daryl asked carefully, wanting it to be a surprise, knowing O'Grady knew not to tell her.

"I went over it earlier, with someone I count as a bigger expert than me. All very satisfactory, Mr Blackmoor. I'm sure she will be…quite amazed."

"Well, hopefully it'll help her forget feeling so ill. If she does do Celeste tomorrow night, O'Grady, I want you to be very vigilant. If you think she can't do it, don't let her."

"I understand, sir."

"Good night, Mr O'Grady."

Disconnect.

Sweet relief.

MYSTY PLACED HER favourite old Madonna t-shirt in the suitcase, the familiar fabric taking her back to that day at the strip club. Jumping in that car. Not knowing just who was driving it. How naïve yet brave she'd been.

Was I stupid to think no one would notice me? Would someone always have found me and pulled me out of my life?

She rested her palm on it for a little longer, a wave of nervous excitement passing through her: her first tour.

But the trip down memory lane also triggered a guilt-trip: she had yet to message Raju back – properly that was. He'd been getting increasingly worked up in his messages, worried about her silence, and she forced herself to rise above her own stretched emotions to reassure him she was okay and would explain when she could. That had at least stemmed the tide of exclamations, capital letters and threats to break their unspoken code of not hacking the other person. She was 99.99% sure he couldn't hack her system as hacking wasn't his forte; but she knew it wasn't fair to leave him in that much distress. She was one of his few friends; she was the one who'd bailed on their Day of Truth. DOT. The day had come and gone in the melee that was now her life, and still she didn't know how to explain it all to him: Blackmoor, the contract, those photos, the TV interviews…

Fuck.

The sheer weight of the emotions involved made her feel like she was made of lead, and the thrill of the tour disappeared. She slumped down onto the edge of the bed. Wherever she went on tour, it wouldn't get her any further away from the issues closest to her heart. Issues that made her feel exhausted they had laid on her for so long. No amount of fame or flashbulbs would erase them.

I used to be such a good friend. I'm not anymore. I'm lost in my own chaos. Will I feel better once I've told him? Or should I just…make something up? I hate the thought of it, but what if he goes to a newspaper? Would he do that, though? Could he? He's in India. He's got no connection to the American press. And what would he give them? A copy of our conversations? Who would give a shit? I'm so lost in my fame maze I'm losing sight of who my friends are. Raju thinks The Butterfly is the most amazing person ever…would he betray her, especially if he found out she's me?

"You alright, kiddo?"

She raised her head at the sound of OG's voice. "Sure. Just thinking."

"You're not feeling ill again?"

Since her days of barely being able to stomach water and dry toast he had been watching over her with a carefully judged joviality that, had she known, she would have realised was a natural fatherly instinct coming to the fore.

"I'm fine, OG, honestly."

Her smile encouraged him to stay a moment, and he leaned on the doorframe. "Don't stress about the packing. Anything you need, we'll get it organised."

"I wasn't…I wasn't worried about the packing. I haven't turned into a full-on diva. Yet."

"You want to talk about it? Whatever it was that put such a frown on your face?"

She opened her mouth to say no, then paused…maybe she could ask OG for advice?

"There's a friend."

"Uh-uh." OG's tone implied one thing, and she shot him a dark look that told him it wasn't *that* kind of friend.

"He…we're pen-pals. Internet friends, really. Whatever the word is. He's miles away…not in America anyway."

"Okay, so what's the problem?"

"Well. I didn't…" An anguished look at the ceiling, then she knotted her fingers together. "We didn't tell each other much…about ourselves. You can guess why I didn't, yeah?" She got a nod of understanding. "We mostly talk computing and maths, and have done for a couple of years now, but we never discuss personal stuff. I don't know why he hides so much about himself from me. I could hack his system but…but that would be wrong. We agreed to have a 'Day of Truth', when we would both explain ourselves to each other. Who we really are…"

Her pause stayed as a pause so long OG prompted her for the next excerpt of the story: "And?"

"And it was hard enough before…especially when he raved about how amazing The Butterfly is etc. How do I tell him, OG? How do I tell him it's…me? Now. After Mr Blackmoor – *the Mr Blackmoor* – and the contract? It's going to sound…" Eyes appealed again to the ceiling for mercy from the hopelessness of the scenario she'd found herself in. "Plus, all the times he's gushed his admiration, and I've pretended she was someone else… I didn't mean to lie, I just couldn't tell the truth. I've trained myself to hide who I am with him. What I do? This is all…really confusing."

OG was once more confronted with how difficult parts of her life had been, and indeed were, and quite without it being her fault. Moving a pile of discarded clothes from a chaise, and other teenager-ish debris like hairbrushes and device chargers, gave him precious seconds to formulate his reply. This clearly mattered to her. A lot. Whoever this friend was, she didn't want to lose him, despite having never met. God. What had her life become?

"He sounds pretty smart…" he began.

"He's mega smart."

"Then he should be smart enough to realise when you tell him that… that you really didn't have a choice, for your own safety. He won't think you lied gratuitously. You've been talking for years, so you must mean something to him too? Think of it from his point of view. He will probably feel more embarrassed about having 'gushed' about his admiration." He saw her expression change to something closer to a bashful. "Plus, he's about to find out he's now friends with one of the most famous and successful sixteen-year-olds on the planet. Why would he get angry at you?"

"Because I worried him. I didn't answer messages for a while. I was too…upset and thrown by everything that was happening with this whole fame thing and…"

"Well, just tell him that. I'm sure he'll understand."

"You think?"

"One hundred percent."

"Everyone else found out through the press because they know what I look like. He's the only person who doesn't know."

"If he knew what you looked like he'd definitely have guessed…

don't overthink this." She groaned: he was right. "I'll leave you to finish packing. Dinner in an hour, okay?"

"Yep."

He got up to leave, his hand on the bedroom door. But something made him pause, and he heard the words he knew she needed to hear. There was no one else to say them. The duty –the privilege – had fallen to him…of all unlikely people.

"I know this has all been a bit crazy for you, kiddo…" he said, "but you are handling it all very well. Anyone would have a wobble or two now and again. I…I'm always here, if you need a chat. Bodyguards make great shrinks."

She didn't look at him, but he knew she heard every word.

"Thanks, OG."

The door shut.

They both paused for a second, reflected on what a difference it made to talk. One in particular wondering how much more he would discover about her over the next twelve weeks of tour. The other…well, she was processing how it felt to share and ask for advice.

DARYL LOOKED BACK over the last five days, so busy, so full of her, and yet now he faced another ten weeks of being apart – except for rare moments at Celeste when their schedules enabled them to see each other. Not that she was bothered about that, he was sure. But then the look that she'd given him when she'd found herself confronted with the sleek silver jet with the Pirate Queen logo on one side had been different from all others so far. He'd also had the MY^2 signature, the Butterfly of Black Magic symbol and a tiger paw print artfully put together in sparkling black. He had enjoyed that moment; enjoyed her complete wonder. She'd looked sharply at him, where he stood calmly watching the revelation dawn that the jet was all for her. He could show her so little of what she meant to him, and the business-related gifts were the closest he could get. There had been no words; she hadn't known what to do or say.

"Do you like her?" he'd asked gently. She'd looked at him again, her eyes asking him what this was all about, sensing it was more than business.

"She's beautiful, but…"

"But nothing. You are worthy of her, and she is worthy of you. Why don't you take a look inside?"

She could use one of his jets just fine, but having her own? Branded just for her? It was a grand gesture, and a personal one. It put her in the same league as him, in a way, and certainly wasn't something he had ever done for anyone else – as far as she knew.

He had ordered a bottle of champagne, and let her have some to toast her maiden flight and the start of her MJ tour. She felt like she hadn't earned this yet, and said so. But he knew she had, because he'd had a few sneak previews, and she was incredible. Nobody would be disappointed.

And so, before he had to accept her absence, he was going to enjoy every minute of their last car drive together, happier knowing she was back to full strength. She'd been weighed every week during her check-ups with Baden, and had regained most of the two kilos lost. He was relieved to know Baden would be going with her on tour. She had the tendency to overwork, just like he did, and Baden would monitor her.

She was dropped at the Vegas town house he had bought for her, so she had somewhere that was a home away from home, and not just a hotel room. It also meant she had the best security available and somewhere lovely to be two nights a week…that wasn't Donny's. Again, she was stunned into silence; the silence screaming *Is this my life now*? as she looked at him.

When she emerged, ready for the evening, she was dressed from top to toe in a deep, gleaming blue, skin-tight with a wild gold belt over her hips and a blue satin trilby – a tribute to MJ fashion, no doubt – and looked stunning.

"Good evening," he said, as she stepped into the car.

"Hello."

"How are you feeling?"

"I have butterflies whirling around in my tummy."

He couldn't help but smile. "You'll be fine once it begins. The nerves are just the hype everyone else is loading onto the first performance. You know what you're doing, backwards, so don't worry."

It was a much kinder answer than she had been expecting and she didn't quite know what to say. She'd barely seen him since their…scuffle…on Monday. And then he'd been so nice to her?

"You know," he said, in the hopes of relaxing her a little, "I had a beautiful Lamborghini in that colour you're wearing, once upon a time."

She blushed gorgeously, colour across her cheekbones.

"I'll buy you another one," she said in a small voice, and he laughed. "I can't understand why you got the jet after I what I did to…your car. I hardly deserve it. Any of it."

"It may surprise you to know that I think I deserved what you did to my car. All of them, in fact. And I have long since decided it was a price very much worth paying. I would do it all again, in an instant, and suffer much worse to have you finally achieving the recognition you deserve. You've earned the jet, and one day you will think so too."

"You're very confusing." She observed him, head on one side. "What is it you want from me?" Her bright eyes challenged him, asking him for truth.

"To be the best you can be. I believe you were born for this. No one else can do what you do, and do it so consistently well. Despite what you think, I have a great deal of faith in you." Would that 'truth' be enough for her?

"I see." She eyed him carefully, taking the answer in. Perhaps it hadn't been what she'd expected. "Do you think, then, I could call you by your first name, seeing as you use mine?"

"And give up using all those other names you have for me?"

The pause hung between them, and then, "Well, as much as some of them are quite amusing, and very satisfying, I do prefer real names." He saw the mischief sneak into her eyes, a smile dancing on her lips. "Unless, of course, it turns you on being insulted…? Does it make you horny, baby?" The English accent was spot on, and the quote perfect, and she laughed when she saw his expression. "Don't worry, I watched Austin Powers last night. I'm going to get a t-shirt with it printed on. Just think…one TV interview of me wearing a 'Do I make you horny?' and half the girls in LA will be wearing one."

"I would request you don't." *But the answer is definitely, yes, you do make me horny!*

"Aw. No fun. How about 'Shagadelic?'"

"No, again. I think it's a little too overtly…suggestive."

"How about 'Groovy, baby'?"

"That one. Just about."

"But I much prefer the 'Do I make you horny?' Would you like one?"

"To wear next time I see the president?"

She laughed instantly. "If you like. I'd be very impressed if you did!"

He could bask in that huge bright smile for hours. "How am I doing in negative dickhead points at the moment, by the way?"

"Not too bad. Only about a fifty-five million at the moment."

"Come on! The jet must be worth a few?"

"It was. That's how you've ended up at fifty-five million. You don't want to know where you were before that."

"I was hoping I was out of the millions by now."

"No, I'm a little harder to please than that."

"Don't suppose you've changed your mind about visiting my penthouse again? I'm sure I could shift a good few million in a few hours."

She laughed again, as he wanted her to, but she didn't miss the quiet intensity in his eyes. She had got used to seeing it, and decided to ignore it.

"No, sadly not. So, first-name terms or Dickhead Billionaire?"

"Your skills as a diplomat astound me as ever." He leant forward and offered his hand. "Hi, I'm Daryl, nice to meet you."

She took it. "Mysty. And you, too."

God how he wanted to kiss the back of that hand. The handshake was firm – good, but soft – but fleeting.

"That wasn't so bad, was it?" he said.

"No. Surprisingly painless."

Another pause, and then, "Daryl."

"Yes?"

"Nothing. I was just checking you answered to your name. Seeing as so few people use it, I didn't want to find that you didn't recognise it."

"You are an irreverent little madam," he told her, with crushing seriousness that he knew she didn't care about.

"Doesn't seem to have put you off any, so tough shit, cupcake," she returned easily, looking just as solemn as he did.

What! No one ever spoke to him like that! And no one had *ever* called him 'cupcake' either. But he looked her full in the face, and smiled, causing her to raise her eyebrows in surprise.

"I love it when you sweet talk me like that," he said.

"Jackass."

Daryl almost laughed, but rolled his eyes. "Heard that one."

"You'll miss me when I'm not here."

Like you wouldn't believe. "You're right, no one insults me as well as you do."

"No one else dares to!"

"I know, you're the odd one out."

"That's because I'm a step in evolution. I'm ahead of the game."

"Exactly."

They sat in brief silence, aware they were nearly there.

"You know you can call me," Daryl said, "when you're on tour, if there's anything wrong or whatever. If I can't answer, I will get back to you when I can. This is a big challenge, and just because I'm not there kicking your ass into line every day doesn't mean I can't do it from a distance." He watched her face go from soft, to mild outrage and amusement mingled together.

"Kicking my ass into line? Since when have you ever done that?"

"Well, I tried, didn't I?"

"Yeah, exactly, tried!"

The car pulled up. Neither of them moved, knowing the moment the door was open these moments together would be over. They were both captive to the magnitude of what lay ahead of her, and that much was likely to come to pass before they got to speak together in such privacy again.

"After you," she said.

"No, after you. Ladies first, after all." But she refused to move. "Shall I come over there and give you a good luck kiss?"

Her eyebrows flew up at the suggestion…and the awareness that he fully intended to carry it out.

"I don't need luck."

"Then I'll just kiss you for the hell of it," he replied with infinite calm.

"The hell you will."

He leaned forward, and she was too stunned to move. He was conscious that the door may be opened by the driver, flanked by security, at any second. That their presence was awaited by the many thousands gathered outside, not least the press. But he tucked a curl back, and placed two fingers on her cheek, moving her face towards his. She was watching him very closely, either too curious or too nervous to move away; most likely, he suspected, a combination of both.

"Just one question, princess," he said. "Do I make you horny? Do I?"

She couldn't miss the heat in his eyes, or the teasing look. In a face so handsome, it was an irresistible combination. From a distance she could cope with the strange magnetism, the attraction she didn't understand; but close up… It was something she had become acutely aware of that night at Celeste, when he'd sat on her sofa and taken the time to tell her that Donny wouldn't be seeing her. Even though she knew from his eyes, and the tension in the room, that he'd wanted her as a man wants a woman, she hadn't felt threatened by him. On Monday, however, in his fury he had shocked her; but somehow the threat had been born of passion, not violence, his anger due to his feeling betrayed – which to him was justified, not mindless. Now, in this car, his face only inches from hers, she didn't know what to say or do. Intense, truly beautiful green eyes held hers without blinking, and she knew she was out of her depth. Always would be if he turned that liquid charm on, on her unprepared defences, offering sensual delight she didn't understand, but rejected instinctively. A hundred different thoughts whirled, and the first one wasn't Donny, though she was sure it should have been. She didn't understand.

She managed to squeeze past him and out of the door, without touching him, leaving him without an answer, and a little surprised but, somehow, not disappointed. She was too innocent to hide her confusion; too inexperienced to know the tension she felt was discernible, and he could read her like a book.

He too stepped out of the car, preparing himself for the noise, and she was there, signing autographs and answering a few questions for one of the cameras, OG and the suits with her. She refused to acknowledge him, and he strolled calmly up the red carpet, letting himself be drawn into a few questions by one of the biggest news stations. He knew how to answer the questions without really thinking, which was good, because his mind was more pleasantly engaged replaying the last fifteen minutes.

MYSTY WOKE UP and rolled over, looked at the time and groaned. How could it be 7am already? She didn't even feel like she'd been asleep for an hour. This tour was going to be the death of her. Three hours and she'd be on a plane again, another Celeste performance, and then back on the plane overnight heading for Madrid.

The plane . . . she even couldn't believe it was hers, with someone to bring her drinks or food if she wanted, and a whole team of others supporting her in any small way they could. And this amazing house too. What had she done to deserve all this?

"Good morning." OG was sat reading the paper in the kitchen when she wandered in, Lazarus by her side.

"Is it really 7am?" she asked.

"Fraid so." He turned and looked at her. She looked tired, and too thin. "How you feeling?" She smiled weakly. "There's bacon in the oven . . . you want a sandwich?"

"I guess." She wanted to go back to bed, didn't really even fancy a bacon sandwich.

"You know you can sleep on the plane? And maybe give the run a miss this morning?"

"The fastest I'll be going is a lazy walk. I'm not running anywhere."

"How about you lazy-walk over to the sofa while I get the sandwich. Oh, and there're some boxes over there for you."

He'd watched her every performance, seen the way she handled the media vultures like she'd done it all her life. But it was taking its toll. She was still just a kid. His girls at her age had needed so much more rest than she was getting. He'd argued that it was too hectic a schedule, but was shouted down. In a week she had a four-day break in the UK, however, and in another three weeks, a four-day break in Tokyo. At least that was something.

"Who are the boxes from?"

"Mr New York." He decided to use one of her names for him just to make her smile.

"My slave driver? Maybe a new pair of shackles to keep me tied to the car or the plane a little more – what do you think?"

She was surprised by the number of boxes. Big white boxes. For some insane reason, she thought of wedding presents, having seen some once piled up on a table. That was not something she was willing to contemplate.

She opened the first and found a fan of brochures laid out on gold tissue paper. There was small envelope on top, which she tore open: What? Was her life not insane enough already? Written in black italics, it said: 'I'm running out of wall space. Have even had to buy a new mansion. These are the new catalogues. Any you like, just say, they'll be waiting for you in LA. Seems I'm not the only one who likes you in print.' Underneath, a graceful bold 'D' confirmed the sender.

Her eyes went back to the brochures. All with the MY^2 motif on the top right, they were separated out, one for the Butterfly, one for the Pirate Queen, one for the MJ concert, one for the Ritz performances. But there were also brochures of her in various other moments, more human ones: with Lazarus, from the Party in the Park, her night in New York, even from the shopping trip all those weeks ago, including – and she almost dropped it – one of her standing on the Lamborghini near the burning Mercedes. Much to her relief, none of them contained any of her in that black string. In another brochure there was a price list for getting some of the images signed – and her eyes widened to see the prices. She'd scribbled on a good few dozen pictures before her before the tour began, and not thought anything of it. This explained a great deal.

Beneath all the brochures there was a sales breakdown, and her eyes nearly popped out her head when she saw them. How many people wanted a picture of her? Posters, framed prints, mounted canvas – it was clearly big business from the seven figures she saw at the bottom. It also showed the top ten most popular. She liked the one with Lazarus, but what surprised her was the one that she couldn't quite place. She was leaning back against a car in bright sunshine, shades on, thumbs in her waistband with one foot up against the car door – a real casual pose, and even she liked the Mysty in the picture. She was looking away, waiting patiently, calmly, for whatever was about to happen – a bit like her life really. She only had to stand still for a moment and something happened.

"Pretty impressive, aren't they?"

She took the plate with the sandwich and took a huge bite, putting the lid back on the box. OG put the next on in front of her, and his smile made her suspicious.

"Do you know what's in it?"

"I was briefed, yes, when I signed for them," he grinned, and she saw the reason for the pun when she pulled out ivory satin, lace-edged briefs with the Mysty signature on the front. There was a matching bra too. Very cute. Innocent, yet a little sexy. She opened another envelope: 'Now you have branded underwear of your own, you don't need to be so jealous of mine.' She snorted. 'Have a look through the brochure and let me know what you think. I'm certain I got your size right, but if they chaff I'll kiss it better.' She blushed bright scarlet and put the note back in the envelope.

OG looked at her expectantly.

"Seems I now have my own line of underwear?"

How . . . intimate. And 'I'm certain I got your size right'! She still hadn't forgotten his 'Do I make you horny, baby?' from the car, and his face inches from hers. Lord, she wished she could go back and slap him. How did he manage to make her flustered?

The next box contained no note but a black satin set of Pirate Queen branded knickers and bra, which she had to admit she also liked, especially as the motif had been used as the clip for the straps. The next contained a brochure that made her groan. Was he for real? Did people really want poses of her in bronze or stone in their gardens, presiding over their spring blooms like a deity of spring?

"I think the world is mad," she said.

"About you," OG finished.

She opened the lid of the final box OG handed her and noticed there was a much smaller box inside that said, 'Open me last', so she put it on her lap. Inside were some more brochures, showing pictures of beaches and palm trees – it looked like paradise. Then she opened the card and read: 'You'll need a holiday when the tour is over. Have a look through and choose somewhere. Let me know when you get back.' Would she really be going on holiday! Right now that was all the incentive she needed to keep battling her way through the hectic schedule!

"Oh good! Are we going on holiday?" he asked.

"Yeah, I guess 'we' are." She rolled her eyes at his boyish enthusiasm as he picked up one of the destination brochures. "You'll get paid to accompany me?"

"I would still go if I wasn't getting paid. But don't tell my boss that!" OG winked at her and she laughed.

She looked down, realised the smaller box was still in her lap, and pulled out a white t-shirt. Opening it up she saw black and gold writing: 'Do I make you horny, baby? Do I?' "Oh Lord!" When she turned it around, she saw that '100% Shagadelic' was printed on the back, and exclaimed, "Oh Lord!" even louder.

"Are you really going to wear that?"

She laughed at OG's face. "Damn straight. I hope he's got it in a catalogue somewhere – I might want another one! I'm off to get ready. How long until we leave?"

"Almost three hours, so don't rush. And give me a shout if you want another sandwich."

"I'm not really that hungry, but thanks."

She strolled off, taking the t-shirt with her.

OG shook his head. If he didn't know better, he'd say Blackmoor had it real bad.

MISSING HER WASN'T getting any easier. It didn't help that every day there was a news item about her. The reception she was getting in the countries she was performing in was absolutely amazing, and the people wanted a chance to show her how they felt, turning out in droves and shouting themselves hoarse at her arrival and departures. And she was magical, doing spontaneous things like stopping the car and getting out to say hi to a group of girls who had all got themselves a Butterfly costume with sequins, like one of hers, and were wearing curly blonde wigs and shades. She had a photo with them, and signed their banner, and then stopped to talk to a group of visitors in wheelchairs, leaving with tears in her eyes that the cameras didn't miss. Kids, adults – it didn't matter, she was just herself, and treated everyone with the same genuine appreciation and the people loved her. The media did too. She was their favourite topic of conversation, and it was driving him mad missing her so much.

Business was crazy busy, but he was more concerned with her, with them, and what might be if . . . if a lot of things. He'd spoken to Donny a few times, as he'd been calling for updates on how she was, and to get order some pictures and a statue for the Capello garden – at a special, heavily negotiated rate, of course! But then she hadn't called him either, despite him telling her she could? He'd enjoyed watching the shows, and seeing her potter about on camera at home, but he wanted to hear her voice, wanted to know what she'd thought of the gifts. He knew she liked the t-shirt, as she'd worn it quite a lot – a cheeky smile on her lips as the press and fans called out to her about it!

They were six weeks in, and it looked like there were going to be three extra dates added so the tour ended in Vegas, where it had started. All of the comments were flattering; but he liked the 'a show to rock your soul' best, because despite the huge audiences, the fact she'd done it countless times, she always managed to make it special, her own emotions touching everybody's soul. That was the general consensus of those interviewed afterwards. There had also been reports of a drop in crime in the cities she was visiting while she was there, and less fighting, and no traffic problems or arguments in and around the shows. Was she really as powerful an influence on people?

"Sir."

"Yes, Mac?" Daryl took the call.

"I have a box here. I've checked it over and it's not ticking or anything – it's from Mysty. Do you want me to bring it up?"

A gift? No one gave him gifts! He just bought everything. What a surprise!

"Yes. I think we're past the trying to kill each other stage."

"I think she'd rather do it in person."

Since when did his bodyguard decide to exercise his sense of humour?

"Thank you, Mac, for that amazing insight. Just bring the box in."

A grinning Mac appeared a few minutes later. It was quite a big box, and the accompanying suits laid it on Daryl's desk at his prompting. They then left, leaving the two men facing each other.

"You know what's in it?" Daryl asked.

"No, sir. But it's certainly nothing dangerous. It's been scanned."

Daryl stood, not sure what to do with a present. It was a big white box, just like the ones he'd sent her. He lifted the lid and leaned in, and stepped back in surprise as a series of balloons floated out and drifted up to his high ceiling, all of them cream and metallic blue – wonderful choice of colours. Encouraging. But when had he ever had balloons before? And how was he going to get them down!

He picked up the small gold envelope and pulled out the message: 'I decided these were long overdue. Sadly, I can't be sure I got the size right, so these are just a pair for you to put on the wall in that empty space above your bed, to make sure everyone who visits it knows they are in the presence of greatness. Let me know what size you'd like. I can get some more. If they chaff, I know you have lots of women who'll kiss it better for you.' Underneath was the signature he knew as well as his own.

He was smiling before he'd even picked up the tissue-wrapped item in the bottom of the box. Pulling the paper off, he saw a framed pair of dark blue pants – boxers, to be precise – with 'Stud Muffin' on the front in gold, over the top of a pair of crossed lightning bolts: Zeus; very nice. Around the waistband read, 'The man, the myth, the legend', with downward pointing arrows in cream and gold stitching. It was the most outrageous thing he had ever seen, and he laughed. Actually, and properly laughed.

"What is it, sir? Not a framed picture of the Lamborghini?"

"No. Nothing quite so tame, Mac." He handed over the gold-framed picture and watched his bodyguard's face. "She has threatened before to get me some; it seems she's decided now was the right time."

There was a moment of silence, and then, for the first time in a good long time, Mac actually laughed too, and then laughed until he had to sit down.

"I didn't think it was quite that funny."

"No, no, not at all, sir." Mac tried to compose himself. And failed, wiping a tear from his eye he had laughed so hard.

"I rather think you need to find something excruciatingly dull to do so you stop laughing. It would be a shame if I had to fire you."

Mac got the message, his smile irrepressible, and went to the door, shutting it behind him. Man, that girl. She might be trouble, but she sure was fun to have around. Finally, his boss had met his match! He'd been waiting years to see it happen, and the result was priceless.

In his office, Daryl rewrapped the frame and put it back into the box. He closed the lid. It would go on the wall somewhere. It would never fail to make him smile.

He pressed the button he had long wanted to press, knowing now he had a perfect excuse. Six rings later, the screen flashed up with a picture at the other end, and there she was, hair all mussed.

"I really fucking hope this important. Have you any idea what the time is?" she squinted at the screen – not such a good start.

"I forgot about the time difference! What is it? 3am?"

"Close enough. So, Stud Muffin, now we're awake, what can we do for you?" She leaned back, feet going up on the table, another cheeky smile on her face.

"I was calling to thank you. Truly the best underwear I've ever had sent to me."

"Are the balloons all over your office?"

"Yes, they are definitely all over the office. Everyone who comes in will think it's my birthday."

"Well, I've probably missed one or two, so take it as a belated birthday present."

"When's your real birthday?" he asked.

"Doesn't matter. The one on my papers does just fine." The humour was still there, but he heard the warning.

"How are you doing? You haven't called me."

"Haven't you got enough to do? You're so busy? I'm not sure I'm high on your list."

He looked at her with quiet amazement. The one woman who he did give a damn about, and wanted to call him, and she was shrugging off his attention like an unwanted sweater. So that was why she hadn't called: she didn't think she was important enough.

"You're my favourite wall-filler. I like pictures of you much more than my usual art, which is far more expensive. You save me money."

"I think I'm also making you lots of money as well."

"Your financial portfolio is looking very healthy, too."

"You know I'm not interested in that."

When would she ever care about money?

"So, how are you? OG was getting a bit worried . . . Baden says your weight has stabilised, though."

"Yeah, well, guess I'm not as good at whizzing around on a private jet as you yet."

They talked some more, exchanging views on the underwear that had been received and just what precisely they thought the other should do whilst wearing it – which surprised him. Was she really so naughty underneath that guard she put up to protect herself?

But then she suddenly said, "Now, was there anything else, or can I go back to bed, because I know you have work to do and I don't think it's a good idea for you to get so excited. Besides, I have some much-needed sleep to get so–"

"How charming. I'm being dismissed," he teased, but he'd seen the sudden wariness in her face. There was only so much teasing and sexual innuendo she could take before she felt it was getting out of control and she didn't know where to go with it.

"You can press Disconnect on me if you'd rather."

He smiled. "You get some rest and I'll speak to you soon."

"Well, you know, if I can fit you in." She rolled her eyes at her own sarcasm. "Good luck with those balloons."

She pressed Disconnect and was gone.

Fifteen minutes and forty-two seconds. He felt so much better for talking to her. Except he had a hard on and it was eleven in the morning. He looked up. What was he going to do with the balloons? Then he smiled. Nothing right now, they could stay, and anyone who asked would get the truth: the most famous girl on the planet had sent him a gift.

DARYL BLACKMOOR WASN'T the only person missing her. There was someone on the other side of a few oceans who was also impatient to get her messages.

She had got used to the one-sided conversation Raju persisted in continuing with her, telling her anything and everything: updates on his calculations, algorithm theories and matrices… But with every message came some mention of The Butterfly or The Mystery Queen as she travelled the world on tour, his amazement at the moments that made the global headlines making her heart pinch, because she knew those moments too…from the inside. Part of her so wanted to tell him, just get it over with, and more than once her hands had hovered over the keys, waiting for the words to come, but each time she would adjust her reply to something non-committal and short.

She realised he probably didn't know or realise just how much he sounded like a groupie. He didn't have lots of friends, and said his family didn't talk to him, so she was getting his full inner dialogue as prose. Nearly every day. An amazing insight into a teenage boy she'd never met. How useful it would be if the other males in her life were so forthcoming with information…

His long messages put hers to shame. And then there was the irony that she was so available for everyone else, appearing on every social media platform and numerous TV channels, and yet didn't have the time or energy left to message friends.

It's so exhausting, this life. No one ever really tells you that.

Her eyes dropped with her heart as another Raju message popped up on her screen, the other nineteen stacked up on top of each other on her handheld.

I should have told him before the tour.

"Showtime, superstar!"

The voice came from one of the studio team, a silhouette in headphones backlit by the bright studio lights, and it startled her. But it brought her back. Back into the glitz and glamour. She thought of Daryl. Saw flashes of him and their meetings, the cameras, the screaming fans. It felt a world away from the quiet, cosy chats she and Raju had shared in her little apartment on her first computer. All that seemed so innocent and childlike now. So simple. So not her life as it was now.

How could he ever understand? But was it wrong to assume he wouldn't?

Passing her handheld to OG, who was hovering close by, watching everything and everyone, a deep inhale-exhale steadied her. Behind the steely calm, however, was the invisible realisation that her commitment to her career had become more than her commitment to friendships.

I don't have the emotional energy and resilience to tell him right now. If he gets upset or angry, I'll get upset too...and make mistakes. I don't want to fuck up on stage. He wouldn't understand that right now, because he doesn't have a job. But he's ok, isn't he, chatting to me like this?

It had to be okay.

Seems there was no other choice.

Was there another choice?

HE HEARD A door open and shut and, as the heels on the floor approached, he finally glanced up: a new addition, and he was curious. He'd chosen her from a picture, and this was her first night; but he didn't really like choosing from pictures, so he had another in reserve. He saw lots of platinum blonde curls, cut to her shoulders, the knee-length charcoal coat and black stockings and heels. He had long ago perfected the art of domination, and this would be no different.

She stopped a good few metres from him. They were always a little nervous, a little awed and wary, afraid of displeasing him when they met him for the first time. It was like breaking in a new horse.

He gestured and the coat was undone and slipped off to dangle from a finger, exposing the generous cleavage emerging from the constraints of the corset which tapered to a slim waist and the curve of her hips. To most men, a centrefold; to him, it was just wrong. He walked over to her, slowly, trying to work out why he didn't like what he saw. She was very lovely, but…he knew she was feeling self-conscious under his silent scrutiny, not knowing what to expect either.

A second gesture and she began to unlace the corset, but it was too hurried and too…inexperienced. And then he realised the source of his discontent.

"They're fake, aren't they?"

He knew real breasts. These weren't. And, just like the painted lips, he found them unappealing. She opened her mouth to reply, but he held up a finger and pointed at the door. She stood frozen for a few seconds, stunned by the abrupt dismissal. And then she grabbed her coat and left. Oh, the shame of feeling his rejection.

Daryl poured himself another brandy, pressed a button to see the other candidate sitting waiting, reading a magazine. She popped her bubble-gum, went back to chewing. No. Definitely not.

He scrolled for a number and pressed Dial.

"Hello?"

"Leanne."

"Mr Blackmoor?" A hint of disbelief, but underlined with warmth.

"Not forgotten me, then."

"Of course not, never. Just surprised."

"Are you available?"

"For you? Of course. When were you thinking?"

"How soon can you get here?"

"Same address?"

"Indeed."

"Twenty minutes."

"I'll tell Mac to expect you."

Disconnect.

One of the few women who had never disappointed him. Despite her one-time dalliance with the press, his monitoring observers reported she had otherwise lived a steady life, investing most of her wealth and enjoying the apartment he'd given her. Now she only took the most exclusive clients, and charged the most exorbitant prices.

He took up his preferred position, leaning against the wall looking over his city at night, the skyscrapers and the lights, the reflections in the pool. Mysty liked swimming. Perhaps he could persuade her to visit him one day for an afternoon by the pool?

A door opened and shut and, again, heels sounded on the floor.

"What the hell are you wearing?" he asked instantly, not sure how he felt about seeing it on another . . . but it did make the fantasy easier to conjure. She was wearing the Butterfly's outfit from the 'Back in Black' return performance, alluring in the sexy, dominatrix-style that suited his powerful tigress so well. Leanne had curled her hair, too, and she was wearing shades. It was the wrong colour completely, but then nothing ever came close to Mysty's vibrant gold, so that didn't matter.

She pushed the shades up and looked at him with a hint of defiance, eyes bright, not retreating.

"I thought you might like it," she purred. "Seeing as she hasn't given you what you want yet."

Leanne wasn't stupid, and she obviously hadn't missed the attention he paid his golden girl. But to get his attention like only one other young woman ever had, was stealing the thunder from the original queen of drama herself, the one and only Butterfly.

"Is that so."

It wasn't a question, and he prowled around her, close enough so that she could sense the tension. The sexual magic was there, already in the air, and she knew she'd won. *Oh God,* she thought, *a few hours with him, to make up for all the useless couplings since leaving his employ.*

Her coat was flicked from her grasp, and he walked her backwards until she felt the backs of her thighs against the familiar table.

"My outfit is a little different," she said, eyes locked onto his, seeing the lust.

He could guess: an entrance, just where it needed to be. He raised an eyebrow.

She knew his Butterfly-Pirate-Queen wasn't a shrinking violet; she'd seen the huge picture of those world-famous indigo eyes on the wall, seen the mischief and the energy. And she knew what this man liked. With deft fingers she unbuttoned and unzipped him, taking the long length of him in her hand, feeling him harden even more as she did so. She then knelt down and kissed from the base to the tip, feeling his hands in her hair as she flicked her tongue in the spot she knew he loved. God, she was wet just thinking about what he'd do next; and, sure enough, he pulled her up, turned up and bent her over the table, found the secret entrance and entered her.

She'd never forgotten what it was to feel the heat and size of him inside her, and the pleasure throbbed through her body, emanating from her core. A moan of pleasure escaped as he grasped her wrists and pulled them behind her. She laid her head on the table and gave herself up to whatever he wanted, loving every flex of his hips, so sure and strong. She knew she was gasping, knew he would soon let go. She didn't want it to end!

But then he stopped, pulled out, and she wanted to scream in frustration – what was he doing?

"Get on the table and turn over."

Her entire body was trembling as she did so, and she pulled her knees up as he moved her thighs apart. And the all the naked splendour of him climbed up onto the table with her, the muscles burned into her mind rippling and solid.

He then reached up and put the shades back over her eyes. She was the wrong woman, and she knew it, but she didn't let that detract from what was about to happen, not for a moment. He pushed her legs up and further apart, taking in every ounce of her flesh with hungry eyes. And she begged. And he did as she pleaded, thrusting into her with a carnal lust that made her shout out. She tried to keep her eyes open, to see his pleasure, to claim even a little of it as her own, but her own pleasure was too great and her climax convulsed her hips against his with such force his own followed soon after, the shriek of her own pleasure not deafening her to the deep groan of satisfaction that left his lips as he shuddered and released himself deep inside her.

She opened her eyes to see sweat glistening on his skin.

"Don't take anything off, we've not finished yet," he said and walked away, returning with swimming shorts on. Letting himself outside, he dived into the pool.

As he swam she moved off the table and sat on one of the sofas until he reappeared, hair slicked back, a towel round his hips. She followed him when he gestured.

How she had missed his bedroom. Now redecorated and refurbished, it still had the colossal bed – of which she had many happy memories. He lay face down on the bed and, willingly, she knelt beside him.

"She must be quite something, to make you want her so much," she said, and massaged his back with rhythmic hands.

"She is."

"So why?" she dared ask, emboldened by his answering, albeit two words.

"She refuses."

"She refuses? Do you want me to tell her what she's missing?"

"It wouldn't make much difference." He sighed and rolled over, leaning back on pillows, looking at her with those green, unfathomable eyes. "She's not impressed with money. Or won over by looks. She has numerous reasons not like me. Aside from which she loves Donny Capello."

"I'm sure an hour in your bed would change her mind."

His eyes lightened slightly at her bold words in his defence. "I offered, but still she refused."

He then raised a hand and rested one fingertip on her lips and she went still. She had never been kissed by him. She knew why. It was too personal.

"I trust you can keep this between us. I have tolerated you talking before; I won't tolerate it again. I hope you don't need me to demonstrate the seriousness of my request."

She shivered at the threat that was as clear to her as a gun pointed at her head.

"No. I swear. Not one word. I wouldn't."

"Good." His fingertip trailed down between her breasts, and she dared not move, feeling its progress all the way to where she was still wet, still wanting. "You seem to be enjoying yourself. I do hope you've missed me."

One mocking eyebrow raised, but she didn't care, as he slipped his fingers inside her.

"No one does it like you do," she breathed. "Everyone has been a disappointment to me so far, despite the vast sums of money they pay."

It was a comfort to know one woman on the planet thought of him like that, and that he hadn't lost any of his skills – skills he was quite determined to maintain and hone until he could use them on the one girl who consistently refused him and make her weep for release.

"Time to be a little more selective with your clientele – you don't need the money."

"Perhaps I should. If you have a twin brother, do send him round." She took his hand from between her legs and lifted it to her lips, sucking the fingers he had used to tease her, aware he was watching her intently.

Her boldness told him she was willing to play the game at whatever level he wanted, and once more aroused he closed his eyes as a leg went over his hips and she lowered herself onto his erection.

"She is very young," she said.

"I know," he groaned as she slid her hand behind to gently grasp his balls. His hands went behind his head, letting her take command.

"She'll know nothing of how to please a man."

"She learns everything very quickly."

"Is she as beautiful as she looks in pictures?"

"More than beautiful. Flawless."

"You have your goddess, then."

He didn't reply.

His hardness encouraged her to move faster, and she was free to do as she pleased as he lay back, eyes closed, until finally he pushed her over and thrust into her for the final climax, heat from both their bodies molten and intense for a few breathless seconds. She was still returning to earth when she felt him push up and away, abruptly and without a word.

"How much do you think I owe you for this evening's entertainment?" he asked, when showered and seated in front of a computer screen. He didn't look round.

"I don't know." She had stripped off the costume and was seated on the edge of the bed in the black robe she had bought with her.

"You're a paid escort, you should know what you charge." He sounded impatient.

"$20,000?"

He didn't answer immediately, eyes on the information on screen.

"If you can keep your lips busy, and make it last half an hour, I'll double that."

She knew what he meant, amazed he wanted more. He was no average man; she'd forgotten just how not average he was.

"Can I get drink first?" she asked softly, knowing he didn't like human needs getting in the way of his wishes.

"Yes. Fetch me a beer as well, would you."

She rolled off the bed, glancing at the clock – almost 2am. Interesting that she was still here, used to being shown the door as soon as he was satisfied.

A beer in one hand, a computer panel in the other, and a head of curls bobbing over his crotch, Daryl Blackmoor felt decidedly decadent. He hadn't planned to be quite so . . . taken over with the night of sensual delight. He wondered whether Mysty would wear that outfit for him, if he asked. One day? Maybe? Not that he cared. He longed to see her naked, knew he would love her naked, as her perfection was always such a miracle to him. Oh, that body. How it held so many secret marvels.

He leaned his head back, daring to imagine the dark curls were golden, and there was a tingling in his spine, a surge of desire so strong . . . He would call her tomorrow and finalise the tour, and the dates, and then he would at least have a set day when he would see her again. He had a great deal planned for her when she got back, but with a bit of a rest period in there as well – she'd earned it, there was no doubt about that.

He finished the last of his beer and tilted his hips a little, enjoying the extended torture of her clever tongue and lips on him. Leanne had been willing, *very willing*, and hadn't disappointed him. She knew what she was doing, no mistake, and even her questions about his golden girl didn't bother him.

Her naked body arched over him, to get the best angle, her glorious femininity in his face. Putting the computer panel down, he stroked her pussy, felt her shudder, heard her moan, her movements getting faster. Boy, she was good. He leaned forward just a fraction and slipped the neck of the empty beer bottle inside her, and she startled in a moment of surprise at the cool glass, but she moved against it, like he knew she would, using it to goad herself to a climax. God, that was a turn on. She gripped his thighs, and kept him deep in her throat as he climaxed.

And then he gave her what she wanted, using long, skilled fingers, and felt her panting breaths of warm air against his belly as she too surrendered to her orgasm.

"The money is in your account. Mac will make sure you are taken home."

It was the dismissal she had been dreading. She moved off the bed, collecting her clothes and going to the door without another word. There was nothing to say. She couldn't complain, and she'd got more than she'd hoped for, both physically and financially. She knew it was all business to him, and satisfying his body was a way of life, efficiently done, calculated and timed to perfection.

But what was he hoping for from this girl who refused him, who had apparently trashed his cars to the tune of $2 million, and argued with him to his face? She knew one thing: she couldn't wait to find out.

HE PLACED THE call he'd been waiting to make all day, recalling his evening with Leanne, and not sure if he was irritated at how well she had read him, or flattered by what she'd said at Mysty's refusal: 'Shall I tell her what she's missing?' Lord, that would get him into all kinds of trouble.

The Receive button was pressed at the other end and there she was, lounging back in the wide chair, one leg dangling over the side. 'Do I make you horny?' read loud and bold across her t-shirt.

"Mysty."

"Daryl."

He liked her using his name. So few people did, that if anyone heard her use it, they would know something had shifted between them.

"How are you?"

Eyes bright, she held up a newspaper: 'Seven New Tour Dates!' "Seven!"

"It's not seven."

"But you want to add some?"

"That was why I was calling, amongst other things, to talk it over with you."

"You've already set the wheels in motion – why talk to me about it?"

"It's clear the show is a big hit, and that's down to you." She snorted at his attempt to implicate her in the situation. "Nothing is booked yet, no tickets are on sale, so I'd like us to come to an agreement that you're happy with."

"I was happy with ending the tour and coming home." Eyes implored him to understand. "I just want to stop. You can't just pull an extra ten miles out the bag when the guys are on the final lap of the marathon, it's not fair."

"I know, and I know you're all tired. I know you want and need a rest, and you will get one. Have you decided on a holiday?"

"I like the pictures of Barbados. It looks like paradise should look."

"Then I'll get something booked. Just think, I get to take you shopping again, for holiday clothes."

"How about I take myself shopping and put it on your account?"

"What if I need your help buying holiday clothes?" he asked. And he was serious. When was the last time he'd been on holiday?

"You're the style guru who never has a crease out of place. What do you need me for?"

"I'm out of practice. I could do with a second opinion."

"Well, I guess that's fair, but I don't know why you want my opinion. I'm hardly an expert."

"You're hardly a novice, either. Your costumes are second to none and your personal style is a big hit. You have a natural eye for co-ordination. I trust you not to choose me a pink suit." His smile almost made her smile.

"I don't see why you have to come, anyway." She eyed him suspiciously.

"Because I need a holiday too."

"Or is it because you don't trust OG to keep the poodle leash tight enough, or because you don't want to miss out on any photo opportunities of me in a bikini?"

"There are nude beaches. Don't feel you have to wear a bikini."

"Very funny."

"It's an ideal time for me to absent myself as well, get away from the press and cameras," he said, getting practical again. "You can enjoy some time away from the cameras, too, which I'm sure you need."

She thought about his answer, unwillingly swayed to see some logic in it. He didn't speak again, just waited calmly for her to reach her conclusion.

"So how many shows?"

He breathed out. Donny was right, she could be reasonable if spoken to with respect.

"Three. New York, Washington, and the final one in Vegas. I chose these because I think it would complete the circle well to end up in New York, and Harlem will be very big audience. Washington as well. And to finish in Vegas, where you started, will tie it all off properly. It's a very significant finish. I doubt anyone will try and top what you've done, so this is a last goodbye, in a way, to MJ. You're the only person able to do that. I know it's not a small challenge, but there is no one better to achieve it."

She was watching him closely, but he was used to her scrutiny. He wasn't lying to her; she could look as hard as she liked, she'd find only truth.

"Whatever you want, if it will help persuade you, you only have to ask," he added.

She contemplated his offer.

"I'd like a drum kit."

"That's it?"

"Well, I'd like a really awesome drum kit, to match the black Pirate Queen guitar, and for one of the apartment rooms to be soundproofed and a sound studio put in, with the full catalogue of every song ever, with all the latest gadgetry so I can work on my music at home. Does that sound better?"

"Much better."

"And can I have another one of these t-shirts? A different colour perhaps?"

"It looks very good on you. But where does one write the answer to the question?"

"Answer on a postcard to my LA address. I'm hoping I'll be able to see the place before Christmas 2045 rolls around."

He heard her loud and clear. "Mysty, it's an extra . . . twelve days, and the very next day you can be back on a plane to LA. I'm cancelling Celeste performances for two weeks, as well. This is my call. You need a proper break, so you're going to have one."

"Wow. Are you really Daryl Blackmoor? You're not a clone?" She peered at him closely on the screen. "Seriously, are you alright? Have you had eight women in your bed again or something, because you're looking disgustingly cheerful."

"No, I haven't. I've barely seen a woman I've been so busy. I've almost forgotten what they look like."

She laughed. "You couldn't possibly forget."

"Why not?"

"Because you have so many goddamned pictures of me everywhere!"

"But you're not any old woman."

"No?"

"No."

"What then?"

"I'll tell you when you get back."

"You're infuriating sometimes."

"Only sometimes?"

"*All* the time." She wanted to throw something at him and laugh at the same time. "You haven't done anything to the apartment, have you? I'm not going to come back and find everything changed again?"

"Everything is just how you left it, except for one extra picture on the wall. The cleaners have been in every two days keeping everything spotless in your absence."

"What is the picture of?"

"You."

"Not you wearing your Stud Muffin undies?"

"No."

"Because if it was I would get on a plane right now. I could do with a giggle!"

"Your flattery is, as ever, like sunlight on my soul. It's a picture I thought you'd like. It captures you very well, but if you hate it you can take it down."

"I'm curious to see what you've chosen. How many pictures are there now?"

"Thousands."

"And how many pictures have you got?"

"Millions."

She laughed.

"How's Donny?" he ventured.

"I've not had much time to speak to him and . . . and I'm tired of long distance, let alone longer-distance. I'd rather see him, so we . . . don't talk that much at the moment."

"I'm sure he understands."

She looked away, obviously not comfortable talking about it. "Anything new and amazing I should know about?" she then asked.

"I have your presidential dispensation."

"No!"

"Yes."

"Really? Oh my goodness! How did you do that?"

"I showed him the data, and the footage. There is a price, however."

"Oh no. Here we go. I get turned into government experiment." She leaned back and closed her eyes, brow furrowing in anticipation.

"Nothing like that. He wants you to go to Washington and meet him."

"You mean I don't . . . he won't try and put me in a jar and pull my wings off?" The fear was real. She was too much of a realist not to have identified a possible threat – and no doubt her experience in the clinic had underlined that – so he owed it to her to put her mind at rest.

"No." He sat forward and leaned his elbows on the desk. "The president thinks – along with everyone else – that you're rather fantastic. He really would like a chance to meet you. He might even be at the last Vegas show, but he's not sure of his schedule. I can assure you there is nothing untoward, no hidden tricks, nothing on the agenda. I've no doubt one day you might be asked to help with some kind of research, but nothing and no one is going to attempt anything while…"

"While what?" she prodded gently, their eyes locked. He could tell she was holding her breath, one hand curled into a tight fist of tension.

"While I'm watching your back. Despite what you think, I'm not a complete waste of space who spends his entire life eyeing up women. You know how Donny's rule of law works in Vegas? I have as much influence, albeit of a different kind, right to the highest levels of government."

She looked at him, with a depth he hadn't seen before. "I don't think you're a waste of space who eyes women up all day." The depth was still there, and he wondered what she would say next. "I know you only chase women after hours, when the office is shut."

He closed his eyes, spirits dropping, fearing he would never win her good opinion. Was she being serious, or . . .?

"Daryl." He opened them again, a soft voice encouraging him to raise his head again. "I'm joking."

"Really?"

"Yes! I repeat: I don't think you're a waste of space! I've told you before I don't know how you do what you do, as there's just so much of it. And . . . I appreciate you watching my back, even though you're just eyeing up my ass. I know I…didn't know who you were before, but I have a better idea now."

"You said all that without swearing," he said, quietly, teasing, but instantly the shutters were up and the moment was broken. *Shit.* "I was joking, Mysty. I'm just aware you see me, and the world, very differently to most people."

"And that makes me wrong?"

"No, it just makes it harder to understand you sometimes, or for you to understand me. But anything is possible if you want it badly enough."

"What do you want badly enough?"

"Home. A free day. To know what it is to relax. You?"

"The same."

"You'll be home soon." Where was home for her? New York? Vegas? LA?

"I can't wait."

"I've got to go, kitten, there's…at least a dozen things to do before heading to the airport and–" Had he really just called her kitten? And she'd not taken issue with him for that?

"I understand, you go do your…keeping the world turning on its axis thing. Just send me the details of the extra dates and consider them done."

She was absolutely the one person in the world he knew he could trust to do exactly what she said, no matter what the problems or issues that might arise. She even lounged back in the chair like she'd been doing it all her life, making him smile; how quickly she had found her feet.

"I should hire you for my office. I could relax, then, knowing everything was getting done as it should be."

"Nah. You'd fire me in five minutes for breaking the dress code. And I'd have to sue to you for sexual harassment." Her eyes twinkled with amusement.

"I'll see you in Vegas."

"You're seeing the show again?"

"Don't you think I should?"

"I'm just…surprised you have the time."

"I'll make the time."

She looked away. Was he for real? Was this friendliness an act to keep her happy and docile, to keep her performing because he could make mountains of money because of her? She remembered how he had called her an 'asset'. Her stomach lurched at the thought.

She reached forward and pressed Disconnect, leaving Daryl with a blank screen and a sense of immediate emptiness. His treatment of her, the words he'd said to her…it was coming back to haunt him. Again. Dammit. He forced himself to move and sent over the dates, venues, details for her accommodation, etc., to OG so all the arrangements could be made, copying her in.

Would she ever trust him?

THE LAST NIGHT of the tour, and it was being broadcast so millions of people could watch it from their homes, too. It wouldn't affect download or DVD sales, as this was going to be something everyone wanted to own, to know they'd been a part of whether at the live show or watching live on their TVs.

He'd watched her arrival. The girl who had claimed to be nothing who now had people so excited some of them cried, who evoked such emotion, such joy and passion through music. There really were scenes captured on film of fans so ecstatic it was reminiscent of the devotion inspired by MJ himself. He'd watched as O'Grady had opened the door, grey suits everywhere, security holding back the crowds. The red carpet dark, edged with gold, and the assembled company of fans and press waited for only one person. Emerging from the car head to toe in pale pearlescent gold, including the trademark top hat and cane, she shimmered like something ethereal. She wore no jewellery – not even the DC bracelet?

At the top of the steps she turned, her face composed. What would she do?

The red lips curved into a smile, and she dropped into a graceful bow to her collective, hushed audience.

"Have an amazing night, everybody," she said, with a smile that sent them into rapturous applause.

"I always knew she had it in her." Daryl turned to the man beside him.

"First time I heard her sing, when she won that school talent show, she was so calm, so cool about everything. I'm glad to see her fulfilling her potential. One day she might even realise how brilliant she is."

"One day. Have you spoken to her?" This time Daryl looked straight at Donny.

"Last night. Not that she was up to much conversation as she was so tired and busy with the set up and preparations. And sad, I think, that it's over." Donny returned Daryl's stern look. "She needs a rest, a proper rest. I hope you haven't got any new hoops planned for her to jump through."

"I have cancelled Celeste for two weeks, and I'm considering adding a third week to give her a real chance to recoup. Her weight has dropped again, which always means she's more tired than anything else. Can you believe she turned down pizza in favour of sleeping?" Daryl didn't see the amused expression on Donny's face, but it was tinged with concern. "She will want to see you."

"I know."

"And? Will she?"

"Don't press me, Daryl, I don't have answers yet. I know what she wants."

"Enjoy the show."

"I always do."

Donny smiled, but there was a touch of sadness in it, and he left, Paulo glancing back at Daryl with a look he couldn't fathom.

Daryl looked back at the scene below. What would she do tonight that would be different?

WITH THE PRESIDENT of the United States of America beside him, there was an almost surreal atmosphere in the exclusive box. And it was all for her, for the spectacle she had created. She had performed the world's favourites – his favourites – 'Smooth Criminal', 'Bad', 'Working Day and

Night', 'Thriller', 'Beat It', 'Don't Stop Still You Get Enough', 'Working Day and Night', and the style, the speed, the ingenuity, the use of her body as an act all in itself as she had danced and tapped and moon-walked her way through each song… Well, she was just breathtaking, and he'd never get tired of watching her. He knew she'd held nothing back, had gone all out to make the most of this last show.

But now they had come to the last song.

He and the world waited patiently for her to reappear. And then there she was, dressed as she had been when she'd arrived, except that the top hat was gone. Against the huge backdrop of famous scenes of Mr Michael Jackson himself, she observed her audience with a face full of emotion, remembering this last night, treasuring each and every face looking back at her in expectation.

"So…" She attempted a small smile, but she seemed a little tense. There was utter silence. "Here we are, thirty-eight shows later, over two hundred hours of stage time, to millions of people, after innumerable hours spent rehearsing and practicing and preparing." She walked slowly along the front of the stage, thoughtful. "You think it was worth it?" She glanced at the audience and the cheer was amazing, a vibration going through the entire building. "Well, I'm glad you think so," she said, and they laughed. "But the reason we're here…isn't me. It's him." She kept her eyes on the audience, but pointed behind her. An image of Michael Jackson, crisp and clear in black and white, appeared and then faded to be replaced with another. "I never came onto this stage thinking I could do this better than Michael, and it has been the greatest privilege to be the person who was able to finish what he started. I hope – *I really hope* – that all his fans believe I have tried to do his memory and his legacy justice, not just tonight, but every night."

She waited until the roars of acknowledgement subsided.

"Like all great men, he was a figure of controversy, both during and after his life, but there is no doubt that he was creative genius, and chose, wanted and loved sharing that gift. It was that passion which drove him to become the star he was, and always will be." The collage of images on the screens returned to a close-up shot of her. "Now I have to be honest, as I have a habit of being, that there were moments on this tour when I didn't want to do another show because I was so tired, and well, I just wanted to stop. But how could I let him down? And now, with it being the last night, I wish we could go back to the beginning and start all over again."

Every eye was on her, every ear wanting to hear this speech. Experience had taught the world that when she spoke, it was worth listening.

"I wasn't alive when Michael Jackson rose to greatness, and I didn't see the start or the peak of his career. I wasn't even alive when he died. But after living and breathing everything Michael Jackson since I first heard one of his songs on an old tape, I've watched TV footage, listened to every song available, and…well, I feel I know him – as crazy as that might sound. Does that sound crazy?"

The response from the audience was unanimous: no, that was not crazy. Daryl glanced at the president. He was riveted.

"And now…now it's the last night…and I feel like I'm letting go of someone I've carried around for months, because this is where it all ends. The party's over, the shows are finished. Costumes will go back in boxes. The seats will be empty. And it feels, in a way, like he will die again."

The screens went blank for a moment, creating a sense of loss, of emptiness. She turned away. The cameras scanned the audience. People were holding each other, some were crying, and Daryl had no doubt that she was crying too.

She turned back, her eyes bright. "But that's not true, is it? Because all of you out there, and everyone watching at home, will keep him alive. In each of you. Like I will. The fact you're listening to me, that you're all watching, proves that his music, his incredible dancing, his amazing clothes and videos, are immortal."

An image of Michael from the Man in the Mirror came up on screen.

"The reason I chose this song to finish the show is because I believe he sang this with complete belief. He struggled with his identity for a complex set of reasons, one of which was that he was so gifted and so sensitive. He was a dreamer, a visionary, a believer in a better world; he wanted happiness not tears, joy not sadness, and he did want a brighter future. And that is the message I hope you all remember. Not the big belts. Not even the huge shoulder pads. But this."

She paused, a soft smile on her lips.

"Ladies and gentlemen, I give you, one last time, Michael Jackson, the man and the legend. Long live the king."

She stepped back, directing eyes to the screen. She then backed away as the video began to play, leaving her audience captive, united, in the emotion she had created and the solace of Michael Jackson in one of his finest moments.

"YOU ALRIGHT, KIDDO?" OG, reliable and ever present, offered her a bottle of water as she wiped the tears from her face.

She needed to let it all go. And it was in her dressing room, alive with colour from a hundred costumes, lights and mirrors, that she leant her head on the desk, amid make-up and accessories, and wept, grieving for a man she would never meet, who she treasured and had brought to life.

She could hear the music; the voice that she knew so well it made her throat hurt. Would any of it ever be enough? Was she, too, destined to live a life in the spotlight and yet so alone? When would she get what she needed? Was this it, being so loved and adored, but always from a distance?

She looked down at Lazarus, who was leaning on her knee, trying to get under her hair to see her face. She leaned down and hugged him, loving him so much for never letting her down, never leaving her. She whispered quiet words of comfort, for both of them, and dried her face. She retrieved her top hat and cane, her shades too, and opened the door.

OG looked around instantly.

"I'd like to leave now."

"No problem. Cars are ready for you."

Trust OG to know she would want to get out of there. She didn't know what she would do without him. She squeezed his arm as she walked past, giving him a small smile of thanks that she knew he understood.

Like a queen she strode through the corridors, with her men around her, opening doors and always checking. She was glad to finally see the grand doors, the red carpet she had walked along in what seemed like minutes not hours ago. This was never going to be a quiet exit, and to slip out of a back door wouldn't have been fair on the fans, and she glanced over at OG, who could only shrug – they couldn't deny the fans or the press.

Mysty slowed, deciding to enjoy the last moments, imprint them on her mind. She gestured to OG, who gave her some space after receiving the all clear from his men outside. He knew what she had planned. One final gesture.

Illuminated by a hundred lights, she stepped calmly through the doors and stood on the top step. Instinctively, the crowd felt quiet. And then she threw up the cane, swept off her hat, performed an elegant final bow and then rose to catch the cane, the tip of which she brought down to the ground with a bang. Gold specks of light sprang into the air from the top of the cane, rising to dance above her like fireflies, creating a MY^2 symbol which hung magically above her.

She almost smiled as she heard the inward gasp of the crowd, but she wasn't done yet. She threw the cane through the gold lettering, and it shot upwards, and then the world burst apart in light and colour as fireworks took over the sky above Soleil in a formation she had designed: the initials MJ. As the crowd cheered themselves hoarse, she slipped away and into the car.

She knew there would be lots of parties out there now, that would probably continue till dawn rolled around, but it didn't appeal to have one of her own. She just wanted silence and rest.

"Want to stop off anywhere for food?" OG asked as she gazed out of the window.

"I just want to go to bed."

OG sighed. She really had given everything, and carried more around inside than she let on. He knew she was mourning for more than Michael Jackson. The sobs from her dressing room were deeper than that.

"And no calls, please. Not from anyone. And I mean *anyone*."

"Sure."

"And no one wake me up tomorrow. I'm sleeping in as long as I like."

"Good plan."

She pulled Lazarus closer. Almost there. Just a few minutes more. But it felt like a lifetime.

Finally the car stopped and she was hustled gently up the steps away from the reporters and the cameras held back by the thick wall of security.

"I'll send cereal up, and milk, just in case," OG said quietly, letting her go.

She might have heard him, he didn't know, as she headed up the stairs. And she might be the most talked about girl on the planet just at this moment, but she sure could do with someone. What a sadness that the man she loved, the one who claimed he loved her back, who wanted her kept safe and well, was never there for her. And the man who wanted her like nothing else, her esteemed manager, who could be there for her, was the one man she would never turn to.

Not even six months in, and another seven and a half years to go? OG wasn't sure she could handle it.

"WELL, MR BLACKMOOR, that was some show. And that's one amazing girl you've got there. Maybe I could borrow her for a while so she could write my speeches – what do you think?"

President Thomas Marshall stood up and everyone rose with him.

"I think she needs a bit of rest for a while, but I'll mention it to her. You'll see her soon, for the dispensation, so you could ask her yourself."

"Of course. Do you think she'll bring the leopard?"

"She rarely goes anywhere without Lazarus, and he doesn't like being away from her, so I assume so. He's very tame, and extremely well trained, so your security team need not worry."

They filtered out, the world suddenly exploding with noise somewhere far above them.

"Fireworks, sir. Mysty warned me earlier," Mac answered, seeing his boss's surprise. "She's obviously just left."

"Oh shame. I was hoping to see her tonight."

Marshal looked disappointed, and Daryl could sympathise; he'd hoped to see her backstage before she disappeared.

"I'm sure she's exhausted, sir. It'll be an early night for our golden girl," Daryl replied, leading them to the room where they would be served drinks and food well into the early hours of a VIP party. "You're glad you came?"

"Best show I've ever seen. Except for Celeste. But they're both very different. I couldn't choose between them."

"There's much more to come. I'll speak to you a little later, Thomas. I have a few calls to make."

Hands were shaken, and the twinkle in Marshall's eye told Daryl the president knew exactly who one of those calls would be to.

Daryl strode down the corridor to the director's office, empty and silent with everyone off celebrating elsewhere.

He put the call through.

"O'Grady?"

"Sir?"

"How is she?"

"Not all that good. She's upstairs. I've just checked on her and she's crying again. She didn't want anything to eat either."

"Crying *again*?"

"Yes. She locked herself in her dressing room after the show. Pulled it together long enough to give the fans and press one last Mysty-style surprise as she was leaving, and then went straight upstairs when we got back here. She's said she's not talking to anyone tonight; not you, or Donny, not anyone, or else I'd patch you through, sir."

"She needs some time alone, I understand. Try and get her to eat something, though."

"I'm sending up some of her favourites on a tray, so it's there if she chooses. A good night's sleep will work wonders, and she's requested a lie in. That and a good breakfast will see her right–"

"Sir?" Daryl heard a voice in the background.

"Yes, Lewis?"

"Erm, sir, surveillance have just phoned in…she's on the roof."

"On the roof!" O'Grady was immediately alarmed.

"Yes. Just…watching the stars."

"I'll see to it. You heard that, Mr Blackmoor, sir?"

"Yes. O'Grady..."

"She really wanted some space," O'Grady replied, anticipating his boss's fear that she would run. "I'll get her back inside, though. Any message for her?"

"No. I'll come in the morning."

"Yes. And enjoy your evening, sir. Great show."

"It was exceptional. Be gentle with her, O'Grady. I know you will."

"I always am, sir. Works far better than anything else."

Disconnect.

He put another call through.

"Bobby."

"Mr Blackmoor, sir! My goodness, I'm honoured! What can I do for you tonight? We're just getting tomorrow's print underway. We held back till after the show, to get the best coverage of it. I managed to watch some of it and I'm still on a high!"

Daryl smiled. His New York editor was always one hundred percent awake whatever time of day or night it was, and his enthusiasm was always welcome.

"Yes. Fantastic show. Tell me, what headline are you running?"

"We've gone with, 'The Greatest Tribute Ever'. That speech she gave, at the end, had two of my girls here in tears. Powerful stuff."

"Yes, it was. I'd like you to move that to one of the inside pages. I have a new headline for you."

"Which is?"

"Long Live the Queen."

There was a long pause. Bobby was too protective of his paper to run something he didn't like without a fight.

But then: "I like it! I do! I'm a bit disappointed I didn't think of that myself! The King of Pop, Michael Jackson, honoured by the Queen of Pop... Yep. No problem. I'll get it changed straight away."

"Make sure the advert for the DVD and downloads is in there, and only use the best pictures."

"Will do, sir."

"And send two copies to my residence in Vegas."

"Of course. And sir?"

"Yes, Bobby?"

"Do you know how she does that magic stuff, with the gold lights and everything?"

"I've not seen what she did tonight, but I know what you're talking about. She tells me it's not magic, it's very clever computer science. She is a genius with more than just her feet and her voice."

"Quite a woman."

"Indeed."

"Well if she needs a hard-working, slightly bald and not-so-handsome-any-more boyfriend, send her my way."

"I'll mention it to her."

Daryl had to smile. That was Bobby. Always the optimist.

"Well, you enjoy your evening, sir, and I'll get all this done."

"Thank you, Bobby."

Disconnect.

Redial.

"O'Grady?"

"Sir?"

"Is she still on the roof?"

"I'm negotiating at the moment. Stay on the line, and feel free to offer any advice." O'Grady sounded slightly frustrated; but Daryl knew it was concern, not annoyance. And his *advice*? About Mysty…?

"Mysty, would it be okay to stargaze another night, not right now? Kiddo, please, you need to sleep."

Daryl sat down at the computer and logged in. He could see O'Grady on the balcony.

"Why?"

"I know you need peace and quiet, but I think you need sleep more."

"Ten minutes."

"Five."

"I just want some peace! Why can't I have ten?"

"Seven."

"You've ruined it now!"

Suddenly she was there, landing with the ease, as if dropping thirty feet onto a balcony was nothing. She strode past O'Grady.

"I promise you'll feel better if you rest."

They were kind, patient words, but they didn't placate.

"You must get paid a hell of a lot to care so fucking much!" she growled, glaring at him.

"I get paid to keep you alive; the caring comes for free. If you want to talk, then you know I'll listen." A standoff. "I've had bigger arguments than this with much bigger people than you. You don't scare me in the least, so just sit your ass down and relax. There's nothing here to hurt you, okay?" Slowly he advanced on her. "Sit down and drink this." He held a glass of milk out.

"I feel sick."

"You always do when you get so upset. See, Lazarus is all worried about you, too."

The leopard jumped up next to her and clambered over her, and there was a low moan from the distressed girl hiding in his fur, forehead against his shoulder. And then she gathered the heavy animal into her arms and marched from the room, this time in the direction of her bed.

"Quite upset, then," Daryl commented quietly.

"Yes."

"Let me know how she is in the morning."

"Will do, sir."

"You did well. Consider your contract extended indefinitely."

Disconnect.

How could he enjoy his evening knowing she was suffering? She clearly needed to talk to someone, but who? Who could understand what she had to say? A girl so extraordinary, so alone? It seemed she didn't want sympathy or soft words; she wanted to be understood.

He was taken back ten years to the first massive achievement of his business career after his inheritance: the celebration dinner, with so many important people, the fine food and wine; the congratulations, speeches, polite words and polite applause. He'd just wanted to leave. How could anyone there – even Harvey – know how he'd felt? None of them knew the burden he carried. He'd wanted to get drunk, but couldn't. He'd wanted to go home, but couldn't. He'd wanted to shout in frustration, but there'd be no one to hear him. He'd needed the instinctive comfort of a mother, or the solid reassurance of a father, but there had been no one.

He knew what that loneliness felt like, and what it had done to him, and he didn't want the same for her.

But she didn't believe he could understand. Wouldn't let him in enough to give him a chance to prove her wrong. And he only had himself to blame, because of how he'd treated her in the beginning.

There was reparation to be made and re-learning for both of them.

She was strong. She would find her way through the night, and hopefully fall asleep soon enough. And in the morning...perhaps they could talk.

Until then, he leaned back as he watched the power of one girl who really did seem to have magic at her fingertips, watched the elegant bow, the golden flash, her signature and then the greater tribute to MJ in the fireworks. The perfect ending to a glorious beginning.

DARYL STRODE UP the steps of the elegant townhouse, pleased that he had bought it for her. She was still the same, though, as unchanged as any human could be moving from a small apartment to a spacious house. But then she was the same about everything, just delightfully honest and appreciative. The only thing that had changed was the swearing; it had definitely receded, and more of her natural English accent and grammar was coming to the fore, adding to the frank but friendly composure she maintained in public, and which won her so much respect from the press and public alike.

He couldn't have been prouder of her. Not that he said it, certainly not to her – she'd laugh in his face. How similar they were. Just as her despair the night before had confirmed their respective loneliness. Which was why he was so impatient to see her.

Mac followed him in. There were three suits in the hall, and all of them gave him nod, just as the two in the living room did, standing smartly to attention. In the kitchen, where he thought she'd be, he found

O'Grady sitting at the breakfast bar with a newspaper, toast and a cup of coffee, munching contentedly as he read. He looked up at the sound of approaching footsteps and finished his mouthful.

"Good morning, sir."

"O'Grady. No Mysty yet?"

"No. Seems she was serious about her lie-in. Which is good, she needed it. Would you like some breakfast? We have…almost everything." He waved a hand at the selection laid out on the shiny granite. Daryl knew it would all be fresh, and tasty – only the best for her, like himself – but right then he had no appetite. How long had he waited to be in the same room as her again?

"I'm fine, but a latte would be good."

Mac went to the espresso machine and started on one, asking O'Grady if he wanted a top up. Everyone seemed calm, relaxed.

"Was she alright last night?"

"Not a peep. First time in months, maybe even years, she's slept past 6 or 7am."

"Definitely a day for the diary. If I had one."

It was the voice he'd been waiting for, and Daryl turned his head to greet her.

"She walks! She talks!" O'Grady teased, hoping it would be received well. It was, and she raised a hand and waved.

"Are you hungry? I've got everything I could think of here in case you were."

"I'm starving. I'm just waking myself up. It's a long way from bed to here."

Mac put a coffee in front of Daryl and leaned against the kitchen unit with his own.

"So," she said, popping bread in the toaster. "You're here early."

"You disappeared last night without a word. I was concerned."

"But you liked the show?"

"The show was superb. As confirmed by the press and the collective opinion of the world." He passed the newspaper to her, revealing the headline.

She was suddenly wide awake.

"This means no run this morning, right?" She looked at OG. "Another treadmill day? How many are outside?" She buttered the toast.

"Probably about two hundred."

She groaned. "Please tell me you have bacon hiding somewhere."

OG smiled and uncovered a dish of sausages and bacon on the hot plate and pushed it over to her. Two sausages got transferred to the toast plate, cut up into pieces like the toast, and put in front of Lazarus. She put two more slices in the toaster.

"The president was very impressed."

"He was there?" Her head whipped around at that.

"Yes, I'm surprised no one told you, but then you were very busy."

"And now I'm totally un-busy and it's the best feeling in the world." There was joy in her voice. The second lot of toast popped up. "You having some, Mac?" she asked.

"I'm fine thanks," Mac said.

The knife was poised over the butter. "Daryl?"

Both O'Grady and Mac looked up, not aware of this 'first name' development, expecting her to be reprimanded, or for her to be using the name disrespectfully. But she wasn't, and Daryl smiled and said, "Sure."

"Mac, have you been feeding him properly? And he looks like he's been working way too hard."

Could she tell he'd lost weight as well, working himself as hard as he could to make the time pass more quickly?

"I don't get to tell him to slow down. And you tell him off much better than I do."

"Jam, or marmalade, or nothing?" she asked, making him want to smile at the English terminology learned from her mother. He doubted it would ever leave her.

"You choose," Daryl replied.

Two buttered slices, one with jam, one with marmalade, slid their way on a plate over the granite to stop in front of him. He looked over at Mac as he started on the toast, raised one eyebrow and smiled. Mac didn't trust himself to say anything. This was all rather...interesting.

She reached over and picked up a slice of bacon, using her teeth to pull the fat off, and took the final slices from the toaster.

"I'll just go make sure the schedule for the plane is all set. Mac?" O'Grady said, and excused himself, Mac following.

"So, how are you this morning?"

She sat cross-legged on the counter, cute as you like, and buttered toast as she said, "Glad to be going home, that's as precise as I can be right now." There was a lot she wanted to say, but she stayed guarded.

"O'Grady said you were a little upset last night."

She offered the dish of sausages and bacon to him, and he took a rasher, his appetite returning now that he was with her.

"I was."

"You want to talk about it?"

"You afraid your asset is going to have a nervous breakdown? That the poodle is going to go the poodle clinic?"

"No. I think you're too strong for that, but the trouble is with being so strong, is you can still feel a great deal of pain without breaking." His quiet answer wasn't what she'd been expecting. She let him continue. "I don't care about the money; I just don't want you unhappy. You've coped brilliantly well, given the changes and the workload over the last four to five months. I'm just saying, if you need to talk to someone…I know I'm not top of the list, but I'd rather you talked than try to cope all on your own."

"I'll be fine. I'm good at coping on my own."

"Just because you're good at it doesn't mean you have to."

"And who do you talk to? Who do you let help you, hey Zeus? Must get real lonely up in that penthouse cloud of a life."

Piercing eyes held his and refused to look away. They weren't angry or unkind, just challenging. And she had a point.

"Yes, it does. My big tip of the day: don't go there."

Her eyes softened and she smiled. "Any other tips?"

"Toast tastes better if you're naked."

She threw back her head and laughed. "Well, you first, you're older and wiser than me, and it's your statement, so I guess you should prove it.

Don't get embarrassed about being naked in front of Lazarus, he's naked all the time."

"No, because if you saw me naked, then naturally you wouldn't be able to keep your hands off me, then I'd have to sue you for sexual harassment, you know that."

He swallowed a mouthful of coffee to silence what he would have liked to say to that, rather than the tame reply he gave.

"There are lots of women out there who'll eat toast with you, naked, I'm sure, and maybe one of them will even marry you, so maybe I'll get to come to your wedding at some point in the next eight years."

"I'm getting married?"

"Of course you are. Imagine the nightmare if you didn't have an heir! Disputes about your fortune could go on for years! It makes me feel queasy just thinking about the complications. So yes, you'll get married and have a little baby Zeus or even many, and I intend to be there to sing all the songs at the reception, and tell your wife all kinds of interesting facts about you to prepare her for her marital life."

"Really? How kind. Do I get a choice of music?"

"Sure. As long as it's not Michael Jackson."

"Damn, that was my first choice."

"Tough shit, cupcake, the Jukebox has rules. You want some cereal?"

"No, thanks."

"Are you sure? It's delicious – it has pineapple in it!"

Her enthusiasm was irresistible.

"Okay, if it's that good I'll try some."

"So. What are you doing today?" she asked him suddenly, while they tucked into the cereal – which was surprisingly good.

"I have a press statement, a news interview, and then lunch with the president and a few others. And then I'm flying back to LA. By the way, I never got to thank you for the balloons. My favourite colours. Thank you."

"How long did they last?"

"Two weeks. Oh, and the drum kit and sound booth are waiting for you. Are you really going to learn how to play? On top of everything else?"

"I'll see how it goes. I've always wanted to try. I might be utter rubbish, in which case the sound proofing will be very useful. As you've realised, perhaps, I love to learn new things."

Once again, he restrained himself from telling her which 'new' thing he would most like to see her learn, and smiled. They'd enjoyed twenty minutes of conversation, and he didn't really want to walk the plank of her annoyance before a busy day.

He thanked her for the breakfast, and left. Soon she would be back in LA and there would be plenty of time for banter and, most likely, plank-walking.

"DID DONNY TRY and ring me last night, OG?"

"Yes. You were asleep at the time. He understood."

"You mind if we go there?"

OG thought about it. Knew she could do with seeing him.

"Sure."

Fifteen minutes later they pulled up outside the townhouse.

Invited into the hall, she saw Mario, Lucio and Paulo looking at her with awe: the twiglet had turned into a princess, and a superstar!

"Where is he?"

"Upstairs," Paulo replied automatically, it not occurring to him that this visit might not be what his boss would want just at this moment.

She smiled, anticipating Donny's surprise, hoping he wouldn't have a shirt on. Slowly, silently, she pushed open the door and saw him instantly, laid out on the bed on his front, partially covered by the sheet and sleeping. It was most unlike him to be asleep at this time of day, so no doubt he had been out on 'business' very long into the night. She smoothed a gentle hand over his hair, and he murmured softly. She lay down beside him and curved into his back, feeling the solidity of his muscle beneath his warm skin. She loved every inch of him. Loved touching him and being so close to his body. Why hadn't she thought to do this before? To take the initiative with him, so he simply could not resist her? She leaned forward and lips whispered over his neck, while a hand slid under the sheet and discovered that he was naked. A wicked smile curved her lips and fingers stroked over his flank again, wishing she'd bargained with OG for a bit longer. Then again, she could be late…for once.

She felt movement, his body awakening, and his eyes fluttered open.

"Good morning," she whispered, placing a kiss on his neck for welcome.

"Mysty?" He tried to turn see her, but she slid on top of him, her chest pressed to his back, her legs wrapped around him. Oh Lord. His dream and his hardest temptation. "How on earth did you get up here?" he asked, in attempt to say something cogent as his body was already reacting to her, and with a force that was barely controllable. He didn't dare try and turn over, as the movement of their bodies would send him over the edge.

"I came up the stairs," she answered in a tone that made him laugh. "I do believe you're naked," she purred, softly biting the back of his neck, sending shockwaves of pleasure through his body. "I could be naked, too, within a few seconds. What do you think?"

"No."

"Donny! I'm seventeen for Christ's sake! I'm plenty old enough!" He was glad he could not see her face, knowing what she had come to give him, share with him, and still he had turned her down, despite wanting her more than he'd ever wanted anything. "I'm not going to change my mind. I'm not going to stop loving you because you put distance between us! Don't you understand?"

He managed to turn and grab her, and held her down, their eyes meeting briefly before he pulled her to him and kissed her. Her body pressed into his, wanting him as much as he wanted her, and it drove him higher into his cloud of desire. He grasped her hair, pulling her head back, placing hungry kisses down her neck, a hand sliding up to cradle her breast, then down over her buttock, between her legs.

She pushed against his hand, arching her back, and he pulled back, not having meant to do more than kiss her.

"Are you going to finish what you've started?" she demanded, the flush across her cheeks as bright as her eyes.

"You know I'm not going to."

"When, then? And when can I come home? I want to be with you, Donny, not anywhere else! You could fight him and insist I come back here, but you don't! Why not? You know I'd rather be here than be some stupid superstar any day! What have I got to do, Donny?" Hands cradled his head, pleading with him, eyes begging him for an answer. "I'd give you anything, everything, you know that. Why won't you say yes? *Why*?"

How could he answer her, tell her the truth, when she was so sincere and so fragile? How could he tell her he loved her and he couldn't have her? He'd known for years that the day would come when he'd have to tell her; but he loved her too much to let her go, and now…now he was paying the price. Or rather she was. He should have sent her further away than LA. But he knew distance wouldn't have dimmed the love. It was unbreakable. It was why he never swayed, was never tempted. He knew he would love only one woman in his whole life and, as penance for his sins, she would be denied him for her own safety…or else he would pay the ultimate price and lose her because of his enemies.

"One day, sweetheart," he said, a shaking hand smoothing her hair, stroking her cheek, wishing he could hold her every day of his life. "One day you'll understand, I promise."

"I hope so, because every day I'm not here with you, seeing you smile and making you laugh, is a wasted day, and my heart is broken just a little more. I love you. Why don't you see?" She took his hand and kissed his palm, and then her eyes sought his, dark as they were in his serious face.

"I love you so much I would sell my soul to be with you, but…I…I already did, years ago, before I even knew you existed. I would give up everything if it would buy me a life with you, you know that. You, are, everything to me, and I need you to be happy, and to stay alive. I'd never forgive myself if you ever got hurt…can you try and understand that?"

He could barely believe he was saying the words that he had rehearsed a thousand times. All the ways he'd imagined trying to tell her, wanted her to know how he loved her, but that they just couldn't…

"I love you more than life itself," he said. "You saved more than just my body, all those years ago. You saved my heart, too, and it is yours for safe-keeping, forever, nothing will change that." And he held her, so tightly, like he would never let her go, the way she longed to be held.

"I'm not giving up. I won't. I can't. I'll wait," she declared as firmly as she was able, succumbing as she was to the sadness that was overwhelming her.

"You're so young, and there is so much life ahead of you, Mysty," he said, but he knew his words would feel like he was pushing her away.

"I'd give it all up in a moment for your ring on my finger."

"What will be will be, but I'm not an oracle. Time is the answer."

"And also the question. I don't know how much I have. He'll come for me, Donny, and I don't want to die not having loved you like I want to." She laid a gentle hand on his chest, over his heart, and he placed his over the top.

"You're not going to die. I won't let anything happen to you. I'll find him and deal with him. No one on this earth touches you while I have blood moving in my veins!"

His fierce words were a comfort, but they didn't erase her fears. She closed her eyes, wishing everything else would go away so it could just be him and her. Somehow, in that moment, the obstacles felt overwhelming, the situation hopeless, and her usually indefatigable optimism eluded her. Donny must have seen it in her face, as she felt a squeeze of encouragement.

"I'll come to LA soon and we'll spend some time together, I swear. In fact, I'll come next week. Alright?"

She nodded, barely, not really believing him.

They heard a shout from downstairs.

"You'd better go. There's only so much a man can take."

"You had the chance. You've only got yourself to blame."

"No, I'm definitely blaming you for this." She managed to laugh somehow, though her throat closed up afterwards. She leant against his shoulder, and he kissed her temple. "I will see you soon, and I'll make sure I have more clothes on."

"No, don't, I like it."

Her roaming eyes almost made him blush, and he said, "Go on, get your ass out the door, before…"

"Before what?" she dared him, but he groaned loudly and manoeuvred her to the edge of the bed.

With a long glance back, she left as silently as she had come, but with an even heavier heart. She didn't doubt he loved her, but…why wasn't he wasn't letting her in?

In the hall, O'Grady was talking to the collected Capello boys. After a kiss on the cheek and a hug for all of them, she was shepherded out of the door.

"Ten minutes?" O'Grady asked when they were back in the car, seeing the paleness of her face and the sadness in her eyes.

"Neither of us was wearing a watch, sorry."

She turned away, closing her eyes, and in moments was asleep.

EVEN THOUGH THEY drove straight up to the waiting jet, there were crowds gathered at a distance, waiting to see their star leave, airport security and her own men holding everyone back. She picked up the stack of signed photos in the car and explained to one of the armed guards on the gate that they were to be handed out. The guard asked for a picture with her and, despite OG's protests, she got out of the car and smiled into his phone's camera with him. She then gave the crowd a wave, and turned to get back into the car.

But as she turned, a sudden gunshot rang out, and the calling, excited crowd broke into screams behind her. Within less than a second she was surrounded, ducking instinctively as security sprang into the action they had been trained for. Her world was tumbling, she was tumbling, and Donny's words 'I won't let anything happen to you' echoed as her hand went to her side, OG moving like lightening to catch her. Just before the world went silent she registered OG's horror, and the blood on her hand. The crowd was gone. The guards too. And security. They were all gone as her eyes blurred and her heart thump-thumped, and she screamed and reached for nothing, grabbing at air as a tall man stepped out from the fleeing crowd and raised a gun. He had something wrapped around his head so she couldn't see his eyes, but she knew, she knew, and then OG was soothing her and rocking her like a child.

"Mysty, Mysty, it's okay, I'm here," OG said, and she saw him, saw she was on the floor of the car.

"He shot me! He shot me!" she screamed, struggling in his arms.

"You were sleeping, dreaming, it's okay, it's okay," he soothed.

"I shouldn't have got out the car! I–"

"I've got you, I'm here, it's okay."

And slowly the world came back into focus

"I'm not getting out of the car. I'm not," she said.

"We're almost at the airport. And you don't have to get out of the car if you don't want to. We can go straight to the plane."

"He shot me, OG, he shot me."

OG knew who she meant, and his heart tightened with anger that she should have to live with such a deep, subconscious fear, but he said lightly, "I'm not surprised you were dreaming such stuff. You've had far too much to deal with, emotionally and otherwise. You're going home. A film, popcorn and bed. Nobody gets shot on my watch. Have a little faith, kiddo!" and playfully ruffled her curls.

His attempt at making light of the situation calmed her; but his eyes were serious as he tried to reassure her.

"Do I have to get out? At the airport, can't I just get on the plane?"

"The boys say that quite a crowd has gathered to see you, but if you're not happy, we'll get straight on the plane."

She could now see the people, some dressed up like her, or wearing blonde wigs, or waving banners and pictures for her to sign. They were so full of joy and happiness, and she cursed her father for always ruining everything. All he'd ever done was destroy and ruin all that was good in the world.

"Oh fuck it, I'm not a coward and I never will be."

Suddenly she grabbed a pen and opened the door, whilst the car was still moving, and OG shouted for it to stop. He and six other suits shadowed her along the line. She could feel her heart thumping in her chest, afraid every second she was out in the open. If it wasn't today, it could be another day, any day; but would he do it like this, in front of people, rather than slowly, privately like her mother and grandmother?

And these were the dark thoughts in her head as she smiled and signed and waved. But gradually the crowd got her full attention. And she knew she had to trust OG, had to have faith in him. She saw the flashes of cameras, both public and press, and the reporters who scrabbled for a few quick words, but these moments were for the public.

She came to a middle-aged woman in a wheelchair. She had a picture in her hands, one of her from Celeste. There was a guy beside her, with his hand around hers so that she didn't lose her grip on it, and Mysty felt a part of her wrench apart at the sight, at the love and the loyalty and the sadness. She gestured for the barrier to be moved and knelt down by the woman, whose eyes were filled half with joy, half with anguish.

"Hey there." Mysty glanced up at the guy, who knelt down as well. "Looks like you made a special effort to come all this way to see me today."

"This is my wife. She really wanted to see you. She's watched everything you've ever done. I'm afraid she isn't able to speak anymore, but she wanted to see you so badly."

There were tears in the man's eyes, and Mysty felt tears fill hers. She looked at the woman who, but for a few faulty cells, would have lived a very different life with this man who so clearly loved her. How could life be so cruel? She reached out and took the woman's other hand from where it lay motionless on the top of the blanket that was keeping her warm in the Vegas sunshine.

"You don't know how much it means to me that you came here today," she said, and she kissed the back of the thin hand, its strength robbed by illness, and she wished, *wished,* she could do something. The crowd around them had gone quiet, realising something far more important was happening here than their own need for an autograph. Mysty then signed the picture while the woman watched in silent wonder and emotion, not having expected this.

And then the world's most beautiful face leaned down close to hers, her hair shielding both of them, and she whispered, "Whatever battle you're fighting, seeing you here proves you've already won. You have a wonderful husband, and you are a wonderful wife. I envy you such joy. Enjoy every second together."

With a soft kiss against her temple, Mysty then stood, aware of both of their tears. And then she walked away with one last wave.

OG glanced back at the couple as they reached the plane and saw them, side by side, both smiling, no longer gripped by the sadness that had been on their faces just a few moments ago.

This kid, he thought, *she really does have a gift.*

DARYL LOOKED AWAY from the computer panels and checked the time. He was on his own jet, but knew hers had left over an hour ago. He wanted to see her get home and he wasn't disappointed when he flicked up the screen and saw her run and jump, depositing herself in a happy heap on the sofa, a big smile on her face.

"How come I left with one case and I came back with four?" she asked OG.

"It's all the Christmas presents you've bought me," he laughed.

"I don't remember having that much stuff?"

There were four large cases on wheels, and several smaller ones, all shiny black with the Pirate Queen motif on.

"Don't forget some of that is stuff from the show you couldn't decide what to do with."

"Oh yes. Did it really all end just last night? Feels like so much longer."

"Hopefully you'll get to relax for a while now. You alright after seeing Donny?"

"Well…to be honest, I wish I hadn't. I feel even less…" She waved a hand and gave up trying to find the right word.

Daryl scowled. She'd seen Donny? When? It sounded like it hadn't gone too well, though… Interesting. Clearly Donny wasn't changing his stance on them being together and her frustration had intensified.

"And the nightmare? You feel okay now?"

"Hell, compared to most nightmares I get that one about getting shot was a walk in the park. I'm fine, really, I'm sorry I worried you."

Nightmares? Daryl didn't know she had nightmares. But given what he'd heard about her childhood, and her father…

"You want a sandwich? Drink? Movie?"

She sat up and put a hand over OG's, where it rested on the back of the sofa. "I appreciate you asking, but you've been looking after me for over two months now, and it's time you had a night off. I'm sorry for getting angry with you last night…it was all just a bit much. I'd go seven shades of loopy if you weren't around, trust me. There's a present waiting for you in your apartment. I promise I'll stay right here in the apartment tonight, so you go relax, okay?"

OG was touched by her honesty, and her apology, and ruffled her curls.

"What is this?" he asked, smiling. "Poodle-watcher appreciation day?"

"Abso-fucking-lutely. As Poodle-watcher people go, you're awesome. I'll definitely insist Zeus give you a pay rise."

"I don't give a toss about the money. I love my job, and you're one hell of a poodle. These presents…they don't tick or growl or anything, do they?"

"Have a little faith!" she exclaimed indignantly.

"What time tomorrow, kiddo?"

"Erm…5am. I want to go outside for a run. I'm tired of treadmills."

"Alright. You know you have your check-up with the doc tomorrow?"

"Yes. Poodle check-up time…doesn't get more exciting."

"I promise to step in if he tries to put a thermometer somewhere personal."

"It's alright, if he does that he's going to get an MRI machine somewhere personal too."

OG laughed, the echo of happiness remaining in the air as the door shut, leaving her alone. Immediately she started looking around for the picture, as Daryl knew she would. She spotted it and carefully pulled the cloth away to reveal the superb shot of her walking through the flames in the black and gold outfit that could seduce a blind man. It was dramatic, fearless and sexy; it was her all over.

She stood back and crossed her arms, tilted her head. He had no idea what she thought. Then she moved away, obviously searching for the new drum kit. Daryl switched cameras. Stepping into the sound-proofed booth, she observed the new kit, the microphones and equipment, but her face was still expressionless. She went back to the kitchen, cheered at the well-stocked fridge, got a glass of milk and then flopped back down on the sofa.

A message came through on Daryl's personal handheld: 'Adjustment to negative dickhead points. New total 34 million. Congratulations!'

'I'm glad you're pleased,' he messaged back. 'Good to be home?'

'Very. I'm not looking at the anything you send me that is heavy-work-related. I'm ignoring everything in favour of ignorance.'

'Don't worry, there's nothing too strenuous. You do have a few appointments with your photographer, though – he's glad to have you back.'

'Do remind him to behave himself.'

'He promises not to be anything other than a gentleman.'

'And I will be going to the Bowl on Saturday night, and I don't recommend you try stopping me because I'm quite certain I could climb up to your penthouse with a loaded gun and four sets of handcuffs.'

'That sounds like tempting evening. However, I realise you'd rather have something other than me between your thighs – sadly. So no, I won't try to stop you.'

'That depends...what horsepower have you got?'

'It's off the chart.'

'Wow. I should call Leanne and get her to confirm that for me.'

'Wouldn't you rather trust your own opinion? First demonstration is free.'

'And after that?'

'For you? I'd probably waive the charge.'

'You generous man. Tempting as it is, I'll stick with the Fireblade.'

'If you ever change your mind, you know where I live. All butterflies and handcuffs welcome. Beer on the house.'

There was no reply this time, and he saw her lay her handheld down. And then she lay down. She covered her face. Was she crying? What made her so sad? And why had she responded so strangely to the picture and the drum kit?

"MR BLACKMOOR, I have Mysty here for you." Carol's voice sounded cheerful, not tense and afraid. Clearly Mysty was in a good mood.

"Send her in, Carol."

He pulled up the information from Baden from that morning. Everything was perfectly healthy. From her toes to the top of her head, aside from being two kilos lighter than before the tour, she was unchanged, possibly a little fitter – if that was possible. It was strange to be able to see so much of her body – the inside as well as the outside – having been sent some of the neuro-layout readings from Baden. Her body was literally buzzing with nerves and sensors; no wonder she was so spatially aware and co-ordinated. He even knew where she was in her menstrual cycle – not that she would be pleased to know that! – something he obviously had knowledge of but had never taken any interest in before, except to see it as a possible inconvenience to his sex life. It helped him understand when she was more sensitive, or tired. But, perhaps more importantly, it was proof her body was fully able to produce another miracle child. It was easy to forget she was only sixteen when he looked at the absolute marvel of her body.

She strolled in through the door, this strange creature of both elegance and raw sex appeal who always managed to sabotage his ability to think.

"Daryl. Are you alright?"

"I'm fine."

"Are you going to invite me to sit down?"

He re-engaged his brain, and smiled. "Sure, make yourself at home."

She sat with the calm poise of a presidential delegate, legs crossed demurely and arms on the edges of the chair.

"So?"

"Well, you certainly are as healthy on the inside as you appear on the outside. Baden gives you a clean bill of health."

"Woohoo!"

"So how are we today?"

"We are fine. We had a run, had breakfast, saw Baden, and we are reporting for duty, sir."

"Excellent. And have we tried the drum kit yet?"

"Tomorrow. I'm having a music-free day."

"I see. What's in the bag? Lunch?"

"No, I ate it already. I had a milkshake and some junk food on the way, as I think there's an alarm that goes off if someone pulls out a hamburger and fries in your office, or Mac would appear and confiscate it and throw them off the roof. Can't have junk food anywhere near his holiness, he's far too healthy."

"Mac wouldn't *throw* you off the roof, he'd just dangle you over the edge for bit."

"Oh well, that's okay, then. I'll bring some next time." She smiled, and it was the best thing he'd seen all day. Forget the reports that told him annual profits on three of his biggest companies had gone up by over 1.5%. "Actually, I brought you a present."

"Another one? I was hoping for more balloons."

"No balloons today. You want them now?"

"*Them*?"

"I travelled the whole world; it would be naff if I came back with only one thing." She went to the door, pulled it open and took something thin and flat and wrapped in pearly-cream paper from OG. She laid it on his desk. She also deposited the small bag she had brought in with her on the desk.

Wow. He didn't know what to do – again. Nobody just brought him presents. Plural.

"It does help to open them, if you want to know what they are," she added.

"I'm out of practice with presents."

"Well, this is training for your birthday. Which one first?"

She perched on the edge of his desk, and suddenly his pristine and rather intimidating office was a different place entirely. He looked at her, saw the gentle smile of anticipation, and pulled out the first item, wrapped in blue paper. He pulled off the wrapping, opened the blue box and removed a heavy glass ball: a paperweight.

"Put it on the desk for moment, and wait a few seconds."

He did as she suggested, and seconds later it burst into life as swirls of light and different colours danced inside it randomly, without order, beautiful and spontaneous.

"It's a novel application of complex physics. The particles inside react with the sunlight. See, it has a button, just there." She leaned over to show him, totally unconcerned about sitting on his desk. "If you press the button it is wrapped in a dark tint, to keep off the sunlight so it'll go to sleep again. I thought it might be a beautiful thing to have on your super-tidy desk."

"Thank you. It's most ingenious!" It was something he would never have found himself, or even chosen if he had, but something rather novel that he actually liked. Like her, he had appreciation of all things scientific, and she had guessed right that he would be fascinated by it.

"Come on, the next one is even better."

He smiled at her eagerness and reached in the bag, bringing out a second box. He glanced at her, not sure what her joy meant. He pulled off the paper and saw the title on the front of the box, as well as the item through the clear packaging. Dear Lord!

She burst out laughing at the look on his face as he undid the box and placed the contents on his desk.

"I can't buy you a new one without you knowing, because I have no money, so I thought this would keep you amused in a smaller way; maybe shock a few clients you don't like by driving it into their shins."

The shiny blue Lamborghini Esporta remote control car sat gleaming on his desk, the control next to it. He looked at her, unable to repress his smile, and switched it on and put it on the floor, 'driving' it around the desk and back. Only she would get him this! She who didn't care about his age, or his status, or that he was so serious-minded that smiling had once been a once-a-week event that required him to forewarn his facial muscles of the occasion.

"You know, this one might manage more mileage than my other one," he said as he parked it up in the corner.

"I might get one of my own, and then I'd have to race you!"

"And what colour would you get?"

"White, I think. I like white."

"Good choice. One of the new ones is white, and it should be ready in a few months."

"I promise not to trash it," she declared, and she obviously meant it.

"That is a relief!"

"Last one, come on. It's something for your wall – that's if you have any space left."

He gave her a curious look, and pulled off the wrapping, revealing a photo on mounted canvas. It was his skyscraper, and the lighting was superb! It must have been taken early in the morning, as the light on the windows and stonework was soft but intense, the sky behind a perfect pale blue, and looping around the very top was a swirl of cloud. It was a stunning picture, skilfully captured.

"I took it while I was in New York on the tour, and quite by chance. I'd not been able to sleep, so I got up to admire the views. It was 4.17am, and there was your office in the dawn light. And that's your cloud. Where you sit and keep the world turning."

It was one of the few moments in his life when he honestly didn't know what to say. He was lost in the picture, and suddenly conscious she was standing right next to him, looking at it with him. It was a beautiful, shared moment. And here she was, close enough to touch, but just far enough away to be safe. He wanted to pull her to him, thank her from the soles of his feet, and kiss her with a gratitude he had never felt before.

But he knew he had to settle for words, and said, "It's exceptional. I insist you sign the back." He reached over and retrieved a pen, offering it to her.

She looked at the pen and then at him. "You don't have to pretend you like it if you don't. You're the expert with the photography, not me."

He could have laughed, but said, "Mysty, it's a great photograph! I meant what I said that morning at the studio; you have got talent for photography, and this proves it. Sign it, and I'll put it on the wall in my New York office."

Slowly she took the pen and leaned forward to sign the bottom right corner with the signature now known across the whole planet.

Reluctant as he was to spoil the moment he knew they had stuff to talk about, and she didn't hide her disappointment when he began to discuss photo shoots and the opening of her brand stores.

"Shucks, I was hoping you'd forgotten about all that," she said.

"No such luck," he replied. "We also need to talk about your return to Celeste. I trust that isn't a problem?"

"No, not at all. Though I only want to do two pieces for a few weeks. I really don't want to overdo it."

"On the contrary, it's good to see you exercising some prudence and restraint." Clearly the MJ tour had taught her something about the boundaries of her own body, and she was learning to respect it a little more.

"Thank you."

"I have arranged for some performances at the Ritz – but so far only three shows each, with a different theme – and the schedule has been sent to you. This is just something to keep the press happy. Your fans might want more of you, but I know you need a break. You can continue to cover songs by other artists, with your own unique flair; but at some point, when the time is right, we will introduce some your own original music. Is that okay?"

"That's all fine."

"Super. Well, that was all fairly painless. The presidential dispensation, by the way, is scheduled for six weeks' time, and he is very much looking forward to meeting you."

"I really have to go? Couldn't it just be sent?"

"The president was rather impressed with the show the other night, particularly your speech, and he wondered if you'd be interested in writing some of his speeches for him." Her face was wonderful picture of utter surprise. "But I told him I couldn't spare you." And then relief!

"Do I have to go on my own, or are you coming?" she asked.

Did that mean she wanted him there, or was it just fear that made her ask the question?

"I'll be there. Not many sixteen-year-olds get to meet the president. I realise this is pretty big."

"I'm seventeen," she corrected quietly.

"Really? When did that happen?" How he wished he knew these details about her, as not knowing simply highlighted the distance that still existed between them.

"A few weeks ago."

"Why didn't you say?"

"It's not important. I don't celebrate my birthday, it just happens."

He could see her retracting. All the sunshine was gone, and the grim seriousness she was capable of was back.

"Why don't you celebrate it?" he ventured, carefully.

"Because it's not a birthday to me, it's a death day."

He really hoped she didn't mean what he thought she meant. Had her family died on her birthday?

"Is there anything you'd like as a late birthday present?"

"What could I possibly want?"

"I'm not a beautiful seventeen-year-old multi-talented female superstar, so I don't know. You tell me."

"What did you get for your seventeenth birthday?"

"A very fine yacht. *The Troubadour*."

He gestured at the model yacht on the corner of his desk. Being ignorant about yachts didn't mean she couldn't appreciate the impressive dimensions the yacht would have in real life, and her expression was compliment enough.

"Wow. I've never been on the water."

"Would you like to?"

"I think so. I like the beach and the sea. But sailing's not something you do on your own, is it?"

"No, not really. Well, that's something else we can fit in sometime. As soon as I have a date fixed for the holiday. I'll let you know."

She nodded, still not quite smiling.

"How did you like England?" he asked.

"I really liked it, from what I saw, which was quite a bit of London and Cambridge, and a little bit of Manchester. I spent most of the time inside the arena in set up, but…I didn't…feel as much as I thought I would. I…I thought it would help me remember my mother, but…no."

"You didn't look up any family?" he asked gently, knowing this was a very sensitive subject.

"No. Aside from the fact they're probably old, and very distant, I don't think they would remember who I was. Besides, it would be a bit of a shocker to have me land on their doorstep with OG and the boys, wouldn't it?" Her smile was sad, but respectful and poignant, always respectful of other people's points of view. "Anyway, I've lasted this long without them, and they never stayed in contact with my mother, so… Lazarus and I will be just fine. Just like always."

"You think Lazarus will be alright doing a photo shoot with you?"

"Sure. You can have as many nudes of him as you like."

Her slight laugh prompted him to ask about Donny.

"Why do you need to know?" she replied. "What does it even matter?"

"Because I know you've been upset, and I'd like to avoid that in the future. If something is wrong, I'd like to know. I don't want you thinking I'm an insensitive, megalomaniac boss. If I know you're struggling I can make allowances. But you've got to tell me."

"I'm sure I could have got 'jackass' in there somewhere."

"I'm paraphrasing your vastly superior descriptions of me," he replied, to a flicker of a smile.

"Things are…confusing. In fact, very fucking confusing."

"Can you expand a little, so I can try to understand."

She looked at him, arms crossing defensively across her chest, clearly deciding what to say, how to say it, and why she was even bothering. She was obviously wondering, too, why on earth he was asking. Why did it matter to him, anyway?

"He's…he's still not giving me any answers about…our future, and I have a feeling it's nothing to do with him being in Vegas. And I don't believe my age has anything to do with the fact he won't touch me, either. There's something else and…he's not telling me the whole truth, which is always a bad idea with me. All I get are more declarations that go nowhere. I don't know what I'm waiting for anymore, as much as I…I won't give up."

It was much more than he imagined she would say and, if he was honest, it made his heart lift to hear her words; but it saddened him too: she deserved more than this.

"I'm sure he has your best interests at heart," he said. "I've known him long enough and had enough run-ins with him over you to know there is little he holds more dearly than your happiness and wellbeing."

"I don't doubt him, I just don't understand."

"Perhaps he was tired and didn't express himself well. I heard from a reliable source that he was up most of that night as, I'm sure, most of Vegas was."

"He was asleep in bed when I got there; but, believe me, he woke up pretty fast when he realised I was lying next to him, and then sat on him. But his explanations didn't make any sense at all."

Daryl tried hard to keep the envy from his face. This was not going to help his concentration for the rest of the day.

"Speaking as a man, being sat on by you – in bed – would not help make any explanations particularly cogent."

"I was fully dressed. I only sat on him. It was not like I did anything else. Well, not much anyway."

"Still very distracting. I'm sure when you see him next he'll be more forthcoming."

"Interesting choice of phrase." Daryl could not believe the gleam in her eye. She didn't miss a thing. But then she never had. "I know Donny, and he's digging his heels in because of something he won't tell me about. Nothing I do or say makes any difference. I don't know what to do, which is unusual for me. Normally I have an answer for everything. Except how to get out of contracts I don't want to sign."

"And do you still wish you hadn't signed it?" His voice was calm, but he didn't breathe.

"I'm still making up my mind. This equilibrium of ours is embryonic. I have every confidence you'll do something utterly stupid and land yourself back into billions of negative dickhead points again."

"And there was I thinking you'd begun to like me. How disappointing."

His reply made her laugh, and it was a proper laugh, not nasty or sarcastic.

"Don't you have at least a hundred other vastly more important people to talk to than me?" she then asked. "So shouldn't I be going already?"

"No one else brings me presents," he answered shamelessly, wishing she'd realise he wanted her there, he loved her there.

"Oh, they're just little. Not quite a priceless Ming vase."

"I've got some of those. I don't ever look at them, and I'm not interested in getting another. Very over-rated."

"Bugger. I'll have to think of something else as a Christmas present. But then I'm on best behaviour for Carol. I don't think she can take too much excitement. Every time she sees me I think she expects the world to come to an end."

"How considerate. Well, let me know how you get on with your new drum kit. I will see you on Thursday for the first photoshoot. Feel free to get naked like Lazarus."

She blushed, but rose and made her way to the door.

"A graceful retreat is not a defeat, nor surrender. Bring on the next round, Zeus, I have thunderbolts of my own," she said and, flashing indigo at him, she left, firmly shutting the door.

He grinned, picked up the remote control and whizzed the Lamborghini around his office, deciding that when he went to collect his new white one he would take her with him. He had to swerve the thing rather suddenly to avoid the huge foot that appeared through the doorway.

"Christ, Mac, you already crushed my other car; can you leave this one in one piece?" Mac stared down at the remote control car, and then back at his boss, who was sat happily behind his desk, now directing it around the chair. "What can I do for you?"

"I brought you coffee. Mysty said you wanted one, and I was checking you were...okay... after seeing her." Mac's voice betrayed his wonder at seeing his aloof, sensible boss manoeuvring a remote control car with the avid concentration of a nine-year-old on Christmas morning.

"As you can see, all fine, and not handcuffed to anything. But I didn't…" – he pulled a tight corner around the leg of the desk – "ask for coffee."

"Well, she handed me a mug with this on it, and I couldn't refuse."

Daryl took his eyes off the car. 'Stud Muffin Extraordinaire' was printed in bright blue on the cream porcelain mug, with a number one in a small star beneath.

"The other side is even better."

Daryl turned the mug: 'For private demonstrations just call…' and a made-up number was printed underneath.

"She's got quite a sense of humour," Mac commented dryly, watching his boss's face fluctuate between annoyance and amusement. No one else on the planet would dare to send him such an outrageous thing.

"Yes, quite. Maybe I won't use this one in the office."

"I'll have it taken back to the residence with the other two, then?"

"Other two?"

"Two more. Very…individual." Daryl sat back and looked at his imposing bodyguard afresh. Where had the ultra-serious, impersonal Mac gone? "She got me one as well." Mac's smile made him look about ten years younger.

"What does yours say?"

Mac held it up. On one side it said, 'Dude-in-Chief' and on the other, 'Don't make me come over there!'

"I'm not stud muffin material, it seems. I was gutted, but…I quite like it."

"Did O'Grady get one?"

"I'm not sure. I do know she gave him some signed pictures of her for his daughters, and a signed picture of his favourite baseball star." Mac then looked at the photo of the skyscraper, and his jaw dropped. "Did she take that?"

"She did."

"Considering everything, and the great job she made of re-arranging my nose, I'd say she has a heart of gold."

"Yes. Definitely a kitten as much as a tiger."

"Just think, after seven years she might even have forgotten you blackmailed her, and it'll be all kitten stuff, without the tiger stuff."

Daryl scowled instantly. "Thank you, Mac. Find the door and shut it after you."

Mac just grinned at him and left, leaving him reflecting on the fact her influence was inciting an unofficial and unsolicited shift in his camp. Since when did Mac grin at anything? And since when did he? But isn't this what he had wanted?

IT WAS THE day of the first photoshoot and his first opportunity to see her that week, and he was determined to enjoy every second. He'd given O'Grady the presents he'd bought her for her birthday to give her, despite her insistence that she didn't acknowledge that day, and watched as she'd opened them. She'd loved the two new ice-skating costumes – one a sparkling ivory with a silk train; the other a sleek sequined black with a high neck, giving her all the elegance of a black swan – together with a new pair of skates that fitted perfectly. It seemed sad that there was no audience to watch her skate, except OG, of course. But she was lost in her interpretation of the music when she skated, and appeared relaxed and happy.

She had no idea he watched her skate, and that was how he wanted it. As for the cameras in her home…she may have suspected that they were there, for security purposes, but probably wouldn't be happy if she knew how he preferred watching her go about her everyday life more than anything at all.

O'Grady was in the corner of the room, watching over proceedings. The room was alive with lots of people, and he'd had his usual team flown over from New York. Various scenes had been set up, including a sofa, a bed with sumptuous covers and gorgeous cushions, and a section with mirrors and an old-fashioned screen. He dropped his jacket on a chair and checked his cameras, looking over the set-up details and conferring with his two main assistants – guys who knew him and the way he liked to work. He wondered how it would work out with her as the subject? Would she co-operate?

"Ask her to come out, we're all set," he said.

"Yes, sir," Malcolm replied, and strode away to fetch their model for the day.

He heard voices and saw O'Grady talking to her through the curtain of the changing room. O'Grady then glanced at Malcolm, and the curtain was pulled back. And there she was, with black heels on and a silk robe wrapped tightly around her. Her hair was loose, just as he liked it, and her face clear of any make-up, just as he'd asked. Make-up had never been part of her image, so it wouldn't be now.

But she didn't look happy and, head down, she let Malcolm direct her to the chaise longue, where she just looked more miserable as he explained what they wanted her to do. She didn't look any closer to taking the robe off either.

"Mysty, we really do need to make a start. Everything is ready, and you've nothing to worry about, we're all professionals," Malcolm said, but she snorted at his attempt at reassurance.

"Mysty." Malcolm stepped back, leaving it to Daryl to take the lead. "Are you okay? What's the problem? You've done underwear shoots before?"

"But not in front of so many people!" she hissed at him, eyes wide and scared.

He had to admit there was a big team in today, nearly fifty people, but only because they had so much to do and because of how important it – and she – was.

"Accepting the fact that the shoot is going ahead, what would help?" he asked, pinning her with his eyes.

"Well, I don't see why I'm the only one prancing around semi-dressed. You want me to stand around with barely any clothes on, then everyone else should get with the theme of the occasion," she declared defiantly, and hugged the robe tighter.

Trust her to come up with that one, throwing the ball back into his court. How could he just tell everyone to take clothes off?

Silence.

Everyone looked at him, then each other, then back at her.

"Well, I'm in."

Mysty looked around at the familiar voice, and Lucy was there, with a headset and some screen clips, which she then put down. She then pulled her T-shirt off, tossing it away from the set, smiling at her old friend!

"Lucy!" What the hell was Lucy doing there? A friendly face in the sea of strangers!

"And me."

"Hope?"

Hope stepped up beside Lucy, and they both smiled, and looked around at the others in the room. Slowly everyone else pulled a T-shirt off, or a top, in demonstration of support for the girl who now stood, watching the impossible happen. In less than a minute, the only one left fully dressed was Daryl, and he looked at his team, who obviously saw nothing wrong with her request – and in fact rather admired her for it.

"Do you need help with your buttons? I didn't think taking clothes *off* was a problem for you, *Mr Photographer*," she declared, and her eyes dared him, having gained a little confidence from the support in the room.

Daryl gritted his teeth and wondered why he was so bothered about this. But hey, he'd be interested in seeing her reaction to his own rather fine musculature. So he unbuttoned his cuffs, untucked the shirt from his trousers, unbuttoned the first few buttons and then pulled it over his head with a nonchalance that rather surprised those who knew him.

Without a word he then picked up his camera, saw her piercing eyes looking over his powerful torso in the viewfinder, a momentary flash of something quickly replaced with an impassive look.

"Well? Time for the robe to come off, cupcake," he said.

She scowled at him, and untied the robe, letting it fall to the floor. Black Pirate Queen bra and knickers and a deep, sultry pout. Perfect. Click-click-click.

She sat down on the deep red velvet chaise and swung her legs up, posing with all the confidence of a sex kitten and all the elegance a woman could possibly have. He was going to enjoy this. But the tension on those high cheekbones told him she was tempted to refuse his commands: head back, arm back, both arms back, legs down, one leg up…and so it went on. Occasionally someone would run up and rearrange a curl or two, or add a cushion or a rose or take it away.

Then it was time for a change, and emerging in the purple set he instructed, "Okay, onto the pedestal," accepting the new camera from his assistant.

She moved across the room, stopping at a table with some of her favourite accoutrements on – a top hat, trilby, cane…and a feather boa? He saw her look twice.

"In case you felt like livening things up a little."

She fixed him with a look. "Can we have some music on? This room is way too silent," she said.

He thought about it for a second. He knew it would ease her nerves – and perhaps help get rid of some of her inhibitions.

"What would you like?" he asked from behind his camera.

"Madonna. The Immaculate Collection. That would be appropriate, would it not?"

"Fine. Charlie? Make it happen, and keep it playing."

As the music began she smiled for the first time. And the transformation was…unbelievable. Gone was the wariness; now she oozed liquid grace and moved her body far more naturally, showing off all the curves that made her sublime. Dancing, but slowly, she paused to allow for pictures, moving into a new pose every few seconds. She was a goldmine of gorgeousness. Why hadn't he thought of putting music on before? The cane twirled, and the feather boa draped. Lips begged to be kissed. She crouched; she bent in impossible angles. Oh Lord.

Another two changes and he called a halt. He put the camera down and saw her head off to speak to Lucy and Hope, giving them a hug, and some excited chatter ensued. It had been a good idea to bring them in on this shoot; he'd thought they might help steady her, and he'd been right.

She then collapsed onto the bed.

"Don't tell me something as tame as a photoshoot has worn you out."

She peered out from under her hair as the male Adonis sat down next to her, looking slightly odd but ridiculously sexy in smart trousers with a bare chest She'd known he would be toned, but there was serious power in that body! How so, when he hardly ever used it? It begged to be used, touched...and something primitive and instinctive inside her reacted to it, far beyond her control or her better judgement. Just like seeing him in leathers, she had no way of denying how attractive he was. No wonder women went stupid over him.

"I'm exhausted."

She went back under the hair again, refusing to indulge herself by looking at him. She didn't want him to see the reluctant admiration in her eyes, didn't want to encourage him, didn't want him to know she might just find him rather...attractive. He was arrogant enough already!

"I didn't realise being so gorgeous was so tiring," he responded.

"You should know," she replied. *Ssshhh, you stupid girl! Don't be so goddamned honest!*

"OG has some snacks for you. You must be hungry."

"Snacks! I'm already underweight. Feeding me is not going to make me fat!"

"You're not underweight, you're perfect."

"I'm practically wasting away. I *need* feeding."

O'Grady came over and handed her a bottle of water and a fruit and nut cereal bar, which she consumed, and then they completed the shoot. Flicking through the shots, they were some of the best he'd ever taken.

Back in the car, she didn't appear to be angry or worried about the shoot; in fact, once she'd given up worrying, she'd almost seemed to enjoy it, instinctively aware of what poses would work, and what he would want. Neither had she argued with any of his commands, even though they had been demanding on both concentration and patience. No, not one murmur of protest, just the occasional raised eyebrow when he asked her to something a little...daring. He had no doubt they would sell thousands of sets of underwear when people saw the new catalogue, despite the high price tags.

"You did really well today," he said. "You're as good in front of the camera as behind it."

"Thank you. Actually, I think everybody should strip off at work. It's a great leveller. What do you think?"

"Interesting thought. It beats wearing a suit to the office every day. I'll make sure I'm wearing suitable undies and lose the trousers, too." She laughed at that, and his heart lifted at the sound. "I'll make sure you get the first copy of the catalogue. I have no doubt the underwear will prove very popular."

"I have to admit, I was surprised by how tame most of it was. Did you really design it all?"

"I had a team of designers, but I had veto over all of it. Too tame? Really? I toned it down to suit your…innocence…but I can add another line with a raunchier edge if you like?"

"*No*! Really, it's fine. I like it just how it is." She looked out of the window, hoping he didn't see her blush.

"Are you sure? Perhaps a few more interesting designs might get Donny to succumb?"

She knew he was smiling one of his knowing smiles, she could hear it in his voice. *Don't look round*!

"I'll think about it," she managed, trying not to think about what sexy items he might dream up – or how it might feel to wear them.

"Are you sure you're sure?" he asked, obviously not having registered the discomfort in her tone or body language.

"*No*!" she yelled. "Nothing would make any difference to that stupid obstinate man!" She shot him a look of pure rage, and frustration, and then turned away again, pulling her knees up to her chest and curling into them.

How could he tell her that Donny was not the only man on the planet? That he would give millions, billions, the world, to hold her how she so needed to be held?

"For one night with you I would part with a fortune. There is almost $800million in your account already. I would double it for one night with you in my penthouse," he said quietly. "Donny is a fool."

Silence. And then she exploded, the disbelief in her voice that he actually thought he could buy her body, as she saw it, equal only to the hurt as she ripped into him with all that she had.

When they pulled up at the apartments seconds later, she threw the car door open and ran.

Shit!

"O'Grady!"

"Already on it, boss."

O'Grady took off up the street after her, with two suits on his tail.

"What did you say to her?" Mac asked, appearing from the other car.

"Don't ask," Daryl snarled.

Goddammit, I'm such an idiot. All the enjoyment from the previous hours was lost; all the good achieved in the last couple of weeks ruined. He was glad to get into his apartment, to be on his own with his anger. He prowled into the kitchen, intending on getting a beer before going back to the pile of work he needed to do. He did not want to go back to the office. He didn't want to do a thing. How the hell was he going to make up for this glaring blunder? God forbid she should tell Donny!

He heard an angry roar and knew it was a motorbike. *Goddammit.*

"O'Grady?" He leaned on the breakfast bar and stared at the chilled beer, feeling too weary in that moment to even raise it to his lips, waiting to hear the noise of other engines gunning it going after her.

Donny Capello, Goddamn you! What is holding you back? Do you not realise you will lose her? Let it be me. I'll be there. I'll be what she needs. Please let her look at me and see what I can give her. And just what exactly would she see, Daryl, if she looked at you?

He snatched up the beer and headed to his study. To do what he wasn't sure, as he couldn't even think straight.

His screen confirmed his worst fears. There she was, screaming along the open road heading out of LA, body bent low over the bike, taking the bends with a reckless defiance that made his gut clench and at the same time… God, how he loved her fearlessness. Her words echoed in his head. She was right. Just who exactly did he think he was thinking he could buy her body? He cursed loudly, and cursed again.

Just get her home in one piece, O'Grady.

TWO HOURS LATER, in the middle of checking through contract documents, a message came through from O'Grady: 'She's stopped at the dance studio.'

He switched on the spare monitor. She was feeding some data into the computer, her leather jacket still on, her helmet on the desk.

He kept the screen open, half reading, half checking on her, until the music started, funky and upbeat, a Michael Jackson 'wooo' giving way the artist of the music: '*Love ain't what it used to be, that is what they're telling me; push it in and stick out, that ain't what it's all about…*'And she began to dance. '*Mother's preaching Abraham; brothers don't give a damn…*' She was then joined by five more Mysty's in gold outline, and they began dancing with her, creating a strange mirage of real and unreal. '*Holy Mary mercy me; can't believe the things I see…push it in and stick it out; that ain't what it's all about.*'

She knew he'd be watching. This was for him. A message.

The mirage disappeared and she was alone. But she wasn't done yet.

MJ's voice again: '*I'm going be exactly what you want to be; the stranger in your eyes… am I amusing you; it's confusing me…am I the beast you visualise…I'll be grotesque before your eyes. Is that scary for you, baby?*' The dancing figures returned, and she flipped back and landed as they turned to face him: '*See a mirror of truth; that the evil one is you…*'

It was the accusation he had been waiting for: his horns and tail were back on.

She stood for one long second, glaring at the camera; she might as well have been in the same room such was the effect of the look she gave him.

Moments later she grabbed the helmet and jacket, the light went off and the door slammed shut.

"OG."

"Yes, Mysty."

“Get me out of this goddamned city as fast as you can.”

Disconnect.

NOT SURPRISINGLY SHE had refused to share his car and they’d arrived separately at Celeste; and afterwards she left with Donny, shimmering in pearl blue, a beautiful figure next to Donny’s Italian darkness, and naturally it had been the picture of them walking down the red carpet that had been on the front page of most newspapers on Saturday morning. Daryl had downed two rather large brandies, availed himself of several women, and barely slept.

He had then spent the weekend musing on the problem she posed, coming to a number of unsatisfactory conclusions, not entirely due to his frustration but because he didn’t know how many more times he could bear to see her on the arm of another man. But here was the thing: Donny was a man the media had decided to embrace because *she* was the nation’s darling. It was Mysty’s influence alone that had Donny basking in the golden glow of her reputation, and that was a situation he was not comfortable with.

He thought back to Friday’s night performance. She’d performed three pieces using music from a new band with a name he wouldn’t forget – Lacuna Coil, all typically dark and menacing. The first ‘I’m Not Afraid’ had lyrics that indeed sent shivers down his spine – ‘*Watch your back because I am coming closer…shivers down your spine, you were not expecting me…are you afraid to see me here? I’m not afraid…*’ but not just because of the words, because of the jumps, the spears, their sharp edges gleaming in the lights as they fell with her in the final jump…

During ‘Spellbound’ she mouthed the words, ‘*You cannot have this control on me; I will break this spell you put on me…*’ moving like she was hypnotised, but then hurling her body into spins that weakened his knees. The final piece, ‘Our Truth’, had her dropping down from the heavens onto one of a maze of moving beams, leaping from one to the next with effortless agility like an Aztec goddess commanding space and sky. As the music had faded, the beams now vertical, she had disappeared into the middle of them, and when they curled open, like a huge flower, she was gone.

But a shout went up, and there she was, striding through flames of white fire that burned in the shape of a butterfly across the arena floor. As she walked, the beams began to spin like a whirlpool and, at a flick of her hand, disappeared into the darkness of the roof space.

The rapturous applause nearly blew the roof off.

Mac had then appeared, his face impassive, as it always used to be. He'd been very quiet since Thursday. As far as he knew, she hadn't told anyone what he had said; but he sure as hell knew which side of the fence everyone was sitting on in this latest dispute.

It was when he'd stepped out of the lift on Monday morning that he was aware there was a problem. Generally, when he arrived, his staff either glanced up at him and nodded in greeting, or occasionally said good morning with the kind of deference he was accustomed to. But, this morning, they just looked…worried.

His suspicions were confirmed when Carol got up, like her chair seat was suddenly very hot, and moved around her desk to greet him, hands clasped anxiously.

"Good morning, Mr Blackmoor."

"Carol. Is anything the matter?"

"Erm…well, it's just…"

She looked over at the highly polished mahogany door to his office. He followed her eyes. A label had been stuck to it: 'Caution: Testosterone-fuelled Jackass Inside. Enter at One's Own Risk.'

When had she had time to put this on his door? And, more importantly, why hadn't anyone stopped her?

"It was here this morning when I arrived. I didn't know whether to…take it down or not."

Why the hell didn't you take it down? Daryl could have thumped the door, yelled at her. But now was not the time to reprimand his secretary, who had found herself in unchartered waters. Again.

Deep breath.

"Take it down."

She nodded.

He deactivated the security and stopped short: everything had been moved. It was all back to front. The yacht, for example, which was usually on the right-hand side of the desk was on the exact same spot, but on the left. He looked behind him, and the two pictures of her had been moved to opposite sides. It had the effect of a sort of optical trick, and was quite disorientating. How the hell had she got in here?

Then he saw something on his desk.

A bright red bowl of cherries – very apt – sat to one side of his screen, with a data card and a note: 'Just press play. Nice chair, by the way. Very comfy.'

His stomach turned over. Please, not another virus? But would she be that obvious?

The video had been made in this very office. Half a dozen males dancers with slick haircuts and tight t-shirts moved around the desks as she sang, '*Stop, slow down, baby; slow down, baby…*' as they entered his office, where she was leaning lazily, her back against the window. '*I can tell that you're into me; baby, it's so plain to see. I can see it in your eyes; you're paralysed every time I pass you by. You're the kind that gets your way, every minute every single day…*' She rested a hand on his computer where a clock and date display were on the screen, the time and days flicking at a stupid speed. And then she gestured at his certificates and awards, proudly displayed on the walls and in cabinets. '*You strut around here like you think that I can't do without you; you got some nerve to think that I would give up everything…and slow down, baby.*'

The camera panned to her dancers, and then back to her: she was sitting in his chair, looking very comfortable and very relaxed. '*After all of the games you played, how does it feel to finally get a taste? I'm not falling for your stupid lines, I know you've used them about a thousand times. I won't buy it; don't you even try…you coming round here like everything's about you.*' It then zoomed in on Ken and Barbie, kissing their plastic smiles together on his desk. She then insolently lifted her legs, her black heels resting on his desk. She gestured at the bowl of cherries on the desk, eyebrows raised in mocking question. '*Listen I don't want to get you down, but I ain't never gonna mess around, so how many ways do I have to say…?*

The dancers then gathered and lifted her, higher, higher, and the camera followed them, her body stretching up to…sign her name on his ceiling. She jumped down, dancing as she strolled from the office, all the way to the lift, where the doors closed on her and her dancing men.

End.

He looked up. And sure enough, as if he needed evidence that she had indeed signed his office ceiling, there it was for real: her signature in what he assumed was a permanent marker.

He took stock of the situation. Compared to trashing a car, strangling a database or making Hitler photos, this was pretty tame stuff. Brilliantly put together as well. And she'd sat in his chair? He actually smiled. Cheeky, outrageous…little…minx. How the hell had she got a camera crew up here, and a dozen dancers? And how had she got into his office?

He went to the security files, saw her and seven 'visitors' logged in at 11.05pm last night. They'd signed back out at 11.27pm. Twenty-two minutes was all the time she'd needed to get into the building, into his office, and make that video? It was choreographed well enough to pass for release! And as for moving things around? When had she done that?

He pulled up the CCTV footage and, sure enough, there she was smiling her way past security, no doubt with some perfectly constructed story on why she needed to enter the building, after hours, with a team of dancers and a camera man.

"Irritatingly smart," he concluded, fast forwarding the video. The office was in darkness, no sign of disturbance anywhere…except that everything had been switched to the opposite side. It was an absolute invasion of his private space, so why was he smiling? And she'd hacked into his security – the best in the world! – and yet he couldn't help but admire her.

He thought about it for a full five seconds, and put a call through. He must be mad.

"You like my chair, then?"

"Yep, rather nice."

In the brief second it took to register that she hadn't hung up on him, he felt a surge of hope.

"The video is excellent. I might put it out for release. And thank you for moving my office around. I was thinking of having a change, and never quite got around to it, so now – wow – it's great."

"You are insufferable."

"You are outrageous."

She hit Disconnect but he clicked back in straight away.

"What? There is *no point* conversing with you," she said. "You don't listen to me, ever, and just try and get what you want from me anyway. Just go away and do all that important stuff you're so very good at doing and leave me alone. Goodbye!"

Disconnect.

Wow. What fun for a Monday morning. He glanced out of the window, smiled. Time he made plans to rock the boat between her and Donny.

PAULO WAS HAPPILY ensconced at the bar talking to Mac. Franny was to his right, and there were another two individuals close by. But it was Donny's presence he was concerned with; it was Donny Daryl had to keep there as long as possible.

Donny was meant to have met Mysty at 8pm at the Ritz for drink. It was now 9.30pm, and every minute he stayed was one more minute Mysty was going to hold against him. He'd hoped for an hour at most, half an hour at least, but an hour and a half? The ploy of keeping the drinks, cards and conversation flowing had worked a treat, and having instructed Mac to keep Paulo contented, and distracted, so there was no reminder of the time or where Donny was meant to be had been a good back up. Despite its ulterior purpose, it was a good evening, and he was even enjoying himself – though some of that was the sense of success in carefully orchestrating the drinks and a hand of cards in a male-only topless casino before seeing his girl who, currently, was still not talking to him.

He'd endured her mutinous silence for most of the week, following their brief exchange on the phone. And he knew she'd given up going to the Bowl because Donny was in town, and instead had been excited at the prospect of seeing him. He also knew she had left the Ritz and was on the way, as the tracker on his handheld had alerted him. Daryl took a sip of his martini, almost smiling in anticipation for the fireworks to start.

As entrances went, it was rather fantastic, and Daryl was perfectly placed to watch events unfold. 'Stormed in' didn't really do her, or her entrance, justice. What exploded through the doorway was one of the most magnificent sights he'd ever seen: a tempest in a dress of black and gold, hair tumbling from where it had been pinned up. She was wearing the diamond necklace Donny had given her; but the fury in her bright eyes dimmed its lustrous glow. Holding her hand out to Giles as she strode past he tossed her Franny's cane. He had been minding from where he stood at the bar, and she caught it in a sure hand without slowing for a heartbeat. Her eyes fixed on Daryl the moment she had flung open the door, and then flicked to Donny. Someone approached her to tell her she had to leave, but the flick of her cane into his gut silenced him. O'Grady, obviously on orders, stepped to one side with two of his men.

Oh Christ.

Silence descended on the room – a silence that alerted Donny to a sudden change of atmosphere, being at a disadvantage with his back to the door. Franny's eyes widened and he slowly put his glass of brandy down. Mac, positioned as he was, put his hand on Paulo's arm and they both stood carefully to attention.

Daryl watched Donny brace himself at Paulo's look, and prepare to greet her. But he'd obviously had far more brandy than he imagined he'd had, and struggled to stand. He needn't have worried, as a hand on his shoulder held him down.

"Don't bother to get up, Mr Capello, please. I can endure a little more disrespect." Her voice was so sharp it as good as slashed his ears. "I had a few ideas as to where I might find you, but this…this really does beat them all. But why should I be surprised, when you have *him* sitting across the room from you? No doubt the devil himself invited you to this little get-together. Am I right?"

Donny looked across at Daryl, who kept any expression from his face.

And then she looked at Daryl.

"You just don't get it, do you?" she snarled, and Daryl met her cold look with one equally as chilling. "You can't bear the thought of someone else having something you want, can you? The one time I get to see Donny and you have to interfere, have to make sure it doesn't happen. You are *pathetic*. I've repeatedly refused your lewd propositions, yet you still don't seem to understand the word *NO*. What do I have to do to get you to understand? What price do you think you can put on me? 'I'll double what's in your account', isn't that what you offered, hoping I would lay down and let you have me? There is no price – NO PRICE! – attached to a broken heart. And that is the price that would be paid in order for you to have your way, you bastard."

Daryl felt his own anger ignite. Their conversations, they were… private. She had no right to air them, and especially not here, in front of–

"You idiot, Donny," she continued. "You sat here and let him play you. How many brandies was it? How many hands of cards? All those words you said to me, they count for nothing. How many times have I believed you, for *nothing*?"

"Sweetheart–"

"Don't you dare call me that!" She tore the stunning diamond earrings from her ears and slammed them down in front of him; then took the glass of brandy from its coaster. "This yours?" She drained it in one swallow and smacked the glass down on the jewels. "Thought you could *buy me* the same way he thinks he can, him over there, who can only get a woman by paying for her?"

She met Daryl's eyes again, but this time they weren't cold, they were scorching hot with rage.

"Shut up, Mysty, you foolish girl," he growled. "Don't you dare speak another word."

Donny looked at him. It was a warning look, but Daryl didn't back down to anyone, certainly not her, not in front of so many.

"Or *what*?" she demanded. "More blackmail? More threats?

Blackmoor…blackmail…my, how similar they are! You are the *fool,* Mr Blackmoor, for thinking you could manipulate me just as you manipulate everyone else, and with a complete disregard for their feelings–"

"Mysty, I'm warning–"

"Tell me, did you get a first at Harvard in manipulation?" Daryl stood, went to grab her wrist and drag her to a private room until she calmed down; but with one smooth motion, a length of steel slid out from the end of the cane and came to rest on his shoulder. "I wouldn't move if I were you." Her eyes stayed on his, full of disgust and hated. Mac went to move, but Daryl stilled him with one look. "I've held you at knife point before. Back then it was pity that stayed my hand. Now it's for my dignity alone." She let her eyes rest on the two men, one at a time. "I see now how similar you both are; now all I have to do is decide which of you I despise more. The truth is, I don't want to have to look at either of you again in my life."

They were strong words, and Mysty felt her heart crumble as they were spoken. She slid the blade back inside the cane and then reached up, slowly, and unclasped the necklace. Stepping back over to Donny, she ripped it from her neck and dropped it in front of him with all the disdainful rejection of an offended queen to a lowly subject.

Franny was the only one who uttered a sound, a tiny exhalation of air. Mysty gave him a nod, and then turned and swept from the room, tossing the cane back to Paulo, leaving silence behind her as resounding as a clash of cymbals.

Donny brought a hand up to cover the necklace, and slid it off the table into a pocket. He looked up at Daryl with fury in his eyes. And Daryl returned the rage, both men as taut as a drawn bowstring under their fine clothes. So taut the air quivered from the tension. And yet still no one moved. All eyes were on the two men now left faced with each other. Donny then removed a gun from under his jacket.

"Back room now or I swear I'll kill you where you stand."

Daryl raised one hand, to keep Mac from reacting. There was no doubt in Daryl's mind: Donny meant what he said. He led the way, aware Donny was right behind him. Mac and Paulo both followed and, much to their horror, were instructed to remain outside the room.

Donny gestured to a chair with the gun and Daryl sat, aware he was guilty of what he was about to be challenged with.

Donny's face was contorted with pure hatred, but he lowered the gun. "She's right, isn't she?" he said. "You planned this. You intended to keep me here so she would be kept waiting. You must really hate one or both of us to intentionally upset her so much." His eyes were dark, their blue intense across the room, daring Daryl to deny the truth.

"That's not why I did it," Daryl replied. He doubted he could lie to Donny, he was too shrewd; but he could try to explain.

"*Then why the hell did you*?" The gun was raised again. The barrel steady as a rock.

Daryl kept his eyes on Donny, not the gun. "Because I'm sick of seeing her hurt. Sick of how she keeps you on a pedestal, despite the fact you refuse to reciprocate the loyalty she has for you. I'm sick of your continuing this charade of a happy-ever after." Some of the anger went from Donny's face, and the gun dropped. "You asked her to marry you, Donny, and she wants to be with you, more than anything in the world. And yet…and yet you barely see her. And where's the ring, Donny? Where's the commitment?" Donny sat suddenly, in a chair opposite Daryl, the space between them closed, his eyes not so intense. "So many words and for what? You know this can't go on forever. When are you going to tell her?"

Daryl waited. He could wholly understand the torture in Donny's eyes, the despair all wrapped up in one girl. He had all the time in the world to talk this through now, with Donny, because he knew he'd already won. The moment the gun had lowered he knew he'd won.

Donny looked at the man he would have happily killed only moments ago, and he wouldn't have regretted it. But now?

"If you had given me any other reason other than that, you know you would have a bullet in your head," Donny said, and leaned back and stared at Daryl. It was obvious what was really happening here. "You want her, don't you?" Donny paused, but did not need an answer. "She told me what you offered her for one night in your penthouse. You really have got it bad, haven't you?"

Daryl had never been confronted about his…his feelings for her before, had never imagined he'd have this conversation with Donny. Harvey maybe. But not Donny. Realisation made him choose his next words very carefully.

"I don't want to see her hurt."

"That's one way of putting it." Blue eyes stayed fixed to green. "There are no guarantees she'll ever look at you in the same way," Donny said, ignoring Daryl's evasion of the question, eyes gleaming with a brightness borne of knowing the truth with absolute clarity.

"She'll never look at any other man on the planet for as long as she believes you're going to be together. Do you know what she did, after the last MJ concert? After a night of brilliance that stunned the world yet again? She cried in her dressing room, got home, and then cried some more. Because she felt so alone. I don't want to see or hear her cry like that ever again." Daryl saw Donny's jaw muscle clench, not liking the accusation in the words. "She hasn't got an easy road ahead, and has never had it easy from what little you or she will tell me, but it doesn't have to get harder. What I'm asking you is, are you going to be there for her… or not?"

Donny's silence was like a dead weight between them. How would he answer? He lowered his eyes.

"I never meant for it to go on so long. I meant to end it, believe me, which is why I sent her away after she saved me from that shooter outside my club. I knew then, that night, seeing her sprint towards the house and climb up, taking him on single-handed with a gun, untrained and only thirteen years old." He shook his head, remembering, still in awe. "I knew then…I couldn't bear to see her hurt. Certainly not for me. I knew I had to end it, but…"

"She'd go to hell and back for you she loves you that much."

"She's already been to hell and back, Daryl. I don't want her to go through that again. Four times over I should be a dead man but for her. She saves me when I'm supposed to be the one protecting her. But aside from the fact I knew how much it would hurt her, I couldn't bear to let her go. Every time I saw her, and every time I see her, well, she's just so…" Donny couldn't find a word, he didn't have to, Daryl understood. "She's always been like that. Ever since the beginning. I don't think the fame or the money will ever change how she is. She's pure…joy. She never stops giving."

"I know. That's what makes her so special."

"I've been thinking about how to tell her for so long, but…I can't think of any way that will make it any easier for her. I can't bear the thought of her being alone."

"There is no way of doing it that won't hurt her, and she is alone. But you know the price for not ending this. She could end up dead, no matter what protection I give her. Because she's allied with you, she's a target, as I know you are aware," Daryl said as gently as he could. "Setting her free and breaking her heart is better than her ending up dead."

"I thought about carousing with women and making her hate me, but…" Donny's sad smile lingered. "She doesn't deserve that. She deserves the truth. Besides, I don't think I could do it convincingly enough."

"You've always said honesty works best."

"It does. Every time. And gentleness works where force does not. She's been fighting all her life, first against her father, then the world, just to survive. She doesn't know how not to anymore. Despite everything, despite you and all your…blackmail and the rest…she's never given up being that fighter, not for a moment." Donny looked up at Daryl with a resigned sigh. "I will let you know as soon as I've decided when and how to tell her. She will need locking in a solid room until she calms down, and it's only fair to give O'Grady a chance to keep her…safe." Restrained. They both knew the effect such news might have on her.

"Yes," Daryl agreed, "she has a tendency to do something reckless after being threatened or upset."

"Reaffirmation of life, Daryl. Once you've cheated death, felt fear like she has, the only way to beat the fear when it returns is to push yourself to experience something worse and prove you can survive. What we see as 'reckless', however, she doesn't see as all that dangerous."

"No, and that's 'a lonely place to be'." Daryl repeated the words he'd once heard her say.

"I'm hoping she has children who can see who she really is: caring, and so generous. She loves sharing. It would be the greatest gift to her, to have someone to share her beauty with."

"Not your children. Not now."

"No. But I would have given everything to be their father, believe me."

"You still haven't laid a finger on her, have you?"

"No. Else I would never let her go."

"She will always love you."

Donny's eyes rose up fiercely bright.

"I love her more. Enough to let her go so she can enjoy living without being afraid. Violence was part of her young life; it was out of her control. I have the chance to make sure she can live without that threat. This is something I can control." Donny wondered why he was being so honest with Daryl; but then she'd always been there, between them, and he had always known Daryl was a potential rival, knew he might see her true worth and want to be there for her. He'd not wanted to share her with him, and had certainly not wanted to let her go knowing she might one day turn to him. But now he had no choice. "Now, seeing as our... discussion is over, I'm going to go find her."

Donny stood up, the gun disappearing under his jacket again. Daryl didn't move. The 'discussion' had turned out far better than he had expected in that he that he hadn't had a bullet put in his head; but had also revealed more about himself than he'd expected either. When had he ever put himself out, at such risk, for a mere girl before?

"And, Daryl, just so you know, I won't forget what you did tonight, but I understand why you did it. Whatever happens, I won't ever stop watching over her. I think you know what that means."

The blue eyes, that had no trace of mercy or softness, confirmed the unspoken promise that Donny wouldn't hesitate to act if he needed to. He turned away and left the room.

Daryl breathed out, rubbed a hand over his eyes and smoothed back his hair, trying to shake off the sense of a...portent. This was not an ordinary evening. That was not an ordinary conversation.

Two powerful men, great men in their own worlds, both overwhelmed by concern for one wild, caring, wonderful girl. In a way it was a comfort to know he wasn't alone in that; but in another a madness that came with the price tag of his own life should he put a foot wrong. So Donny was going to end it, and she would heart-broken. But she was young, and she would move on. Daryl just had to make sure it was to him she moved on to.

The door opened and Mac stepped in looking anxious, and angry too.

"I'm in one piece, Mac, you can stop looking at me like that."

"Why didn't you just talk to Donny straight off? Why did you have to get her riled up and have him pointing a gun at you? This isn't Mexico, for God's sake!" Mac had been convinced he would hear twelve years of faultless protection go down the drain when Donny shot his boss between the eyes. "I hope you know what you're doing," he declared, refusing to be cowed by the warning look that said, loud and clear, that his criticisms were not appreciated.

"I don't think I've ever not known what I'm doing, and I had hoped you'd have a little more faith," Daryl replied, standing up and moving to the door. "Where is she?"

"While you two had your little chat, she went home and then straight back out again to the Bowl. Very fast. Naturally she won, breaking the track record, again."

Daryl grimaced, knowing that meant crazy speeds, ramp-jumps and turnovers on curving bends, but said, "It is an unusual trait for a woman to have, but I do believe she is actually more beautiful when she's angry. What do you think?"

"I think I prefer her when she smiles, give you gifts, and doesn't put a blade to your throat," Mac growled back, shadowing his charge down the corridor, not amused by the tiny smile on Daryl's lips.

"It wasn't near my throat at all. It was my shoulder."

"From where I was standing, it was close enough."

"She wouldn't hurt me."

"You sound very sure. I do remember you being punched quite impressively."

"But nothing serious or fatal."

"Excuse me while I hang the fucking flags out. Sir."

Daryl just laughed, feeling the aftereffects of the adrenaline that had flooded his blood stream only minutes ago, and strolled back into the bar to apologise for the interruption to the game and to say goodnight. Then, with the lightness of step belonging to a man well-pleased and much invigorated, he made his way to the car.

His good humour dimmed, however, when he remembered just how upset she was, and was going to be. He promised that for every second she spent in tears of misery, he would replace them with tears of sweet ecstasy.

Just give me a chance.

Lord, what a wife she would make. And she wouldn't need a mile-long pedigree to be deemed suitable for his hand in marriage; she was making herself his equal without even intending to.

MYSTY GOT OFF the bike and accepted the congratulations with muted response and glanced around with dispassion. She couldn't even enjoy the Bowl she was so angry. How dare he interfere? After pretending to be so considerate and asking how she and Donny were!

"Man, one night with you here and we're heading the leader board again!"

Rusty's happiness managed to drag her attention back to the present, half of her still in that topless casino feeling like the world had turned over. She forced a smile to her lips, but her distance and sadness weren't hard to see; and that she had turned up out of the blue, then ripped the opponents to shreds in three consecutive races going at speeds no one else ever dared, they knew something was wrong.

"*What the fuck?*"

A procession of Bentleys was driving down the track towards her, number plates giving away who was inside. Everyone backed up to let them through, their progress only ever leading to one person.

She leaned back against her bike. One false move and she was going to trash every single car. Rusty and Slick stayed with her, every eye watching or glued to screens as the black Bentley stopped in front of her. One tall black suit got out, looking grim, and opened the rear door.

So they thought she would just get into the car, right?

"Kiddo, get in the car. Talk it out. I'll get the bike back for you." Mysty looked over at O'Grady, who nodded at her: *It's okay. I got you.*

"Mysty, please get in." Donny's voice was soft, almost tired.

She pushed off from the bike and walked slowly over to the man she loved more than life. Her stomach was tight, her heart beating so fast. What was this?

Paulo glanced at O'Grady, who saw the look: there were going to be no witnesses to this conversation.

Inside the car she took the seat opposite.

After several agonising seconds Donny took a breath and said, "You know I wouldn't deliberately hurt you–"

"You stood me up so you could go play cards and drink in a topless casino. I'd say that was deliberately hurting me."

"Dammit, Mysty, it was all engineered. Daryl admitted it. I wouldn't be here now if I didn't love you. And I wouldn't have pointed a gun at his head if you weren't the most important person in the world to me."

"You held a gun to his head?" she repeated slowly, wavering on being impressed.

"Yes. Luckily for him he gave me an answer I liked as to why he did what he did tonight, and I didn't put a bullet in his brain. Though I was incredibly tempted."

"And what answer did he give you?"

"He…he challenged my treatment of you. He doesn't think I deserve you."

"Coming from the most debauched and selfish man in America I find that utterly offensive."

Her disgust was a comfort to Donny. Perhaps Daryl would never be loved, or even liked, by her?

"He doesn't think I spend enough time with you, amongst other things."

"Why the fuck couldn't he just talk to you? Why did he have to make his point by keeping you away from me?"

"I think he thought a demonstration of how I would prove him right was more effective."

"Maybe I should give him a demonstration of how to breathe through a different hole in his head!" she tossed back, riled and now confused. Just being angry had been easier. None of this was making any sense! Why was Daryl doing this? And why was Donny so calm about it?

"As much as I would love you to hate him, he doesn't deserve it, sweetheart. Trust me, in a strange way he does have your best interests at heart."

"Are you joking? How much did you drink at that club? The only thing that man has any interest in is getting me in his bed!"

"I've no doubt he would like to, but he did what he did this evening knowing you were going to be incredibly angry with him, knowing he was taking a huge risk. If he was out to seduce you, he wouldn't have said what he said tonight."

"I think you're all mad," she said in utter disbelief. Donny was actually trying to redeem Daryl after he derailed their evening, having already pointed a gun at his head and then seemingly forgiven him? There were too many conflicting scenarios here. What the hell was going on?

"I think we probably are," Donny agreed gently, seeing she was struggling to make any sense – and little wonder. He reached out a hand and took her wrist, pulling her towards him and settling her in his lap, kissing her without restraint because he knew she needed to feel it, knew it would calm her. But he kissed her because he knew, even as her arms slid over his shoulders and her legs slipped either side of his hips, it was most likely the last time he ever would. Donny Capello, Lord of Vegas, could have wept it hurt so much to know the truth: this was going to end. Not even because she was dead, or he was dead, but because of who he was to the world.

Finally he released her.

"You're staying with me tonight, alright?"

A nod.

He wished he'd been able to hold her in that dress. She'd looked wonderful in it. But then she always looked wonderful, even when she was furious. He remembered the fiery little ball of pluckiness that had shown up in his life; he looked at the fiery woman of passion and courage she had become.

"That was quite a diatribe you threw at me tonight. Most impressed."

"You know I have a temper."

"I don't think anyone has ever dared to confront Daryl like that in public. The legendary tiger was certainly out for all to see," he teased.

"He should be used to it by now."

Donny smiled at her answer, bittersweet as it was. Whatever Daryl wanted from Mysty, he was determined to see it through. And at least, Donny consoled himself, at least if Daryl did win her over, he knew he'd had to fight for her. Every step, every inch. Because money did not buy this girl, not at all. Daryl would have to earn her trust and respect through his words and actions, the hard way.

"Have you stopped being angry with me now?" he asked.

"I'm not angry with you anymore. I love you too much."

They were gentle words that eased the ache in his heart, yet made him so sad. Would she still love him after she'd heard what he had to say? Would she hate him? Would she ever say those words again?

"I love you more," he declared, stung by the reminder of having said this to Daryl, and knowing that, because of that love, he'd have to let her go.

"If that's what you like to think," she mocked gently, and pulled off his bowtie as she kissed him again, fingers seeking beneath his shirt to feel the warmth and strength of his body. And, for once, he didn't stop her. He wanted his memories of her passion for him to last him long, lonely years, and sustain him when she fell into the arms of a man she could trust as she had trusted him.

He'd always known she was too good to live in a world like his.

IT HAD BEEN a long week. Too long. Made worse for the fact she'd refused to speak to him, taking none of his calls to the point he had given up. And right now it was impossible to relax, because tomorrow morning, Sunday morning, was when Donny was going to tell her. He had chosen Sunday because there would six days before the next Bowl, and he was hoping that this would give her time to calm her down. O'Grady had been apprised and was, at first, angry at their collusion, arguing that it would upset her far beyond anything that had gone before. Donny had stepped in and reaffirmed that it was for the best that they were all in agreement beforehand so as to keep her safe, which O'Grady had to agree with, and knew he'd need to use the time to comfort and protect her. They had made discreet changes to her bedroom door and windows while she was absent at the dance studios, which meant she couldn't get out.

The intercom buzzed and he looked at wearily at it, thinking that the five metres from the window to the device was five too many. With a sigh he sat down in front of the screen and pressed the button.

"Daryl, where is she?"

"She's mostly likely at the Bowl, where she goes on a Saturday night when she's not working." *Until I call a halt to it because it's impossible to keep her properly safe there.*

"She's not answering! I've tried calling her three times and no answer. I can't get hold of O'Grady either!"

Donny's tone immediately made Daryl's back straighten…why was he so agitated?

"It's very noisy there. Wait, I'll try O'Grady."

Daryl pressed some buttons and the call went through.

He looked back at Donny and knew immediately there was a problem. He froze. "What's wrong?" he managed.

"We've had a credible threat confirmed. There's a hit planned on her. Tonight," Donny said, his face so grim Daryl swallowed hard.

"Shit. Oh God."

"Sir?" O'Grady took Daryl's call. He had never heard such panic in his boss's voice.

"OG, where is she?" Daryl asked.

"She's just leaving the Bowl with a group of Pirates."

"Get her out of there, out of sight and into a secure unit. Get her out! I have Donny on another line. We have a credible threat on her confirmed for tonight."

He heard O'Grady's rapid orders to his team. Apparently, they were about a hundred metres away from her, with over a thousand people between them.

"Do we have any intel on who they are, what they're planning?" Daryl asked Donny.

"They knew she was going to be at the Bowl. They could have been in the crowd, watching. Being a biker would be a perfect disguise and an easy get away."

"How many are we talking?" Daryl looked at Donny. His blue eyes were intense, his body motionless.

"At least two dozen."

"Holy Christ! O'Grady, did you hear that?"

"Mark! Baz! Start running! Get to her however you can! And get the fucking people out of the way!"

O'Grady rang through to her, praying she picked up.

"OG? You okay?" she asked. He could hear laughter in the background.

"Mysty. Are you alright?"

"Of course." He heard a bike start up. Hers? He knew it was fast. It would need to be, if they couldn't get the car to her first, and thank God she was perfectly able to handle the speed. "What's wrong?"

"Kiddo, we need to get someplace safe. Donny's just called. Someone's called out a hit on you – tonight – we need to get you out of here!"

"What the hell? OG!"

"I need you to stay where you are and give us a chance to catch up. The car is on its way. Failing that, get the bike started–"

A sound of gunshots; a sound that turned the hearts of all concerned to ice. They'd found her. They were too late.

"Slick!" she screamed. "Don't! Get back!"

And then the sound of screaming and shouting.

"Fuck! Fuck!" Both Donny and Daryl were on their feet, cursing, hands tearing at their hair.

And then they heard her voice: "It's me they want! Everyone just stay back!"

And then the call was disconnected.

"Fuck! Fuck! Oh fuck! O'Grady!" Daryl cried, pulling up the satellite view and sending it to Donny, pressing the buzzer for Mac. He zoomed in on her in the crowd of bikers now outside the venue, on the last stretch of dirt track before hitting tarmac that would take them back towards central LA. Oh thank God, she was alive. She was gesturing to everyone, to get them to move away from her. He scanned the area. There was another group of bikers up ahead of her, blocking her exit, leaving her trapped in front of a dense crowd of black-clad bikers who were starting to panic as a wall of bikes appeared about fifty metres away, the pillion riders with raised guns. She whispered to the people around her. He couldn't hear her over the roar of engines and shouts of fear.

Mac appeared at the door. "Mr Blackmoor, sir?"

"Mac. The chopper. To the Bowl. Now! Call me from the roof."

"Yes, sir." Mac was gone. There was no time to get the pilot; he would fly it himself.

Her helmet was on with the visor down. He heard the deep rumble of an engine, and knew it was hers. There was only one thing she could do. But she'd never get past them. A second later every light on every bike went out. As did every light in the stadium. And he lost her in the sea of black leather and helmets. He heard the twist of her throttle, distinct over the sound of a thousand others that roared until he could hardly bear the noise. What was happening? What was she doing?

And then a shadow roared out of the darkness, heading straight at the gunmen, who didn't fire because they couldn't see her as every bike now turned their full beam on them and blinded them, and revved engines so that they couldn't hear her. He saw them raise their arms, shielding their eyes. Clever girl. But how would get past the wall of metal they had formed?

He searched the screen. Where was she? He could no longer see her or hear her; and then a pulse of blue light rippled out from her bike, making contact with the first bike, toppling it into the second, which slammed into the third. She didn't stay to watch and, avoiding the bullets of those firing blindly into the night, she disappeared.

"Dear God," Donny whispered, saying the words Daryl was thinking.

What was that she had put on her bike? Thank God that she had.

"Sir!" Mac came in on Daryl's earpiece. "We're on the roof."

"I'm on my way."

"Sir? This isn't safe!"

"You just fly the thing, Mac. This is my choice. Donny, we're on our way in two."

The force from the rotors buffeted him as he made his way to the powerful chopper, his suit jacket flapping madly. He was handed a headset and clipped in as the bird lifted off into the darkness. The satellite feed showed her heading through the suburbs towards the open road, where a car would meet her.

He rang through to O'Grady, and heard their conversation.

"Where are you, OG? Are you close?" Calm words from the hunted.

"Following as fast as I can. Bentleys don't go as fast as your superbike."

"Keep eyes on me. I'm going to stop soon. I'm being followed, but I have a plan."

What! Followed? Daryl panned back on his handheld. In the dark he spotted at least another dozen bikes, probably about a mile behind her.

"Mac! Move it!" he yelled.

"Mysty, you are not to stop! You keep–"

But OG's protest was lost in a screech of tyre rubber as she stopped in the shadows, pivoting the bike with her foot, now facing the way she'd come. She cut the engine and lights.

"Bobby, bring out the pins, lights up on my mark, scatter pins as soon as I move."

"Mysty!"

"OG, I've got this."

Daryl felt his hands clench into fists. Clearly she had more tricks concealed in that bike. And people on her team.

The gunmen were almost on her, a small army of bikes hurtling around the bend and into the straight where she was waiting.

She let them come on, so close.

Five seconds.

Four.

Three.

"Mark."

Her full beam flicked on.

And then flicked off.

In a chaos of exploding front tyres and blinded, catapulted riders the metal pins claimed their first victims as the bikes bucked and skidded across the tarmac. The front ten or so had no time to react, and the back markers swerved through the mayhem as she calmly restarted her bike and roared off back the way she had come without a single glance back.

"Bobby, are we good? Are any of them following?"

"You have twelve following. The rest are on the ground."

"Great."

"Kitten, are you alright?" A new voice joined them.

"Donny? Yeah, I'm good. OG, where are you now?"

"Less than thirty seconds. But we're not fast enough to get you away. Wait for the chopper."

"Bobby, get me a map up of the area. A ten-mile radius."

"We have enough fuel left for twelve miles at this speed." The onboard computer was succinct. Everyone heard the information.

"Shit," OG cursed. "Hang in there, kiddo."

Mac's voice cut in: "We have the chopper. We're almost on you."

"You got some rope?"

"Of course. Get off the road, as far away from the guns as possible. We'll get you out."

"Bobby, bring up sector seventeen and zoom in. Okay. OG, I've got a rather large building site coming up. I should be able to find somewhere to hide while you fellas catch up. You found it on your system?"

Daryl brought up the site as well, a jigsaw of heavy machinery and mounds of dirt and temporary cabins.

"Sure. Get in and get out of sight. You've bought yourself a bit of time. Turn off your lights as soon as you can. You might be able to lose them when you turn into the place."

"Will do. Mac, you got an ETA?"

"Five minutes, max."

"Longest five minutes of my life."

The lights went off as she turned in, swerving around the barricade designed to keep out cars, but not bikes. She began cruising among the shadowed world of giant diggers and trucks parked alongside huge earth piles. She rode between two monster vehicles and cut the engine and lights. Then came the sound of bikes approaching and, shit, they turned in, where, like two-wheeled jackals, they prowled the site.

She heard them. "Bobby, give me an expanded view of this place and show them to me."

Where was OG? Had they got him? Who were these people?

Abandoning the bike, she crept through the darkness, her visor showing eight moving red dots, circling, surrounding.

"Kitten, you just hang in there," Donny whispered.

She held in the whimper of frustration and fear inside her chest, the leathers feeling suddenly very tight as she dropped low, trying to navigate her way to a point where the chopper could drop a rope. In the darkness she saw a raised mound of earth.

"Mysty, we have you." Mac's voice was the best sound in the world just then.

"The northwest side, there's a bank of dirt. Fly over, get the rope down, I'll be there to catch it."

"That's not safe. What if they see her?" Daryl hissed, not liking the look of the huge, open mound where she would be shot at. Even with her skill, getting to the top and catching a rope fast enough to avoid their bullets was a slim call.

"News flash, Mr Manager, *I do this for a living*! I don't have another play. It's a calculated risk, but I know what I'm doing." The snarl in her voice for Daryl did not escape notice, least of all by him. "Mac, are you in?"

"On it, kiddo."

"Drop the rope as soon as I break cover. As soon as I'm going up the slope start peeling away. Don't leave it until I'm on the rope to move or we're all a target. You got me?"

"Are you sure?"

"I'm sure," she sighed. "Bobby, download into the mainframe as soon as the bike's in the air. Everyone else, it's been fun. Mac – buckle up."

As last words went, it was concise, and hardly anyone was breathing.

"Ready when you are." Mac forced his voice to stay upbeat, despite the lump in his throat.

The riders had seen the chopper circling and, thrown into confusion, unsure whether its occupants would fire, they took cover.

Mac stayed high, just out of reach of their possible bullets, ready to swoop in for the pick-up.

The rope was uncoiled. This was insane.

Mysty pulled her helmet off, pressed in her earpiece to make sure it was secure, and put her shades on, pressing the switch for night vision. She loved these shades. She'd never shown them to anyone. Maybe she never would.

Taking one last breath, to calm her fear, she crouched, ready to launch herself up the mound, eyes on the position of the chopper.

She didn't want to die.

Didn't want this to be the end.

Running had saved her life before. Would it save her again?

Daryl watched as she twisted the throttle and urged the bike up the mound of dirt that suddenly felt like Everest. The bike's engine was loud from the revs, the noise giving away her position, and the hunters turned their guns in her direction as she headed towards the rope that would carry her to safety or to death. Bullets began to pepper the air, their desperation to snatch at her equalled by her need to reach the summit. She saw the rope swirling in the air, and a quiet instinct kicked in, all the hours of practice on trapezes and beams high above the arena at Celeste.

The top of the dirt mound levelled off a fraction, so the bike valiantly picked up enough speed to take them both into the air as she launched up and off. With practised moves she knew so well, her hands found the rope and she held tight, feeling the chopper swerve away as she did so. She knew Mac had this, but still flinched as the bullets rang out as they climbed, the stars above witness too to her rescue. She used her strong leather-gloved hands and booted feet to climb the rope as they hurtled upwards, her eyes flicking down just for a moment to see what was left of her bike now resting brokenly at the bottom of a rocky ditch. Although processed in seconds, it felt like much longer.

Daryl let out the breath he had been holding in. "Donny, we have her."

There was an inaudible sound from Donny, and Daryl glanced down to see innumerable cars pile through the barrier and into the site, a hundred men unloading and unloading bullets as they did. Franny. And OG, now that he had back-up.

"Hey, kiddo, it's a bit windy out there, you want to get in?" Mac's voice in her earpiece sounded more than a little relieved.

"I'm happy with an outside seat," she said, and Daryl swore softly as he looked and saw her dangling off one of the legs, the rope safely tucked around her so it didn't unfurl into the blades.

"Let me rephrase that for you: get into my fucking helicopter," Mac said.

Donny's voice came in: "Mac, get her out of there. Thank you…"

"Yes, sir."

The chopper leaned away and headed back towards LA central.

Daryl opened the door so he could see her, watching as she raised a hand, swinging up to sit on the chopper's leg with such easy grace he felt that sense of wonder he always felt when she was at Celeste. Looking up, she went still; even with shades on, he could tell she was surprised to see him.

"You know, I think this is the first time I can honestly say I'm pleased to see you," she said.

Holding on tight to the handhold, he offered his right hand to her, sweet relief flooding his body as he felt her grasp not his fingers but his wrist – a much safer place to grip. But then, of course, she knew what she was doing.

Pulling her up, they knelt on the floor for a few seconds, the adrenaline pumping in both their veins. After two deep breaths, she pulled off her shades and looked at him in a way she never had before. Lips parted slightly, but no words were uttered.

"Always a first time for everything," he said softly, marvelling at how huge her eyes were. Somehow in those few seconds, amidst the noise of the rotor blades and the gusting wind through the door, there was a silence, a stillness that held them both captive.

Then he felt her fingers retract, and the moment was over, reality reclaiming them from the giddiness of survival. Daryl pointed to one of the seats and she settled into it. But he noticed her hands were shaking uncontrollably, and reached forward to secure the clips on the straps. It was then that he felt a wetness on his hand. Even in the dimness there was no mistaking what it was.

Blood. Her blood.

"You're bleeding," he said slowly, careful not to panic her, and her eyes flicked down to see the blood on her gloves and on his hands. She felt sickened, the red gleaming in the dark, but still distinctive. This time her blood. He saw her pale. "You've been shot… where? Where are you hurt?"

"My shoulder, I think. It just caught me."

He moved her blooded hair away from her shoulder, gently unzipping the jacket to take a closer look. She couldn't look, and closed her eyes as he called for the onboard medic. She kept them closed as he unclipped the safety belt, carefully pulled her t-shirt away, swabbed away the blood…

Then she heard the gunshots.

Not just one. Not just a couple. A cacophony of firearms unleashed all at once. There was only one reason why: the men who had tried to kill her, probably in waiting all over LA, had been found and dealt with. She opened her eyes, needing comfort in that moment of horrible realisation, and saw Daryl's face, as serious and troubled as her own. How he hated seeing such fear in her face.

The medic didn't pause, but cleaned the wound and applied a dressing. Her gloves were removed too, and her hands cleaned.

She looked away, and heard someone say: "It's alright, sir, it was nothing serious, just a graze. She'll heal."

And then gentle hands clipped her in again. "It's alright, Mysty, it's over. You're safe now." Daryl hoped the words would comfort her, but she didn't react, her face still chalk-white and expressionless.

She could feel her hands still shaking, and clamped them between her knees, hoping he wouldn't notice. But Daryl had seen. Only now, in the safety of the helicopter, would it really hit her that the last horrible thirty minutes of her life could have been her last but for her own intelligence and bravery.

They touched down, and Daryl unclipped her, easing her out of her seat to stand next to him, his arm around her ready to hold her if she stumbled. She didn't seem to be wholly aware of what was going on, the shock taking over completely. It was only when she had been shepherded down the steps and along an unfamiliar corridor, surrounded by a phalanx of guards headed by Mac, that she came out of her daze of silent horror and looked around her with wide eyes.

"Where are we?"

"My apartment. It's safer here. The chopper is on its way back to get Donny."

She didn't fight as an arm guided her forward, through the door and into a distantly familiar apartment, and to a sofa. She didn't argue as her jacket and boots were removed and a blanket laid over her. So many emotions. They were welling up enough to drown her. She just wanted them to go away. She wanted to feel safe and not sick with fear. This wasn't like last time, when death threats had been made. Last time they had been for Donny. This time…this time they had been for her. She felt like a rat in a maze, turning this way and that to endless dead ends.

Daryl looked over at Mac, who was standing silent and serious at the other end of the sofa, both of them unsure what to do with a Mysty who looked so fragile and lost, just a young girl, dusty, injured and shaking. A hand raised up to cover her mouth and she choked on a sob, but forced herself to swallow it. He felt utterly helpless. He didn't know what to do, how to comfort her. He was, for once in his life, completely out of his depth.

"Donny will be here really soon, alright? Just take it nice and easy. Mac, can you bring her a glass of water?"

He doubted she'd even heard him.

Mac held the glass out, but she looked at it without seeming to recognise what it was, so he handed it to Daryl.

"Have some water, Mysty," Daryl urged, trying to put it into her hand.

Nothing. Her hands were cold and clammy, her eyes too wide.

Moments later he heard the front door open, and rapid footsteps on the wooden floor, and then Donny appeared, eyes looking for only one person, face like a death mask. His gaze touched on the split on her shoulder in her black top, where the hint of pale skin and the stain of blood marred the perfection. Daryl saw his eyes close as he went past, heading around the sofa, needing to see her face, check she was alright. Eyes that closed with resignation, relief and regret. Eyes that opened with solemn, heart-breaking resolve.

"Sweetheart?"

Donny had been here; he knew what this felt like. He also knew how to deal with her; he needed to break the spell she was trapped in. Those beautiful eyes full of tears, but now with a spark of hope.

"Donny?"

"You're safe, sweetheart, you're all safe. It's over now." He smoothed her hair, pulled her forwards into his arms and laid her head on his shoulder.

But she pulled away, as if needing to confirm it was him. And after scanning his face and chest said, "Donny, there's blood on your shirt. Are you hurt?"

He knew she hated the sight of blood, and whispered, "It's not mine. I'm not hurt." Mentally cursing himself for not checking this before rushing in, he kept his self-recriminations hidden as he focussed on comforting her, his voice low and soft. "It's finished. No one will come after you again."

"I'm cold. Really sick."

He pulled the blanket up around her shoulders and put his arms around her. At that moment Baden arrived, and Donny rose quickly, eyes going to Daryl, recognising him.

"The doctor just wants to check her over. It'll take a few minutes, that's all," Daryl explained, and Donny nodded, relaying the information to Mysty.

Whilst Baden carefully attended to Mysty, Donny went to Daryl. "Do you have a room she can stay in tonight? One with a lock? It has to be now while the fear is still in her," he whispered.

Daryl knew what he meant. The sadness, almost desperation, in his eyes spoke volumes. He hadn't expected this. Not here, not now, and right under his own roof. He'd been prepared to support Donny from a detached distance, and to oversee her care and safety after it was done, but not this.

"Yes. Down the corridor behind you, fourth door on the right. The room…has no window and the door is very solid, and secure."

Donny turned back with a curt nod, his face drawn, the obvious weight on his heart sickening his soul. Her evening was about to get much worse.

Baden was talking in low tones to Mysty that Donny was relieved to see were calming her. He closed his bag and stood. "The wound is clean and will heal quickly," he said, "and my thanks to whoever attended so quickly to avoid infection. Her vitals are good, too. The symptoms of shock will ease. I recommend quiet and rest, now, for a full recuperation, and plenty of fluids. Keep her warm. She can eat as soon as she feels able."

Donny held out his hand. "Come on, sweetheart, let's go somewhere quieter and get you settled for the night."

He could have said anything he liked as, glazed and unsteady on her feet, she allowed herself to be helped from the room.

Everyone else watched them go. Paulo and Mario stood grave and silent. O'Grady glanced over at Mac, and then his boss. Baden left after a few low words were exchanged with his employer, with the demand that he be called should they need him. The atmosphere was like that of a funeral. Even Daryl, who was infatuated and selfish enough to want

Donny to end it with her, found himself struggling when faced with the reality: the task Donny had before him, and why, and her imminent heartbreak.

There was one crazy moment, a little after they had left the room, when he felt like marching in and making Donny change his mind; then he remembered the guns and the moment he'd heard the words, 'There's a hit planned on her. Tonight.' A hit. A kill. A painted target on her back. Rage burned at that. She was just a kid. And someone had tried to end her life, after she'd struggled so hard to survive. He didn't want to see her risked like that again. Ever. She'd done nothing to deserve it.

Please God, let Donny find the words. And please God, take care of her.

DONNY WAS PRAYING the exact same thing as he settled her into bed. He was about to hurt her, so badly. And to do so meant he was going to have to tear out his own heart too. How could he not see her? He loved her. He loved her so goddamned much. Here she was, trusting him, and there he was planning on breaking her heart again when she deserved to be loved. To be comforted in every way a man could comfort his woman. This time he lay her down, knowing…this was it.

The thought made his hands a little unsteady, a little desperate, wanting to touch her satin cheeks and memorise every curve of her lips and face, her cheeks, and the feel of her hair.

"I'm so sorry you had to go through that."

"It's alright. I'm here, you're here. Nothing else matters."

He squeezed his eyes shut, lay down next to her and dropped his head to her chest. She cradled his head, stroked his hair, comforting him. *Oh God, don't make this any harder…*

He forced himself to think about the gunshot wound, the blood on her shoulder, and he knew: next time she might not be so lucky; there mustn't be a next time. He'd seen death a thousand times. But her death was one he could never live with.

"But it does, sweetheart. I was so scared for you. I've never feared for anyone more than I feared for you tonight. I'd rather have someone try and shoot me."

"Donny, please, I don't…I don't care. It's over now. Please just hold me, help me forget."

He listened to the solid throb of her heartbeat, proof of her vitality, understanding why she liked listening to his when they lay together in the quiet of his room…a room that would be forever haunted by her magical presence, never to be known again. How would he ever survive without her golden loveliness and beautiful laughter? She would haunt his rooms for ever.

"I can't do that tonight."

Her face registered her alarm at his words, and the sorrow in his voice.

"What do you mean? What are you saying?" she demanded, trying to struggle up, but he was stronger. "Donny! What are you talking about?"

"I have to end this, sweetheart. I have to end it now, before it gets you killed."

She heard the emotion in his voice, and cried, "Why? Why? Don't, Donny! Please!"

"Please listen. I have to set you free, to find your own way, without me, without the association of what I represent. I can't see you anymore, sweetheart. This is it. No more open-ended promises, no more maybes. I should have been more honest with you sooner, but…" She cried out; a long, strangulated sound that ripped his heart open. "I couldn't bear to let you go. I love you so much, kitten, I always have. There's nothing I wouldn't do to keep you safe, including putting you first…and…and that means giving you up. You don't…you've never belonged in my world. I've always known that, but I fooled myself into thinking we could still make it work somehow–"

"No! Donny, please!" She twisted underneath him, fighting against his weight. "You're everything to me! You're only saying this because of tonight! How can I not see you again? Just tell me what I have to do! I'll wait! I'll do anything! *Don't do this*! *Please*!"

"I ask only one thing of you: don't hate me."

"I couldn't ever hate you! *I love you*! I'd die for you! How can I bear to be apart from you, not knowing if you're safe, or if you need me? I'm not afraid to die for you! How can you make this choice for both of us? It's my life too! I've made my choice! Why won't you accept that?"

"Because I would sooner put a bullet in my head than have you die! *Because of me*! Can't you see? I don't want you to be afraid of anything, and all the good things I wished for you are finally coming true, and all the recognition I always believed you should get for your talents is becoming real. You're *seventeen*, Mysty, you have so much ahead of you! I won't let you throw it away for me."

"I don't care about the fame! I don't care about any of it! I'll give it all up! Please, Donny, you're all I want, all I'll ever want!"

"You don't know that."

"*Yes I do*! *Yes I do*!"

Pure rage bucked against his body weight, and he almost smiled at how he loved her tiger side, that passion, that strength…but everything now was moving into the past tense, and the joy was tainted with anguish.

"You're not old enough to know that, kitten. I made a choice, too young, and now I wish, more than anything, that I could just be the man who could marry you, and have a family with, and love you every day of your life. But…I can't."

This couldn't be real. These beautiful words made ugly by their truth, a bittersweet cocktail of honesty and heartbreak. Tears now poured down her cheeks; but he knew he had to finish this.

"This can't be happening…" she sobbed, shaking her head from side to side. "I don't believe it. I won't believe it."

"I'm afraid it's very real. But I'll always be there, in the background. If you ever need me, you know I'll be there. And I'll let you know when that man, that fath–"

"Don't say that word! Don't say his name!"

"When he is gone, I'll let you know, so you know you're free of him. I'll always love–"

"Don't, Donny!"

"Always know you are loved, sweetheart, as much as a mortal man can love a woman."

Donny could not believe he would kiss her, now, for possibly the last time, but kiss her he did.

But she broke loose. "Love me now, tonight, please? Don't say no. I don't want to die not having loved you like I want to."

His whole body mourned and ached for her. He knew her passion for him, knew how she longed to be loved like that.

"If I love you once, I'll never let you go, kitten. You'll find someone, I know you will, someone who loves everything about you just like I do. Never forget, I would love you a million times over if I could." He kissed her again, her body shaking as she sobbed and fought him yet surrendered to the kiss. "My heart is still in your keeping. You're the only one I would ever trust with it."

His eyes were so sad, his whisper so soft. She could barely breathe. She gave in to the kiss as he unleashed all the passion he dare use, drowning in it like she might die from it. On and on until she opened her eyes, and he was up, and then he was gone, and she screamed as she heard the lock turn.

"*No*!" She dived off the bed and grabbed the handle. "*Donny, don't do this! Don't you dare leave me! Not here! Don't leave me! Please, Donny! Open the door! Open the door*!"

Donny stood for a long moment, staring at the door. And then he glanced at Daryl, who looked like he might vomit. Mac and Paulo stood like silent bookends either side of the door, their faces rigid with control.

They could all hear the panic and the distress, the hard thump of her body as she slammed it against the door.

"Sweetheart, please don't hurt yourself. You've been through enough tonight, because of me; fuck, all because of me. Please lie down and try and rest."

"This isn't fair and you know it! Open the fucking door!"

"I love you." A hand laid flat on the door for a few moments, feeling the vibrations from the thumps and shakes as she fought to get out.

"Donny! Donny! Don't leave me here! Not with him!"

"Goodbye, sweetheart."

"*No*! *No!*"

Donny broke in a silent moment, his face wracked with grief, his hands clenched, and Daryl put a hand out to him, but it was waved away as he turned to the wall.

Daryl nodded, and Mac and Paulo followed him into the living room.

Moments later Donny joined them.

"Everyone out. Paulo, I'll be there in a moment."

The command clearly excluded Daryl, because Donny was looking directly at him with eyes that said, Not you.

"So. You have what you wanted, after all."

"I didn't want this. I admit I might have, once, but…I'm sorry it's ending this way, Donny. I know how much she means to you."

For Daryl they were genuine words; but for Donny? Well, winners can be as generous as they like with losers.

"*You don't have a fucking clue how much she means to me*!" The blast of anger silenced whatever Daryl might have considered saying next. Even the thumps against the door down the corridor stopped. "You have your pictures, I see! *So many fucking pictures*!" There was little point in defending their presence; they were on the walls in all their gorgeous clarity and colour, for all to see. Donny prowled around, incensed by them. Pictures of his girl! His girl! He turned to face the silent figure that didn't attempt to explain or protest, didn't back away from Donny's rage. "You have your chance, Daryl. Not that you deserve it, after all you've done to her. You'll never deserve her. But don't you dare waste the chance I would give *everything* for, because I promise, if you do, you'll hate yourself for the rest of your life. There isn't a woman on this planet like her. If you're too stupid to see that and how goddamned precious she is, you aren't the man to claim her."

Donny then walked right up to Daryl, well inside the boundaries of personal space, eyes fixed dangerously close to his.

"I'm trusting you, with her," he snarled. "Don't forget, I'll be watching, and if you hurt her, I'll kill you slowly with my bare hands and then have you thrown from your own fucking skyscraper."

With one last furious look, a look that would have made a lesser man's guts turn to jelly, Donny strode away. He allowed himself one last glance towards the corridor where she was, but forced himself towards the door before he changed his mind; nothing could be worse than the next second.

Daryl sat down heavily, exhaling long and slow.

Two figures entered the room.

"You alright, sir?"

"I don't think it's me you need to worry about, Mac," Daryl replied tightly, leaning elbows on his knees and rubbing his face as he opened up the view of the room she was in on his handheld.

She was sitting on the floor with her back against the door, a tumble of curls falling over her shoulders as her head leaned against her knees, hands wrapped around the back of her head. The tremble of her body told the three men she was weeping, silently, as she usually did. They'd seen her defy everything, survive everything; now she was a vulnerable butterfly with broken wings.

Daryl remembered his own words: 'I don't want to see her hurt.' Now it felt more like he would do anything on earth to see her smile again. But right now? Right now he had to keep her safe.

"It's not the locking her in a room you have to worry about. It's what she'll do when you let her out," O'Grady said quietly, as if reading his mind.

He closed the screen, too saddened by the sight of her misery. He knew he couldn't go to her now. She would have to be left alone in the hope that time might cauterise the wound carved into her heart.

"You can go, Mac," he said. "I'll wait until she's asleep and then go to bed. We'll see how she is in the morning. Let Baden know we may need sedatives if she's still as upset tomorrow. Warn Craig Roberts Celeste on Tuesday may have to be cancelled."

"Yes, sir."

"O'Grady, you too. Go and relax, I'm sure tomorrow will be busy enough. I'll call if I need you."

"Are you sure you'll be okay, alone?"

"Yes. Thank you."

"Sir."

He'd dreamed of having her here, in his apartment, but not like this. Oh God, not like this. What he wouldn't give, or pay, to take away the grief that consumed her and have her here because it was something she'd chosen.

What on earth would happen in the morning?

SHE WAS STILL asleep, laid out by the door, face obscured by her hair. What the hell was he going to do with her today? He was the last person she'd want to speak to, but, aside from O'Grady perhaps, there was no one alive she would want to see. The reality sunk in: her family were dead, and her other family, the black and white suits, were all going to have to keep their distance now. She was absolutely alone and she knew it.

The frantic shout of protest from last night was clear in his mind, 'Don't leave here! Not with him!' Not to Daryl Blackmoor, the man who had earned only her distrust and her enmity, who had never bothered to understand her, who thought he could buy her affections, who was so used to having his own way he didn't know how to put in the effort when it came to a person and not a business?

He drank a glass of orange juice, hoping the chill and the taste would wake him up, and there she was, on his wall. He'd seen her brilliance a hundred thousand times before he'd met her, and wanted her for himself. He hadn't cared who she was, not really, and the fact that he hadn't even known her real name didn't matter either, he just wanted her for himself.

He took a shower, hoping the blast of the water would relax him, and there she was, in his mind. He could still her shouts, the thumps on the door, and crying out for Donny. Would she ever feel anything like that for him? What did he have to do?

He looked back at the screen. If it would help her trust him a little, he had to let her out. Besides, she must be starving. She was awake, sat back in her position against the door. Her face was pale, expressionless. He pressed in the command and the computerised locks slid back. He heard them from the kitchen, and she heard them too. She got up, slowly, and opened the door, looking a little unsteady, and his eyes left the screen to watch her walk down the corridor towards him. Not that she saw him. She looked and moved like a ghost.

She got to the lounge and paused, blinking at the sunshine that poured in through the panoramic windows and huge doors. There was nothing angry about her posture, just weakness and defeat.

"Is there anything you'd like?" he asked gently, anything to break the spell.

Her eyes turned to him, but she didn't answer. Her silence was worse than her tears, and he wished she would react, in any way at all. Instead she moved as if in a trance towards the windows and, before he could react, had flicked the concealed lock on the doors – of course! she'd been here before! – and was through them and heading for the impossible drop on the other side of the pool.

He dived round the breakfast bar and went after her, and grabbed her, and she reacted with automatic reflexes. An elbow caught him in the face and a foot kicked out his leg, leaving him face down on the tiles.

"No!"

Instinctive reflexes, reflexes he didn't know he even had, forced him up, and this time he was ready for her. He hauled her back against him, locking her into a hold which she fought like a wild animal. But she was a weakened wild animal, and he felt her tears on his bare arm as he held her.

"*Let me go*! Please just let me go!" she cried.

"No! You know I can't do that. Mysty–"

She emitted a growl of rage, and fought him again.

"Please, *please* let me go!"

He didn't want to hurt her. He grappled with her, backing them up, and then hurled the pair of them into the pool. He didn't lessen his grip on her as they fell, and they emerged, gasping for air. His feet found the floor and he stood; but she slipped from his grasp and, shorter than he was, sank again. He pulled her up, held onto her.

"*I don't want anymore!* Let me go. Oh God, let me go…"

Her pleading, broken voice cut him so deep it was agony to hear the pain and the despair.

He held her tight. "I won't ever let you go! *Ever*!" he growled, the words close to her ear, feeling her body finally lose its tension. And then the moment of surrender: she leant back against him, her head on his shoulder, close enough for him to hear her next words, that were little more than a whisper.

"No one ever keeps that promise. No one ever keeps it."

And then the grief poured out, her body convulsing as a sob after sob broke loose. It felt like she would break apart, and he laid his hand against her forehead, gently, and waited, his other arm secure around her waist so she didn't slip back under the water. He wanted to lower his lips to her hair, her temple, and kiss away the grief, but knew it was not the time, knew it would confuse her even more.

Facing nothing but the sky above, it was the single most surreal moment of his life. They could have been the only two beings on earth, and the city noise drifted away as he absorbed the sadness of why they were standing like this, and the responsibility that came with it. It was an honour, a gift, and he wanted that responsibility…more than anything he'd ever known.

He could feel her lack of resistance, knew the fight was over, for now at least. He lifted her up, arms under shoulders and knees, carried her to the edge of the pool and walked up the steps, seeing their reflection in the glass door. His eyes drifted over to the point where he had almost lost her. He didn't know if she could have made that jump; he didn't even want to think about it. He had a feeling she hadn't planned to, but he hoped her natural reflexes would have saved her…somehow. Not that he was going to test the theory.

Inside he sat on the sofa, not caring that they dripped half the pool in with them, perfectly content to have her in his lap, her head still resting against his shoulder.

"Why…why does it have to hurt so much?"

"If it didn't, you couldn't have loved him very much. But you do, so it hurts." He paused, not sure if that was the right thing to say, and not sure what to say next. "It will fade. In time. You'll find a way. You always do."

"I'm sorry about the sofa. I think we just ruined it."

He smiled. "I don't care about the sofa. All for the best reasons."

He dared to push the wet hair from her cheeks; but there was no protest.

"Can I say something?"

She nodded.

"Mysty…he didn't make that decision lightly. I've never seen a man more tortured. But he didn't do it so you could throw yourself to your death. He wants you to have a life. Don't make the sacrifice worthless."

He knew he was very close to saying more; but this was neither the time nor the place. She didn't react, just sighed. He wondered why she hadn't removed herself from his lap. Was she still in shock?

He heard voices, and reached over and pressed a button, waiting in their silence for the inevitable footsteps, not wanting to share her but knowing she needed more than him just then.

O'Grady and Mac appeared, barely hiding their concern, and surprise, at finding them soaking wet on the sofa – and she in his arms.

"Did someone make my Pirate Queen walk the plank or something? Kitten, you're soaking wet," O'Grady ventured.

"Expedient measures for exceptional circumstances," he replied, but softly.

"You should have let me jump," she said sadly.

"I don't think so," Daryl returned, gently, without hesitation, and eased her up so she sat next to him.

O'Grady crouched down to look her over. His wayward, half-drowned prodigy looked a sorry sight indeed.

"You're shivering. You need to get dry and warm. How about a hot bath? We'll bring some clothes over, and Lazarus, and then we can get some food inside you, hey?" A finger tipped her chin up a fraction, hoping to see something register in her eyes, but there was only sorrow.

"Are there cameras in the bathroom?" she asked quietly, not looking round, but Daryl knew the question was for him.

"No, no cameras."

And there weren't.

"Come on." Mac led the way to one of the guest suites, OG bringing her with a gentle hold on her arm, down the corridor and out of sight.

Daryl looked down at himself. He and the sofa were soaked. Not that he cared. He'd done something right by her, even though she might not thank him for it for a while.

Mac and O'Grady then reappeared, but O'Grady got called back, and her words made his heart sink.

"OG. I can't…I can't be on my own. I don't feel safe with myself. I just want to lie in the sunshine. Please?"

A drowning soul asking to be saved.

"Sweetheart, can we…can we trust you on the roof?"

"Cuff me to something. I just want to be in the sunshine."

He nodded. "You still need to change out of these wet clothes."

There was a robe hanging in the bathroom, and he waited outside while she put it on. He then picked her up, carried her through and laid her on a sun lounger, reassured when she made no bid for freedom. But he still pulled out the cuffs and snapped one on her wrist, one on the frame. "And can I have Lazarus, please? I need to see him."

"Of course."

She lay on her side as if she never wanted to rise again.

"You going to have a drink for me, some orange juice?"

"I don't want a drink."

"This isn't about what you want, kiddo, this is about what you need. You need a drink, and something to eat, as much as you need to see Lazarus."

No reply.

"I'll get you some orange juice, and when you've drunk that I'll get Lazarus."

She sat up, unwillingly, and drank it.

"Will you eat something for me?"

"I'm not hungry."

"You're shit at lying, you know that?"

"Yeah, I know. But I still can't eat anything."

"The moment you can, you can have whatever you want. I won't be far away. Alright?"

She just nodded.

Minutes later there was a blur as the leopard ran past OG and leapt up beside her, instantly lying down next to her and licking her, letting an arm pull him down to lie within the shelter of her body.

The three men watched as they lay together, unmoving except for the occasional flick of the leopard's tail.

"Shall I call Doctor Baden?" Mac asked Daryl.

"No!" a stern voice answered him from outside.

"I guess that's a no," Daryl said dryly, wishing he had remembered she had exceptional hearing. "I'm going to put some dry clothes on. Mac, get my press officer here. Get Gloria over here too. I also need to talk to Franny to check…a few details. O'Grady…"

"Yes, sir?"

"Make sure she has some shade after a while. It gets pretty warm out there."

"Will do."

Daryl finally headed to his room, bracing himself for the fallout. You didn't get to field an attempted hit, create a pile-up of motorbikes, hear gunshots fired, and see choppers dropping ropes to rescue people without the press getting hold of the story. The physical evidence might be gone, the blood might have been washed way or dusted over, but the stories were there, and explanations would have to be given.

THE MEDIA FURORE that had blown up in such a short space of time – with all kinds of crazy stories and theories – was hardly surprising given everything that had been witnessed. It certainly had been an exciting night in LA, and now the rest of America was hearing about it because there were fears that the Butterfly was dead or fatally wounded.

As he stepped up to the podium, where he would to make his press statement in the cavernous auditorium usually used for business presentations in his LA offices, he knew that she was still lying by the pool; that she hadn't moved, hadn't drunk anything, and hadn't eaten. Nor had she spoken. For four hours.

He took a breath and with one last glance at Mac, who was doing his best to support his weary boss, both physically and emotionally, stepped up to the microphone.

"Good afternoon."

The room was packed, and cameras flashed as others began filming and recording, everyone waiting in silent anticipation.

"As you all know why we're here, I'll get straight to the point and take questions afterwards." He didn't have a script; he hadn't wanted one. "It has come to my attention that there are rumours and stories being shared because of events last night, and I want to establish a few key facts to remove the fiction from what, for the most part, is conjecture." He paused, gathering his thought. "First of all, I can confirm that Mysty – as we all know her – is alive, and I'm sure, when she feels able, she will make a statement of her own. At the current time, however, we would appreciate it if the media would be respectful of our need for privacy. Mysty is just seventeen, has survived a traumatic event, and must be allowed to recover in her own time and without harassment."

There was a hum around the room as low words and comments were exchanged. The questions remained, however, on people's lips as they restrained themselves from asking, knowing better than to interrupt when Mr Blackmoor himself was speaking. One of the reasons he had chosen to do this himself and not leave it to Gloria, or someone from DB Entertainment, was that there would be no interruptions from those too impatient to wait until the Q&A at the end.

"The events of last night are undoubtedly very serious, and there are certain legalities that must be cleared before we know what we are able to reveal. Suffice to say at this moment, Mysty was attacked without provocation outside the LA Bowl by over thirty gunmen, also on motorbikes, and a chase ensued in which she managed to shake a number of them off and outpace them, heading out of the city to avoid involving anyone else. Shortly after, she was rescued by helicopter, and sustained a small graze from a bullet. It will come as little surprise to many, but the gunmen were sent by someone with a mob-related grievance."

He took a deep breath. This next bit was not going to be easy. None of it was easy.

"For those of you who are aware of Mysty's relationship with Mr Capello, it's clear her death was intended as revenge, despite her innocence."

Silence.

"It is because of the risk by association that Mr Capello has discontinued all contact with Mysty. Last night proved just how serious revenge attacks can be, and for her long-term safety and wellbeing, this was his only course of action. Mr Capello, I know, found this decision far from easy, and I greatly respect his choice. She too is struggling to come to terms with this change of circumstance, so I again repeat my request for privacy and discretion from the media."

The burning look in his eyes was warning enough to all news stations and newspapers that anyone who stepped over this line was going to get themselves into deep, career-ending shit.

"Now," he said, "are there any questions?"

A forest of hands rose from the sea of faces, but he knew already who he was going to pick: reporters he knew would not ask stupid questions.

"Mr Blackmoor, you said she sustained a small graze from a bullet. Where was she hit and how will it affect her performances – particularly at Celeste?"

"The bullet grazed her shoulder. The wound has been checked by her personal doctor and there are no complications. It will not affect her physically in anyway whatsoever, and will heal within a few days. As for Celeste, I will speak with her later today as to whether she will be able to fulfil Tuesday night's performance. If she says no, I will not hesitate to cancel. Anyone with tickets booked must not worry. If the evening is cancelled they will be contacted and an alternative date given."

"Mr Blackmoor, sir, there are reports that her bike gave off an energy pulse which helped her get away from the initial attack of the gunmen outside LA Bowl…what technology is she using and how does it work?"

"I'm afraid that is a question for the girl herself. As you may know, she is particularly good with technology and is able to develop software that goes beyond projects that even I have people working on. I'm hoping at some point she'll consent to share her inventions; but at the moment

I'm just glad she had them last night because it means today she is alive."

"Sir, do you know who it was who took out the hit on Mysty? As you said, she's a young girl and innocent but for her association, so they would have to be pretty heartless to pick her as a target. Are they going to face prosecution?"

"Heartless is certainly the right word. As for the details of who orchestrated the attack, I do not know. I was involved with getting her out of last night's attack, not dealing with those who organised it. Mob business is best left to the mob."

There were plenty of arms in the air, but he invited one last question. They had enough for their headlines, and he'd just had enough.

"Mr Blackmoor, you said Mr Capello has ended the relationship. Does that mean Mysty, the most beautiful woman on the planet, is single?"

Daryl stared at the man, wondering how he could be so callous, so crude.

"All press must be advised to remember that privacy and discretion are paramount. I refuse to answer the question due to its intrusive nature. Thank you."

He stepped away, feeling about a hundred years old, letting Mac and five others shield him as they exited the room. Outside the press clamoured with their cameras, shouting questions. He didn't respond.

Once inside the car he immediately pulled out his handheld, scanned the pool area.

"O'Grady!"

"Excellent press conference, sir."

"Thanks. Where is she?"

"In the car. We're going to get some milkshakes. And today is a big day as, apparently, she's going to try something other than strawberry. Life's too short, she says, not to try a few others."

Daryl felt some part of him let go. Thank God.

"And how is she?"

"Quiet, but not as quiet. I'll let you know how we get on. I've already told her she's having a night at home, and got no arguments. Lazarus is doing everything he can to cheer her up, but it's going to be a long road."

"Try and get her to talk if she will. She has a habit of pretending she's fine when she's not. Last night scared her, of that there is no doubt."

"Will do, sir. More good news, though, aside from milkshakes."

"What's that?"

"That graze on her shoulder, it's healing really quickly. I'd say that's another feature of her uniqueness."

"Wouldn't surprise me in the least." Daryl had prayed it would heal well and leave no scar, no physical memory of something so violent. The psychological scars would have to be dealt with over time. "Enjoy the milkshakes. Keep me posted."

"Yes, sir."

Disconnect.

Daryl looked round at Mac.

"New milkshake flavours. Today is a big day," Mac said with a smile.

Since when did Mac care about milkshakes?

"Why is it such a big deal?" Daryl asked.

"She only ever has strawberry. She won't eat anything sweet, like cake or chocolate, so that's the closest she gets. Something to do with her mother. That's all O'Grady knows at the moment."

Daryl mused on his answer, surprised. He'd not known she didn't touch anything sweet; but then he knew very little about her at all, which was entirely his own fault. How deep did those scars of her past go? They must be very deep if it took a scare like last night to shake her enough to break one of her own rules.

WHEN HE TOOK the call he was more than relieved to see she was eating, stretched out on the breakfast bar on her tummy next to a bowl of grapes. There was also a half-demolished bacon sandwich on a plate, which Lazarus was eyeing up.

"Daryl."

"Mysty. How are you doing?" He put down the book he was reading, which was an indulgence for him, even for a late Sunday afternoon; but he was still more interested in talking to her.

"Can I defer answering that question for at least a month?"

"Sure. No rush."

"I just rang…to apologise for hitting you this morning. I didn't mean to, exactly, I just…well, I'm sorry if it hurt."

He had completely forgotten. His temple was sore where she'd elbowed him, and his shin too, where she'd kicked him, but she had been his only concern and his pain had been inconsequential at the time.

"I'm fine, really. I know you didn't mean it maliciously. It was reflex, I understand."

"And I'm sorry about the sofa."

"As I said, I really don't care about the sofa. After what's happened to you in the last twenty-four hours, you don't need to apologise for anything."

"I saw your press conference."

"I couldn't have the world going crazy thinking you were dead."

"No, well, I don't want you to cancel Celeste. I'm okay to do it."

"Are you sure? You don't have to."

"I'm sure. I need the distraction, and I don't really want to feel like I'm letting everyone down as well as feeling so…miserable."

"It's not letting anyone down to take some time for yourself."

"So why don't you take time for yourself? The weekend has nearly gone. What have you done to relax?" And then she realised what she had said. "I'm sorry…about your weekend. It's my fault, isn't it? I kind of screwed it up, didn't I?"

"It's not your fault. None of us could have predicted what happened." He didn't think it best to mention that Donny had already planned to break it off with her that morning.

"Tell you what, send me your schedule and I'll put on a suit, go to your office and do my best Daryl Blackmoor impression for a whole day. You can go dance around, play with Lazarus and bang on the drum kit."

It was a huge relief that she still had a sense of humour in there, and he really wanted to laugh. He hadn't thought he'd be able to, not ever again.

"That's a nice thought, but I think there are a number of flaws in the theory."

"Oh come on, I promise to behave. I wouldn't re-arrange anything, not again, I swear. I'd just spend the whole day sitting in your awesomely comfy chair, scowling at everyone, looking serious and drinking lattes. I think me and Mac would have a great time, too. We could even play darts or something, at lunch time."

Daryl looked up at the ceiling, wondering why he could never resist her irreverent teasing.

"It's not you I'm worried about."

"No?"

"No. For one, I don't think I'd look good in black leggings and a Pirate Queen t-shirt. Two, I can't dance. And three, you know Lazarus doesn't like me."

"Can you play the drums?" she asked, ignoring all of that.

"No."

"Well, I guess we are stuffed, aren't we?" She gave a big sigh of disappointment. "And there was me thinking I had an easy day tomorrow. Then again, I doubt Carol would let me through the door."

"Not after she found that sticker on my door." A snort of laughter. She couldn't see his glower, but it was obvious in his tone of voice. "Thank God she didn't see what you'd done on the inside."

"You see? I *can* be discreet when I want to be. And you deserved every bit of it, anyway, so don't think I'm going soft on you."

"I wouldn't dream of it."

"Seriously, though, if you do need a hand with anything…like if one of your databases goes belly up, just call me. I owe you a Sunday afternoon…well, pretty much a weekend really."

He didn't know what to say; he was touched that she was being so generous. It wasn't the time to mention what he had in mind for a Sunday afternoon. Nowhere near.

"Okay, sure. I was hoping I might persuade you to upgrade all the firewalls and tell me how on earth you hack into everything."

"Why would I do that?" she laughed. "But I will upgrade your firewalls. For a price."

"A price…"

"Well, you see, I learnt from my manager never to sell myself short. So I'm thinking whatever figure is offered, plus an extra twenty percent, minus ten percent – that's his cut anyway – and then maybe if he's polite, I'll give him a ten percent discount, and we can reach a fair price. What do you think?"

"I like the sound of this guy. He sounds very smart."

"He has his moments," she replied darkly – a warning to not get ahead of himself. "I hear he still hasn't got a home computer system like Toby."

"No. Sadly he hasn't."

"But he must have looked into it?"

"And then business takes over and he has no time to finish looking into it."

"Well, if he does, even just the initial stages, tell him to send his stuff over. I can check it for him, point him in the right direction."

"I'm sure he'd like that."

"Yeah, well, he works too hard. He could do with a break every now and then. He should clone himself, really."

"What? You really think you could cope with two of me?"

"Actually, no!" Lazarus jumped up onto the breakfast bar and she reached out a hand stroked him. "I don't want to do a press interview yet," she said quietly.

"They've had enough to keep them at bay for now. Shouldn't you be going to bed soon, young lady?"

"Says you? And 'young lady'? Don't say that in front of anyone or you'll ruin my reputation."

"You're every inch a young lady, despite your 'alley cat' wildness, and you know it." It had been a risk saying that, knowing she would remember.

"I can't believe you did all that. Even leaving Mac behind somewhere, which I bet he didn't like at all. How did you find me?" she asked, and it was honest curiosity not anger on her face.

"It was pure chance. I'd worked out you were in LA, but nothing beyond that. Then there you were, running down the street."

"Fate is a kind mistress to you, isn't she. How did I end up so unlucky?"

"You're seventeen. You have to wait till you're my age to start being that lucky."

"Very funny. I don't feel seventeen. I feel more like a hundred. I want to wake up and find that…that…"

He knew what she was thinking: that this weekend hadn't happened, that she hadn't had a hit taken out on her, that Donny hadn't broken her heart. Her face darkened and he wondered if she might cry, or end the call, or both. She had been remarkably okay during their conversation. Was she really okay? He searched her face.

"I'm leaving tomorrow afternoon, for Seattle," he said quietly. "I'll be flying around for most of next week, but…if you need anything you only have to message me, or tell OG. You had him pretty worried today, you know. You had all of us pretty worried. Even Mac, and he's usually impervious to everything."

"No he's not, he just pretends he is because…he thinks that's part of his job. I think Mac needs a bit of TLC as well."

"Oh really?"

"Yeah. When did you last take your head of bodyguard out for a milkshake?"

"When did you last take your manager out for a milkshake?"

"He wouldn't drink one."

"How do you know?"

"Because it's not…expensive or sophisticated or swish…that's why!"

"You could try asking him."

"Maybe. He can be quite horrid, though. Though sometimes I don't think he realises he is."

"No, he thinks you're probably right there."

"I know."

"What do you mean 'I know'?"

"I know I'm right. There's no probably about it. Hadn't you noticed, I'm rarely ever wrong?"

"Yankees game, Thursday night. What's the score going to be then, my little oracle?"

"Ooooh…" She sucked in a breath as she thought. "I'd say…8-5. Yankees win by three points."

"If you get the final score, or the score difference right, I owe you $50."

"Only $50?"

"If you get it wrong, you owe me a milkshake."

"Ha-ha!"

"Not cherry flavoured."

"Good God, are you feeling alright?"

"Absolutely fine."

"I think you just made a joke at your own expense."

"Wonders never cease."

"I'm glad I'm lying down."

"Which reminds me, you said you were going to bed."

"I did? I know I didn't commit to that. Don't try any Jedi mind tricks on me, Mr Manager. Anyway, I go to bed when I want to not when I'm told."

"I'm going to bed…" he tried reasoning.

"That isn't going to work either."

"You need to rest."

"Au contraire, monsieur. I know what I need, and he isn't here. Won't ever be in fact."

Disconnect.

The abrupt end to the call made him inhale sharply. It was going to be one hell of a week.

MYSTY STARED, BUT it didn't even matter what at because she wasn't looking at anything anyway. She was far away, lost in the whirling maelstrom of pain inside her head. It felt like a maze in there. A labyrinth she feared she wouldn't ever find her way out of.

Waking up felt like a burden. Getting up felt pointless. Forcing herself to continue breathing, as if everything was going to be alright when it felt very much like nothing would ever be alright again, felt like a waste of energy. The whole basis of her world had gone. Ripped away. Again.

How could life be so cruel? It just didn't make sense. Every time she tried, it just hurt to think about it. Hadn't she suffered enough? Donny had been such a lifeline! She'd heard once, listening to a random podcast while tinkering with her bikes, that the way to really fuck with someone's mind wasn't to punish them for doing something wrong, but for doing something right. That totally ruined a person's sense of justice, of right and wrong, of fairness… And by God did she feel punished. And all for loving someone? Had she lied, or cheated or behaved badly? No! What on earth could justify the dice of the fates rolling against her so harshly that they would take away the one person – *the one person* – she loved above all others?

The cursed child. Destined to lose everyone I love. My mother gone. Not allowed Donny…

And yet people expected her to carry on. She saw it in everyone's face. They all wanted her to dance, and sing, and inspire.

I feel dead.

A vibration next to her on the sofa told her someone had sent a message. She'd had thousands. Mostly got Toby to filter the ones from the public now, so she only heard from close friends, but even then… she still didn't always have the energy to reply. She was vaguely aware she was wallowing, but so what? What did she care? Why did she have to be strong anymore? She'd never wallowed before. So why not now?

She tilted the handheld with a single finger, just enough to see who the message was from: Raju. Again.

She closed her eyes. Why not now? Why not just call him right now and get the thing done? Even if the worst happened, and he flipped his lid at her, she couldn't feel much worse than she did already. The months of agonising over this now felt irrelevant. She felt so numb inside, like someone had filled her with anaesthetic. A bomb could have gone off outside the window, and it would barely have raised an eyebrow.

Now. Do it now.

Hitting the video call button, for the very first time to Raju, she lifted the handheld up to her face. All she saw looking back at her were the saddest eyes in a dishevelled halo of hair, which was what Raju would see when he picked up, which he did, after six rings. Had he seen her number and hesitated? What had been going through his head? No matter. It was done now. And making that call had suddenly made her feel empowered. She had made a choice, rather than have choices constantly taken away from her.

A rich brown face, in huge glasses, and slightly crooked teeth in a dropped jaw looked back at her. The slant of his body was acute, and she looked more closely. He was not leaning because he was slouched on a sofa…he…he was in a wheelchair. *Oh God…* One hand rested on the armrest, and looked like it didn't work. The other was hovering near his keyboard, twisted but maybe okay.

A hundred thousand thoughts crashed in, and her mouth opened to speak, but then the hovering hand came down and hit a button: he'd ended the call.

Reeling, she tried to call back…and again. She pressed some buttons. Raju had blocked her.

Looking at their message chat, she saw the option to reply had also gone. She started typing commands into her handheld. She could easily find a way around this, take another route.

But then she stopped. What was the point? If he didn't want to talk to her, she couldn't make him. And then came the realisation that even in her dishevelled state he would have instantly recognised her. All the things he'd said about The Butterfly would have come back to him and…he would have been so shocked, embarrassed and…angry? Maybe he needed to calm down, to recover.

She dropped the handheld back on the sofa, dragged herself and her loadstone of sadness to the window and looked out.

"You okay?" OG asked, looking up from the paper.

"I rang my friend. To tell him…I am who I am"

"Oh? How'd it go? I bet he was surprised?"

"He cut the video call, and then blocked me."

"Very surprised then. Maybe intimidated? You are…pretty famous."

"He knew me before I was famous. I thought that would count for something."

"Give him a bit of time to calm down. It'll be okay. He'll call you back."

She didn't reply. Didn't want to hear hope, or positivity. She felt like just another victim to the fame train. And Raju was yet another person in her life she wasn't allowed to hold on to.

But remembering the feeling when she'd pressed the call button she decided wallowing was overrated, and the only way out the maze in her mind was to smash through the walls.

"I want to go to the ice rink."

"Sure. I'll make some calls. Have some lunch while I get it arranged, okay?"

She nodded, despising the idea of eating alone, again, even though she knew her body was hungry. Eating reminded her of some of the happiest meals of her life in the Capello household.

If it had been possible to remove her heart and spare herself the fresh rush of grief that flooded in like water into a new cavity in the ground, she would have taken someone up on it.

HAD IT REALLY been a week since the hit? Some parts of that night still seemed hazy when he went over them in his mind; other parts crystal-clear. He never tired of recalling the moment he'd reached out and pulled her into the chopper. He'd never been so glad to see someone alive.

The buzzer went on the intercom, and he was tempted to ignore it, but it was from one of the few people he would never ignore.

"O'Grady."

"Sir. I'm sorry to bother you on a Saturday evening."

There was a controlled politeness in O'Grady's voice, even an uneasiness, and Daryl was immediately concerned.

"What's happening?"

"I'm afraid we have a problem."

"Not another threat?" His stomach turned to ice. Why had he let her go!

"No. Not that."

"Then what?"

"She's had four beers, and is now on her fifth. She, erm, also helped empty a bottle of vodka after celebrating winning the first race. She's also…kiss-testing."

O'Grady was clearly uncomfortable saying the words, and there was a hesitancy as he waited for the explosion from his boss.

"*What*?" Daryl exploded. The drinking was one thing, but he could only imagine what 'kiss-testing' was, and it did not conjure welcome images.

"She doesn't realise the danger of the game she's playing, or else she does and she doesn't care."

Daryl's mind ran through a hundred hoops: one extremely beautiful, famous, talented girl who was completely off limits, suddenly back on the menu and showing herself to be…free with her affections? And in the testosterone-fuelled atmosphere of the Bowl on a Saturday night where eighty per cent of the attendees were male and definitely up for it? This was not only foolish and dangerous, it was a PR nightmare. It could sully her reputation. She was the media's daring darling, not a sluttish vodka-drinking wild child.

"You've asked her to stop?"

"Of course, but she doesn't seem to care what I say. As far as she's concerned, being good never got her anything but lonely, and everyone else has a bit of fun, so why shouldn't she? I've got the boys all around her, and I'm trying to get Rusty to convince her to stop, as she seems to respect him, but he's reluctant to get involved…" O'Grady paused, not sure if he was out of line saying the next bit, which was the real reason he called. "I, sir, I was wondering if you would come down here yourself? She won't listen to me, and perhaps I shouldn't involve her friend Rusty, but she might listen to you."

"That would be a first," Daryl replied.

"Sir…"

"I'll be there as soon as I can. Keep her off the bike."

"Yes, sir, of course. Thank you."

Disconnect.

Daryl headed for the wardrobe, knowing the leathers were in there somewhere, putting a call through as he did.

"Mac!"

"Sir?"

"We're going out. LA Bowl. Seems our kitten is tangling with some tomcats, and not with her fist this time. Time to get her out."

"You need the bikes?"

"Yes. And get everyone on alert. We might need them."

Disconnect.

By the time the Jackals roared up into the Bowl, alive with noise and people, he was part furious, part exhausted. It had been a frenetic week, and he really didn't need this.

He parked up, surprised at how easily the skills of riding a motorbike came back to him once the leathers were on, and he was already striding away towards the track calling O'Grady when the excitement kicked off.

He had no idea where she was, but the cameras were on her – she was their queen and a celebrity now, so anything to do with her was instantly on camera, and numbers at the Bowl swelled to almost 100,000 if people knew she was there.

He saw her standing on the seat of her bike, waving her helmet and laughing. Some of the Pirates were around her, but they fell quiet as another rider rode up close, aggressively, and spun the bike to a stop in front of her. Daryl could see from his body language when he got off the bike what it was he was after. And, from the look on her face, she did too. He vaguely recognised him, but was not sure why.

"Pirate Queen."

"Washington. Nice to see you again. Sorry, I didn't know you were visiting."

"I came back to see you. I heard you were now…in need of someone for some after-race excitement."

"Really? What you and the rest of the male population?" She observed him for a moment, her face arctic-cold. "I'm not in need of anything, or anyone, except another beer. Excuse me."

She jumped off the bike and went to go past him, but a hand caught her wrist, her black leathers a sharp contrast to his white and blue. Leonine eyes looked down at her across the short space of air, eyes that told her what he wanted, what he offered.

"Not so fast, Queenie. I came a long way to see you; I'm not so easily put off."

"Is that so?" she scoffed. "And I'm supposed to be impressed that you can catch a plane?"

"I'm happy to impress you in a completely different way, if you'll let me." His lips glided closer to her ear and almost brushed her cheek, the tension between the two bodies visible on camera.

Daryl clenched his fists at another man staking out what was his. No one around him had a clue who he was, or what she was to him; he was just another figure in a crowd with their eyes and ears on the screens.

"I hate having to repeat myself, but no thanks."

She pulled her wrist from his grip and stepped away, but Taylor James wasn't so easily put off. He tossed his helmet to a friend and took her wrist again, intending to pull her back, but a hand whipped round and smacked him round the face, a knee caught him in the guts, and the swipe of a foot left him on his hands and knees, tasting blood.

He'd just about registered the shock and speed of her when a hand gripped his hair and pulled his head back, and a fiercely beautiful face glared down at him.

"What is it you want? My fame, my face or my money? Tell me?"

"I don't give a shit about the fame or the money. I-I just thought you were awesome the first night I saw you. I'd be a fool not come back."

"You think you have what it takes to tame the Pirate Queen?" She let him go with a dismissive snort of disgust and walked away.

Daryl felt himself relax. Clearly she wasn't completely drunk; and clearly she was not about to let anyone try it on. And he knew OG and his team were close by should she need back-up.

But no one expected Taylor James to get up, wipe the blood off his lip, and focus his eyes on the tumble of golden hair disappearing into the crowd. Nor for him to stride after her and bring her down onto the track before she'd had a chance to turn and defend herself.

He pinned her arms to the ground and smiled down at her, using his body weight manoeuvre himself between her thighs.

"Not everyone is afraid of a bit of a fight, you know. A little pain doesn't put me off, Queenie."

Daryl was at breaking point, but Mac gave him a look that said not to interfere. Just yet.

She glared at him, feeling compromised, embarrassed. And then, from somewhere, something sparked and she embraced it. It was better than misery, better than despair. Being this wanted was actually okay; it was something mindless and primitive, something irresistible that demanded satisfaction.

"So, you going to spend all night talking to me or what?" she replied.

Her answer brought his lips down on hers, ignoring the cut on his own, and the whole of LA Bowl was given a real-time view of another side of the Pirate Queen. And it wasn't a chaste kiss; it was a kiss that made people want to know what it was to be kissed back with such passion. TJ's hands slid down her arms and over her leathers, and one of her thighs crept up around his hip, a hand against his cheek, then in his hair, back arching against the weight above her.

In the body-hugging leathers, it was…erotic, to say the least.

Daryl was, by now, incandescent. How could she just let herself get ravished on the goddamned track? What was she thinking? And God, she looked hot. And fuck, how he wanted it to be him.

In a moment, she was on top, body straddling his, as they kissed. His hands went to undo her jacket, but abruptly she broke away and sat up.

The crowd were glued to the screens. What the hell would she do next?

"Well, it was a good effort, but it didn't quite do it for me," she said and patted his shoulder, and then got up in one lithe move and walked away, leaving him stunned, aroused, his face registering utter bemusement.

'It didn't quite do it for me?' What the hell was she looking for? That had been a hot, passionate kiss, and it didn't get much deeper or full on than that! Daryl looked around, expecting to see a certain amount of disapproval for her actions, but no, it seemed her ability to command and demand respect had gone up a hundredfold! It didn't take a genius to see the looks of admiration as she headed for the Pirate's pitch up on the balcony. It was time to go and get her. She may have got away with it this time, but on the loose in this petrol and testosterone-fired crowd she might not be so lucky next time. He and Mac followed her, his other guys too, and he approached her before she'd had a chance to immerse herself in her teammates, and just as O'Grady turned up.

"What the fuck are you doing?"

"What the fuck are you doing?" She stepped up to him, not afraid of the fury that made his head hurt. "Don't be such a hypocrite. It doesn't suit you." Eyes glittered dangerously at him, and then she stalked around him, so close he could smell the sweetness of her hair, the warmth of her leathers. "Nice leathers, Mr Manager. Good to see you still have them. You know, I think there are quite a few ladies here tonight who'd take you home for free, to save you paying for it. How does that make you feel?"

"You're drunk and you're embarrassing yourself," he told her, without sparing her feelings, using as much scorn as he could.

"So what? I'm seventeen. I'm meant to be young and stupid! You didn't have to come over here and get yourself all upset watching it."

"OG rang me because he said you were drinking too much and weren't listening to reason."

"Listening to reason! What did listening to reason ever do for me? Nothing!"

"Donny wouldn't want to see you doing this."

It had been a gamble to mention that name and, a single second after using it, he knew it had been a mistake.

"*Donny? Donny doesn't want me!* So why can't I have a little fun of my own finding someone who does?"

"Donny wants you to enjoy your life free of danger, not turn yourself into a slut and invite it with your legs wide open!"

A blush and outrage both raced across her cheeks at the crudity of his accusation. It was a little too accurate.

"A few kisses don't count for anything! There's plenty of time for me to do something *really* sluttish before dawn rolls around!"

She delivered her threat with a wry laugh, and eyes that said, Watch me! And then she turned on her heel and disappeared into the crowd of bikers, all of whom closed ranks against the guys in leathers who all looked very much the same: all sober, all clean cut, all serious.

"Shit," Daryl muttered, knowing this was the rebellion that had been triggered by a dozen things, not least losing her beloved Donny.

"She's been working herself into a real state all week. I should have seen this coming," O'Grady admitted, feeling helpless but responsible.

He'd thought going to the Bowl would help exorcise some of her anxiety but, no, it had provided the perfect environment for her to stick two fingers up at everything and everyone. And it wasn't that he didn't understand. She'd been responsible and hard-working since she was a kid, and all she'd got was trouble, grief and a broken heart. Of course she was going to throw the bridle off and bolt.

"She...she had a call from Paulo earlier," he added. "I think it pushed her just a little too far. Donny's not doing so good, and he only called to check she was okay. I've told him to not call again. She was inconsolable. Then out came the leathers."

"Mac, see that that particular tomcat gets a little chat before he leaves," he said, seeing a replay of the kiss appear on the screen. "He isn't to go near her tonight, and make sure he knows not to speak to the press, or his riding days are over. Permanently. Speak to management, too, and make sure they get the same message. One word, and I'll have this place shut down. We can't control what this crowd will say amongst themselves, but this is damage limitation, so get them to make an announcement that if anyone shares this with the press, we will hunt them down."

Mac nodded and disappeared.

"What are you going to do, sir?" O'Grady asked.

"I need her away from this crowd, for starters. And then she must be brought back into line."

"Yes, sir." O'Grady didn't know what he was planning, but she'd slipped through his net tonight and he knew for her own safety he was right.

"I'm going to call to someone, and have them call her, request that she goes somewhere quiet and safe. Make sure you know exactly where she is at all times, until we leave, understood?"

"Yes, sir."

Daryl stepped away and went to the edge of the balcony as he placed the call, watching Mac and a good crowd of his men swamp the Washington visitor's patch. The group were quietened by muscle stronger and in greater numbers than theirs. Taylor James was bundled out of sight. Mac had a way of saying things.

"Benjamin."

"Mr Blackmoor? Are you alright, sir? It's very late. Are you on your way to the hotel?"

"No, I'm not on my way. Benjamin, I need you to ring Mysty and get her to go somewhere quiet. She's…well, you may have heard about her and Donny. She's upset, understandably."

"She visited for half an hour the other day. Sat on my sofa for old times' sake, I guess, so I know how upset she is – though she tried pretty hard to gloss over it. Are you…are you at the Bowl, sir?"

"Yes. Wasn't planning on it, but she's acting a little crazy. I need you to call her and have a talk with her, get her away from the noise by asking her to go somewhere quiet…do you understand?"

"I do, but why?"

"That's not important. Just rest assured you're doing her a favour because, right now, she's creating a world of trouble for herself."

"That kid's been as steady as a rock. It's hard to believe this has her so thrown."

"I know. Will you call her?"

"Sure. Now?"

"As soon as. Patch me in."

"Yes, sir."

"Disconnect.

He waited, and whilst he did he caught sight of her bright hair in the lights.

"Mysty?"

"Benjamin? Wow! What a time to call. Are you alright? You staying up late working?"

"Well, you know me, especially now my star has left me and my poor hotel to carry on without her."

"Ben, you know I didn't want to leave. How are you doing?"

"I'm okay. Mysty, could you go somewhere quieter? I can barely hear you and I have a huge headache already. Us old people, going deaf, you know."

"Sure, hold on." Daryl watched as she moved out of the dense crowd and headed towards the quiet of the main building. "Wow, the music is loud tonight. No wonder you can't hear me!" She was complaining about the volume? That was a first! He slowly moved after, tracking her into one of the tunnels under the grandstand. She leant against the wall. "That better?"

"Much. Thank you. So, how you feeling? As great as it was to see you the other day, it was hard when I could see how upset you were."

Daryl hung well back, knowing how good her hearing was. Above them the arena rocked with the muffled noise of bikes and music.

"Yeah, well." Her voice was immediately choked with emotion. "It seems nothing ever turns out the way I want it to, not when it comes to men. I think I'm cursed, like my mother."

"It's going to be tough, to begin with, but it will get better, I promise."

"You don't need to promise things like that, Benjy, I know you mean well, but I think my chances of being loved are zero."

"No, they're not. You're seventeen, kiddo, not seventy. Everyone gets their heart broken, at least once. It's part of life."

"Twice is too many."

"You're the one who told me that if I lost the belief in something wonderful happening, then I'd have lost an integral part of myself."

"Well, I was wrong. I was fucking wrong. And I don't believe in wonderful anymore."

"You may not right now, because part of you wants to give up believing, but you don't want to. Not really."

"I don't want to believe in anything at all. It's far easier that way. Anyway, why did you ring?"

"Just because. And to tell you I had a letter arrive for you – from Alice. It has a picture of her standing next to the photo you sent her. It's on her wall. Her parents are over the moon. Her mum brought the letter in herself…figured giving it to me would be better rather than sending it to the fan mail address."

"I'll stop by sometime next week. Maybe call in at your restaurant for some lunch. But I'm not wearing a cocktail dress."

"I hope you do. And cocktail dresses are overrated anyway."

"Exactly."

Benjamin could tell she was on the verge of tears, knew it was time to let her go. "You know my sofa's always here if you need it. Hang in there, Jukebox."

"I don't think I ever want to sing again."

"You will. I don't know when, but you will." No answer. "You take care, kiddo."

Disconnect.

She didn't move for a few seconds; then she turned around to lean against the wall and hide her face, hair falling forward over her face. Perfect. She didn't move fast enough and he had her pinned against the wall in a moment, his feet pushed hard against hers apart to weaken her stance, his full body weight against her back, her face to the wall as he gripped a handful of hair and pressed her forehead into the concrete. He wanted her to feel the fear that would make her remember that, despite her fighting skills, like this she was a good as helpless.

"Get the fuck off me!" she gasped.

He could hear the fury, but not fear, and realised this would have to get worse before she understood the reality of her situation.

He didn't speak, not wanting her to realise it was him.

Her hands and arms were absolutely no use to her, and therefore no threat to him either, and her legs were pinned by his. He took out her earpiece and tossed it away to let her know no one was coming to help.

Daryl had so often been forceful with a woman, with his Cherries, but he had never assaulted one before. He was shocked at how easily the aggression fused with the almost uncontrollable desire. The primal lust a man has for a woman rose and would not be denied, raging through his blood and driving him into a frenzy. With his free hand he stroked down her thigh and up the inside of her leg, making her buck to move him off her. But she was going nowhere, and every time she fought him she would get weaker. He gave into the temptation and slid his hand between her parted legs, driven now by something more than just wanting to teach her a lesson.

"I hope to God you have something to kill me with, because if you let me go I'm going to leave you choking on your own blood, you fucking sicko!" But her voice was muffled against the wall, and she must have realised that no one could hear her. "Fucking get off me!" Finally, there was a hint of panic.

Maybe he'd done enough, but his body had other ideas, the need for her so strong he knew he wasn't fully in control of himself. Breathing hard, he reached around and pulled the zip down on her leathers, heard her cry of protest as he slid his hand over the velvet-smooth skin of her belly. He'd never been so aroused, could feel his pulse throbbing hard and his erection harder as his fingers found the top of her knickers and slid underneath the lace, longing to find the secret parts of her that meant ecstasy. Feeling her soft warmth, he let his fingers linger, lost in the feel of her as she cried out, "No! Stop it! Please!"

He wasn't so out of control that he could not hear the acute panic now, and the fear in the begging, half-screamed 'please!'. This wasn't the way he wanted her to scream that word. No way. Lesson time over; back to business.

Mysty felt the fingers pause against the parts of her she didn't fully understand, parts that didn't belong to this attacker. *Oh God, please help me*, she prayed silently, panting from the panic.

"After your display tonight, I would have thought this was what you wanted? Is it not?"

That voice! *His voice*!

She desperately tried to move.

"*Let me go*! *Let me go, you fucking bastard*!"

"Careful, you're not in a position to throw insults around just now." He moved his fingers against her, gently, and she stilled instantly, overwhelmed by shame and anger, fear and anguish. "Do you have any idea the danger you place yourself in with the kind of behaviour you've shown tonight? Do you think you can cock-tease eighty thousand guys and no one will ever try anything? They'd risk blood and broken bones to have you, Mysty. *Do you understand*?"

There was a pause and then her head slammed backwards into his, the pain registering instantly. But he still had hold of her, too hard for her to move, and took a handful of her glorious hair and yanked her head round harshly, not caring if it hurt, far enough so they could see each other.

"That *wasn't* the answer I wanted."

"Fuck you! Fuck you, Daryl! You're enjoying every second of this, I can feel it! Don't pretend this is for my benefit!"

The fight was back in her eyes, despite the horrible fear, and Daryl felt a part of him sicken inside, knowing he was going to have to make this worse to get through to her.

"I'm still a man. Most men would feel something in my position. And you're not exactly displeasing to the eye."

He slid his fingers further down, and felt her body tense, her eyes fixed on his, angry, fearful and defiant. As he caressed her he watched for some reaction, any other reaction other than rage and fear. There was none.

"Donny would kill you for this."

Nothing was working. He knew he had to go in for the kill.

"Donny left you to my keeping. And, for the record, I'm not scared of him. I just don't want to have to fight him. It's far too time consuming, and no doubt expensive. Anyway, seeing you behave like a common tart certainly wouldn't have impressed him tonight."

"Strangely, to impress wasn't why I did it!"

"Then why?"

"Why not? Why should I care?"

"*Because you're better than that*! Because the reason people respect you is because of who you are, because of your amazing talent, not just your beautiful face!"

"So what! I'm just a performing poodle, remember? Eight years and the press will chew over my life regardless, and then what? Why should I care about being good when it doesn't get me anywhere?"

"Because you owe it to yourself. Even if you can't see it."

He relaxed his grip on her hair, let her recover from the pressure the hold had on her throat and neck, part of him glad to escape the glare of her eyes.

He took a deep breath, stilled his fingers, tried to get some control back.

"I want your word that you'll stop this madness. No more kissing, no more flirting like a bitch-in-heat. No more drinking and trying to race like you're immortal. Promise me you'll start behaving like a responsible woman and I'll let you go."

"Why should I promise you anything? I don't owe you! You're no better than the fuckwits in the bar fight, you fucking bastard!"

He pushed her back against the wall, hard enough to hurt, and the dormant hand between her legs came to life again.

"I told you to keep the insults to yourself. And you should be grateful I took the time to show you this lesson myself. I could have sent someone else to do it for me," he growled in her ear, using his bodyweight to push down on her, leaving her totally unable to move. "You don't owe me, you're right, but right now you're not in a very good position to refuse me anything." His middle finger played where he could slide it right inside, and he heard a whimper. "Promise me, or your precious innocence is going to come to an interesting end beneath my hand, and everything you were keeping for Donny will be gone. You'll be used, and you won't enjoy a second of it." His moved a fraction closer, making the threat very real, not surprised to find her dry and tense. "I should be at home being fucked by one of my girls, or maybe even two, so I'm figuring you owe me."

He could feel her whole body trembling now, and felt horrified at what he had said and done to bring her to surrender. Words so different to the ones he so wanted to say.

She sobbed once, short and breathy and panicked.

"Do you wish me to continue?"

"No! No!" She sobbed again.

"Promise me, then."

The finger moved deeper, just another a fraction, and her body jerked in terror.

"I promise! I swear! Just let me go!"

"You break that promise, I will finish what I started."

"Please let me go. *I promise*!"

She was close to collapse. He had her.

"But I don't think I'm quite satisfied yet."

"What do you mean? I promised, didn't I?"

"Your promise was for your own good, not mine."

"What do you want? I promised!"

I only want what you've been giving out so cheaply to everyone tonight: a kiss. Surely you can manage that?"

"It wasn't everyone!"

"It might as well have been!"

"Don't do this. Please."

"I think it will help make this experience more memorable for you."

"It's memorable enough! Please, Daryl, don't do this!"

Her plea was genuine, and her using his name a nice touch, but his desire was burning bright and it was far from sated. He closed his eyes and the image of her beneath those leathers taunted him.

"Just pretend I'm Donny. I'm sure it won't be a problem for you, then." Jealousy had wormed its way into his frustration.

"*Pretend*? No. I'm no good at pretending. I'll kiss you knowing *exactly who you are*. And I'll kiss you so you know exactly what you *won't ever have.*"

He removed his hand and pulled up the zip, turned her round, keeping his weight on her as much as possible so she didn't have a chance to hit him. Her face was as fierce as her words, and her eyes glittered at him. He felt like the devil, but he couldn't leave it now. He needed to see this through to the end.

"Let me have one of my arms, at least," she demanded. "They're almost numb!"

He considered it, decided the risk was worth it just to have her hands on him. He unzipped her jacket, dropped it to the floor, watching her face, seeing her wince as she rubbed her arms, trying to get the blood flowing. They were so close, his hips pressing against her. She had to be aware of how much he wanted her, not that he could have stopped it if he'd tried.

Her eyes came back up to his, glaring, angry, accusing. He took one of her wrists and held it against the wall, warning her he didn't trust her and that he wasn't about to let it go.

"You're such an idiot," she told him with breathtaking disgust, before she took hold of his hair with her free hand and pulled his head down swiftly and her lips claimed his.

He hadn't been kissed for a long time; and he hadn't been kissed like that in his life. He responded without having to think, seduced by her yielding lips, the tongue that teased, demanded and delighted, open-mouthed and passionate. This was not the kiss of a virgin, nor the kiss of a child or a girl. Hungry and heady, he was vaguely aware of her fingers moving through his hair, and forgot to hold onto to her wrist, moving his hands down to clasp her around the waist, his fingers reaching to feel her ribs expand with her every breath. It was everything he'd imagined it would be; there was nothing wrong, nothing wanting. His blood pounded hard and fast, and rational thought was left behind as he tasted her mouth, felt her move against him, falling into the sensations like he would never be able to let her go.

Mysty knew she must be mad. She hadn't meant for the kiss to go so far; couldn't believe her body was betraying her so much as to want the hands of the man who had so threatened her, again, to hold her like this, to kiss her like this. What magic was it? Why had she let this happen? She couldn't even imagine how it felt to kiss Donny her senses were so alive. The revulsion she'd expected hadn't been there. And the kiss she had offered to silence him was being matched touch for touch, instinctively, the hunger in him rousing something deep inside herself. She should have bitten him, and then kicked him to the floor. She couldn't find a single word to explain this, but she couldn't give in to it either.

She pulled back from the traitorous lips and pushed, finally sending him back with all the force she could muster, her breath laboured, her body shaken by the anger, the shame, and now the confusion. She watched him push himself off the opposite wall with hands that had delved and touched parts of her that no man had ever touched like that. How dare he? How could he abuse her so deliberately, knowing her fears? She knew she was blushing with the shame of just thinking about it. How would she ever look at him without remembering what he'd done?

"*You bastard*. I'll *never* forgive you for what you just did."

He rubbed the back of his head where it had smacked into the concrete – the least, he suspected, of what he deserved.

"You should be glad. Someone else might not have been so gentle."

Her eyes nearly fell out of her head at his words.

"*You are a monster*!" she yelled, stepping towards him. He could see the intent in her eyes, and he kept his hands ready to fend her off. "You didn't have to do that! But you wanted to, didn't you?"

She feigned a left cut, but it was her right hand that struck him, hard enough to throw his head to the side, the pain instant as his neck cracked. Next second a knee landed in his groin and he doubled over, gasping and instantly on his knees. He looked up and saw her watching him, eyes he adored now shuttered with hate.

"Why is it every time I start to *trust* you, start to believe there's a man beneath that mask you wear, you go and prove me a fool again. You make Harvey look like fucking saint. I should do far more to you for what you just did, but I don't think you can help yourself. You don't know what you've just done. All I know is, you always think you're right."

She grabbed her jacket, pulling it on and zipping it up. "But you know, there's one thing you didn't make me promise not to do." Her smile was wide and dangerous. "And it's worse than anything else you've seen so far. So just know that whatever happens, *on your head be it*."

She strode away, leaving him hurting, empty, and disgusted with himself. She was right. He could have tossed her in the back of the car, handcuffed her down and made her listen, battered her with words and threats, but his male instinct had been too strong, and he'd wanted the excuse to get his hands on her. He couldn't deny it. But he'd gone much further than he'd wanted to; treated her far worse than any other woman in his life, despite the fact he adored her. No one else had ever made him lose control like that.

What the fuck have I done?

He heard a shout: "Don't fucking touch me, you Goddamn Judas! Don't anyone try and touch me! Ever!"

She must have seen O'Grady and his boys keeping people away from the tunnel whilst he dealt with her. His 'dealing' with her had been little better than rape. He had to go after her. What had she meant by 'on your head be it'? What was she going to do? Oh God.

He limped out of the tunnel to be met by a furious O'Grady.

"*What the fuck did you do to her*?" he demanded as soon as he was level with them, too angry to care one iota how he was speaking to his employer.

For the first time ever, Mac stepped between the two of them, his men on alert too.

"Just get the fuck after her, O'Grady. She's just threatened to do something stupid, and I don't know what it is, but standing here isn't going to help. *Go*!"

The fear in Daryl's green eyes and the cut lip told O'Grady enough. He shouted to his boys, who took off after her. He turned back to Daryl, opened his mouth to speak, thought better of it and left.

Mac had seen her face when she'd fought off the kind hands that had reached for her, knew blind rage when he saw it. But it was more than rage. She fled like a frightened mouse fleeing a hawk. What he saw was blind fear, not rage. What the fuck had Daryl done?

Daryl touched a finger to his lip, not expecting a word of sympathy. He didn't receive any. Mac stood silently by his side. And just as he was about to say they should leave, a whole gang of Pirates appeared, and some of the heavies that patrolled the front gates and the arena, the unofficial police force with their massive bodies, bandanas, tattoos, and fists the size of plates.

Mac held up a hand for restraint and, much to his relief, the silent force parted to let the Blackmoor party leave.

The message was clear: *you upset our girl.*

"SHE JUST SAID what she would do would be worse than anything she's done so far," Daryl said.

"You can't stop her," Mac replied matter-of-factly. He resisted from saying what he was really thinking; that she would go looking for a fight, just like the Saturday morning when the contract got signed. "And I don't think your presence would be beneficial. O'Grady has gone after her. You are not going downtown."

Daryl didn't argue. Her words were rotating in his head, making him feel weak with shame: 'You make Harvey look like a fucking saint,' and, 'You're like the fuckwit in the bar fight.' And that whimper, the half-scream for him to stop. What terrors a man could unleash with his own hands was now a question Daryl knew the answer to.

"Sir?" The voice was a welcome distraction.

"O'Grady?"

"She's just gone into a bar. It's a real shit hole – excuse my language. I'm going in to pull her out, get her home somehow." Daryl was about to answer him when he heard, "Oh Christ! Get in there! *All of you*!"

Disconnect.

Mac looked over at him and together they pulled up the satellite feed. The bar, which was most likely a total dive to begin with, was now wrecked. Furniture and battered bodies and smashed bottles lay everywhere.

"Are you done now?" O'Grady demanded, and Daryl realised the girl with her feet up on the bar, her back against one of the roof supports and eating crisps as calmly as if she was sitting under a tree, was her.

"Hell, no. I'm just warming up." She upturned the packet of crisps and poured the last broken pieces into her mouth, screwed up the bag, tossed it, and then hopped back down onto the floor, littered with broken glass and smashed furniture. "Why? Too much excitement for you?"

Her smile was sardonic as she stalked past O'Grady and headed for the door, that now swung on its hinges, pushing through it with the confidence of a victor. O'Grady followed swiftly, while ordering his men back out.

"Where the hell are you going now?" he called.

"Why don't you come and find out? She swung a leg over her bike. "It's going to be worth a watch."

She pulled on her helmet and was away.

OG shouted his boys back onto their bikes.

A BUILDING CALLED 'Fight Club' didn't bode well. But the heavy-duty figures that stood outside talking, all male, boded even worse. The stir she caused when she pulled up, took off her helmet and strolled in in that long, easy gait of hers, was obvious.

O'Grady swore loudly, and ran in after her.

"Mysty you're not doing this."

He tried to grab her arm but she flicked him off without looking round.

"Fuck off, OG. My night, my body, my choice. *Back off.*"

She kept her eyes on the guy at the desk, big enough to fill a small room, muscles standing out on every part of him, just like the guys outside.

The guy raised his eyebrows at her. "That your dad?"

"No. He's the world's most useless bodyguard. You got issues with a woman taking part in a fair fight or what? You want to take those issues out of your little box and discuss them out front now? 'Cos I'm in the mood for it if you do?" She slammed some notes down on the desk.

It was the same defiant talk Daryl had heard so many times before, and it put the fear of God in him.

"Save it for the cage, beautiful. You paid, you're in."

He let her through the wire mesh door by pressing a button under the desk, and it swung shut behind her, stopping O'Grady from following.

"Have you any idea who she is?" he roared. "You must recognise her!"

"I know who she is. And maybe she stands a chance. I'm not stopping her if she wants to fight. Most exciting night of the year getting a girl that pretty in here. You wanna watch or you gonna wait outside for whatever's left to get put out there when we shut?"

OG ignored the attitude, the Rage tattoo across the knuckles, the flexing muscles. "How much to get in?"

"Spectators is only $40."

O'Grady got all of them in, using the expenses card he always carried, half wishing it had cost a hundred times more just to hit Blackmoor harder in the wallet. What the fuck had that man done to her? She'd have been better off at the Bowl just getting drunk and then sleeping it off. Why the hell had he rung Blackmoor thinking he'd know what to do? Donny had understood her, better than herself sometimes, knew how to talk her down. But Blackmoor? Fucking fool. But he cursed himself for being a fool too.

He led the fifteen-strong troop through the dark corridors, hearing male voices, smelling the stink of sweat and blood. The lighting was poor, so when they got to the end of the tunnel-like corridor, the brightness that met their eyes was all the more stark, and the truth more blindingly awful.

There was a huge metal cage centre stage of the room, the floor covered with sand, stained with blood in some places, and they arrived just as the last defeated guy was dragged to the cage door and pulled to the side. The spectators were all men, some bare-chested, some bloodied from previous fights. It was alpha-male paradise, the air thick with testosterone and aggression. This was far more dangerous than the Bowl, and far more lethal and focussed than any bar fight. Men were watching from all sides.

There was nowhere to hide.

"Where the hell is she?" O'Grady muttered, sending men in all directions.

But it was too late.

With all the purity of the first woman created by God she stepped through the cage door. A deep hush fell on the room. Her face grim, she was beauty and danger epitomised, joined and made one. She stopped just off centre of the cage, pulled a leather thong from her arm and tied her hair back, ignoring the wolf whistles and the catcalls that tore the hush to shreds.

Another body stepped through the cage door, and Daryl felt his heart thud to a halt in his chest. '*Know that whatever happens, on your head be it.*'

Her challenger was huge. He looked like he could snap her in two with two fingers. And he was clearly highly amused at the sight of his opponent, and glanced back at the official, who merely nodded. He was barefoot, like her, and had tape over his knuckles, just like her.

The cage door shut, OG's attempt to prevent it being shut getting him shoved in the chest, hard enough to throw him back a few feet into one of his guys.

"Wait."

She raised a hand.

The giant before her rolled his eyes, as if expecting her to change her mind and want to get out.

"I came here for a real fight. Not some fucking one-on-one shit – no offence." She held up what looked like a cash card. "There is twenty thousand dollars on this card. It goes to the man who can break my face. I'm not afraid to lose it. Anyone else who wants the chance to win it had better get in the cage now 'cos I ain't offering twice."

She held it out to the official, a sign she was willing to hold good to her word, and the guy took it, but paused. "Are you sure about this?"

"More sure than anything else. Should have done it years ago. Might have saved me from so much," she answered, and stood patiently, unmoving, ludicrously relaxed as another six guys came through the door.

It was closed again, and Daryl felt dread consume him. This was it. This is what she'd meant.

"Get Baden!" he barked at Mac. "Have him taken there immediately. Have everything on standby. Send more guys to help O'Grady."

How could he watch this? See her get torn apart? He felt sick to his stomach and his head and his heart. *This is my fault.*

"O'Grady. Use whatever force necessary the moment she's down to get her out of there. I don't care what it takes."

"What are the rules?" she asked calmly.

Her original challenger answered for the rest of the room: "There are no rules."

Her instant smile was a thing Daryl tried to imprint on his mind, to remember her how she was. And then something else flashed across his mind: hadn't Donny told him that she does this? that when the fear takes her, the only way she beats it is to find something bigger and scarier to prove she is still alive, still stronger? And then a horrifying realisation: she was there because she was too restrained to take her fear out on him, like he deserved, because she didn't think he could fight.

The sound of her voice jolted him.

"Wow, I like this place even more," she said.

"You want out, you have to raise a hand, but that's surrender. There are no timeouts, breaks, rounds. One cage. One fight. To the end," the original guy replied.

"So anyone who doesn't raise a hand to tap out is fair game?"

"Yes. Unless they're…unconscious." Or too pulverised to know how to raise a hand.

"Lovely. Who starts?" She glanced left, then right, letting herself gauge where all of them were.

"I've heard of you," he then said. "They call you the golden tiger. Amongst other things."

"You're about to find out why."

He eyed her up and down, as if unsure of her statement. The tension was reaching breaking point, everyone frozen, waiting for the first blow to get thrown, and the violence to start.

"Don't tell me you're all afraid of trying to hit a girl?" she mocked gently, looking over all of her opponents. "I'm sure a few of you like smacking your girlfriends around, don't you? Like you…" She singled one out. "I'm pretty sure you do. I can see it in your eyes. Tell me, does she ever try and hit you back?" She strolled a little closer, prowling like the tiger she was so named as.

"No," he replied, sneering, not afraid of this slender bitch with attitude.

"No, I bet she doesn't. I'm sure you wouldn't like that, would you?"

She turned away, smiling, everyone distracted by her beauty, or her control.

The next heartbeat, her foot slammed into his face and then his chest, sending him flying backwards to slam into the solid mesh cage ten feet away. In silence he slumped to the floor, blood dribbling down his face, which was a mess.

"Holy shit," Mac muttered, realising the force she'd used on him that morning all those months ago was nothing to that which she was capable of. Even from the angle of O'Grady's jacket camera, the damage looked impressive.

She stalked back to the centre of the circle of men, knowing the scent of blood was what they'd need to get them in the mood. One down, six to go.

She brought both arms up, crossing her forearms in front of her, palms facing each other, the pose angelic and peaceful, pausing in silence for the storm to unleash.

O'Grady could have sworn he saw her eyes shut.

And the dance began.

Daryl thought he knew how well she could fight, but nothing compared to this. The control, the precision and the speed left him speechless. Mac too. Their physical strength was useless, as they were too slow to get near her; and her skill far too great to ever put her in an insoluble situation.

She ran at the cage wall, sprang off, flipped over, landing blow after blow. It was almost beautiful to watch. And the insolence with which she fought proved time and again that she had the edge, had more than enough time to plan her next move as they lumbered around the cage. All the fitness of the Celeste athlete coming to the fore, gravity was defied as she leapt and kicked, span over, landed behind her victim and kicked him again in the back, sending him face first to hit the cage mesh with force enough to send the crowd into roars of approval, and shock.

There was blood, but none of it was hers; and there were broken teeth and bones, but none of them belonged to the girl.

When the last man fell and stayed down, she paused, tilted her head to the side and waited to see if anyone changed their mind and wanted more…but no one launched themselves at her again.

She let out a long, dissatisfied sigh, reached and pulled the thong from her hair, looping it over her arm with practised ease, and stepped through a cage door that was held open for her. Her cash card was held out for her to take, and she took it.

No one spoke. No one touched her. No one in the hundred-strong male crowd outside the cage moved. And the expression on her face when she walked past O'Grady was devoid of any emotion. No satisfaction, no joy, no sadness. Nothing.

The room was still in silence when she left.

O'Grady hurried after her, and the Blackmoor boys flooded out into the car park, hurrying towards her.

"What time is it?" she asked, throwing her leg over the bike.

"One thirty in the morning," O'Grady answered.

"I'm going home. Lazarus will be wondering where I am. He is the one joy in my life."

O'Grady stood and watched for a second, as she rode away, his heart still beating hard in his chest. He'd been so afraid for her. And there she was, talking like she'd been having dinner with friends, not pulverising seven men.

"Everyone, back to base."

O'Grady disconnected his comms and Daryl leaned back and closed his eyes. Alive. Untouched. Not beaten to a bloody pulp.

"I'll tell Baden he isn't needed," Mac said quietly.

"Yes, thank God."

"You sure you don't want to tell me what happened tonight?"

"No."

Daryl could feel eyes on him but refused to look round. Mac stood up and left, leaving Daryl feeling the most wretched he could ever remember feeling. He was why she had stood there, daring the muscle-mountains to pulverise her into the sand in that cage. To break that beautiful face because all it did was bring her grief, not joy. Why had he lost control so badly? How had his judgement been so impaired?

He showered and pulled on a dressing gown. At first he couldn't see her when he logged on, and then he did. She was huddled by the window, her back against the wall in the corner, her head laid against the leopard's body.

But her face was not relaxed. She was facing into the room, facing the door, afraid someone or something might come after her, even there, in her home. But she also looked sadder than he'd ever seen another human being look before.

He didn't know what it was to have a broken heart; he didn't know what it was to love so completely as she had loved Donny. How could he have been so arrogant? He should have found a better way. Once more he felt sickened to think of how he had threatened her innocence, used it as a weapon to get her to surrender to him.

Finally she stood, eyes on the door. Slowly she made her way to her bedroom, the lights went out, and there was silence.

Oh God, what had he done?

For the first time in living memory, Daryl Blackmoor knew he was going to have to apologise.

RELUCTANT TO LEAVE the peaceful painless oblivion of slumber, she knew now she was awake there was little chance she would fall back to sleep. The night before came flooding back, and she felt sick just thinking about it. His hands, and his words. Threatening. Taunting. And then that kiss! She wished she'd never gone to the Bowl in such a reckless mood. She dragged herself out from under the duvet.

"My, that is colourful." Her head snapped up and she stopped, all sleepiness gone, her eyes focussed on OG, who was sitting at the breakfast bar, a cup of coffee in front of him. "Did you think about getting a matching one on the other side?"

He was referring to the fabulous bruise on her arm, all bright yellow and purple. She had no energy to reply. Why couldn't they all just leave her alone?

"Emergency room must have had a night of it putting them back together," he added, and pushed a glass of orange juice along the breakfast bar. "Hungry? I might be the world's worst fucking bodyguard, but I can still fix you breakfast."

She took the juice and retreated again, not wanting to be anywhere him. He'd betrayed her. Again. Put his boss before her. Again.

"Kiddo, are you…" he attempted. "It's so hard seeing you like this. Half the time I don't know what to do. If bacon makes you in the slightest bit happy, then I'll make you a sandwich. But if toast is better, I'll make you some toast."

She still didn't reply, not sure how to take the concern and the sincerity.

"Toast?"

She nodded.

"Bacon?"

Another nod.

He got up, rubbed a hand over his face and then went to the fridge, pulling out bacon, tomatoes, eggs, butter. He was a man. If there was one thing he knew how to do, it was a fry up. And the simple kind, just how she liked it.

She headed back to the bedroom to fetch a sweater and, as she disappeared, he heard the door go. He turned, seeing Blackmoor and Mac.

"Hey, no! *No way*!" he protested as Blackmoor immediately followed the oblivious Mysty out of the room. "You can't be serious!"

Mac put a hand up to halt O'Grady's progress across the room.

"I know, I said the same, but he's determined to speak to her and apologise." Mac was calm and immovable.

"Apologise?" OG repeated in disbelief. Were they talking about the same man?

"Whatever he did, I don't think he's feeling very good about it."

"Good! Because *she isn't either*!"

Mac looked pained, agreeing whole-heartedly with the sentiment. But he'd been greeted with the unusual sight of his forbidding employer looking very sick that morning, and had been talked into coming over here.

"It has to be settled, whatever it is between them, you know that. Best to give them a chance," he said, to OG's snort of disgust.

OG returned to preparing breakfast, keeping one ear open for any sound that would give him the excuse to go to her, regardless of what Mac said. Mac got a coffee and sat down, rubbed a hand over his eyes, much like he had a few moments ago. The man did look tired. they were all tired.

"I still can't believe what she did last night," Mac said.

"No. I'd rather not live to witness that again."

"Christ, no."

Both men stared at nothing, going over the images that had kept them holding their breath for the entire time she had been in the cage.

The bacon and tomatoes went into the pan.

The next few minutes were going to be a similarly anxious wait.

MYSTY FOUND HER favourite baggy Yankees top and pulled it out, held it up to pull over her head. She caught sight of herself in the reflection of a picture frame and, in a moment of complete despair, she took it down from the wall and lay it flat on the bed. The older she got, the more she looked like her mum. Why did that have to be? She dropped the sweater and hung her head, just wishing the pain would stop.

"Don't do that. Your mother wouldn't want you to be ashamed of how you look. You're beautiful. When will you see that?"

She froze, then whirled round to face the voice she hoped was the remnants of a nightmare.

But it was real.

He was standing there, in dark blue trousers and a white shirt, in her doorway.

Neither of them moved. She stared at him in abject horror, her mouth frozen in the shout that wouldn't come.

Daryl looked at her, seeing everything he wanted, knowing once and for all that he didn't deserve a solitary thing. It was the feeling that had dogged him all night. The sense of unworthiness against her goodness. He didn't know how long he could live with feeling so guilty for what he'd done. A wretchedness had seeped into his very bones. His only recourse was to try and undo some of the damage. He stepped in the room and closed the door gently.

She backed away instantly, terror etched into her face. "No! No more!" she whispered.

Daryl raised his hands slowly, hoping to calm her, not drive her nearer to complete panic.

"I'm not here to hurt you, Mysty. Just sit on the bed, please. I'll stay over here. I just want to talk to you."

His gentle words were the last thing she expected, and she sat slowly, not taking her eyes off him. He picked up her fallen sweater and handed it to her.

"Here, put it on, don't get cold," he said.

She looked down at it, took it and pulled it on, the bold slanted script of 'Yankees' across the front tugging at him, reminding him they could share so much, except he always seemed to ruin everything.

Guarded eyes turned back to him, waiting, the silence surrounding them loud and tense.

"All I wanted, last night, was to pull you back from the madness you were getting into. I couldn't stand by and watch you throw so much away, no matter how upset you are," he said quietly. When she didn't respond, he continued. "You deserve so much more than fumbled kisses with strangers, than turning yourself into a wild-child celebrity relied upon to do the most outrageous things. You owe yourself so much more than being killed in a bike race. You are not a cheap little piece there for everyone's entertainment. You are so much better than that. Why else have you been fighting so long?"

He thought he was going to drown in her eyes, the tears so bright in them, the colour so strong.

"Despite what you think, I respect you, and care about you, which is why I won't let you destroy yourself. You're so gifted it's hard to believe sometimes that you're real. But you are real, and people love you for being you. You don't need to change. You haven't done anything wrong." He indicated the end of the bed. "Can I sit down?" he asked. When she nodded, he sat slowly, carefully, a good distance from her. "Mysty, you didn't lose Donny because you failed in any way at all. Life is just unfair sometimes. Sometimes very unfair, and for the most undeserving people. But that's no excuse to give up. You never have before, please don't start now."

She blinked and the tears fell, saddening him. No girl of this age should have to cry so much.

"Please hear me. I need to tell you that, last night, I shouldn't have treated you the way I did, and I apologise for having scared you. If I could undo it, I'd give anything. It wasn't what I intended to do. It got out of control, and I lost control. You seem to be the only person, in the world, who manages to…to make me lose control."

His eyes dropped as he forced the words out, hoping she'd understand, that she'd see the sincerity and his regret, wondering if it might douse the flames of hatred a little.

"I know I used force last night, which was wrong, but I still want you to keep that promise. And I want you to promise not to put yourself in danger again, ever again, like you did at that fight club. I know why you went, and I know you only part-found what you were looking for. But there are other ways to find the peace you need so much. Don't go risking yourself like that again, promise me?"

Four long seconds passed and then she nodded. The memory of her in that cage was horribly fresh in his mind, as was the image of her huddled in the corner with Lazarus when she got back, her eyes fixed on the door in fear. He'd never been so emotionally embroiled in the life of another person before in his life, and he knew he was on a learning curve far steeper than any that had gone before.

"I'm leaving LA in less than an hour, and I'm sure you'd rather I was as far away as possible, but I couldn't leave without talking to you." He smiled sadly. "I don't care what you have to do to work through your feelings, just don't do it thinking you're alone. You're not. Even if that's how it feels right now."

He looked back at her, knowing she was barely breathing she was so still, her eyes still on him. Every business meeting, every conference… they'd been a walk in the park compared to this.

"You once told me you were nothing. You couldn't be nothing if you tried. Never will be. I wonder when you will see your true value. The future is unwritten, waiting for you to make your mark. You've already started, but there is so much else before you. Do you really want to throw that away? I don't think you do."

He stood up, and after one more moment of silence, one more look at her face, he went to the door. He stepped out into the hall, half praying he'd hear her say something, knowing he didn't deserve a single word, never mind her forgiveness. But at least she had listened. Now he had the long wait in purgatory, however long that was, until she was ready to deal with him again.

It was no surprise to find Mac and O'Grady watching for him, both looking worried, not sure if the lack of shouting was a good thing or not.

"She might want a bit of company, O'Grady," he said, and the man nodded. "Mac." He couldn't bear to be there a moment longer, else he was going to walk right back in there and do what he'd wanted to do last night, which was hold her until she lost the fear and trusted him again.

O'Grady went straight to her room the moment the front door closed. He knew what she needed and there was no one else to do it.

"Come on, kitten," he said, sitting down next to her, holding her tightly while she cried it out, as he would with his own daughters.

When she finally went quiet, he asked, "Did he talk to you? About last night?"

She nodded against his shoulder.

There was something he needed to ask, as he would with one of his own daughters. "Did he…did he rape you?"

"No. Not quite," she whispered. "But what happened, I don't think he meant to…do what he did. I…I…someone had to stop me."

Indigo eyes lifted up to his and his heart melted. There was no answer to her words, and he pulled her against him again and let her finish weeping the sorrow and fear into the safety of his shoulder.

They still had a way to go, but he sensed the worst was over.

The healing could begin.

DARYL LOOKED OVER at the skyscraper photograph she'd given him for the thousandth time, wondering what she was doing, how she was feeling. It had been three weeks now. He'd watched the rehearsals for the first performance of 'Ladies' Night in LA' show, which was as organised, efficient and friendly as ever, if a little quiet. It had been a relief to see she hadn't lost anything of the magic which she brought to the stage; in fact, her recent heartbreak seemed to add something. The all-female audience had loved the women-empowering songs, and the show had been a huge hit, with every night selling out and attracting brilliant reviews. Compared to the MJ tour, this was much easier to organise and execute, and she was taking it all in her stride.

Without him.

He felt useless, and lonely. Despite his hectic work schedule, and putting his charming social face at corporate dinner parties, he wouldn't be at peace until things between him and Mysty were resolved. Even if she was determined to hate him, he would rather know than not.

Speaking to OG on a daily basis, he had regular updates on her recovery from the hit, and Donny. She was chattier, made a lot more jokes, and made lots of trips to the ice rink, which he had enjoyed every second of watching. She'd not gone to the Bowl once, spending Saturday nights in her computer room or on the sofa with Lazarus, not showing any sign of missing the bike-fest. But he wondered what she was really thinking. Had the place just become yet another place of bad memories for her? He'd never know unless he got to ask her…

He only had to think of that tunnel, and how he'd groped her, and how he'd demanded that she kiss him, to feel great shame and horror at what had happened. Lord knows what she was thinking. He'd wanted to kiss her so badly; but he'd ruined that too. No kiss that ever followed – and there was no chance of that now – would ever be a 'first' kiss again, and he hung his head. Why did he get everything so catastrophically wrong with the one person he wanted everything to be so right for, and with?

The intercom beeped, dragging his mind back to the present.

"Harvey."

The image of his reliably positive, carefree and handsome friend smiled at him from behind his own impressively large desk in his Manhattan office.

"Daryl, how are you old chap?"

"Good, how are you?"

"Super! But you're not good, are you? Lord, man, what's wrong? And don't lie because you missed my birthday party, which is never a good sign. If you're not in the mood for very fine wine, wonderfully loose women and entertaining conversation – and very fine cigars, I might add – then there is definitely something wrong."

Daryl just smiled sadly, not really wanting to talk about anything with his overtly cheerful friend, as dear as he was to him. He couldn't really help, anyway, and nor could he be trusted to keep his mouth shut.

"Thank you for my presents, though, they were fantastic!" Harvey babbled, filling the silence. "I have all the pictures up. Devoted one huge wall to them. And the wine. I promise this time I won't give in and open it. I'll save it for a special occasion."

"Good, I thought you'd like them."

He'd sent a set of three large Butterfly pictures, mounted in glass, from the pieces she'd done the night of her return. He had a feeling it was the 'Back in Black' picture with her in that sexy black outfit with flames dancing around her that Harvey would have put in the centre.

"How is the tiger-taming going? From the demoralised look on your face I'd say it was not good, which I find amazing considering Donny is now removed from the picture. Hasn't she fallen head over heels for you yet?"

Harvey's whimsical flattery was hard to listen to considering how different the reality was.

"No. And I don't think she will. She's a bit too sensible for that. Besides, I don't think you appreciate just how close she and Donny were. I was there when he told her; it wasn't good."

There was no reason for Harvey to argue with him considering the look on his friend's face.

"What happened that weekend? I heard about the hit taken out on her, and some wild motorbike hunt through LA. Was it as close as everyone's saying? I saw your press conference but–"

"It was close enough. She got grazed by a bullet. She had one chance to get out and it involved hurtling up a hill and catching a moving rope from the chopper. I don't want to go through that again; I don't think she does either."

"*You were there*?"

"I pulled her inside the helicopter from where she was sitting contentedly on the leg of the damn thing. No fear of heights."

"Bloody hell. How did you persuade Mac to let you go?" Harvey knew how protective Mac was of his boss.

"Mac does what I tell him. No, he didn't like it, but I think he was too worried about her to waste time arguing with me."

"Christ. She is exciting, isn't she?" Harvey saw his interest wasn't going down too well, or even raising a smile. "Well, there's everything to play for, surely? Early days. Not like she's going anywhere, is it?" he then said.

"No, I suppose not." *Unless she falls in love with someone else while I'm not there.*

"Why don't we go out for dinner, have a chat? I'm certain you've been working too hard. Come on, my treat, anywhere you like. Let's just leave the office in the office for one night." Harvey sounded like Mysty, Daryl realised, having missed her teasing about his over-working. No one except a close friend, someone who cared, would dare say anything like that to him. Harvey didn't like Daryl's long pause, and said, "You owe me, Daryl, you missed my birthday party! Come on, it's not like pulling teeth! Just say yes for God's sake and have the night off."

"Alright, fine. I'll be free from eight onwards. Let me know where. I'm really not bothered. I trust your choice."

"Oh, wow. After knowing each other for twenty-odd years he tells me he trusts my choice of restaurant." Harvey rolled his eyes, teasing his quiet friend just a little more. "Shall I invite anyone else, or is extra company not something you want?"

"No, no one else."

"Good, excellent. Well, I'll let you know the location and I'll see you later. I'm sure it can't be as bad as you think, whatever it is you're brooding on," Harvey chided him sternly, then disconnected, leaving Daryl to smile unwillingly, touched that his friend refused to give up on him and leave him in his doldrums.

"KIDDO, YOU GOING to take a break soon?"

Mysty appreciated the carefully chosen tone in OG's voice. Not nagging, not sharp, just concerned, reminding her that she needed to make the choice for herself.

"I will, promise. Just finishing this last bit of code."

She looked up from the three computer screens she was working on, and saw for herself the affection behind the question, and the one that followed: "You want to go to the rink again?"

The rink had become her regular solace lately. She'd spent hours skimming over the ice, ignoring the bright happy sunshine in the sky, preferring to be in the chill inside with her wounded, bleeding heart. They'd been evenings spent with music and the blades on her feet, wearing herself out so she could sleep a little, before having to do it all over again.

"Sure. 5pm?" she said.

"We'll stop at 9pm tonight. Four hours is plenty." She rolled her eyes. "We can get a pizza on the way home."

His eyes rested on her a moment longer. No pizza, and she might not be so compliant at getting off the ice.

"Deal. Pizza on the way home."

Careful not to crowd her, OG took a couple of steps closer. "You can tell me what you're working on over the pizza."

"Come back in twenty minutes, after I've made my sandwich, and I'll explain it for you then if you like?"

"Okay." Surprised at her offer, but not about to turn it down, OG felt he was doing well at communicating with his complicated, grieving, truculent charge. "Oh, and how's your…friend?" he risked. "The one who blocked you when he realised you were the girl he sees on the news every day?"

Even with her face in profile he could tell that hadn't been the right thing to say.

"Still blocked." But then she softened. "I…I hope he's okay."

"Sure you could hack around it somehow? I mean, you're so good on these things…" He gestured at all the kit surrounding her. It was a genuine compliment.

"I could. But…he's a friend. And if he's blocked me then… Well, I feel I should respect that."

The weariness in her voice told OG she'd already debated this issue with herself a number of times.

"He'll come around. I thought about it some more, after you told me. If he's a bit of a nerd…" He left that trailing as a sort of question. "Then he probably isn't the most confident of guys. And you're you. You're stunning, Mysty, and he'll find that intimidating. He's not Donny, or Slick. He won't have that self-assurance. It would have been quite a shock to see you. Give him time. He'll come back. It's not like you did anything wrong."

"Thanks, OG. I admit I miss him, even though we've never met. Stupid, I know. It's just…we've been talking for years… I don't have a huge circle of those kinds of people in my life."

"Don't beat yourself up. Come on, finish your code, get that sandwich. I'll see you in a few minutes for my computer science lesson."

He dared to give her a pat on the shoulder, and then left her to it, closing the door.

She realised that was the first time someone had touched her in God knows how long.

TRUST ONE NIGHT out with Harvey to end more raucously than anticipated. Daryl turned the screen off, wishing he hadn't seen the unfortunate news headline. Somehow they'd become the focus of attention for a number of women and, Harvey being Harvey, he had encouraged them. Somehow someone had got a picture of one of them leaning forward to kiss Daryl's cheek, showing off ample cleavage, and later two of them getting into his car. Having 'Billionaire Playboy Back in Town' posted large and bold across the broadsheets was not really the way he'd wanted to remember the night.

The two hours spent idly chatting about nothing in particular with Harvey had been quite relaxing, but they never remained inconspicuous wherever they went, and the restaurant chosen was a popular eatery for those of their elevated circles; and with two of the most eligible men in the world out for the evening, it had been like putting sweets in front of children.

Daryl couldn't even remember their names it had been so fast and frivolous. Going back to Harvey's apartment the other side of Lexington, the party had continued and then the clothes had come off. He hadn't intended the evening to turn out the way it did; but the good company, the flirtatious women who were asking to be taken to bed, and not fussed about sharing the two men between all of them…well, after feeling so miserable and hopeless for weeks there was only one thing that was going to happen. He must ask Harvey if he wanted him to replace the vase that got broken when the woman of the moment had reached to grab something as he'd fucked her against the wall in the guest bedroom. Of one thing he was certain: the women would keep their mouths shut.

Money and reputation could buy certain things.

But that headline wasn't something he wanted Mysty to see.

"Sir?"

"Yes, Mac?" He pulled up the contract for the next appointment in half an hour. He had to know it backwards because he knew the client was going to argue with a number of the terms.

"I have a…box for you."

"A box?"

"Mysty sent it under guard. Apparently it's rather precious, so it's currently handcuffed to someone. Would you like me to have it brought in?"

"Sure. I'm free at the moment."

He tried to sound casual, as though he hadn't spent the last three weeks desperate to have some communication from her – any form of communication from her. A box? She'd put gifts in boxes before, when things were…different. But what on earth had she sent him this time?

Mac appeared at the door two minutes later, followed by another grey suit who was, sure enough, handcuffed to a wide, square box, the casing designed to protect the contents very securely.

He pointed at one end of his desk and the case was put down, released from its guardian, and turned to face its new owner. The grey suit left and Mac leaned forward to put something else on the desk in front of Daryl – a data-chip.

"She sent this as well, to be seen first…apparently it'll explain what's in the box."

This seemed an awful lot of effort to go to when the most he would have expected was a long email of insults and another demand he end the contract. Ideas that had frequently kept him awake staring at the ceiling in the small hours of the night.

"Is it…safe?"

"OG watched her pack it himself, by all accounts. Yes, it's safe."

Mac smiled and left the room, leaving Daryl in a state of utmost curiosity. He picked the chip up and slotted it in to his computer, opening the only file on the chip marked 'MYDB'. At least it wasn't named 'Jerk' or 'Fuckwit.'

"Hi."

Those indigo eyes looked at him, and he let himself absorb how healthy she looked. There was no trace of misery; her eyes and hair shone. She looked beautiful. He was stunned. She recorded a video? For him? He held his breath. What on earth would she say.

"I'm sorry I'm not calling you. I…I don't like leaving messages, but I'm not quite up to talking to you yet, so I hope this will suffice." She took a long breath. "I…appreciate the fact you came to apologise for what happened. We both know even God couldn't make you do something you didn't want to do, so I'm assuming you meant it, which was very honest of you, so I owe you that honesty in return." She closed her eyes, as if gathering her thoughts. "I don't hate you. And I'm not angry anymore. I was hurt, yes, but…looking back…I understand my own part in what happened, and I know I shouldn't have gone to the Bowl while I was that upset after speaking to Paulo. I know I pushed you into doing what you did to teach me a lesson. And at the end of flying everywhere, and meetings, and working too hard, as usual. We need to work on how you spend your Saturday nights."

Daryl didn't break eye contact with her, even though she was on video, watching her every move. He smiled at the gentle chiding about his overworking, again, and his Saturday nights.

"So, what the hell is in the box? Well, I spoke to Mac a couple of times, and he says you've been going around looking all moody and grim, so I thought I'd do something to give you a little less to worry about. Inside the box are twelve data cards, all individually labelled and designed. They're new firewalls for your twelve largest corporations. I've already gone in and had a look around – and I didn't do anything *wrong* before you start worrying about that – so they're all designed to load, install and integrate without any glitch in the system or incompatibility. There will be no downtime, and nothing needs to be uninstalled or deleted. I've designed them so that it will be a seamless upgrade, like a glass of red wine with a little water added. The colour will change, but at no point will there be no liquid in the glass." Obviously it's a little more complicated than that, but that will do."

He paused the video. This was incredible. How had she done this? He pressed Play.

"I should point out, these systems are far beyond what you have at the moment, and the only person who could get through them is me – but I have no interest in doing that and, frankly, it would be self-defeating. So, there we are. They're there if you want them. The code to the box is 2749. I figured I'd use a code you already knew."

She paused, giving him a chance to work out where the code was from…his BMW! That first car ride! She'd remembered? Of course she'd remembered.

"But that's all rather serious stuff so, in about sixty seconds, Mac should bring you the other box, which is far more exciting. It's called the Mount Olympus, and it seemed the most appropriate one I could get you. I'll leave it to you to decide. Any problems, you know where I am."

The screen went blank, and he immediately wanted her back. The relief to hear her voice and, more importantly, to hear her say that she didn't hate him…

He put in the code and opened the lid, and a dozen miniature balloons floated out in the trademark blue and cream, going to sit on his ceiling. He just grinned. He wasn't going to get them down. He didn't care who saw them. He threw the catches on the box inside and opened it, and, sure enough, there were twelve data cards inside. How much time had she spent putting this together for him?

The door knocked and a second later Mac came in with another box, smaller, white, and when it was put in front of him, he could see 'This is definitely not a milkshake' written around it, repeated in five different lines, forming an attractive pattern.

Mac was hovering, clearly wanting to stay and see what was inside, so Daryl didn't dismiss him. He opened the lid and the sides fell down, revealing the drink in a usual plastic cup with a domed lid. What was inside was off-white with swirls of brown, and looked creamy. The note read: 'Vanilla, coconut, caramel and double cream. You'll need an extra thirty minutes in the pool. I can't have you blaming me for losing your crown of the World's Most Handsome.'

He couldn't remember when he'd last drunk a takeaway drink, at his desk, with a straw; in fact, had he ever?

One taste of the milkshake told him he should have. She was right. It was heavenly. Rich, creamy and sweet, but not sickly. It was just... delicious.

"That bad, huh?" Mac asked him as he leaned back in his chair with the milkshake and groaned with pleasure.

"Awful. I won't offer you any. I don't want you to suffer."

Mac pulled out his own milkshake, from behind his back, and took a slurp.

"That's okay. She sent a whole load. Everyone in the office has one – even Marlene. I got the Mr T milkshake – peanuts, chocolate and caramel. I can't believe it's existed all this time and I've only just tried it!"

Daryl had to see this, and got up and went to the door and peeped through the gap. Sure enough, everyone was happily taking slurps from their own milkshakes, and other people's, sharing a rare moment of multi-coloured and multi-flavoured joviality in the minimalist, state-of-the-art office. It was such a great sight he couldn't be angry. God knows he worked them hard enough every day.

He went back to his desk, removed the FKY data card, and asked Mac to put the case in the safe. Then he strolled through the office with his milkshake. Everyone ground to a halt, seeing their boss had emerged, worried they might get in trouble for the impromptu milkshake party, and then noticed that he was drinking one too!

Mac followed him moments later, highly amused to see the looks on people's faces.

They got into the lift, getting out at the database epicentre. Daryl knew Simon would be there, and probably wouldn't like what Daryl was about to tell him to do.

"Simon."

The man looked around instantly as Daryl entered the room, screens on every wall showing data reads, the database coding, any attempted breaches or points of weakness. Simon could see his boss was drinking a milkshake.

"Mr Blackmoor, sir." Simon stared at the milkshake, then his boss, and then the drink again. "You're drinking a milkshake…" he ventured.

"What of it?"

"There is a company policy of no drinks or food in this room," Simon answered uncertainly, uncomfortably.

"Yes. New company policy: the boss can drink milkshake in any room he chooses. Now, I want you to insert this into the main data hub." He held out the data card and Simon looked at it as if it were a live snake. "New firewalls."

"But…you never said anything about this. We'll need to schedule downtime for the transfer, lock down all systems, certify integration…"

"No, that's already been done by the person who designed it."

"Who designed it?"

"Mysty."

"The same girl who put a retraction nebula in the database, froze everyone out and strangled it for a whole weekend."

"There was no permanent damage. Just do it." Simon didn't have much choice, and took the data card, looking at it suspiciously. "Today would be good, Simon. I have to leave in a few minutes and I want to see what she's created."

Simon kept his horrified protest zipped up and went over to the main console and connected the data card. Every screen went blank. Simon swallowed and felt sick. Daryl took a calm slurp of his milkshake, seconded by Mac.

A blue light appeared, pulsing in the middle of the screens. Five seconds, and then every screen showed the new data feed, the original red still streaming, but gradually being replaced by blue. When there was no red left, there was a stillness on the screens as activity paused for one imperceptible moment, and then the coding began to move. Daryl stepped forward to look at the large screen more closely, trying to understand what she had done. It was like nothing he'd seen before. The codes rippled across, like waves across an ocean. So many numbers and letters, all moving in harmony, despite the density. So much movement in tight formation. How could anyone hack past that?

"Download complete. Welcome to Halicarnassus System 1." The female voice, low and unhurried, was almost like Mysty's, but not quite.

The screens then went back to showing the original data reads as before, but this time in blue.

"Database integration complete. Please enter nominated systems controller ID and nominated system users."

Daryl looked down and saw the appropriate spaces on the screen for the ID numbers to be added in, every employee with their own ID card, pass and clearance. She'd actually done it. Spot on perfect. He would have kissed her except she wasn't there, and the only alternative was Mac, or Simon, and that was a definite no. He would have to contain his celebration.

"We're able to put our ID numbers in? Are we able to change any of the details?" Simon looked up at his boss, completely thrown at how seamless it had been.

"You can change all details provided you have the necessary clearance. System controllers will have access to all areas. All entered ID nominees can be edited, deleted or suspended. It is fully operational."

Everyone's eyes swung to the screens.

"Did the computer just answer my question?" Simon asked in utter disbelief.

"Does the human need the computer to answer that question?" came a slightly terse voice.

Daryl had to grin. "Simon, congratulations, I think you've finally got a girlfriend."

"Are you serious? Like he's the best I could do? No thanks." Simon continued to stare at the main screen. "I'll enter the data myself then, as 'Simon' is too busy doing a goldfish impression."

The screen for data input disappeared, and Simon's open mouth snapped shut.

"How is this even possible? Or fair! I now have a database that argues back?"

Daryl removed the data card and slipped it in his pocket. He patted

Simon on the shoulder. “A healthy degree of respect can go a long way, Simon,” he said. “Try being nice to her. It might help you get a date when you finally decide to get a life outside the building.”

For the first time in weeks Mac followed the relaxed shoulders of his boss from the room. Fingers crossed, things would stay this way.

“O’GRADY.”

“Mr Blackmoor, sir, how are you?”

“I’m very well, and you?”

“Just fine, sir. You got your case alright?”

“Yes.”

“Good. She spent hours on those data cards.”

Daryl had worked that out, realising what she had been doing on her Saturday nights in.

“The first one is already installed and, so far, I am very impressed.” And he was. He’d gone back into the database and seen the subtle changes she’d made, as well tweaks to the firewalls, all designed to improve performance. He was annoyed that he hadn’t taken the time to look himself and spot the areas that could be worked on, or that his staff had missed them, but was glad that she had. She hadn’t just designed an upgrade, what she’d done was a step up completely, and he doubted even the government had anything to rival it, despite the man hours and investment to come up with something unbeatable.

What had intrigued him, however, was that the programme the computer voice came from was not operating out of his system, his database. He knew she had one of her own, and clearly she was devoting some of her resources to it, but she was keeping the software a complete secret.

He would definitely pay her for her work, even though she hadn’t asked for anything. Such security was effectively priceless, but he hoped they could settle on a suitably large figure so he could transfer the monies over. He wanted to get her something else though; something that meant something…to her. He’d buy her half of Tiffany’s if he thought it would please her, but he knew she wasn’t that kind of girl. He’d have to think of something else.

"How is she?"

"We're a good couple of thousand miles from LA at the moment, and she's currently stacking shelves in a small food store, talking with Mr Matthews and eating cheese sandwiches."

"She *what*?"

"It's a little road trip, sir. She met Mr Matthews when she was nine, when she was travelling on her own. She helped him for two days with his delivery, and stocked up his shop, apparently. He's an old guy, with really bad arthritis that makes him very stiff, and he's quite moody, except for when he's with her. You should have seen his face when he saw her. It lit up like Christmas."

"Right."

"And yesterday we went to Louisville – bit of a sad old place, really – and went to visit a Mr Gibson, who has a boxing club."

"She was fighting?"

"No, not at all. She's not fighting. He's retired now, same as Mr Matthews, and knows her from way back. He first gave her the idea of going to Vegas. They went for a walk, talked a lot, then sat on the bridge and ate a bag of fries. He's a nice guy. Shame he's on his own in a town that's slowly dying."

"I see. Well, if I'd known that would make her happy I'd have bought her a bloody food store and a bag of fries." O'Grady chuckled. "From what I saw of her in her message, she seems a lot better."

"Yeah, definitely. She's a lot calmer, and most of the hurt is dealt with, I think. Not gone, but she's working through it."

"That's good. Good news."

"And her drumming is amazing. She's put in the practice, and it's paid off."

"I shall have to remember to ask for a demonstration at some point."

O'Grady smiled at that, amused that Mr Blackmoor was going to *ask* not demand to see a demonstration.

"You do know she has the press conference tomorrow?" he said.

"No, I'd not heard. This is her choice?" Daryl had to be sure.

"Yes. One hundred per cent. She's arranged for it to take place outside the city hall, where there's plenty of space. No doubt there'll be a crowd."

"I'm surprised she's going ahead with that. She hasn't mentioned it to me, and Gloria hasn't mentioned it either."

"Mysty and Gloria don't really get on. In truth, they never have, but lately it's become more pronounced. Gloria doesn't seem to get that Mysty has her own way of doing things – which always end up as a success – and always wants to shove pre-set speeches in front of her. Mysty is the most spontaneous person you could find, as you know, and she'd rather just be honest, which always works just fine. Short story, Gloria refused to get involved hoping Mysty would come unstuck and need her help. Again, completely underestimating the girl who organised a concert tour."

"Yes. I'd hoped Gloria had learned that after the first press release and was adapting to the new type of role she has play when it comes to Mysty. I'll have words. Is Mysty alright about it? She does know they'll be asking all kinds of questions about Donny?" He needed to ask again.

"She's bracing herself for it. I think that's partly why she wanted to come here for two days, for the trip down memory lane. Needed to remind herself where she came from, to see how far she's come."

"Yes. I think you're right." Daryl paused, spiralled the latte in front of him. "Is there anything she wants, or needs?"

"No, she's happy."

"That's not very helpful, O'Grady. The girl hands me a couple of hundred million dollars-worth of security software and you tell me there's nothing I can get her in return."

"I don't think she sent those to you expecting anything back, sir. She just wanted to make sure you were protected, and had one less thing to worry about."

"Well, she's going to have to learn not to give things away for free. You let me know if she mentions something she'd like."

"A lesson on how to fly the helicopter." O'Grady felt compelled to mention it, and it made Daryl roll his eyes.

"No."

"Sky-diving?"

"No. If she asks for something that isn't dangerous, let me know. Knowing her, though, I'm guessing she only talks about doing dangerous things, to test herself."

O'Grady laughed. "Yes, sir, I'll let you know."

"What time is the press conference tomorrow?"

"Scheduled for four in the afternoon here. She wanted it to be at a time when people were more likely to be able to get away from work, and after school hours. Having regular people there, and not just the press, will keep her calm."

"I'll be watching. She'll be upset afterward, no doubt, so get her home quickly."

"Will do, sir."

Disconnect.

Staking shelves? He pressed in the commands for her satellite location and it came up, showing the dusty sun-bleached strip of street. He could tell which shop it was by the cars parked out front and the grey suits hovering around. As he watched, O'Grady smiled at an old man walking towards them, his grasp firm on Mysty's arm. They stopped and she gave him a hug, his walking stick raised for a moment as he used both arms to embrace her back. He couldn't hear the exchange, but could tell there was warmth in the words spoken by both. O'Grady then shook Mr Matthews' hand in farewell and he and Mysty got into the car. The grey suits into a second car, and they drove away, a hand raised by the stationary figure outside the shop in goodbye as the dust rose in their wake.

Was there anyone untouched by her kindness?

It was good to know she was okay, that she was fine without Donny, as much as it must still hurt.

When would he speak to her again in person? That was one question he didn't have the answer to. But he knew he was going to enjoy watching her message again. And hopefully by the time she returned that damned headline would have disappeared.

CITY HALL HAD been chosen because it had huge steps, and a large pedestrianised area in front. However, the appeal she posed had been underestimated again, and it was another last-minute mission to get screens up for those in the crowded streets to be able to see her when she appeared.

Daryl was waiting for her to appear, like so many others, Mac and he sitting in his office counting down the three minutes until she was meant to step in front of the camera. He had checked with O'Grady she was alright, and had been assured that despite being a little nervous, she was, which was the most anyone could ask for just then.

Finally, at 4pm, the double doors opened and two grey suits emerged, followed by Mysty, then O'Grady and two more suits. It was only she, however, who stepped behind the podium, her hair loose and bright in the late afternoon sun, shades in her hair. She was wearing a pale gold bodice, metallic tiger stripe leggings he'd seen once before at the casino, the night she had beaten him at poker, and the spectacularly expensive necklace Donny had given her. It was her only adornment. And her outfit was intended only for one man. Her face was serious, and the cheer that greeted her obediently came to an end when she raised both hands with gentle grace, asking for silence.

"Good afternoon. It's lovely to see so many here today. I know I've kept you all waiting, and you no doubt have a number of questions. You have the bare bones of the situation, and I will answer them as best I can. Questions are open to members of the press and those of the public who have taken the time to come here today. I also have a couple of questions from people who have emailed me, which I thought would be useful to be answered today, so if they don't come up I will use those also. First question please."

Daryl leaned back slowly in his chair, amazed, even knowing her as he did, at her composure, which was as steady as a presidential delegate. But the girl also had all the poise of a lady, not letting anything or anyone phase her. He knew from having faced so many cameras himself how important the initial greeting was, to get an audience's attention, their respect, and to set the tone for whatever followed.

There were many hands raised, but she calmly pointed to one person.

"Mysty, the bullet wound, are you alright? Has it healed okay? We know you've been doing Celeste and your LA shows, but do you have any concerns at all?"

"The bullet wound was not so very much. It healed weeks ago, and I can't even tell where it was now. Not even an amazing scar to go with the story, I'm afraid. I'm as fit as I have ever been and see no reason why that will change. I have no plans to cancel any Celeste performances or to change the schedule of any shows at all."

She smiled briefly and then pointed to another.

"The hit that was taken out on you, you had no warning of what was going to happen? Can you tell us what exactly happened that night?"

"The warning when it came was rather late. As you know, it began as I was leaving with the Pirates. My first concern was to make sure no one tried to be a hero and got themselves hurt, or that the gunmen shot anyone just to get to me, which was why I took the chance and rode straight through them." She cleared her throat, bracing herself for having to divulge that which she did not want to have to. "I have…an energy pulse built into my bike, wholly non-fatal, and it saved my life. It's my own design, and no doubt someone will ask for more details at some point, but the salient fact is it meant I could get clear of the line of gunmen and get away. I was low on fuel, with it being the end of the night, so after creating the crash I pulled in at a construction site." She paused, realising the memories were taking a grip more than she'd anticipated, and reigned back her control. "I then hid, waited for the chopper, and then hurtled up the bank and caught the rope." A shrug, as if it was simple. "Best catch of my life."

"This hit – so far the claims have been that it was taken out on you as a means to get to Mr Capello, and you are innocent of any wrongdoing. Is this true, or is there some other reason why someone would want to take revenge against you?"

"Despite being unconventional in many ways, I have never involved myself with mob business in such a way that would make me a target. Sadly, it is the danger that Mr Capello's business entails that casts a shadow over me by association, and that is the reason he decided it was no longer safe for there to be any contact between us." The words were forced past her lips, and Daryl could see she hated saying them.

"Does that mean you'll never see or speak to him again? That seems a bit harsh considering how close you were before?" The question surprised her, particularly as the reporter chose to imply support for her after perhaps hoping to find some wrongdoing in his first question.

"Yes, it is harsh. But a bullet in the back of my head would be even harsher. I won't pretend I like his decision, or that I agreed with it at the time, but I have to respect his choice, as much as I would wish it different. This is an imperfect world, and we all live with what that means."

"So does that mean you're single?"

She scowled for second, and then a patient smile curved her lips.

"Let me rephrase your question for you: Does that mean I'm looking for a new man? No, it doesn't. So sorry to disappoint, but I'm not looking for anything or anyone, and I'd appreciate it if all you press people would stop wasting ink making up stories, because you don't have anything to base them on."

"Then can you explain what happened at the Bowl a few weeks ago? There is footage of a very…exciting embrace on the tarmac."

"That was someone who needed a chance to finish something they thought they'd started. Nothing more. I doubt I'll see him again, and I think he knows there's nothing for him in LA, so he should stay in Washington."

Daryl was relieved to hear this.

"Is it connected that your manager Mr Blackmoor has been absent from LA since that night?"

One momentary pause, and then a look of slight irritation.

"Have you forgotten just who he is? I think he has more important things to do than worry about one of his contracted star's broken heart. He has a global empire to run, with more things to do than I even want to think about. He goes where he has to, to get the job done. I figure very small in that scenario."

Daryl refused to look round at Mac, who had glanced at him. *Oh,*

Mysty, if only you knew.

"Do you know when he'll be returning to LA?"

"No, I have no idea at all. When he wants to, I suppose. I am not his keeper or his secretary."

She chose another reporter with a nod in their direction.

"There is a story going around that you were involved in a bar fight and then a cage fight downtown a couple of weekends ago – is this true?"

"Do you know how many bar fights happen across America every night? A good number. If I was involved, it would have been with a good reason. The cage fight was for personal reasons. And exercise." A tiny smile of mischief.

"Exercise?"

"Sure, it really stretches the muscles out. Tests my reflexes."

She shrugged, and Mac snorted.

"Apparently it was you against seven huge muscled guys, all of whom came worse off for the experience."

"Yeah, well, speaking as a fairly small person who has had to fight to defend herself since she was much smaller, as I see it, muscle just gives me a bigger target to hit. If they can't reach you, size can't hurt you, and some of those guys are so bulky it impairs the way they move. Muscle isn't everything." She sighed. "And I'm not condoning fighting, either. The cage fight is in a controlled environment and consensual, it's voluntary, and the guys who go, go to fight. I don't see why it's okay for them but not for me. If anyone wants to have the sexism argument, please, I've got all night."

No one dared comment, though she gave them a chance by looking around, waiting for someone to try it.

She pointed to a new raised hand.

"You haven't gone to the Bowl in three weeks, though you've been in LA. Is this for any particular reason, or because of the scare the night of the hit?"

"No, no reason in particular. I've been very busy working on a few things, so I've stayed in. The trauma from the night of the hit did affect me in some ways, like not sleeping so well, so if I end up feeling tired and

I can sleep, I do, regardless of what night of the week it is – unless I have a show, of course. I will go again when time allows and the fancy takes me. I haven't stopped loving bikes or speed but…you can't ride the same road forever, things change."

Wow, wise and mature words. What had happened over the last three weeks?

Mysty pointed to a girl sitting on her father's shoulders.

"Is Lazarus okay?" she asked.

Instantly a smile blossomed on her face.

"Lazarus is fine. He's been brilliant, in fact. He's very good at knowing when I'm not happy and he's been fussing over me lots."

Another member of the public got the go-ahead for a question.

"Do you know what will be coming next, after your current shows?"

"No, not at the moment. I'm still concentrating on them, but no doubt I will be appraised of my next challenge at some point soon, and as soon as its finalised I'm sure there will be an announcement made, as well as a posting on my website."

She nodded at a young guy in the crowd, refusing any more press questions.

"What were you thinking, before you went to catch the rope from the helicopter?"

"Wow. Good question. It's funny, I remember exactly what I was thinking, aside from *I don't want to die*, which was about my shades. They're the ones I made for myself, and they're actually a lot more than just shades and…I've never shown anyone. I was thinking how maybe I never would."

Silence.

"And have you?"

The guy made the most of the silence to ask the obvious.

"Shown someone? No, not yet. But I'm sure I will."

Daryl wanted her to show him. For her to amaze him again, as she usually did.

She let the press get another word in.

"It was mentioned you were going to take a holiday, but so far you haven't, and you didn't take a break, even after the hit-attempt. Is this by choice, or are you under pressure to perform?"

"The holiday is being arranged, and I wouldn't tell you even if I had the dates, because I don't want to see a camera let alone a newspaper headline for the whole time I'm away, so no clues from me. But as for taking a break, it was my choice not to cancel Celeste. I've never missed a performance of any kind in my life, and I didn't want to start then. I felt miserable enough after everything that happened, and I didn't want the knowledge that I'd disappointed so many people who'd got tickets, or had to put up with the types of headlines I've no doubt would have made it into print. I do not feel under pressure, or that my feelings are being ignored in favour of any commercial endeavours."

"Do you know what happened to those who tried to kill you?"

"I know a good number ended up kissing the tarmac pretty hard, but not long after making it into the chopper I went into shock. Quite a bit after that is a little unclear. I have not been told what the eventual outcome was, except that the threat was dealt with. Beyond that…I doubt I'll ever know."

It was a clever, careful answer, but honest all the same. And Daryl knew she didn't know; he'd made sure of it.

One more nod to a reporter.

"You've made clear your feelings for Mr Capello, and I doubt you'll speak of how you feel about the loss now that contact has been cut off, but…I know from what you've said before, you find answers in music. Is there a song that encapsulates it for you? Would you sing it?"

Again, a moment of silence, and she looked at the speaker, who shrank a little under her gaze, not sure if she'd overstepped the invisible line.

"You know, I had a feeling someone was going to ask me that. I'll answer your question, but is it the last I will take." She walked around to the front of the podium. "You're right, I won't speak about that. I'm happy to share many things with you, as I've demonstrated, but aside from the fact I don't think I have the words for how I feel, it's my business, not anyone else's." She strolled along the top of the steps and then back.

"There are lots of songs that came to mind, some of them angry, some of them…utterly miserable; but now, admittedly four weeks' later, there is only one I have left. Some people will think it inappropriate, and some people will understand the true message of the song, because they know what it is to love someone more than life itself – and those people are the lucky ones. Those who can't, or don't, I hope one day you will, because it's a revelation; it's beautiful and sad in equal measure. Anyone who wants to join in, you are welcome. It's not a song for one person, but for everyone who has something to be thankful for."

The crowd stood silent and waiting, the atmosphere intense, intimate. How did she always find the words? How did she, a seventeen-year-old, have the courage to stand there in front of all those people and talk openly about her feelings without shame or fear. Daryl doubted few people would ever be able to speak like she did.

She closed her eyes and sang 'Amazing Grace', every note pure and long, strong and true, beautiful and sincere. The cameras stayed on her face, and it didn't surprise Daryl when two tears slid out from beneath the long lashes. What was even more special was that some of the audience joined in with her. There were no instruments, no backing vocals, just her flawless voice soaring, carrying them all a little closer to God. When she sang the final note, there was silence. This wasn't a moment to clap and cheer; this was a prayer to be respected and honoured.

"Donatello Raphael Capello," she whispered. "I know you're watching. And you always will be."

She raised the necklace to her lips and kissed it, then left, O'Grady at her back.

Only then did the cheering start, the only way the crowd could show its approval and its support, thousands of voices who wanted her to know they were there.

Daryl didn't move for a second. It was the best tribute she could have given Donny. He felt a strange pressure in his chest, and he looked round at Mac, who was similarly affected. That hadn't just been a press conference.

God help Donny. Daryl couldn't imagine how he was feeling.

PAULO LOOKED OVER at his boss, who was standing pensively in the middle of the room, too tense to sit, too emotionally knotted up to be comfortable in his own skin. From the moment she'd appeared in front of the cameras, neither of them had moved. It was just the two of them. Paulo hadn't wanted Donny to be alone, but it wasn't a moment for all the boys to crowd in, either, although he knew they'd be watching downstairs.

The notes had rung out clear and true, all the beauty of her voice made heavenly with the sentiment of a song chosen to represent her love for him. Paulo could see how intensely Donny had been staring at the screen, like he would never look away, and couldn't look away despite how hard it must be for him to see her.

"Leave me, Paulo."

Such a calm voice hiding a wealth of pain.

Paulo knew it was useless arguing, and he didn't want to add to the grief as much as he didn't want to leave him. God knew the Lord of Vegas had been drowning for weeks, restless, angry and depressed. Would this give him the chance to find some peace, now he'd seen her acceptance of their split? her unashamed declaration?

Donny heard the door shut, glad to be alone. But he wasn't alone. On the sofa was the young girl who'd taught him tenderness, compassion, and how to be touched by another person. At the table behind him was the girl who'd made him laugh, surprised him and cooked him dinner. In the other room was the girl who had made nights and afternoons unforgettable with freely given love and comfort. Next to him was the girl who'd never let him down, who'd saved his life. That was how it felt. Like she was there, so potent in his mind. Oh God, it had to get better, didn't it? He couldn't spend his whole life feeling like this. Like he was torn apart in every direction for the single need of wanting to have her back.

He went into the other room and opened the drawer in his desk that held the gift she'd sent him a few days ago – the gift that had come with a ring that told him so much, and prepared him for what he'd just seen.

Part of him had wanted her to rebel, to have her turn up on his doorstep and demand to see him, storm in and kiss him like she had before. Part of him had been afraid if she had, he would have given in, and refused then to let her go. Ever. Come what may. Part of him was glad she hadn't, because she was safe now.

The rest of him mourned.

He went to the sofa upon which they had spent so many hours of joyful togetherness. He put the glass paperweight down on the coffee table and sat down. Inside were two figures – the two of them skating, just as they had that first time, her hands holding his on her hips, head leaning back against him, safe in his arms, and so wonderfully close. He pressed the button on the base that had the inscription, '*The only man I ever wanted by my side. I love you and I always will*', wanting to hear the music that would be forever theirs; the music she had played in the car before going to LA, that he had listened to so many times. He looked down at the ring on his finger, the gold band with the alternating black and white diamonds, to match her necklace. He didn't need to take it off to know the words that were written on the inside: '*No one can touch what we have*'.

He kissed it, and it felt so bittersweet. He then lowered his head into his hands and finally, finally, gave in and wept, the music drowning out the misery that consumed his every waking moment.

How could he never see her? He loved her. How would he live the long empty years without her?

He knew in that moment it didn't always take a bullet to send a man to hell.

He would never be happy again.

O'GRADY STEPPED INTO the lift.

"O'Grady."

"Sir?"

"How is she doing?"

"Not so good. For two hours she's been moping around. One hour was spent sat on the floor leaning on one of her bikes trying quite hard to get drunk. I'm just on my way down to try and get her to come back upstairs."

"I see. Has she said anything?"

"Not much. I tried to give her a hug when she looked like she was going to cry, but she refused. She said Donny wouldn't have anyone to hold him now, so neither should she."

Typically selfless and compassionate. She knew Donny enough to know he would be hurting, badly.

Daryl pulled up the camera and watched as he walked through to her lock-up. She was, as O'Grady said, sitting on the floor leaning on one of the bikes with a six-pack of beer bottles for company.

"Do what you can. Everything considered, this is fairly…tame."

"I know. I think this is the last of the storms, and it'll blow itself out. Today was quite hard. Poor kid can't take any more."

"Good luck. Try and get her to talk about it."

"Will do, sir."

Disconnect.

"O'Grady! My most favourite bodyguard in the world! What a surprise to see you. You want to get drunk with me?"

Daryl had to smile. She looked tiddly, and actually quite adorable. Though he didn't like the wetness on her cheeks, and the red eyes.

"Hell, why not? Long time since I've wallowed. Did plenty of it when I got divorced." O'Grady sat down on the floor and leaned back against the door, accepting the bottle of beer from her with companionable ease – as if he'd gone to a friend's house for a ball game.

"Why did you get divorced?"

"She decided, after fifteen years, that my career was the wrong one and she'd had enough, despite enjoying the pay it brought home and the lifestyle she led. She'd married me when I was a soldier, but…I guess she got sick of the hours I work. She started getting nastier and bitter. Used the kids to vent her frustrations. I took a step back because I couldn't ever win her over, no matter what I did. She decided to chuck my bags in the street one day – out of my house, that I'd paid for by working my backside off at not a little risk of life and limb. Anyway, I got drunk, ended up sleeping with someone I'd never met before, and woke up realising that, actually, I didn't have to put up with her crap and there wasn't anything worth saving if I didn't even feel guilty. I arrived at the meeting with the divorce lawyers first." He sighed and took a swig. "And that is the sad story of my marriage. I don't recommend you follow my example."

"I think I'd make an awful husband." Her attempt at levity was noble; but her face betrayed her sadness at O'Grady's story.

"Yeah, I think you would too."

"I don't think I'll ever marry."

"Oh come on, you can't hold a torch for one man forever."

"No? Well, I never really wanted to get married anyway, even to Donny. It's…I guess because I know what it did to my mother, so I don't want to be tied to man. Donny was the only man I trusted enough to marry, but no…not even him."

"Not every man beats his wife, sweetheart. Even men with a temper would never turn a hand against a woman. My wife drove me insane. We had arguments I'm sure everyone in the next zip code heard, but I never touched her."

Well said, O'Grady, Daryl thought, wondering how on earth he was going to change her mind on the subject of marriage.

"Lots do. Knowing my luck I'd end up with the one that did." She smiled sadly and stared at the bottle in her hand. "The saddest thing about it all, is I think she still loved him. Despite everything he did to her, it wasn't just the fear that kept her quiet, or the inability to get out of the situation because there was no place where he wouldn't find us, despite all that…I think she still hoped he'd change, that he'd go back to being the man she'd fallen in love with. Crazy. Why did God invent love? It just… screws everything up."

"It makes good books. And films and music."

"You telling me God is a DJ, a writer, or secretly owns every movie company!" O'Grady chuckled. "Why does God do it, though? Wasn't losing my family enough? Why let me find Donny and then take him away?"

It was the most natural question in the world.

"Maybe Donny was the best person to look after you during those years. He was who you needed just then. What you had was very special.

Some people go a lifetime and don't feel what you do." *Exactly*, Daryl thought, hoping the crease of pain on her brow would clear. "What's this I hear about you saving Donny's life, how many times? Three? What happened? As saving people is my profession, I admit I'm curious."

"The first time was the first time I ever saw Donny. I was standing on the opposite side of the road. He was angry, and had four of his boys trailing behind him. He didn't look, just headed across the road. A bike, a car and a truck all got tangled up, one trying to overtake, and didn't make it. It was only a narrow street. I could see the truck was going to hit him, and I just ran. It's a miracle I managed to push him out of the way, I was such a twig, and I ended up getting more hurt than he did.

"The second time was outside his club. I was so tired. He made a joke as we went out to the car, and I looked round at him – and saw something on the roof. I pulled him out of the way and the bullet smacked into the pavement. All hell broke loose. Paulo bundled Donny into the car, the boys all pulled out their guns, and I was so pissed off that someone had tried to kill him – so cowardly, you know, trying to kill someone from a distance like that – that I took Paulo's gun from his back holster and ran to the building, jumped up to the balcony and climbed up to the roof. The fucker got away over the rooftops."

"And the third?"

"The third is the most dramatic, and horrible. It also prompted my exile to LA. It was Friday night, and it was going to be a beer, pasta and movie night, and I was going through the tunnels the back way into the house when I found Pepe…his hands cut off and an eyeball gone. I thought I was going to be sick. I can't take blood, and that was… Anyway, I added the pieces up, and instinctively knew what was happening. But I wasn't just going to leave, was I?"

She looked at OG, asking him to understand. He nodded.

"So I went through the door, which was stupid, because I had no weapon and I didn't know who was behind the door. Five seconds later, a guy showed up, on the phone to whoever, so I got a good idea of the SOP. He saw me. For once in my life, I was glad to look like I do, as the bastard let me get so close he didn't even see my motorcycle helmet coming, the first or second time. I also dealt with the second guy, and took his earpiece. I then found Fabio and half a dozen others locked in a room, and Giovanni bleeding out across the floor – it's horrible how blood pools when…when there's so much of it. God, I hate red.

"Donny was in his usual room at the back of the house, with someone in with him. I figured there wasn't much time before this guy would shoot, so I ran back downstairs and grabbed some explosives and an assault rifle. I climbed up the roof, shot at Paulo to stop him going in the front door, went over the roof and down the side of the house. Then it was just make the window explode in Donny's room, and jump through.

"The guy had a gun right on Donny's forehead, so I aimed at him. Luckily I had leathers and my helmet or most of me would have been toasted in the explosion. Donny couldn't believe what he was seeing, and looked horrified. I didn't kill them, any of them. I hate guns. I wish they'd never been invented."

"What happened then?"

"I went into shock and…Donny took over. I just remember him making me wait behind the sofa in the smoke-filled room, with plaster and glass everywhere, while he removed everyone from the room and went to make us safe. That is one night I won't forget."

"No. Sounds like I should hire you for my team: I have this girl, she's only young, but amazingly talented. She can be quite funny, works a bit too hard, can be a bit of a pain in the ass, but generally has a heart of gold… You want in? I could do with you helping me keep her safe."

"Very funny."

"You and Donny go way back, don't you?"

"Yes…"

"It's an incredible bond you share. Especially you being such different ages and him being…a mob boss."

"He's not a mob boss to me. Trust me, if that was all he was, things would have turned out very differently. I still remember the first time he sat me on his sofa, after sending all the boys in to catch me at the hotel. They bundled me into a limo and I got taken to his house, which I thought was the most amazing place I'd ever seen – and this was not what

I was expecting at all, as I thought they were going to hold me prisoner in a cellar, or something. I got taken to his rooms, by Paulo, and he was standing there, leaning on his desk. I really was the mutinous prisoner, and we just looked at each other for few seconds. He said something about me finally 'agreeing' to come and see him. I told him I didn't remember being asked. He then asked me if I wanted to sit on the sofa, and I told him I wasn't planning on being there that long." She laughed, and so did OG. "Man, I had an attitude back then! God knows how or why he put up with me."

"*Had* an attitude," Daryl mused.

"I don't think it's rocket science to work out why," O'Grady said slowly, feeling like she had unwound some to be able to talk about this. For her, that was a lot of talking. "How about we go upstairs and finish these beers sitting on something other than concrete?" he then asked. "I know you're a superstar and everything, and being a little eccentric is par for the course, but my ass is going numb."

"Sure. I know you're getting a bit old and all," she laughed, and got to her feet and offered him a hand.

"Right, that's it! Tomorrow, we're getting a hoop! I'll show you who's old. You can get your ass handed to you by a basketball pro!"

"Bring it on! I can fly, remember, so make sure the hoop is pretty high."

OG smiled and pushed her towards the door, letting her lock up, watching the blue lights and automated security bolt into place. He wished he knew how she did that.

"I do have some good news," he said.

"Really?"

"I brought pizza."

"No!"

"Oh yes."

"Did I mention you are my favourite bodyguard ever?"

"I think so, but I don't mind you repeating yourself. By the way, you going to need spirits not beer if you want to get drunk, you know. Your metabolism is too fast, and beer will just give you gas!"

"I know. But I can't stand spirits. I hate the smell. It makes me think of my father. I'll stick to beer."

"Ladies don't drink beer."

"And you think I'm a lady?"

"One day I'll remind you that you said that, and you're going to blush. Actually, I think I'll do it on your…wedding day." He gave her a friendly shove as they headed along the corridor, two grey suits giving OG a nod and a smile for her.

"I just told you, I'm not getting married."

"Yeah, well. Life is full of surprises!"

"Please can they be good ones? I've had enough crap lately."

"Oh, I think your luck is definitely due for an upward turn."

"Thank goodness! Lazarus, sweetheart, will you marry me?" Paws danced and a tail wrapped around her thigh. "I'm taking that as a yes. Super. All sorted. OG, you can be best man. Now where's the pizza?"

Daryl turned the screen off, and went back to his emails, the knot of jealousy an ache in the pit of his stomach.

HOW STRANGE IT felt having not seen or spoken to him for so long. *Please let him have forgotten that night, and that kiss,* she thought. She leaned back in her chair, determined to stay composed. If only she could understand him, be sure of him in any way but…things were always so volatile between them, and it was so hard to put any faith in what he said when he was so distant and guarded – and the rest.

His image came up on the screen. He was at his desk, in New York, as she'd seen him so many times before.

"Mysty."

"Daryl."

Warm green eyes looked at her, and she felt a quiver, not sure if she was glad he was pleased to see her or not.

"How are you doing?"

"Fine. How are you?"

"Tired. And yes, I have been working too hard," he admitted.

She paused for a second, not expecting the admission, not sure how to respond.

"When's our holiday?"

"Four weeks. We'll have seven to ten days, depending on the weather and how long our location remains a mystery to the press. It really ruins things to have cameras poking out of coconut trees."

"I can imagine. I'd be more amused if they tried to dress up as the coconut tree."

The twinkle was back in her eyes and he relaxed, realising her reticence was more to do with her own nervousness at talking to him than his having done something wrong. Or, rather, something else wrong.

"Actually, I think you have a point. Finding myself being stalked by a suspiciously short odd-shaped coconut tree would definitely be a story for my grandchildren."

She smiled. The ice was broken. "Goodness, do we need to get the auditions for the new Mrs Blackmoor started?"

"I'm not quite ready for that yet."

"By the time you are, and you find someone to fulfil your undoubtedly lofty standards, we could be nearing the next century."

"How about I waive the lofty standards and you marry me, then I won't have to waste time finding someone new. You're already very good at telling me off about how hard I work, so I think you'd be great." He felt the tingle of nervousness just saying the words in jest he meant far more seriously.

"Aside from the million things about me that drive you nuts, and the fact that you regularly want to strangle me."

"I'm used to big numbers. Millions don't bother me at all."

"How gallant. Can you remember how to be gallant when you come back to LA, whenever that is? I'd like to see it with my own eyes."

"Just for you, maybe."

During the slight pause, a flicker of a smile passed across Mysty's lips, and he dared to smile back.

"Anyway, the reason I called," she began in earnest, the moment passing. "I…I've drawn up a proposal for a charity. I've already scouted for various locations, and looked at what we need in terms of recruitment, costing, legalities…everything I could think of. It's for a woman's refuge, as you might have guessed, but it will be a little more than that, because as well as women having somewhere they and their children can go and live safely, they will be able to get help with prosecuting abusive spouses, and improve their lives in a much wider sense. I've sent everything over to you, for you to look through, of course. I'd like to make it happen, but I know you have to say yes as well."

Daryl noted the acknowledgment of his authority over her funds, acceptance even.

"I will look at it tonight and call you tomorrow. I'm sure it'll be very well done if you drew it up. And Mysty…" She looked at him, waiting. "We'll get it started as soon as we can."

Her face broke into a huge smile. "Thank you."

"Do you have a name for it?"

"The Butterfly Foundation. It seemed appropriate, but not because of Celeste. It's just…all the women and children the charity will help will all be butterflies. People are fragile things. They'll need to learn how to spread their wings, and this project should help them feel safe enough to be able to do that." She held his gaze.

"I should have known you'd think of something so apt."

"Sadly this is a topic I don't find it hard to be inspired by."

"I realise." So much more than you think. "I will be back in LA soon. There are things to discuss as regards the future."

"I realise."

He smiled. They were so similar sometimes. "How is everything?"

"I'm experimenting."

"With what?"

"My voice. Celeste. Physics. It's all very exciting."

"I look forward to being amazed." He leant back in a gesture of easy confidence, making her lean in.

"How many times have I amazed you?" she asked.

"Countless."

"Wow. You owe me big time, then. You've not amazed me that much."

He smiled. He hadn't anticipated that coming. "No? Oh well, at the risk of getting glared at, you know where I live."

She just laughed. What did he have to do to get her to take him seriously?

"I'd better go. I'm sure you're busy."

No I'm not. Stay, talk to me! "Don't forget I want to be *very* amazed when I see you next."

"I'm sure I can rustle something up. How was your milkshake?"

"Fantastic. Sinfully so. I did forty-five extra minutes in the pool, just to be sure I'd burned the calories off! I'm going for the ten-year record."

She smiled widely, pleased he had read her note. "I'm sure you can think of other ways to work them off that would seem less burdensome. How are the firewalls?"

"Superb. I should tell you, I transferred $100m over to your accounts. Those system upgrades are invaluable; the firewalls unbreakable. I tried to get in, just for curiosity's sake, and I only got so far. I can probably get you a government contract to work on national security."

The quiet admiration in his tone didn't seem to register, and instead a ferocious frown creased her forehead.

"Why did you do that? I didn't want paying for it! It was a *gift* – don't you understand?"

He was completely taken aback. Why was she so angry?

"It's ground-breaking, what you did – and for twelve huge databases that I would usually have whole teams of people working on. I only paid you what was fair."

"I didn't *want* any *money* for it!" she raged at him. "Why do you always have to throw money at things? I did it because I wanted to…to try and make things just a little easier for you, and I didn't want anything back! Why is it so hard for you to accept something that doesn't have a price tag? Or are you still trying to buy me? Even now?"

He was too surprised by the heat of her rebuke to reply quickly enough.

Disconnect.

Damn! He shouldn't have told her. It was a fair price, but he should have thought about how she'd see it. He was a businessman. She was a young girl with more morals than most, and with a nature more giving than most as well. And she was a girl who had every reason to be suspicious of his intentions involving money. He'd upset her again, goddammit. Why hadn't he just accepted she'd meant it as a gift? And those sweet words telling him she'd just wanted to 'try and make things just a little easier' for him. When had anyone ever done that? Only she seemed perceptive enough to understand the pressures he was under. Others saw them as part of his life, his remit, and assumed he was just fine dealing with everything. She, of all people, had the least reason to care. So why did she? Was she transferring the care she had for Donny? Or was he reading too much into it?

A week, and then he would be back in LA. He couldn't wait.

He opened the attachment she'd sent him and found a thorough, well-researched and realistic business proposal, complete with logo, mission statement and funding requirements. She'd even included proposed buildings for purchase and renovation in two locations, suggestions for workshops to teach skills women could take to the workplace so they would be able to support themselves, and activities for the children to help build confidence. There was a security programme designed to protect the women, and access to legal advice. Everything.

He had no problem approving this and releasing the funds to make it happen, and he was proud of her for wanting to do this.

He sighed. When would she realise he was on her side?

"BOSS."

"Yes, Toby?" Saturday afternoons were the best. Celeste was over with – and after last night's debut of three new pieces the media was hailing her performance as one of the best ever – and now she had time to kick back and relax.

"You've just had an email. You might want to look at it."

She had been heading for the music room, but then turned and went to the computer room instead. Five minutes and a phone call later, she grabbed her jacket and patched through to OG as she called Lazarus and headed for the door.

"OG, I need the jet. We're going for a quick trip. I'm on my way down now. Any reason why we can't leave immediately?"

"No. Can I ask why, though?"

"I'm getting a baby."

"You're what?"

The horror in his voice made her smile.

"A baby leopard. I'll explain on the way. Please can you get the car and organise the plane."

Disconnect.

Three hours later they were in a car borrowed from one of Mr Blackmoor's San Francisco offices, which swung through wide gates into the private grounds of a large white-painted house with paradise-like gardens. It reminded her of Franny's house and she instantly liked it.

OG held out a hand to still her, insisting on getting out first, and she huffed quietly but stayed still. There, waiting at the top of the steps, was a woman in her fifties in the arms of her husband, who was probably around sixty, both smiling, never imagining they would ever get to meet the amazing girl they'd only ever seen on their television screen. But there was a sadness, too, and Mysty took a breath and looked down at Lazarus, who looked back, trusting her as ever. She was familiar with the heartbreak they had endured, and climbed the steps.

"Mysty." The woman held out her hand and grasped the one offered to her, taking it as if it were more of a lifeline than just a greeting. The husband offered his too. "I'm so glad you got our message. I'm Anna, and this is Jon."

"Hello, it's so lovely to see you. This is Lazarus. I couldn't not bring him. I hope you don't mind?"

Lazarus sat, and looked up at the new people before him, and offered a paw that Anna took, delighted but bordering on tears.

"No, it's lovely to see you together, for real. Seeing you on TV is so lovely, but this is so special. Do come in."

The foursome went into the house, Anna chatting to fill the quiet and try and make her superstar guest feel at home. She soon realised she didn't have to. With a drink in everyone's hand, sitting in the conservatory that looked out over the garden and the swimming pool. Lazarus nosed about and then settled between Mysty's legs and rested his chin on her knee, making the couple smile.

Anna leant closer to Jon, needing the comfort of his presence. "So, Mysty, I still can't believe you're here," she said.

"I can't believe I got your email. I'd almost given up hope. I am sorry, though, for the circumstances that have brought me here. I…know what it is to have violence in one's home and to be attacked. I was horrified to hear what happened. It must have been awful. I don't know what I'd do if anything happened to Lazarus."

Hearing his name, the big cat looked up, always alert.

"Seeing you together brings back lots of memories. Penny was… well, she was our baby from day one. We had accepted the fact we couldn't have children, and she was our girl. We loved her so much. We decided it was unfair to not let her have any children, though, and gave her the chance to breed. There are a few people in the US with leopards now, which is a good thing if you ask me, as they are so endangered. We were so thrilled when she became pregnant. We had everything planned. We were so excited…" Anna gave up as the tears welled, and Jon covered her hand with his own and accepted her unspoken request that he finish the story.

"She was almost full term," he said, "and nothing was amiss. There were four healthy cubs, as far as the ultrasound made out, and she was so happy, so contented. It was like she knew what was coming. Then that night… that changed everything. I can't help thinking if I hadn't gone and disturbed them they'd have managed to take her without hurting her and she'd still be alive."

Anna shook her head and added her other hand to the contact between them.

"They abandoned her, but the damage was done. Combined with the trauma of the attack, and the drugs they used to sedate her, she haemorrhaged and lost all of them except one. She's beautiful, and perfectly healthy – somehow. We haven't named her yet, and as much as we thank God she's alive, we…we can't keep her. It brings back too many memories of Penny. She's still very young, obviously, only two weeks old, but already very used to us. I remembered your interview months ago and what you'd said. I thought I would contact you first. It seemed the perfect solution."

"I'm so glad you did. She is very precious for having survived so much. I can assure you I would care for her and love her. I would never let anything happen to her."

"We believe you. Lazarus is proof of that." Jon reached out a hand and offered it for sniffing. Lazarus reached forward with his nose and enjoyed the interesting smell. "So, why don't you come and meet her? She's probably wondering where we are."

Anna led the way through the house. OG waited by the front door. When she stopped outside a door at the end of a long hallway, Mysty asked Lazarus to stay outside. He obediently sat, and they entered the room. The tiny occupant looked up from the fluffy towel in the cushioned bed she was lying on – in a pose Mysty knew well from Lazarus, body on her side, legs splayed out. Her big eyes were instantly watchful and alert, curious and just a tad fearful. The fear of the lost and the lonely. How Mysty knew that feeling.

The little leopard was the loveliest little thing she had seen for so long.

"Why don't you say hello?" Anna invited, seeing the way Mysty's eyes settled on the leopard, and vice versa.

With slow, unthreatening movements, Mysty walked forward and crouched down. Familiar with how curious leopards were, she knew it wouldn't take long before she was investigated – also prompted, no doubt, by the smell of Lazarus. The small creature sat up and regarded her calmly. Mysty offered her hand, waiting for the cub to decide whether to approach. The deep, dark blue eyes looked from the hand to those of the new two-legged person with lots of hair and eyes as brilliant as her own.

Mysty held her breath, willing her to make the journey, wanting to hold the little animal and let it feel the safety of an embrace she would never know from her natural mother.

Sniffing, she inched forward, and examined the outstretched hand. She gave it a small lick. Mysty slowly lay back, and the cub moved closer, looking, testing, and then put two small paws on her chest. And then she climbed up and stood looking into calm indigo eyes, curious and searching. Mysty spoke quietly, and the eye contact was held, and then the cub flopped down and closed her eyes. Anna and Jon could scarcely believe it, and Anna reached for Jon's hand again. Mysty laid her hand on the cub's back, softly, feeling the heat of her little body, and gently stroked.

"I think she likes you," came a voice from behind her, and Mysty almost jumped. She'd been so absorbed in the cub she'd forgotten they were there.

"I think I like her too."

The cub peeked at her, and Mysty smiled. She wasn't stupid; she knew when she was being talked about.

"Please, we would love you to have her. It's so obvious she'll be going to a good home," Anna whispered, her voice breaking a little.

She cradled the cub as she sat up, keeping her firm and safe against her chest, remembering how Lazarus had liked to be held. "You must let me pay you for her."

"No, why would we want any money? It is enough to know she'll be happy. Just some pictures would be nice, as she gets older. And, if she ever has any cubs, please let us know," Anna replied quietly, a little embarrassed at the emotion that had brought tears to her eyes. It was going to be hard to see the surviving baby leopard go.

"I promise you I'll send regular photos and, fingers crossed, if the two of them have a family of their own, I'll let you know so you can come and visit. You'll always be welcome. And I'll make sure you have my personal email, not just the fan-mail one. In the meantime, if you're ever in LA, just let me know."

"You're not quite what I…we expected," Anna said slowly, surprised and pleased by the offer.

"I never am, usually. I'm more a person than the performer you see on TV." She looked round at them. "Do you mind if Lazarus comes in? To introduce them?"

The door was opened and his name spoken. He trotted in and came up short, faced with his mistress's eyes, and the blue eyes of the cub. The moment was magical. He approached slowly, his eyes intense, checking with her, then darting back to the cub. Their noses touched, sniffing. Mysty put the cub down and let them interact, knowing Lazarus wouldn't hurt her. The cub raised a paw and Lazarus lay down, so she could explore him. There was a little more staring and sniffing, and then the cub clambered onto his leg, and then his shoulder, and tried to chew one of his ears, before dropping down to lie close to his chest.

Laughing, Mysty picked her up. It might just work having Lazarus on baby-sitting duty, but it would have to be a carefully managed process. He then stood and moved to her side to be hugged, sniffing the new face that was held tightly as well. Like a child with a new baby brother or sister, sharing her love might be a tough concept for him to accept at first, and she wanted to reassure him.

"Well, I think we're going to be just fine," she announced, looking up with a smile, and finding both adults watching her with teary smiles. She also saw OG standing in the doorway with two suits. They had obviously been too curious to wait any longer!

"What do you think you'll call her?" Jon asked.

Mysty paused and looked down, the cub looking up at her instantly, excited by the attention and the company.

"Lula."

"Oh, that suits her so well," Anna said, and Jon nodded. "I'll get her things, and her papers, too. She's had the first lots of vaccinations. All of the details are in her records. It'll be strange for her to be somewhere different tonight…"

Anna disappeared, and Mysty looked over at O'Grady. He had to smile. Her face was so happy. And, in that moment, he was so glad he'd accepted the job of caring for this wonderful, kind girl.

"SIR?"

"O'Grady."

Daryl stepped out of the New York offices and nodded at Mac, who was keeping the press back so he had a clear run to the Bentley. He ducked as he stepped into the car, glad to be going. He would soon be on a plane back to LA, the place that had been calling him for so long.

"I just thought I should let you know that we will shortly have a new addition to the family."

Daryl froze and his stomach turned over. When had this happened? How could O'Grady have let her? And why hadn't Baden told him?

"*How the hell did that happen*?"

Mac was taken aback by the sudden anger in his boss's voice, and glanced at him.

"Pardon, sir?" O'Grady sounded alarmed and confused.

"How the hell did she end up pregnant?"

"She's not pregnant."

Daryl breathed out, his shoulders slumping, halting the storm of emotion that had exploded, hot and fast.

"I'm talking about Lula. Our new baby leopard."

"A new baby leopard?" Daryl repeated the words, mostly for his own benefit, his pulse climbing back down as the relief flooded in.

"Yes. We're just flying back from San Francisco. Her mother miscarried and died after thieves tried to steal her, and she lost all of her cubs, except this one. She's an orphan, which couldn't be more appropriate considering the girl who she's currently asleep on."

Daryl leaned over to the computer console and pulled up the image from inside the plane. Sure enough, there on a sofa was Mysty, Lazarus under one arm, and a cub sprawled on her chest, all with their eyes shut. Amazing, and utterly adorable.

"They're all getting on like a house on fire. Well, they were before they fell asleep. Just thought you should know."

"Thank you, O'Grady. Just tell me things like that straight off next time. I'm trying to avoid high blood pressure."

"Yes, sir, sorry about that. Are you still planning to arrive tomorrow?"

"We're on the way the airport now. How is she? Not too tired after the last performance?" It had been another night of sheer glorious skill and creativity in Celeste, that had held the world spellbound. He watched as one of the cub's ears flickered and her tail twitched, and a sleepy hand rose to stroke her back, providing instinctive comfort.

"She's a little tired, but she's had a good day, including a run, a skate, four hours working on various things…and then we were off to San Francisco. If I hadn't got the plane ready quickly enough, I think she'd have probably tried to fly it herself, such was the authority of the instructions!" O'Grady didn't sound upset, just amused.

Daryl smiled. That was his girl alright. "I'll see you soon."

"Yes, sir. Shall I tell her you'll be in LA soon?"

"No. Just let her enjoy her new baby." Daryl couldn't wait to get some pictures of them together. What a perfect idea as a present for her – that didn't have a price tag.

"Will do, safe journey."

Disconnect.

"A baby?" Mac repeated, looking curious, but instantly realising the reason for Daryl's outrage at the beginning of the conversation.

"Lula, our new baby leopard." Daryl turned the screen towards Mac so he could see.

"*Our* new baby leopard?" Mac repeated.

"Yes. Be careful, or you'll get demoted to leopard-sitting duty," Daryl replied tartly, not liking the fact he had given something away in his phrasing.

"I don't know, sounds like fun, and I bet Mysty would get me milkshakes."

"If you'd like to tender your resignation and apply for the position, don't hesitate."

But Mac wasn't intimidated by the acerbic tone. "Like I could trust you to look after yourself," he snorted, and looked out the window.

"She really has rubbed off on you, hasn't she?"

Mac only smiled, and looked round at his boss, who had lost some of the ferocious scowl. He was glad to be heading back to LA, not least because he hoped that seeing Mysty might mean his boss would relax and lose some of the tension he'd still been carrying around with him. "Oh shit, you mean to say I've morphed into a seventeen-year-old beauty-queen lookalike? Damn. That could ruin my reputation."

"If I didn't know better, I'd say you were looking forward to going to LA," Daryl commented lightly, but scrutinising his bodyguard, who looked far too cheerful – and certainly not the silent and unapproachable man he had once been.

"I think that would make two of us."

It was Daryl's turn to snort and look away, and he refused to confirm Mac's supposition, or its implications.

The downside to a highly intelligent bodyguard, who went with him everywhere, was it was hard to keep secrets. At least he had the consolation that Mac wouldn't tell the girl in question and even if he did suspect anything. She'd probably fall off her chair laughing, anyway.

"TOBY?"

"Yes?"

"How does that feel?"

Daryl was alerted to her presence by her voice and the sound of the door shutting, then various computer-tinkering noises.

"It feels fine. All working one hundred percent. Multi-task capacity now at one hundred and twenty percent from what it was."

"Good, just don't tell Joey 'cos he'll want his upgrade doing and I've not finished it yet."

Then there were sounds of footsteps in the hall, and he turned the volume to mute on the TV. He'd been watching the Yankees match while he waited for her to appear, sitting casually on her couch. It had seemed a non-threatening way to start, but suddenly he felt very conscious of being uninvited, and that it would appear arrogant to make himself at home. He'd just been so keen to see her he'd chosen to arrive unannounced rather than wait.

"Erm, boss, there's just one thing you might want to know."

Toby's voice told Daryl the shit was about the hit the fan.

"Oh, don't tell me Lula's chewed up my drumsticks again."

"No, that's not it."

She rounded the corner – and came up short she saw the figure standing behind sofa, the TV on mute, and pause, his eyes intense.

Her heart thudded in her chest. What was he doing there? She didn't even know he was back in LA, and he was in her apartment! Uninvited? Since when did he treat her home like an extension of his own? Because he owned it? Just like he thought he owned her?

The look on her face made him feel distinctly unwelcome. This clearly wasn't how to bridge the divide between them after her being upset about the money for the upgrade.

Long seconds and no one spoke; then she turned and headed for the door again.

"Wait." She stopped, her back to him. "I didn't come here to drive you out of your own home. I just came to see how you are. I'll go. Don't walk out."

She turned, watching him, defensive.

"Just so you know, there's a pizza in the oven for you. It should almost be done – not that I'm the expert on them."

He just wanted to leave now, self-recrimination already loud in his head that he should have done it differently. He started walking towards the front door.

She said, "Wait," just as he had. He paused, not really wanting to hang around to witness her anger. "If you leave I'm going to feel like a right bitch. And I can't eat pizza on my own. Come back in and we'll try again."

He didn't move. Did she mean it? Or was she playing with him?

"Well, come on, then. It's been five weeks since I've seen you. I've practically forgotten what you look like." He looked back at her properly, still disbelieving. "Choose a peg," she said, and pointed at the row of hooks for jackets and coats by the door. "You can be in charge of the pizza; I'll get the drinks organised."

She disappeared into the kitchen, leaving him to follow. Just like that.

He removed his jacket, and hung it up. He frowned. Were they really going to have pizza and beer together?

She had a bag of ice in her hand, which she plonked down on the counter, and then rummaged in the back of a cupboard and pulled out a champagne bucket. God, the backside on her…but he wasn't going to jeopardise the evening by saying so.

"Are you going to amaze me and tell me you made the pizza?" she asked slowly, pulling out a wooden chopping board and opening a drawer to get out a pizza slice.

"No, I wish I had. It is fresh, though. I managed to get Raffi to make you one to heat up at home."

He dared walk forward a little way, not sure what would be deemed too close, where the boundaries were. She didn't seem to mind, even when he was within a metre of her. No fear clouded her face.

"Wow. He doesn't do takeaways usually." She held out the oven gloves. "Come on, let's get her out."

He took the gloves, removed the pizza and slid it onto the wooden board, desperately hoping he wouldn't drop it.

"I know. That would be why I had to pay so much. Plus the fact he thinks I'm a jackass."

She put the tray in the dishwasher and handed him the pizza slice as calmly as if they did this every day, then went back to her bucket and ice.

"Oh no. How much did he sting you for?"

"Enough."

"Come on, tell me! I'll make sure he doesn't do it again."

"$500." He grimaced, and waited for the ridicule.

"*For one pizza*? Good God, you crazy man! I'll have words with him!" He managed to slice across the pizza; but his second cut went skewed when he looked around and admired her backside again as she put the rest of ice back in the freezer. "Why on earth did you agree to that? It's exorbitant!"

It was true, but it wasn't as though he couldn't afford it. Besides, anything for her. He turned the board to slice the pizza the other way whilst she loaded beers into the bucket. And then, with two plates under her arm, she transferred it to the table in front of the TV, along with a tea towel for the drips.

Pizza, beer and a ball game, *with her*? His dream evening had arrived all in one.

"When one requires an olive branch, it doesn't matter how much it costs as long as it's the right one," he answered carefully, following her with the pizza, hoping she'd heard him. He put it down on the table, and she observed it.

"Could you tell me how you, of all people, managed to slice a pizza into an odd number of pieces?" she asked, looking at it, and then him with much amusement.

He looked from her laughing eyes to the pizza and studied it for a moment. It was true! He had! Moderately embarrassed and irritated at himself, he wasn't sure how to react, but she did, and burst out laughing.

"You've never cut a pizza before, have you?"

He watched her laughing. It was a most beautiful sight.

"No, I admit I haven't."

Her eyes held him captive. He didn't have any defence against the power of them.

"Wow. A virgin pizza slicer. Don't worry, I won't tell anyone you fluffed your first try." She winked and picked up a plate, and he followed suit. Despite the outrageous tease, this was a side of her he liked very much. All the fear he'd had about being here evaporated in that moment. Just for a moment.

She plonked herself down on the sofa, and by the time he'd deliberated over where best to sit, and how close, she was reaching for a beer and pulling the cap off. She handed it to him, and un-paused the unmuted the game.

"5-4," he said.

"Close. Should be good." She took a swig of her beer, her eyes on the screen.

Daryl made himself concentrate on the game, wondering why he even found the way she drank beer from the bottle sexy. So uninhibited.

She put pizza slices – very odd-sized ones! – on to their plates. When had he last eaten pizza? He carefully picked up a slice, turned it a bit, and took a tentative bite, afraid the cheese would drip, or an olive would slide off. She, however, had no hesitation, and sitting crossed legged on the sofa took a huge bite.

"You're hungry, then?"

"I usually am!" she answered, without looking round.

"Good to know some things don't change."

"I can't believe you brought me pizza! Or was it just an excuse to have some yourself and blame me?"

He took another bite. Raffi really did do good pizza. Why the hell hadn't he eaten one long before now?

"You guessed it. Milkshakes, pizza…I'm having to double my training regime just to keep trim."

She giggled, and then jumped up over the back of the sofa and ran from the room. Daryl didn't know what was wrong. It wasn't something he'd said, was it? The next second she was running back with her Yankees cap on her head. He turned back to the TV, relieved it was something so simple; then something landed on his head, and she landed back on the sofa next to him.

"If you don't wear it we'll lose," she told him seriously as he looked round at her, aware of two things. First, that she looked very cute in her cap, and second, she'd put a second cap on his head, back to front. "Wow, what a dude," she said. "You should try that look in the office. Marlene would fall off her chair." He calmly put down his pizza, licked his fingers, and then turned it around.

She just laughed and retrieved her pizza.

"So how you been?" She rested her feet on the table, leaned back and tucked in.

"Busy, as always. Bored, too, sometimes. And tired and irritated. Which is why I thought I'd come to LA and let you cheer me up."

"Oh, really. I thought I infuriated you."

"Most of the time you do. The rest of the time you can be quite nice."

"Wow, don't hold back on the flattery, I'm going to blush."

"You never believe me when I say anything truly flattering."

"Hmm, that's true."

"So how have you been?"

"Is that question really: Are you going to throw yourself off a high building?"

"No, not at all. I already knew that. I'm just asking. Not ticking boxes."

"Okay I guess," she said. "Sometimes I feel alright, almost normal. I'm used to getting on with life on my own, and I'm not unhappy, but then I feel sad, and a bit confused."

"Human beings aren't designed to cope with prolonged periods of misery, or we'd go insane. Having bad moments is nature's way of helping us through. Don't feel guilty."

Their eyes met and he knew he'd surprised her. Hers had narrowed with obvious suspicion.

"Are you really Daryl Blackmoor?"

He smiled. "No, I stole his body. I'm the much nicer version he keeps locked in a cupboard most of the time."

"Yeah, I thought so."

"So, any exciting news?"

"You know about Lula?"

"I do. O'Grady rang me to tell me." And almost gave me a heart attack thinking you were pregnant with another man's child! "How is she?"

"Fine. Exploring everything. We're getting on just great. Lazarus is doing his big brother impression, and the press keep trying to get pictures of her every time we go outside. She's asleep at the moment, but I'm sure she'll come and investigate you when she wakes up."

"Wow, I've never been investigated before."

"One of the few things you've not experienced, then." He smirked, and took a swallow of beer. He checked the score. The Yankees had scored twice, and neither of them had noticed. "I had another look at the Butterfly acquisition today – it's very exciting. I can't wait to see it all finished, though I know it's a long way off. What's even more exciting, is someone made a twenty-five million-dollar donation – anonymously!

How amazing is that!"

"Yes, clearly they think it's a good idea," Daryl replied carefully.

"Not many people would give so much. Not many people *could* give so much."

He took another bite of pizza and accepted another slice from her, not sure what else he could say that wouldn't give anything away.

She let the silence run on, and then spoke again, watching him so completely that any reaction would be noticed. "I wish you'd just admit it was you. I'd like to know it was."

"How on earth do you know it was me? What have you been hacking into now?"

"Nothing. It was a guess. You just proved me right." Her grin countered his scowl; but his eyes were soft. "Why did you?"

Daryl took a silent moment to appreciate what was happening: they were talking, discussing, asking, answering… This was bonding, friendship, wanting to know, wasn't it? With that comforting revelation, and Donny's advice as his guiding light, he was happy to be honest in his answer.

"It's a subject I had no real awareness of before, though not intentionally. What little I've learned, and from bits that you've told me, it's a hard thing to take in. The rest I can guess at. I don't like the idea of what you went through, so if the money helps other women and children avoid the same, it is well spent." She considered his words, and smiled. Had he been judged and found not wanting? "Will you tell me what happened?" he dared to ask.

"Maybe. One day. Though I don't know why you care to know. It's not like it matters all that much really."

"It does matter. It would help me understand you better, and then I might put my foot in it a little less often." She looked at him curiously. "Mysty, I didn't intend for the money I paid you for the databases to be seen in…in the way you saw it. If was far too generous of you, to do all that, and I paid you a fair price, because your talent warrants it. That was all."

"My talent is mine to share, how I wish. It is for me to choose how generous or ungenerous I am. Why are you so rubbish at accepting gifts?"

"I don't usually get any."

"What? What about Christmas, or your birthday?"

Her horror at his answer was sweet, and his expression was grim when he answered. "What do you get the man everyone assumes has everything?"

"A remote control Lamborghini," she replied instantly, her smile irresistible. "Surely Harvey and the boys get you something?"

"Sometimes, but it's usually a little pointless. Fine wines? I have them. A racehorse? I have far too many. A car? More than I will ever drive. Priceless art, sculptures? I have so many I can't even list them anymore."

"I'll get you some really awesome socks for Christmas. Does that sound suitably mundane?"

"That sounds great. Some to match my mugs would be excellent."

"You still have them?" she asked, her eyes wide.

"Of course. They have their own shelf."

"I thought you might just chuck them out! They were just a bit of fun."

"No, they were definitely the most exciting mugs I've ever had. And you know I like excitement."

"Oh, yes. The more the better." She handed him a fresh beer and a new slice of pizza, taking the same for herself. "Well, I will try and think of something for you for Christmas that is utterly original, just to surprise you."

Daryl managed to avoid mentioning the one thing he wanted, that was utterly original and quite priceless, and the only thing she could give him that he truly longed for.

"I look forward to it. I'm hoping I might be in fewer negative dickhead points by then."

"A new, record low has been achieved this evening, despite the epic fail with the pizza slice." He looked at her. When had he had an 'epic fail' at anything? It still felt uncomfortable! But her eyes were bright with… what? "So, what with the delicious pizza, obtained at great cost, and the donation, I think…wow…we have a new low total of twenty-two million."

"What happens when I'm not in negative dickhead points – just so I know?"

"You're assuming you'll actually get there?" She looked at him with a deadly serious face, and then laughed as he looked so crestfallen.

"Well, it would help to know what it would mean. I could try being on my best behaviour?"

"Well, you could try that. I guess I would have to officially like you. And that might even go so far as calling you a friend. But as you always do something new to upset me, I don't think I need to worry for at least another six years."

"Huh? *Six years*?"

Before she could reply, Lazarus strolled around the corner and eyed him suspiciously. Then a little face peered around, too, and the cub crept forward to sniff him. He looked at Mysty uncertainly, not sure if this was okay or not, but she just smiled as Lula put two front paws on his leg and gazed up at him.

"Lula, meet Daryl. Daryl, Lula," she said.

The cub then climbed up and onto Mysty's lap, and immediately settled down.

"She is fond of you already."

"She knows she's loved. Most animals do." At her nod, Lazarus trotted over and settled down next to her, on the side away from Daryl. "I just have to make sure Lazarus doesn't feel left out. He's finding it a bit hard to share me."

"I can understand that." He'd said the words before he'd realised, and she looked round at him, amused.

"Really. Can you now?" she said.

"Absolutely. I wouldn't share you if I was Lazarus." She just smiled, and the moment passed. *Phew. That was close.* "So, when do you want to go shopping for your holiday?" he asked.

"I'm sure I can fumble my way though. You must be far too busy to bother with such things."

"I need to be less busy; I need some time out the office."

"I haven't seen you check your devices once tonight."

"I didn't bring them." *Because I wanted the time with you. I've waited so long for this.*

"Golly. Careful, I might take that as a compliment."

"You should. I've never done that for anyone else."

"I bet no one else has threatened to steal it off you and lob it out the window either."

"Well, there is that…" She chuckled. "I have a present for you. A gift of sorts."

"Really? What is it?"

"A photo shoot, for you, Lula and Lazarus. So you can get a few pictures up. And some memories to keep."

She looked at him, face a little surprised but soft. "With you as the photographer?"

"Only the best for you." He smiled.

"Such modesty!" She smiled back at him. "That would be great, thank you."

"And, we need to sit down at some point and talk about what happens next. Your shows are almost finished and you need a new direction. Perhaps we can do that this week?"

"Fine with me. Idleness isn't something I do well. I'll only get myself into mischief."

"I could volunteer to help?" She rolled her eyes at him, and would have thrown a cushion but didn't want to disturb Lula. "I'm very good at mischief as well. But we can see who's better."

"You!" She threw an olive at him, but he caught it and ate it, amused at her outrage. "Didn't you and Harvey get up to enough mischief in New York?"

"I wish to God I hadn't accepted his invitation to go out that night!" He shook his head, remembering how the quiet evening had been derailed, having thought she'd missed those headlines.

"I thought that's what you did, and enjoyed it?" she asked curiously.

"It's not quite that simple. I went out with Harvey for a quiet evening because I missed his birthday party." He tried to find words that didn't sound arrogant, aware she was watching him closely. "Present company excluded, most women…" He waved a piece of pizza in the air, struggling to phrase what he wanted to say.

"Only want a trip to your penthouse," she finished for him, her tone not condemning, which was something at least. If she understood, then maybe she'd hate him less.

"Yes. Despite not looking for it, it's all very easy. For Harvey, too. Always has been. When you start going to parties you'll understand how it all works. You'll end up with the same problem."

"I don't have a penthouse to invite them to. And I have no hesitation in saying no. I can't imagine anything worse," she replied calmly, surprised she was so unflustered by the subject or his explanation. Somehow it all made sense. Why should he turn down what was made freely available to him? "Do I really have to go to parties?" she then asked. "I like being at home."

He smiled, knowing how that felt. Sensible girl.

"I'm afraid you will. Being a celebrity does require a certain amount of socialising. Not every night, but sometimes. There's nothing to worry about, though. You get on well with practically everyone, except me, and you won't be on your own."

She looked about as enthusiastic as having been told she was having her fingers removed.

"Will you be there?"

"When I can." He didn't like the way the happiness had faded from her. "But that's for the future, nothing immediate. Don't get worried about it now."

"You'll make me wear dresses and earrings and all kinds of paraphernalia. I'll look like fucking candy floss."

Her disgust was obvious, and he grinned at her reluctance. She would, and she would look stunning.

"We can definitely get your ears pierced, seeing as you're so keen."

She looked round at him. "I got them pierced weeks ago."

He tried to look, but her hair was in the way. He pulled off the cap, and dared to lift her hair, and, sure enough, there was a double piercing, one at the top of her ear and one in the lobe, where a small infinity symbol hung. A fine chain connected the two, all in gold. Normally he'd hate anything like this, but it suited her; it was sort of tribal and primitive. He was annoyed he'd missed the occasion, but he could now buy her some earrings as a gift.

"Twice?" he said.

"I'm a rebel. You know me." She didn't care for his disapproval, or him touching her hair, and the cap went back on. "The top one really hurt – just so you know, in case you want one. Not as much as my nipple piercing, but…"

He choked on his beer, but she just smiled wickedly at him, not missing the fact his eyes dropped to her breasts as if seeking proof.

"You are joking?" How had O'Grady not stopped her, or warned him?

"Why does it matter? It's not like anyone will see it," she shrugged, and he could have groaned. "But yes, I am joking. I have no intention or wish to pierce anything else. I like the chain, though."

"Anything else new I should know about?"

"Nope. Have you got any piercings? Any rude tattoos from nights out with Harvey? A nice big 'Stud Muffin' on your shoulder or a 'The Man From New York?' across your backside?"

"No."

"I bet life was really easy without me around to question you every five minutes."

"Easy, but boring." He let himself say it with an element of affection, wondering if she'd pick up on it.

"Wow, I think you missed me," she teased.

"Maybe. Just a little." *Like every hour of every day.*

She just laughed and settled back, putting her plate down. He kept his eyes on the TV. The football game was almost over, and neither of them had paid any attention.

"There's another ball game a week on Wednesday that's pretty big. You want to come over for pizza again? I'll get it, seeing as Raffi will most likely overcharge you again!" He didn't know what to say. This was not the kind of invitation he'd ever had, and definitely not one he'd ever expected to get from her! But his pause was misinterpreted. "Actually, it's probably not a good idea. Your poor body probably couldn't cope with junk food twice in less than a year, and you're probably busy, so…never mind."

"I'll check the diary, and unless you hear otherwise, I'll assume my seat is booked for the match. This is a nice sofa."

She had a think about that. She was not sure if she was pleased or not, if it had been the right thing to do or not. But…it was never boring being with him, and it beat watching it on her own, despite the fact he still unnerved her sometimes. She'd had Slick, Rusty and some of the guys round once or twice, but they were clearly struggling with who she was… She'd lost more than just Donny and his 'family' recently, and she knew going to the Bowl would eventually become impossible. It would never be the same now she was…who she was.

"Great," she eventually said. "What beer do you like? Nastro?"

"That or Leffe."

"Ah yes, I remember. That was nice, a fine choice."

He couldn't help but smile as she referred back to the beer she'd had in his apartment that night.

"I still can't believe you did what you did that night," he said.

"I still can't believe you didn't work out the code on the damn cuffs." She glanced over at him, and their gaze held. "I really didn't think you'd be there all that time."

"I was far too distracted to think of numbers."

"I bet you were." She gave a naughty little laugh, which would have got her kissed if he'd been free to. "Go on, have the last piece," she said. "I'm stuffed."

"You sure?"

"Totally."

She stroked Lula as he ate. "I'd forgotten how much they like sleeping when they're young."

"You're very good with her. It's a gift you have, looking after them so well."

"All it takes is a lot of love, and…well, I have no family, and they have no family, so I guess it works for everyone."

You're so lucky to have them, Daryl thought, watching.

"Do they sleep on the bed?" he asked.

"Sometimes Lazarus does. He's never far away even if he doesn't. Lula does at the moment. She's still a bit unsure and settling in."

"Bit tough on your boyfriend."

"I'm afraid I come with the leopards, so he'll have to learn to live with them, too, when he turns up in my life. Your wife will have to share you with other women."

"Not necessarily."

"Oh, come on, you're the man who needs – how many? – five women to keep him satisfied? With maybe a few extras thrown in, for good measure? She'll have to be tough, and forgiving, whoever she ends up being."

"It's not quite that straightforward. Not that I'm going to explain it to you. You've clearly made up your mind on the subject. As for my wife, I don't think she will have any complaints."

"Oh really?" She sounded wholly unimpressed. "Please explain. I promise to be as open-minded as I possibly can."

"No."

"Daryl, you prude!"

"Not tonight. Ask me another time." She huffed and sat back. "Did you really just call me a prude?"

She blushed, refusing to look at him. "Last five minutes of the match. I'm concentrating. Seeing as you've distracted me for the last seventy."

"Makes a change. Usually you're distracting me."

She glowered at him for a second, and then looked back at the TV.

The game commentary switched to the interviews, and Daryl noted how relaxed he was. He'd enjoyed every moment, but he really ought to get going now and do some work. He turned to her and smiled… She was asleep, long eyelashes casting shadows on her cheeks, her hands still around the cub, who had wriggled up to lie on her chest, and Lazarus by her side.

He wished he had his camera. It was such a priceless moment. They were so at peace together, and he was somehow touched that she'd fallen asleep with him next to her. Surely she wouldn't have done if she was still so uncomfortable with him, and afraid?

It was a miracle. And as much as he would happily carry her to her bedroom, he knew she wouldn't like him to. And if she woke up, she'd probably think the worst of him – and he couldn't blame her, either. He got up and carried the plates, the ice bucket and the empties through to the kitchen. He then returned, and lay his jacket over the sleeping threesome. The only reaction was her snuggling her head against the sofa cushions a little more.

At the door, he turned back for a moment. When had he wanted this with anyone? Never. And now he had to walk away from it.

"Goodnight, Toby."

"Goodnight, Mr Blackmoor."

"So…" O'Grady said slowly from his position just outside the door. "All okay?"

"She's asleep on the sofa. I didn't wake her."

"She's not been sleeping so well lately, so that's good news. The pizza went down okay, then?"

"Very good suggestion, O'Grady, it certainly helped." Daryl looked at Mac, who kept his thoughts to himself; but the twinkle in his eye gave him away, making his employer scowl. "I'll see you tomorrow, O'Grady. Mac, if you wouldn't mind being useful for once, let's go."

Mac rolled his eyes after Daryl, making OG smile. He didn't ask where his boss's jacket was.

SHE STEPPED OUT of the Bentley after OG and onto the dark blue carpet of the exclusive LA club. It beat being summoned to his office any day. The waiting photographers got their shots, and then OG led her inside the dark blue and chrome interior, smartly dressed staff standing to attention to each side. Past the beautifully lit fountain of water she spotted him waiting for her. And then she did a double-take. There appeared to be an image or statue of her in the water?

She didn't know how she felt about this. She wasn't sure how to be with him after waking up with the warmth of his jacket draped over her. Anybody who did sweet things like that, they couldn't be a complete monster, could they? How could he be so nice, and yet she knew he had a darker side…and she didn't know if she could trust him. Experience told her to beware, and her instincts warned her he was trouble; yet the natural response she had for the new friendly side of him made her want to know more. Was she desperate or lonely? Or mad?

"Mysty." He indicated that she join him.

"Daryl." She stepped up onto the raised dais, and sat in the chair pulled out for her. "Is that me in that fountain?"

"I'm afraid so." She scowled. He was so predictable. Yet somehow it was flattering that he never gave up. "I see you almost got dressed up for me," he teased.

If he was honest, she looked fantastic and supremely sexy in silky black leggings and high boots. Her hair was up, piled in curls, making her look regal and much older than seventeen.

"Why is it you always want me to wear a dress? You should be glad I accepted your invitation, dress or no dress."

"I think you look great. In fact, you never look less than beautiful." She threw one leg over the edge of the chair and one arm over the back. "I know you're unconventional, but is that totally necessary?" He said it as calmly as possible, trying valiantly to keep his eyes on her face, not the rest of her.

"I'm comfortable like this."

A waiter appeared at the table, and she smiled and looked up at him. "Madam, can I get you a drink?"

"I'd love a glass of milk."

"Milk?" he repeated, as if she'd asked for a live snake.

"A white Russian without the vodka, does that sound better? Full fat with a straw, if you have it, please."

"Just get her what she asked for, and next time don't question it," Daryl snapped, sending the man hurriedly from the table. "No alcohol? I was sure you'd have a beer."

"I don't drink very often. Last night was a once-a-week occasion. And I have Celeste tomorrow night."

"You don't feel unwell?"

"No, just these new pieces are pretty hard. I don't want anything making it harder. I'm sure Ying has reported back to you that I'm letting him feed me one of his drinks occasionally."

"Despite the disgusting taste?" he teased, her grimace telling him everything.

"I just hold my nose and think of England."

He almost laughed at her phrase, and how often it was used for quite a different reason, but settled for a wide smile, unaware of how his exceptional good looks and boyish grin were playing havoc with her composure.

"Well, you look as healthy as a person can be, so it must be doing you good."

"You sure you don't want Ying to get you a couple of his swamp concoctions? All that rushing around and travelling?"

"You're saying I don't look well?"

"No, I'm saying you need to take extra effort to stay looking well, that's all. Can't have you not winning World's Most Handsome, can we? I thought you were aiming for a ten-year reign at least."

"You're so right. You could be my personal trainer? Make sure I'm up to scratch?"

"I'm afraid I'm all booked out."

"Shame. I'm sure my performance would improve with you around."

He saw her struggle to ignore his comment, and enjoyed it. So she wasn't immune to him at all.

"I sent your jacket for dry cleaning, just in case Lula had dribbled on it."

"I didn't want you getting cold, and it wouldn't have mattered, it's just a jacket." With an exorbitant price tag. "Though why I was feeling so generous, when that was the first time in my life a woman has fallen asleep on me, I don't know."

She laughed. "I was tired. All the excitement of pizza and the game. I apologise."

After the drink had been placed on the table he said, "O'Grady mentioned you'd not been sleeping too well. Are you having nightmares again?"

Her eyes snapped open in surprise, both at his question and because she wasn't used to genuine concern like that from him. "How do you know I have nightmares?"

"I pay O'Grady to look after you, to keep you safe and inform me of anything important I should know about. Not that he wouldn't do his job for free. So, was it nightmares?"

"Yes." She blinked rapidly a few times, and then looked away.

"Can I ask what about? Is it because of the hit?"

"It always goes back to…what happened…before. Certain things trigger the memories. Like blood and gunshots. I knew it would happen but…I thought they'd have gone away by now. I guess I never realised how much I assumed – subconsciously assumed – Donny would be there. Of all people, I knew he understood. He is no stranger to…to violence and everything that goes with it."

She swallowed and went very pale, swinging her leg down and crossing it over the other, the body language suddenly defensive – and vulnerable. She probably wasn't aware of how obvious it was.

"Would you like to talk to someone about it?"

"A shrink? Some psycho-something or other who can make sympathetic noises as if they know what it is to see their family butchered? No…thank you. There was no one to help me when I was nine, so I don't think I need anyone now."

She said the words so simply, but he knew the cold tone was an ice-cap over a wealth of pain. What had she seen?

"If you change your mind." He didn't argue with her, as he knew it would only upset her. It meant more to him that she trusted him rather than try and prove he was right.

"I doubt I will, but yes, I know." There followed a moment of silence, and the tangible message to leave the topic alone and move on. She raised a finger to indicate the surroundings. "Lovely place. You only ever go to the nicest places, of course. Do you own it?"

"Yes."

"And the Coliseum?"

"Yes." He raised his Martini to his lips.

"Wow. Free drinks and free food. That must be great. Do you get free lap dances in those topless clubs you own as well?"

He forced himself to swallow the liquid that was about to choke him, her wicked smile telling him she'd timed it just so. "Yes."

"It really is good to be you." Her lips wrapped around the straw, and her fingers played with it, and for the thousandth time he remembered the feel of her lips on his. "Which brings me to another point… Your time is very important. You must have asked me here for a reason?"

"My time is important. And so am I. But you must understand, I have no one else I can joke around with about free lap dances. I have to make the most of such light relief."

"There are numbers you can call for that kind of thing."

He chuckled, not realising the effect it had on her. It was a rich sound, and it stirred something in her somewhere to realise there was a real man behind the mask.

"You're right," he said, "and I have a plane to catch soon so I don't want to run out of time."

"Where are you going?" He liked the fact she asked, and the way the light caught her hair as she tilted her head in curiosity.

"Washington. A state dinner and a meeting with a number of ambassadors and dignitaries. There is an important conference tomorrow discussing various economic and environmental issues – very exciting, as you can imagine."

"No wonder you wanted to talk about lap dancing. Are you sure you can't get out of it?"

He looked down, and groaned, and then had a thought: When had he ever let anyone see the side of him that didn't take on every business meeting or commitment with utter command and conviction? The side of him that wanted a life away from matters of high importance?

"Sadly, there is only one of me, and I have to go, but I'll be back on Thursday. I've checked your schedule, and you have Thursday morning free. We can go shopping then?"

"You don't have to take me shopping. I promise I'll buy some dresses. How many miles do you clock up on that jet? It's not good. I could fly to Washington instead, or something?"

"I really don't notice it anymore."

"We could meet somewhere in the middle, then?"

"Mysty, sweetheart..." – how did that endearment come so easily to his lips? and how would she react? – "I'm fine. I'll be in LA for over a week when I get back. I don't want having you flying such distances when you have Celeste on Friday."

She didn't know how to take such consideration, or the 'sweetheart'. Who was this man?

"Okay. Though I still don't think it's good for you. New York to LA is a long way and you do that enough."

"Which is another issue, tied in with what I'd like you to work on in the coming months." He looked at her, trying to anticipate how she might react. "I'd like you to consider moving to New York, for a little while." She looked stunned. "Not forever, just...a change of scenery for a while, which might be good after everything that happened, and... because of the new project I have for you."

He waited for the outburst, but there was none. He let out a little of the breath he was holding, not wanting their current truce to disintegrate.

"What is this new project?"

"There is a very important meeting in New York in a few months, and the dinner tomorrow is a prelude to it. A summit has been arranged to agree various economic sanctions and treaties to be updated, and representatives from all over the world are meeting to discuss, agree and hopefully sign. The summit will last one week, and the day everyone arrives I would like there to be a performance, to greet and amaze everyone. The whole point of economics isn't numbers, it's people; in short, making it possible for more people across the world to live a secure life with a job and assured of food, etc.

"The mark of any civilisation is its culture, and the expression of its people through music and dancing. I'd like you to put on a show incorporating different styles of both, and to make it as inclusive and inspiring as possible, so that the morning everyone sits down for the first day of the talks they're on a high, they're positive, and cooperation is the order of the day."

He paused, giving her the chance to speak, but she was sitting very calmly and looking thoughtful.

"You may or may not be aware, but crime rates in the cities you visited on tour recently dropped significantly. Reported incidents while you perform at Celeste, particularly on nights you do new pieces, have seen record lows. You are a symbol of much more than you realise to many people, even if they don't quite recognise it themselves – that and how distracting you are for a number of reasons."

She ignored the final statement and simply said, "I think it's a great idea. No problem, I'll do it."

"Excellent! I'll send you the information, of course. The location has already been chosen. I've already booked a dance studio, like the one in LA, so you'll have lots of space for practice and rehearsals. Whatever you want, you can have. I'm leaving it to you."

"Well that's nothing new," she returned cheekily. "And rather presumptuous to assume I would say yes." Which was true! "You really have put yourself to a lot of trouble for me, haven't you, planning things…"

"That's why I'm here: to organise things and leave you free to do what you do best."

"Which is?"

"Amaze people," he said simply, not looking away.

"Not make you money?"

"I don't need it."

"You're very confusing sometimes."

"I know. When I'm dealing with someone as smart as you, it helps keep your attention."

"What's your IQ? Just out of curiosity."

"189."

A tiny twinkle in her eye showed how close it was to her own. But there was no gloating. She wasn't the type.

"Ah. Did you do the same test I did?"

"No. I was impressed with yours, though. I've never known anyone else play around with maths or physics as well as I do."

"You had a number of incredible breakthroughs in both software and hardware design when you were…a little older than me," she replied. "Why did you stop? The Blackmoor Empire took over?"

How did she know that? He was pleased she knew that. "In a word, yes."

"Don't you wonder what else you might come up with if you went back to it?"

This was a question no one else had asked him, not even Harvey. "Yes, often. I hope one day I'll find some time to do that."

"You should. Goodness knows what magic you might create."

"I'm rather interested in what magic you're creating. Feel like sharing yet?"

"Nope." But she said it with a big smile.

"How's the palladium doing?"

"I've barely had a chance to work on that project, but it's in the pipeline, don't worry." Her smile faded a little for some reason, and he wondered why. "If I go to New York, when do I have to go and where will I be? Can I take…my stuff?"

Ah, that was why. "I have an apartment ready for you. It's maybe a little larger than the one you're in now, and, yes, you can take whatever you like. However, there are duplicates of your guitars and drums, and two bikes in the lock-up, so you don't need to take everything."

He saw her eyes widen. "You really do think of everything, don't you?"

"I've lived in numerous places for most of my life. I know it makes things easier, to have things set up in each place just how you like it. I realise you prefer a home to feel like a home."

"Have you been taking anything I should be reporting to the police?"

"I'm not a monster. And I'm not heartless."

She looked away, almost afraid to see the reaction to what she wanted to say next. "Daryl, I don't think you're a monster, and you're evidently not heartless. Sometimes you go the wrong way about doing things, which means I get hurt, and then I say…things." And then she turned to face him. "I wouldn't say them now."

A large knot unravelled in his stomach and finally set him free.

"Good," he said quietly. "That is the best news."

The moment hovered between them, and then settled.

"Is there anything else you need to talk about?" she asked, breaking the trance.

He took another sip of his drink, and shot her a small smile. "Yes, actually. If you could come up with some of your own material for your debut album, that would be great." His smile widened at her look of surprise. "It's okay, I have people working on it. By the time the summit is finished we should be ready to hand it over to you."

"I'd rather do it myself. I don't like the idea of people 'working on it'. Doesn't that make me a fraud?"

"I'd rather you did it yourself, but it's a big task. Getting some lyrics or pieces of music written for you to put your own stamp on doesn't make you a fraud, it's how the music industry works, to a large extent, and has done for decades."

"I still don't like it. I'm sure I can come up with something. If I'm in New York can I use the sound box to make some recordings?"

"To experiment?"

"Yes."

"No problem. I'll let Armstrong know and you can book yourself in." The magic wand was waved again.

"And there's something else you should know."

"Which is?"

"I have twelve other MJ songs ready. I'd like to get them recorded, and videoed, and then they can become a bonus DVD or download, with something inside to commemorate his birthday, or the day he died – whichever you think. It just seems a shame to not do anything with them…"

She looked a little unsure about taking the initiative with this. Would she ever stop surprising him?

"Of course. It's an excellent idea," he said, and she relaxed. "I'll send a team over to help you and you can arrange everything with them, both PR and on set. No wonder you fell asleep on me."

"It wasn't quite *on* you."

"If you had been on me, I wouldn't have left."

The twinkle in his eyes brought an instant heat to her cheeks.

"Mac! O'Grady! How are you?" she said, and jumped up and gave each of them a hug, glad of their intrusion.

How come they get hugs? Daryl thought, as everyone in the room turned at the spectacle of the two huge security guards with two leopards in tow.

"I'm very well thank you, kiddo, how've you been?" Mac said.

"I'm good!" she said, and bent down so Lula could jump into her arms. She rubbed Lazarus's head, and he closed his eyes appreciatively.

"Sir, we should make a move," Mac then said. "The plane is ready."

"If you don't want to go, I can go stand in the way so you can't take off? Blame me, I can take it," Mysty suggested.

Mac smiled, as did O'Grady, and they looked down at Daryl, who suddenly felt there were far too many eyes watching him.

And then she glided away, back through the club and down the steps, one leopard by her side and one on her hip, and every eye in the room on her.

The three followed her moments later and caught up with her at the entrance, standing in the shadow of the door after finding a host of reporters and cameras outside. A plush silver Bentley waited, with a company of serious-faced grey suits she didn't recognise, and she knew it was his car not hers.

"Well, I'll see you Thursday. Good luck tomorrow night. Not that you need it," Daryl said, attempting to sound indifferent for the benefit of the present company. But she saw the look of slight sadness in his eyes.

"Fly safe. Enjoy your swish party – and make sure Harvey doesn't turn up and lead you astray again. Hope all goes well in the Oval."

It was a mingled response of teasing and concern, and he would have kissed her cheek had it not been for bodyguards and a hundred cameras snapping away. Plus there was a leopard cub in her arms, who might object. But he carefully offered his hand to Lula, who sniffed it and then licked her nose.

"She doesn't bite," Mysty whispered, touched that he'd made an attempt to get to know the cub.

"Doesn't take after you, then," he whispered back, and with a flash of a grin then strode to the car, never wanting to walk away from a woman less.

He was right to have worried. The papers the next day hadn't missed the interaction and he was treated to 'LA's Golden Tiger Tames Lion of Manhattan' spread across the breakfast table when he picked up the newspapers. He didn't mind that; it was if they started taking bets on her being the next Mrs Blackmoor he needed to worry…she might realise what the game was, then.

IT WAS THE MOMENT he'd been waiting for since leaving her on Monday night.

"Good morning."

"Hello." She pushed the shades up and smiled.

"No leopards?"

"Wore them out already. They're both flopped out on the sofa watching the Disney Channel."

It sounded like she was talking about the kids, and he couldn't wait until she was – providing they were his, of course.

"You've been for a run already?"

"Yep. Then we had an hour of playing catch and chase, and then it was bath time and breakfast. You're lucky I have the energy to get in the car! How are you? Was the flight okay?"

"Fine. Take-off wasn't delayed – a miracle to say the least with the security around the airport – and I slept most of the way." His handheld vibrated in his palm and he flicked it on to silent and slid it inside a pocket. There were things he'd much rather see than another stream of emails, and she was sitting opposite him. "How are you?"

"Dandy."

"Not peachy?"

"That too."

"Good. I might make it to Vegas on Friday to see the show live."

"Terribly shabby of you not to have made it already. That would be maybe…the third you've missed?"

"I know. Almost enough to make you fire me and get a new manager."

She laughed. "I think I'll let you off, just this once."

"Eternally grateful." She was intrigued. He was in a good mood. Again. So good, in fact, that it was hard to remember what a complete arsehole he could be. "Anything you specifically want to get for the holiday?" he then asked.

"Flip-flops, bikini, sarong, beach towel. And I'll be done." She shrugged, happy with her short list. Daryl remembered taking Rachel shopping. There was such a difference it was untrue. "I can't imagine I'll need much else, will I?"

"Maybe a few summer dresses, some shorts. Sun hat perhaps. Don't worry about the bikini, I'm not offended by nudity."

She rolled her eyes, but wasn't annoyed, and he just leant back contentedly in the seat, happy just to have her there.

"I've never been on holiday before. I don't really know what to take."

Never been on holiday?

"You can take whatever you think you might need – preferably not the drum kit, though, but if we really must, we can. Anything you forget we can grab while we're out there, no problem."

"When did you last go on holiday?"

"I can't remember. I gave up years ago when they always got interrupted or cancelled because something happened that required my attention."

"But you must go away for boys-only weekends with Harvey and your merry men?"

"Sometimes, but that never feels like a holiday."

"Debauchery is such hard work. And it never feels like a holiday, because?"

"Because when you're me…" He looked out of the window, uncomfortable talking about himself, and not sure why she wanted to know. Perhaps she was trying to understand him more, so he took a deep breath.

"Because when you're you, you have to be the life and soul of the party, the one everyone looks to for leading the way?" she then said, beating him to it. "I can imagine how that would not feel like a holiday at all." He looked at her. She had worked it out. "I promise I won't expect you to lead me anywhere. In fact, if it would help, I can boss you around instead, and make sure you're only doing things to relax?"

"How about a lap dance?"

"No."

He laughed, and not for the first time did she feel its power, feel his power. He was so good-looking, and had a magnetism that even Donny didn't possess, despite how much she loved him.

And that kiss still lay unspoken between them, simmering away under her skin. Did he remember it? Had he felt anything? Why was she so distracted by him, and so goddamned curious? Whoever had coined the 'curiosity killed the cat' adage certainly must have known about people like Daryl, and the girls so intrigued by them.

She lived with the uncomfortable fear she might do something stupid, like start believing she meant something to him, which was number one on the Don't Do list, above the 'jump into a snake pit' and 'go out with no clothes on'. It was on the top spot for a reason, and she was not going to forget it.

The car pulled up and the door opened.

"This is a shop for me, I'm afraid, so feel free to stay in the car if you think it'll be a bit dull for you."

"No way. You get to harass me, so I'm going harass you. Get going, pin-up boy, I'm right behind you."

A large 'DB' stood proud in gold and cream above the highly polished glass doors, and she realised they were at his store. She followed him in, the security guard nodding, and the staff opening the door to welcome him, clearly alerted of his coming. Mac and OG stayed outside in the cool shade of the blue and gold canopy over the doors. The shop was tastefully done, of course, and catered solely for men.

"You must need more branded underwear."

"Would that surprise you?"

"No."

"Because?"

"Because I think you've more than likely worn yours thin in a certain place, what with all those pictures hanging in your various apartments."

He absolutely did not know what to say to that. Decorum, propriety, whatever you want to call it, went out of the window and he swung around, grabbed her, and slung her over his shoulder, much to the shock of the attending staff.

"I do not appreciate this!" she cried, thumping him on the back.

"You are far less bother up there," came the firm reply.

But her hands reached around his waist and, before he could stop her, she started to undo his belt and trousers. His arousal was instant; as was his verbal reaction – anything to avoid her seeing the truth in her statement for real!

"Do the trousers back up and I'll put you down." He held his breath through long seconds of pleasurable torture as she complied, and he swung her back down. "Do the belt back up, too."

"*No.*"

"Alright, I'll take your shades then until you do."

He plucked them off her head and put them on – and found far more than he expected when he did so! Numbers and lights were dotted over the inside of the shades, and 'Unidentified User – Fuck Off' immediately flashed up on miniature screens.

"Jesus Christ." He pulled them off and looked at her, but still held them up high, where she couldn't easily grab them. "What are these?"

"My shades," she said dryly.

"My belt," he said, and she finished fastening it, the soft blush on her cheeks unmistakable.

He handed them back. "They have face recognition, distance logging and data scanning built in, connected to my mainframe," she said. "These are a prototype. I'm not happy with them yet." She pushed them back up and looked at him, seeing pure amazement etched into his gorgeous face. "I'll do you a pair, when they're ready. I was going to give some to Mac and OG, anyway, so it would be rude to miss you out. I know you're really just a big kid who likes gadgets."

Never mind *him* liking gadgets, even from the short seconds he'd seen them operating, they looked impressive. The possibilities were huge.

"You could patent those!" he said, truly stunned. "It's brilliant that you've done this, and they work so well."

"You do that if you want to. I just wanted to see how well they worked, so I could refine them. Are you getting some of these or what?" She indicated a display of cotton boxer shorts, in subtle shades of blue and cream.

"No…"

"Oh dear. Mr Prude is back. Don't tell me you've gone all shy, too?" she said, sliding an oversized windbreaker from a model and slipping it on. "Where is everyone, anyway? The staff are here, but there are no shoppers?"

"The shop has been closed for security reasons, so I – we – will be left in peace."

"Wow."

"You're wearing my initials," he said slowly, pointing at the 'DB' embroidered on the front of the windbreaker.

"Oh, I didn't notice that. I was just beginning to like it, as well."

She actually looked adorable in it, despite its size, and it felt like she'd borrowed his. It was what he'd wanted to see for so long, something on her that connected her to him.

"Most women would be proud to wear my initials; but…I know you would rather wear another's."

His soft voice surprised her, and she looked at him. "No point dwelling on what cannot be." She blinked. "I'll go wait in the car, if that's alright."

She went to take the jacket off, but he stopped her, and reached down and did the zip up, all the way to the top.

"We can always take the label off. Keep it. Use it out on the ocean. You look cute in it."

Her sudden pain was so acute, so raw, he couldn't be jealous or angry. He questioned himself for saying what he'd said, but then reasoned that Donny couldn't be left unmentioned for ever. Perhaps it would help her to know he was aware of her pain?

"I guess if I get washed up somewhere, at least someone will know where to send the body back to. Simple rule of logic."

She sent him a tight smile, but then turned and walked away. He followed a short while later, after making a few quick decisions about clothes he needed. The staff knew his sizes, and would send them on.

"Is she alright?" he asked when he got to the car.

"A bit emotional, but pretending she's okay," O'Grady answered calmly, sensing nothing malicious had happened. "Very fetching jacket she has on."

"Yes. Indeed." He climbed in, and the door was closed. "I was hoping today might be a day when I didn't make you cry," he said.

"It wasn't you. It's just not a good subject for me."

"Have you really never been on holiday?" he asked.

She closed her eyes, knowing it wasn't a question designed to hurt. He was curious, just like she was about him.

"A family that can't afford enough food to eat doesn't go on holiday. And a child running for her life doesn't go on holiday, either, because every day is about survival. With Donny...I never wanted to be far from him, and he never left Vegas, so we never really went anywhere. Best we managed was the ice rink a few times. I don't think it bothered him so much before...before he met someone he wanted to walk in the sunshine with, if that makes any sense."

Daryl could see in her face how deep in her memories she was, which explained why she had mentioned the ice rink...she still had no idea he already knew.

"It does. Perfectly."

"And he's not a monster, either. People assume so much about him."

"I've never thought he was a monster. We've known each other for years. At one point we were good friends…well, as far as time and business allowed. I've always respected him, despite the clashes we had from time to time over you. He is an honourable man, especially with regards you."

It was the right thing to say, and he saw some of the tension ebb.

"I wish he'd been a little less fucking honourable," she groaned. "Have you ever had a dream come true?" Her eyes were as open as the question was forthright.

He didn't have an answer for a second. She never asked the mundane or predictable. Dreams? He was too busy for dreams. Except the one that took over his consciousness whenever it could, and he could hardly admit to that.

"I've been so busy for so long I don't think I know what my dreams are."

"I guess being you means there's not much to dream about, you just make things happen every day in some way, in a business sense."

"There is that. And you? Any dreams come true?"

"No. I stopped dreaming for a long time after my mother died. All I ever wanted was to somehow save up enough money to get us out of there. It didn't happen. I ran out of time. Things like Harvard, Donny…well, after those two things didn't happen either, I officially gave up dreaming."

"Don't do that. One day a dream will come true. Simple rule of logic." Her eyes slid up to his, because he'd used her words, employing a sensitivity she hadn't thought him capable of. Neither had he until a few weeks ago. "I can't believe you undid my trousers."

She blushed and laughed. "Neither can I. But you put me over your shoulder and walked me across the store! How could you?"

"Easily. You're not very heavy."

"I'm so glad so few people saw that happen."

"I think my staff would love to have you back. They don't usually get exciting customers."

The car pulled up and she followed him out again. Once again the store had been closed to the public so they could shop privately.

"What about this? With these?" After ten minutes of browsing the racks she held up a dark green t-shirt and khaki shorts with stylish but functional pockets, and similar navy-blue pair. "Not for *you*, for *Mac* and *OG*," she added when she saw the frown of disagreement on his face.

"Mac and OG?"

"Sure. It's a holiday for them, too. I bet Mac has never taken a holiday, as he's so busy watching over you. OG neither. Wouldn't it be a nice surprise for them?"

Her generous nature was something he was going to have to get used to. He'd never thought of it like that. They did a job; they got paid. Story over. Or not, as it turned out.

"Yes, I guess it would."

"What size are they?"

Daryl patched through to Mac.

"Sir?"

"Mac, what size waist and chest are you?"

"Sir?"

"Your clothes sizes, what are they?"

"Forty and forty-four."

"And O'Grady, can you ask him?"

Mute.

"Thirty-six and forty. Why do you–"

Disconnect.

"I definitely think it's time to look at bikinis," he said. As lovely as it was buying for Mac and OG, there were more interesting things to choose.

"I can do that on my own."

"No, I really think you need a second opinion." She saw the determined glint in his eye and knew there was no point arguing. "OG says you like swimming. A high diving score of straight tens."

"I do wonder how much he tells you about me," she responded.

"Not nearly enough. Did your mother teach you to swim?"

"We didn't have money to go swimming. The first time I went

swimming I was on my own, somewhere in the middle of America in the middle of nowhere, when I was trying to get to Vegas. It was boiling hot. I came over the top of a hill and there was this amazing lake below me, and not a soul, a building or a road in sight. The cold water was bliss. I stayed for two days there, splashing around, trying not to drown myself, daring myself to swim all the way across and back. Looking back it was remarkably dangerous."

"You were nine."

"Yes."

"It's a miracle you survived."

"It didn't feel like a miracle." *It felt like an unending nightmare.* Time to change the subject. She held up a bunch of bikinis. "What do you think?"

"Those two, that one, and those two."

"Five?"

"Actually, anything in white looks good on you, so those two as well."

Two more stores and an hour later he was ensconced on a sofa, sipping a latte, when he heard, "I don't know why you're making me dress up like the first lady of goddamn America." The curtain swished back to reveal a Mysty in a very smart dark blue dress, ending just above her knee, the sleek material hugging her all the way up to her neckline. Simple, but timelessly elegant and, on her, beautiful. The next Mrs Blackmoor.

"If the shoe fits."

"So you're trying to marry me off to the president now, are you? I feel like a complete goose! This isn't me at all! I feel like a fraud!"

"He won't think you're a fraud. And it is you – just an undiscovered side of you."

She glowered at him; but she had to look the part when she met the president, and he dug his heels in.

"Try the cream suit on." When she emerged, he almost gasped. "Stunning. Definitely that one."

"But it's not very proper to meet the president wearing no knickers, is it?"

"You're not wearing any?"

"No. Can you see a VPL?"

"A *what*?"

"Visible panty line."

"Wear a thong."

"I hate thongs."

He swallowed. Oh dear. The topic of conversation had awakened a certain something.

"It's up to you. Try the last one on and then we'll go."

"Promise?" she whined. "I'm hungry and bored now."

"I promise. We need to work on your shopping stamina." She came out wearing a pure white blouse and deep blue satin pencil skirt. "Beautiful. Any underwear?"

"No."

"I'm not sure I believe you."

"Don't think for one minute I'm going to prove it to you."

"Looks like Little Miss Prude is in the room."

"You want to apologise for calling me that, because I haven't seen you change your clothes once, let alone prance around in swimming trunks? Why don't you? It might get me as excited as you are right now."

She stretched a high-heeled foot towards him, until it almost touched his shin.

He moved suddenly, grabbed her foot and pulled, landing her in his lap, the skirt riding up as one bent leg wrapped either side of his thighs, the sudden contact almost bringing him to a climax. Her face was pure outrage and shock, and he was too aroused to keep the tension from his face.

"Would you like a demonstration on what happens when you get me this excited?"

"I wasn't trying to. Let me back up!"

What was he doing? She could feel his hands on her waist, pulling her down closer to him, to his… Did he have no self-control? How could he get so excited with her in such prissy clothes!

"I know you weren't. Shall we see if I can get you as excited?" A hand trailed down over her backside, threatening to slide under the skirt, and she knew it. A quiver of anticipation ran through her traitorous body, his eyes holding hers, promising all kinds of things she didn't understand. Part of her wanted to; a much larger part wanted to run a mile, or twenty. He was far too potent! That any man could send her senses into disarray like that was far too dangerous to contemplate.

"No, Daryl, please let me go."

He paused, and sighed long and hard. He let go of her and she swallowed, afraid of the intensity in his eyes as she backed off, tugging the skirt back down as far as it would go.

"Sir, would you like the car brought around?" Mac's voice in his ear broke the stare that kept them locked together.

"Yes. We'll be ready to go in a few minutes." He looked at her. Dare he? "Sweetheart?" he said softly.

"Yes?"

"I'll meet you by the door, alright? No rush."

"Okay."

Inside the changing room she sagged against the wall. Why couldn't he just be horrid, or lewd? Then she could just be angry with him, or offended. But this?

What was wrong with her? Why was she even tempted? She *loved* Donny, didn't she? But she couldn't have him. She hadn't dared look at his lips. Knew he'd been looking at hers. Why did she even want to kiss him again, never mind…? She could feel him, pressing against her, and Oh God, what was her body doing responding like that? This was his game, at which he was the master, and who played just for the sheer hell of it, and she the innocent novice!

She left the changing room, thanked the woman who handed her the windbreaker, and slipped it on, wanting the comfort of its softness and the sheer size of it to hide her body from the eyes that would be waiting for her.

Oh God! What would he say? She'd been sitting on him! Very much *on* him!

She threaded her way through the store to the door.

"Ready to go, kiddo?" OG smiled and she nodded, arms coming

around to hug herself.

"Are you cold?" Daryl asked, and reached over and, for the second time, did up the jacket, all the way to the top, pulling the collar up as well so only her nose and eyes peeked over.

She didn't miss the gesture; it was both concern and an indication that she had nothing to fear from him. Which she knew was only half true. She couldn't hold him accountable for the reactions of her own body.

"Let's get you home," he then said, and he stepped back, indicating that O'Grady open the door. He did, with a curious frown on his face, trying to work out what had gone on between the two of them.

Still, there was no shouting, swearing or tears in the car, which led OG and Mac to conclude that whatever had happened hadn't been that bad, and that considering the individuals in question, dealing with each other was always going to a steep learning curve.

Daryl asked to be dropped at the office. He knew from having held her in his hands that she'd felt something, but she didn't want to, or didn't trust where it might take her. But there was something else. This time she had not been completely resistant or even repulsed by him. Quite the opposite.

The door opened and he looked over at her, hoping for a clue as to what she was thinking. There was nothing.

"I'll see you at the weekend, for some leopard pictures?" he asked. "I trust you'll amaze me, on Friday night at Celeste?"

"Of course. It's what you rely on me for."

She sent him a small smile, but with guarded eyes.

He got out, nodded at O'Grady and walked towards the glass doors, with Mac at his shoulder.

She had no idea how he relied on her for far more than that.

TWO PAIRS OF eyes popped up to look at her over the back of the sofa. The apartment was too quiet, and if a shopping trip with her manager was a highlight of her day, then what the hell was that all about?

Going over to fuss her double-trouble jungle pile of furriness, and ending up on the floor with Lula chewing gently on her thumb, and Lazarus playing with her hair, his tail wrapped around her thigh, she found herself staring at the ceiling. The room felt like it was moving a little. How was she here? No longer scrounging for food. No longer afraid of shadows. (At least not as much as she had been.) No longer hiding under the radar. Living this life…but alone. Well, not quite alone…

Minutes passed as she mused the recent exchanges, the emerging emotions, noting the changes she saw in herself. Despite losing Donny, despite the contract that changed every second of her life, here she was… in her home. So many things she hadn't chosen, and so many things had happened, things she thought would break her, and yet…here she was.

A tongue licked her face, just to reconfirm her three-dimensional existence, and she smiled. But it faded a touch when she remembered Raju, because she felt so powerless.

I can't make him unblock me. I feel bad, but should I? He didn't even give me a chance to talk.

She frowned. It wouldn't take that long to hack in. Not do anything intrusive, just make sure he's…alright. Alive. Kicking. And then a thought, based on such a common expression…kicking…just how damaged was he? What had happened to him?

The next best thing could work. Then at least she'd know she'd explored all avenues before taking the final solution of hacking.

Pulling out the chair to her computer desk felt good. It had always been a skill she felt very familiar with. Confident, thanks to the Capello boys for corrupting her when so very young. An apprenticeship to last a lifetime, that was for sure.

Logging into her Ecce Facebook account, she thought of the few people from the group she had shared with Raju, who she knew he talked to, if infrequently. Trying to sound casual, she messaged one of them, just saying that she hadn't heard from Raju much recently, which had been unusual, and if they'd heard from him and if he was okay. Mentioning that she respected his privacy, and aware she was messaging another introvert, she knew her respect of his boundaries but genuine concern would be understood. She hit the send button, and felt hope swell around her heart.

I swear to God, if I can just sort this thing out with Raju, I'll never pretend to not be myself again in my life. Please. I just want to talk to him.

She hoped for a quick reply, but knew it might take a few hours. Not everybody was glued to their computers and devices. Raju was the one who seemed permanently online. Now she knew why. Was he paralysed from the waist down? Had he ever walked, or had he had an accident? All the questions she had thought already, about four dozen times, had made her feel guilty at unforeseen moments when enjoying her own ability to move and dance and run and skate.

As she went to log off, she saw a reply pop up: 'Hey, Ecce! I heard from R last week, discussing an algorithm. I was surprised, as I know you're the maths genius, but he said you were really busy with work at the moment. I was flattered to be his second choice! HAHA! Good to hear from you. I'm sure he appreciates you watching out for him. I know how private he can be. You're a good friend to have.'

Busy with work. An excuse that gave nothing away. Clearly he hadn't told anyone what had happened. Or who she was. But if he'd wanted to tell their circle they were no longer speaking then he could have, easily, and that would have made it more final, more definite. But he hadn't…

You're a good friend to have. She so wanted to be. Could she be? Again?

Maybe OG was right: he just needed some time to calm down, to get over the shock.

She typed a cheerful reply, offering to help with the algorithm anytime, if they needed, as she now had a gap in her work schedule, which was true enough. She hit Send and logged out, reassured Raju was okay, just pissed off with her, and embarrassed, maybe even ashamed – which he had no reason to be.

Perhaps it would okay.

The leopards trailed her as she headed to the kitchen to get a juice.

WHERE WAS HE? The game was starting in five minutes, and she thought he'd arrive at least a few minutes before. Then again, maybe he was tied up at the office. She turned the oven off and put everything back in the fridge. She fed the two bundles of fur, both of them circling and rubbing up against her legs. The photoshoot had gone well on Sunday afternoon – the awkwardness from the previous shopping trip having faded – and all three of them had flopped down onto the grass at the end and snoozed in the sun. When they'd stirred she had seen Daryl sitting just a few feet away, and he took some shots of her all sleepy, which she'd protested about. He seemed relaxed, and nothing she had done had annoyed him; in fact, he appeared to have enjoyed the slight chaos of trying to organise two leopards – one of whom was particularly lively! There had been so many she liked, but had chosen five to go in the New York apartment, at his suggestion. She glanced at the TV. Seeing the game paused was depressing. She wanted to watch live. Where was he?

She dialled. The call connected after two rings.

"Mysty?" He sounded happy to hear her voice.

"Daryl."

"Is anything the matter?"

"I was going to ask you the same. The ball game, it's already started. I just wondered what time you were coming over, or if something has happened that means you can't."

She held her breath, not sure if this was stepping over a big invisible line by questioning him. She could hear water. Not bath water, or the pool, but the ocean. Somewhere in the background a woman laughed. For some reason it rattled her.

"I'm afraid I'm going to have to miss it. Something came up to do with work. I should have sent a message, but this week has been so busy I didn't remember." It sounded like a weak excuse, but why did he sound genuinely unhappy?

She didn't like the lump of disappointment in her chest, and forced herself to ignore it, keeping her voice cheerful and relaxed – which was not how she felt. How could he forget to let her know? He, the most organised person on the planet, and he just forgot?

"That's okay. I understand. I'll…leave you to it."

Disconnect.

Five seconds later the phone buzzed.

"Mysty."

"Daryl."

"Can I take you out for dinner next week to make up for it? I honestly forgot." She heard more laughter, and the chinking of glasses. He was obviously on a yacht somewhere.

"Don't bother. Really. I'm not fussed. Enjoy your evening on the ocean."

Disconnect.

She glared at the phone and then strode back into the kitchen, grabbing a slice of pizza. She hadn't realised she'd been looking forward to it so much? Why was that? Why did she enjoy the teasing, the laughing a little? It had been fun watching with him last time. How could she have let herself be fooled into thinking he wasn't a complete selfish dick? And why did the idea of him lying to her make her so riled?

She lasted half an hour with the game, ate all the pizza, and switched the TV off and went into her computer room. She quickly accessed the security database and scanned through the signals being sent, knowing there would be a satellite watching Mr DB as much as one was always watching her. She found it and looped into the feed.

What a beautiful boat. Not a yacht, but a pleasure cruiser, sleek and white, with multiple decks and walkways. She saw a hot tub and a small pool. And there he was, on a sofa, still dressed, though with jacket and tie gone, champagne flute in hand. There were five naked women in front of him, either in the hot tub or sitting on the edge, all with a glass of champagne, glancing over at him occasionally to make sure they weren't wanted. They all looked happy, and were all very beautiful – of course. From his pose, she would say he did not look happy, however; and the way he finished the champagne in one swallow and dangled the elegant glass from his fingers revealed more frustration than enjoyment.

But she was feeling far from sympathetic. Something came up 'to do with work'…that was one way of putting it. Why couldn't he just have been honest about where he was? She felt the ache in her chest again. Why would he want to watch a ball game with her, and eat pizza and drink beer, when he could have champagne and a choice of five women to satisfy him? Or all five, for that matter…

She was tempted to ring him again and ask him outright if the 'work' thing was going okay. But she didn't; she didn't want him to know she'd been curious (or nosy) enough to look.

As she watched he stood up, strolled over to an ice bucket and poured himself some more champagne. The women joined him, five pairs of hands removing his clothes easily, until he was left in nothing but his swimming shorts. Mysty knew the image was many miles away, but she still blushed. That torso, so strong; the long, toned legs and slender hips. Dear God, what a man. Donny had been gorgeous, but he was… She couldn't even think of a word to do him justice.

His hand rested on the head of the woman who had gone to her knees to remove his shoes, and she looked up at him. The rest drifted back to the hot tub with their champagne.

He went to the sofa and sat down. The woman crawled across the deck to him, sensually, and used her teeth to undo the buttons on his shorts. He didn't look at her. He was staring at something far off in the distance, his drink poised in a hand. And she couldn't look away, even as the woman swallowed him in her mouth and her head bobbed over him, his legs parted as she feasted upon his flesh.

Mysty felt ill, but her eyes were fixed on the screen as the woman's hands crept over his thighs and she moved her body to get a better angle, and ramped up the tempo. From the ripple that went through his body she guessed he had climaxed. He hadn't even touched her. He took a sip of his drink, his other arm draped along the back of the sofa. Even from the angle of the satellite feed, she could see there was no expression on his face whatsoever.

It all seemed so wrong. So meaningless.

The woman remained kneeling on the floor before him, and retied his swimming shorts, and he handed her his champagne glass. She drank, but still received no word. And then he got up and dived in the pool.

Mysty got up and went to get a drink, the ice-cold orange juice refreshing but almost harsh on the back of her throat. She sat back down in front of the computer and searched around in the database, looking at different camera feeds on the boat. She saw Mac sitting in one of the rooms with a number of other guys, watching the game.

She flicked again, and there in the stateroom, she saw him again. Two of the girls were drying him off with a towel, his face dark and serious, not the charming Don Juan more suited to the naked frivolity on offer around him. They then removed his shorts, without a word. Mysty refused to look at his…and instead concentrated on what was going on around him. She'd heard he was a legend in the bedroom – and how many times had he as good as told her himself! – and that he was insatiable.

And then her jaw dropped. A figure appeared in the room, dressed from head to foot in black. But not just any black…the outfit from her Celeste performance of Back in Black, complete with shades! The woman prowled in front of him, wearing heels higher than Mysty could ever wear, teasing him, daring him. With one hand on her wrist, he turned her and manoeuvred her towards a table, with controlled force and breathtaking arrogance. The other two stepped up and secured the imitation Butterfly's wrists with cuffs and bent her over. Her insides shuddered as she saw him step up behind her and, after doing things to her with his hands that she couldn't see, he thrust into her, and her back flexed as a small cry of pleasure broke the silence.

Mysty knew this was not what her innocent mind wanted to see, but she had to know, had to gain insight into this man who had hurt her and trapped her and shown her kindness, sometimes, and who she now couldn't tear her eyes away from.

The other women then slid down beside him, lips nibbling over his buttocks, rocking themselves against him. The woman in the cuffs gripped tightly onto the table edge, her face pressed against the surface. She gasped and he moved faster, and the women wrapped around his thighs gasped too, there appearing to be no shame in using his thighs for their pleasure. With a low moan of pleasure, his final convulsion deep and strong, and the woman on the table cried out too. He then stepped away as the black-clad woman was released from her cuffs. He was handed a robe, which he shrugged on, leaving the women to amuse themselves for a little while.

Don't stop now, she heard herself thinking, *I've heard you can go all night, you bastard.* What was he thinking, having one of them dress up as *her*? What kind of game was this? She could not believe what she'd just seen. This was like a porn scene, one in which she knew the porn star. She felt used without even having been on that boat. Was that what he thought of doing to her, whenever he looked at her?

She leaned back in her chair and took another swallow of juice, her mind a tumble of thoughts and feelings. She thought he'd enjoyed spending time with her, despite not getting fucked. Clearly that was a lie. That was all he wanted. No doubt the few hours spent with her had been rather empty and tedious for him. She felt so foolish she could have cried. But worst part was, she'd *wanted* to believe he was a better man than the arrogant asshole who had taken over her life and blackmailed her into signing a contract; that behind that was the man who just wanted to enjoy pizza and a ball game. Why? Why had she wanted to? She didn't quite know.

It wasn't long before he was naked again, and this time he was joined by all five women. She peered closer. What was that sparkling around their necks? She zoomed in and saw the 'DB' in what must be diamonds on platinum chains. Only the best for his whores. Thank God he had never given her jewellery. And she would never wear that stupid windbreaker again.

They gathered around him, one boldly sliding her tongue over his hip to his groin and then straddling him. Once again she pondered the fact that none of them seemed bothered being naked in front of each other. It was surreal. There was something else… And then it hit her. They were all blonde-ish. They all had some resemblance to herself. And they were all wearing shades.

Her hand went unconsciously to her mouth, to keep the horror and the words she couldn't quite believe she was thinking in check. What the…?

He put his hands behind his head and let her ride him, finally moving to turn her over, obviously not satisfied with the pleasure she was giving him. She held her hands away from him, so she couldn't touch, and her legs wrapped around his hips. Pure surrender. Mysty felt some inside her move watching the first powerful thrust, his face taut, devoid of any joy, intense with desire but not happy. The woman beneath him writhed, hips arching to meet his, to let him deeper. Another woman put her face to the once place Mysty could not believe anyone would, using her lips and tongue to tease him, whilst the others played between each other's legs, use their mouths and fingers. It was beyond her wildest imaginings.

Mysty didn't realise until she felt a drip of wet on her knee that she was crying. Eyes huge and transfixed on the orgy of carnal pleasure before her. Part of her didn't understand at all; part of her rejected the overt surrender to the purely physical. It was so debauched, so decadent, so… unloving.

The woman beneath Daryl was begging him to fuck her harder, and then she screamed, body rocking with her ecstasy, his own fast on her heels.

She couldn't take any more. She turned the system off, glad of the empty silence. But she couldn't forget the scenes in her head. Something dark and primitive called her, despite the fact it repelled her. Why did some part of her want to know what it was that felt so good that she, too, would scream?

She had to get out for a while. She was too trapped in the jungle of fame he had created around her to go wherever she wished, so she made a call.

"OG."

"Kiddo? You alright? You watching the game?"

"No." She pulled on her boots. "Listen, I need to go out. Just an hour. You can follow in the car if you like, but I'm going anyway."

"You want to go for a run? Now?" he asked in surprise. She could hear him getting up from wherever he had been sitting down. Her voice had obviously given her away. "Mysty, what's wrong?"

"Doesn't matter. Don't worry, I won't be going far. Not as far as I'd like anyway."

Disconnect.

She went and stood on the balcony, loving the ripple of air around her. One push of her legs and she was standing on the railing. She glanced down. It was not the first time she'd done this, from here, and it was well within her abilities. She spread her arms, just as she heard the front door open, and pushed off. It was beautiful, just like always, the air pushing against her, and she turned, curled and dived, as fearless as ever.

Safely on the ground, in a low predatory crouch of readiness, she heard a shout from high up. She only smiled, pushed her shades over her eyes and started running. In the distance she heard two Bentleys roaring after her.

"Is she going for some kind of fucking medal!"

O'Grady watched the satellite feed in the back of the Bentley as she soared from one building to another, crossing huge divides without hesitation. It was a tense fifty minutes later that she somersaulted over a high fence and finally slowed to a jog, and then sauntered towards the entrance of her building, where a row of grey suits was waiting for her. No one tried to speak or touch her. She pressed the button for the lift. OG came striding through the door, looking angry but concerned.

She felt so much better. Satan could pay for whatever he liked to keep him amused. What she possessed was far too priceless for him to understand.

Before OG could say anything, she said, "I want to leave at 8.30am tomorrow morning, and we won't be coming back. We'll head straight to Vegas, and then to Washington."

"Fine. I can get that sorted. Will you tell me what's wrong?"

"Maybe. Right now I don't have the words." She saw such concern on his face that it almost undid her. She gave him a quick hug. "I'll see you in the morning."

And she was gone.

Half an hour later she got a message. From him: 'What was the score?'

She messaged back: 'Curious as to why you should ask me when you have more computer access than anyone on the planet. Mac watched it; you could ask him. Or one of your harem girls could check for you – unless of course they're only good with knobs, not buttons. Either way I can't say. I didn't watch it. I don't know.'

Daryl read the message in the hot tub under the starry sky, one girl under the water, another massaging his shoulders. He hurled the phone across the deck and watched it smash impressively, the rush of the ocean around him only highlighting the violence. Hands hovered over his skin for a second, then continued as if nothing had happened.

Shit! And he'd spent most of his evening wishing he'd been with her, on her sofa eating pizza and sipping beer, waiting for her to smile at him as brightly as a sunbeam as they chatted and teased each other whilst half-watching the game. Not that she would believe him.

Fuck.

"O'GRADY."

"Mr Blackmoor, sir."

"I'll be round in half an hour. I want to see her before she leaves. Is she alright?"

"We're leaving in twenty minutes according to schedule, sir. She brought it forward last night, after going for a…run. As to the other point, she would say yes, I would say no. Something upset her last night but she won't tell me what."

Well that was something. She was upset about having been stood up! A zing of anticipation and excitement shot up his spine.

"I'll be round in five minutes. Don't tell her I'm coming."

Disconnect.

As he went into the apartment, OG simply said, "Computer room."

He'd never seen this room before. It was crammed full of stuff. Not just stuff, but machines he couldn't always identify: screens, electrical items, tools, lights, magnifying lenses, a dartboard, wires, boxes of parts, tall cabinets with multiple drawers, a sewing machine, scraps of cloth…

"Toby, is the download complete and the case fully charged?"

His eyes rested on the jewel of the eclectic collection of items, her body bent over, typing into the keypad.

"Yes."

"Disengage and check voltage."

"Disengaged and all safe."

She whizzed across the room on the chair, picked something up with the utmost care and laid it in a box, securing it down and snapping the lid closed. A call came through.

"Richard."

"Mysty."

"You have my five minutes?"

"I have three and a half."

"You know I need a minimum of five. Ideally, I'd like seven. Three is no good."

"I know it's just…we're a little stuck as to where to take this next… to get an improvement."

What is she talking about?

"Send over the latest results and I'll look it over. It won't be till Sunday, probably, when you hear from me. I'm a bit busy until then." She pulled over two other computer panels and checked some details.

He was captivated seeing the genius at work.

"Oh yes, I heard. Meeting the president, no less."

"Trust me, I'd take a pass on it if I could. So…" She began typing again. "Have you tried layering? Alternately? And elemental substitution?"

"Err no. I'll do that today and get those results to you as well. If I break five minutes do I get to take you out for lunch?"

"Break five minutes and I'll take you for lunch, how about that?"

"I think you'll get your five minutes very soon."

"Good, because I've been waiting a long time. Go be useful. I'll speak to you soon."

"Enjoy Washington."

"Yeah, like a hole in my head. I'm sorry, I have another call…ciao." A breath. "Maria."

The next conversation was in fast Spanish.

Something trundled past Daryl, and he looked down to see Lazarus towing a case by a cord, with Lula next to him. He ducked out of sight as she rolled over on the chair and fussed them both, before telling Lazarus to take the case back out into the hall and putting it with the rest. Lulu jumped up to be fussed, and it was then that she noticed him. Well, his shoes.

Her eyes rose up to his. "What are you doing here?"

"I wanted see you before you disappear. I didn't mean to royally screw-up last night's ball game and pizza."

"Royally screw. What a choice phrase. Must have been a very important *work* event…"

"Quite important, yes, but I'd much rather have been here."

"Oh…I think we both know that's not true." She switched the main computer off, and everything in the room shut down, and sturdy barriers descended from the ceiling to partition off all the work benches and computer equipment. Everything designed just so, and operated at her command. "I think it's fairly obvious that I am nowhere near exciting enough for you."

He stayed very still. And quiet.

"You lie so well, don't you?

She stepped around him.

In the kitchen he watched as she finalised the details of her departure, in between fussing the leopards – and praising Lula for finding her dance mat, which was tucked inside a suitcase.

"You're going to be a great mother one day; you're so organised," OG said cheerfully, watching from the side lines.

"As long as it doesn't involve an actual male and actual intercourse." They were harsh words, which startled both men. "Are you going to leave, or just continue staring?" she directed at Daryl, who had fallen silent, wondering just what she knew, and the implications…

"I wondered if you might play the drums, before you go, so I can see how well you're getting along with them."

Was he insane? "*You want me to play the drums for you*? Are you asking, or telling me?"

"I'm asking."

"And there was me hoping you'd give me the wrong answer and give me the perfect reason to tell you to go to hell. Fine. I'll assume your ears are the *one* part of your body not subject to overuse."

Daryl's head was in turmoil – Oh God! What exactly had she seen? Please not all of yesterday's…

"It gets pretty loud," OG warned him, and the bodyguard indicated two screens. "This screen is the original of whatever song she chooses to do; this screen shows her drumming patterns."

The music started: Fall Out Boy's 'America's Suitehearts'.

As was usually the case, he couldn't take his eyes off her as she absolutely became one with the music. Her hair was loose, her hands so sure, and her voice joined the male lead, the power and the mournful conviction needed all there.

At the end of the song she went straight to another: 'Thnks fr th Mmrs'. He felt the lyrics as deeply as sang them: '*I only think in the form of crunching numbers, in hotel rooms, collecting pay sheets, lovers. Get me out of my mind, get you out of those clothes. I'd find a way to get you in the mood… one night and one more time…*'

The last piece was one he recognised, and her take on Pink's 'U + Ur Hand'. He was pretty sure the 'hand' in the chorus got changed to 'harem', and the message was loud and clear. His behaviour had landed him right back to square one.

She put the drumsticks down and got up to leave.

"Mysty wait."

"Why?" She strode from the room and picked Lula up.

"Don't just walk away…"

He dared to touch her arm and her reflex was so quick it was scary, her eyes flaring bright at him in warning. "*Don't touch me* or so help me *God* I will break your hand."

She nodded to OG, called Lazarus and left, a wake of men carrying suitcases behind her.

Fuck. Even the expletive reminded him of what he'd done. Going after her was not a good idea. She would probably – definitely – hit him. Hard.

"How did she manage to see what happened last night?" he asked Mac.

"You know how good she is. She would have hacked into the private cameras on the boat. Why did she doubt you when you said you were working?"

"She must have heard the sound of the waves." He'd forgotten about her superb hearing.

I'm such a fucking idiot. He'd never lied to her before. Why had he this time? How the hell was he going to pull Washington off, the presidential dispensation, now?

He glanced at the sofa, the one he should have been on last night, with her, and a wave of weariness washed over him. He was sure he would never be invited back. Why hadn't he just told her the truth? She might not have liked it, but at least she would have respected him. He'd so badly needed the physical release…but all he'd wanted was her.

Mac followed him out of the now silent apartment and shut the door. Any assumptions about a straightforward conquest in the wake of Donny walking away were now thoroughly blown out the water.

HE'D JUST WATCHED the recording of her special MJ performance for the fourth time, and decided for the hundredth time that she really was the most creative person on the planet. He was very tempted to go over there and try and speak to her. What he saw on camera, however, told him it would not be a good idea. She was still quietly fuming; she would not listen.

He had only one alternative. He pressed in the call.

It was answered, but there was no greeting, just silence. He could see her quite clearly, sitting on the sofa, with Lula on her shoulder, working on something on a laptop.

"Mysty. You can't stop talking to me."

"No, I know, so I'll just talk to you as little as possible."

"How are you feeling?"

"Okay."

"The press release from Celeste is saying incredible things about tonight's performance. I trust it's not anything like Fortuna?"

"Nowhere near. I'm just giving the world and the press exactly what they want."

"And what is that?"

"A goddess."

"I see. I might need somewhere new for some more pictures."

"Was that it?"

"Yes."

Disconnect.

Only one set of claw marks. Not bad, considering.

He walked towards the bathroom, intending on having a long relaxing soak in the deep tub – alone – before getting ready for the event that was sending the media wild with anticipation. What did she have planned? Craig was similarly in the dark, telling him she had been illusive and secretive – which always meant she had something brilliant tucked up her sleeve. He wondered if she knew the president was going to be there tonight? This was the reason why Harvey and the boys wouldn't be with him tonight, as he would be entertaining slightly more elevated company in his private box. Hopefully she wouldn't send any more spears up at the glass, as it would be an awkward conversation explaining why she was so angry with him.

He disliked many things in his life but above all, he decided, pulling off his shirt, he hated it when she was so angry with him he felt they might never share another moment of laughter again. She'd been pretty angry before; but this time…this time they'd shared something, and he'd trampled it, and he had no idea what to do about that.

He hoped their well-earned holiday wouldn't be seven days of her cold shoulder.

DARYL RUBBED A hand over his eyes. How the hell had she done that? If this was her entrance, what was she saving for the show? The car had pulled up, and the door had opened, but no Mysty emerged; instead, a gold cane floated from the car, followed by golden butterflies that danced in the air around it. The last one spiralled faster, and expanded and then flashed, until there she was, in gold from head to toe, hands on her hips – to a collective gasp from the waiting press and fans. A single butterfly danced in the air beside her, and she let it land on her finger as she took the cane in her other hand.

What followed was one of the most amazing shows she'd ever done. In an outfit of pearl-white, she whirled to 'Promise' by one of her favourite bands, Within Temptation, stretching and contracting in amazing shapes and twists. Utterly breathtaking to watch, wholly impossible to fully comprehend, with effects that involved air born red roses and the gaping red mouth of a volcano, Daryl found it hard to breathe as she finally fell, a broken figure under a pair of wings, like a glorious bird struck down in flight.

A pool of red began to spread across the floor.

The lights dropped, and then rose again.

She was gone.

President Marshall looked around at Daryl. "Is she real?"

"Very much so. You'll be meeting her tomorrow. I'm sure after that you'll be more than convinced."

"I think I need another drink."

Daryl smiled and raised a hand for the waiter.

This was going to be one hell of an interesting weekend.

When 'Deceiver of Fools' began, Daryl felt a horrible creep along his spine. Despite her having told him it wasn't, he realised this was going to be another Fortuna-style performance. There was nothing he could do except sit it out as the music and voices swelled around the arena, haunting, portentous, a breeze wafting through the air as if there was something there around them. The hairs stood up on his neck. Had she done that?

There was just enough light in the darkness to pick out a huge 3D skull hovering above the arena, made of what looked like smoke and cloud. It dropped, and moved over the audience, as if looking for someone or something, prowling, feeding on the fear in the people below. As they shivered under its spell, it suddenly broke apart, turning into a swirling vortex of light, like an entrance to a wormhole in a sci-fi movie, or a tornado of satanic cloud. A flaming pentagram etched itself into the floor. The atmosphere was crackling with tension, but aware of imminent doom or deliverance.

'*No light in the darkness is too small to see; there's always a sparkle, if you just believe...*' A bright crystal light glowed high up in the darkness, and Daryl knew it had to be her. The voices faded and the music rose, drums beat their rhythm and trumpets beckoned. The single light moved and dropped fifty feet, and she was there, landing on a beam and suddenly illuminated, in a costume that looked like it was made of a million diamonds. She ran as the music began to pound and soar, diving off the beam into dark nothingness, taking her light with her.

'*But darkness is looking; he will sell your soul...*' a thunderbolt and she high up again – how the? – and she jumped, falling fast, twisting and turning, aiming at the very centre of a swirling vortex of black cloud. Another thunderbolt and she disappeared into the darkness, the lights whirling in a writhing mass around her. Like a mirrored vase breaking apart, the blinding effect made it impossible to see where she'd gone. Only the Butterfly symbol remained in bright white lights on the floor of the arena. No trace of the pentagram; no trace of her.

This time it was Daryl who looked at the president, who was obviously trying to process what he had just seen. He stood up and patched through to OG as he manoeuvred past the second line of presidential dignitaries, who were equally speechless.

"O'Grady," he whispered.

"Sir?"

"Is she alright? These pieces are exceptional, but they must be tiring her out."

"She has a forty-minute break now, and she assures me she's okay. She's a bit wobbly, but nothing too bad. I've got the chopper on the roof to get us to the plane. She can sleep on the flight, and eat if she's able to. I don't think we'll do a crowd-walk tonight."

"Sound plan. How did she do that...with the butterflies...when she got out of the car?"

"Honestly, sir, I have no idea. And I really don't think I'd understand the physics even if she told me. However she does it, it's well, bloody miraculous."

There's a quote for a newspaper headline, Daryl thought.

"Let me know if you're worried about her, and message me when you're safely on the plane. Aside from that, I guess I'll be seeing you at the White House tomorrow."

"Yes, sir."

"Take care of her, O'Grady."

"Always, sir."

Disconnect.

Daryl sighed, saddened by the reminder they would be flying separately, and that he couldn't even call her to congratulate her. She wouldn't want to hear his praise.

He prepared himself for another conversation with the men of state. He'd much rather have her next to him exchanging teasing insults and smiling. At least tomorrow he would see her.

Until then he had one last act and then his cameras to rely on.

The third set. Before them was a tropical rainforest, full of colour. Birds flew and called to each other; butterflies rose and insects buzzed. He knew it was all computer generated, but it was so real. 'In Perfect Harmony' by Within Temptation filled the air.

From the floor rose the vast bud of a flower, opening slowly, the petals curling to reveal her lying, foetal-position, in the centre. '*In a world so far way, at the end of a closing day, a little child was born and raised... deep in the forest on a hidden plain; mother never saw her face; ancient spirits of the forest made her queen of elves and trees... She was the only human being who lived in harmony...*' As delicately as one of the butterflies around her, she rose, and stepped onto the branch of a tree – one of her amazing, moving beams – and moved, as if in slow motion, through the forest. No corner was missed, allowing every one of her rapt audience a chance to see her. Tree branches followed her progress, and colourful birds swooped and flew with her, truly a being of harmony.

'*A thousand seasons they passed her by; so many times she said goodbye. And when the spirits called out her name, to join for ever a spirit to stay, so a spirit she became...*' She was in the centre of the arena now, and flew into the air, arms wrapped around herself as she turned, and a golden light covered her, like the weaving of a cocoon.

And then, as if an ancient spirit herself, reincarnated many times over, the gold light fused, swirled and then faded away, and she was gone. A moment later she re-emerged, clothed in a Grecian dress of shimmering gold, a garland of flowers in her hair. Her beauty was that that it almost hurt the eyes it was so pure and bright.

She stood, letting the audience catch up with her re-appearance, hands gracefully by her sides, and then dived backwards to land in the flower she had emerged from. The sunlight faded, and the petals closed over her, and lifted away, like an immortal being taken back to the heavens. The simulated forest disintegrated slowly, everything turning to gold, and a hundred thousand butterflies rose like a cloud to the roof of the arena. And vanished.

Wow.

There was a full five seconds of utter silence, and then the cheering broke out, the audience's reaction astounding.

What a night.

"You know, Daryl, I really didn't think I would see anything to top her MJ performance, but actually, she's outdone herself. That was out of this world. I can't believe she does all that herself," President Marshall said.

"I agree with you. I should warn you, though, there will be a bonus set of MJ songs available in a few weeks. I've seen it, and it's incredible, to say the least."

"Good God. I can see now why you've been out the office a bit more lately. Must be quite tempting having her so close at hand." Marshall gave Daryl a knowing look.

"Hmm. Well, just to warn you, she might not be in the best mood tomorrow."

"Why ever not?"

"She's not too happy with me at the moment."

"I've heard she has a temper to reckon with. I'd have thought you'd enjoy that. Only so many times a man wants a woman to roll over. A bit of a fight is far more satisfying, not to mention interesting both long and short term – not that you need me to tell you that, I'm sure." Marshall stood, leaving Daryl slightly stunned. He had certainly not expected him to say anything like that. "I'd better go, I'm sorry I can't stay longer, but I'm looking forward to brunch with you tomorrow at the White House as agreed, yes?"

Daryl stood and took the offered hand. "Of course. Mysty will be arriving as little later, as arranged."

"Excellent. Well, enjoy your evening. Good luck with the tiger-taming."

And with a wink, he was gone.

Dear God. Were his intentions so bloody obvious, even to Marshall? The man didn't know him that well…or did he? Or was he just a perceptive enough man to see the determined, possessive look in his eyes, and recognise in her a woman any sane man would want to call his own, but few would attempt to make so. What would happen when she recognised that look in his eyes as well? Would she understand or reject it completely?

He downed his martini in one swallow and put the glass put down.

Only time would tell.

But, just as the song had said, no light was too small; there was always a glimmer of hope, even in the darkest night.

He sat back down and watched the arena empty, in no rush to go anywhere after that visual banquet. A short while later message beeped. It was O'Grady telling him they were safely in the chopper, and that she was exhausted but alright. Mostly.

'Mostly?' he messaged back.

'The bright lights have made her eyes ache. No appetite. Just wants to sleep.'

'Does she want to see Baden, to get her eyes checked?'

'No. Nothing wrong with her vision, just that they "hurt like fuck" – her words not mine.'

'Make sure she gets all the rest she can.'

'Don't worry, she's in good hands.'

She would be in even better hands if I could care for her.

"Mac, get the car, we might as well make a move."

Time to leave the magic of the arena behind.

SEATED IN THE secretary of state's chair, behind a large and organised desk, he dialled through.

Three rings and the screen lit up. It was Lula, her big searching eyes reminding him of the girl he so wanted to see instead. Lazarus joined her, and growled at the screen. He was just glad they were across town.

"Lazarus, don't teach Lula to growl at the screen." She picked the cub up and flopped down in the chair. "Oh. Well, now I completely understand."

Lazarus jumped up onto the seat next to her and kept his eyes fixed on Daryl.

"Good morning. How are you feeling?"

"Fine. What do you want? Aren't you at the White House already?"

"I am, but I wanted to see how you were. O'Grady mentioned a couple of things that concerned me. How are yours eyes now?"

"Better. Only very bright lights irritate them now. And having to look at you."

He ignored the barb; knew there would be more of them.

"Good, I'm glad. I trust you'll think of a way to avoid that next time?" A nod. "It was an astounding show. I think the press are struggling to find words for you."

"I can sympathise. I have that problem talking about you."

Yep. There was more.

"The president was immensely impressed. He's very much looking forward to meeting you." No reaction. "I hope whatever your personal inclinations are towards throwing me off a bridge – preferably not in box – you will still be your polite self with him?"

"Is that a tactful way of asking me not to swear, throw insults at you, and generally make my true feelings about having to be in the same room as you abundantly clear to the assembled gathering of dignitaries and senators?" He almost smiled at the clipped words. He sometimes forgot her mother was English.

"Yes."

"Well, just say it next time. You know I have no problem with *honesty*..."

He should have seen that one coming. "Mysty, I didn't want to lie, I just–"

"Didn't want to tell me the truth, either. No. I can understand that. Still doesn't really make it any better. Whatever you've done to me before, you've never lied. I think that takes you to a new low in my estimations. Only cowards lie."

"I didn't lie about forgetting about the ball game. I did, and I wish to God I hadn't, alright?"

"Oh, come now, don't perjure yourself in the White House; leave that to the president. You expect me to believe you'd rather watch a ball game with me than fuck your little troupe of harem women forwards, backwards and upside down? No. I may be young, and I may no longer be innocent, but I'm not stupid."

He didn't miss the wording. He could well imagine her innocent horror at the orgy that played out before her.

"You stayed watching for a while then."

"I figured you owed me some entertainment, given how much I've given you over the years. You really must pay them a great deal. They're very convincing lesbians, aren't they? And the black outfit? And the blonde hair? How do you fit all those requirements on the advertisement?"

Heat in his cheeks and a sick sensation roiled in his stomach as the extent of what she had seen became clear. His guilt was undeniable.

"It's not what you think."

"No? It's just a coincidence they all have blonde-ish hair, then? And that black outfit that I designed – wow! – that is commitment. You do like your handcuffs, don't you?"

"It's not just me who thought it looked rather attractive. You'll find wives and girlfriends across the country dress up to look like you. You're not just a star, you're regarded as the sexiest women on the planet – what did you expect?" A hand covered her eyes and Lula looked away from the screen to her face, sensing the distress from the tightening of muscles in the body she was sitting on.

"Shame I didn't think of trying that outfit out on Donny…" The sarcasm was at least aimed at herself, giving him some respite from her rapier-sharp tongue.

"He wouldn't have touched you, no matter what you did. It wasn't anything you lacked; it was only because he loved everything you were that he had to walk away."

"It's like bloody Shakespeare, with his 'star-crossed lovers'. Romeo and bloody Juliet. Everyone thinks it's so fucking romantic and they have no idea."

Lula decided the tension was reaching critical, and made an attempt to get into the black robe to snuggle closer to the soft warm skin, making Daryl smile.

"Lula…no…why must you…

"I can wholly sympathise."

"Shut up. Have you got an office in the White House as well?"

"No, I'm borrowing one from Charles Brentford."

"The secretary of state."

"Yes."

"Wow. Such important friends. Do you lie to them, too?"

"Mysty…"

"Did you choose that tie you're wearing?"

It was gold and ivory; simple and classy. He wasn't fooled; he knew it looked good. She was just irritated because he was wearing her trademark colours.

"Yes, but I admit I was distracted by the screaming of my housekeeper. She can't help her enthusiasm and appreciation when I bend her over my desk. Best way to start the day. After fucking my chambermaid, of course."

She knew he was only saying it to irritate her, but a blush still coloured her cheeks.

"Would you just stop this, for God's sake? Stop pretending everything's okay, because it's not!"

Disconnect.

She really didn't get it, he knew that. He would give them all up for her; for one week with her, one day, one night. Even one hour. He'd lain on that bed, with all the hands caressing him, pleasuring him, and had actually just wanted it to mean something. He'd actually just wanted to be with her, talking and occasionally laughing.

"Daryl?"

He looked up in surprise. "Charles."

"We're about to go through for brunch – are you finished?"

Daryl turned off the screen and moved around the desk. "Yes, of course."

"How is she this morning?"

He regarded the older man. Charles refused to be intimidated by the raised eyebrow and quelling eyes, his quiet smile still firm on his lips. He didn't know what to say, but knew he'd already given himself away, so denial was pointless.

"Feisty, to say the least. As per usual." He nodded at Mac, who had been waiting outside the room, and he fell into step a few feet behind them, with another three behind him.

"Just imagine what it'll be like you're married; all that daily excitement to keep you busy."

"Have you been hitting the brandy a bit early, Charles?" Daryl looked round in amazement at his colleague, not sure how he felt about someone being so forthright.

"No, Daryl, just promise me I get an invite to the wedding. Don't worry; I know how to keep my mouth shut."

Charles winked and opened the door, and Daryl found himself in a room with some of the most important men in government, all of whom stood to greet him. No time to say any more; the charming sociable mask was pulled down.

Everyone was in good spirits. All still on a bit of a high, he guessed, after seeing her spell-binding performance last night.

Please let her be in a better mood when she gets here.

Please let her wear what we agreed upon.

OG AND A troop of six grey suits led her from the underground car park under the White House. The secret service guys waiting for her arrival followed them in, deeper into the labyrinth of tunnels and rooms beneath the great building devoted to governance and surveillance. OG knew something was in the air. Her determined march didn't help his unease, or the defiant gleam in her eye.

"Well, here she is, in all her glory," the lead security officer said, perhaps a little too exuberantly. She regarded him, quietly, intently. She was obviously in no mood to respond. "Er, welcome to the White House, ma'am," he corrected, and began the standard protocol for admittance, which included a pat-down of all present for weapons – something that elicited barely restrained enjoyment when it came to Mysty, who received 'extra-special attention'.

When they had finished and indicated that the party proceed, the same officer eyed Mysty up and down.

"Seems you're clear," he said.

"Seems you're not so good at your job," she replied, and removed the knives she had concealed in her boots. She handed them to him, and his previous sneer somewhat froze on his face. "I'll collect them when I leave."

OG observed the men as they passed through the barriers, and saw the exchanged looks. They were cocky, and had obviously enjoyed the search, and the power it gave them to touch her, despite the disgrace of not finding the knives. OG looked at Mysty. Her mood was worsening.

She stayed centre of the group, who now escorted her up into the building itself and down long corridors, bound for the company of the most influential man in America: President Thomas Marshall, not Mr Daryl Blackmoor.

"Sweet Holy God, some days it's good to be the president."

Daryl followed the president's gaze, and there she was, all around her captivated.

Daryl groaned inwardly, as much as the sight of her stirred every cell in his body. What the hell was she wearing? He should have guessed she'd throw his 'recommendations' back in his face.

In the white shirt – but tied at the waist, with the collar up and the sleeves rolled up – and black hot pants that were as good as sprayed on, she strolled towards them in death-defying black, thigh-high, high-heeled boots. Her hair tumbled and curled around her face. The hat was on. The shades were on. Utterly beautiful, but utterly inappropriate!

"I'm so glad she came as herself. I was worried her wardrobe people would make her wear something vastly dull, but no, here she is, just as fantastic as she is on stage."

Marshall's words caused him to turn and look. The president meant every word. No doubt. He then glanced at O'Grady, who looked unsettled, and attempted a silent message which was not understood.

She stopped a few feet from Marshall, her leopards stopping with her, and then raised a hand and removed the shades.

"Mysty. So good to meet you finally. You are certainly the most beautiful guest to visit the White House!"

She let go of the cane and took his offered hand.

"Mr President."

The cane stayed where it was, a white butterfly hovering above the tip. He wanted to know how she was doing this. He wasn't the only one a little taken aback. Marshall faltered for a second as he observed it.

"I see…you really are everything you are on stage and screen."

Her hand calmly reclaimed the waiting cane.

"Indeed. I would not wish to disappoint."

"Well, let me introduce you." Marshall took a step back, indicating the men gathered around him.

"I was not aware I was going to get such a welcome. Half the Cabinet is here," she said.

Daryl kept his surprise to himself. He hadn't known she paid any attention to politics. Or else she had done her homework.

"I don't think I could have kept them away!" he said. "Mysty, may I present Charles Brentford, Secretary of State."

"Mysty, delighted. Truly, you're a wonder. I now understand why my daughter and grand-daughters are so obsessed with you." A blush tinted her cheeks, and the tension in her face relaxed a little at the genuine compliment from the friendly older man. "Personally, I have heard all about you from Daryl."

Her eyes briefly touched on his, then returned to Charles. "Dear me. I wonder what on earth he could possibly have been saying. He can be a little grumpy sometimes – too much work."

"That is why I rely on you, Mysty, to distract me." He dared to step forward, wanting to be closer to the brilliance of her.

"And what, might I ask, do I rely on you for?"

Charles was grinning like a Cheshire cat and looked over at Daryl, who was not enjoying being put on the spot.

"Keeping you busy and out of mischief."

"Ah. Such a devoted manager."

Charles actually laughed. The President reined his chuckle in. He hadn't missed the dangerous glint in her eyes, and decided to distract the duellists by introducing her to the rest of the party.

"Will you introduce us to your companions," he then said.

"Lazarus," she gestured, and the larger cat stepped forward and offered a paw. The president bent to shake it, and Daryl knew the reporters at the end of the garden who would be clicking away, loving this. "And Lula." She stepped back and patted her hip, the smaller leopard not needing a second invitation, and she jumped up into Mysty's arms. "She's young still, so very curious. But she won't bite if you want to offer your hand."

The president did so, and he was sniffed and licked.

"She's fantastic! I can see she is more than happy." She got a wide smile from the president, and regarded him with bright, intelligent eyes. "Why don't we go inside and get a drink."

The party progressed into another room, and Daryl followed at a distance, feeling the familiar bite of jealousy as he watched her with the president. Even with Marshall she was relaxed and confident.

"Apparently you've done another twelve Michael Jackson songs, Mysty? How do you think they compare with those you performed at the concert?" Marshall asked.

"I did all of them to the best of my ability, and with every consideration towards the original work. They should all be equally as good."

"I have to say, I thought the concert was absolutely brilliant. A long time since I've been to such an occasion, as you might imagine, but… truly fantastic."

"That's very nice of you to say so," she replied.

"Would you do one now?"

"Would I what? Sir?"

"Would you do one of the songs now? Here? The sound equipment is all ready, so just sing whichever song you want."

Her eyes – wide and surprised – then narrowed in accusation as she looked at Daryl. Had he planned this? But, in reality, he was as surprised as she was – and a little annoyed. How could Marshall just land this on her? She wasn't there to entertain!

"Well, I doubt there's any way I can refuse," she responded politely, but there was an edge to her voice that those who knew her well enough would recognise. "Do you have a request?"

"'Working Day and Night' – that was my absolute favourite."

"Fine. Let the sound people know." She turned away and she touched a finger to her ear. "Mason, come in. Seems I was right." Daryl stepped forward, planning on intervening, but with a click of her fingers the leopards went to the side of the room then sat down. One look from her silenced him, and all in the room waited while the sound people did their checks. A few moments after that four guys, all in trousers, braces and shirts, were ushered into the room – her band. How had she known?

She stepped up to the mike.

The music began.

So did the magic.

It had to be one of the best performances he'd seen of that song – and he'd seen plenty over the months. It was only when his eyes reached hers, as she rose from her bow, that he realised she wasn't absorbing the applause with her usual grace. She was fuming with anger.

"I'm so glad you enjoyed that, because I shall be leaving now." Her voice brought instant silence. "My welcome here, from the outset, was not ideal. I was invited here as a guest. But as a performer I exercise my right to leave, now that the show is over."

With another click of her fingers, the leopards came to her, and she turned to leave, but not before glancing at the once-jovial unsuspecting face of the president, whose hands were still raised to clap. Daryl felt the shocked surprised at her words work its way through the room. They had no idea just who they were dealing with. They had perhaps imagined they would get the pussycat today, not the tiger. Was that the warning look OG had sent him?

"Mysty, you haven't had lunch, and what about your dispensation? Do stay," the president called, trying to find some way to salvage the situation.

"I have no appetite, sadly. I am sorry, but I will have to politely decline. As for the dispensation – give it to him." The gold tipped cane was pointed at Daryl, who knew arguing the point was no good. "He owns everything, anyway. Let him have that as well. My life is so minutely engineered I doubt I'll remember what a bike looks like, or what a beer tastes like, in a few months, so it doesn't really matter."

OG glanced at Blackmoor, and then went after her with his men.

"Damn it! I'm sorry, Daryl, I didn't mean to upset her. I…I thought she'd take it as a compliment," Marshall said, clearly upset.

"It's not me you need to apologise to, sir." Daryl was touched by the utter regret in Marshall's voice, but he was annoyed for her, not with her.

"I told you it wasn't a good idea, but you never listen to me," Charles threw in for good measure, earning himself a scathing look from his president.

"Thank you, Charles. Please keep your 'I told you so' to yourself. Daryl, I'll make amends. You can take the dispensation for her, can't you?"

"Of course. I really wish you'd told me what you'd been planning. This could have been avoided." Daryl was surprised at the severity of his own words, with his, albeit carefully bridled, defence of her. Now he was stuck at the White House for a dull lunch, during which she would have been the only source of joy. Something else was bothering him: her comment about her welcome not being 'ideal'… What did that mean? What had happened?

"Let's go through for lunch. You can think of something I can send her by way of an apology."

Marshall led the way, without waiting for agreement, obviously intensely annoyed with himself.

SHE DID NOT need a secret service agent to tell her where to go, she had memorised the way.

Her favourite person was there to greet her.

"Leaving so soon?" he said, that same cocky edge to his voice.

"My knives, if you don't mind."

He nodded, and they were handed to her. She swiftly slotted them back inside the boots.

"Are you sure you want to leave?"

"I wanted to leave the moment I got here. Excuse me." She brushed past him, but then paused and turned, holding out the cane. From the end of a twelve-inch blade, now protruding from the tip, dangled his ID card. "Agent Boscum, you really need some more training. And I think you may need this back. At least until you get your ass fired for incompetence." A flick of her wrist and the ID card was at his feet. He made no move to pick it up.

There was a silence in the car on the way back that OG didn't know how to break. Idiots. And even the President, asking her to sing… Why had he done that?

"What are you doing?" he asked when she reached for a computer panel.

"Agent Boscum is about to get his ID *adjusted*," she said. "And then we can get on that plane!"

OG felt his earpiece buzz; he knew who it was before he heard the voice.

"O'Grady."

"Sir."

"Has something happened I don't know about?"

"One of the guys in security had very keen hands, and an attitude to match." Daryl felt his fists clench in rage. "Add that to being asked to sing – even though she'd anticipated it – and she feels slightly abused."

"And?"

"She's currently doing something to Agent Boscum's ID." This didn't surprise Daryl at all, and he controlled the smile. "I've no idea what it is, but I'm disinclined to stop her. The jerk was totally unprofessional. He was so busy with her body, he missed the knives in her boots, and didn't even check her cane, which incidentally has a retracting blade."

Daryl was too angry to say anything immediately, and a number of thoughts skittered through his mind, mostly centred on how to exact a pound of flesh from this Boscum. He'd never thought The White House would be somewhere he had to worry about her visiting. He should have been there to protect her. Why the hell hadn't he gone down to greet them?

"We're on our way to the airport, sir. She'd like to leave."

"Don't! Please." He controlled his voice. "Take her somewhere she wants to go and get her to calm down. I'll meet you on the plane as soon as I can extract myself from here. I'll let you know when I'm on the way."

"Yes, sir."

Disconnect.

He summoned Mac on his way back to Charles's office. Twenty seconds later they watched the replay from the security cameras as she received her extra warm welcome.

"Make an example of Agent Boscum," he snapped. "Make sure it is clear to him, and all with him, who is watching over her. No one treats her like that." He then placed a call to Charles himself. "And, Mac." The big guy paused. "Don't be gentle."

A nod, and then he was gone.

"I JUST WANT to go *home*!" she cried on the news that they couldn't leave immediately.

"I know, kiddo, we'll be on our way in just a few hours. Until then, we'll kill some time, okay? How about a museum or something? Hungry?"

"I don't want any food."

OG sighed. He knew that was going to be her answer. Any kind of upset killed her appetite stone-dead. He took an executive decision and spoke to the driver, and the car turned off the highway. She looked away, not caring enough to ask where she was being taken, and went back to the laptop, a little smile lighting her face.

"What have you done to Boscum?"

"Oh, nothing much. But his ID is now instructing others that he is armed and dangerous and needs apprehending immediately. He's facing a court martial, naughty boy."

She then hacked into the camera at the security gate – and gasped. Several suits swept into the frame like the horsemen of the apocalypse. And then she saw Mac go straight to Boscum. She'd never seen Mac hurt or fight anyone, only attempt to defend himself from her, and his demonstration of controlled violence was something to behold. He took Boscum by the collar – and he was not a small man – and forced him up and back against the wall. The anger in his face seemed to say that anyone who had crossed Mysty crossed him also, thus making himself an instant enemy. He then grabbed the man between the legs in a crushing grip, making him yelp in horror and pain.

"Agent Boscum, I believe you amused yourself this afternoon at someone else's expense. It is my understanding that you took it upon yourself to welcome a certain guest *very* personally?"

Mysty could hardly breathe. She couldn't believe what she was seeing.

"You do know who her boss is, don't you? Did you really think he would turn a blind eye when he discovered your behaviour?" Mac squeezed, and this time there was screech from the victim. The words were as merciless as the hands: "I wonder why I bother leaving you with your dick attached as you show little sign of being able to be trusted with it," he whispered through clenched teeth, and Boscum's eyes rolled as he pulled down, hard, on the man's genitals.

But then suddenly Boscum was released. He fell to the ground at Mac's feet, his legs failing to hold him up as the pain spread up his spine and down his thighs.

"As you've discovered, she's not the kind of girl to let such liberties go unmentioned. Believe me, your record is thoroughly trashed, and hopefully your ability to father children, too, for a long time."

Mac then grabbed a hand-full of hair and pulled his head up and smacked it into the wall.

OG took the panel from her and turned it off. She'd seen enough.

"Come on, time to relax. He's been dealt with."

"Where are we?"

"The zoo. Just make sure you hold onto Lula."

It was surreal. An hour ago, she'd been with the President of the United States, in the White House; and now she was strolling in a zoo, Lazarus and Lula by her side, wide-eyed at all the fascinating sights and sounds and smells. Her arrival created quite a stir, but OG and her boys made it possible for her to relax and turn her mind away from those images on screen for a few hours. What on earth would happen next?

"SO, HOW WAS the zoo?"

His voice was surprisingly calm. She'd been worried he'd be angry with her – for walking out on one of his closest friends – the President, no less – and for carrying knives, and for not wearing what he'd asked her to wear.

"Interesting," she managed, her eyes on the floor, hoping it would put him off conversation.

"Good. Didn't come back with a few more leopards, did you?"

"Not this time."

"How are you feeling?"

"How do I look?"

"Angry. Hurt. Afraid."

She looked up at him and he saw her eyes ablaze with emotion that sparked defensively at him. "Spot on. Congratulations."

"Mysty, I'm not angry with you. I didn't know Marshall was going to ask you to sing. I didn't think he'd be that insensitive. If I had I would have vetoed it. He intends to apologise, and he gave me this to give to you. You should have it."

Daryl took a breath and sat down on the next sofa, the nearest he dared let himself go, hoping that it didn't panic her. He held something out to her. It was the official presidential dispensation in a beautiful and very expensive frame.

"As to the other…matter… I have had him dealt with."

"I know. I saw."

"Good." Of course she'd hacked into the camera. He should have guessed.

"How can you get away with that? In the White House! How can you get away with it? Won't you get in trouble?"

Her concern utterly surprised him. He needed to explain.

"Perhaps you don't quite realise," he began, and stood, somehow uncomfortable speaking to her about the influence he had. He didn't want it to add to the distance between them, if she looked at him differently because of it. "I have no reason to fear the President. He would not dare offend me, nor challenge my authority. I am…too large a cog in the American machine. Without me, too much would fall apart. There is no one better to watch over you, and keep you safe…no one." Their eyes were locked together in seconds that felt like eternity, hers filling with tears.

The frame was put on the seat beside her, and hands covered her face as the implications, the real power of the man who stood before her, became abundantly clear. He didn't speak; just let her take her time. He had all the time in the world for her. Daryl could see her struggling with the truth, the reality of his words. Maybe she was wondering how on earth she'd got away with all her insults, and hacking into his mainframe, and breaking into his own apartment and handcuffing him… If only she knew.

Finally she moved her hands away from her face, but kept her elbows on her knees. He hoped the tears on her cheeks were tears of relief, but he couldn't be sure.

"You'll understand why that worries me as much as the other?"

He saw the appeal to understand, for some reassurance. He owed her that. He sat back down, carefully.

"I know you have a good number of reasons to doubt what I am about to say, and I know you don't think much of me at the moment, but I assure you, you have nothing to fear from me. I don't like to see you cry, and I don't like your fear. I will keep you safe, as I always intended. No one will ever treat you like he did again."

It wasn't easy for him, sitting there knowing he was guilty of far worse than Boscum. But it didn't change the fact he meant what he said, and he realised from her body language how much she needed to hear those words from someone. There was no one else anymore.

"Did he hurt you?"

She shook her head, and drew in a sharp breath. "Not the outside. Every time someone – a man – is like that with me, it's like all the other times come back and it's… I hope every time it's the last time, but there's always someone else."

"It won't happen again."

"How do you…how can you be so sure?"

"Mysty, it won't happen again." She looked up at him, surprised by the surety, and the care, in his voice. "We're on the way back to LA. You can go home and rest."

"You're not Daryl Blackmoor. Go away and get the other one."

"One day you'll realise we're the same man."

Feeling exhausted by regret, he stood and left it for OG to go in with a blanket and the leopards, going to sit in his usual seat so he could stare out of the window. Would she ever trust him? Believe him?

Glancing at the camera feed in her cabin to check on her he saw her blink. She wasn't asleep; she was thinking. Please, let it be something good…

HE PRESSED THE button on the paperweight and watched the colours dance in the LA sunshine that streamed through the windows. In less than a week he would be on holiday. In Barbados. With her.

It made the tedium and the weight of the matters yet to be dealt with bearable. He really wanted to see her; to heal the breach and be able to start the holiday on friendly terms. He thought about how he must appear to her. The scumbag 'Mr Photographer' who followed her to a dance-off and into a filthy strip club were her first impressions; the man who stood unchallenged and revered in the White House was quite another. It seemed she had noticed that, and perhaps found some reassurance in it.

He could only hope.

He knew she had been packing for the move to New York, and smiled at the thought of having her in his city. It would make his life easier, her being there rather than LA; but more than that, it meant she'd be further away from Donny and Franny, and perhaps that would be easier for her, in the long term. Her next shows at Celeste had been rescheduled, after a discussion with her and Craig, to avoid the excessive travelling. It was the first time they had done this, and he knew her fans would understand. He didn't want her performing whilst in the throes of jetlag, and to run them consecutively, Friday and Saturday, would be much easier on her. He had already secured the purchase of an ice rink, so she would be able to enjoy one of her favourite things. And he'd had a couple of interesting conversations about her skills on ice. Her talent would not be a secret forever.

He also knew a large bunch of flowers, along with a beautiful pearl and diamond necklace, had arrived from the President, with a letter of apology. He'd included an invitation to return for dinner, when she was able. He knew the necklace was beautiful because he'd picked it himself, choosing something particularly expensive just to sting Marshall in the wallet a little. Her surprise had been wonderful; but the look she'd given O'Grady had made him laugh. 'Does he think I'm a princess or something?' she'd asked, and OG had laughed, and put it in the safe.

He pressed the Receive button.

The screens connected and a familiar face popped up, looking as handsome as ever; yet there was a dark, wounded misery in Donny's eyes that Daryl had seen in Mysty's often enough to recognise.

"Donny."

"Daryl."

"How are you?"

"I'm not thinking about that. I have a pulse. How are you?"

"Not bad."

"Don't tone it down for my sake. You look disgustingly happy and relaxed."

"I'm okay, yes. It's been weeks."

"They've been very long weeks. The reality of it is sinking in now. I sometimes forget she won't just appear through the door again. Part of me can't quite accept it. Is she…is she alright?"

"We've had a few interesting moments, but yes, she's alright. She's keeping herself as busy as possible, so as not to dwell on how things are. She's strong, but she still can't talk about you without crying."

"And how are you getting along with her?" Piercing blue eyes fixed on the green with the sharpness of a hawk.

"I've been slapped, ridiculed, insulted… Occasionally we get on quite well. I was even allowed to eat pizza and watch a ball game."

"Franny told me about the world's most expensive pizza." Donny almost smiled. "She has a new leopard?"

"Lula, yes. They're kindred spirits. You should see them together. She's an orphan, like Mysty, so I guess they share a bond. I can send you some pictures, if you like…?"

There was a slight pause, and then Donny said, "Sure. Pick one and send it over. That would be nice. You're going on holiday with her next week, I hear, and she's moving to New York."

"Voluntarily. She agreed, after we discussed it."

Donny nodded slowly, relieved by the new approach.

"And the holiday?"

"Her choice. Barbados. It'll be a nightmare keeping it off the press radar, but it makes sense to go to the same place. I'm sure she'll find plenty to enjoy. She'll have an entire private beach and a piece of sea as a playground."

"And you?" The question was rather loaded.

"Apparently I'm getting pushed in the pool." Daryl knew he was dodging the question and tried again. "Donny, it's a holiday for her. I'm not taking her out there to seduce her, for God's sake. She barely likes me, and she still loves you."

"But you're going, despite the fact you won't get her into bed?"

"You never did, and you still enjoyed every second with her. Do you really need me to answer that?"

There. He'd admitted it. Of course he wanted to take her to bed, but he loved her company more, just as Donny had.

"You do have it bad…" Donny replied slowly, not sure if he was reassured or saddened further.

"Thank you for pointing that out."

A smile suddenly appeared on Donny's face, and he actually laughed at Daryl's obvious frustration but newfound, simple love of her company.

"Isn't life ironic?"

"Thank you, Donny, yes. I hadn't missed that either."

"You'll forgive me if I don't wish you luck."

"Even if it means she might be safe, and perhaps even happy?"

"If you can make her happy, then I will be able to bear it. I have yet to see some proof of your ability to manage anything lasting and meaningful, however, and she's a lasting and meaningful kind of girl."

"That is something I rather like."

The pain in Donny's heart deepened, and he knew he had to change the subject. "Send me a picture from last Friday's Celeste. I'm still getting over it. How does she vanish like that?"

"I have no idea. She's not sharing yet. Hopefully she will one day."

"Hopefully? One day? Where is the blackmail, Daryl? The demands and the threats?"

Daryl wasn't about to let the mockery dim his mood. "What can I say? I've learnt that it doesn't work. If it does, I feel like I've lost."

The signs of just how much his own girl was having an effect on Daryl, the one man he never imagined would unbend enough to show even five minutes concern for another human being, was almost too much. He needed to find a large bottle of something strong to drown in.

"I am reassured that your attitude is now somewhat more co-operative," he said. "Look…I had better go. If she needs anything…"

"You know she is well looked after, but of course."

Disconnect.

Why was it so hard to see Donny's distress? Maybe because it was there, right in front of him, just how he would feel if he made such a huge mistake he lost her completely.

He ordered a coffee and turned off the paperweight. Back to business.

He wanted as much out of the way as possible so he could enjoy next week. Saturday couldn't come soon enough!

THE NEWS THAT she was leaving LA to live in New York for a few months had hit the airwaves, and the web, and there were equal amounts of delight and dismay.

Thankfully there was only a small audience in the studio, decked out with a big curving sofa. OG gave her a reassuring smile from behind the camera crew, knowing she wasn't looking forward to another grilling by the media. To everyone else she looked calm and confident.

"Mysty, thank you so much for joining me today. You don't know how excited I am to see you again." The female presenter, Janice, leaned over and offered her hand, and Mysty smiled and shook it. Her male co-presenter was not there. Both women settled, and Mysty demurely crossed her legs rather than sitting in her usual pose of an ankle resting on a knee. "So, wow, since I last saw you so much has happened."

"I know. We'd better start talking faster if you want to get through it all."

Janice laughed. "So, the big news, of course, is this move to New York. Can you tell us a little about it? I know LA is sad to lose you. Is it forever, or what?"

"No, not forever. It just makes sense given the show I'm working on at the moment, which will be taking place in New York. I guess moving around comes with the territory, though I am sad to be going."

"The move has nothing to do with your relationship with your manager?"

"My manager has put me in charge of putting on a show in New York for the summit on the economy in a few months' time. That's all."

"It's a very prestigious event. Are you nervous about it, at all?"

"Not at the moment. Everything is on schedule, and the costumes and choreography are all fine. Five minutes before the opening piece, maybe. But no, right now I'm very happy with how it's going."

"And moving your Celeste performance night? That's a first in the history of your Butterfly career. Is this a sign of a big commitment to move to New York permanently?"

Mysty eyed the women, knowing what she was trying to imply.

"It's a long flight, so it makes sense. I don't want to sacrifice the quality of the Butterfly pieces because I have jetlag."

"The Butterfly shows are becoming even more world renowned for their excellence and their complexity. How you do it is a constant mystery to everyone – except you. Of course. How do you do all your… disappearing? On top of the physical side of things, which is equally astounding?"

"Are you familiar with particle physics?"

"No, I can't say I am."

"Because any explanations I give you will be wasted unless you do, so I'm afraid it's going to have to remain a mystery. It's not magic, its science. Just not science anyone else possesses at the moment."

"And has Mr Blackmoor asked you to divulge your secrets?"

"Not as much as I think he'd like to. He seems to be fairly happy with how everything is going. I suppose he doesn't wish to rock the boat by demanding answers."

"By which you mean the equilibrium between you?"

"That's an interesting way of putting it. Simply put, we are…getting along better than we did."

"No more trashed Lamborghinis?"

"No."

"And your new companion – I think you brought her with you today? – could she come on set?"

"Lula? Lazarus?"

Lazarus trotted over, while Lula bounded, full of enthusiasm. Lazarus calmly seated himself on the sofa in between the presenter and Mysty; Lula jumped straight onto Mysty and settled on the back of the sofa, her front half hanging over Mysty's shoulder, eyes bright and alert. There was a collective 'Aaaawww' from the audience, that most certainly would be echoed in every home tuned in to the show.

"Wow. She is so cute! Where did you get her?"

"From a wonderful couple in San Francisco. Anna, John, hey! How are you? Lula give them a wave." The cub obeyed, after a fashion, and the audience laughed. She was clearly too excited about the new surroundings, the cameras and the lights, to pay much attention. "She's an orphan. Her mother was almost full term when thieves broke into the house to steal her. The rest were stillborn, due to the shock to her mother, and the drugs they used to stun her. Lula is the miracle survivor, and she is very well loved."

"How is she getting on with Lazarus?"

"Fantastic. He stops her getting into too much mischief, and they've not had one fight, which is a huge relief. I'm hoping when she grows up she'll be the companion for him he might have found in the wild."

"And end up with lots of little leopards."

"Maybe. They are an endangered species, so that would be amazing. I couldn't imagine life without them around. Lazarus has certainly been happier now he has leopard company, and Lula has blossomed now she has a 'family'."

"Are you training her to do anything? I know Lazarus goes on your motorbike. What kinds of things does she like doing?"

"She's a bit young to ride on the bike, but she likes dancing. She follows me and tries to join in with what I do. She likes the drums, too, and whenever I play she runs in to watch."

"You play the drums?"

"Yes. I taught myself after the MJ tour. It went better than expected."

"Do you think we might persuade you to come on the show and give us a demonstration, when you're back in LA?"

"Perhaps." *I'd rather not.*

"And how are you, after…the split with Mr Capello? It must be strange returning to Vegas and not seeing him. Or has that changed?"

"No. Not as far as I know." For the first time she looked away. "It's not what I wanted, but I'm living with it."

"So, no new romance on the horizon, then?" Mysty was stunned when the kiss with Daryl flashed up in her mind, intense and bright for one second – no!

"No. There won't be for a good while. I was blessed to know and love one man; to find another would be rare…and asking a lot of the universe."

"Well, something else that is rare is an audience with your manager. Mr Blackmoor, if you would like to join us?"

Mysty's face was pure shock for one second; then she remembered the cameras. Janice stood to greet him respectfully, while Mysty made no move to welcome him. She watched as the familiar impeccable figure moved towards her, dressed in a cream suit, with a blue shirt – had that been deliberate, to wear similar colours to her? That was really going to fire the media up. What was his plan? She eyed him covertly as he sat down. He was smiling, and looked relaxed.

"Mysty."

"Daryl."

She almost blushed.

"So – wow! – the first ever joint interview with the two most famous people in the world! The two people considered the most beautiful and sexy! Mr Blackmoor, you've been in receipt of such accolades before. It's impressive you're still at the top. Almost ten years now, isn't it?"

"I'm flattered so many still think so; I'll be impressed if I can make it to ten, though I'm sure Mysty will easily equal that over time."

Mysty realised it was going to be a case of who could field the attention to the other the quickest. He didn't like the questions any more than she did.

"Mysty, you are relatively new to the world of fame, and yet you've scooped two of the biggest prizes out there – 'World's Sexiest Female Performer' and 'World's Best-dressed Performer' – how does that feel?"

"Very strange. I still find the fame – or notoriety, whatever you want to call it – rather hard to understand sometimes, so those titles feel a little uncomfortable. But I also consider it a compliment, and I'm grateful for people taking the time to show their appreciation. I certainly don't mind giving Daryl a run for his money on taking the title for ten years. Though recently I don't think he's put enough effort into earning it."

"No?" Janice didn't know what else to say.

"Not at all. Perhaps he needs to concentrate on his own modelling career, not mine." Her eyes slid round to his, and her lips curved into a smile that he wished he could kiss, but he could only look at her with the calm, unshakeable composure that years of exposure to the media had taught him. "I think he's getting a little shy as he gets older," she added, and the presenter's eyes almost fell out her head. Daryl Blackmoor *shy*?

"I assure you, my dear, I'm not at all shy, and with age comes experience." His voice had dropped to a level only she could hear, his tone dangerous and intimate, and Janice flicked her eyes over her cards, looking for an appropriate question.

"Well," she said, "it is good to see you getting on so well – certainly a step up from the trashed Lamborghinis, Mr Blackmoor?"

"Oh, a few steps further than that."

She fumed, and he smiled benignly, perfectly aware he may have been hit with a cushion had there been one to hand.

"Lucky, considering you're going on holiday next week, together? Whose choice was that?"

"It was mutually agreed, so we had the best chance of a week away from the media and the press," Daryl answered calmly for both of them, to prevent Mysty saying anything outrageous.

"Mysty, how do you feel about it? Looking forward to it I hope?"

"To having a holiday, definitely. But I'm not so certain about the location. I'm used to LA and Vegas, so I don't know why Daryl chose somewhere with minus temperatures, and I don't even know how to ski."

Daryl fully understood the need to throw the press of the scent. Not a bad plan. "You'll be fine," he said. "You'll pick it up in no time. You might even keep up with me by the end of the week."

"I'll freeze to death before then."

"Stay in and drink hot chocolate by the fire, then," he countered easily.

"What about the kids?"

"They'll probably want to stay in and drink hot chocolate as well." He reached out a hand to Lula, who recognised his smell and gave him a lick. Mysty's face relaxed into a smile. To anyone watching closely, both he and Mysty appeared contented in that moment, displaying an easy closeness that neither were aware of.

"I don't suppose you'll tell us where you're going?"

"No," Daryl replied decisively, leaning an arm on the back of the sofa and turning his body towards Mysty, under the guise of paying more attention to the presenter – a presenter who was struggling to deal with the interview that was not quite what she expected. This was not the Daryl Blackmoor she had anticipated meeting.

"Aren't you a little worried letting her ski when she has Celeste performances, and everything else? What if she gets hurt?"

"Compared to her performances at Celeste, a bit of skiing is rather tame. You are talking to the girl who would happily sky dive out of her own jet if I said she could."

"You're just jealous because Mac wouldn't let you jump out of yours."

"Absolutely. It's his job to keep me safe; my job is to keep you safe. So no sky diving."

"So mean."

"I know."

The exchange was typical for them, but jaw-dropping for everyone else.

"Mr Blackmoor, you must be so pleased with how everything is going? I don't think we've seen a star of Mysty's calibre for years. It must be rewarding to know you were right to choose her for such celebrity."

"She has proved my faith in her abilities was well-founded countless times, and risen to every challenge with all the commitment I could wish for, and a maturity of someone far older. She is a credit to herself."

He didn't miss the blush that raced over her cheekbones, his words reminding her of the promise he had coerced from her with his hands in intimate places, and the words he had spoken the next morning. Perhaps she might actually start believing them…

"So you're glad you persuaded her to sign the contract, despite her initial unwillingness?"

"Yes. And I hope one day she will think so too."

They were calm words, but there was so much was wrapped up in them that he felt a rush of emotion having said them. He glanced at her, looking for some sort of reaction, but there was none. It was all hidden behind a perfectly neutral face.

"The recent trip to the White House, what actually happened? I understand Mysty left sooner than planned."

"There was a misunderstanding of sorts. It's all been resolved now, of course. As I understand it, the President is keen to have Mysty back for dinner one evening. I'm obviously not at liberty to divulge anything further."

"Of course. And are you looking forward to having Mysty in New York? Will you be returning more often?"

"I'm planning on being in New York more, and hopefully travelling less for a little while. Recent months have been incredibly busy. Naturally it will be great to have Mysty just across the street, and I've no doubt New Yorkers will delight in having her."

"Just across the street? She'll have her own apartment?"

"It's not exactly just across the street, but compared to LA, it is much closer. Every effort has been made to make the move as easy and stress-free as possible."

"And when will Mysty be making an appearance on the party scene? So far she has been noticeably absent from celebrity bashes."

"She is young. There will be plenty of opportunities in the coming months for her to make her debut in those circles. I doubt there will be any she does not get an invitation to."

"So, roughly six months into the contract…how do you feel, Mysty?"

"Ready for a holiday."

"And you, Mr Blackmoor?"

"The same, but very confident about the future."

"She's certainly a star that seems to rise higher and higher. Whatever will happen next? I can't wait to find out. I do hope you'll come back and tell us all about your holiday when you get back. When will that be?"

"In about a week, depending on how long our location is kept secret, or until frostbite sets in."

"Well, it certainly shouldn't be lacking in excitement."

"No. Mysty does create an atmosphere of excitement wherever she goes."

Lula chose that moment to pounce, launching herself towards Daryl's lap, and Mysty reached out and grabbed her mid-flight, not sure quite how that would be received.

"Looks like you were about to become a landing pad!" Janice laughed.

"Could have been worse. She might have bitten me as hard as her mistress does," Daryl whispered, and offered his hand for another lick.

"You were warned."

"Well, Mr Blackmoor, Mysty, it's been an absolute pleasure to see you today!" Janice trilled, unsure what the whispered exchange was all about. "I'm sure everyone here and at home has thoroughly enjoyed seeing and hearing from you. Just one last thing before you go, Mysty…we have a gentleman here who has something for you. He got in touch before the show. I believe you know him."

Mysty froze, and her eyes went to someone just beyond the lights, trying hard to see. The figure came forward, slowly, clearly a little embarrassed, and intimidated by the cameras. When their eyes met, she could see he was emotional as well. Her fear receded immediately and was replaced with bittersweet joy as she recognised him. She got up without hesitation, stepping forward to greet the man who didn't need words to tell her the worst. It was the man she had stopped to speak to as she'd been leaving Vegas, his sick wife by his side.

"She was so happy those weeks afterwards," he began, as Mysty led him from the shadows. "I don't know what you said to her, but she was… like she had been before. It was the best way for it to end." The cameras were all around them, capturing this special moment. "She was at peace when she died, and I know part of that was because of you. I can't thank you enough for that. She asked me to give you this – you'll understand when you open it. She said not to let you refuse. It was her wish that you have it; she hoped it would bring you luck." He pressed a small envelope into her hand. He leaned a little closer. "She kept the picture, the one you signed, by her side. It gave her courage. I'm so glad you were there that day. I wish you every happiness." The man took Mysty's hand and kissed the back of it in a beautiful, old-fashioned gesture, and left, a hand covering his eyes.

Silence fell throughout the studio.

Mysty looked down at the white envelope. She knew she wouldn't open it then. She was glad she had seen him, so sad at his news, and wondered how they had arranged for him to be there at such short notice. She sat back down, scooping Lula into her lap. Being on camera was the last thing she needed.

"I understand you met Mr Gregson and his wife when you left Vegas?" The presenter gently broke the silence, seeing that Mysty was too stunned to volunteer any information

"Yes. His wife was there. I was so touched they had taken the time to come and see me off at the airport. She was an amazing woman, incredibly strong in the face of such…impossible circumstances."

Daryl's heart was beating hard in his chest, aware of his jealousy, again, at how easily she responded to all but him; but also because the exchange had been so emotional. She looked at the envelope and then at the presenter. He gave Janice a look: it was time to wind this up.

"I think one thing is for certain: LA is going to miss you, but New York will be honoured to have you. Thank you for coming in today. We look forward to talking to you again soon."

Both guests smiled as the cameras panned around, and a few minutes later they were given the all clear to leave.

Mysty went straight outside into the corridor, away from the glaring studio lights and the intrusive cameras, and Daryl followed, past O'Grady, not afraid of her tears anymore. He knew behind them was the need for comfort.

"Mysty," he said softly, and she couldn't really avoid him, he was so big and tall in front of her. "She knew she was going to die. What you did changed everything for her, and she died in peace."

"But *why*? She was so young! She didn't even have children! What did she do to deserve that?"

They were impossible questions, to be asked only of God. He dared to smooth a curl away from her face and tucked it back.

"We can't know why, and I doubt she did anything to deserve it. It's just life, and it's unfair, but she was happy before she died, you should be glad of that. You were a part of that."

She let out a quiet groan of sadness, and looked down at the envelope. She slowly opened it. Inside was a note that said, '*I hope it brings you luck finding that which you envied of me. You deserve to. Eternally grateful, Edith.*' The single carat diamond ring caught the light and shone brightly, even through the blur of tears.

"An engagement ring," Daryl said quietly, watching her face.

"I told her she had a wonderful husband, and that I envied her. It was obvious he loved so much," she whispered, staring at the ring, remembering the warm sunshine, the beautiful woman the only one who needed a blanket to keep her warm. She slid the ring onto the third finger of her right hand, wiped the tears away and looked up at Daryl. "I have to go."

She gave him a half smile and slipped past him, her eyes on the ring on her finger, and her heart both saddened and warmed by its significance.

"SHE'S QUITE SOMETHING, isn't she?" Mac said, rather impressed with how his boss had handed the situation – clearly he was learning.

"She is that."

Daryl started down the corridor after her, half hearing Mac sending orders for the car to be brought round. He'd been on camera thousands of times, and in countless interviews, and never seen anything like that. How was it life flowered around her like cherry blossoms in spring? She had managed to touch the lives of two people she had met once, for only a couple of minutes at most, and had somehow found the words to make such a difference. Whatever had scarred her as a child had become a generous and sensitive spirit that brought out the best in people. Was it also bringing out the best in him, too?

IT FELT WRONG to speak to Mysty when he had another woman in his apartment, but he still took the call.

"Mysty."

"Daryl."

"You look exhausted."

"You win first prize for that. I didn't wake you, did I?"

"No, I'm just finishing some work off so I can leave tomorrow with a better chance of being left alone. I'm wide awake. Is everything okay?"

"Everything's very okay. I've been exploring the New York apartment and it's amazing. I just wanted to call and say thank you."

"Your New York apartment, it's all yours, and I'm glad you like it."

"It even has a Jacuzzi!"

"I know." He'd hoped she'd like that.

"And the MJ piece up on the wall is fantastic! And the pictures of Lazarus and Lula!"

"Good. It should make it easier to come back. How are the kids?"

"They're fine. They love their room, but I have a feeling they'll still be jumping on my bed for a while. It's great that they have their own space." He smiled, enjoying the relaxed Mysty. "I should go. I'm going to fall asleep any second, and you should get some rest as well. You have an exciting week ahead of you, after all."

"Doing what?"

"Having a holiday!"

"Ah yes, a holiday…"

"I'll see you on the plane. Don't work too late."

She was gone.

A whole week together. What on earth would that be like? Would he finally get bored, or find something not to like about her?

He sent some final messages, instructions for his staff mainly, and headed back to the bedroom. With Lucile he now could play out the fantasy that Mysty would fall in love with him whilst they were away, let him teach her all the secrets of her body.

Lucile looked over her shoulder and smiled in welcome, arching her back and raising her bottom in a way he knew he wouldn't be able to resist, wanting his ecstasy again. He didn't disappoint. He gripped her hips and he filled her, and she surrendered to his lust.

IT WAS EXACTLY what he needed to see: one jet, four Bentleys, a row of grey suits, two trusted bodyguards, two leopards, and one gorgeous superstar.

"Daryl. Wow. Still in a suit? I'm feel rather underdressed," she said when they boarded, and flopped down in the seat opposite him, a wide smile on her radiant face. She was in a short white summer skirt, a silky gold top with a white silk scarf tied around her neck, and gold sandals. Her shades were in her hair. Simple, and gorgeous.

"You look…great. It will take a little while longer for me to relax, to get into the holiday mood."

She just laughed, eyeing him with amusement. "Well, seeing as you're not quite in the holiday spirit yet, these might help." She reached into her bag and pulled out a small, shiny blue box and placed it in front of him. It was shaped like a Lamborghini.

"A present?"

"I did promise you. Go on, open it. I had them made for you."

He lifted the top half of the car off and inside was a pair of very cool-looking black shades, a thin dark blue metal band curving up the arms ending in a small dark blue DB. Very nice.

"You like them?" she asked, logging on to a tablet.

"Yes, very much. I might even look as cool as you."

"Nah, you'd need to wear your leathers more often to be that cool." Was that a compliment? "Try them on. I need to initiate them for you. Have you got a personal mainframe or database you'd like all the files to go onto?" He slipped the shades on, wondering what would happen when they came to life. "Can you type it in for me?" She handed him the tablet and he looked over the page, the complexity of the programme she was running quite obvious. "It's perfectly safe, and I'm not going to hack into anything. I've only done that for a good reason, never just to be nosy."

"Wow. An interesting set up," he said and typed in the database of choice. She then reached forward and put a finger on each side of the glasses, and the inside of the lenses came to life, a red box appearing on each lens.

"It'll just do a quick retina scan, as it has to confirm it's you the first time." A soft light scanned down, and then gone. "If you put the tip of each forefinger on the sides, just back from the initials, that is where you'll be able to turn them off, secure them, or reactivate or turn them on. They're very sensitive so you don't need to press too hard." He did as he was told and 'Welcome Daryl' flashed up on the screens. "They run on solar energy, and have wireless connection to your database. Facial recognition and gathered data will download automatically. You can take visual images of what you see in front of you by pressing on the DB on the right. Images will download like everything else, but if the signal is poor images will be stored until it improves. The left-side DB is the off. Clear?"

"Yes." The red lines inside the lenses picked up her face and her name appeared at the side of the screen. "Do they come with a manual?" he asked.

"Sadly not. The girl who made them had to go on holiday and ran out of time. On-hand assistance is available, though. Mac, how are you finding yours?"

"No problems at all. They're great." Daryl looked over at Mac, who had a pair in his breast pocket, and again the lines fixed on him. 'Mac the Dude' came up at the side.

"Mac the Dude?" he said. "What am I saved on his as?" He could see she was enjoying this!

"'The Boss'," Mac answered.

When O'Grady appeared he came up simply as 'OG'. "Ah, great, the shades presentation," he said. "How do you like them, sir?"

"So far, so good."

OG smiled, and the two bodyguards left the room.

"Once the system sees a face regularly, it will not need to scan him or show his name, so it won't keep reminding you like you're ninety and senile."

Daryl slid them off and looked over at her, a naughty smile on his lips. "Do they have the ability to see through clothes?"

"No!" she said sternly. "Well, mine do, but you can't be trusted so I took that function off yours."

"Really? That's not fair!"

"You're so going to end up in the pool. In your clothes."

"I've survived ending up in a pool with you once before. I will again."

The sudden reminder of that day, when he'd said things she'd never expected him to say, and fought to keep her on the roof, not once resented her for the disruption, made her look at him with soft eyes.

"I think we both survived because of you," she said.

"You're glad you did?"

"Yes. But at the time, no. I thought there was no hope; but now? Now I have Lula, and…"

"I'm happy to hear that. I wouldn't want you, of all people, to lose hope in tomorrow."

She broke into song, laughing. "'*Tomorrow, tomorrow, I love ya, tomorrow, you're only a day away…*'" making him smile. She then put away the tablet and pulled out two milkshakes, sliding one across the table to him. "It's called Pirate Island, and has coconut, banana and a dash of rum – the most appropriate one I could find. Happy holidays, Daryl." She raised hers in a toast.

Had she any idea just how much her twinkling eyes and pure smile were all he needed to see? Why had he thought there was nothing on earth that would surprise? He raised his in answer, and then tried it.

"You know, this is definitely the way to start a holiday. Cancel the hula girls!" he declared. It was delicious.

She laughed, just as Lula launched herself into Daryl's lap, eyeing both him and the milkshake with curiosity.

"Lula! Hello!" he said.

"She's not quite made up her mind about you yet, but I think she likes you."

"A bit like you then?" he dared.

"Yeah, I guess… But don't go getting ahead of yourself. Seven days, with you, in one place…and you really think you won't manage to do something dickish?"

"I'll try not to."

"Are you working during the flight?"

"No. No work. I've not got a single device with me. Are you going to be working?"

"Nope."

"You play chess?"

"I can. Though I haven't played for a long time."

"I will take that into account when I beat you, then."

"I'll remember you said that when I beat you. I bet that's the dullest offer you've ever made to woman, isn't it?"

He had to admit she was probably right. "I can offer you something far more exciting, and you wouldn't even have to move from that chair if you didn't want to."

He smiled while she drowned in her natural reaction to his bold words – a deep blush – and the eyes that offered to do all kinds of things to her. Visions came back to her from that evening on his yacht – very real visions that did funny things to her insides.

"Dull is good for me," she managed, and he gave a long dramatic sigh, indicating she had made a disappointingly poor choice, and reached over to press a few buttons on the side of the table. A virtual chess board appeared on the table, complete with pieces.

"Your move. You're white. It's voice recognition."

She paused for a second, immobilised by a gaze that was as deep as it was strong, her instincts telling her to beware, as much as she enjoyed it. She then looked down at the board, and tried to concentrate. She had a game to win.

MANY HOURS LATER, after drawing at two games of chess, they disembarked from the plane into bright hot sunshine. Before them were a row of gleaming Bentleys, one a convertible, and Daryl took the keys from the driver.

"You can ride with me, if you promise not to trash my new car."

"That's an easy promise to make. Are leopards allowed, too?"

"Leopards, tigers and butterflies, all welcome." He got in the car and put on his new shades, waiting whilst she got Lazarus and Lula into the back. She then joined him in the front, just as vital and beautiful as the first time she had got into a passenger seat next to him. "You used the door," he said. "You didn't last time."

His smile made her laugh, and their eyes met. It was a look she knew she'd never forget, playful and happy, and then with a raised eyebrow of fun as he hit the accelerator. If she'd said, she knew he would have slowed down, but she didn't.

A while later he pulled up to a set of security gates, and she noted the high walls and the smiling people there to meet them. They were admitted and he drove down a palm tree-lined road, and her eyes widened at the landscaped gardens, and the smells and sounds of the place. He pulled up in front of a group of sandy-coloured stone buildings, and she stared at the sheer beauty. She knew it would be lovely, and that the villas were fitted with every luxury imaginable, because she'd read the information when she'd chosen it; but reading the words and seeing the pictures was quite different to actually being there.

She didn't realise she was being watched by her driver, who was enjoying her quiet wonder. Daryl tossed the keys to the valet, and she slowly climbed out, followed by the leopards. How had she ended up here? In this paradise?

"Come on, let's look inside."

She blushed, and was glad he had looked away. Was she really here with him?

She felt like Cinderella must have felt when she stepped into the palace, and picked Lula up, as much to hide behind. Each villa was so beautiful, with airy corridors and large spaces to eat and relax in. Sometimes there was a roof, but otherwise she looked up into the stunning blue Barbados sky. So many rooms, and then gardens, with a spotless pool, and access to the beach and surrounding land.

"What do you think? Do you think you made the right choice?"

"It's amazing. I can't quite believe it's real."

She couldn't look at him, feeling embarrassed, afraid her wonderment might be ridiculed.

"Now you know how everyone else feels about you," Daryl replied quietly, and her eyes came up to meet his. "Why don't you pick your villa? The butlers will bring your cases through."

"Which one do you want? It's your holiday, too."

"I insist you choose first."

"The middle one?"

"O'Grady, can you instruct the butlers."

O'Grady nodded, and Mysty wandered into the villa that would be home for the next seven days. It felt like they were in their own private world.

When she stepped back outside, she spotted Daryl. He had changed into tan shorts and a white summer shirt, and was sitting on the luxurious sofa that overlooked the pool area. He couldn't look more attractive if he tried. That he was her boss…well, it didn't quite fit.

He beckoned her over, and as she sat she was handed a glass of orange juice by a waiter who appeared out of nowhere. Then Mac and OG appeared, and Daryl smiled when he saw their apparel. Gone were the suits. Mac was in the khaki shorts Mysty had picked out for him; and OG was in the dark blue ones they'd both agreed on. Both had on a white t-shirt that said, 'Chief Bodyguard on Holiday – Behave!' He guessed who had given them the t-shirts!

"Well, Mac, you're certainly getting in the spirit of things," he said.

"Me and OG, we figured you guys can't have all the fun," the bodyguard replied.

When had he last seen Mac in anything other than a suit? And now O'Grady was 'OG' to Mac as well? Was there anything or anyone she couldn't transform with her magic?

"You like them?" Daryl nodded at the shorts.

"Yes, You two can go clothes shopping for me any time," Mac answered with a cheeky grin.

"It was Mysty's idea, so you should really thank her."

"Daryl, don't ruin it. You helped pick everything. I refuse to take sole credit."

"Only here thirty minutes and I'm already getting told off." His grin was utterly lacking in repentance and she just shook her head at him, refusing to rise to the tease. "So, what would you like to do?" he then asked Mysty. "There are still a couple of hours of sun left."

"Can we have a look around the island?" Mysty looked from Daryl to OG to Mac, who conferred with various looks.

"We can go for a whiz round the island if you like," OG answered.

"In the car?"

"No, on a jet-ski. Far more fun. What do you think?"

Her huge smile said it all.

"Are you coming, sir?" OG asked.

"No. I think I'll stay here and enjoy not doing anything at all. Go if you'd like, Mac. I'll be fine just here."

Mysty put her empty glass on the table and reached down and picked a tired and relaxed Lula up. "Can you watch Lula? She'll go to sleep in a few minutes' time, most probably. But if she starts exploring, don't let her in the pool on her own." She then laid her on his lap.

Daryl, however, was not the pillar of tranquillity the cub was. "Could Lazarus watch her, perhaps?" he asked. He wasn't sure he was okay being left in charge of the young leopard.

"Lazarus is coming on the jet-ski with me."

"But what if she…gets hungry or something?"

"She can eat when we get back, and if she needs the bathroom she knows where it is." A leopard that took herself to the bathroom? Did Lazarus do that too? So that was why he'd never seen any mess. She must have trained them to do that. Seeing his worried face, she said, "You'll be fine. She's a young, naked female. Aren't they your speciality?"

His eyes shot up to hers and she grinned, turned, and followed Mac and OG, Lazarus trotting beside her.

He looked down at the bundle on his lap. He'd never even had a puppy or a kitten as child. What was he supposed to do with a leopard? Lula looked up at him trustingly, then put her head back down, able to feel the reassuring warmth of him. He felt her body relax, could feel every breath she took, in and out. He recalled their conversation on the plane, just hours ago: 'She's not quite made up her mind about you yet, but I thinks she likes you'; 'A bit like you then?'; 'Yeah, I guess…' Was this a test? A way to show she trusted him? She wouldn't leave the precious cub with him if she didn't…which meant she might trust him with other things, one day.

He slowly stroked the cub. She didn't stir, except to move her tail so it curved around his body. How amazing.

Her rhythmic breathing and the peace of being trusted by an animal so completely worked its magic.

He couldn't say who fell asleep first.

MYSTY SAT DOWN next to the sleeping individual who, for all his greatness, slept just like any other man.

"Daryl?" He didn't stir, his head back, his body relaxed, and the cub contentedly sprawled on his front. "Don't wake him; I've got to get a picture of this," she whispered to OG and Mac, ran off to grab her camera. This was a completely different side of Daryl, the man who never stopped, never relaxed, who was always in control. "He really is tired, isn't he?" she murmured to Lazarus, who was watching as closely as she was. Lula's ear flicked at the familiar voice and opened her eyes. When she saw Mysty, she stretched and jumped off Daryl's chest to be with her mistress. Daryl, too, opened his eyes as her voice welcomed him back to the world. It was a familiar voice, but not one he associated with waking, or sleeping. "First-class leopard-sitting. You have qualified as an expert," she said.

He sat up and smiled. "How was the trip round the island?"

"Amazing. It's all so beautiful."

"Just enjoy it."

"Are you alright? You were sleeping for quite a while."

"I'm more tired than I realised, but I'm fine."

"It's not like you haven't earned a rest. Can I get you anything?" Her concern was genuine, and her offer to get him something, ignoring the legion of staff there to wait on them hand and foot, very touching.

Yes, I want you to put Lula down and come over here and lie in my arms while we both fall asleep.

"No, I'm fine, thank you. I think I'll have a swim before dinner. Are you hungry?"

"I'm nearly always hungry," she reminded him shyly.

"I know. That's why I had three times as much food organised!"

He stood up and headed towards the pool, stretching his arms out as he did. It felt good though to have slept. He was so relaxed it was incredible. And happy. And he knew why. He stood for a moment, watching the light on the water, but turned when he heard footsteps.

He was too slow. With a huge splash she honoured her word and sent him flying into the pool, fully dressed. He rose to the surface, flicking water out of his eyes and his hair to see her, laughing, the sound magical. The laughter turned into a scream, though, when he lunged and grabbed her leg, causing her to lose her balance. As she tumbled he caught her and lifted her above his head, and then threw her in. She curved in a natural reflex and then disappeared, coming up laughing.

Another splash, and Lazarus was in the water swimming across to her. "Oh, my hero, come to rescue me!" She held her arms out to him.

Daryl pulled off his shirt and looked up at Mac, who had come to watch their boss – as they'd never quite seen him before. "Thanks, Mac, fantastic bodyguard you are!" He threw the wet shirt at his amused bodyguard.

"I'm sorry, sir. I'm not used to rescuing you from beautiful young women!"

He looked round for her, but she had disappeared. She then reappeared next to him, as proficient at swimming as a seal, wet curls plastered to her head, skin gleaming with water.

"Do you mind if Lula comes in? She'd love it in here."

"Why not? Lazarus is already in."

She swam to the edge of the pool, where Lula was watching and half trying to touch the water. She gathered her into her arms and dipped her slowly in the water, getting her used to the wet. She seemed reassured to see Lazarus, and thus commenced Lula's first swimming lesson. OG and Mac drifted away, leaving them to it.

Daryl pulled off his shorts and chucked them on the side, fascinated by the cub and her curiosity of the water. He managed ten lengths before he was drawn to watch them again. But he stayed at a distance, so as not to spook the cub. Or her.

"Come on, Lula, swim to me." Voice and hands beckoned and the cub valiantly swam, snorting water from her nose, small strokes bringing her closer. When she arrived she was lifted high and congratulated.

"Was she alright with you earlier?" Mysty then asked.

He took it as encouragement and swam over to them where they were playing in the shallower end of the pool.

"One look at me and she fell asleep. I make a good pillow, it seems," he laughed.

Lula rubbed a wet cheek against his offered hand, and Lazarus swam up for some attention, appearing under Mysty's arm.

"Can you hold her for a minute, while I give Lazarus some fuss?"

"Sure."

Lula happily settled against his chest in seconds. And it was bizarre, but it felt perfectly natural. Mysty hugged and then wrestled with Lazarus and they disappeared in an explosion of bubbles and re-emerged seconds later further up the pool. Daryl almost found himself talking to Lula, as they watched the play-fight that progressed all around the pool and ended up with them back with him.

"Forget your personal trainer! This will keep you super fit!" she said as he handed Lula over, and she floated on her back, Lula on her tummy, her hair a cloud of gold on the surface of the water.

"I would prefer a water fight with a tiger rather than a leopard."

"You would *lose*."

He smiled and went back to swimming, enjoying smooth lap after smooth lap as she ducked under the water, taking Lula with her, the leopard trying out swimming underwater. He then got out and dried off; but Lazarus had the same idea, and shook himself, all the way down to the tip of his tail. Their eyes met, and the leopard somehow realised what he'd done and looked a little apologetic. Daryl offered his hand, wondering if Lazarus would thaw to him as well. Sure enough, after an investigative sniff, he got a lick, and that was that. He then strolled over to Lula, who was now snuggled inside a towel, and plonked himself down next to her.

Mysty dived in and swam the length of the pool without coming up, and back again. Why was he surprised, given her level of fitness and lung capacity?

He picked up her camera and took some pictures of Lula and Lazarus, smiling as they began to doze in the evening sun, realising he'd not thought about work from the moment he'd woken up to the sound of her voice.

He brought the camera round to capture her as she emerged from the pool and walked up the steps, a dripping wet goddess, the low sun catching her hair and skin. Beautiful.

"More pictures?" she groaned, when she turned and saw what he was doing.

"Absolutely." Daryl kept snapping.

"There are some on there you might want to see." He was curious, and handed her the camera. She flicked back through, smiling when she saw the pictures of Lula and Lazarus. She turned the camera around, and there he was, with Lula, both fast asleep. "I'm going to get it framed for you and put it somewhere really obvious, so when you get all bossy and rude you can see that and remember."

"Remember what?"

"You're not a god, but a man."

She then took back the camera and got picture of him, far too quickly for him to have stopped smiling. She then slipped the camera over her shoulder, picked up the tired cub and disappeared through the archway to her villa to shower and get ready for dinner.

He did the same, a little afraid of just how much he was enjoying himself.

AN HOUR LATER, at a table overlooking an ocean view that would ever cease to impress, Daryl sat nibbling olives, enjoying a glass of white wine while he waited for her.

"Is she ready? I thought she'd be here by now?" he asked OG when he appeared, alone.

"She probably would be if she was awake. She's currently fast asleep with two leopards sprawled over her. You want me to wake her up?"

He was torn between disappointment and tenderness. She, too, really needed to rest.

"No, let her sleep," he said. "There's plenty of food. She can eat when she wakes." He held in the sigh, having so badly wanted to end the day with a meal spent chatting and laughing with her, like he had seen her share with so many before. But the memory of their time in the pool and unexpected afternoon siesta – when had he ever done that? – with Lula snuggled into him – and he'd certainly never done that! – kept him mellow. After all, he reminded himself, they had a whole week ahead of them…

THE FIRST THING that registered was the dark. The second, that she was absolutely famished. Great! She had fallen asleep and she had missed dinner! The time read 12.49am.

There was no way she would be able to go back to sleep this hungry. She gently moved the leopards.

The villa seemed strange in the darkness, and it took her a moment to get her bearings. She felt a brush against her leg and knew it was Lazarus. Together they wandered along the paths, past the pool and into the communal rooms where she knew the kitchen was. It was all in darkness, apart from the lights on the various appliances, and she looked around the spacious room, big enough for ten chefs without anyone getting in each other's way.

"There is a prize if you can find the fridge," she whispered to Lazarus, and crept over the cool tiles. She found it eventually. "My God, who makes fridges so big? I think we need one," she grinned, and Lazarus licked his lips. She stood for a second, hands on hips, starving but unsure what to eat. She reached out and pulled out the milk. "Now we just need a bowl, spoon and cereal. Easy." She shut the fridge and looked around, trying to guess the logical home for things.

Daryl watched from where he was enjoying the cooler night air and the sound of the ocean. Having slept earlier he wasn't very tired, and his brain was a little too alive to lie in an empty bed. She sat on a sun lounger by the pool, content in the silence and the moonlight eating cereal with Lazarus lying by her feet. The temptation to join her was strong, but he didn't want to interrupt the peacefulness. She then stood up and laid her bathrobe on the lounger, and went to stand by the diving board.

Would she? In the dark?

The answer was yes, as she stepped on to board, paused for a second, took three steps, bounced, and then flew into the air, somersaulting twice, twisting, and entering the water with barely a splash. He remembered Donny telling him about the high-diving competitions, and watched as she emerged back where she had started. In the soft moonlight she was breathtaking. He wished he had his camera.

She returned to the sun lounger to reclaim her bathrobe and found a towel on it. She looked around, trying to see the deliverer, but there were only shadows and plants. Her cereal bowl was gone, too. She hesitated, before picking up the towel and slipping it around her shoulders. She then tiptoed away to her bed.

Daryl nodded at the silent night porter who was on hand to keep watch and do whatever was required, without a word or a sound. He, too, then headed off to bed.

HE REFRAINED FROM asking where she was until at least a quarter of an hour had passed, and sat on the terrace beneath the shade of the large umbrella sipping a latte pretending he was quite content to be there on his own. It was a complete sham. The silence around him felt so loud it grated on his patience, so expectant was he for her voice or her laughter.

Mac was standing by at the edge of the terrace, also with a cup of coffee.

"Can't believe she'd want to go running," he said conversationally.

Daryl looked up from the newspaper – flown in especially for him from the mainland by sea plane – and frowned. "Running?"

"Yes. At 6.30am this morning. Bright as a button. OG's boys are trying to keep up with her."

Sure enough, fast footsteps were then heard on the path beyond the terrace wall, followed by several others, that sounded far less speedy.

"You should be glad I don't do that, Mac," Daryl commented, smiling.

"It is a mercy, for sure. Though you make up for it in other ways."

And then she appeared, in a black bikini top and shorts. She pushed her shades up and grinned.

"Good morning. Enjoy your run?"

"Absolutely. We went for a trot round the island, didn't we, OG?"

OG rolled his eyes at the use of the word 'trot'. "Yes. Could we keep it at a trot, please, because I don't think the boys could cope with a gallop."

She laughed and turned to Daryl. "How are you this morning?"

"Excellent. We laid out extra breakfast for you, seeing as you slept through dinner."

"I'm sorry, I didn't mean to at all, it's just…" An orange juice was poured for her, and she was presented with a plate of toast and another of hot, sizzling bacon. Waiter service at breakfast was a bit different from sliding things across polished granite! "I must have been more tired than I thought."

"I guessed as much."

At the appearance of the leopards she asked if he minded if they ate on the terrace, or if she should take them back to the room.

"Here is fine," he said. "It would be cruel to separate you all, even for five minutes."

She looked at him curiously for a second, reassured but intrigued by his words, particularly as not long ago she had been threatened with extended periods of separation as a form of control. Since when had he changed so much? Had he really changed? He didn't miss her look.

She chopped toast, bacon and, to his surprise, some grapes and orange. She indicated two chairs, and they jumped up, both clearly very keen to eat breakfast. They ate quietly, without squabbling and with surprising delicacy, and Daryl smiled. It was like having children – incredibly well behaved four-legged children – and he tried to remember when they'd started referring to them as 'the kids'.

"So, what would you like to do today?" he asked.

"I don't know. What can I do today?"

"Would you like to go out on a speed boat? See some more of the ocean and take a tour round the islands?"

"Wow! I've never been on a speed boat. Are they super-fast?"

"Yes, for boats. Not compared to your bikes, though… You found the cereal alright last night?"

Mysty froze and looked at him. "How do you know about that?"

"I was out here when you had your fridge raid."

"Well, you could have come and told me where everything was."

"You seemed to manage perfectly well. Anyway, I didn't want to startle you stepping out into the darkness."

"You're not that scary," she dismissed him casually, though she seemed to appreciate the thought.

"When would you like to leave?" he asked.

"As soon as we've finished breakfast!"

"Sure, alright. Make sure the boats are ready, Mac. I trust there are no objections?"

"No. They'll be ready in ten."

LOOKING OVER THE controls, Daryl was satisfied. He'd ordered that the boats be overhauled and prepared as soon as she'd chosen her destination, and arranged for them to be delivered. It had been a year and a half since he'd been to the villas – he hadn't confessed to her that they were his, and had been thrilled when she'd chosen them – but had never felt quite as happy to be here as he did now. He also allowed a very select few friends to stay here occasionally, as gestures of patronage and goodwill.

"Permission to come on board, captain?"

She had Lula in her arms, who was wearing a small black lifejacket, and a slightly wary Lazarus was by her side wearing a much larger one.

"Permission granted. Please leave all clothes on the jetty."

She rolled her eyes and he fired her up, the deep, throaty noise of the engine causing all three to startle slightly. She pulled two leads out of her bag and secured Lazarus and Lula to the side of the boat. He waited until they were secure, pulled down his shades, and then he eased down on the throttle and manoeuvred the boat out of the harbour.

She dared to glance at him, her own shades safely down. He was enough to make most women's hearts race. Strong, sure hands held the wheel, feet solidly placed, legs tanned and muscular. It was almost impossible that he was real. She looked at his firm jawline, his face serious but not tense, dark hair ruffling in the breeze. He turned to see if they were okay, and gave her a slow, slow smile, the gaze intense, albeit from behind shades. What was he thinking? She was pretty sure she didn't want to know. She smiled back, a smile which widened when he cleared the harbour wall and increased the power. She returned his thumbs-up, and he turned back to the ocean, not scared, just loving the feel of the wind rushing past, the scudding of the boat over the ocean. She could tell he was confident, knew how to judge the waves, and he took them around two small islands, pointing out the huge palm trees and white sands. He then headed towards the clear blue ocean, and an empty blue-blue horizon.

Sure that the leopards were safe, she crawled along the cushioned seat running along the edge of the boat to the bow and peered down into the water. The colour was astonishing, like nothing she had ever seen before.

Daryl couldn't resist, knowing it would be safe to do so, and swung the boat to the left. She laughed, and held on. He swung to the right, and this time she shrieked a little. He then cut the revs and, sure enough, the momentum carried her forwards, but not enough to send her overboard as he obviously didn't want her dropping into the path of the boat.

"That's not very gentlemanly!" she laughed.

"You don't think I'm a gentleman."

He killed the engine and joined her, but in his relaxed state wasn't ready for the swift move she deployed to send him sideways over the edge.

Five seconds later, he emerged and blinked the water out his eyes. "You…!"

She laughed, and a second later joined him. "It's so warm!" she said, splashing him, and then ducking beneath the water.

His hand went to his head. She'd better not stay long down there… It was then that he realised his shades were gone.

"What's wrong?" she asked, seeing his face when she appeared by his side.

"My shades have gone!"

"Oh bollocks. Hold on."

Before he could stop her, she had dropped beneath the surface again. Damn. He should have made her wear a lifejacket. As far as he was aware, she'd never swum in the ocean before. There were currents to deal with, not to mention the possibility of sharks.

"Mac!" he shouted after a few long seconds. "Mac!"

"Boss? Where is she?" Mac and OG had seen them go overboard from their boat and hadn't been overly concerned. Their boss was a strong swimmer; and judging by what they'd seen in the pool, she was too.

"She's still down there. She's looking for my shades. Goddammit!"

Mac steered the boat over to Daryl's and tied on. They then hopped over and scanned the glittering blue. She couldn't be trusted for a second. Where the hell was she?

Seconds felt stretched into hours, and dark looks were exchanged, as were comments muttered under the breath by the two security men: she had been under the water for well over two minutes.

Mac bent down to offer a hand, so his boss could get back into the boat, but it was obvious Daryl didn't want to leave the water without her. The three men fell into a tense silence, the sound of the splashes against the boat the only thing to be heard. Eyes stayed fixed on the water, waiting…

Finally, there was a different splash, and like a mermaid from the depths, contentedly treading water, her blonde hair spread around her, she surfaced.

"Get her on the boat. *Now.*" Daryl's tone was icy-cold.

"Come over here, where I can reach you, and give me your hand," OG said.

"What?" she asked. "What have I done now?"

"What have you *done*? This isn't a pool, Mysty, it's the *ocean*. God knows what might be down there, and there are strong currents!"

"I could see where I was. My shades have lights. And I just wanted to find yours."

Daryl reached out and pulled her shades off so he could see her eyes…they were wide, and a little scared. "I don't care if you had a fucking chandelier with you! There are all kinds of dangers in waters this deep, and we have no way of getting to you! Don't you dare take such foolish risks again! Splashing about on the surface is one thing; to dive down there is entirely another!"

She didn't dare move or breath or answer. It was so long since he'd shouted at her, and this was fully fledged anger – and she could see that OG and Mac were on his side. She felt outnumbered, and very foolish. She then realized Daryl was angry because she'd scared him, and dared to look into the fierce green eyes.

"I'm sorry. I didn't…mean to…" She swallowed and looked away. Her hand went to her bikini bottoms, and she fiddled with the ties on the side. She then turned back to Daryl and handed him his shades. "I…I caught them as they were falling. I tied them onto –"

"Promise me you won't do that again. Not for shades, not for anything. Nothing is as important as your safety."

"I promise."

Daryl pulled a lifejacket from a cupboard and passed it to her. "Put this on, please." The ocean had claimed his parents; it would *not* claim her. "And, Mac, if you could fit these too."

"Daryl! Do I have to be cuffed to boat? I promise not to go anywhere!"

"Yes." He didn't look at her, aware that she had curled into a ball, the way she did when she felt stupid or lonely or sad. "It's for your own safety."

He nodded at Mac and OG, who climbed back into their boat and unlocked the cuffs. He then restarted the engine and eased down on the throttle.

Ten minutes later he heard a shout: "Dolphins!" He looked over at her. She was pointing with her free hand. Sure enough, there they were. He dropped the boat into neutral and went to her.

"I haven't seen dolphins for years," he said quietly, hoping it was enough for her to know the storm had passed.

"I haven't seen dolphins ever!" she replied with unashamed enthusiasm, and he almost smiled. "Do you think they'll come closer?

Have we got any food they like?"

"We could throw you in. I'm sure you're quite tasty."

She looked round at him slowly. "You're bigger than me. They'd much prefer to eat you." He was saved from replying because a face appeared out the water, and she gasped, and then another, and another. She laughed in delight and looked round at him. "Can we touch them?"

"I don't think they'd mind."

She manoeuvred herself so she could reach, and stretched a hand down.

"Come on. You too." He leaned over, not at all confident with animals, but placed his hand on the grey-blue head. One of them let out a high squeal as it rose from the water, and others appeared. "They're amazing! Feel their skin. It's so smooth, and strong. You can feel it, can't you?"

She looked around at him, and it took his breath away. She'd thought it the most natural thing in the world to try to communicate with them, by reaching out, by touching them. It had never occurred to him to do that. She wanted to experience everything, to get close to everything. Even the way she was with him, challenging him to step outside of himself, to relax… Had he ever been that free? He wanted to freeze-frame the moment.

"We can't go swimming with them, can we?"

"No," he said softly. He didn't want to break the magic, but knew it was not safe to get into the water with them.

After a few more minutes, they swam away, and she smiled. "That was so beautiful."

"Yes."

"Can you move me that way, so I reach Lula and Lazarus? Please?"

He sighed, and took the cuff off completely. He wanted to trust her. Her glance of surprised gratitude was enough. She'd learnt her lesson.

"Are there any drinks onboard?" she asked.

He smiled. "Come with me."

He pressed a button near the controls, and a panel slid open to reveal a whole array of spirits and mixers and equipment for making cocktails.

"Wow!" Her face was a picture. "Would you like a cocktail?"

"Can you make them?"

"Weekends spent in Donny's club with the bar staff…it had to be good for something, right? What can I get you?"

"Sex on the Beach."

"Why would I imagine you'd pick anything else!"

"What will you have? Do you like spirits?"

"No. But I'll have a Pina Colada."

"A good choice."

"There is beer."

"I know, I just don't fancy beer."

"Why don't you like spirits? Mind you, they're pretty strong."

She looked away. "My father. He stank of them. Do you know any jokes?"

"Jokes? No. I'm no good at remembering them."

"I was hoping you were! I'm rubbish at them too." She finished mixing the drinks and took a sip of hers, and handed him his. "Why don't we play a questions game. We ask questions alternately, on anything, and the other person *has* to answer or…there's a forfeit."

"What's the forfeit?"

"Fifty laps in the pool."

"You'd do that for fun."

"So would you."

"True." He took a sip of his drink. It was great. But then of course it was going to be great. "Who starts?"

"You can. Though I won't answer any questions about my mother. You can pick one topic you won't answer on either, to keep it fair. And before you say anything, this is between you, me and the ocean."

"Of course. Okay…" He dropped the boat into neutral again and sat down. "How did you end up so close to Donny? I know you saved his life in the street, because he told me, but how did you end up best friends with a mob boss?"

She smiled sadly, and leaned her head back, the sun glorious on her skin. "Man, do you know how many times I've asked myself that very question? Especially after coming to LA and having Franny and Giles adopt me as well, and Don Salvadore, who was hoping I'd go to Harvard so he could have me in Boston." She took a deep breath. "I didn't want to know Donny in the beginning. After the truck incident, he tried grabbing me once at night. I ended up on the railway bridge, with his boys pointing their guns at me. He said he just wanted to talk to me, but I ran.

"A couple of months later he saw me on camera, thanks to his surveillance team who saw my first public jumps in Palm Square. He had me followed, and a few days later he sent Paulo and the boys to come and 'pick me up' from the derelict hotel where I was 'living'. Eventually they got me – not because I surrendered, mind you. Paulo was crushing me under his arm, which wasn't hard because I was so small and skinny. They took me, handcuffed, in a limo to see Donny. I was so scared, but it wasn't at all what I expected. He made me sit down, took the cuffs off and introduced himself…and we had dinner and talked. He told me he wanted me to go to school, that I wasn't going back to the hotel, and I didn't have a choice. I argued, of course."

"You don't do debts." Daryl's interjection made her smile.

"No, but he reminded me I'd saved his life, and told me it was the right thing to do to help me, just like I'd helped him without being asked. I thought he'd change his mind and kick me out, but he didn't. He was so kind, but I saw in his eyes the same sadness I had in mine. If I'd wanted someone who understood, I couldn't have found a better person."

Daryl didn't know what to say. His own deep desire to be so understood haunted him. But now was not the time to talk about that.

"Mario called you twiglet, right?"

She looked surprised that he had remembered this from one of their crazy conversations, so long ago.

"I was so skinny, for years. As a kid I never had enough to eat, and with my metabolism – which I now know about – no wonder I never gained any weight. I spent most of my life starving hungry." No wonder she hated starving herself when it came to her performances at Celeste… "When I was with Donny, everyone was always trying to feed me in the hope I'd stop looking like a collection of arms and legs. I was such an ugly duckling. I was about thirteen when I stopped looking like…like I could slip through a drain cover or hide behind a lamp post."

"I can't believe you were ever ugly, my future 'blonde secretary'."

She blushed, and then laughed. "Oh Lord, that was one joke I shouldn't have started."

"I couldn't believe it when I heard you answer Donny's comm. He's always been so careful."

"He trusted me. No locks, no bolts. That's how I learnt to trust him and, in answer to your original question, how we became so close."

That hung in the air between them, uncomfortably, but with an honesty he had to respect.

"So, erm, it must be time for you to ask me a question."

"Where did you grow up?" she asked simply, which surprised him.

"Early on, in Philadelphia. My family have a large estate. I still go there, when I can. I used to think I'd live there one day, with a wife and kids, because it's the place where I have my best memories from childhood. My mother and father were busy, but happy, and I remember we had some fun times. After a while, my father was nearly always absent, and if I saw him it would be for quick conversations about my studies, or my friends – checking up on me, I guess. Mother and I moved around a lot with my father's work, and private school became home tutoring. And then came Harvard, and a bit of military training in the summer holidays in the navy – 'character building', my father called it. I never questioned it; it was just what life was."

"Did you ever have the option to do anything else other than become the world's richest and most successful businessman? You must have wanted something?"

"When I was a kid, I loved science – hence all the computer gadgetry when I was a bit older. I could spend days working on something and not even notice the time. Apparently, that was 'indulgent' and I had wider responsibilities and talents that needed to be put to good use. At college I loved football, and could have turned pro. I was good at it. Better than good. But my father said no. 'This is Mac Terry,' he said, 'your new bodyguard. He's going to keep you safe, and that includes no football.'

I think he was scared I'd get hurt in a hard tackle and end up with brain damage… I was the only heir to the Blackmoor fortune, so…"

He fell silent. Lost in thought.

"Dreams are hard to give up, aren't they?"

"Yes. They are."

"Would you like another cocktail?"

"Absolutely."

She smiled at the subtle compliment: she had done a good job. "Same again?"

"Please, yes."

"Mac's been with you a long time," she said, tipping ice into the shaker.

"Yes. He has disapproved much, but said little. He is reliable. I know he intends to keep me alive and safe until Judgement Day. He's irreplaceable."

"He used to be so grim. He's a lot happier now."

"He was always grim, and silent, and obedient, until someone turned up and started buying milkshakes and answering back."

She had her back to him but he could tell she was smiling. "Wow. They sound awesome. Who was that?"

"A mutinous rebel called the Pirate Queen."

She handed him a second cocktail. "I think I've heard of her. She sounds like fun."

"She's lots of fun."

"What you said about football… Is that why…?" She looked away.

But he wanted to hear her thoughts. He wanted that honesty she'd had with Donny to belong to them too. "It's okay," he said. "Finish your question."

"You might not like it."

"Honestly, it's okay."

"Because your father put a stop to the football, and no doubt everything else he considered 'too dangerous' – like sky diving! – is that why you…why you always watch and never join in?" She held his gaze. "Only, there's nothing wrong with you physically, and it's hard to understand why you are so strong and do nothing with it, except keep fit. I would go mad if I didn't have a way of using my strength, even if it is in bar fights…" She laughed, and he rolled his eyes. "And…

"Go on."

"When you take all those women to bed, is it a way of getting rid of all the energy, despite the obvious, well…obviously you like doing it… and a way of getting over the fact that you couldn't be a footballer? To reconnect with the physicality of life after so long stuck in offices and meetings?"

"So what you're saying is that all those women are actually a type of therapy? In that case, you should pity me for my affliction." He smiled at this new theory.

"Pity? Affliction? Therapy? You scandalous rake! Don't start playing the sweet and innocent card *Mr Blackmoor* because we both know you're the world's most notorious womaniser! And you enjoy every second of it!" His tease had totally backfired. "I grew up surrounded by twenty-odd hot-blooded Italians who all thought they were God's gift, so don't think I'm falling for that." Her eyes scorched him, challenging him.

"I've just been trying…" He searched for the right words. "To find the right woman."

And that hung in the air between them.

But he sensed she still wasn't convinced, because she arched an eyebrow at him. He was right: "By sleeping with so many? Prince Charming with a glass slipper looking for Cinderella? Poor you," she said.

The challenge in her eyes dimmed not one iota, and Daryl became aware he was playing verbal, mental and moral chess, and he wasn't doing so well. Diversion seemed a good tactic. "Was Donny one of that twenty-odd?" he asked.

"He had his moments, but he realised that wasn't the approach to take."

"What is the approach to take?"

Their eyes locked again.

"I can't tell you. It only works if you work it out for yourself," she replied, refusing to give an inch. "Your turn," she then said.

"Donny said you had a sister," he ventured, knowing she had said she wouldn't discuss her mother. But maybe she would open up about her sibling? "Was she anything like you?"

He could tell she was contemplating the question, considering the answer. The water lapped at the boat, gently rocking her and the cocktail in his hand.

"No. And yes. She was dark-haired, but thin, like me. She never ran around and played games, even when were really young. She was two years older than me, and so serious. I know I didn't smile very much either, but she…she'd been witness to our lives for longer than me, and I think she'd given up hope of it ever getting better. I often wished she'd been more of a sister, like showing me how to do things, like plait my hair…but I think she was too…worn down by it all. Anyway, when our mother needed help, she would hide in the wardrobe or under the bed. I used to plead with her to help me, but she never did. Not once. She'd still be there when we got back from the hospital…"

"How young were you when you first took your mother to hospital?"

"Four. I called an ambulance, somehow knowing that was the right thing to do. My mother was unconscious otherwise she would have stopped me."

"Why?"

"We couldn't afford the ambulance. My father had to settle the bill, and he took it out on me. I didn't go to school for two weeks."

Daryl could hardly bear to hear those words, let alone try to process them. How had she lived like this?

"What…? But why…?"

"Everyone in the town knew who we were, and at school. It wasn't such a very big place. Everybody knew who the 'disaster family' was. The sheriff used to come and sit with me outside the hospital room. He wanted my mother to press charges. But we had no money, so no lawyer. There was no way to get away from him. Even if he got charged, he would have lied and been freed…and what he would have done when he got home… I know the police let him off DUI a couple of times. Nobody challenged my father."

"What did your sister like? Did you have anything in common?"

"No, not really. I went to every possible after school club, for sports and dance. She just hid in books. She started to get into magazines, and loved the glossy pages and the photos – one of our neighbours used to give her the ones she'd finished with. She loved looking at all the famous, beautiful people. There was some free lipstick with one of them. That was a night I'll never forget. I don't know how my father found it. My mother tried to get my father to stop…hitting her, so he did, but then…" Her eyes darkened with the memory. "I'm not sure if it was worse being broken on the floor, or being the one to try and put everyone back together."

Daryl stayed silent for a moment, sensing she hadn't shared these parts of her past for a very long time, which was why the emotion in her voice was still so raw.

"Is that why you don't wear make-up?"

Her silence answered the question.

"You don't need it."

"Can I ask you a question?" She pushed her shades up.

"Yes."

"Why didn't you marry Rachel?"

His heart fell at the reminder of betrayal and misjudgement, as well as the emotional scar tissue of his one attempt to make someone a part of his life.

"That's probably the one question I choose not to answer."

"Sure. You don't have to."

"Suffice to say I realised there is far more to marriage than merely finding a woman who can act and look the part. I was wrong; very wrong, in fact. But I am eternally grateful I found out before I married her. I went completely off the idea after that…experience. But I admit I do want to marry, and I do want a family, despite what people think. But I don't want to get divorced, for so many reasons."

"Did she sign a pre-nuptial?"

"Of course."

"Most very rich men need pre-nuptials, I guess. You could get married and divorced and remarried seventeen times over and women would still line up to marry you."

"I'm sure you mean that as a compliment..."

"Daryl..."

"It's okay."

"I did mean it as a compliment, but I'm sorry, I sort of know how that sounded. I guess...well, in your position there are countless other issues to consider, not least your vast fortune. If you want something meaningful, and not just a trophy wife, how could you ever be sure it was real? Some women can act well enough to win an Oscar when they need to. And either she will have to love you very much, or not at all, to have to bear you constantly disappearing on business. Or utterly stupid, of course."

In the long pause that followed her soft words, while they sipped their drinks, he wondered if, as in the world of his deepest dreams, they would look back on this conversation as man and wife. He imagined the life they might have, the ring he would love to put on her finger, the children...

"I could never imagine the burden you carry," she then said. "And frankly, I don't think one man should have to bear it." Her eyes rose gently back up to meet his, his heart beating painfully loud in his chest to witness the next second, not having expected such soft words. "Which makes me wonder why you got yourself a whole other load of hassle with me! I've not exactly been a walk in the park!"

"I don't regret making you sign the contract. How I did maybe, but I still would have done it."

"You are insane."

"Quite possibly." He smiled, amused at her easy acceptance of his answers, and happy there was no longer any fury and bitterness in her voice. Sitting there with her now he felt even more sure of the rightness of his previous decisions, even if his methodology had been sometimes wanting.

"Mac must have thought I was the biggest load of trouble that ever breathed, what with you going out in LA on your own, the Bowl, the trashed cars...it's a wonder he didn't drop me out of the plane when you weren't looking."

"I think he'd agree with me now that it was worth it. Especially after you got him a mug and a t-shirt. His mean-spirited boss never did that; he was very pleased with them." A smile flickered at the corners of his mouth.

"He's a great guy, once you get past the serious face. I still feel a bit bad I hit him so hard."

"I think he needed a good fight. He's far too well-behaved, and he enjoyed the excitement."

"Well-behaved? Are we talking about you here? Mr Playboy Billionaire himself?"

He tried to scowl at her feigned disbelief, but he was enjoying himself far too much. It wouldn't have had any effect anyway.

"Can I ask you another question?" he said, happy to leave this subject alone. For now.

"Yeees…" She squinted at him, clearly braced for another deep question.

"Would you like to try taking us back?"

Her face blossomed like the sun bursting past the horizon.

"Really? Can I? You're going to trust me with a speedboat?"

"I've had to learn to trust you on your bikes, haven't I? I'm sure it's not beyond you. Just take it as slowly as you like, no rush."

He stood up and placed his glass back in the box for empties and led her to the controls. He was going to enjoy this.

"Hold the wheel like this," he said, and she copied. He then moved behind her to show her the controls, the pitometer, the depth finder, start button and throttle, and she didn't flinch when his chest brushed her back as he leant in.

"So the handling is quite light or heavy?" she asked.

"It's light," he said, surprised, "but even lighter when you're at the higher speeds." She nodded, taking it all in. "Why don't you take us over to Mac and O'Grady, to get used to how she handles."

She fired the boat up, as she had been shown, and gently eased the throttle, just a touch, taking the boat smoothly over to the second boat.

Mac and OG were playing cards with two others. Unbeknown to them, both Mac and O'Grady had lost their bets as to how long it would take until there were raised voices.

"You're letting her drive?" Mac exclaimed, as if Daryl was a little touched in the head.

"Well, thanks for the vote of confidence, Mac! Much appreciated!" she laughed. She looked around at Daryl. "Do you think it's time they got a bit wet, too?" For once the twinkle of mischief in her eyes was colluding not confrontational.

"Absolutely."

"We'll see you back on the island. Don't bother trying to keep up!"

Like a pro, she spun the wheel and the boat took off in a roar of revs, sending an arc of spray over the four men and their playing cards.

"You're sure you've never driven one of these before?"

"Nah. But I've watched James Bond enough times."

Cocktails in the sun and Mysty at the wheel.

Life didn't get any better.

"SHE MADE IT for dinner!" OG laughed as she appeared on the terrace.

Mac pulled out a chair for her, next to Daryl, and then another two for the leopards, who bounced into theirs happily, excited by the smells in the air.

"To the champion of the cricket pitch!" Daryl toasted, and handed her a beer.

"Joint champion of the cricket pitch," she corrected, and toasted him right back.

Their afternoon beach cricket match had been a huge success – for them; less so the poor guys they had beaten! – and they were now hungry and looking forward to some great food. Mac and OG sat, and they tucked into the dishes that were brought over, one after the other, each as delicious as the next.

"This place has an excellent reputation, as you can see. I'm sure the kids will write rave reviews about it," Daryl said, indicating the two leopards. "If they're happy, you're happy."

"And are you happy?" she asked.

"Very."

And he was. He was wonderfully happy. How had that happened? But as the evening progressed, he felt the urge to be closer to her, so strong it hurt. How badly he wanted to pull her into his lap, to not have to share her with Mac and OG, or have any of the guys there at all. How he wanted to hold her, kiss her, make her moan with pleasure as he kissed every inch of her soft skin.

He found himself feeling a little distant after a while, and needed a distraction. He politely made his excuses and wandered over to the quiet pool area. But the pool only served to remind him of her earlier playfulness. He could still hear her laughing as she ducked in and out of the water, the two of them sparring like kids. When had he ever had so much fun? He'd never imagined it possible. But it was she who made it possible, like she made everything possible. Even burying Mac in the sand and shaping it to look like a mermaid, his incredulous face peering out at the pair of them when he woke up. There was a moment when the temptation to hold her, feel her, had been too much, and he'd dared to grab her. Of course she'd squirmed and struggled against him – against his hip and not his front, as despite the cool of the water he'd been highly and visibly aroused – but she hadn't fought him that hard, not even when he'd lifted her above his head. Instead she'd threatened him with further drownings, of course, but with neither malice nor rage. The feel of her firm body against his, of his arm around her waist, had created a pulsing desire that was too much.

He'd grabbed a towel, needing to wrap it around his lower half, and climbed out of the pool and headed straight for the shower. Hands braced against the wall of the wet room as powerful jets sent cascades of icy water over him. He could have growled in frustration the need was so strong. Could she not see? Could she not sense how much he wanted her? How much he wanted to taste every inch of her body, gorge himself on her, awaken her until she clung to him? The insistent pulse in his groin hurt, and he knew he was far too aroused for it to just go away. Why the hell hadn't he discreetly brought a woman with him? He could have installed her in a nearby hotel. He might have known it would get unbearable.

He had moved a hand down from the wall, wishing it was her hand, wishing she would touch what she had secretly admired – he'd seen the glances and the looks from behind her shades – and wrapped his fingers wrapped around his erection. What hold did she have on him to drive him to this? He despised every motion of his hand, knowing it should be with her, just as every meaningless coupling with his 'harem girls' had been wasted, selfish moments. He heard her saying his name, like she had on the boat, when she'd mentioned marriage and divorce, soft and full of concern. He saw her hands on the wheel, her hair in the water, the water on her skin in the sunshine. The explosive orgasm caught him by surprise, its force both painful and pleasurable.

God knows, if she ever did let him have her, he was going to struggle to control himself.

He'd turned off the jets and stepped out, hungry for her and for dinner.

He pulled out his handheld. While they had been out on the boat, a call had come through for him from Charles Brentford. Perhaps a brief conversation with the secretary of state might be the distraction he needed.

"Daryl?" He turned, and saw her peeping round the foliage. "There you are. Are you alright? You disappeared."

"Fine. Apologies. I know I shouldn't have, really, but I had to call someone back. It was important."

"You look like you need cheering up? We have coconut ice cream, and apparently its fantastic."

"I have good news," he said, and she looked round expectantly. "The press is still convinced we're skiing, and no doubt hunting every known ski resort and every unknown one trying to find a pair of leopards wearing earmuffs and thermals."

She laughed at the image he created; he silently realised how much he loved making her laugh.

It was true, the ice cream was delicious, and the still night air carried the sounds of laughter that rose and fell as easily as the waves on the distant shore.

DARYL COULD SEE her, lit up by the soft lights on the stage, the big white lotus flower in her hair. They'd somehow been invited to an island wedding – well, Mysty had after she'd been coconut 'hunting', as she called it, with some locals early that morning – and had in turn 'invited' him, Mac and OG. She was now singing with them. Some others were dancing. He knew no one there. The song came to an end and he turned to Mac. She was having a fine time, and he wasn't needed. She made friends so easily, and he could hear her laughing as naturally as if she was with a bunch of lifelong companions.

"Mac."

"Boss."

"Think I'd like to call it a night."

"Sure."

The big man looked surprised, but orders were orders. They made their way through the crowd.

"You're not going, are you?"

Damn: spotted. He turned to her. "I think I'll just go back. It's not really… I'm sure you'll have a great time." He didn't add 'without me'.

"Daryl Augustus Bartholomew Blackmoor, there's nothing wrong with doing something a little different, with different people. Please stay."

"It doesn't sound like you're asking me."

"Lots of people would like to meet you, and they may even be persuaded to join your excellent cricket team. You visit their world when you come here, and they don't even know you. Come and join in?" She gestured at the crowd of dancing bodies in the firelight.

He sighed.

Hours later, with another cup of a fruity cocktail in his hand, and after talking to lots of people he didn't know but who seemed genuinely happy to meet him, one very sleepy girl came to sit next to him.

"Wedding parties are hard work," she said, "let alone driving speed boats and winning cricket matches. Have you enjoyed yourself?"

"Yes. More than I expected I admit."

"Really?"

"It seems it is your personal mission to see that I enjoy myself."

"You're doing just fine."

But instead of going to bed when they got back, they began a big poker game, everyone playing for matchsticks, laughing in between the straight poker faces. It was too much for Mysty. It reminded her of nights with Donny and his boys, or with Franny and Giles, and she found her happiness ebbing from her, every second bitter-sweet. She couldn't bear it; she didn't want to have to face the pain of losing any sense of belonging and security all over again. Tears that had nothing to do with tiredness pricked at her eyes, and she knew she needed to be alone. Slipping away from the bonhomie, she thought she'd made her exit unnoticed before a voice behind her made her pause: "Mysty, are you alright?"

She stopped. She'd almost made it to her room.

"Yeah, fine, just tired. And I should check on Lula."

Mac didn't look convinced. Just like Paulo and Giles hadn't, those big men with their thick skins and big hearts.

"You're crying."

"I yawned and my eyes leaked."

"You're shit at lying, you know. Are you going to tell me what's wrong?"

"No, Mac. If it's okay, I really don't want to talk about it."

"Did someone say something?"

"No, nothing like that." It squeezed her heart how protective he sounded.

"You know, my dad used to hold us kids up in the air if we wouldn't tell him something."

"You wouldn't dare."

But he dared, and she hung like a ragdoll, too tired to fight him.

"Talk to me."

"I don't want to."

"Come on, kiddo. Talk to me." The gentleness was her undoing, the persistence hard to resist, tempting her to give up her pain and share. Mac felt her body relax, then the fight left her mind as well and she surrendered her truth she had tried so hard to hide.

"I don't. I'm not very good at being happy. Not like this. I'm afraid it'll all disappear again, like it has before, and I'm tired of fighting to be alright. I don't want to lose everything and end up alone again, with nothing."

"Why would it disappear? You have the best people here, to keep you safe, and we are your friends. You're not going to be alone."

"I thought I was safe before, and then I found a good friend in a dark tunnel with a bullet hole in his forehead and his eye plucked out. Next day I'm on a plane to LA, and my life changed forever. Things just happen. I never seem to hold on to anything."

It was a succinct argument. Her life had been a rollercoaster of discontinuity.

"None of what happened was your fault. It's nothing you've done, kiddo." It was OG.

Mac put her down as the man appeared next to him.

"You can't live like this, not enjoying yourself for fear of something happening. Isn't that what you've been lecturing Mr Serious about?" OG added.

She stayed quiet.

"And like me or OG would let anything happen to you, when you're the one who gets us playing cricket in Barbados? We're having far too much fun we don't even deserve to get paid!" Mac said, and saw the twinkle of amusement in her eyes. "How about some football tomorrow morning. Early. When it's not hot. Yes?"

"Okay…"

"Right, you, bed. Now. You're far too tired," OG said.

"You're just making the most of bossing me around because I'm too tired to argue."

"Yep, that's me. Really mean bodyguard."

She gave him a look, but it only made him smile, and after a soft pat of gratitude on Mac's arm that probably felt like the brush of a butterfly's wing, she headed off beneath the bowing foliage to her apartment.

Daryl joined the two men who waited to hear the door shut.

"She alright?"

"She will be. A few ghosts to deal with. Kid's had a pretty rough ride so far even before we all turned up." Mac answered quietly, not excusing himself from the comment. "We have another ball game planned in the morning. You want to help O'Grady try not to lose?"

"I like your optimism – what time?"

"6.30am, before it's hot."

"See you then."

"Losers get thrown in the pool apparently." O'Grady added, just for the hell of it.

Daryl just smiled and walked away to bed, reflecting that having her running around in a bikini would make such an immersion in cold water an incentive.

"COME ON, KIDDO, boats are ready."

"The boats? We only just finished playing football? Where are we going?"

"Fishing," OG said, trying to sound encouraging.

"You mean, you're going to kill the fish?"

"Can't eat them if they're still alive," Mac commented, and OG sent him a look.

"Will there be blood?" Yes, that was what he suspected she would ask.

"You won't see anything," Mac said gently.

"You know, I think I might sit this one out. I'm…I'm sure I'll be rubbish at fishing. You guys go and have some fun. I'll stay here by the pool, I promise. OG, you don't have to stay."

Daryl noticed how she hugged herself, and knew then wasn't a time to push, despite feeling sad he wouldn't get the afternoon with her as planned.

"You sure?"

"Yes, really, I'm sure."

"No, I'll stay. I'm not a big fan of fish," OG said equably, refusing to leave her or make a big deal out of it. "We can always go out on the jet skis instead, yes?"

She nodded. "You two go and catch dinner and argue who caught the bigger fish."

"We'll be back soon."

But she strolled down the beach in their wake, glad to see Daryl relaxed. Every day she'd woken up and realised that the day before hadn't been a dream, and he really was relaxing, and quite funny even, especially when they'd been playing about in the pool. She had learned so much more about the man he really was, seen him talking with the other guests at the wedding, people he didn't know, and watched them respond to him. He still had the quiet command and authority – she didn't think that would ever change – and the strength of his mind was mirrored in his body, in equal measure. He was intriguing, still a mystery to her; somehow becoming a man different to the one she was used to, dressed in a suit, and yet the same.

She'd encountered men in her life, lots, some almost naked back when she was a performing tiger. Some of them were totally uninhibited; some a little more reserved. But him? All that muscle. He didn't show off exactly; it was just…well, he couldn't help the way he was built. And the way he made her feel. She didn't feel anything burying Mac in the sand, or when OG gave her a hug, but Daryl? She would have to keep her distance. She was far too inexperienced to play any kind of game with him, because she would only lose. He had been respectful, anyway. Teasing and even admiring, and not afraid to grab her in the pool, but he'd never once taken advantage. Clearly, he was a gentleman, to a degree.

She watched him help load up the three fishing boats, and eventually all was ready and they set off, waving as they did.

And then the world day changed as surely as a cloud covering the sun.

There were shouts, and the boats circled. And then the engines died.

Mysty looked at OG. What on earth could be the matter?

One of them was carried on the current to the jetty, and the guys jumped off, calling and beckoning to the others. The guard appeared, after hearing the shouts, and called out to Daryl, who pointed into the water.

"Come in! Come in!" the guard shouted, and Mysty and OG stood to try and see what was happening. Why had they cut the engines? And why was the guard shouting for them to come in?

And then the water erupted. It was so sudden that Mysty barely had time to gasp in horror as a large shark shot upwards, his jaws wide. Mac was too late, and despite grabbing Mark, one of his men, and pulling him backwards, blood sprayed from a large gash on his forearm.

"Sweet Holy Jesus," O'Grady muttered, as Mysty shouted out.

But there wasn't one shark, there were many, and the water churned as the huge animals circled and butted the two remaining boats.

"Come in!" the guard shouted again, but Mac was shaking his head and now pointing at the engine. The other guys were doing the same in the other boat. There must be a fault? But why? The vulnerability of those on board was too much for Mysty to bear. Without engines they had no way of moving to safety, and she watched as Mac and Daryl cowered in the centre, and ducked down by the wheel as they jumped again.

She ran.

"Mysty! No!" OG got to the mooring just as she pulled out in one of the speedboats, one hand steering, the other hard on the throttle. Oh God! His worst nightmare had just materialized. He ran Lazarus and Lula back up the beach and ordered that they be taken back to Mysty's room, and then hurtled back down, pulling his service weapon as he did. Daryl's men had done the same, but hesitated to fire indiscriminately into the water, such was the positioning of the boats – and Mysty on the way out to them.

Daryl looked up at the sound of a motor…and froze, seeing the banner of her golden hair. What the hell was she doing? He went to go to the edge of the boat to yell at her, but Mac pulled him back.

"Don't fucking move," he growled, the wrath of God etched into his bloodied face. He finished tying off the t-shirt he had stripped off and wrapped around the injured man's arm.

Mysty pulled alongside the second boat. The three guys on board didn't need asking twice, and jumped across, and there was an almighty thud as she pulled away, making contact with one of the large, angry animals. They fired, and the beautiful blue water coloured with red.

"Holy Jesus, O'Grady, grab her! Get her off the water!" Mac yelled, as OG jumped into another boat and fired her up. But she had a different idea, and steered a wide arc in the opposite direction, both of them forming a frothing circle of water around the main body of sharks.

"Any bright ideas, Mac?"

"Let's go skiing next time." The big guy then reached for his gun and went to the edge. "I think I could cope with a yeti or two, but not a sea of maniac fucking sharks…" He shouted for everyone to get down, as the pair came back around for another swoop. It was impossible not to appreciate her skill, despite the situation. Face expressionless, she was doing what she did best: responding to a life-threatening situation with calm action.

"Anything on the motor?"

"Dead as a fucking dodo!"

The coil of fear in Daryl's stomach solidified into pure unadulterated terror. He concentrated on watching O'Grady, to distract himself, who then swung around and pulled next to them while she circled, confusing the sharks who dropped beneath the surface. In a swift role reversal, O'Grady zoomed around as she arrived to take the remaining passengers so neither vessel was overloaded, and Mac grabbed the wounded man and half threw him across. He then reached for Daryl, but as he did the boat lurched violently as a shark smashed its way between the two boats.

"Go, Mac! I'm right behind you!" Daryl shouted from where he had been thrown to the floor of the boat.

Mac hesitated, and then jumped over, reaching across to hold the two boats together. But the shark hit again, breaking Mac's hold and throwing him backwards.

As Mysty came around again she caught sight of the nose and jaw of the enraged shark and felt her gut coil in dread, angry that her efforts had been frustrated again by these unpredictable, scarily powerful monsters of the surf.

Daryl scrambled back up, the lilt of the ship now obvious, his face pale with horror as he realised the hull had been breached by the violence from beneath. He knew the boat was only going to be an island for a few seconds longer. There was nowhere to go. Nothing he could do.

Mysty saw his face, and the recognition of his perilous position. The water was getting in fast, and would soon have him under. She had seconds.

"Mac! Get up here! Take the controls! Tell OG to get on the other side and be ready to take some passengers!"

Mac scrambled up and over, patching into OG as he went, vaguely understanding what she was saying but happy to try anything as he stood to see his sole charge, his life's work, about to disappear into the frothing saltwater. Holding off as long as possible, Daryl was right up on the back lip of the boat, eyes on the water that churned towards him as if it was hungry to claim him.

She looked over at OG who was skimming round in a perfect arc to intercept as she hoped. Glancing back at Mac, their eyes locked for a second.

"You sure about this?"

"Get me on the fucking boat!" Her face said, 'Don't ask me again'. She heard the revs and the thrust of the boat forwards, she braced herself to move.

The boat scythed in, Mac lining her up perfectly…and she jumped, landing on the back edge of Daryl's boat. He was vaguely aware of her being in the air, and then the collision of their bodies as his brain registered her body slamming into his, and her hands grabbing for him. And then the world became a blur of sensation, physical chaos, as the second impact stunned him, this one harder than the first. He lay still, crumpled against the floor of the boat.

The loud noise of the speedboat called him back from the brink of unconsciousness, and he groaned with the ache of his body against the hard surface and the shock of hitting it so hard.

"You alright? Sir? Mysty?" OG shouted down at them as Mac sped away, also heading for the shore.

Daryl didn't answer. Moving felt like he was in treacle, his co-ordination clumsy and slow. He was winded, but she was there, right next to him…thank God. But there was no smile of triumph, of relief. Her eyes were closed. She was unconscious.

"Get the medics on the beach! Call Baden. Get the chopper! Get him to meet us at the mainland hospital," Daryl yelled over the roar of the engine.

She was like a crumpled doll, pale and battered in his arms. There was not a mark on her…no blood…she was breathing, but ~~so~~ why was she so still and so lifeless?

"Sweetheart? Open your eyes," he murmured, eyes desperate for a sign of movement. "Say something." Fingers smoothed over her cheek, a caress he had waited for months to make; he hadn't dreamed it would be like this. "Mysty. Please. Speak to me, so I know you're alright."

Once again with her he was in unchartered territory. All the concerns of his father flashed up in his mind, and it was there, under the hot bright sun, he had the realisation that had been a long time coming. He suddenly felt himself in his father's shoes, and he as his only son, and for the first time understood the deep, instinctive need to protect. Only it was not him and his father, it was his most precious girl, and she was not responding. This innocent girl who had risked herself to save him from a most awful fate. It was almost too much to take in. It was a mercy no one could see the storm of emotion on his face.

The boat came to a halt, and Daryl reluctantly stood up and took a step back as the two medics from the villa complex climbed onboard and a stretcher was lifted into the boat. Far more capable hands than his secured her and covered her in a blanket. OG moved closer as others secured the boat, needing to see her.

"Has she said anything? Woken up at all?"

"No, nothing." *I wish to God she had.*

His eyes met Mac's…they mirrored his concern…and the unspoken question of whose life was more valuable hovered in the air: that Daryl had needed rescuing, against the price of her getting hurt, sat as obvious as the bloodied waters before them.

The mood on the beach was so different from half an hour before it was like night and day. He felt sick, and watched as they checked her neck was stable. Medics accepted the helping hands from the security men on the boat to lift her carefully onto dry land; men who then hung back, solemn and shaken, all staring at the girl who had so recently beaten them on the football pitch, who had just saved a good number of them thanks to her own immense bravery. Finally, after what felt like too long, the group around the stretcher were moving as fast as they dare to the waiting chopper, OG next to her.

Knowing he was with her allowed Daryl to take a breath. "Mac. Find out how the sharks got past the barriers, get them out, and have the barriers reinforced. I want answers. This shouldn't have happened."

Mac nodded. His boss had switched into default mode for survival, too angry to communicate any more.

Please God, let her be alright. Don't take her away. Not now. Not like this. Not ever.

LIKE WAKING UP in the clinic after she'd taken the terrible dose of drugs, she struggled to orientate herself. She heard someone whisper, footsteps, buttons being pressed, and more whispering. She forced herself to open her eyes.

Daryl was beside her, his eyes straight on hers when she tentatively moved an arm.

"Hello."

She saw the drip stand, the fluid going into the back of her hand, and lifted it. He laid it back down, slowly, and she didn't argue.

"How are you feeling?"

"Like I ran into a truck and then got run over by another one."

"That's pretty accurate, though I'd rather be described as a Lamborghini than a truck." His humour made her smile but pain shot up her neck and ballooned inside her head. Her grimace prompted another question.

"Are you in pain?"

"What's wrong with me?"

"You took quite a knock to the head, and were unconscious for a while. You've got an impressive bruise." Her eyes closed as she winced. "Baden's going to come and take another look at you soon to make sure nothing else is wrong." *Like bleeding on the brain, or a haemorrhage, or memory loss, something else that could kill you silently and without warning and steal you from me.*

"Baden?"

"He was close by." Daryl kept details to a minimum. She was in no state for an overload of information. But there was something else he had to say, the words burning to be said: "You saved my life."

She frowned. And then it all came back.

"You don't deserve to be eaten by sharks, not you."

It wasn't the most cogent or eloquent explanation, but it proved one thing: her short-term memory was okay, and he suppressed a sigh of relief.

"You risked yourself."

"Nothing new there, then."

The sad smile tugged at him.

"The chances you take, you shouldn't…"

"Never do nothing if you can do something. I would do it again if I had to."

And he knew she would. Knew she was too courageous to leave a soul to a terrible fate if she could at all help it.

"Is everyone alright?"

"Yes, everyone's fine, remarkably. Mark had surgery on his arm, and there's no reason why he can't regain complete use." She turned away, the image of the attack rather too vivid. "I think I know how Donny felt… when you saved his life."

"And how does it feel?"

"Like a gift." *Like no other gift I've ever been given.*

"It's free, so don't try paying me for it."

She managed to muster the energy to glare at him, and he smiled.

"I would pay anything to take away your pain. I was furious when I saw you in that boat, as much as I'm glad to be alive."

"I'm young. I bounce. Are Lazarus and Lula alright?"

"They're good. Missing you. But they're being well looked after, so don't worry, just get better."

"You know, Mr Manager, I think you're in very great danger of showing me what you really are."

"And what is that? God, Satan…a regular man?"

"No."

"What then?"

"Maybe I'll tell you when I'm better."

"I look forward to it. Get some rest."

She would be fine. She was right. She was young, and would bounce. The nightmare scenarios that had played through his mind finally faded, and he began to believe she would be back to her usual self soon enough. He was just not sure when.

He stepped out of the room to get a coffee while she slept, finding Baden with O'Grady. Both men looked up expectantly for a report on how she was.

"She has no loss of memory, and no sign of anything more than a bruised head."

"God be praised." Baden then muttered some German curses, and bustled off to check her vitals again, leaving Daryl sure that the good doctor would undoubtedly monitor their miracle girl, their study in evolution, over him any day.

"Sir." Mac's voice patched through on his earpiece.

"Mac."

"I'm afraid I have something disturbing to report."

Daryl slowed slightly, knowing it must be bad if Mac used a word like 'disturbing'.

"Go on."

"The motors in all three fishing boats had been tampered with, so that they would fail after they had been running for a few minutes…"

"What the…"

"There's more, sir."

"Tell me."

"The barriers around the island had been weighted down, enabling the sharks to get into the bay. And two small canisters were discovered in the water and, from what remains, it seems they had a timed release valve. Inside we found traces of blood, as well as additives and steroids that would have sent the sharks into a frenzy. Whoever planned this knew exactly what they were doing. What we don't know is who, and which of you they were after."

Daryl's blood turned cold in horror, dread, disgust. Could someone really want to kill her that much? Or him? And then the dreadful realization: Was he a danger to her, just like Donny had been?

"Get divers in the ocean around the bay. Get any information you can. Go back over the surveillance videos and satellite feeds. We have to find out who is behind this. Get video footage from people arriving at the airports, and any ferry landings from the last month, and check everything against the passenger manifests."

"Of course, sir."

"Is everything else ready?"

"Yes, sir. The chopper will be back to collect you after Mysty has been moved to the new location. We have secured three villas, and they have been searched thoroughly."

How could everything have gone so wrong when it had been going so right? Daryl couldn't escape the knowledge that it had been her he'd been thinking about in those moments of terror, trapped on the back of that fishing boat. Not his wealth. Not his businesses. Thoughts that hadn't been cogent, but fleeting; desperate declarations of consciousness, when all he knew was that he didn't want to die, and wanted more time on this earth because…he wanted more time with her. Because the last three days had proved to him just how good things could be with her. The thought of someone making an attack on that happiness…on her made his blood run cold despite the heat in the air.

As they flew over their 'home' of the last three days, he glanced down at the pool. What he would give to enjoy it all over again. What would things be like where they were being moved to? For once, he would have been glad to have his holiday interrupted purely for business reasons.

LIKE A COCOON for a butterfly, that's what this bed felt like, with the fine gauze drapes and all the feather-soft white pillows and sheets. And as for the ivory satin pyjamas… Who had put her in those?

The pain in her head was gone. The drip had gone. There was just this big, soft bed and a room full of gilt-edged furniture and deep-piled rugs. And two pairs of eager eyes waiting for her. At her welcome they came forward and any fog of slumber was lost as tongues licked her face and bodies snuggled in close for the hugs they had waited days for.

She got off the bed, feeling the cool of the marble floor under her feet, and wandered through the vast room into a large, airy living area with her two shadows in tow. She stopped short in the doorway of the kitchen, seeing three very serious-looking men seated at a long table toying with a vast array of breakfast items, the mood morose and deflated.

"Where was my invite to breakfast?" she said, and they all turned.

Seeing her standing there, a cheeky look on her face, like a pyjama-clad pixie who'd crept out of the forest, was just what they needed to see, smiles blossomed to match hers.

"Hey!" Mac said. "Come and sit down!"

"Hey, kiddo, come join," OG agreed, patting the seat next to him.

Daryl just drank in the sight of her, and finally found his appetite seeing her tuck into a laden plate of food.

"Wow. How long did I sleep? What time is it? My first holiday *ever* and I spent half the time sleeping! Have I missed anything?"

"Your holiday is extended indefinitely. You won't miss out on anything," Daryl said, watching her digest this piece of news. "Though I will request you spend the next few days taking it gently…nothing strenuous. If you feel sick at any point you tell someone immediately so we can check again. O'Grady, please send a message to Baden so he knows she's awake and he can downgrade his panic level."

"Where are we?" she then asked, glancing towards a window.

"Sicily."

"One minute we're in Barbados, now we're in Sicily. Just like that."

"Just like that."

"Is there *anywhere* in the world where you don't own something?" She rolled her eyes.

"No." He smiled as he said it. She was back. He'd missed her.

"I see. Why did the engines cut out?"

"They were bought new, for this trip, and someone used the wrong fuel mix by mistake, thinking they were the same type as before. It was an accident, and very unfortunate, but we're all here. Thanks to you and your quick thinking," Mac replied easily, and convincingly, trying to bring the focus back onto her, which was casually rebuffed.

"Anyone would have done what I did. Right time, right place." While her eyes were on her food, a look was exchanged over her head. She was still paying attention, then, and asked the next most obvious question: "And the sharks?"

"We've got teams out checking the barriers to see how they got so close to the island. It's never happened before, so just unlucky, I guess. Even paradise comes with a few catches."

She seemed to buy that too, and it was with no little relief that they continued eating, glad to have averted what could have become a meltdown of fear and panic. While they all knew she loved honesty, the lie seemed a much kinder option given what she had been through.

"YOU'RE NOT WORKING, are you?"

"I'm afraid so."

"That's not good."

She got up and stretched, and then sat down on the sun lounger next to him. For the very first time he didn't know if he was happy with the attention, despite craving it. She was dangerous to him, made him feel so desperate, and incomplete. She turned her indigo eyes on him, calm and beautiful, and he could tell she had no idea how he felt. None whatsoever.

"Can I help?"

"You're meant to be resting. No."

"Perhaps it would be done quicker if you had a secretary. I can follow instructions and write emails just as well as Carol. Come on, I'll pretend to be your secretary, just today, and then you'll finish sooner."

He smiled, and handed her a laptop and a panel. How was he supposed to resist her? "The laptop has my email set up on it, and the panel has the list of people and messages that need sending. If you get bored, you can stop."

"I think my brain will abandon me for neglect reasons if I don't do something with it. I won't get bored." She adjusted the cushions and leant back, the laptop on her knees, and started reading. For twenty minutes there was just the sound of two people typing. Someone brought two drinks and set them on the table and disappeared again. After another twenty minutes she stopped. "Daryl, do you have anything more to do?"

"There's always more," he replied, swapping panels with her.

"I think we'll need lunch soon."

He almost laughed. Her mind was never far away from a thought about food.

His handheld buzzed, and he glanced over and then ignored it.

"Who is it?"

"Charles. Brentford. Secretary of State. He called before."

"Why don't you want to speak to him?"

"I'm tired of talking about the same issue with him. I've told him my stance, and it will not change."

"Why don't I speak to him?"

"Fine, I'm sure he'd love to hear from you."

She took the call. "Charles Brentford. What are you doing calling Daryl while he's on holiday?" Daryl looked at her in surprised horror, but her smile and mischievous eyes told him she knew exactly what she was doing. He obviously couldn't hear the other half of the conversation, but he rather enjoyed her half.

"It's lovely to talk to you, too. And all was going really well, thank you, until we had a bit of an incident with some wildlife, but everyone's okay." Very wise of her not to give their location away. "Currently, he's working," she continued, "and I'm pretending to be his secretary… Now, Charles, what is it you keep calling him about? Daryl has made up his mind about whatever it is, so unless you have some spectacularly exceptional argument, I don't think he's going to change his mind."

There was a pause as Charles was talking, and perhaps not used to such straight talking.

"Have they been warned economic sanctions will be used otherwise? Okay, so it's the next logical step. Are they invited to the economic summit in New York? No? Then why not offer the first olive branch rather than making them walk the plank. Invite them. Being amongst other people who are co-operative could very well achieve what threats can't. No one wants to be on the outside, really, yet some people feel they have no choice. Backing them into a corner won't work. Give them a chance to make some friends and don't give them a chance to stylise themselves as a victim, either in their own minds or in the eyes of their people or sympathisers."

There was another pause.

"What does Daryl think?" Mysty pressed the speaker facility.

"He thinks it's worth a try," Daryl said. "It can't hurt to have a delegation come to the summit. Extend the invitation; make sure they know who else will be coming."

Mysty was pleasantly surprised by his answer.

"Excellent. We'll get that organized," Charles replied. "Mysty, I owe you dinner."

"You'd better check your expenses account, Charles, she gets very hungry!"

"He can be such a bully can't he, my dear."

"He tries to be, but I don't let him win."

"Oh dear, I hope he's a graceful loser."

"He's learning, though it doesn't come naturally."

"I think Mysty has a date with the pool, Charles. I haven't thrown her in for days, so it's about time. Speak to you soon."

Disconnect.

But by the time he'd made a swipe to grab her she had run and jumped into the pool.

"DO I HAVE to go back, too, if he's gone?" She could barely hide the disappointment that he'd left at 4am on the jet, called back on urgent business in New York. This was not the news she had expected to wake up to. She had got used to having fewer surprises.

"No, you're still on holiday, and he wants you to have a proper rest."

"Right."

"So, what would you like to do today?" She didn't know. She pushed her plate of toast away. "There must be something?"

There was one thing. "I was wondering…"

"What?"

"Could you teach me how to drive a car? I mean, I kind of know what to do, but I've only ever ridden bikes. Is there a car here I can try?"

OG smiled. He'd taught his daughters to drive, amidst much yelling and disapproval from his wife, who wanted them to learn with a paid instructor. But he'd had specialist driving training; he knew what he was doing. He would enjoy teaching Mysty, and had a feeling she would be a quick learner.

"I should think so. There's a whole row of cars in the basement."

"Is there a Ferrari?"

She looked hopeful and OG smiled, suspecting it would be a case of the faster the better with her.

"I think so, but you'll have to work up to that one."

"No problem. Can we have a go after breakfast and a swim?"

"Absolutely."

She drained her glass of orange juice, and raced off to change into a bikini. Mr Blackmoor might not be there but O'Grady didn't think it was going to be dull.

WOULD THE TORMENT ever end? He'd left in the hope it would, but it hadn't got any better. Why had God created human beings to feel such emotions? He should have left the moment he knew she was going to be alright, not stayed a whole extra day basking in her beauty and that smile.

The flaw in what he felt for her had made itself clear, and he could not escape the facts: she made him forget himself, made him fearful of losing her, she made him weak, vulnerable, made him feel…out of control of his emotions. Nothing and no one had ever done that to him. He wanted everything she was, but how could he bear to have any more of her when she already meant so much to him? How could he live with that potential loss? He thought about his parents, and the hole they left in his life… And his feelings for her, should he allow them to grow, how would he feel when they were washed away like writing on a beach?

He dragged his hand across his face. Oh, the conundrum of mind versus heart. He didn't have time for this emotional turmoil.

Was it too late to wean himself off her? He could still manage her career, but he could keep her at a distance?

No wonder Donny looked a broken man.

He glanced over at the shades, the ones she'd made for him, and they reminded him of a dozen priceless moments… Yes, he'd have to put some distance between them, and not just miles. But surely he had every right to know how she was?

"O'Grady."

"Mr Blackmoor."

"How are things?"

"Just fine, sir. She's riding on the beach at the moment."

"A horse? I didn't know she could ride?"

"She couldn't until two days ago. She tried it, and loved it. Her natural balance really helped."

The camera feed came up and he saw her, body bent low over the horse, her hair and spray flying up behind them as she galloped through the shallow water on the shore. No riding hat. No saddle.

"Why the hell is she galloping full pelt with no riding hat?"

"What? Oh Jesus."

O'Grady started running down the beach, his hand raised for her to stop, and she slowed, pulling the white horse to a stop and nudging her with her knee to bring her around. What was wrong? Was it because she was riding in a bikini?

Daryl could have pulled his hair out. When would she understand the word 'risk' or 'danger'?

"OG? What's wrong?"

"Nothing strenuous, remember? What happened to walking and trotting? And where is your hat?"

"We did some of that, and then I discovered Megan has other gears. Fast ones! Isn't she fantastic?" She dismounted, and the same hands that caressed Lazarus and Lula now stroked the horse's strong neck, and Megan breathed hot air against her skin.

"You know Mr Blackmoor is not happy about you taking such risks. You're a novice rider. What if you'd fallen off? He doesn't want you hurt again." *Thank God he doesn't know I let you play in a Porsche and then a Ferrari.*

"I'm perfectly fine! Why is he so bothered? I do far worse at Celeste?" She swung back up onto the horse. "We can get the plane back to New York, if he would prefer. I'd rather work than continue this charade of being free to enjoy myself when clearly I'm not. What's wrong with him!" She turned the beautiful creature and gently kicked her into a walk, which became a canter. There was nothing 'novice' about the way she handled the animal.

Daryl let out a sigh as OG raised his hands in despair. *This is good, Daryl. Remember, you don't want her good opinion anymore. If she's cross with you it'll make it easier.*

"If she wants to come back, let her. But she's clearly not suffering in any way physically after her ordeal in the boat."

"No, she's not. She's running, swimming. Baden has checked her every day, and there's nothing amiss whatsoever."

"Fine… I guess I'll see you at some point."

Disconnect.

He glanced at the time, knowing his Sunday evening 'entertainment' would be here soon. Just enough time to get a beer. He hadn't touched a woman since he'd been back. He took a sip, remembering the beers on the terrace only three nights ago, watching the moths dance under the lights, Lula choosing to sit in his lap for a few minutes before jumping over to Mysty. How it hurt to know he was putting all those moments in a box and slamming the lid on them. It felt almost impossible, but he had to do it.

He heard the door open and close, and there they were, one in bright red, one in white, and one in black. They were all wearing shades, their hair curled and dyed the closest they could get to the kind of natural highlighted gold he so preferred. They were holding various chains and handcuffs, and they understood the look they received and immediately undid buttons and removed clothes. By the time he was naked, his beer was finished. The one in black sank to her knees and nuzzled him, lips working over him as hands slid up his thighs and gripped his buttocks. He didn't want that just then, and pushed her away. She looked up at him and obediently backed off. He guided the one in white to the breakfast bar, and lifted her onto it. She lay in the middle. Her legs parted for him, inviting him, and her back arched to beg him for fulfilment. He didn't need asking twice.

How many times had he imagined making love to Mysty? He couldn't say. He adored her in the morning, sleepy but gorgeous from the moment she awoke.

He heard the woman moan, and her hands reached for him. But he didn't want her to touch him; he wanted to see her climax, and brought her closer and closer, wishing it was Mysty, wishing he could give her the gift of ecstasy, to join them together, to wipe away all the sadness he'd made her feel.

A startled cry of pleasure from the woman distracted him, and he pulled her forward and lifted her body to receive him, wanting now to bury himself in the physical, erase the thoughts that hounded him and gave him no solace. The women had picked up on his mood, and the one in the red came to him from behind and wrapped her leg around him as he rammed into the woman in white. He felt her muscles tighten around him in welcome, her loud intake of breath turning into a groan of pleasure as she tried to fight against the force of her second orgasm, but surrendered. The woman in black joined them, weaving her hands between his buttocks and teasing him to a powerful first climax.

And then he turned, and indicated they continue in the bedroom.

He lay back on the pillows, and the three women used lips and hands to pleasure each other and him, panting, wanting, an uninhibited display of desire and sexuality. He too used knowing hands, feeling them climax against his fingers. His cock was deep inside one of them, then another, then inside an eager mouth, his hips thrusting, his groin aching, searching for that joy that seemed to elude him.

But always it was her he wanted. And then a thought: she was innocent. She might learn quickly, but she would tire. She would never keep up with him, never know how to keep him truly entertained. He would have to find other ways to satisfy himself. He would have to let her go.

That would be, by far, the simpler option.

He would be fine.

SHE WAS CUTTING it fine, and he was in a bad mood. It had been almost two weeks since he'd last seen her in person, and his attempt to forget her and cease wanting her wasn't going too well. His Cherries probably thought he'd taken ill, or that they were losing their touch. Even as he made them writhe and beg him to finish what he'd started, they were all the wrong woman, and he was disinterested and distracted. It was all wrong.

The right woman should be here, any second. If she was late, he would probably lose his temper he was so on edge. But he had to behave like she absolutely wasn't the right woman, which wasn't too difficult with the frame of mind he was in.

A glance at the time, his fingers curling with impatience and frustration, wishing he felt less like he was lying to himself. *When will this purgatory end?*

He heard a glass break, and then another, and heads started to turn and a hush fell across the restaurant. He could guess why. Only one woman had the ability to cause such havoc just by entering a room.

When he saw her he could see why.

Oh God. He had the beginnings of an erection already, and she hadn't even sat down.

"What the hell are you wearing?"

She flinched as though he'd slapped her. She hadn't expected a warm welcome, but…

"I only got the message to be here twenty minutes ago. I just about had time to shower and throw these on and get the Firebird out, or else I would have been horrendously late – a crime I thought greater than not wearing some fancy dress for you, but clearly I was mistaken. I'll go." Her biting tone matched his and she began to turn away.

"Sit. Down."

She sighed then and sat, and pulled the zip down on the tight red leathers just a little, slouching in that way that annoyed him, one ankle slung over her knee, yet turned him on. Insolent yet undeniably sexy. Why did she have to make this so difficult for him? Couldn't she at least try to look unattractive?

"I sent the message an hour ago. Why did you only receive it twenty minutes ago?"

"I was at the end of a rehearsal. OG couldn't speak to me until it was completely finished."

Fair enough.

"Well, do you want to at least take your jacket off so you don't look like you're about to leave?"

God, he was uptight.

"That's not a good idea."

"Why not?"

"There wasn't much time. I don't have anything on under the jacket."

He shifted uncomfortably in his seat around his increasing erection and irritation. One of New York's most exclusive restaurants and she was not only breaking all dress codes by wearing red hot leathers, but she had nothing on underneath? He closed his eyes. It didn't help: images were waiting for him.

"I didn't know 'I'll be there waiting' was…here. If I'd know it was a restaurant as posh as this, I'd have told OG to let you know I would be late while I found something more appropriate to wear I just…well, I know you don't like people keeping you waiting."

He was aware of a number of other diners looking over, their status in the fame stakes so high. But what was going on at the table? One of them looking disgruntled was enough to cause a tremor; both of them together was a potential earthquake off the Richter.

"Well, you're here now. No point wasting any more time dwelling on it."

She stayed silent, disconcerted by his troubled face and the crushing put down. Clearly nothing she said or did today was going to be adequate. A waiter approached and asked her what she would like to drink, and then backed off.

"So. How are you?" he asked, knowing it was almost pointless. She looked good enough to eat, and the doctor's reports said she was as healthy as the horse she had galloped along the beach; and her performance last weekend at Celeste had proved without a doubt that she was very much okay.

"Absolutely fantastic. How are you?" she answered without any expression, her eyes hard: *you can keep your token gesture of concern.*

"Super." *Awful.*

"Did you get it sorted?"

"What sorted?"

"Whatever it was that dragged you away from a holiday and back to New York?"

Ah. Of course. His need to return for *business.*

"It's being dealt with." His impatient tone was doubly insensitive when compared to her genuine inquiry.

The waiter arrived with her glass of sparkling water and she nodded her thanks.

"That's good."

How could he resist her, her genuine kindness and sweetness? He had not calculated this into the equation.

"I've already ordered for us."

"Thank God. I'm starving." She took a swallow of water as if she hadn't tasted water for some time. Her ability to take such pleasure in simple things rankled.

"All going alright with the rehearsals?"

"Very well. Though I may need a slight extension on the budget. The costumes are costing quite a lot."

"Not a problem. It was a conservative budget, anyway. I half expected you to need more."

"It does seem a shame not to do the show more than once, as such effort has gone into it."

"It could be done again as a standalone show – if it's good enough to warrant it."

She raised an eyebrow, not enjoying his unexpected, subtle attack on her professionalism and talent – the one part of her that he usually supported without fail. "Really? Good enough? My, you are feeling ungenerous tonight, aren't you? What's happened?" She crushed an ice cube mercilessly with her teeth. "Stubbed your toe on your mile-wide desk? Had to go six hours without fucking someone?"

Their eyes locked, each daring the other; their old game of brinkmanship engaged upon without a flicker.

"I'd forgotten how irritating you are."

"I'd forgotten what an arrogant jerk you can be, so I guess we're even."

She smiled, but it was a warning. He knew the signs.

Luckily the first course arrived.

"Can I ask what this is?" she asked, looking at the plate like a miniature alien had just been placed in front of her.

"The world's best and most expensive caviar."

He sampled some. It was delicious. Even more so because he knew she'd hate it.

"Caviar being fish eggs. Raw fish. Which you know I don't like." She sat back, crossed her arms and looked at him as if he were a bizarre species. "What are you trying to do? Starve me? Poison me? Or just insult me?"

"Try it. You might like it."

"I can smell it, and I feel sick looking at it. I hardly think trying it is a good idea. Can I just go? I…I really don't think you want me here."

She was so wrong and so right. He hated the fact that she wanted to leave, get away from him, even as much as he tried to tell himself it was best.

"Try it. Don't be such a child," he snapped.

She went pale. His tone was unkind, and she realised he wouldn't give up unless she did. This had to be the worst dinner experience of her life. She tentatively picked up the fork. And trying to close off her senses put some into her mouth, and immediately swallowed huge gulps of water to wash it down. On an empty stomach the sensation of it sliding down her throat was almost too much. She raised her eyes to his when she was sure she wasn't going to vomit.

"You tried it. Congratulations. Hopefully, when you try sex, you'll get on better with unusual things in your mouth."

"We both know you don't like using your mouth during sex. Why is that? Too much effort to use more than one body part? I don't think I'll have any problem using all of mine." Daryl almost choked on his food, his mind conjuring images thanks in part to her confident tone of voice.

"Give me a demonstration and I'll grade you."

It felt suicidal to continue to bait her like this, but somehow he heard himself speaking the words. He came to life feeling the heat of her anger, that familiar, much-missed challenge of stepping up to engage with the tiger.

"I won't need grading. I'll pass with distinction. I'm just waiting to find a suitable candidate to major with." Her eyes glittered dangerously with the message: It won't be you. "I heard you have a new one. How much do they earn nowadays?"

Daryl couldn't believe she was even asking him this. She was punishing him for his crude comment. Male pride made him answer with flippancy: "Eighty-thousand a year, plus the rest…bonuses for extra special performances."

"Such an expensive indulgence. Hope you're saving something for Mrs Blackmoor, when she comes along. If would be very disappointing to have heard all the legendary talk and find out it was all such a let-down. Very deflating."

"I don't think she needs to worry."

"Then again, if you choose a Mrs Blackmoor that swings both ways, your harem girls could look after her as well. But then I bet you've already thought of that, genius that you are."

He pushed his plate away, his appetite ruined by his own acid-tinged comments and her constant looks of deep disgust at him.

The waiter collected their barely touched plates of food.

Just a couple of weeks ago he had been laughing, and they'd been talking…really talking.

Was it really only two weeks ago? It felt like a different lifetime. The next course arrived.

"Braised duck," he said, seeing her uncertainty.

She'd never had duck. Still, it wasn't fish… She cut into it and the nausea she had fought to ignore before rose up again. Blood.

"I think mine is…undercooked. It's bleeding."

"That is how it's meant to be done. Too much cooking and the meat is ruined. Try it."

"I really don't think I can. I'm sure it's very nice, but I just can't. I'm not being rude, it's just…" She closed her eyes and tried to force away the images, red, bright red, blood, everywhere…

Daryl didn't have the heart to force her when she was so clearly distressed.

"OG said you've been having nightmares again."

"Yes."

"Do you know why?" He leaned in, his eyes intense.

"Yes." She mistook his concern for anger, though. "It's my problem. I'll deal with it. I don't need you asking me anything."

He was back to wearing the horns and tail again. He wasn't allowed to care. But based on his behaviour tonight alone, why should she believe he cared?

"How are Lula and Lazarus?" he attempted.

"Why?"

This was what his attitude had brought them to. How easily they slipped back into their old ways of sniping at each other. When she didn't trust him.

"I hope OG knows where you are, and you rode with a helmet."

"He's right outside and, yes, my helmet is at the front desk. Although from the look on the guy's face I might as well have put a live skunk in front of him. Maybe I'll bring one for next time, so he doesn't flinch at a simple motorcycle helmet. I bet he doesn't realise just how bad they smell."

He didn't reply. Fought the smile and ate some duck. She hadn't touched hers.

"How's Mac?"

"Fine. As always."

"How's his sister doing? Any results yet? I meant to ring him, but this week has been insanely busy."

"His sister?" Daryl barely remembered Mac had a sister. She was never mentioned, and he'd never met her.

"She has breast cancer? She's had an operation and waiting on results. He's really worried for her." She sat back and looked at him. "You didn't know, did you? The man spends his entire life watching over you and you never knew. You probably didn't even notice he's been worried."

"It's his job. I don't have time for personal questions."

Her beautiful plate with the bleeding food on was removed. Daryl laid down his cutlery and they took his too.

"I've just realised something. It wasn't me who came wearing the wrong clothes. If I get Mac to bring you some shorts, will you cheer up? Or are you going to stay like this indefinitely?"

She wasn't making this easy at all, alternating between answering his rudeness in kind and appealing to him to return to being how he had been.

"That was a once-in-a-decade sighting. Should have made more of it when it was around."

"Yeah, I figured that much. Ah well, his loss. I think he'd actually started to enjoy himself, despite not having something to fuck."

"A leopard rarely changes its spots."

A few moments of silence and then dessert arrived. The red cherry cheesecake with biscuit base and summer fruits ice cream had got rave reviews, but she looked unimpressed.

"Did you completely forget who it was you were going to dinner with when you ordered? You know I don't eat seafood, bloodied meat or desserts."

"This childish collection of eating habits you have. Are you ever going to move on? It is a superbly ungrateful performance you're putting on tonight. Do let me know when I'm supposed to applaud, won't you?"

The muscle in her jaw jumped.

"Amazing you judge so much, yet know so little. I would say that kind of ignorant superiority is childish. Though I don't know why you're bothered that I haven't eaten. I'm sure you worry that somehow I'll lose my figure, and a fat butterfly doesn't sell well, does it?" She kept her voice low, despite the anger adding a fiery edge to it that warned him to be very careful what he chose to say next. "If you'll excuse me, I'm going to the ladies' room."

She knew her abrupt departure from the table and their exchange – even from a distance – would have told anyone watching that they really weren't getting on. Her glass of water most surely should have turned into a block of ice.

She had no intention of going to the ladies' room, and didn't care if he worked it out or not. She was leaving.

At the desk, which she had already calculated was out of sight, she didn't need to say a word. A couple, dressed in best dining finery, stood frozen to the spot as the shiny red sex goddess picked up her helmet, zipped up her jacket, and exited the restaurant. The Butterfly – the super-famous starlet – was leaving? Without having barely touched her food? What had gone on between them?

Outside, everyone – public and press – came to a standstill as she marched down the steps, instantly recognising her. OG and Mac noticed the hush and turned around.

"Mysty, you alright?" OG asked.

"Worst meal of my life." She didn't break stride, and threw a leg over her bike, firing up immediately.

"I knew this was going to happen," Mac growled. "Man's been like a bear with a foot caught in a snare for the last two weeks. God knows what he's said to her."

"I'll speak to you later. Find out what's going on."

OG walked over to the waiting Bentley and got in, intending to follow her back, though she was already disappearing down the road at some speed.

Mac patched through. "Mr Blackmoor, sir?"

"Mac."

"The car is ready, sir."

"We're not quite finished."

"Sir?" Silence. "Mysty just left."

"She *what*?"

Mac cleared his throat, preparing himself for the onslaught the dangerous tone indicated was imminent. "She just left, sir. Going home apparently. She looked pretty upset."

"Jesus Christ."

She'd actually walked out on him. No one, in his life, had ever walked out on him.

He left without speaking to anyone, looking at his handheld, pretending he'd been called away on business, that everything was under control.

Like hell it was…

They sat in silence in the car. Mac almost wished his boss would shout, or do something to let the frustration out rather than combust slowly by his side.

"How's your sister?"

It was the last question Mac expected, and he struggled to keep a neutral face.

"She's doing really well, sir. An appointment has been made for reconstructive surgery, so hopefully she'll be back to her old self soon."

Mac knew he'd not mentioned his sister. Mysty must have done.

"Good. I'm pleased." Daryl pulled out his handheld, as a distraction. "If you need time off, to go and see her, you only have to say."

The big man could have fallen off the seat. "She'll be visiting New York soon, with our mother, so yes, I'd like to see them. Thank you, sir."

Silence.

"How was Mysty?" Mac dared.

"Very much as you'd expect." Daryl didn't want to talk about her, or rather his failure at dealing with her.

"She not like the food?"

"I wasn't really thinking when I ordered for us. Caviar was the wrong choice, as was the duck, cooked rare, which had blood in it and, apparently, she 'doesn't do desserts'. She drank water." Daryl's eyes swung around to Mac. "Why doesn't she eat desserts?" There was obvious frustration in his voice.

"She told OG about that…" Mac hedged, but Daryl wasn't fooled for a moment.

"Who told you? Tell me what it is. Believe me, right now she needs all the help she can get."

Mac sighed. It seemed they'd gone back seven months in the space of half an hour.

"The last thing her mother ever made was her birthday cake. The first and only one she'd ever had. Something happened at her ninth birthday party. A couple of hours later, everyone was dead. That's why she hates sweet things. Milkshakes are the closest she gets."

Mac held Daryl's gaze, daring him to deny it, or the horror of it, forcing him to take in the words.

Daryl closed his eyes. How he despised himself for not bothering to find out more about her. She had attempted a truce by being her kind, caring self, and received only more hostility. So she did the only thing left: she'd walked away. Other women might have got weepy; some might have begged him to tell them what was wrong, and how they could make amends, but she? She had nothing to make amends for. Knowing her temper, it was a wonder she hadn't slapped him or tossed a drink in his face. That was some small mercy and testament to her self-control, not his.

The silence in the car was like a tomb.

"Should I expect anyone to arrive tonight, sir?" Mac asked at the front door.

"No."

Daryl didn't want anyone. He was glad when the door shut and he was alone. Immediately the shoes were kicked off and jacket thrown, wanting to shake the day off, to relax, to find some peace. Yet he knew he was unlikely to know that any time soon.

Giving in to the need to know the aftermath of their epically poor dinner experience, he pulled the feed up for her apartment, throwing himself into the chair behind his desk and fixing eyes on the main screen.

She was already in jogging bottoms and Yankees sweater.

"Maybe he had a bad day," he heard OG say.

"Doesn't give him the right to take it out on me. I didn't have such a great day either, but I still got ready and went over there to see him, and I was ready to have a meal and just chat."

"No. You're right. But he's a split personality trillionaire, sweetheart, he can't help it."

She looked at OG from where her head rested on her arms on the counter, eyes sad. Clearly humour wasn't going to cut any ice tonight.

"Why don't you go get on the sofa, put a film on, and I'll bring this over when it's done."

Daryl zoomed in. OG appeared to be frying some chicken.

"You're far too nice to me."

"No, I'm not. Pick something good to watch and I might stay."

"*Bourne*?"

"Excellent choice."

Daryl switched off the screen. What was he doing? Just because he was retracting – for necessary reasons - didn't mean she had to suffer. She hadn't done anything to deserve his disrespect. He couldn't believe he'd made that comment about sex, and putting things in her mouth. Had he really been so tactless? So crude? He'd deserved every one of her barbed replies. And now she was beginning to mistrust him again, he could see it in her eyes.

He'd had enough of today. Time to go to bed, and try not to think about who he wanted to be there with him.

It was never going to happen.

LYING ON THE bed in the dark, Mysty accepted the presence of fur and whiskers without question, and stared wide-eyed trying to make sense of the evening. Of the past month.

Why had he reverted to being such an asshole? What had she done? She'd saved his life, the bastard, and he'd barely spoken to her, and then, within twenty-four hours of waking up, he'd gone?

Exhaling so deeply that Lula slid a little from her position over her ribs, Mysty apologised and waited for the cub to settle again. Men. Did they ever make sense?

"Toby."

"Boss."

"Has Raju unblocked me yet?"

"No. Not as far as Facebook and Messenger are concerned."

"Great. Thanks."

Another exhale. She finally gave up looking for answers outside of herself and lids closed…yet her senses and thoughts were suddenly louder, more intense. She tried to put herself in alternative viewpoints, to get a new perspective, to find what she must have missed to have ended up on the receiving end of so much contempt.

Think logically. Did I do something to upset Daryl? Not as far as I can see. So, it's not for me to try and fix whatever is up with him.

Raju. He's still angry at me, which I can't help. I guess I surprised him more than I thought. I should think of his pain, his emotions, not mine.

She flopped her hand over her face. Logic hadn't alleviated the pain in her chest or the confusion in her mind. She hated problems she couldn't fix.

She'd been at work so long, and the dinner had been a battle. She hadn't really switched off or had a proper conversation to unwind. She really needed a friend. Her thoughts tumbled. Had Raju ever been on holiday? Did he miss their chats as much as she did? Was he reading all the headlines instead of talking to her?

Familiar, dark thoughts crept back in from the shadows she convinced herself she wasn't afraid of anymore, familiar demons that taunted her attempts to achieve peaceful oblivion in sleep. And then the voice she knew too well reminded her that she hadn't deserved that holiday. That she shouldn't have gone. Every smile had been unworthy. All those swims in the paradise pool hadn't really belonged to someone like her…the lost girl tainted by blood from a broken home, whom clearly, as evidenced by her current lonesome state, no one really wanted.

SHE LOOKED AT the screen and froze.

'*We bring you a story, just breaking this morning. It is believed that the world-famous Butterfly, known simply and unmistakably as Mysty, has had an abortion in a private clinic in Sicily following a holiday with her manager, Mr Blackmoor. Sources report he returned to New York while she remained for a few days in the exclusive villa complex, owned by Mr Blackmoor, to recover, before returning also. Furthermore, while no sightings of them have been made these two weeks, last night they were sighted at the exclusive French restaurant, The Orange Window, also owned by Mr Blackmoor. Witnesses say they were not getting on at all for the duration of the meal, and it would appear Mysty walked out on him. We can only guess at what they were arguing about.*

'*As the star of Celeste, and at the beginning of a career with Mr Blackmoor as her manager, it is unlikely Mr Blackmoor – who remains single and childless, despite his fortune – would want her to remain pregnant and have his love-child after a holiday romance. We cannot help but wonder how long this 'romance' might have been going on, and some credit the romance as being something of a flight of fancy after the recent split with Mr Capello. Staunch Mysty supporters do not believe she would have agreed to an abortion, given the star's obvious love of children. We are hoping to hear from either one or both of them today, though all the evidence is pretty convincing, don't you think, Clive?*"

The front door banged and she tore her eyes away from the screen.

"Now don't flip, alright?" OG said, trying to prepare himself for the fact that she might do exactly that.

"What the hell is going on?"

"I don't know, but they were always going to suspect something. You went on holiday with the world's most notorious womaniser."

"I can't believe this is happening. I was in hospital because of a shark attack, not…" She looked her bodyguard straight in the eye. "I'm not going to go mental. I'm going to deal with the problem, okay?"

"Okay."

"Good. So, I'm going to have a quick shower now, and then we can go out. Make some toast if you fancy some."

The moment she was gone, he patched a call.

"Mac."

"OG. You've seen the news?"

"Yes. So has she. What the hell is going on? Is he going to make a statement?"

"He seems to find it amusing. He's not made any arrangements to make a statement."

"Shit."

"She alright?"

"Surprisingly so. I don't know what she's planning."

"Well, whatever she does, I think I'm going to enjoy watching it happen."

"Yeah, you and me both. I'll keep you posted."

Disconnect.

Her stride was sure and confident as she walked from the elevator to the doors, beyond which there was a double line of suits creating a corridor to the waiting Bentley to hold back the press and cameras.

"Mysty! Why did you have the abortion? Were you forced into it?" one of them cried.

"Did Mr Blackmoor force you to give up the child?" called another.

She paused. "I will be making a statement this evening, outside my studio. Until then, I have no comment, except to say you've all wasted your time coming here, and your ink printing your newspapers." But her eyes settled on one man. "OG, bring that man to my car." He was someone she recognised from similar press moments, including some in LA, and knew the news station he worked for was big enough, but not owned by her nemesis.

When they were seated, she flanked by the leopards, and her guest in a state of awkward, awed, apprehensive excitement, she began her interrogation.

"Peter Macon, miss…ma'am…" he said as the car pulled away.

"Mysty will be fine, Peter, I much prefer first names."

The man was star-struck, and obviously struggling with the reality of being in the car with the mysterious Butterfly.

"What, erm, do you want? I mean, how can I help, if I can?" he asked.

"I have some questions for you. You know how it works, but this time it's this way around. Answer my questions and you can have a half-hour interview with me next week."

"Alright, sure, okay." He could barely breathe. He could practically smell the promotion that would come his way after such a career break.

"The first question is very simple. I want to know who started the rumour about an abortion? Who is the source?"

"I can't say…they…if I told you…it's part of the agreement with sources…we don't name names."

At least he hadn't just lied to her. Then again, he looked too nervous to construct a lie, never mind a sentence.

"Let me re-phrase that. Is this person someone who is currently paid by Mr Blackmoor?"

She watched him weigh up the rights and wrongs of the 'yes and no' option she was giving him against that exclusive interview. After an extended silence it ended the way she knew it would:

"Yes."

"Are they in my staff?"

"Yes."

"Are they part of my bodyguard?"

"No."

"And you can't give me a name?"

"No. I'm sorry."

"You can have your interview, Mr Macon. I'll be in touch with possible times. The location I'll leave to you, but preferably it needs to be private and with comfy chairs."

"I'll get the best chairs I possibly can. Do you want my card?" He reached into a pocket for one, deciding this had to be the best day of his career ever. An exclusive interview with her was a ticket to the front page!

"No, it's fine. I can find out everything I need to know in a few minutes on a computer. As I said, I will be making a statement this evening from outside my studio. I recommend you be there to get the story. It's about time someone started talking truth, not fable." The car pulled to halt and the door opened. "Peter, thank you for your time. The driver will take you where you need to go." She offered her hand, and he took it, wondering if he was meant to shake it or kiss it. After the pause of his indecision had expired, she took it back, and she was out of the car and striding away, the leopards with her.

"Sir?" He jumped. "Where do you wish to go?"

Peter Macon gave his office address. Everyone was going to hate him.

IT WAS LATE morning. Daryl saw the caller ID and resented the jolt of excitement at seeing who it was. After last night, he really should have no expectations whatsoever.

"Mysty."

"Satan." Ah, back to being the Devil. "You've seen the news?"

"Of course. Very disappointed. Apparently I got you pregnant. I don't even remember it. You must be a very unexceptional lay."

She blushed, but the indigo eyes turned dark with fury.

"Works both ways. I don't remember it either. Clearly we're equally bad, but at least I have inexperience on my side."

Touché.

"When are you going to make a statement and end this pointless speculation?" she then asked.

"Why would I? It's selling newspapers and it's on every channel. The world is getting the juiciest intrigue for months."

"It's a lie! It's tainting my reputation! And like I want to be associated with you any more than having you as my manager? Sorry Zeus, even the mention of my having apparently conceived your love-child makes me feel sick!"

"Your reputation? You didn't seem to care about your reputation when you were lying flat on your back with your legs wide open on the tarmac at the Bowl."

"You have no right to bring that up. Would you like me to remind you of the reprehensible behaviour you were responsible for that night?"

They both paused, knowing this was old territory they had laid to rest. If they kept this up, things were going to get very nasty.

When Mysty broke the strained silence she kept her voice low and steady, to try and bring them closer to some kind of accord. "I want the truth known because I don't want Donny seeing that headline."

"He'll already have seen it," Daryl dismissed, surprised he hadn't had a call from Mr Capello.

"Then he'll see it corrected! How do you think he must be feeling seeing that? You think I'm going to let him feel hurt and betrayed and do nothing?" she demanded, willing him to grow a conscience.

"I don't really care, to be honest. I don't owe Donny anything."

"You are so full of shit, aren't you? You say you respect me, but look at how you're treating me again. You say you respect Donny, and yet you can't be moved sufficiently to feel any consideration for him about a matter you know full well means a great deal to him." She shook her head in wonderment at him, and then a steely determination crept into her face. "You think I will be the whore to your Babylon? No. You have *one hour* to make a statement, and it had better be good. After that, well you'll discover I'm a quick learner at the game you play, and I can play as hard and as dirty as you can." She gave him a look that startled even him, not sparing him any of her disgust. "I thought you were worth saving. I should have let the sharks have you. It would have been interesting to see the species kill one of its own."

Disconnect.

Daryl sat perfectly still for a second, his last image of her imprinting itself in his mind; her eyes so bright and fierce. For the thousandth time he asked himself what he was doing, and received no answer that helped.

He was never going to be able to concentrate.

WITH OG BY her side she then went to stand at the top of the steps, the thick line of security holding everyone back. But they could all see her. And she could see them. She was going to give them plenty. Back straight, head up and shoulders back, she didn't cower from the cameras, she welcomed them. They would allow her to tell her truth. The actual truth.

"I know why you're all here, and we are all aware of the rumour that started this furore amongst all the news stations," she began. "I have a preference for the truth, which is why I'm choosing to stand here and address you now, rather than let you all continue in ignorance and this speculation go uncorrected." She wasn't going to be rushed, however, and took a few moments to gather her thoughts. "I am disappointed that the cowardly Mr Blackmoor has not had the decency to make a statement himself. I had hoped he might prove me wrong in my estimations of his character, but no." He was going to hate her for that; he would hate her for the whole thing. "All I can tell you at this current moment is that whoever started this rumour was, without a shadow of doubt, lying. There was no baby; there was no abortion. The reason for being in Sicily near the clinic – which wasn't an abortion clinic – was because they had the equipment to monitor a head injury I sustained in Barbados. My personal doctor has all my medical records, and they reveal there was no pregnancy or abortion. These will be made available after this statement."

The crowd was captive to her oration. No one shouted out, and instead listened, knowing she would most likely allow questions at the end.

"The head injury was sustained saving Mr Blackmoor's life, which makes his tolerating these insulting and insane rumours today even worse. I had chosen not to accompany him on the fishing trip that day, but shortly after they set off sharks began attacking the three boats, and his boat was sinking, so I did what most of us would do, and went to his rescue. Perhaps I should have just let him sink into the water."

No one spoke. This was one serious statement.

"There is no relationship between my manager and myself. There was no fling or holiday romance. There was no love-child. If ever I am fortunate to become pregnant in the future, for the record I would never let anyone bully me into an abortion. Not for money, and not for a career. Not for any reason. Now. Are there any questions?"

"If all this is true, why hasn't Mr Blackmoor said anything? Why not make a statement this morning?"

"Aside from the fact this story is selling him lots of newspapers and broadcasting, proving him the media whore that he is, he doesn't appear to care. I am the only female to turn down the chance to experience his sexual expertise, and I think this story, despite being false, has gone a long way in mending his bruised ego." Members of the press started to smile. "I am surprised, though, that despite sleeping with countless women, not one of them has ever become pregnant? This is interesting. One might even go as far as to consider the reason why Mr Blackmoor might not be able to conceive a child… That would explain why he rather liked the rumour, and why he is dragging his feet as regards clearing it. Far be it for me to know the mind of the man, but for one who is so rich, so powerful and so revered in the eyes of the world, would it not be the greatest irony if he isn't able to father his own children? Especially when he requires an heir to such a fortune. I wonder if he is our very own modern-day Henry VIII…"

Mysty felt a wicked sense of glee at this little trump card. The reaction through the press told her that tomorrow's headline was going to be quite different from one they had envisioned.

"How would you describe your relationship with Mr Blackmoor at the moment? Your dinner last night was reported to be not at all amicable."

"I don't think relationship is the right word. There is barely anything between us except contractual ties and a good number of insults or grievances. I am responsible for the former and he for the latter. There used to be toleration; but now, whatever it is, it is tenuous in the extreme. I choose not to comment on the dinner."

"And what does Mr Capello think of all this?"

"I have no doubt he found the headlines this morning very disturbing, and disappointing – though he may have worked out that they were a load of complete nonsense. I very much hope he did, because I hate the idea that someone's rather imaginative loose tongue has caused him upset. I haven't spoken to him, but I know he will understand when I say that distance and time only makes the heart grow fonder."

"How will this tension between you and your manager affect your work for the summit?"

"It doesn't. I'm not performing for my manager, I'm doing it for the delegates who will be there, so that they might understand it is the expression of a strong, positive culture that is ultimately the purpose and the proof of success of a country – or indeed, the world's economic health and happiness."

She nodded to OG. She'd had enough. She'd later find out that millions had tuned in to watch that statement, and she hoped Daryl Blackmoor was absolutely fucking furious.

Man, that had felt good.

A COWARD? A media whore? And to top it off – *infertile?*

He looked at the screen: 'Recipient Denied Access.' She had blocked his number? Blocked it! *How dare she*?

The intercom buzzed.

"Yes?"

"Mr Blackmoor, sir? It's Simon, from the database department."

"What is it?"

"It's Hali, sir. She's…disappeared."

"The software? Or the security? What do you mean 'she's disappeared'?"

"The firewalls, programmes, systems – they're all fine, all operating, sir. But…she's gone. There's no answer."

"Surely you don't need someone holding your hand! Earn your exorbitant salary, Simon, and get on with some work. I'm so sorry your little cyber girlfriend has gone, but maybe it's time you went out and got a real one. Don't bother me unless you have a real problem."

Disconnect.

And then he realised what he'd just said to one of his most trusted employees. Oh God. He couldn't remember the last time he'd been this angry. Hali. Part of him knew what it meant, her disappearing. Hali had been a gift; a symbol of her forgiveness of him after that awful night at the Bowl when she had correctly called him out on his reprehensible behaviour. No wonder Mysty had made her 'disappear'.

He forced himself to remember that having her on the wrong side of him was good; it meant she would hate him and it would be easier to extract himself from what he felt about her. But there was a small, persistent voice that told him it wasn't right. How could it be the right thing to do when it felt so wrong?

The intercom buzzed again.

Oh shit.

"Donny."

"Daryl." A pause. "Well, is she right?"

"About what?" he asked, genuinely thrown by the conversational tone in Donny's voice. Why wasn't he furious?

"About your inability to father a child."

Daryl controlled the impulse to hurl the intercom system across the room, and send the screen after it. He now knew exactly what tomorrow's headlines would be. She was taking a most apt revenge. He forced himself to take a slow breath.

"No. She's not. And I'll no doubt get no end of grief now she's started that goose chase off."

"Give the press a sample to analyse. I'm sure you'll have no problem filling up a few pots for them. Better keep it guarded, though. It would probably fetch a decent price on in the black market."

Daryl pressed two fingers to his temples. "Donny, I really would appreciate it if you left that subject alone."

"Really? Just like she would have appreciated you coming out and telling the world the rumours were false?"

The words pricked at Daryl's guilt. "For God's sake, Donny! They're always going to come out with rubbish like that every once in a while, given who we are. And the fact we went on holiday together, well, it was bound to happen."

"A love-child and a secret abortion are a little extreme." Daryl knew he was right and didn't bother arguing. "How was the holiday?" Donny then asked.

"It was…" Should he be honest? "It was great. The first few days were great."

"You lucky son-of-a-bitch."

"Yes, I am." Daryl started at the photograph on the wall. *Yes, I was.*

"And the accident?"

"I was a dead man. We had seconds before I was in the water. She launched herself across from another boat, to grab me. She hit her head when we crashed to the floor."

"That sounds like her." A wistful fondness graced Donny's strong features, softening them for a moment. "It's quite something, isn't it, having someone risk themselves for you."

It wasn't really a question; it didn't need to be. The power of the thought was enough to humble.

Daryl could remember hearing Donny talk about her saving him, wishing he knew what it was to have someone care that much. Now he'd felt it too, and he was trying to push it away, so he could stop suffering. Of all the people in the world, Donny would know how that felt.

"Donny. There's something you should know."

"Go on."

"The shark attack. It wasn't an accident. It was a trap."

"What?" The change in tone was subtle, but there.

"The engines had been tampered with, so they would cut out and leave us all stranded in the bay. And the barriers around the island had been weighted down, so the sharks could get in without alerting security of a breach. Even more damningly, in the clear up, time-lock release canisters were found that still had traces of the blood released into the water to attract the sharks. The blood had been doctored with various drugs, hormones and steroids to make it more potent, to send the sharks into a killing frenzy."

"Christ."

"Mysty hadn't wanted to come on the fishing trip, because she didn't want to see the fish get killed or see any blood. But whoever planned the attack couldn't have known she'd decline. We don't know if it was me, or her, or both of us they wanted to target. She was amazing. She didn't just save me. Her quick thinking most likely saved a number of my security too. I would have called you, only…I didn't think to, and then, when she was on the mend, I…had other concerns."

"Christ." Donny sounded weary.

"Why are you not angry? I imagined you would blame me, for my team missing something?"

"I've been expecting it, Daryl."

Daryl felt his heart thudding in his chest and a pain lanced through his head. Again, something beyond his control or his knowledge was turning his world to a new angle on its axis.

"Not another hit, surely?"

"No. Nothing mob related. I would have dealt with that before they got the chance to make an attempt."

"Then what? Jesus Christ, Donny! You've been sitting on this information and you never thought to share it with me? When I'm the one meant to be keeping her safe?"

Donny did not fight his fire with fire, and instead asked, "Did you ever find out why she didn't want to be famous, Daryl?"

Donny had asked him that before. This had to be significant. Everything significant always came down to her family and the past shrouded in blood and shadow. And the not wanting to be famous, instead desperate for anonymity…why was that? And then it hit him.

"Her father killed her family, didn't he?" Even saying the words felt surreal.

"Yes."

"Are you telling me he's *alive*?"

"Alive, free, and thanks to you and your interfering, all too fucking aware as to where and who his daughter is!" Donny's temper finally broke its hold. "Do you know how much she looks like her mother? *One picture* – even a *bad* picture – is all it would have taken and he'd have known who she was! Did you think she didn't *know* how talented she was? Did you think she didn't know how far she could go with that voice? Of course she did! But she knew the price of fame was too great. Why do you think she fought you so hard? Why do you think she hacked in and deleted herself off the FID at fourteen years old? For a *joke*? No, in the hope her father couldn't find her! You've made her a *target*, Daryl, and she knew it as soon as she signed that fucking contract. Do you know how afraid she is on stage, terrified he'll be there, watching from the crowd?"

Terrible seconds passed, as all the pieces of the picture fell into place like shards of a broken mirror, knife-sharp and so, so bright, shattering the image of safety he had thought he'd built around her.

"Why? Why would he be so intent on killing her?" he asked, his head in his hands.

"If you knew what he did to the rest of her family, you'd know he wouldn't rest without having killed her as well. He is not a man who wants to see his beautiful daughter successful and famous. No. His daughter is the image of his wife, if not lovelier, the woman he killed in the most brutal fashion. He wants to kill her, just like he intended to when she was nine years old. But you know, I was never worried about a bullet. He wants her to die an awful death – that's why getting torn apart by sharks would have been so fitting. Congratulations, Daryl, now you know it wasn't you they were after."

Daryl stared at Donny, his mind tumbling, his heart beating loud in his chest.

"The threat of her father was the only reason I agreed to the tracker, and the only reason I got her to agree to it as well. She knows he'll come for her. She knows I'm dealing with the issue, but so far he has proved remarkably illusive."

Donny's face was a mask of control, showing no shame about speaking of the hunt to kill the man who stole Mysty's childhood.

"You should have told me. I have people who could have helped you."

"I don't need your help having people hunted down and shot, Daryl, it's more my sphere of expertise. Trust me, everything that could be done has been done, but, as you might guess, as her father he's not stupid." Yes, that was quite clear. "Do not tell her I told you this. She only told me his name after she signed the contract, because I insisted, because I knew he would come for her. Before that she refused to tell me anything because she knew I'd kill him and she didn't want to be responsible. OG needs to review all security measures. Do whatever can be done to protect her. I live in fear of the possibility that her father will find some way of kidnapping her. If he does, there won't be any hope she'll survive."

Daryl sat back, dragged a hand over his face, like he always did when faced with the seemingly insurmountable. All this time. All this time, when she'd had the best reason – and the worst reason – on earth to hate him for making her sign that contract, and despite everything that had happened afterwards, she had still forgiven him, treated him like a…a friend. Bought him presents. Milkshakes. Tried to lighten his load by building the firewalls. Had taken the time to understand his workload, and alleviate some of the pressure he was under. And now he'd left it to her to resolve the shame of the world thinking she'd aborted his baby, as an inconvenience to the progress of her career. He would love her to have his baby! Oh God.

Donny stayed quiet, seeing the horror and realisation dawn on that arrogantly attractive face.

"Oh God."

"Yes. Quite."

"I wish you'd told me."

"I wish you'd controlled yourself and left her the fuck alone."

"I wish I had too."

"Pardon me?" Donny jumped on this new admittance like a hound sensing blood, his temper still flowing. "You've spent God knows how long and fuck knows how much money manipulating her into your world, and now you're wishing you hadn't? What are you saying, Daryl? That because she's in danger – because of you, your arrogance, and her sadistic father – you're now abandoning her to the wolf?"

"No, Donny! I'm not going to let anything happen to her. I will spend as much money on security as I have to, you know that!"

"Then what?"

"I've decided it's…not a good idea."

"What isn't? What!"

"Even if I ever managed to convince her I'm not a complete bastard, it's not going to happen, with me and her…" They were words he'd only ever thought. Putting them into the air was not easy.

"What the f…? '*It's not going to happen*?' All of this has happened *because* you wanted her so bad, and now you're telling me you're just letting her go?" Donny didn't believe him; Daryl didn't believe himself when he heard is said like that. "You said the holiday was great. What changed your mind? And there was I thinking you might actually have grown a sense of decency and decided to treat her better than just a thousand trophy-photos on your walls!"

"Maybe, once. But it's not a good idea." It almost closed his throat to say the words.

"Oh really. Why?"

"I really don't want to talk about it."

"No, Daryl, tell me why. You owe me that. You put her through hell to get your chance, and now you're just giving up?"

"It's not because I want to."

"Then *why*?"

Daryl stared into the blue eyes, knowing Donny would work it out. He did. Heartbeats thudded by unnoticed, a numbness affecting him in a way that felt very unfamiliar.

"Oh dear. You have it so bad you don't know what to do, do you? You're scared she really means something to you, aren't you?" Donny leaned back in his chair and dropped into the shock of that truth, part of him not surprised given the girl in question. "You got so shit-scared when she got hurt in that accident you didn't like it, did you? Not being able to control it, or magic everything better by throwing money at it or giving orders. Very unpleasant to be so dependent on another for one's happiness, isn't it? Even worse if you have to give them up because what you've created around them is a danger to them."

Daryl didn't respond. He knew there would be more. There was.

"And from a man renowned for his expertise with economics and physics. Did you not grasp the simple concept of input versus output, good versus bad? Did you really think it would all be easy? That it would be about enjoying her smiles and jokes for a while, and then her body in your bed? No. Sorry, Daryl, it takes a little more than that. You want the smooth, you have to take the rough. You've barely scratched the surface of who and what she is; if you can't cope now, I doubt you ever will, and you'll never truly understand the joy of her and her trust, in marriage or otherwise. You're right to back off. Like I always said, she's too good for you, anyway. This is cowardice, Daryl. Cowardice."

Disconnect.

Daryl stared at the blank screen. *Cowardice.* The second time in as many hours he had been called such. So be it. He would see her safe, but he couldn't afford to lose himself to a woman who may be taken from him.

"O'Grady."

"Sir."

"I want you to call Mr Capello. He has information you should know, so should Mac. She must not know you have spoken to him or what you discuss. She must never suspect you know. You'll understand why."

"Sir."

"Tomorrow I want you to begin a full security review. I want every second of every day accounted for. Are we clear?"

"I understand."

"Her life is at stake, O'Grady. I trust you don't need any more incentive than that."

He looked at the girl snuggled on the sofa with her leopards. "No, sir."

"Good. And you can tell her from me, if she ever comments negatively on my ability to father children in private or in public again, I will personally see to it she is locked in a room and kept there until I have her pregnant, irreversibly."

"Yes, sir."

OG stood in the uncomfortable silence of the news, and his boss's outburst, feeling like he was unfortunate witness to a domestic argument that should have been private.

"Ring Capello, and keep her safe. Nothing and no one gets close, understand?"

"Yes, sir."

Disconnect.

It was time to go home. He needed to be alone. Properly alone.

The door knocked and Mac looked in.

"Sir?"

"Get the cars, Mac. I want to go home."

"Yes, sir. Sir, there are a number of reporters outside. Would you prefer to take the chopper?"

It was tempting, but her accusation of being a coward rang in his ears.

"No. This media whore will face the press and deal with their questions. It's not like they'll go away otherwise."

"She was just angry, sir. You know that."

"I know."

Daryl stood. Love. It really did screw things over.

At the time it didn't register with the imposing figure of a man who stepped out into the night air and the forest of waiting press, with his usual godlike composure, that he'd even thought the word 'love'.

OH GOD, THE headlines: 'Billions in the Bank but Not Where it Counts' and 'Blackmoor Empire Needs an Heir', not to mention 'Billionaire Fires Blanks'. One newspaper went so far as to put his face in the place of Henry VIII, the English monarch rumoured to have been infertile. And this despite negating the aspersions cast on his ability to have children last night by addressing the clamouring press. He had simply confirmed her statement that the romance/love-child rumours were not true, adding that the reason for his silence had been that he'd considered the stories 'too fantastic' for anyone to have taken them seriously.

But his failed engagement to Rachel had been aired again, and did not reflect well. And the fact that he had six Cherries and King Henry had had six wives was suddenly a most unfortunate parallel that, on any other day, would mean absolutely nothing. Some small part of him had to admit, however, there was some justice in it, and he had to admire her fight.

And yet still he couldn't resist the temptation to check on her.

"O'Grady?"

"Yes, sir."

Daryl peered in at the screen. "Can I ask what you're doing?"

Mysty was lying on the sofa, peacefully asleep in the arms of the man still wearing his suit.

"She won't tell me what she sees, and last night was bad," OG whispered.

The man in the multi-million-dollar skyscraper didn't know what to say. He felt completely responsible, and utterly useless. The meagre enthusiasm he'd had for the day fled from him like heat through an open door in winter.

"Let her sleep as long as she needs to. That's far more important than getting to a rehearsal. I'm sure she's already got the performance down to a thing of perfection, anyway."

"I've already let the studio team know she'll be late."

"With respect to the other matter, you have free rein, no budget. Let me know any problems. Oh, and show her some of today's headlines; I'm sure they'll cheer her up."

Disconnect.

He was tempted to ignore the intercom and just zoom in on her angelic face, glad to see her resting. But what the hell was he doing? Telling OG to 'let her sleep', like he cared. This was not part of the plan. He closed down the screen, angry with himself, and pressed the button.

"Daryl."

"Harvey. What a pleasant surprise."

"I've seen the news, friend. What on earth is going on? You've never said anything to me about firing blanks? I thought I was a good enough friend that you'd share something like this with me, you know. How are you? Are you okay?"

Daryl pinched the bridge of his nose, closed his eyes and exhaled.

"Harvey. There is nothing wrong with me. It's her revenge for the headlines I didn't do anything about, the ones that dragged her name into the mire. Believe me, she says anything else about it, she's going to be having my baby nine months from the moment she opens her mouth."

"I see... You two don't half know how to wind each other up, you know. Lord above, I actually spilt my coffee down my tie yesterday, seeing the news about the abortion, and today I luckily only got it on my shoe, hearing you were, you know..."

"I'm a little insulted you were less surprised by today's erroneous revelation." Daryl found his lips actually curve into a smile. It felt so strange. "Buy a new tie, and send me the bill."

"Hell, no. Most exciting day of the week so far. Is she going to apologise publicly?"

"I think it'll be a cold day in hell the day she does. She did warn me she would do something if I didn't make a statement. I can't complain."

"So, when's the wedding? I am your best man, aren't I?"

"What wedding?"

"Come on, Daryl. You and her. It's so bloody obvious!"

How was it other people saw this, and she didn't? Besides, having other people thinking 'they' were a great idea was not going to help his resolution to leave her alone and pick someone else he preferred far less who he would never feel anything for.

"And why do you think we're going to get married? She's not from our circles, for God's sake." The words sat uneasily on his tongue, such was the gravity of their irrelevance.

"Daryl, my friend, I've known you for a very long time and I've never see you enjoy being with a woman – outside of the bedroom – like you do with her. You're so suited to each other. Surely you must see it? Who cares if she's not from a dull, pedigreed family. What does that matter? She's beautiful, smart, talented, has a great sense of humour. And, judging from her relationship with Capello, as honourable as a girl can be. She's also widely respected, liked by the president, the world and the press. And she's only seventeen. And would bear you the most amazing children! What more could you possible want? Thank God you never married Rachel!"

Oh, for the love of God shut up, Harvey. Like I don't know all this.

"Why don't you marry her yourself, then, seeing as you're so keen to extol her virtues?" Daryl's voice was tight and low, far removed from the jovial tones of his always upbeat friend.

"Like she'd even look at me, after what happened?" Silence. This was true. "Fine, Daryl, you just keep pretending and I'll keep my mouth shut. Hopefully you'll realise before she walks off with someone else." Still no argument. "The boys are out on the town Thursday night, starting off with dinner at the Windsor, if you'd like to come? We'd all like to see you. Feels like an age."

"Probably. I think I'm free that night." He would make sure he was. A night of immersing himself in his bachelor ways would help no end, and he wouldn't be able to give in to temptation to check on her.

"Did she really walk out on you at The Orange Window?"

"Yes, Harvey, she did."

"What did you say to make her do that?"

"A number of things."

"Lord. If I could only have been a fly on the wall. You are going to invite her to that big party on Sunday night, aren't you?"

"I've been thinking about that, but I'm not sure it's a good idea, particularly if she's still on the warpath. I might end up with a number of drinks over me."

"She'll have calmed down by then. Go on, it'll be so much more interesting if she's there. Put the golden tiger amongst the pampered Persian pussies. I'd love to see what happens."

Daryl rolled his eyes at the innuendo, and the pun. He had been toying with the idea. Having Mysty in a ballroom with the perfect coiffures, manicured nails and ball gowns of the women who fell at his feet? That would be a sight to see.

"I admit it would be interesting…"

"Great. Super. Well, got to go. Do give me a heads up next time, if there are any more superb headlines on the way. I can't keep throwing liquid over myself. My secretary already thinks I'm a delinquent."

Harvey, the joker, always on top form.

"Thanks for calling, Harvey. You've actually cheered me up."

"Any time, old chap. I'm not as useless as you think I am."

"I'll see you Thursday."

"Roger that. I'll let the boys know and arrange a time."

Disconnect.

Just keep going, Daryl. Don't give in.

He glanced at the photograph on the wall, again. When on earth would he be able to give up his pictures of her?

HARVEY'S VOICE WAS unusually animated, even for him.

"Harvey?"

"I'm calling because I've managed to wind up some business earlier than expected. I just wondered if you fancied a few drinks before heading over to the concert hall?"

Daryl was confused. What concert hall?

"Harvey, are you sure you're asking the right person the right question?"

He waited, growing suspicious, and the immediate person who sprang to mind was the very one whom he had spent a whole week trying to ignore.

"She hasn't invited you, has she? Do you mean to tell me you don't even know?"

"Invited me to what? Know what?"

"The Light and Dark Show? Over on Fifth?"

None of this was making sense. Daryl knew the theatre that was putting on the show. It was exclusive, and expensive, and quite intimate compared to most theatres, with only five hundred seats at most.

"No, I don't know. Are you telling me she's putting on a show there?"

How the hell had she found time to do an extra show when she had the summit dance to prepare and rehearse? Daryl knew one thing: he was going to find out.

"Yes! You're her manager? How can you not know she's invited five hundred of society's rich and famous to this exclusive show?"

He chose to ignore that. "What time does it start?"

"Eight o'clock. Doors open at seven thirty."

It was a quarter to seven. He could cancel his final call of the day.

There was no way he was going to miss this.

"Fine, yes."

"Are you going to gate-crash this show? I assumed you knew about it and would have the option to attend anyway, as her manager?"

"Absolutely."

"You've never gate-crashed anything in your life!"

"There have been a lot of firsts since meeting Mysty Reverie, my friend. Don't worry, I've learnt to live with the excitement."

"I'll be waiting."

Disconnect.

Thank God for Harvey.

THE ARROGANT MAN just couldn't keep away, could he, not even for one show. She didn't want him in the audience. Typical he should turn up with Harvey and make sure they had the best seats in the house. Insufferable bastard.

She heard the audience quieten as the lights dimmed, and then she stepped through the folds of curtain and walked on. It felt strange to have fabric around her legs, a pure white soft material that fell from her shoulders in two halves to the floor. Hair up, coiled and bright, one single long curl left to trail over her shoulder, she was a goddess, requiring no other adornment.

She stopped in the centre of the stage where the spotlight gave her a circle of light to stand in. She looked around, seeing the eager, expectant faces beyond the lights, some of whom she recognised, some who she would never forget, and some quite new to her.

"Well, good evening, everyone. I'm most flattered that no one turned down their invitation. Even those I didn't invite have turned up. I will try and take that as some sort of compliment." Her eyes rose to where she knew he would be. "As you know from the invitation, this evening is purely for fun, and the songs chosen are a collection of my favourites and those of the people who mean a great deal to me. Possibly they are favourites of yours too. I hope very much that you enjoy yourselves."

There was an unconscious inward gasp as her audience watched the miracles of light and science at play, crafted it seemed like magic in the darkness of the hall where suns became moons that shimmered and faded in showers of light shards above each table.

Daryl looked down at the programme. The first song was 'Benedictus', and he had no idea what to expect. It was exceptional, from the full piece orchestra in front of the stage to the Latin verses that made each word a prayer echoed by the male choir. She made it look effortless, hitting the high notes and holding them in waves of impassioned praise followed by bare whispers. He glanced across at Harvey, who looked back with raised eyebrows and a quiet smile of amazement. This was a very different Mysty.

The next two hours passed in a dazzling medley of songs, from Lord of the Rings, Phantom of the Opera, and Don't Cry for me Argentina, Time to Say Goodbye, and Nessun Dorma, which soothed and soared and, yes, he could feel his heart pounding. The accompanying light show was spectacular, a 3D creation of the universe, echoing the lyrics – '*A star shining in a universe far away; my heart knows that we shall meet again some sweet day. And you, you will be the flame that burns in my breast; and though I know just by knowing you I was blessed…heaven…heaven…oh waiting there for me…heaven…heaven…oh always let it be…*'

The necklace Daryl recognised as the gift she had received from Donny sparkled, each diamond picked out as a star in the darkness, and he felt heavy, felt her loss, felt too much… Was she really only seventeen, and a heart so broken already?

She was flawless, spectacular, and her audience loved her. Her orchestra stood, and she led the applause for them, so too her incredible choir. And then with a wide smile and a wave she turned and strode away, the white gown flying behind her.

What Daryl hadn't expected was for people to come up to him to congratulate him on such a brilliant evening – and he tried to make it clear that tonight the credit was all hers. He had not known about this event, and they needed to know this had been of her making alone.

He left with Harvey after chatting with these astonished, grateful people, but returned home. He had to ring her. He had to tell her.

After the expected abuse, and her outrage at him being there uninvited, he managed to ask, "How did you do all that? And when did you organise it? And how did you pay for it? Haven't you got your hands full with the summit performance pieces?"

"The concert hall was free provided I gave the owners tickets and a signed photograph. The rest…wasn't that expensive."

"And I trust it was recorded?"

"Of course. It's released tomorrow."

"I see."

"I don't need your PR people sitting on my shoulder. I can handle things perfectly well."

Obviously.

Lazarus chose that moment to walk into the awkwardness, plonk himself down and raise a leg to lick his manhood. Daryl had a ringside seat and he looked at Mysty as if to say *Can you stop him*?

"Oh come now, Daryl, no need to be all prudish. You're both boys, aren't you? You're just jealous anyway, as I'm sure you'd like to be able to reach that part of you yourself. It might give that arrogant mouth of yours a break, not to mention your hand. Might even save you some money."

"A knowing hand is better than an untutored one, whether mine or that of a woman."

Her face remained remarkably impassive.

"What more could a man possibly want? I'm amazed you lasted so long on holiday without your special women. Or was that why you left without saying goodbye? Gosh, you must have been desperate. All that time without your harem. No doubt they satisfied you upon your return, and then you kicked them out of your bed as an inconvenience."

He gritted his teeth. "Anyway, I just wanted to congratulate you, it was a sensational performance."

"Why should I believe you? You know, when we were in Barbados, I actually believed you were a real person, with a sense of fun and humour. I'm so glad I discovered the truth."

"What do you think the truth is?"

"That you have more issues than I do. I thought my father had messed me up pretty badly. Yours did a pretty good job on you too, didn't he?" Wow. He hadn't expected that. What the hell did she know about his father? "Good night, Mr Blackmoor."

Disconnect.

He ran a hand through his hair, turned the chair around and looked out into the nothingness of a starless night.

He thought about his coming meeting with one Dawn Ferguson, who, from reports from his investigative team, was reliably proper and lovely in all the requisite ways, everything a sensible man would want in a wife. She was no Mysty. But then that was the whole point.

THE FIVE MEN carrying the boxes were quite aware that what they were bringing was unwanted, and looked at OG for permission to go. They were dismissed.

"I don't want to go. I don't know anyone and I'm not a party person. Not that type of party anyway."

"How do you know? You've never been to this 'type of party'."

"Exactly! And I'm happy with that!" She lifted the lid of one box with a single finger. "Pink? He knows I hate pink!"

"I'm sure they're not all pink." OG opened another box. "Look, this one is black."

"It's probably transparent, knowing him."

"It's just one night."

"It'll be hours, OG. Thousands of seconds. It's going to feel like a lifetime." She sat glumly in a chair and tossed the invitation away. "Is the plane ready?"

"Of course."

"Let's get to Celeste." She strode away, clearly keen to leave New York and her manager far behind, not even looking in three of the boxes.

Whatever Blackmoor had done, he was reaping what he had sown with a very fruitful harvest.

THE SOONER HE was married with a pregnant wife the sooner he would realise just how insane the idea to marry Mysty had always been. Dawn had been unchallenging, ladylike, quiet and reliable. But she was also uninspiring, unexciting, and not all that smart.

"Daryl!"

"Harvey."

His friend looked in fine spirits, a glass of champagne already in his hand, tuxedo pristine. It was hard to believe they were all in their late twenties now, but some moments it felt like they were all teenagers again, when life was less full of concerns and the world was waiting to surprise them. Tonight was one of those nights.

"My, you all look remarkably happy," he said, noting the warm smiles and handshakes of his friends.

"Of course! You said she was coming, did you not?" Harvey replied, with a wink, and Robbie and Guy raised their glasses to that.

"She's not here yet, so you can all calm down," he said with mild amusement, and a touch of irritation. He no longer intended to claim her, but it still felt wrong to passively accept the acute interest of the group of males who would be sniffing round her skirts like a pack of rampant dogs.

"Like you're not keen to see her, either!" Harvey scoffed.

"Not for the same reasons you are."

Daryl sighed, receiving a nod from Mac, which was noticed by Harvey. "For what we are about to receive," his eager friend said, and Daryl's eyes went to the double doors.

Which dress had she chosen? He'd heard she'd been disgusted at the pink one he'd thrown in just to annoy her. What about the black? And the white was spectacular. The answer was, however, none of them.

She was dressed from top to toe in a silky red skin-tight bodysuit, her hair a glorious piled up in a mass of plaits and curls decorated with red ribbon and twinkling gems. Jewels glittered in her ears and a single red pendant hung from the choker at her neck. She was no blushing debutante. She was there, on her terms, and she didn't look like she gave a quarter.

"May the Lord make us truly thankful," Harvey murmured.

Why the hell had she dressed like that? Like some red-clad Pirate Queen on an outing to parley with the colonials.

"Are you going to go and say hello?" Harvey then said, to no response. "Super. I will then."

Harvey handed Robbie his champagne glass, his eyes fixed on his target.

Daryl was fuming. She had broken every rule of accepted etiquette and dress code for an event such as this. Yet she looked so, so gorgeous. Seeing Harvey step forward pushed another set of buttons he hadn't even been aware existed until that moment, and his fingers curled into a fist.

"Mysty…you look ravishing! Welcome to our little party."

Surprised, she took his offered hand, and watched him kiss the back of it. His eyes stayed on hers; they were warm eyes, friendly, and shared a look of mischief with her that she had just rendered the entire ballroom speechless.

"Just ignore them; they're all thinking exactly what I'm thinking."

"Which is?"

"That we're all bloody glad you came, and you look good enough to eat. No other woman could wear what you're wearing half so well. Don't worry about Daryl, either; he's impossible to please at the moment."

"He's always impossible to please. Though I should tell you…I wore this with the intention of annoying him."

Harvey had not expected such a frank declaration. "I see. Still not very happy with him at the moment, then?"

"I would have put it a little stronger, Harvey, but no, not happy. And I have no expectation of that changing any time soon."

Harvey contemplated this as they walked further into the room, which was stirring back into chatter, albeit all eyes on them. She wasn't playing hard to get, this was real animosity.

"Thank you for coming to say hello. I know you didn't have to, considering. But I would have looked a complete goose if you hadn't."

Her voice was soft, her eyes grateful, and Harvey found himself captive to them, not expecting the tiger by his side to turn into a kitten. It was also subtle apology for her part in what had gone before; an apology she didn't need to give when he had been in the wrong. He knew that now.

"A tiger should never look like a goose. On any occasion. It was my pleasure, honestly, don't mention it." He'd done it because he'd wanted to be the one to meet her, as a direct challenge to Daryl. But he was now doubly glad he'd done it now, for her own sake, her sweet confession the last thing he had expected to hear. How much more was there to discover about this unusual creature that had intrigued him from the first?

"Good Lord, Harvey, are you doing an impression of a gentleman?"

That gorgeous smile made his eyes dip to her lips – lips he'd never forgotten, despite the torrent of abuse that had poured from them all that time ago.

"Just for one night."

"I'll make the most of it, then."

He laughed, and held out his hand. "Mysty, I think you know everyone. Robbie, Guy, Claude, Luke, oh, and Johnny – all as disreputable as each other, I'm afraid, so steer well clear of them." She looked at him, as if to say *Aren't you forgetting someone*? But Harvey knew exactly what he was doing. "Oh, and Daryl, of course, though he doesn't look too sociable at the moment. But…" – and he plucked a glass of champagne from a passing tray and handed it to her – "I don't suppose that bothers you."

Blue eyes met green over her head, Daryl promising Harvey a short, sharp exit from the room via a balcony if he continued his attitude, distracted by a new irritation as he saw how easily the flute sat in her feminine hand.

"No, I'm quite used to that. He has only a very limited capacity for being sociable. I wouldn't want him to waste any of it on me."

"Lovely of you to *dress* the part yourself…" Daryl said, ice-cold and loaded.

"I didn't feel like wearing a dress."

"Another stunt like this and you'll suffer the consequences."

She hadn't expected him make that kind of threat in front his friends, and was instantly incensed he should dare to humiliate, making her out to be a naughty child he had to discipline.

"You do that and there'll be consequences for you too."

The face-off was excruciating, unbearable.

"Mysty, would you like to dance?" Harvey dared, finding the perfect excuse to take the most beautiful girl there for her first spin around the dancefloor, and to separate these two before Lord knows what kicked off.

"Dance? Really? Where?"

"The other ballroom, through there. It's all very tame, I know, only a waltz or a foxtrot, not anything quite up to your standard, but fun all the same – what do you say?"

"Bit of an issue who leads when you're both wearing trousers," Daryl threw at them.

"Harvey, why don't you take your shirt off and we'll see who has the nicer breasts. In fact, where's Mac? He could join in. He had a fabulous pair on holiday, albeit made of sand. He can be the judge, and whoever does can be the lady, the other can lead."

Daryl nearly choked on his champagne. But Harvey burst out laughing and shook his head, delighted with her suggestion.

"You definitely have the nicer breasts, any day of the year."

"Then I am the lady?"

"Most definitely. But what's this about Mac?"

"Oh, he fell asleep on the beach and I covered him in sand, in the shape of a mermaid, complete with tail and beautiful breasts. He was not impressed."

Harvey eyed the serious man standing a short distance away. He couldn't imagine that at all…and, in truth, didn't want to. "Shall we?" he asked, extending his hand.

"Yes." She turned her angry eyes on Daryl. "Keep your eyes off my arse, please. Harvey, lead on, and amaze me with your foxtrot."

"Wow. Still not in her good books, then?" Robbie asked quietly as they walked away, none of them missing the fact that despite her asking him not to, their esteemed friend still enjoyed watching her derriere as it disappeared into the crowd.

"You make the assumption I wish to be," Daryl replied blithely, threw back the rest of his champagne and stalked off in the opposite direction. He was not going to pay her any more attention, and she could damn well cope all evening on her own. But why the hell was he letting

Harvey have the honour of dancing with her, a thing he had wanted so much? *Don't even contemplate it.*

On a second glass of champagne he scanned the room. Dawn. In a classic long black dress. She looked rather lovely. In fact, she looked very lovely. She was a little older than he'd wanted, but at least she wasn't some defiant seventeen-year-old with an unpredictable temper. He admired her straight dark hair, and patrician features, the smooth skin and high cheekbones. What was there to find fault with?

He strolled over and was immediately welcomed into the circle. Her parents were there, whom he knew, as well as other family friends. All of the same social standing, he could be assured of respect and polite conversation without lewd implications or blatant insults. The exchange was remarkably un-extraordinary, like one of a hundred thousand conversations he had just like it. Very safe, very meaningless.

He made the mistake of glancing away at the sound of familiar laugh, and spied the golden-haired beauty back in the company of his friends, a merry party of almost fourteen now. She was the centre of their attention, and they were obviously having a very amusing conversation.

Harvey caught his eye, and sent him a look questioning why he didn't join them, because it was obvious where the most fun was to be had. Daryl looked away.

No.

"CHARLES, SO GOOD to see you. I wasn't sure if you'd make it."

The two men shook hands, and then Charles joined Daryl, leaning on the balustrade looking out over the assembled gathering.

"Late, but here at last. You're not with Mysty, I see?"

As before he said, "And you assume I want to be?"

"Ah. Like that is it. She's still not forgiven you over that abortion story in the news, has she?"

Daryl bridled just slightly. Charles could be rather forward with his comments on occasion. "I don't care for nor need her forgiveness. Whatever you thought was between us is now not the case."

"Oh. Well, that's a disappointment. I came over to see when the wedding might be, so I'd know to expect my invite. But if you're going to marry one of the unexceptional selection you just danced with, then I think I'll pass. You'll be bored out your mind within five minutes and despise them in less than ten, but what do I know? I've only been happily married for forty years. I'm an old man. Out of touch."

He went to move away.

"And what makes you think we are at all suited? Given who I am and who she is?" Daryl asked, and Charles turned around in surprise, looking at the man who was obviously not at all in the party spirit.

"You really need me to tell you that you'd find life with any of those 'suitable' women down there interesting? It would be no more interesting than choosing a pair of shoes from your wardrobe. Mysty's in a different league, Daryl, and you know it. Who cares who she isn't in terms of family or pedigree? She's brilliant, and respected for who she is." Charles paused, eyeing his young companion more seriously, a furrow in his brow. "What happened? Last time I spoke to you it sounded like you two were getting on very well?"

"We were." It wasn't easy to admit, and it brought back memories of sunny days by the pool. It seemed like a lifetime ago.

"Then what went wrong? She saved your life, didn't she? Why are you now so set against her?"

"I decided it was the wrong choice. She didn't do anything wrong."

Charles digested this piece of information. "You know, I was so pleased. It seemed you'd found someone who made you happy. It's a rare thing in this world, especially for men like us, and especially for a man like you. I'm disappointed, Daryl. I thought you had the sense to realise how precious that is." Charles smiled sadly. "Never mind, a girl like that won't be wanting for offers; and once she's over Capello properly, I'm sure she'll have no problem loving again." He turned to Daryl. "Well, I'm going down to speak to her. Had a lovely chat with her the other day, as did the president. Very bright young woman. Going to go a lot further than just the stage, I think. Superb party, Daryl, good to see you."

Charles toasted him with his glass, and trotted off down the stairs and across the ballroom, making for the scarlet goddess across the room.

Why the hell had she been speaking to Charles and Thomas? What was she up to? There would be no point asking OG, as she most likely wouldn't have told him, in case he was asked. He watched Charles ask her to dance, after a brief and very friendly exchange, and she was once more led through to the adjoining ballroom, for the twelfth time or so, not that he was counting. He was conscious of what Charles had said, as so many had in their way: she in a different league. He been watching her, despite trying so hard not to, and once the ice was broken, everyone relaxed in her company. Harvey, or one of his other friends, was always on hand to make an introduction if she looked a little worried, and once more the beautiful smile would be back.

He strolled with fake nonchalance to the balcony in the next room so he could continue his observations. There was nothing inelegant about her dancing in that outfit. She looked unorthodox, but never less than beautiful.

"You know, old chap, I really thought you were keen on her." Harvey was there next to him, having approached silently, and alone. They viewed what was going on below with critical eyes, as they had done so often before.

"I was. For a while. Then I realised that it wouldn't do."

"Why?"

"We don't suit."

"Bollocks. That last time at Celeste, I've never seen you look so happy. Why are you turning your back on this?"

"Because it's for the best, now please, just leave the subject alone. I didn't ask you for any advice. And besides, what makes you of all people such a fount of wisdom regarding marriage and suitability? Have you got some hidden wife somewhere I don't know about?"

"Because I don't want you to throw away the chance to be happy. You must have been serious to have contemplated it. You've successfully ignored it, for years, and then suddenly you're changing your schedule, even moving your main office to LA to be near her? You've tolerated her destroying your cars, and God knows what else, and you're telling me it means nothing?"

"It does to her. Absolutely nothing. And you haven't answered my question. You seem to expect a whole lot of answers from me, it's only fair you answer one for me."

"I'm not a total wastrel, Daryl, and I know I chase women as much as you do, but it doesn't mean I've never felt I was…in love."

"When? You never told me?" Daryl looked at his friend with acute surprise, dismayed to have missed out on this significant episode, not thinking to refute the idea he was 'in love'.

"It was years ago, I shouldn't have mentioned it," Harvey replied, annoyed at having admitted it. He finished his drink in one swallow.

"No, tell me, what happened? Who was she?"

"Some girl, you don't need her name. We met at Harvard. I thought she was fantastic. Fun, gorgeous, witty and smart. We went out for drinks and dinner, and even sat in the library and actually did some work. Ironic, I never got past first base, and I was already thinking of taking her back to meet the parents and…all kinds of stupid dreams. I actually wrote her a letter over Christmas, when she was away visiting relatives."

"So what happened? Why don't you find her, whisk her off her feet and send me a postcard from Vegas telling you've tied the knot?"

Daryl hoped the outrageous suggestion might make Harvey smile, but the sad twist on his usually laughing lips was the response, and the blue eyes refused to meet those of his green-eyed friend.

"Why? You want to know why?" Harvey shook his head, as if that was the wrong choice, or representative of what felt like many wrong choices. "The reason I never took it any further was because she went to a party, a party on the roof of a skyscraper for my best friend's eighteenth birthday, and it only took one look from him and she walked off, without so much as a glance at me, and blew him while he lay on a sun lounger. Then disappeared with him to do goodness' knows what else. That was a good party wasn't it, Daryl? You must have had a good night, right?"

Daryl felt himself pale slightly as the truth unfolded before him like some grotesque porn poster, with him centre stage.

"Oh God. That was why you suddenly disappeared off to Maine, to visit family I'd never heard of?" Daryl vaguely remembered what had happened, but couldn't recall a face or anything exceptional about her; he just knew Harvey had left before everyone sobered up the next day and didn't see him again for a month.

"Did you even know her name?" Harvey demanded, finally having voiced the grievance that still stung so sharply now it had been aired.

"No. I admit I didn't." Daryl paused, feeling awful. He'd hurt his friend, so long ago, and Harvey had never said anything. Why? "Harvey, I'm sorry. I wouldn't have, had I known. You know that."

"I know. I was angrier with her, not you. And myself." Harvey glared down at the ballroom, suddenly despising all the people laughing and smiling, his mind on another party a decade ago that had smashed his heart into messy pieces, like a dropped punch bowl. "I was angry she hadn't noticed me at all, that she went and prostrated herself for you in front of everyone there, and you'd done nothing for it. And me? What a fool I felt. An utter fool."

"Harvey, you're not a fool. You couldn't help how you felt. And we were all so much younger then. If she didn't reciprocate, then she wasn't the one for you, despite how much you… If I could undo my part I would. You know how much you and your family mean to me. At least when you do find the right one, you'll have parents to introduce someone to, one day. That's something to look forward to." Daryl dared rest a tentative hand on Harvey's shoulder.

Harvey's head swung around. Daryl never mentioned his parents, or their death, even in passing. What was going on? There had to be a link somewhere.

Damn. He shouldn't have said that. He might know Harvey would jump on it. He took his hand back and rested both elbows again. "Harvey, just leave it, alright?"

"How badly was she hurt, when you were on holiday?"

Daryl looked away, irritated that his friend, who specialised in tomfoolery and excess, could be as razor-sharp as himself when the opportunity presented itself.

"She was unconscious. We thought she had serious concussion, or… worse. She banged her head, so hard." It had been absolute torture, and the memory must have shown on his face.

"Had you pretty worried then."

"Had all of us pretty worried." He hoped the mention of 'all' would shut his friend up, but no.

"You were scared of losing her, like you lost your parents."

"There's no need to read so much into this, Harvey." Daryl stood up and went to move away but Harvey caught his arm and made him stay to hear it all.

"You were. And you didn't like it at all. So you decided to give her up. Just like that. And yet…and yet you've spent the *whole night* keeping an eye on her, feigning interest in various others. Doesn't look to me as though you're in agreement with your own choices."

The tension in Daryl's face was enough to tell him if his friend spoke again it would be to tell him to fuck off. Harvey retracted his hand, knowing the touch was more than unwelcome.

"Well, you're right, in as much as you have to decide something when it comes to her," he continued. "Just remember, though, it's a decision that will affect the rest of your life. I wish to God I'd grabbed Amanda back then, taken her to Vegas, sent you that postcard, then told my parents, even if they disowned me – for a short time, anyway." Harvey began walking away as quietly as he had arrived, but he turned back. "Just so you know, I've invited Mysty to my New Hampshire estate to go riding, and she accepted. Apparently, it was what she enjoyed most about Sicily – aside from the fact you 'buggered off and left her in peace'. Her words not mine." Harvey's taunt was designed to rile. It was his parting shot.

Daryl glared back at the ballroom below. He couldn't see Mysty anywhere. How perfectly apt.

He spotted Dawn again. Saw her talking to friends; saw her kiss another man's cheek in greeting. And felt nothing. Wasn't that what he should want? Wasn't that the safe option? To feel nothing?

TUESDAY AFTERNOON, AND she was on her way to see Harvey. Goddammit.

He watched the car make its way up the long, winding drive through the beautiful parkland. He had every anticipation of her loving it there. Anyone would. And the house was worth an absolute fortune. He knew Harvey preferred it to any other property he owned. One day, like Daryl to Philadelphia, maybe he'd imagined taking a wife there, and bringing up their children. Only it had better not be this particular woman… But then why not? If he didn't want her, why shouldn't Harvey be happy with her? He was a lot more fun that he was.

Harvey walked down the steps to greet her, dressed in jodhpurs and riding boots and a polo shirt. He looked fit, and well, the familiar handsomeness irritating. She was in jodhpurs too, and looked fantastic. Mysty took his offered hand, which he slid to the small of her back as he guided her up the steps. It was the lightest of touches, but intimate enough to make Daryl's stomach clench.

Her face appeared at the large sash window, and it was obvious she was admiring the garden. Harvey naturally opened the French windows, and they stepped outside. She gazed in wonder at the flowers, the fountains, the view, OG and the five-man bodyguard hanging back to give them some privacy but never letting them out of sight, as per his recent drilling. Her host was clearly pleased to see her, and looked enraptured to have her there.

They reached the stables, where the stable boys had prepared a grey Arab for her and a stunning bay for Harvey. It wasn't difficult to see how at ease she was on the horse. Harvey brought them to the top of the first hill, at a steady trot at first, and then a gentle canter, and pointed out various things. He was a confident horseman, relaxed and in charge. Daryl watched him instructing her, showing her how to move the reins in her hands, and then they were off, galloping down the hill and then on.

Daryl felt sick just witnessing the simple enjoyment. He should turn the screen off and leave them to it. Work intervened, requiring his presence in the boardroom and his full attention. By the time he got back to his office, the feed from OG's jacket camera was unhelpful. He appeared to be waiting outside a set of double doors on the first floor, standing patiently in the corridor with the rest of the suits on the polished marble. Where were they, and what were they doing?

"SO, HARVEY, WHAT is it you'd like to learn? You already know ballroom. Do you fancy something more exciting?"

"I know it's ballroom, but I've always wanted to know how to tango – properly – but I'm not too sure I could, so it might be better to stick to something easier?"

She watched him talking. He was clearly on his best behaviour, warm but not flirtatious. She was glad she had forgiven him.

"Why not? You're a passionate man, yes? I would say the tango was made for you. Don't shy away from expressing that part of yourself in dance." She walked towards him, held out her arms. He looked suddenly quite coy, and she laughed. "I'm not thirteen anymore, Harvey, and I have danced far more passionate dances than a tango. I can handle you."

"Right…" He was still uncertain, but he also didn't want to back out.

"So? Do you want to learn or not, Mr Lincoln?"

"Yes." He smiled at the use of his surname.

"Great." She looked him up a down. "The shoes are fine, but you might want to lose the jacket. We're not at a ball now." He smiled and slipped the expensive sports jacket off. He'd changed out of his riding gear into jeans and a shirt. She was wearing black leggings and a Pirate t-shirt, and pulled off her trainers and changed into heels suitable for performing a tango. "And roll the sleeves up. Once we get into this, you'll get a bit hot!"

He obeyed, and she connected her beloved, ancient iPod to the sound system in the room.

"So, first we'll go over some of the basic steps, fitting them to the rhythm of the music. The beauty of the tango is that it is – as with most truly passionate moments – made up of lots of different elements that all go together to make something brilliant. Does that make sense?" Harvey nodded. This wasn't going to be like any dance lesson in his life. "I can teach you the steps, but as the male lead it will ultimately fall to you to drive the dance. If things go well, you should get to a point where you can communicate where and what you want your partner to do by the way you touch her, your body language, your feet and with your eyes." Harvey really did not want to make a complete fool of himself and fall short of her expectations; but he was also very nervous about being so close to her. This was Mysty, for goodness' sake! How on earth was he going to be able to touch her without…? And what if his feet forgot how to work and he trod on her foot? Mortifying! "I will teach you the steps now, and then we can play around with them, maybe create our own sequence of steps to some music you really like, okay?"

"Yes."

He was co-ordinated, graceful, and had the strength to move fluidly and confidently, and three quarters of an hour later she was satisfied he was doing well enough to put something to music. She played the first thirty seconds of a tango piece. "Tell me what you think about it," she said, playing it again. "What do you think the music is saying?"

He felt like he was back in school. "It's…strong," he ventured. "And forceful. And passionate. Almost…aggressive?"

"Yes. Exactly. This isn't a foxtrot and it isn't a waltz. It is a declaration and a claiming. A statement of wanting. You wouldn't dance the tango with your gran – or at least I hope you wouldn't."

"She's sweet, but definitely not!" he said and laughed.

"So, Mr Lincoln…" He didn't know why but he liked her calling him that, and the way her eyes twinkled at him when she said it. "I want you to leave all your polite foxtrot learning over there somewhere. Here, you are a man. Passionate. Wanting. Nothing matters except what you say with your body. Clear?"

"I think so." He knew what she was asking of him, but he didn't know quite how to, erm, access that part of him and use it without, well, becoming somewhat aroused.

"Good. Reach for me, like I showed you." He tried and she looked sternly at him. "Too weak. Do it again." Her eyes were on him. He stepped up to her. "No. Do it again. Where is your passion? Where are you? I know you have this in you, I've seen it, remember?"

"I shouldn't have done that."

"No, you shouldn't have, because I was a child, but the emotion was real. That's the point. Again," she commanded.

Oh hell, he thought, *she's not going to give up on this.*

Again she stopped him.

"Do you need some help getting your blood pumping a little harder?" she asked.

"I think that would help."

"Fine." And to his astonishment, she slapped him reasonably hard on the cheek, and then ripped his shirt open, exposing his chest. "Take it off," she said. He didn't take his eyes off hers as he yanked the shirt out of his trousers and tossed it away, not ashamed to be topless in front of her, feeling heat flow in his veins, and his breath push through his nose. "So?" she said.

The single word was a mockery, and his hand darted out, grabbed her wrist and pulled her in against his chest, his naked flesh against the soft fabric of her t-shirt and her gorgeous breasts. There was a moment of silence as he caught up with the sensation of having her so close to him, and he breathed in the smell of her fresh clean skin.

"Perfect. Well done." She stepped out of the embrace and into her starting position. "I'll buy you a new shirt, by the way."

"I don't give a damn about the shirt," he laughed.

She laughed too, glad to see he was getting in the mood, but not in a threatening way.

"Now, when the music begins, use the steps we've already gone over, but move me with your hands. Really move me. I will be able to anticipate your moves, but you need to be the lead. I'm sure you won't have trouble with that now, will you?"

"I will try very hard not to disappoint."

She waited, and their eyes met, the silent duel was engaged. She hit Play and once more she was expertly grabbed and this time spun, held against solid muscle, his forearm firm across her stomach. Good. They moved together, his moves strong, demanding, hungry, but not frightening.

He definitely had the right idea.

HIS LATTE HAD been ignored as he stared at the screen, waiting for it to come back to life. Would he care what Dawn was doing this much? No, he most definitely would not.

Suddenly there was the sound of a door opening, and OG turned, and there they were. His jaw clenched. Harvey was topless. And she was flushed and laughing. What the hell had they been doing for so long? They went to the foot of the stairs. Why were they going upstairs together?

"I'll see you downstairs in a few minutes, when you've showered or whatever," Harvey said. "I've ordered high tea out on the terrace, so you can enjoy the garden."

"What is high tea?"

"Everything. With tea. Though you're welcome to have coffee if you'd rather."

Thankfully they parted ways, and OG shadowed her to a guest room, where she disappeared into the bathroom. His blood pressure dropped a few notches. But he was going to call Harvey the moment she left.

"HARVEY."

"Daryl, what a surprise to hear from you. Mysty has just left."

Daryl braced hands against the desk and glared at the intercom, too tense to sit.

"So? How was your afternoon?"

"Fantastic. She's a great girl, isn't she?" Harvey was smiling as he spoke, Daryl could tell.

"What did you do?"

"We went riding first off, after she admired the gardens. Never thought she was the type, but she absolutely loved them. Made me glad I pay a small army a small fortune to look after them while I'm not here. Then she gave me a dance lesson. Best dance lesson of my life. She's a very good teacher. Has she ever taught you any dancing?"

Daryl's mind went into freefall. Harvey had had a dance lesson with

Mysty? One on one? One of the things he'd longed to do was to dance with her alone, and Harvey had already done it!

"No."

Harvey was happy to notice the quiet voice on the end of the line.

"She taught me to tango, like nothing I've ever done before. Seriously, she can dance."

Daryl closed his eyes. As if he needed Harvey to tell him that; as if he hadn't watched her a hundred thousand times already. The mental anguish was like needles in his brain.

"You were topless when you emerged from the room, apparently."

"Well, you have to get into the mood of it, and I was failing miserably, so she kindly offered to help. Slapped me round the face and then ripped my shirt. Very, very effective."

I bet it was, you bastard. "I trust you behaved yourself?"

"Oh, absolutely, though it's very…hands-on this dancing. I have never needed a cold shower more!" Daryl could sympathise. "She wasn't afraid of me for a second, and didn't seem to hold anything against me, from before. She's very grown up. Not at all like a seventeen-year-old."

"She's lived through a lot, in a short space of time, and she's highly intelligent."

"I realise that. It's just refreshing, but takes some getting used to." Because she is so much more than the women we know. "I can't wait to have her back."

"Have her back?"

"Yes. She loved the riding, and I definitely need another dance lesson. Maybe even three or four. Maybe see if she'll consent to let me take her out for dinner – not at the Orange Window of course, I don't think she'd like it there – to say thank you?"

"What are you up to, Harvey?"

"Up to? Daryl, old chap, you make it sound like a conspiracy. I'm up to nothing except embarking on a most interesting friendship with someone quite exceptional, and whom I would like very much to see more of. What is so difficult about that? Just because you decided you don't want her doesn't make her out of bounds to every man on the planet.

How can you complain, given your recent treatment of her?"

"She is not someone to toy with."

"I'm not toying with her. And I don't intend to. I genuinely like her, as aside from her beautiful self, she's excellent company. Didn't bore me for a second, didn't do anything stupid or pathetic. Just because you're too much a snob concerning the lack of rich parents, and breeding. She's superb just as she is. I would happily marry her tomorrow, except she'd laugh at me if I asked her."

"Yes, she probably would."

"But I intend to change her mind."

Daryl felt something squeeze his heart. Breathing became painful. Thinking was a struggle, apart from two immediate thoughts: *Harvey cannot marry Mysty! She belongs to me!*

"Daryl? I do hope you're not offended, old chap. Nothing personal, but she's one in a billion. I'd be a fool not to try."

"No, not offended. You show remarkably good taste. I have to approve. You're right. One in a billion." *Despite the agony, perhaps this was the answer…*

"Just think, if you find a suitable Mrs Blackmoor, it's odds on who has the first baby."

As if her marrying someone else wasn't painful enough, the thought of her having children with someone else felt like a knife in his heart. It would be the same hell he had lived with knowing she loved Donny. There was no reason she would dislike Harvey, really, and it was obvious how well they got on. And there had been no blackmail, no threats, no injections, no moving her home…topped off with the painful realisation Harvey had only come back into her sphere because of Daryl's involvement. The cruel ironic circle of events was just too much to contemplate just then.

He forced himself to speak through the pain: "Yes. That would be interesting."

"What if they were born close together – they'd be best friends, like we were. Oh Lord, just imagine two small boys like us. I'm not sure I could cope!"

"No, me neither."

"Tell me about Dawn? How are you getting on with her? Are there others you're considering?"

"She is one of them."

"Fine choice. No danger of…a repeat of what happened before."

"No." It was a good job he'd forgiven Harvey his misdemeanour…

"Well, I'm afraid I'm going to have to go. I've a business dinner in an hour so I had better ready myself. I may have asked her to stay had I not been going out. Any exciting plans for tonight?"

Daryl looked at the intercom in shock. Ask Mysty to *stay*?

"Not really. It's been a long day. I need to go home and relax."

"Sure. I'll catch up with you later in the week. Don't work too hard. I mean it."

"I'll try."

Disconnect.

How could Daryl hate his best friend for imagining a future he had wanted so badly himself? Particularly as Harvey had always had to settle for second best, after he'd helped himself to the very best. But had he ever faced a decision as difficult as this one? Would she really fall for Harvey? Was that the kind of man she really wanted? She had been laughing and smiling, and there had been no unease between them at all. But she did with lots of people, didn't she? Was Daryl Blackmoor having some kind of crisis of confidence?

'PHOTO SHOOT FOR MY^2 brand' was all the entry said in the diary, and she'd been given no more information, only told when and where to present herself. She knew her tension was rubbing off on the leopards, and left them at home with a Disney film; she couldn't really leave OG at home, and he was just as aware of her anxiety.

The room was furnished in dark red, with various spotlights set lights. There were at least ten other women in a changing room to the side, having elaborate hairstyles created and make-up applied. What the hell was she supposed to be modelling? And then she saw the outfits.

"You've got to be kidding me."

"I'd get changed if I were you. And then your hair and make-up will be done. I've made arrangements if you don't comply." Daryl felt a small sliver of satisfaction at seeing her horror, and sauntered back towards his cameras.

Going over to look at what she would be wearing, it was obvious she was about to pay the price for her insolence in walking out on him in the restaurant.

Eyes skilfully darkened, as were her lips, she emerged in a state of abject rage, having been forced to sit in front of the make-up mirror almost naked and watch as her reflection was altered for her in ways she'd ever have chosen for herself. The room ground to a halt as she walked onto set, a black leather army cap on her head, black heels on her feet, and a riding crop in her hand. The black bra and panties were cut to a minimum, and decorated with studs and chains. She had a studded collar around her neck, and black gloves to her elbows.

Her eyes told him she hated him.

His eyes told her he didn't care.

He began to direct her, getting her up onto the dark red pedestal, feet apart, tip of the riding crop between her teeth. After the cameras fired – and only his camera on her – he demanded that she go and change into the next outfit. She glared at him and strode away, flicking the crop hard across through the air. The atmosphere was charged, like a lightning storm, waiting for the strike to hit and the thunder with it. Daryl welcomed it. Not only was it making for some excellent photos, he hoped it would trigger a final showdown between them, so he could get on with his life as his role as manager, and nothing more.

She reappeared in thigh-high boots, all in red this time.

He could hardly wait to get the photos downloaded. The rage was manifesting in poses that couldn't be contrived; her simmering defiance giving her a powerful allure.

When she appeared in the penultimate outfit, she stared at the two poles and handcuffs waiting for her. Where were the other women?

"Don't argue; we don't have time."

She glanced at OG, and Mac, both silent, palpably uncomfortable. They didn't seem to be enjoying seeing their boss like this at all. It gave her a bit of courage: she wasn't the only one who thought this was going too far.

Three men appeared, built of solid muscle, hairless glistening bodies in the most minimal underwear. Her hands were raised up, and her legs parted so that one booted foot rested on each of the poles, and then she was handcuffed into position. It was an impossible position to escape from, weakening the body at every angle. Thank God she was facing away from the camera.

And then the pedestal was turned around.

Oh God. Oh no. She closed her eyes, refusing to look at him. She felt one of the men move behind her, his body pressed against her back. One hand slid across her stomach, the other pulled her head against his shoulder, so his lips could find her neck. She wanted to scream, to shout for him to stop. She could feel his thighs against her, his hardness pressing between her buttocks. Even her treatment by Baden, that first time, was preferable to this far more personal violation of her body.

In the final outfit, of black leather, and barely covering her breasts and crotch, she was instructed to get back on the pedestal. Her hands were chained behind her back.

"Get on your knees."

"What?" she whispered, unable to comprehend why he was doing this to her, why everything so far hadn't been enough…

"You heard. Get on your knees. Pretend you're going to put that pretty mouth to some good use for a change."

Somewhere, the words echoed in her brain. She'd heard them before, she knew, but she'd blocked them out. She didn't move. This was too much. This would break her.

"Move!"

"No!"

"Boys."

She heard OG's angry words, but he was silenced by a look from the devil behind the camera.

"Let me go! You have to let me go!" she screamed, but a tug on the collar around her neck pulled her head back.

"For God's sake, you frigid little bitch!" Daryl's frustration broke its hold. "Grow *up*! Do everyone a favour and get laid, so you can lose your fucking pious attitude! You think you're so goddamn precious, don't you? Anyone would think you'd never got on your knees for a man. Surely you didn't deny Donny the pleasure of those lips of yours?"

The whole room turned into a photograph; no one moved, no one breathed.

Mysty felt a part of her crack, like she'd been hit by a truck. He'd hit her where she was most vulnerable. She hadn't even known how vulnerable she was until the words were in the air. It felt like a body blow, winding her. Her throat was so tight she could barely draw breath.

She felt a surge of hatred. God knows she would have given Donny anything he'd wanted, but he'd barely let her touch him. She'd had enough. The world was too unfair and unkind to comprehend. She didn't want a part of it. With the strength she reserved for occasions such as these, she wrenched her arms apart, and there was the sweet sound of metal snapping: her hands were free.

"You can get on your own knees before I get on my knees for anyone, let alone you!"

Their eyes locked in pure, unbridled anger, the heat and the mood in the room as dark as the fury that roiled around the softly furnished room like a storm in a rainforest. There would be no more photos that day.

The room stayed still as she swept out of the room like a force of nature.

In her wake, the team started packing up, the ordering of the equipment an illusion given the invisible emotional carnage that had taken place.

"I have to admit, that was the stupidest thing I've ever heard you say." Mac's glacial voice cut through the silence that followed her outburst and exit from the studio. OG was too disgusted to speak, and followed Mysty without a backwards glance.

Unacknowledged but resolute, the usually stalwart bodyguard headed for the door as well, leaving his boss to finish up – or rather, finish being a complete asshole, leaving him standing conspicuously alone; the kind of alone that spoke volumes; the blood and shame rushing loud in his ears.

Daryl had done it again. Harvey was going to look like a goddamned saint.

ANNABELLE FLEURETTE, AND another very exclusive restaurant – and a world away from the photo shoot that had put the nail in the coffin of Mysty's respect for him. It was a very pretty name, and she was a very pretty woman, with flame-red hair, a pale complexion and pale blue eyes. He watched her walk over, and saw that she had rather too many freckles for his liking. Never mind. He was willing to enjoy the evening anyway.

She smiled nervously and was seated, Daryl remaining so himself, not wanting her to think he was enamoured with her, only vaguely interested. His eyes skimmed critically over her while a waiter took her drink order. Her breasts were a little too large too, and she seemed such a demure female – she couldn't be all that exciting bed either, could she? He imagined how she would look after one child – he'd seen her mother, and that told him a great deal – as her body was slender but not toned. Hers would be a body that would pad out easily and, out of nowhere, he found himself thinking that she'd never have the strength to rescue him from a shark attack, let alone the courage to try. Hmm, she was like a very lovely daisy, a lily maybe, but hers was not a lasting kind of beauty. Still, he would finish his analysis of her over dinner. She might just amaze him.

The charming exterior was employed, and he forced his mind to concentrate on the woman in front of him.

"Annabelle."

"Mr Blackmoor." She inclined her head in a ladylike fashion, careful to be respectful, as they always were.

"You look lovely."

And she did, in a crisp winter-blue gown that trailed wonderfully round her body as she walked. It certainly had been chosen with care. Not flirty or outrageous, but still very stylish. Proper, even. Yet he remembered a very different girl, with indigo eyes, telling him she'd only had twenty minutes to throw clothes on and get across town to meet him, and she'd looked twenty times more tempting with far less effort.

"Thank you, and for the invitation, it was a surprise, to say the least."

"But not unpleasant I hope?"

"No, not at all. Though my mother did insist on taking me shopping."

Daryl could well imagine her mother getting very excited at the fact her daughter had attracted the attention of Mr Blackmoor.

"Then you can thank your mother for me. It suits you very well."

A blush stole over pale cheeks, and the pink clashed with the red hair. Another thought: the vibrant red would no doubt be inherited by her children. Daryl had thought it rather unusual, but he was fast changing his mind. He decided to shorten their dinner arrangement and opted for the four-course option – and of course she didn't mind; she understood he had business matters to attend to.

When Annabelle excused herself to go to the ladies' room, he used the opportunity to check on Mysty. She was still at the dance studio. She'd been there since leaving the photo shoot. She'd been there for hours? Still, it was better than having her zoom off on one of her bikes.

His dinner companion returned, threading through the tables, shyly keeping her eyes on the floor as people looked at her and judged, knowing with whom she was dining. Were they too critically appraising her as to her suitability for such a man? He had to concur with most of the expressions: she was not.

MAC WAS STILL in silent protest over his treatment of Mysty, and Daryl wasn't in the mood to reason or argue with him so he called O'Grady.

"O'Grady."

"Mr Blackmoor."

Daryl grimaced at the same chilly greeting he would have expected from Mac.

"Where are you?"

"On the way to LA, sir. She asked that the plane be readied."

LA? "Did she say why?"

"No."

"And when will she be back?"

"I believe she's intending to stay in LA tomorrow, and then go to Vegas for her show at Celeste."

"No disappearing, no nothing, you understand?"

"Of course, Mr Blackmoor. Her wellbeing and whereabouts are my sole priority." O'Grady's tone implied that Daryl's priorities were far different.

"What time will you land?"

"Approximately 9:30."

"Fine."

Disconnect.

He was left in a resounding silence.

Why on earth was she going to LA? But then was it any wonder she was going to LA? He'd ignored just who she was, again, and everything he respected about her. He behaved disgracefully at the photo shoot. What right did he have to prostitute her innocence like he had? And what had he been thinking, ordering for her, knowing she hated raw fish. As usual, she had suffered, having done nothing to deserve it.

He knew he should take her pictures down. All of them. His wife would need to tolerate a lot of things, but he doubted numerous photographs of a younger more beautiful girl would go down well.

He poured himself a large brandy and ran a deep hot bath. Anything to try and clear his head and ease the tension in his muscles. For a man who usually made so few mistakes, he seemed to be racking up quite a few.

SHE DIDN'T KNOW why there were tears in her eyes as she stared into the box. It wasn't quite like any emotion she'd felt before; it was almost grief, but with a huge sense of despair and shame all mingled in. And there somewhere, glimmering brightly, was anger, and she'd focussed on that to get her through. He was going to be furious. Serve him right. That would be the last time he spoke to her and treated her like that.

She had already told Mac to expect the item. It was tempting to put a camera in the box, so she could watch his reaction, but she really didn't want to look at him, even on a screen. She closed the lid, securing it with a chain.

Attention to detail was key.

The computer told her there had already been over ten thousand downloads – in only twenty minutes of it being released. She hoped the site didn't crash, as that would rather ruin the moment.

Time to get on the jet, have some dinner, and look forward to landing in LA.

Then she was going to see a friend.

THE BOX MADE him stop in his tracks. Dark red, the same colour as the underwear he had made her wear. But bound in chains?

He paused before opening it, immediately aware that this from her.

There was a note, handwritten on a red card: '*Half of America has probably seen this by now. As the most perverse man alive, I decided it was only appropriate you have your own hard copy. I'm sure it'll give you hours of pleasure.*'

What the fuck was she talking about?

He flipped the clasps on the small silver case. Inside was a single data card, with MY^2x squared on it.

What had she done this time?

The camera panned around to her as she spoke, standing in a kitchen, quiet music in the background, in the softest, huskiest voice she'd ever used:

"*There's something I have to say to you, if you promise you'll understand. I cannot contain myself when I'm in your presence. I'm so humble, touch me. Don't hide your love, woman to man.*"

The camera moved to the silhouette of a man in a stairwell, his feet slowing as he heard her words. He reached a door, his back to the camera, and pushed it opened – and there she was. She turned, surprised to see him, and her eyes locked with those of the man. Her phone hit the floor at the same moment he pushed the door closed on the camera with a slam, and darkness descended as the music changed, now pulsating with a strong beat. The lights came back on, and she was standing tall, in the first outfit he had made her wear at the shoot, all black, with chains and studs.

The leather-clad figures that now appeared all moved together, with her at the centre. It was arousing, to say the least, to see her gyrating hips and flawless flesh moving against and in sync with those of the men, all built like the models he'd hired: hairless, handsome virile men.

The scene flicked back to the kitchen, showed her lifted up and laid back on a breakfast bar, the man between her legs, leaning into her. It was obvious what he was about to do.

Another cut and he was taken back to the gyrating bodies, the female moving with the allure of a goddess, singing the timeless invitation that would entice any man: "*She's just a lover who's doin' me by… It's worth the giving; it's worth the try…*"

Two of the men knelt at her feet, lips trailing kisses towards her thighs, two others up her arms towards her neck. In her hands she held the chains to each of their collars, her head tilted back, lips glossed and slightly parted. A male head came into view, kissing her stomach, up and up towards her throat; but her hand came up and pushed it back down, guiding him, the camera staying on her face as she closed her eyes.

She raised one heeled boot and rested on his shoulder; another came up behind her and took her weight as her knees weakened.

"*She wants to get it on; she wants to get it…*'

The scene then cut to shots of passion, male hands smoothing her thighs, her back arching, her hands reaching to pull the men kneeling before her closer with a brutal hold on their hair.

"*One thing in life you must understand… The truth of lust; woman to man… So open the door and you will see there are no secrets. Make your move; set me free…*"

The kitchen scene had now moved to a doorway.

"*Just promise me, whatever we say, or whatever we do to each other… For now we'll make a vow…to just…keep it in the closet…*'

And in a tumble of lust they made it through the door of a bedroom, which also slammed shut.

The words of the song were almost irrelevant now, as the brilliantly choreographed orgy unfolded, cut with scenes of her in the bedroom with the man the identity of whom remained unrevealed. Soft words were exchanged by the lovers, now naked, but artfully shot to exclude the watcher from the intimacy unfolding. The final shot was of her legs around his hips, her head back, the lights catching the gloss of her lips, the camera capturing her cry of ecstasy.

The screen went black, and stayed black.

After several moments of stunned silence, his erection throbbing, Daryl went through to the lounge. He switched on the television, her words 'half of America has probably seen this by now' inducing a mixture of horror and curiosity.

"*After the release of the 'Light and Dark' album and show, Mysty has today released a one-off Michael Jackson rendition of 'In the Closet', which has so far had over ten million downloads. I hardly need say it, but this is a new record but, given the content, it is hardly surprising. Clearly earning her place in history as the world's sexiest, most beautiful woman, but one who we are led to believe is still a virgin, we are all at a loss as to what to make of this… exhibition. Does it have anything to do with the recent animosity between her and her manager, the so-called 'heated words' that took place at a photo shoot? Danny, what do you make of it? The girl I see in that video does not look like virgin. And what about Mr Capello? What do you think he'll make of this?*"

How the hell had they heard about that!

"*Well, Jane, I know what you're saying, I really do, and clearly there are a lot of people who appreciate the, er, unique representation of the song… The download has a fifty-dollar price tag! The 'heated words' as you put it were apparently because she was furious at some of the poses she was expected to do during the shoot, with Mr Blackmoor insulting her innocence. I would say this was her way of showing her manager precisely what she thinks of him and his insults.*"

"*And Mr Capello? Are we really to believe there was nothing between them in the bedroom department?*"

"*Capello loved her enough to put her aside when his association became a clear danger to her. There is no question of his attachment to her, but as beautiful as she is, I suspect being the elder of the pair he'll want her to make her own decisions as she gets older herself. She's still only seventeen, but this is clearly one of those decisions.*" Danny held up a hand. "*I know it sounds a little crazy, but if there's one thing we know it's that Mysty inspires great loyalty and respect in all kinds of people, myself included. And it would be especially so with a man she was so close to."*

"But the video… I mean, there's nothing innocent about that. It comes with a R rating!"

"She may be young, but I'm sure she's well aware of what people get up to, even if she hasn't herself."

"Well, we know she's in LA at the moment, so hopefully we can get her to come down to the studio tomorrow, before she heads off to Vegas. Goodness knows how many downloads there will be by then, when the rest of the world wakes up and finds their favourite superstar has just made herself the ultimate male fantasy. James, over to you for the business news…"

The speed dial wasn't fast enough.

"O'Grady."

"Sir?"

"Where is she now?"

"Staying at a friend's house, sir."

"A friend's house? Not her apartment?"

"No, sir."

Daryl gritted his teeth; clearly O'Grady was going to be obstructive.

"Which friend?"

"Slick. One of the Pirate bikers. Nice guy. You met him I think."

Daryl's heart began to beat a little faster. The guy was young, and very good looking. A sensation passed through him, like he was running down hill and his legs weren't going to keep up…running towards a disaster he couldn't stop. "Why? A bit of a sudden decision when she has a perfectly good place to sleep tonight?"

Don't say the words I'm afraid of hearing. Don't tell me she's going to do something even worse than releasing that video to the world.

"I don't think she went there to sleep, Mr Blackmoor, sir."

He was aware that O'Grady was taking great delight in telling him that; but he didn't want to believe it, didn't believe she really would.

"O'Grady, what are you saying?"

"I would have thought it was fairly obvious. I think she's gone to rid herself of that which you found so abhorrent. She's gone to get laid, in other words, with someone she trusts. And I hope she enjoys herself. The girl deserves a good time, don't you think? Especially after all the enjoyment she's given other people."

The anger in O'Grady's voice was hot and sharp, the 'people' including one significant individual, and Daryl felt the sting on his conscience. This couldn't be happening. Not after all that waiting for Donny; not after all her talk about love and… But this was what he'd done. He'd been a part of ruining this dream of hers, of having something precious and meaningful with a man, by implying her innocence was worthless. She'd obviously given up waiting for another Donny; she was just going to sleep with someone, anyone, and make it as meaningless as the sex he had with his women. She deserved more than that! She deserved something beautiful and precious, not just a roll in the sheets for the hell of it! And certainly not to just get back at him.

He felt sick. How was he supposed to stop her? Could he order OG to get her out?

"OG. You can't think this is a good idea?"

"I didn't think that photo shoot was a good idea, but I still had to watch it. I hardly think this is going to do any more damage. Don't worry, we're watching every side of the house, and we'll be here in the morning when it's time to leave. Goodnight. Sir."

Disconnect.

OG hadn't spared Daryl one syllable of his disrespect. It was enough to get any other man fired.

Goddammit! *She was his*! She belonged to him! Her strength, her composure, her everything, it was his! He closed his eyes, the video replaying in snapshots, which played out in whatever was going on with her and Slick.

"Mac."

"Sir?"

The man's unfriendly voice wasn't going to put him off. He'd made his decision.

"Get the plane. We leave immediately for LA. Do it. Now."

A moment of silence.

"Yes, sir. The chopper will be quicker."

Daryl thought he heard a change in Mac's voice? Something like approval?

"Good."

Disconnect.

Daryl didn't stop for a change of clothes, a final call, a quick email. He just went straight to the door. Mac was waiting for him, looking slightly less angry. Despite it being too late, he was going to put right what he'd made wrong.

"MYSTY?"

The disbelief in his voice was painful. So much time had gone by, and so much had changed.

"Hi, Slick." He looked down and back up to her face, not quite believing she really was there. "I promise I'm real." She smiled self-consciously. "Can I come in?"

"You want to come in?"

He still wasn't quite computing, and his eyes went to the three silver Bentleys in the street, and the collection of grey suits that were watching them.

"Well, I would rather speak to you inside the house, but if you prefer the doorstep…" She was starting to think this was a really bad idea.

"No, no, sorry, I'm just…so surprised to see you." He stood back instantly, beckoning her in. "I just…it's not exactly the Ritz, you know." She hated the waver of uncertainty in his voice, fearing inadequacy because she was famous now.

"Slick." She turned to him suddenly, desperate not to lose this friend because of the way her life had been taken over. "You're talking to someone who grew up in poverty and spent a year sleeping on roofs and in trees. You know where I used to live. I don't give a shit about the money or the rest of it, but if you're not the friend I knew because this fame thing means so much to you, I'll leave right now…" Her voice broke, and he realised this wasn't just a social call; it was a cry for help.

"No. No, I don't care. I just…I'm just really surprised you're here. I've not seen you for so long, and then you're here, on my doorstep. I'm still your friend, okay. You need a beer. Get yourself sat down and I'll get you one." He gave her a gentle push towards the sofa. The news report was still playing on the TV.

"You saw the news, then," she said when Slick returned to the lounge. The casual proximity felt alien but welcome to her.

The beer was handed over as if it was an essential part of having a conversation; no glass, just a bottle, just like they used to. It made her smile inside. They both kept their gaze on the TV, getting used to the presence of the other. Mysty became acutely aware of the impact of the video content, that had seemed like such a good, righteous idea at the time, but now suddenly felt awkward.

Slick cleared his throat. "Yeah. Quite a storm you've stirred up. $50 and over ten million downloads? Must be some video."

"Yeah, I suppose so. You haven't wasted $50, have you?"

"No."

"Because I can give you a copy of it for nothing, if you want it."

"I'm not sure it's the kind of video I should see, given the fact you're my friend."

"That's a nice thing to say."

"Is it true?"

"Is what true?"

"About…what Blackmoor said to you? That you're a virgin? Even after how close you were to Donny?"

Mysty closed her eyes. She wanted to talk, but every word seemed stuck in her throat.

"Yeah. Feel free to laugh any time you like. I'm sure millions of people already have."

"I don't think it's funny," Slick replied, voice low but steady, realising how upset she was. He knew her control well enough that she could hide all but the most intense emotions. "I know how much he meant to you, and I saw you give a feared mob boss a piece of your mind without hesitation. He loved you, I know that. It's just hard to imagine it never went any further."

The quiet in the room continued for a moment. He didn't want to push it, but he knew she needed to talk it out of her.

"The video sounds pretty…steamy," he then said, trying to soften the silence.

She burst out laughing at his attempt at being subtle, at the enormity of the understatement, and put the beer down on the table. She already felt she had cheapened herself, though. But she'd been so angry, and wanted to do something outrageous, not caring about the consequences.

"What made you do it? And how come you came to LA last night, out of the blue? I thought you were in New York for the next few months?"

"There was a photo shoot. I have to do a few…things. Anyway… Well, Blackmoor had arranged a whole new line of bondage-style underwear, S&M stuff, all studs, black leather, chains, handcuffs…things…well, I didn't want to do it, but he made clear if I didn't…I would be forced to."

"But you're *you*? You're the one person in the world who wouldn't hesitate to tell him to fuck off."

Slick's belief in her ability to stand up for herself was bittersweet, but it did make her smile.

"Believe me, if I thought that would work, I would have. But he's done things to me…you don't understand. If he doesn't get his way, he has people who will do his dirty work for him, or he makes my life hell in other ways. He's stuck needles in me, threatened to take Lazarus away, and left me in agony and unconscious for days, because I wouldn't let him do what he wanted to me. These last few weeks he's been so angry, and I don't know what he'd do to me in fit of temper."

Her eyes were begging him to understand. He'd never seen her like this, and he reached out and pushed a curl back, telling her he was happy to listen to whatever she said in that one simple gentle gesture. Reassured that she was safe, she started talking, the words spilling in a torrent of what she'd been made to wear, the male models, the poles and the chains and the insults when she wouldn't do as he said.

"He told me to put my mouth to a good use for once, after calling me was a frigid little bitch, and saying that I should get laid, lose my innocence, so I didn't think I was so precious. And then he started talking about Donny…"

Slick leaned back against the cushions, taking her with him, drawing her in to curl against him.

She continued, but her voice was muffled into his chest, but he heard the words 'stupid' and 'wrong'. Slick had three sisters, who were all younger than he was, and he was well trained in the art of comforting them when they'd had fights with their boyfriends or had fallen out with each other. He stroked her hair.

"You're not stupid, Mysty," he said. "Blackmoor was completely out of line making you do that shoot and saying what he did. And there's nothing wrong with being innocent. I wish my sisters had waited until they were at least seventeen until they hooked up with a guy. There might have been fewer broken hearts." He eased her away from his shoulder, not letting her hide. "You've nothing to be ashamed of. Nothing. Blackmoor is just jealous because you're not desperate to get into his bed, like everyone else. Walking out was the best thing to do. Spineless fuck should know better than to bully a young girl like that."

She looked at him, the sadness clouding her eyes. "Can I stay tonight?" she asked softly. "Here, with you?"

"Mysty, I don't know if that's such a good idea…"

She sat up a little, bringing her head up, level with his. Slick swallowed, not expecting the girl of his dreams to be sat here, on his couch, looking as gorgeous as an LA sunrise. His surprise gave her the upper hand, and she leaned forward and kissed him, and whatever protest he might have managed to make was forgotten as her soft lips pressed against his, willing him to respond. She put her hand in his hair, ran it down the back of his neck and over his chest, stroking the muscles he'd worked on for hours in the gym.

He was only mortal. Fantasies so long buried came alive, and Slick kissed her back. He slid his hands around her body, soft yet firm, and his reaction to her was instantaneous. She moved, and a moment later she was across him, her hand sliding lower. He needed to slow it down, and grasped her hand. This wasn't the kiss of a virgin, of an amateur, and he was already feeling far too aroused. But then she had his t-shirt over his head, and she stroked his bare chest, her lips and hands hot against the naked skin, her body flexing and arching against him.

He moved her onto her back, held her hands in one of his so he could control how much she touched him. He didn't want to rush this. His hand was on her ribcage, and his eyes went to hers. Her unspoken yes gave him permission. He unzipped her top, and she wasn't wearing a bra. He could feel only flesh, and she watched as he moved his head down and gently lifted the t-shirt and closed his lips over one nipple.

His groan of appreciation was welcome reassurance that he liked what he saw, and the sensation was so strange, but not unpleasant. She was happy. Whatever he wanted to do, he could do, and she didn't want him to stop. She didn't want to be ignorant and unloved anymore. His tongue then danced over her other nipple, making her draw in a sudden breath, one hand in his hair, her eyes shut, not wanting to see, only feel. She could feel the heat of him against her, and the hardness, and the heat in her own body was a new thing, mysterious and potent, and she arched against him.

And then he stopped.

His face was tight, his breathing was fast. She could see the hunger, the passion, in his eyes, but he didn't move. What was wrong?

"Mysty." She shook her head, knowing what he was going to say. "I can't do this. Jesus Christ." He sat up. "You're upset, you're emotional. If I do this I'm taking advantage of you." He carefully zipped her top back up.

"I want you to take advantage of me!"

He smiled sadly at her angry answer and pushed her back down, a hand either side of her head, his eyes above hers, knowing he had to make her listen.

"Ever since I first saw you, sitting in the corner of that café after wiping the floor with Troy and his boys, I've respected you – let alone what you can do on a bike. I respect you too much to just give you what you're asking for, as much as my body would clearly disagree." He glanced at the unmistakable shape of his erection. "I'm flattered I…I was your first choice. You being you, it's a big compliment, and I know it took guts to come here tonight. But…" He sighed and closed his eyes, trying to find the words. "You know I've always liked you, but regardless of that, we're friends, right? I don't want this to be just one night and then watch you walk away, maybe thinking afterwards that I was an asshole for letting this happen when you're upset. I'm not that guy…"

She choked on a laugh as the tears crept from her eyes. She raised a hand and pushed a lock of his hair back.

"I don't think you're an asshole, not at all. That was why I came here. Because I knew the moment I saw you in that café that you were one of the good guys and I could trust you. I'm sorry. I didn't think of it from… your point of view. I should have." The gorgeous lips closed into a tight line as she cried a little more.

"No, don't apologise. You did the most natural thing in the world, and I'm glad it was me you came to. But I won't let you throw away this precious moment so easy. You didn't wait this long just for this, did you?"

She covered her eyes and groaned. "I'm such an idiot. And you're such a good friend."

"You have always been a good friend to me, the best in fact. What do you always say? 'No debts between friends'? I don't want this to be between us."

He pushed her chin up with a finger, and she managed a smile. The easiness between them was just like it always used to be, before her world changed and she was no longer able to live a regular life.

He grabbed his t-shirt, pulled it back on, and she stood up.

"Where are you going?"

"I had no right really to just land on your doorstep like this. I'll go. It's okay."

"No, stay. I have beer, and I'm sure there must be a pizza around somewhere. We can put a movie on. It'll be like old times. Just you and me. You need to unwind, with a friend. For one night just be Mysty, not the superstar. You can have the bed. I'll take the couch." He could see she was tempted. "I'm not taking no for answer, by the way, so you'd better sit down and pick a film."

She laughed and let him pull her back down onto the sofa.

"Stay!" he instructed.

Twenty minutes later they were both on the sofa, scoffing pizza with the uninhibited relish of hungry people. It was like going back in time.

"You alright?"

She looked at him, saw the concern, wishing she could love him like he deserved to be loved…if only her affections were so easily transferred.

"Yeah. I have the best friend in the world. I'll be fine. I'll have to pop by a bit more often."

"We might need to pick somewhere else. Three Bentleys aren't a regular occurrence outside my house."

"Oh yeah. Sorry, I don't have any choice about those. Next time I'll have you smuggled over to my place. I don't want your life turning into a media circus, though, even for a day. Trust me, it's no fun."

"I believe you."

"Are you alright?" she asked.

"Yeah, I think so. Though part of me is still stunned that I just turned down the most beautiful woman on the planet. I'm going to wake up tomorrow and wonder what the hell came over me."

She laughed, and blushed, and elbowed him playfully. He wrapped his arm around her shoulder and pulled close, and they went back to watching the film, both relieved there was no tension between them. It could have broken them apart, but it had only made them stronger. It was so simple, and so blissful.

She didn't want the morning to come.

She reached up and smoothed a hand from his brow to his jaw, sleepy eyes blinking open and the hand on her belly contracting, moving to the far side and pulling her against him a little more.

"DON'T TELL ME it's morning," Slick groaned, his eyes still shut.

"It's 6.30."

"Oh crap." She smiled. He looked so young, so boyish, so utterly harmless, and she stroked his hair from his eyes. "Well, you are officially the best pillow I've ever woken up with on this sofa."

"Wow, thank you!"

"So does that mean I did 'sleep with you', after all?" He grinned, hoping it was okay to joke about it now.

"Yeah, you stud," she laughed. He chuckled, and pulled her close. "When are you leaving for work?"

"In about half an hour," he said. "Though I can be late if you want me to stay?"

"No, no, it's okay. I just…I really wish I didn't have to leave. God knows what'll happen today."

"You'll be fine. And you know where I am. My sofa is always available. And come by the workshop anytime."

"Thank you. That means a lot."

"And Mysty…"

"Yes?"

"What happened last night is between you, me and the couch, okay? No one needs to know."

"You trying to make me cry all over again or something?"

"No, no I'm not. I need a shower. You want to go first?"

"No, I'll get some coffee on and get breakfast going."

The world's most famous girl and she was making him breakfast?

He paused in the doorway of the kitchen. She was barefoot, in her leggings and top, no makeup and hair wild, and she was the loveliest thing he'd ever seen. What would have happened if he had done as she'd wanted him to last night?

"LA hasn't been the same without you, you know. I've missed you," he said, unable to keep the words inside.

She turned to him, eyes warm, trusting.

"I've missed you too. I've missed a lot of things. I wish I could go back to how it was before, I really do."

"LA and me ain't going nowhere. You ever want to change career, I'll give you a job at the garage."

She smiled instantly. "Awesome! I might just take you up on that." She watched him for a moment, happy and safe in his company. "I promise when I'm back we'll have pizza and beer at mine. I'll find a way of getting you there without being seen."

"Better invite Rusty. He misses you too – all the Pirates do."

"They were good times, weren't they?"

"The best. I still remember that first night. You didn't stop surprising me, even when we got you back home and Lazarus came out to say hello. How is he?"

"He's great, and Lula – did you know I got another one?" He nodded, aware the catch-up chatting would be endless if they kept going. "She's fantastic. Reminds me of me, actually, always getting into trouble without meaning to." He laughed at that. "They're probably getting worried about me; they're generally with me all the time. This will be Lula's first night away from me. She'll be clinging to me for the rest of the day!"

"You'll make a great mom."

"So I've been told." She smiled sadly. "Go shower now. Can't have you blaming me for being late to work!"

"I'm the boss. I can be as late as I like, especially on a Friday!" He put a bit of swagger into his hips as he turned away, and she laughed.

"I'm the boss, for certain things, and I always seem to be there first and last to leave."

"Wrong job then."

He returned ten minutes later to toast, bacon, scrambled eggs, tomatoes and mushrooms. It smelt fantastic. She poured him coffee and sat down, one leg pulled up against her chest, a bowl of cereal waiting for her.

"Not hungry?" he asked, seeing that she wasn't eating much.

"I have Celeste tonight, so I need carbs not proteins. Don't worry, Sunday I'm going to eat half a pig of bacon for breakfast."

As he tucked in and she ate a pile of toast they exchanged stories, as if they did this every day. Slick wished they did.

"Are they all going to be out there waiting?" he asked.

"Yep. Where I go, they go. But it's for my protection, and I've given up arguing. It's not so bad now. OG – O'Grady – he's a gem of a bodyguard and I love him to bits. Most of the guys are okay, too. Mac – Blackmoor's chief dude – he's great. It's just his boss who is the asshole."

"Yeah, world's biggest."

"You said it. I hope he has the world's biggest headache too, from seeing that video!"

"I might just have to see this video, you know. Looks like the rest of the world is going to."

"I'll send you a copy. Just don't ever mention it again. I wish I hadn't done it, really. I was just so angry and…wanted to shove his insults back in his arrogant face. I really should kick the shit out of him and leave him hanging from his own skyscraper."

"That's my girl."

She laughed at that. "I'd better go." She got up and put everything in the dishwasher, turning to take his plate and coffee cup. "What's wrong? Think us famous people don't know how to cook or clean up?"

"Something like that," he replied, admiring her bottom as she bent over, knowing it was safe to as she would be gone soon, and the temptation with it.

"Yeah, well, this famous person didn't want to be famous. She wanted to be a normal girl with a normal life."

"There's nothing normal about you, Mysty, never has been. You've always been extra special."

"And you're extra special to me. Promise me you'll take care at the Bowl?"

"I'll be fine; but feel free to come by and check me over any time."

The cheeky grin was irresistible, and she pushed him playfully out of the kitchen, grabbing her boots and heading for the door. He opened it just a fraction, the light spilling in, and they both glanced out. Sure enough the cars were there, as were the suits. OG immediately noticed the door had opened and gave some orders. She swallowed, not wanting to go, knowing time was running fast through the hourglass.

"Thank you, for last night. Your 'no' wasn't what I came for, but you were right, and it was perfect." She reached up and kissed his cheek, her hand flat on his chest, his resting briefly on the small of her back. "I'll see you soon. I hope."

The soft look held, both wishing they had more time. Reluctantly he opened the door.

"I hope so."

Lazarus and Lula ran over to greet her, and she rubbed the bigger cat's head, and lifted the smaller into her arms. She looked back for a single second and smiled, just before the car door was closed, the pure happiness he always associated with her there in that one moment shining back at him. Her look told him that happiness had been down to him. He shut the door and leaned on it. Wow.

O'Grady was relieved to see her so relaxed, and watched as the leopards vied for her attention, her smiles and soft words of love all they wanted to hear…a world away from the bundle of nerves that had got out of the car the night before.

"Home?"

"Yes please, OG."

"You alright?" he asked, unable not to. He'd been working when his daughters had decided to lose their virginity, and he didn't remember it being too happy an event when his wife had told him. She, on the other hand, looked perfectly happy.

"I'm fine. Better than fine. I'm great. Really."

She sensed his disbelief, and looked at him with eyes that couldn't lie.

"Good. Excellent. Am I going to get more conversation out of you now?"

"Yes, I promise. I'm back to being me again."

"Great. I missed you."

She looked at the man, saw the worry lines in his face. "I missed you too, OG. I'm sorry, I know you were worried."

She leaned against him and his arm went around her shoulder.

"WHAT DO YOU want?"

She might as well have thrown another spear.

"Where have you been?"

"Losing my innocence. Isn't that what you wanted? You must be sorry you missed the performance, as my manager of course."

She sipped her water, watching him, waiting for a reply, but he looked too furious to speak, glaring at her with those hard eyes that made her feel so worthless. Not anymore.

"What? No reply? Surely you have something spiteful to say? No? Oh well. I'm going for a shower. I need one. I'm sure you know what I mean."

Disconnect.

This was torture. *He had to know.* He had to hear it from the guy's own lips, because she'd never tell him herself.

"Mac?"

"Sir?"

"The car."

He knew as he strode towards the waiting Bentley that he could have sent someone else. But this…this was personal.

ANYONE WATCHING THE unexceptional house on the unexceptional street in LA would have been intrigued by the three silver Bentleys that had remained outside the house all night. Seeing four more arrive less than an hour after they'd left they would have been pressing their noses against their front windows, without a doubt.

Only one man approached the house, leaving behind a collection of grey suits, and an enormous black guy in charge.

Daryl had never wanted to punch someone more. Could not ever remember feeling this level of possessive anger before. It made him forget who he was, that he was meant to be in New York attending a long list of business meetings. Hell, he couldn't even remember what day it was. Right then, he was just a man, a mere mortal, and he wanted another man's blood.

The door opened. The guy was younger than he was, and had the LA tan and the spiked hair, the casual clothes, the ease…everything that added to the bonfire of resentment centred around the fact that this man, this average nobody, had had his girl!

"What the hell are you doing here?" Slick asked, recognising Daryl immediately, expecting a sharp retort, or a well-aimed insult.

What Slick didn't expect was for the guy in the creaseless business suit, with his hands in his pockets, to look at him for a second, and then shove the door hard with one foot, throwing him off balance. It was just enough to give Daryl a chance to step through the door and slam it behind him, with the same ruthless efficiency he used to shove the younger guy hard up against the wall.

Slick felt the hand on his throat at the same time his eyes connected with the dangerously furious green ones of Mr Daryl Blackmoor.

"*What am I doing here?* You really need me to answer that?" Daryl growled.

And then Slick was yanked away from the wall and punched, hard enough to throw him backwards, blood instantly seeping from his nose and his lip. He'd underestimated his guest because of the suit, not thinking he'd lower himself to fight in such a fine thing; but he was horribly wrong, and another blow to his face and darkness closed in on his vision.

Slick raised a hand, sensed the pause in the storm of aggression currently holding him captive, and he opened his eyes, his legs just about keeping him braced against the doorframe.

"Why do you care if she was here or not? You told her to get laid, didn't you? This is what you wanted!"

Slick's questions required far bigger answers than Daryl was prepared to give.

"Did you sleep with her?" A hand pulled Slick forward and then slammed him back against the doorframe.

"Sleep with her? Yes, all night, right there on the couch!" Slick waved a hand behind him, and Daryl's eyes flicked to the sofa. "Did I make love to her? No. She's as innocent now as she was when she arrived at my door."

He felt the hold on his neck loosen, and he bunched his fists. Time for a bit of payback. He used both hands to shove the larger man off him, and Daryl lost his balance. Reaching out to steady himself, Slick dealt the handsome face a beautiful right, and then a left, and then slammed the unwelcome visitor hard against the wall as he had been moments ago.

He backed off, judging that fair payback, leaning against the opposite wall and glaring at the man, watching him for any move he might make while a hand inspected his bloodied face. But the mood had changed; the storm of aggression had broken. The guy in the suit didn't seem to care about the wounds to his head.

"You didn't sleep with her?"

"No. Not that she didn't ask me. She needed a friend, not sex. Needed comfort, not more misery. I respect her too much to use her like that, when she was so upset – not that you would be able to understand why, the way you treat women. How could you say what you did to her? I've known her for years, since the beginning, when she saved my sister – who she didn't know – from getting dragged off by a gang of blokes twice as big as her. She's one of the most selfless and courageous people I've ever met! Can't you see that? Is all you see on the outside?"

Slick was surprised at how easily the words came to him. He was not one for talking about someone when they weren't there usually, and wasn't one for aggression, but then he didn't usually have house calls like this.

"She said you had."

Daryl's voice wasn't angry. There was only relief. Somehow the impossible had happened. It wasn't too late.

"Good. And I'm glad it pissed you off so much. Serves you right for what you put her through. Handcuffs? Bondage underwear? On an innocent seventeen-year-old? Why?"

"Believe me, I wish I could undo what I said…"

"She saved your life, apparently." Daryl nodded wearily, feeling so unbelievably worn out, his perfectly fitted suit feeling twice as big as he sagged inside it. "She saved your life, and *this* is how you repay her?" The disgust dripped off the words. "Well, ain't you the most undeserving son-of-a-bitch?"

"Yes. I think you may be right about that." Daryl closed his eyes for a brief second and winced as the pain from his eyeballs connected with the ache in his jaw.

"She doesn't care about all of the fame, you know. Or the cars or the glamour or the money. You know what means most to her? *Belonging*. She doesn't have a family. She doesn't even have Donny anymore. You ripped her out of the little home she made for herself. You took her away from all her friends. You fly her all over the place doing God knows what, singing, dancing, her magic in Celeste. And what have you given her back? Tell me, Mr Blackmoor, what have you given back to her?"

"Not enough."

"That's one way of putting it." Slick eyed the man he had expected more resistance and arrogance from, but he was seeing…surprisingly a self-deprecating, almost apologetic man. "What is it you want from her? Because if it's favours in your bed, you've gone completely the wrong way about it."

Daryl had to smile, though it hurt to do so. "Yes, I have realised that."

"Answer the question dammit, as you've managed to step-side all the others. *What* do you *want from her*?"

"You really want to know?"

"I would like an answer that makes sense, yes. One that might allow me to let you walk out of here as you are, rather than pulverising your face a little more."

Daryl had to admire the fighting talk. It reminded him of her, and he sighed, wanting to say the words, feeling strangely like he owed it to the man who'd taken the hits for her, who was totally loyal to her.

"In short, everything. I want it all. I want her so much I decided it wasn't safe to. But it's no good. Nothing changes how I feel. Even her insults and her mockery… God knows I'm used to that by now." Daryl watched Slick contemplate his answer. It was an admission he wouldn't have spoken out loud, even to his own reflection. Saying it made it real. "I shouldn't have told you that."

Their eyes met.

"Yes, you should, and I know what you mean. But like I told her, her being here last night never happened. Neither did your…confession. She won't hear about it from me. I'm not going to help you any." Slick took a step closer towards the door, though his eyes were still on his guest. "And I'm not going to apologise for your face, either. I think it's the least you're owed."

Daryl knew it was time to leave. He had his answers; he had no right to stay.

"I apologise for yours. I'm glad she came to you last night. You're a good friend," he said, hardly believing he'd said such a thing given the rage he had arrived with.

"The things she's done for me over the years, I'll always stand by her."

Daryl offered his hand, but said, "I understand if you don't want to shake my hand, but if it means anything, I'd like you to."

Slick thought about it, not sure of the man's intentions; but there was no trickery, no animosity in the green eyes now. It was an olive branch; he would be foolish to turn it down, considering the man. Hands clasped for a few moments, and then Slick went to the door.

"You've set yourself a real challenge, you know, with her."

"Yeah. Still doesn't seem to put me off though."

Daryl saw a smile flicker across Slick's face. "Tiger-taming is a dangerous pursuit."

"Don't I know it…"

Slick had to grin at the rueful words as the impressively built but wearied man in his elegant suit stepped back out into the sunshine, one hand going to a pocket and the other to his mouth as he strolled back towards the gleaming car, clearly already deep in thought. He had to admire him for that at least, for taking the blows like a man. Blackmoor could have waded in with his heavies and ripped Slick and his house apart. But he hadn't. In fact, Blackmoor hadn't been anything like the complete jackass he'd imagined he was – after the billionaire, or whatever he was, had finished punching him that was.

The giant of a man, who hadn't taken a single step towards the house, looked curiously at Slick, before getting into the Bentley after his boss. Finally all four cars moved away, almost silently.

He shut the door and exhaled.

Mysty was definitely back in LA.

THE PENTHOUSE WAS completely silent, so the footsteps were easy to hear. Daryl cursed under his breath. He wanted to be left alone, damn it! Just some peace and quiet so he could reflect and wallow in peace – was it too much to ask?

"Mac, I don't want anything, please. I left orders I was not to be disturbed."

His neck hurt, his face hurt, and his eyes ached like he'd not slept for forty hours – which was pretty accurate. The idea of looking in a mirror revolted him.

"Last time I checked, my name wasn't Mac, and I never do what you tell me to do anyway."

His head whipped around, the reflex overriding the pain. What the hell was she doing there? Why had Mac let her through the door? To give him another black eye? He was too stunned to move as she kept coming towards him, took a seat on the sofa to one side of his chair, and put a case down on the table and calmly flicked the catches.

She looked radiant. Composed. It hurt his eyes too look at her.

"It's funny. I just had to go patch up my best friend across town, and he looked in a remarkably similar state to you." She put some antiseptic onto a small cloth. "How about that?" She turned his head to the light. "My, you are looking pretty, aren't you?" She cleaned the blood from his lip and the cut near his eye, gently touching the bruise that was swelling around it. It stung, but oh how he was grateful for every second of her attention.

"You didn't sleep with him."

"No." She didn't look at him, despite how close they were. "Seems I always pick the good guys, that I am the one woman no one will take to bed." She observed her handiwork. "And please don't say anything. I do not want to hear any more lewd propositions, thank you very much."

"I shouldn't have said what I did. I do know that."

"*Good.*"

He dared look at her, then. He saw the tension in her face. But there was no anger. The way things were between them, he knew it wasn't what she wanted. It never had been. It was he who'd ruined everything with his behaviour after the holiday.

"I take it I'm in minus a couple of billion dickhead points territory."

"Like you wouldn't believe."

"No, I really would."

The eyes glittered dangerously at him, and he smiled sadly, then put a hand over his eyes, wishing the pain would go away. The physical and the mental. If only he could somehow make things closer to being okay again.

She moved his hand away, and something wonderfully cold was pressed against his bruised eye socket and cheek.

"You might want to have a quiet day at home, unless you want to prompt a million questions from the press about your beautiful black eye. What the hell were you doing, going over there like that? It was none of your business."

"I thought…I thought he'd taken advantage of you, and I didn't want anything going out to the press, to shame you anymore. I…I didn't want any of this to happen."

Would she hear the sincerity in his words?

"Slick would never say anything to the press. He's not the type." She sighed out a mixture of sadness and frustration. "Why are you always saying you don't mean for things to happen to me? Don't you ever think about what you're doing or saying? Why have you reverted to being such a dickhead all over again? Are you actually going insane?"

How good it felt to have her back. Her frankness and fearlessness in dealing with him felt so right. She was the one person who was always so honest with him, and it made him face the truth about himself, as painful as that was.

"Possibly."

"Hold this." He lifted his hand to the cold compress and she left him, striding decisively back across his apartment. The relief was immense. Knowing that she just might not hate him… Minutes passed. Where was she? He closed his eyes.

"Mac is worried about you. Apparently, you've not eaten anything for God knows how long, and he says you've not slept for even longer. You look as shit as I feel sometimes, which is pretty bad, so I'm assuming you don't feel that great either." A tray was deposited on the coffee table in front of him, and he was stunned. She took the cold compress from him. "I know you eat everything that's on the tray because I've seen you eat it before." She took his free hand, and put two white tablets in it. "Ibuprofen. It'll take the ache away." She then held out a glass of water. He obediently swallowed both, and she took the glass from him.

"Now," she continued. "I've called Marlene and explained that you are unavoidably detained – a bit of cold – to give you time for bit of LA sunshine. The Butterfly Foundation, which is nearing completion, had a problem only you could solve, so I hacked in and sent emails to all of the necessary people." She handed him a computer panel that he took wordlessly. No one in his life had ever taken charge like this. How casually had she just hacked into his supposedly secure system? He tried to roll his eyes, but it was impossible due to the pain. "They all know today's meeting is cancelled and you'll rearrange. Marlene will sort out tomorrow's meetings and find somewhere for them next week." She looked at him sternly. "You need food and sleep and fresh air, so make the most of the next couple of days. I've told Mac to lock the door on you, and I'm cutting all communications for eight hours so you have no choice but to relax – unless you want to try some semaphore from the roof. Wouldn't that be an enlightening experience for you?" The tilt of her head reminded him what an idiot he had been.

She turned away and closed the lid on the first aid kit.

"You got me breakfast…" was all he could say.

Was this a dream? It felt like it could be, sitting there in the comfy chair, the light spilling through the windows, illuminating her beauty. The sun had dawned after a most awful night.

"There is a selection of food in the fridge for you, so just rest and eat. Your face, I'm sure it hurts, but the pain will be gone soon enough. I have to leave now."

He didn't speak. Knew if he did he might ask her to stay, as he so desperately wanted her to. With one last look at his injuries, and satisfied they were clean, she was gone. Even after he heard the door shut behind her, he stayed perfectly still, taking it all in.

A minute later he heard a helicopter fly over. He knew without turning his head who was on it.

His future wife.

After the nightmare of denial he'd been living, the last ten minutes had erased every possible doubt from his mind. Groaning at his stupidity rather than the pain, he moved to pick up the glass of orange juice, remembering too late about his split lip. But the sting was barely noticeable his mind was so busy unravelling all that had happened in the last hour.

One day he would lock them in his penthouse with no outside communication.

That was the day to aim for.

A DARYL BLACKMOOR he rarely saw was walking towards him wearing a pair of chinos, nothing else, and rubbing his hair with a towel. Whatever she'd said or done it had worked. He couldn't miss the black eye though, which had deepened in colour over the last twenty-four hours.

"Very nice," Mac smirked.

"Not bad, is it?" Daryl even smiled. "Nothing wrong is there?"

"No, I was just checking on you. How do you feel?"

Daryl was relieved Mac was talking to him normally again. "Human again. Did you send her in?"

"She called me after she'd seen Slick. I told her that you pretty much looked the same and she came straight over. Seems she's too nice to kick a man again when he's down."

"Far too nice." He surveyed the contents of the fridge, feeling hungry again after his long sleep and half-hour in the pool. "Is she alright?"

"Pretending to be, you know."

"The communications and network, have they been turned back on?"

"Yes."

"Can you get me copies of every newspaper from yesterday, and today. I have some phone calls to make, and I need to wake my legal team up in New York. I'll no doubt have some work for them shortly."

"Yep, sure." Mac had a feeling the sleeping lion was about to roar; a good number of people were going to get fired or sued. "You hungry?"

"Starving. Why?"

Then he smelt something familiar, and saw various items on the counter.

"She had a word with Raffi, so you didn't get over-charged this time."

"Pizza and a milkshake!"

"Certified recovery food. Caviar is over-rated."

He didn't know what to say; but he had a whole lot of questions.

"She's very confused, but she can't quite hate you, sir," Mac said, reading his boss like a book. "For some reason, she still thinks there's something to like about you, and that you still need taking care of."

"I'd better start proving her right then, hadn't I?"

Daryl sat down at the breakfast bar. "Help me eat this lot, and then let's see what we can do about the press, if they got wind of her night… away, and the photo shoot." He also needed to do something about the video she had released, which she now regretted according to OG. "That is something I can fix."

"As you wish, sir."

SHE DIDN'T KNOW what got her thinking about it again as she rode home in the Bentley, with OG only feet away. The city flashed past as the thoughts in her mind flashed just as fast inside her mind, taunting her: it was going to be all over the news, her video. For weeks. No question. And that had been what she'd wanted, to make her point.

Be careful what you wish for.

Those words made her squeeze her eyes shut for a moment, keeping her face turned away from OG. She was unable to escape like she used to. Now she was front page news. She thought she'd be okay with it by now. Turns out she wasn't.

But worse: people she knew and cared about would see it: Donny, Slick, Rusty, Benjy, Leisha…and Raju. A lance of pain at that thought. Now it would be even more impossible to talk to him. Was he sat there wondering what had happened to the girl he used to talk to every day? If he had been thinking of unblocking her he definitely wouldn't now. She wasn't sure if she blamed Blackmoor or herself for the mess anymore, and she wished she didn't care less. She wished she could feel less.

What would my mum think? Would she understand?

"You okay?"

OG touched her arm, and she immediately forced a smile to her lips and gave an affirmative, the pain too great for her to confide.

This loneliness, of feeling like no one understands, is a special kind of lonely.

SOME OF THE headlines were shocking and he was furious. She would have seen them too, and he was worried. 'Bondage Queen…Is She A Virgin?', 'What $800 Million Would Have Bought Him', 'Venus' Darker Side', 'Lock Up Your Sons' and 'The World's Hottest Download…Ever', all with scandal-mongering articles to go with them. The worst had been 'The New Linda Lovelace?', 'Stage Beauty Forced?' and 'Manager or Pimp?' all of which raised the question of whether what she did was voluntary or whether she was forced into it. The reference to the abused star of the 1970's pornographic *Deep Throat* film was the very last thing he wanted.

So far there was a twenty-four-person headcount and eighteen lawsuits underway for libel, amongst other interesting and imaginative charges to make it a punishing experience for the newspapers responsible. He was not willing to have his reputation tainted by the smears and, more than that, he would not stand by and see her name dragged through the mire again.

Please keep your cool, Mysty, don't let them upset you.

He'd given her the option, via O'Grady – he didn't think talking to her directly was a good idea at the moment – as to whether or not to do an interview, and whether or not the line of underwear was pulled. She had opted for the interview and to keep the line, typically refusing to be a coward. They were supposed to be finishing the shoot for it on Wednesday, and he was trying to think of something he could do to help improve her opinion of him, and make the shoot go smoothly.

"And so, ladies and gentlemen and everyone at home, it's the moment so many of you have been waiting for. I know little else has been talked about since last Thursday evening, so it is my great pleasure and an honour to welcome to the show once more, Mysty, our multi-talented queen of the stage…" The two presenters stood up – the original interviewers from the very first time. He had hoped that would help, flying the familiar faces in from LA to the New York studio.

Her face, he was pleased to see, was remarkably calm.

Hands were shaken and she sat down on the long couch, crossing her legs and stretching her arms along the back, as if she'd just walked into a bar for a quick beer and a chat. She looked stunning, and there was nothing about her body language to suggest she was there to apologise or felt one ounce of shame.

"Wow, Mysty, it's so good to have you back on the show. How are you?"

"I'm okay, thank you."

"It's been an interesting couple of days for you. If we can go straight to your video, it's the fourth day since it was released and its download rating stands at two hundred and ninety million. It's the biggest selling hit in history! How does that feel?"

"Quite amazing, really."

"Fifty dollars, though, for one download, that's six and a half minutes long, that is not cheap."

"I'm not cheap."

"No, clearly. That is a lot of money off the back of one song."

"It is. However, it is my intention that ten percent goes to charity: five percent towards the Butterfly Foundation, and five percent to helping start a dance foundation that will – hopefully – run throughout the US, and maybe even further. I'd like to take dance and music to people and places where it isn't given a chance to unite people. And I'm hoping the profit margin means my manager won't argue with me over this…"

No way he could now she'd said it live on TV. Not that he would have anyway.

"Mr Blackmoor controls your finances to the point he could stop you making that donation?"

"He controls everything; but I can't see that he'll refuse me this."

"I see. The profit margin on this video must be pretty high? You shot it in less than a day, I hear?"

"Yes, I started making arrangements during the flight to LA, but it took nine hours from the start of shooting to the final editing and release. I had two amazing people who helped me with editing. There was no CGI. I wanted it to be filmed on location with real people."

"It's not only the biggest selling but also the hottest video-single released; it's pretty raunchy stuff, too, you have to admit."

She looked at the guy who asked this as if to say, *No shit…* "I know, that's what I intended when I put it together."

"But why did you do it? Did it have anything to do with the run-in with your manager at the photo shoot on Wednesday?"

"I'm sure you all know what was said, and I won't pretend it wasn't said. I didn't want to do the shoot, but I wasn't given any choice…"

"How can you not be given a choice? Surely the shoot was discussed and agreed? And you must have seen what you would be wearing before the shoot?"

"I don't know how you think it works, but what I think doesn't feature in a lot of what I do for Mr Blackmoor. Compliance is the safest option. I didn't know what the shoot was for until I arrived."

Daryl groaned; this wasn't going to score him any respect in the manager-star working relationship department.

"I see. But what was said – it made you do the video?"

"Yes. If nothing else just to prove I could."

"You must be aware of the interest in the fact that Mr Blackmoor implied you are still a virgin?"

"I find amusing that so many people are so interested in such a trivial matter."

"So are you a virgin?"

"You really want me to answer that question, don't you?" She actually smiled. Were people really on the edge of their seat to hear this?

"It would put an end to the speculation," the female presenter said.

"Fine. If it means so much for people to know, yes, I am."

"But your relationship with Mr Capello…?" the male presenter dared to ask.

"Donny was always conscious of two things: first my age, and secondly that from the age of ten I'd been attacked, assaulted, and suffered more than one attempted rape. He's one of the most honourable people I know and insisted we wait until I was eighteen, but…we never got that far."

"There are a number of people on various forums voicing their support for you. Do you realise just how many people – despite being amazed – are actually inspired by the fact you've waited?"

"I find it sad that girls feel so much pressure, and I know a lot of girls who wished they waited, but got drunk and ended up doing something they didn't want to because all their friends were doing it. Be proud of your innocence. It shows you have respect for your body."

"I'm sure thousands of parents out there will be very much encouraged by your words, and girls too. The video is very passionate. Many might find it hard to believe you're as innocent as you say you are…"

Daryl had known this question would come up, and was unsure how she would answer. He had spoken to Gloria and knew she'd refused to discuss anything in a pre-interview coaching session.

"What is passion? A feeling? A sensation? A state of mind? People – the media – have described my Celeste work as 'passionate', and use the word to describe my commitment to what I do and what I bring to music or my dancing. I guess it's a part of me. I feel it in most of the things I do, that sense of breathlessness and not quite understanding the power of the sensation. Just because a man hasn't made me feel that yet doesn't make me feel I'm missing out. I believe passion is an expression of love for what you do, and that is one thing I do understand. Sex is merely a different physical expression of it. And passion can die…"

They waited for her to elaborate.

"What about the man who once upon a time made his wife blush remembering the night before in the bedroom, but who now spends late nights in front of the TV, maybe watching a bit of porn and pleasing himself when his wife is upstairs in bed on her own? And what about his wife, who can't quite remember why she married him? He doesn't make her heart race anymore; she never feels like she wants to push him down onto their bed and seduce him either. Why do you think the video is so popular? Because people see something they want to feel themselves. It is lustful, wild, uninhibited, passionate, wanton – all of these things and more – and seeing it makes them want to bring that back to their own life. I might be young and innocent, but I'm not unaware of what goes on in the bedroom. What you see in the video is like dancing to me, which is as easy as breathing. It's a musical interpretation of what I feel passion is."

Satisfied with the mature, insightful answer, they moved on. "The underwear you objected to, is it still going on release?"

"Yes. The catalogue will be available in about two weeks and can be purchased from the MY^2 website. Apparently the pictures are quite… racy!"

"I can imagine. Does this mean your feelings about the type of underwear featured have changed? Has doing the video changed you mind? Do you think bondage is something you'd maybe like to get into when you're…older?"

She scowled at the guy, who obviously hadn't been able to resist the question judging by the smirk on his face.

"I was shocked by the outfits, initially. I'd never encountered anything like them before. What made it worse was being forced into wearing them. Doing the video made me realise that…well, they're all just a collection of various fabrics. It only has meaning if you want it to. It felt like more of a costume in a sense, and I've worn enough of those. I guess when I did the video I was proving to myself that what I wore on the outside didn't matter, I'm still the same person. As to the last question, I don't know. I believe it's something you discover along the way, and certainly whoever you're with should have a say too. Everything should be consensual. It should be fun. And I know I'll get to have that fun one day, if I choose."

There was no denying the sound reasoning in that.

"And is there anyone on the horizon for you?"

"No."

A pause, and a slight change of tack.

"And how are things between you and your manager now? Are you aware he has spent the weekend reading the riot act to those he felt went too far in covering this story of your video and your virginity?"

"No I didn't know that. I guess maybe I can leave off the tail, though the horns can stay."

"Pardon me?"

"When I'm angry with him, I call him Satan."

Daryl almost smiled, and glanced over at Mac, who kept his eyes on the screen but was already grinning.

"Since the holiday you seem to be quite distant from each other and apparently there's been a fair amount of…hostility?"

Something in her face flickered, pained by the reminder of the holiday.

"I'm hoping he'll carry on being really busy and leave me to do what I do best."

"How was the holiday?"

"Great, thank you."

"So the reason for the disharmony when you returned…?"

The female presenter was not going to give up on this.

"I have no idea. I can't explain his unfriendly attitude these last few weeks. I only hope whatever work or business that has been worrying him so much is eventually resolved. He works too much as it is; being miserable with it is just unfair."

Wow.

"A very…considerate answer in light of his treatment of you recently."

"I'm not good at hating people and I'm monumentally awful at holding grudges."

"Luckily for him," the female presenter threw in. "How are things going with the summit?" she then asked. "Everyone is intrigued as to what you're preparing. Will the general public be able to see the show at any point?"

"The performance at the summit will be recorded and I'm hoping it will be judged as worthy of a least a couple of repeat performances. Naturally, as soon as this is decided, there will be a press release to let everyone know. I think it will be a great show for anyone, of any age, of any nationality."

"Excellent. We can't wait to see it, just like so many people at home. So, I think we've run out of time. Thank you, Mysty. In your usual candid way you've given everyone far more to think about than expected. I hope we'll see you soon. Good luck with the summit, though I'm pretty sure you don't need it."

"Thank you."

Mysty kept a quiet smile on her face as the camera finally zoomed in on the presenters, and when she received the signal she breathed out, and was led offset.

"So, there you have it," the male presenter said. "Always a girl to set the record straight, we now know the truth and have a rather enlightening alternative perspective on the video and the reasons behind it."

She didn't hear anymore.

"You okay?" OG whispered.

"Glad that's over."

"You need to go home and have a rest."

"I'd rather go to the studio."

"Not today."

"OG! Just for a few hours? Then I'll go home."

"How are you sleeping at the moment?"

"I'm not really. Not properly."

"That bad? You want me to get Baden to give you something to help you sleep? You've got to rest, kiddo, you know that."

"No. Absolutely no."

"What if I sit with you until you fall asleep. Having someone else there might make all the difference?"

"It's not in your job description to do that."

"No, it's not. I'll write it into my contract myself if you think it might help, me being there."

In truth, it had made a difference someone being there, as despite being slightly cramped on the sofa with Slick, she had slept so well, and with no nightmares.

OG looked at her, her face clouded by his boss's treatment of her, again.

Blackmoor needed to do something to make amends, and soon.

"SHE'S NOT DOING too good, then…" Mac commented dryly, and Daryl knew he was held responsible.

"No. All suggestions welcome."

"You know, she always feels better when she does something a little wild. We might think it's crazy, but to her it's not. Why not let her do something to…let her hair down?"

Daryl thought about it for second and then swung around in his chair. It went in the face of every instinct to bundle her up and keep her safe. But he had to learn to trust her. Donny had.

"Sky diving?"

"I think that might work." Daryl sensed Mac had been waiting for him to say the words.

"Good. Tell O'Grady. If she wants to do it he makes sure she knows all the safety procedures*, to the letter*. And make sure she only goes if she's not too tired and she's been eating regular meals. She needs to have stable blood sugar levels. If anything happens to her I'll have O'Grady dropped out of a plane without a parachute."

It amused Mac to see his boss so protective, without an inkling of shame for being so. "Yes, sir."

"And keep the cameras off her. Go somewhere she won't be spotted. Give the poor girl a chance to breathe. They've had their fun with her, now they need to back off."

"Absolutely. Anything else?"

"Send her a milkshake at the studio. Pick one you know she likes."

"Will do."

Mac turned to leave.

"And Mac."

"Sir?"

"You let me know when they're going, if they go."

"Of course."

In the wake of the chaos he'd created yet again, there was a resolute determination to make things okay. Donny had been right. If he threw this away he'd never forgive himself.

"SIR? I'VE JUST checked with O'Grady. The plane is in the air and they're about to jump. She's been drilled."

Daryl flicked to the camera feed in time to hear OG say, "When I say, you pull your chute, and don't try being clever on the landing. Do it the way I showed you, alright?" He could see the prospect of jumping out the plane at goodness only knew how many thousand feet wasn't bothering her in the slightest. He would rather she wasn't doing the jump at all, but this was the whole point: letting her do something she really wanted to do.

"OG, can we jump now, or would you like to go over the drill *again*?"

"Fine. You go first." OG nodded for the door to be released.

She smiled and moved to the door, the view from which showed cloud and sky, and bright sunshine, and below a world that looked much too far away. He held his breath. He must have been mad letting her do this.

She took a step, right to the edge, and OG made a mock salute. With a final glance at her bodyguard, she stepped, and the sudden rush of air around her blurred her final words, flipping over backwards to launch into the sky then diving down headfirst into the clouds.

"Jesus Christ," OG muttered, watching her perform a perfect arc, and threw himself out of the plane after her, knowing two others were going with him. He tried to manoeuvre, to get her back in his sight. When he spotted her she was on her back, smiling into the sky, arms and legs outstretched as if on a lie low in a pool.

"Bloody hell," he heard Mac say next to him.

He could see her heart rate read in the corner of the screen and it was only 86 bpm. His heart rate, he was pretty sure, was far faster watching from his office!

After a few moments she let her hands lead her body, and arched backwards into a dive, still elegant at however fast she moving as she enjoyed the freefall.

"Time to pull your chute," OG called across the rush of air.

"Yeah, yeah..." she replied.

"Don't make me come get you."

She laughed and pulled the cord, the blue canopy blossoming above her, and her descent slowed, as did Daryl's heart rate.

"How high are we?"

"Four hundred and fifty feet."

"What's my heart doing, OG?"

"It's 91 bpm," Daryl said.

"Yep, 91 bpm," OG repeated.

"Let's get it a bit higher, shall we? See you on the ground."

Time slowed in the seconds that followed as Daryl and OG saw her reach into her boot, pulled out small wickedly sharp-looking blade, and before their shouts made it from their lips she'd cut the cords to the chute, and dropped. So fast she was gone from OG's sight that his camera simply could not track her.

"Fuck!" OG swore as the loosed parachute hovered momentarily in thin air, and then began to float downwards.

"What the fuck does she think she's doing? I let her do this and this is what she does?" Daryl was on his feet, his own heartrate leaping with panic.

Mac didn't answer. He knew it wasn't safe to do so when the fury in his boss's voice was so apparent. He had dived before, and knew it would be impossible to catch her. Was this her revenge? To kill herself?

Daryl switched feeds and found her, dancing with gravity, letting it bend and twist her body, half using the force of the air, half controlling it.

Her pulse was 165 bpm.

This couldn't be happening.

In the final seconds, Daryl forced himself to watch the one person he could never get enough of. In a blur of motion she curled and then uncurled, and suddenly she was spinning across the grass, her body rolling too many times to count and too fast to fathom. Finally she stood, an unsteady miracle of humanity, and her face broke into a huge smile of pure joy.

"Well, I'll be damned," Mac muttered, as she lay down in the grass, hands behind her head to watch OG and his men complete their descent. She had no doubt intended to do that since the jump had been scheduled. He was as dumbfounded as his boss was furious, but patched through.

But it was Daryl who spoke: "O'Grady, you will get that girl in a car and back to her apartment immediately. And you can tell her from me she's lucky I'm not there, or she would get it from me with both barrels!"

"I think I might just do that for you, sir. Damn it!" OG touched down, and they heard the thump of his feet and saw his chute falling around him. He unclipped and pulled off his helmet, and removed the parachute harness. "How could you be so fucking irresponsible! What the hell is it with you?"

"OG, you know I don't do anything I haven't first calculated. Four hundred and fifty feet is fine. I was going to find some way to test it anyway, but if I'd asked you if I could do it today, you'd have said no, wouldn't you?"

"I'm not in the mood for your cocky answers! You shouldn't have done it and that is the end of it! Boys!"

"OG! I will suffocate!" she yelled as she was bundled into a chute and karted off to the car.

"No, you won't. You can hold your breath for a very long time. You know that I know that. You'll be fine."

But she used the knife to rip through the fabric, pulling in several large gasps of air.

"You are out of control. You are…a bad girl!" OG told her, eyeing her with great disapproval.

To his surprise she laughed, and then kept laughing, and flopped back into the chute that she was being carried in.

"Why on earth was that so funny?"

"Donny told me that once. For a completely different reason." The laughter kept coming all the way to the waiting vehicles.

"If you two have kids, and they can do what she does, I will expect a pay rise," Mac said quietly, crossing his arms and turning to Daryl with a grin. "And OG and I are going to need therapy."

"Mac, you can name your price. Keeping her and my children safe will be the most important thing in the world. I might even have to clone you," Daryl said, stunned at his forwardness on an issue about which he never spoke.

"I'll get the cars ready," Mac said, deciding against quizzing his boss on the subject.

The door was shut and Daryl was alone; alone and able to indulge in a wide smile, imagining what sort of children they might have, contemplating the making of them, and then the girl herself. He closed his eyes and there she was. How he admired her control, the fearlessness, trusting herself to make the landing and that her calculations had been right.

It had been good to hear her laugh, see that big smile, but God, when would she stop terrifying and infuriating him?

HE WASN'T QUITE sure which Mysty would walk through the door that afternoon, exactly a week on from the first awful photo shoot – the worst of his life professionally and personally – and had been tempted to pull out and find the next best person to do it instead. But he didn't want her to think him a coward, and didn't want to miss out on directing the shoot; but, most of all, he wanted to prove to her he wasn't the ogre he'd been last week. There was a long road of reparation to walk but, like a pilgrimage, he was driven to undertake it by a belief and a need far stronger than he could explain. He had to trust the ecstasy and peace of redemption would appear somewhere at the end of it.

Daryl analysed the look on her face. It wasn't one of fear, or hate. More…a silent challenge. What was she'd she said at the interview, about the items feeling more like a costume? It seemed she'd conquered her dislike of them by making them something she could relate to, but how would she be today?

"So? Where do you want me?" she asked simply, appearing in the first 'costume' and for some reason eating cherries from a paper bag.

What a question. Daryl forced himself to keep his answer professional, and gestured towards the set.

"Cherries?" he asked carefully.

"I find them immensely satisfying," she replied, a glitter in her eyes.

He controlled his reaction to her comment, just, and watched her lick some juice from her fingers. It was a beautiful shot, and he immediately asked that someone find a bowl for the cherries that would match the set. He then ordered that more cherries be fetched. This was inspirational. Why hadn't he thought of this?

The shoot began, and it became obvious this girl and the one last week were two different creatures. The one before his camera was now unashamed, eyes watching him through the camera lens, every pose enticing, so sexy he knew the results were going to be superb. This was a girl who now knew her own body's capacity for attraction and played it to the full, and eyes that had previously been full of misery were now impossibly bright, curious, seeking, teasing, as if she knew the torture she was putting him through as she posed with the male model, one leg across his body as he lay between her thighs.

Click-click-click. Perfect.

"I bet you couldn't wait for today to roll around," she said, emerging in a second outfit.

"No."

"I bet you wish you'd designed a dozen more outfits."

"Absolutely." She moved into another pose, and Daryl could barely breathe imagining it was he kneeling before her on the bed. She focussed on the camera lens, her eyes intense. She knew what she was doing, and the ache in his groin was almost unbearable. "I think you like torturing me."

"It's pay back."

"Would you like some music on?"

"If you can think of something appropriate," she said slowly.

He smiled, dropped his hand to the bowl and put a cherry against her lips, the moment silent and erotic. She glared at him for a second, and then opened her mouth and accepted the fruit, taking it in her teeth.

He strolled off to talk to someone about playing some music, choosing P!nk as he already knew she liked her work, and it was suitably feisty and empowered.

She had come fully prepared for the dickhead billionaire to make a nightmare out of today, but here he was, being charming and…something else that was stirring all kinds of sensations. He returned, and she was joined by another of the male models. She sensed that they were all quite wary of her, like she was the most dangerous creature in the room, capable of ruining not only their career but their professional composure. She hooked a leg round the guy's hip and he placed his hand on her chest; there was something feverish about his touch, and she could feel his arousal against her leg. But it didn't scare her anymore; it was natural. In fact it was a compliment. She had also realised they couldn't help it. The frames were shot, and the guy removed himself from the scene. Rather hastily.

"You really are having fun, aren't you?"

She looked over and saw an amused and warm pair of green eyes watching her from a few feet away. She was lining cherries up in a neat row along her stomach.

"Getting to lie on a bed for a few hours and rest, and eat cherries, and getting paid – it's great."

He took a cherry from the bowl and ate it, still watching her. She took one too, and spat the stone neatly into the bin. She placed another at the end of the row she was building, that now extended to just below her breasts.

"I see you prefer to spit, rather than swallow," he said. The flare of colour over her cheekbones was instant, as was her sudden jolt upright as he sat on the end of the bed. He glanced at her body, his own responding beyond his control. "You appear to have lost all your cherries." A delicious smirk curved his lips. "I think I'll have this one." He reached over and picked up the one that had rolled between her thighs, his fingers a hair's breadth from her skin, and the blush deepened. He popped it into his mouth, his eyes on hers.

Mysty felt her heart beating very hard against her ribcage and looked away. How dare he? But her skin burned where his fingers had been.

The afternoon took another twist when, in yet another outfit, she was led to a bed strewn with thousands of deep red rose petals. She watched him work, 'seeing' each shot before it had even been made and directing accordingly. She was surprised, stunned even. He was an artist at work, the images in mind becoming a reality as he called 'hold' and the shutter fired.

Laying in the roses, she felt her eyes close.

"No falling asleep just yet, Venus. We're not done."

A feather was whispered over her cheek and her hand shot out and grabbed a wrist, knowing whose it was because of the voice.

"No one ever tell you not to disturb a sleeping tiger?" she murmured.

"You know I like excitement." His unrepentant eyes smiled down at her, liking her hold on his wrist, and she let him go as if he'd burnt her. "Don't move."

"Daryl!" What the hell was he doing taking pictures from that angle? She was barely wearing anything! "These better not go in the damned catalogue or I'll drop you off your roof!"

"No, these are for somewhere very particular."

"Which is?"

"On my ceiling, in my office."

She threw a cherry at him, and he caught it and placed it inches away from the part of her that longed for ecstasy.

"Why are you doing this? Haven't you got enough already?" He didn't answer while he concentrated on the shot. She picked up the nearest feather and laid it between her legs. She didn't want him photographing her so…close-up. And yet she was burning inside…his eyes on her, there, where the heat was almost unbearable.

But he had the shot he wanted.

"You're not really going to put it in your office, are you?" she asked.

"No. I have somewhere else in mind."

She sat up and moved over the petals to the edge of the bed, and took a slow prowling walk towards him. She stopped. The camera was still in his hands, and her eyes went to his obvious arousal. He was on the edge. He prayed she wouldn't touch him. But she stepped closer, and placed a cherry against his lips, as he had done to her, and he accepted the fruit from her fingers. And then she stepped past him, so close that the edge of her hip brushed against the erection he hoped she hadn't seen, as lightly as a butterfly's wing but enough to send a jolt through him. He knew he was going to have to control the urge to follow her, but he also needed some relief, and fast.

She gave him a curious look when she reappeared, before stepping through the door held open for her.

Once home she received a message: Due to the quality of the shots the price tag on the catalogue had been doubled. And a thank you from the one who'd worked so hard behind the lens.

The monster had been replaced by a man, and one who hadn't hidden his admiration of her or his hunger for her, but at the same time hadn't let it get the better of him. This time.

"MYSTY. SO GLAD you came. I wasn't sure if you would."

"No, I wasn't either."

She let Harvey take her hand, relieved to see nothing lewd in his eyes. After the video release some people had treated her slightly differently – and usually in a negative way. Given the type of man Harvey was, there was a good chance he might have been the same, so she was pleasantly surprised. He did, however, warn her to watch out for all the men who would now be after her and her money. She thanked him, and told him she was on the lookout, and that she didn't have access to any of the money from the downloads anyway.

He led her through the gardens and towards the stables, letting her stop and admire them when she wanted to. He was delighted to have her back, and he wondered what today might bring. He was also aware that he would be presenting her with a very special surprise, rather than the man himself who, it seemed, had done a 180-degree turn and decided he wasn't going to let her go. Not that he'd come out and said it, but Harvey could read between the lines of Daryl's flight to LA and apparently – as rumour had it – dropping everything to go to see her. It wasn't hard to see why Daryl had reassessed the situation, and unsurprisingly found the idea of Mysty belonging to another man utterly unacceptable.

Harvey wasn't about to give up though. He figured he owed Daryl a bit of competition and, frankly, he really did like her. He had discussed this with himself and found nothing he could object to – except her hectic schedule and the sad necessity of a bodyguard. But he wasn't overly worried about either of those things; in his circles, it was the norm.

"You're rather quiet." She pulled him from his quiet thoughts with her own quiet words, and looked round at him curiously. "Is something the matter?"

"No. I was just pondering. I know you probably won't believe me, but I do think about things sometimes, you know, exercise the grey matter. Not often, I confess, but occasionally."

She laughed. "And what were you thinking about?"

"What a little miracle you are."

"OG, Mac and Daryl would probably correct you on that. I think they think I'm a right royal pain in the ass." It was Harvey's turn to laugh and she smiled. "I was allowed to go sky diving on Monday. I was amazed, to say the least, as Daryl is always so controlling. But I ditched my chute to land on my own. Man, they were so pissed off with me."

"You *ditched* your *chute*?"

"Yeah, it made it a little more exciting. It takes a bit more than a regular sky dive to get my heart racing. I was in big trouble when OG caught up with me."

"I can imagine. How high up were you when you, erm, let go?"

"Quite high. I'm forbidden telling anyone. It's nothing personal, just for my safety. You can always ask Daryl. I guess he might tell you."

"I still say more of a miracle than a pain in the ass. Just about." She laughed again, and they rounded the corner into the stables. "And I would say Daryl agrees with me, which is why we have someone quite special here who wants to see you." She looked intrigued, and followed Harvey to one of the stalls.

"Megan?" Mysty looked at Harvey in disbelief. Surely not? "But she was in Sicily? How on earth is she here?"

Harvey indicated that the groom allow the horse to walk over, if she wished, and she did, making her way willingly towards the welcoming hands.

"She was flown over for you. Daryl asked me to keep her here, because you were coming to ride. She'll be here whenever you want her. He thought you might like it. I think it was his way of…apologising."

Mysty didn't know what to say. It was a grand gesture, as it was not easy to transport a horse halfway around the world, but he'd done it because he'd thought she'd like it? Like letting her sky dive on Monday? He hadn't thrown jewellery at her, or sent a dress or flowers? On top of the photo shoot yesterday, she was most confused. Was the mask off again? What did all this mean?

Harvey could sense her confusion as she stroked Megan's mane and cradled the soft velvety nose, the easy affection between horse and girl obvious to see.

"He's not a monster, Mysty. He just…sometimes he makes mistakes, like the rest of us do. He's not too good at apologising for them or even admitting them, though, as you know."

"Yes, I know. I accepted that a long time ago. It's just… Well, he was being such an asshole, and now this? Is there any history of split personalities in his family?"

Harvey smiled at her blunt way of putting it.

"No, but I'm sure he'll explain one day. Daryl never does things without a reason. It's just not always obvious at the time."

"People say the same thing about God." She leaned a head against the mare's neck and the horse snuffled her hip.

"That may be the case, but she's here to enjoy, so let's go riding – and I expect another expert dancing lesson afterwards, so we'd better get moving. Unless you're too worn out after all those rose petals and cherries yesterday?"

"How the hell do you know about yesterday?" It was a cry of dismay.

"Daryl wanted me to help him pick some of the best photos for the catalogue. I have expertise in the field of buying underwear, so it was good to put it to use."

This was putting rather a gloss on the truth, as it was part of an agreement to let Harvey keep the horse at his stables – though he would have said yes anyway. It worked as the perfect excuse to see the pictures pre-catalogue.

"Hasn't he got enough expertise himself?" she demanded, outrage putting even more colour in her flashing eyes.

"Second opinions always help."

A groom walked his horse over, and he pulled himself into the saddle.

His eyes were warm, and it was hard to be angry with him. She vaulted up into the saddle. "Right, that man's horns and tail are back on. You'd better be careful lest you grow a set of your own, Harvey Lincoln! The world's most debauched pair of perverts who ever lived and I end up knowing both of you!"

With a flick of her wrists the mare twirled expertly on her hind legs, and they were off out of the stables heading for open ground.

Harvey grinned and spurred his horse after her, deciding this afternoon was going to be just as enjoyable as the last.

"SO, HAVE YOU been practising?"

They were back in the ballroom, Harvey once again in trousers, shirt and smart shoes. She was in a simple little dress that swung from her hips, the curves of her upper body delicious as she tied up her mane of hair.

"I confess I did try, but my butler gave me funny looks when I asked him to play the female! I don't think I've forgotten anything. It was rather memorable."

"Could you not tempt a woman into practising with you rather than your butler?" Harvey laughed easily. She liked that. "Anyway, once you have all the steps you will stun everyone at those mind-numbingly polite parties you go to, and women will fall at your feet when they see you dance so well."

"Are you saying they don't already fall at my feet?"

"Even faster than they already do."

"That's not why I wanted to learn."

"But there's no denying it would impress them!"

"We definitely should. Dance I mean. At one of those parties. I'd love to see the look on Daryl's face."

She saw the twinkle of mischief that matched her own. "It would be criminal not to showcase your talents, having gone to the trouble of learning," she agreed.

"Exactly. We'll choose an occasion."

They went over the steps from before, and the images he had previewed yesterday, coupled with that phenomenal body so close to his, meant he didn't need his shirt ripped this time. But he did pull it off after an hour and used it to wipe the sweat from his brow. This was hard work! But they had one sequence perfected, and he was happy.

She looked at him. He was breathing hard, and had a hungry virility to him. "Too much for you?" she asked, and tossed him a bottle of water.

"No."

"You want more?"

"Absolutely."

"Do you want to learn the lifts and throws?"

"Do you trust me to throw you around?"

"You're strong enough, and I am better able than most to land safely if you get it wrong. But don't let being afraid of getting it wrong and hurting me put you off. You've done very well so far. I think you can do it."

He wasn't going to pass up the opportunity, and soon she was explaining the holds, the best places to grip, how hard and how to release. One huge incentive, aside from the obvious desire to get it right, was that one day he might get to dance with her where Daryl would see them – and for once his friend was going to find himself second best.

OG COULD SEE them both on screen. Wow. This was some dance lesson. They were breathing heavily, as the moves were fast and furious at times. Yet there seemed to be a natural harmony of movement between these two relative strangers.

He waited for a suitable pause in the dance. "Mysty?"

She looked around, still breathing hard, though not as hard as her partner. "OG. Is everything okay?" Normally he didn't interrupt.

"Sure. Just it's half past seven already, which was when we were planning to leave."

"Really? Have we been in here that long?"

"Better get you home. We can get some food on the way?"

"You can stay for dinner, if you like?" Harvey offered, grabbing the opportunity to keep her a little longer. "We can eat in the garden, so you can enjoy it a little more?"

"I…" Mysty looked at OG, not sure if this would be allowed. She loved the idea, but… "I don't want to put anyone to any trouble."

Harvey loved her humility, her concern. "It's no trouble. My staff are underused as I so rarely get a chance to come here. I think they'll rather enjoy the chance to cook for a guest such as yourself. I'll get a gazebo set up. What would you like to eat?"

She looked at OG, who nodded his consent and left the room.

"I really don't mind, just not raw fish or duck. I don't eat desserts, so don't worry about that."

"Oh dear, well aren't you just the most specific person ever?" he mocked her gently. "I think we'll find something you'll like. Come on, I need a shower. You're an excellent teacher, but you certainly make me sweat for it."

They both turned at the sound of the door opening again, and two excitable leopards came bounding in.

"They were getting a little restless in the car and insisted on coming to find you," OG commented.

"Do you mind, Harvey?" she asked, crouching to welcome the cats into her arms. "They're fully house-trained, and they don't bite."

She looked up at him and he smiled. "I have no objections, as long as I get a formal introduction." He dropped down next to her, and OG stood back, not surprised that she had managed to attract the attention of not one but two powerful men. One of them at least seemed to know how to treat her properly.

In his apartment, Daryl glared at the screen, for once very much hating his friend. The brandy burned down his throat and he leaned back in the chair. He needed to get her away from there. But anything he did would look obvious. He gritted his teeth.

MYSTY BREATHED IN the smells of the garden, so pure, the air so clean. It was beautiful sitting under in the gazebo on the lawn, the beautifully lit fountain a few metres away on one side of them; a multitude of blossoming rose bushes on the other. The night was still, and she could hear birds singing – something she never heard in New York.

"You like the gardens, don't you?"

She looked round at the handsome man who had proved charming and witty over a dinner of simple marinated chicken with new potatoes and salad. A fruit salad with cream had then been brought to the table, and she'd dared to try a little. It was delicious and, to her surprise, she hadn't felt a moment of unease or pressure – but then she hadn't had someone sat opposite so ready to pick fault with her.

"Yes. I think they're beautiful. You're very lucky to have such a place."

"Why do you like them so much? I never had you down as a girl for flowers."

It was an honest question, and she smiled sadly. "My favourite place as a child was my grandmother's garden. It was always so full of colour, with plants and flowers of all kinds. She loved it, and was so good at making everything grow. There was even a little stream running through it, so we used to look for little fish. There was a miniature bridge across it, and we used to lie on there and stare into the water. The birds so tame they didn't fly away. It was my heaven. It was the one...safe place I could go to. I've often thought about finding it on Google Earth, to see what it is like now, but...I don't want to ruin the memories I have. They're all I've got."

"Daryl mentioned your family...are dead. I apologise for being so blunt. Do you have any photographs?"

Again, that warmth in his eyes. It made her want to answer him.

"I ran away. I had a box of biscuits, a blanket and my grandmother's handbag, with a hundred and fifty dollars inside, that was all I could take. It was the most money I'd ever seen in my life. I thought it was last forever it was so much. I was running for my life. I didn't have time to stop for pictures."

"Can I ask how old you were?" He had to place her properly in the picture, imagining her as a young girl.

"Nine years old. Exactly."

Nine? How the hell had she survived? "I was right then," he said softly.

"Really? How so?"

"You're definitely more of a miracle than a pain in the ass." His smile was gentle.

The conversation might have progressed a little more down the road of memory and heartache, but there was a splash, and they looked over and saw Lazarus peering into the fountain.

Mysty jumped up and ran over. "Oh Lula!" There sitting in the water, looking very innocent but rather surprised, was a soaking wet cub. Harvey joined her, with his wine glass in his hand, looking somewhat amused at the new use for his stunning fountain. "Trust you to get into mischief!"

She slipped her shoes off and climbed in, Lazarus following her, obviously deciding this was a pool party. He jumped at her, pushing her backwards to land in the water next to Lula, and she squealed and laughed out loud, looking up at Harvey, who was grinning widely.

"Hold this," he said, and handed her his wine, and she watched in amazement as he pulled off his rather nice blue shirt and tossed it to the ground, along with his shoes, and stepped into the fountain with them! He reclaimed his wine glass and leant back against the edge of the fountain as if they were in a hot tub, as if this was the most normal thing to do. One of the waiters brought her orange juice over from the table and handed it to her from a silver tray.

It was so ludicrous, she ended up laughing in utter astonishment.

"I find it offensive if my guests are having more fun than me!" he declared. "And I'm still hot from all that dancing!"

They lay happily in the fountain, discussing New York, and the coming summit, and Harvey recommended places she should visit and answered her questions, enjoying her innocent curiosity and appreciation for his answers and suggestions.

There was a polite cough, and they both looked up.

"I'd like you to get out now," OG said. "You're shivering. It's time to dry off."

Mysty looked over at Harvey, who shrugged, knowing it had to end at some point, and knowing OG was right. She stood and let Harvey help her out of the fountain, and everyone wrapped in big white towels, including the cats. And then they all drifted back to the waiting Bentleys.

"Do you want to borrow some clothes?" Harvey asked.

"Don't tell me you keep ladies' clothes in the back of your wardrobe, Harvey? Really, I never thought you were the type," she teased. "I'll be fine, really. I have clothes on the plane and it's not very cold. I'm not so fragile."

"But you are very precious. No amount of care is ever enough."

Daryl cursed his friend's easy charm, and for always finding the right words. He watched her smile at Harvey's solemn voice and kind eyes. "I'll see you in New York, next week. Don't work too hard," she said.

Harvey shook OG's hand, and watched from the steps as the convoy of Bentleys rolled away down the long drive and into the night.

Daryl didn't know what to do with himself. He couldn't let Harvey lay even one little claim on her; he did not want him to think he'd even got one foot through that door; he must not be allowed to even kiss her. He wanted that first special moment; he wanted every first to belong to him. How could he stop this?

SHE LOOKED BACK at the collection of photos she had fixed to the back of his bedroom door, sent a disapproving scowl towards the one over his bed, and returned to the kitchen to make a Pina Colada. She left the music playing – well, a recording of waves washing on the shore – and placed the note next to the cocktail. Time to go.

She watched the numbers read down in the lift and, as the doors opened, there he was, striding back into the building. She smiled, knowing he would be confused and no doubt surprised to see her. She wasn't disappointed.

Daryl came up short as the vision he dismissed as a daydream kept walking. She was smiling slightly. What the hell was she doing there? And why was she carrying a crossbow and a rope?

She walked straight past him, as if passing a stranger in the street. Mac and the rest of the boys, none of whom intercepted her progress across the polished marble floor, all followed her with their eyes.

Daryl turned to see OG get out of the Bentley to meet her.

"That and that are confiscated," he said, pointing at the interesting items she was carrying as easily as any other woman would carry a handbag. She sighed, and handed them over. As she got into the car she glanced back at Daryl for a split second over the top of her shades, eyes full of mischief.

What had she been doing?

OG gave him and Mac a look, shook his head and got in after her.

Mac came up with him to the penthouse, to check for what might be amiss. Daryl was about to join him when was distracted by the sound of waves, a cocktail on the breakfast bar, and the folded note with a large letter 'D' on the front – an improvement on '666'.

'As you appear to have no comprehension of the word "discretion", I felt a demonstration was in order. PS – The cocktail isn't poisoned, I'm just hoping it turns you back into a man I once met in Barbados – he was much nicer than the jackass prowling around New York recently. PPS – Did you really have to put that picture above your bed…'

Oh God, what had she done? And what did she mean about having no discretion? Oh, of course: asking Harvey for an opinion on the pictures… As for the latest installation above his bed…what man wouldn't want such a gorgeous image to gaze at, the feather tantalisingly placed where he most longed to explore?

Mac reappeared looking rather amused. "Can't find anything amiss," he said, "except…"

"Except what?"

"There are some pictures on the back of your bedroom door. Very nice. Definitely worth keeping." Mac saw the frown of curiosity. "Will that be all, sir?"

"Yes. Have the cars ready at quarter to nine."

Mac nodded and left, pretty sure his boss would want to be alone when he saw the photographs.

The memories of their time in the sun came flooding back. The largest picture was of him asleep, with Lula on his chest, the light perfect, the focus excellent. It was so real he could almost feel the warmth of the cub against his skin. The photo of him smiling – a rare sight he had to admit – tugged at him somehow. How happy he looked. There was another, of him on a sun lounger, a book resting on his chest, again asleep. Since when had he been so relaxed he read a book? On the far left was a shot she couldn't have taken. It was them together, surrounded by the island children after the cricket match. The dust in the air was flecked with light, which reflected in the eyes of the child in her arms, and the child who was holding his hand. He couldn't take his eyes off the beautiful simplicity of the moment. No wonder she had chosen this picture. She didn't want a god. And she certainly didn't want the devil. She wanted the man.

He strolled back to the kitchen and sipped the Pina Colada. And then a thought: What on earth had she been doing with a crossbow and a rope?

He pulled up the satellite feed on her and back-tracked an hour. It was 6pm and quite dark, but he could still make her out scaling the side of her building, her hands and feet finding holds he was sure no other person on earth would be able to find, until she was on the roof. Calmly, as if she did she did this every day, she attached the rope slung over her shoulder to the end of an arrow – and fired it across to his building. The cocktail was forgotten as he watched her test the hold and, satisfied, strap the crossbow to her back. Surely not? He could barely watch – despite knowing she was perfectly fine, having just seen her – as she then wrapped the rope around her body, stepped up onto the ledge and jumped into the gaping emptiness between the two buildings. He could hardly breathe in the long seconds that saw her brace and use her strong legs to take the impact just beneath his balcony. She paused for a second, and then used the rope to climb up and over the high railings. A few moments later she appeared to use a key card to enter his apartment through the sliding doors. The rest he could guess, but he watched it anyway on the internal cameras, amused at her consternation at finding *that* picture above his bed.

He didn't doubt OG would have given her a major lecture when he'd seen her with the rope and crossbow and realised what she'd done. He felt like putting a call through and delivering a rather strong lecture himself. But as he picked up the cocktail again, and listened to the sound of the waves, he felt something else – astonishment and, as always, admiration. He would talk her later on that night, at the party.

"My goodness, you look happier!" Harvey declared. "Not surprising, though, given all those photos you have, hey?" Harvey nudged Daryl playfully as they greeted each other, the collection of society's most eligible gradually gathering in the chandelier-lit ballroom, all eagerly awaiting the arrival of one girl. He had already greeted Charles, and numerous other politicians, all of whom wanted to know when she would be arriving.

"Absolutely, though I'd prefer the flesh and blood version."

"Oh, really? So you've changed your mind again?" Harvey dared, and Daryl didn't miss the just perceptible irritation in his voice.

"Sorry, Harvey, old chap, what can I say? You were right."

"Damned rude of you," Harvey laughed, but again sensed exasperation.

"I know, but a very good friend's advice finally sank in and I decided some opportunities really can't be passed over." Daryl was trying to be as gentle and tactful as he could, but there was a chance this was going to test their friendship to the limits.

"I was rather enjoying the fact you'd, erm, given up on her," Harvey remarked, unable to keep the frown from clouding his convivial face. He focussed on his champagne to dim the intensity of the moment, aware this was unchartered territory…when had they really competed against each other?

"I realise that, but it is still her choice, Harvey. If I lose, I lose. But I don't want to lose her because I didn't try."

Harvey regarded him calmly, losing the scowl and smiling just a touch, knowing his reserved friend was being as open as he dared let himself be, and fair minded.

"May the best man win," Harvey said, and raised his champagne glass. Daryl followed suit. He had no intention of losing, but the game was on.

He sensed a reaction in the people around him, and turned to the ballroom doors at the top of the magnificent flight of stairs.

Like the dress she had worn for the opening piece at the Light and Dark concert, this one was a midnight black version, in soft material draped over her breasts in a deep V to her navel and flared from her waist. Her hair was piled high and secured with black ribbons. She was exquisite.

Daryl engaged his brain a second faster than Harvey this time, and the guests parted as he went to meet her.

He stopped at the foot of the stairs and watched, mesmerised, as she made her way down. He caught a flash of smooth thigh, almost to the curve of her hip, as the dress fluttered and parted as she walked. The music played, but no one spoke. He offered his hand, and she took it wordlessly, eyes silently asking if all was okay. If only she knew just how okay everything was in the moment he felt her fingers in his.

"I do believe you're wearing a dress," he whispered, absorbing her beauty, the bright eyes, the tiny smile that flickered on her lips. He allowed himself to lower and raise his eyes, taking in the vision she was. He lingered on the jewelled clip between her breasts, holding the soft fabric; it was the symbol for infinity, and he knew then she had made the dress herself, exactly how she'd wanted it to be. The contact in their fingertips sent a heat through both of their bodies, and her eyes rose to meet his. "You look…beautiful."

"Compliments, and after I've visited into your apartment uninvited?" she half teased, a slight wariness in her voice.

"It was an excellent cocktail. I'm easily won over," he said, wanting her to relax.

"And the rest?"

"The pictures are great, really."

She was handed a glass of champagne, and he let go her of hand to take her elbow, dropping back slightly as he led her into the room. The dress had a deep V at the back too, to well below her waistline, and the same infinity symbol but at the base of the V, in black and purple jewels.

"Are you wearing any underwear at all?" he managed to ask her before they reached Harvey and the waiting group of friends, threading through guests who smiled in adoration at the woman by this powerful man's side, slower to move than normal as they took in the surprise image of them together.

She merely sent him an infuriating, delicious smile, and then they arrived amid his circle of friends. Harvey kissed her hand, compliments and champagne waiting for her, as well as a tease or two about her wearing a dress that she pulled off beautifully, with a wide, genuine smile. She could more than handle the disreputable group of rogues he was happy to call his friends.

He left her in their safe hands, knowing they would take care of her whilst he circulated. He found himself, once more, on the balcony overlooking the room with the secretary of state.

"It would appear you've changed you mind," the man remarked, eyebrows raised. "Again."

Daryl smiled. It seemed Charles took far more interest in the developments between he and Mysty than the rest of the issues they needed to talk about.

"I'm afraid so." Daryl turned and saw the older man smiling too.

"Excellent. There was I thinking you were going to make the most monumental mistake. Wholly out of character. I await my wedding invitation."

"I'd go to the altar tomorrow; it's getting her there that's the issue." Daryl said the words quickly, but then realised he meant them. He would. No hesitation.

"She seems to have a great deal of patience for the follies of man from what I've seen, including your own, and yet she took your hand tonight. There is hope."

"Thank you, Charles. I'd like you to know that she tells me I'm an idiot, or worse, frequently, so no need to join in." Charles laughed loudly at the thought of Mr Blackmoor, a man respected and also feared by so many, being taken to task by a beautiful, fiery seventeen-year-old. "Tell me, what has she been talking to you and Thomas about? I hope she hasn't been up to any mischief?" Daryl then asked.

"I'm not at liberty to say at the moment, though it's nothing terrible. Far from it."

"She's a resourceful girl and puts that to good use. As you might have noticed, she's not someone who needs telling how to make a success of a thing. Which is why I trust her to handle the performance for the summit without interfering, as I trusted her to do the MJ tour."

"Daryl, I promise you it'll surprise you when you find out. I think you'll be impressed. But I'm sure she'd tell you if you ask her *nicely*." Charles's mischievous grin made Daryl roll his eyes. "Which brings me to another point – are you going to ask her to dance?"

"I was thinking about it."

"*Thinking* about it? What are you waiting for? Mr Lincoln and your friends seem rather content to entertain her. Never leave your prize filly running loose in the herd, Daryl."

Charles patted his shoulder and wandered off, happy with his admonition – and the news that Daryl had finally seen sense in respect to the finest filly in New York.

Daryl spotted her easily, in the centre of a large group of gentlemen. Time to extricate her.

As he approached, the black jackets separated for him to let him pass, and he found his best friend and his tiger in an exchange that seemed to intrigue and shock her at the same time.

"Mysty."

"Daryl. Please tell me Harvey is lying and you didn't really go into your first lap dancing bar when you were fourteen?"

Wow. He wasn't prepared for that! But her amusement was infectious, and he looked over at Harvey, who shrugged as if to say *Who cares? She knows what we're like!*

"Yes, well, we managed to get ourselves in, but then Harvey managed to get us thrown out trying to tuck some notes inside a certain woman's thong. She was the manager of the establishment, not an employee. Luckily my father wasn't around. But yours was, as I remember." Daryl looked pointedly at his friend, who cringed remembering the severe reprimand, the sore buttocks, and being grounded for two months.

"Yes, sadly he was. My father had strict rules about such places: I definitely had to be fifteen, and I should have used $100 bills, not $20s."

He was glad to see she found that revelation amusing, but said, "Mysty, I would like to save you from hearing any more debauched stories. Would you like to dance?"

Her eyes betrayed a little nervousness when she looked up at him. Was she afraid of refusing him, or afraid of being so close to him?

"Yes, why not," she suddenly said. "I would like to rate your dancing, Mr Manager. If you're any good I might offer you a small part in one of my productions."

"Excellent. That's very kind of you."

"Make the most of it."

"I will. You may lead."

Daryl smiled, and he held out his hand once more. She took it, and as they joined the guests on the dancefloor they turned to face each other and his hand came to rest on her waist. He could feel the warmth of her skin under his fingers, and his heart beat faster. He forced himself to breathe slowly. He wanted to enjoy this moment, something he had waited for for so long.

Mysty didn't like the way her body reacted to him. She felt self-conscious under his gaze, and she knew she was blushing, her entire body heating up not just her face. Damn him and the green eyes that held hers with such…warmth. There was an intensity in just those few seconds she hadn't felt in all the hours of dancing with Harvey.

"How are you feeling?" he asked, as they moved together, so close. Too close, or not close enough, depending on whose thoughts you listened to…

"A little tired," she confessed, her eyes dropping away. "Celeste is demanding at the moment, and I have a rehearsal at 6am tomorrow."

"You can leave whenever you wish. Rest is far more important than a party."

The fantastic eyes lifted back up and he felt the full power of her attention, just like that first time during the pall-mall car ride in the back streets of LA.

"Daryl."

"Yes?"

"Why are you being nice to me again?"

He paused before answering, looking into the large eyes that begged him to explain. She had no idea why he'd put them both through so much. But he felt she wouldn't believe the truth if he dared tell her.

"Because you didn't do anything wrong. I pushed your buttons and you got angry. What happened when you got back from Sicily is my fault."

"But what happened? What business did you have to come back for that bothered you so much you turned into an ogre again?"

"I'll explain it one day."

"I hope this 'one day' isn't so far away?"

"But it rather depends on something else."

He glanced at her and saw the look of frustration. He knew such a vague answer had earned him that, and he wished he could explain. Just not now.

"Well, as this conversation is clearly going nowhere, how are you otherwise?" she asked bluntly, making him smile; who else demanded answers from him like she did?

"I'm fine. Much better than last weekend. How is Slick? I trust he is as fully recovered?"

Damn. Why had he asked that?

"He's okay. He's a tough LA boy, not some pampered New Yorker," she said with a rather penetrating look.

"Nurse Mysty. Thank you for repairing us both. Can you wear a nurse's outfit next time?"

"Next time? Are you planning on knocking on people's front doors every time you think I might sleep with someone?"

"*Every time?* Should I be expecting a repeat performance?"

"No. Not that it's any of your business."

Oh but it is. "But say I got badly injured somehow… Would you wear one for me then?"

"No! Get Baden to put one on."

"That is a very disturbing image!"

"It is, isn't it? Quick, think of something else!"

"That isn't difficult." His eyes dropped to the swell of her breasts, the curve of her back, as he spun her a slow spiral. "I do like your dress. You didn't answer my question about your underwear, or lack of."

"Maybe I am, maybe I'm not."

"I'd like to find out. May I?" He smiled that rare, irresistible smile.

"Not unless you want to lose a hand," she smiled back, aware they were being watched by an awful lot of people.

"It would be worth the sacrifice." He moved his hand slightly on her waist, and slid two fingers under the fold of soft material. Her grip on his shoulder tightened, her expression warning him not to do anything else. "Easy, tiger. No harm done."

"We might be in a ballroom in front of all these people, but I wouldn't hesitate to put you on the floor," she whispered, and he knew enough was enough. He knew she would. He sighed and moved his fingers to where they had been. He felt the tension in her hand decrease; he also wondered if anyone had noticed the momentary intimacy that had sent the blood rushing to his nether regions. Had she felt the same? They danced in silence for a few moments, and he hoped he was doing okay. He was no Harvey, but he knew his way around a simple waltz.

"Very nice cocktail, by the way. Stop by anytime and make another."

"You're only hoping I get you drunk and take advantage," she derided, narrowing her eyes.

"Of course. Anytime. Anywhere." His smile was impish and irresistible, and she was taken back to when they had been at another party, a wedding reception, with the waves on one side and the palm trees on the other.

Taking a breath, he addressed the real issue he had wanted to broach through his segue in conversation, inwardly praying she would listen.

"What you did today, getting up into my penthouse, I would like you to promise you won't do it again. I know you're very capable – I saw

– but it's not safe. O'Grady can't protect you when you're doing things like that, nor is it impossible that something might go wrong. None of us want to see you hurt, let alone anything worse."

Mysty could feel the intensity of those eyes even though she didn't look up at him; and she could hear the seriousness in his voice. She knew she couldn't refute the truth of what he'd said. How did he always make her feel so…responsible? How did he have so much power over her?

"Even you?"

"Even me."

"Why?"

"No one makes me laugh like you do." That had clearly surprised her, for her eyes came up to his. "No one else has ever made me breakfast, either. Or told me off like you do. Or helped me with my emails. One day you might start believing you're as special as…I think you are. Promise me you won't take those sorts of risks anymore."

"Or what?" She held his gaze, and saw real concern there. "I promise," she said when he didn't answer, compelled more by the lack of threats than anything else he could have said. In that split second she realised he didn't want them to go back to those old ways of dealing with each other; in truth, neither did she.

"Thank you."

The music came to an end.

"Thank you," she said. "For Megan. I couldn't believe it when I saw her. You really…" She looked at him. He knew what was coming.

"Didn't have to? I think I did. I don't like the horns and tail, you know."

Realising they were still in hold but the music had stopped, she slid her hand from his shoulder, and he removed his hand from the warmth of her waist.

"I do believe you've removed your mask," she said quietly. "Welcome back, Daryl, it's good to see you again."

And then she reached up and kissed his cheek, lips as soft as a butterfly's touch. Just for that second he smelt her fragrance; it was light, flowery; something he recognised but couldn't quite place. By the time he had registered all these things, she was gone, and he caressed the line of her spine, and the curve of her shoulders and neck with his eyes. He watched as Charles came to greet her, kiss her cheek and draw her away, handing her a glass of champagne as they walked. But she turned back, for a brief second, and their eyes met. And then she was enveloped by the crowd of guests.

She had kissed his cheek. Such a simple, chaste thing. But the most significant thing to have happened in the entire time he had known her. Her words echoed in his head. Was there hope, yet, for them?

"SO, HOW WAS Charles?" he asked when she was seated. He had tried to speak to her last night and found out from OG she was indisposed because she was having an early dinner with the secretary of state… But not only this. While he had been out of the country on business, she and Harvey had had another dance session. He was impatient to speak to her properly, but kept his tone casual – as much as he could – determined not to ruin the fragile progress they had made on the dancefloor by losing her trust with a badly judged comment.

"Very well. In good spirits."

"And what, may I ask, do you two need to discuss in such detail? You were thick as thieves at the party…"

Her brow lowered at the pointedness of his questions.

"I don't know why you can't have a little more faith. Why do you always act as though I'm disappointing you?"

A waiter appeared and took their drinks orders, quietly, discreetly, as was fitting in the exclusive club he had chosen for their rendezvous.

"You've never disappointed me in your life. Worried me, but not disappointed me. And as someone who has witnessed some of your more unpredictable moments, I am at a loss as to what you need to discuss with the secretary of state."

Pausing, she absorbed his answer, and seemingly judged it acceptable as she explained: "It's more Julia Jefferson I'm talking to now – the culture secretary – but there are various things I'm also discussing with Charles, and then he speaks to the relevant people on my behalf."

It seemed it was her turn to be deliberately vague…

"And why are you talking with the culture secretary?"

She looked at him, obviously trying to decide whether he was genuinely interested or annoyed. He hoped his face showed the latter and not the former.

"Because I persuaded the president and Julia that it would be a brilliant idea to buy the old Harlem concert hall, where MJ started, and the surrounding buildings. They came up at auction, and are in dire need of refurbishment, but I want to turn them into a museum of Michael Jackson's career and my tribute tour, which is still breaking download and sales records. It will be a benefit to New York in terms of tourism, and a place of pride for the US to pay tribute to their star."

She paused to give him the chance to comment, but he didn't.

"As you may know, most of the items from the tour are in storage – the original costumes and parts of the sets, as well as the new bits I had built. These will be displayed, and the staff will all be dressed in character, showing off his work and mine. There will be a small auditorium showing many of his old videos, and some of mine, and there will be interactive sessions, where people can try on the costumes or learn some of the dance routines. It will be great for kids on school trips. I've also suggested talks on how the special effects work, both then and now, and we'll schedule recordings of his interviews. We want to preserve as much of the original building as possible, but some parts need to be rebuilt in line with health and safety regulations. The designs are all coming together, and I estimate it will be about ten months until opening night."

She waited again, finding it hard to read his reaction.

"And you're the architect of the project?"

"Essentially, yes. I'm being left to design the project as I see fit. I have free rein and a generous budget."

"And in return?"

The waiter returned, and with a small bow left them to enjoy their drinks.

"I have a half share with the state as a financial enterprise in which I am the directing force. Well, just over half, at fifty-one percent."

It was a noteworthy undertaking, to be sure; but the fact that she'd obviously bargained for a majority share... She was no fool. She was a visionary and a businesswoman. He was impressed.

"Some of the profits will go towards the dance foundation I mentioned before," she continued, "the details of which I have drawn up already and will be ready for you tomorrow."

"I see."

"You're not angry, are you? I started talking to Charles and Thomas about it when...when we weren't speaking. And then you continued being so horrid that I didn't want you involved."

He considered this and it made sense, sadly.

"No, I'm not angry at all. I'm impressed. It's an excellent idea. It will be a landmark of creativity for many generations to enjoy, and as an idea it is quite typical of you, for all the best reasons."

"Wow. The mask is clearly still off. Now it's my turn to be impressed."

"Only for you. Can't have everyone else thinking I've gone soft. My stocks and shares would plummet and I'd be bankrupt by dawn."

"I've got plenty of money – apparently – so you can have that, start over," she laughed.

He was surprised by the offer, and touched by the easiness of the words. Was she really that generous?

"You do have plenty of money. Even more than my estimates for this financial year after the unexpected video release..." She bit her lip and covered her eyes with a hand, wishing the intensity of his green eyes would lessen. "And the catalogue comes out on Friday. There are already over three hundred thousand requests in the US alone, and we upped the price to sixty dollars."

"Sixty dollars!"

"You're not cheap and, frankly, considering the quality of those images, that is a bargain. Porn magazine sales are going to hit a new low over the next couple of months, is my feeling."

"No doubt this prediction comes from personal experience."

"Of course. I had to test the theory."

"You are joking?"

"And I can afford as many copies as I like, so laminating won't be necessary." She groaned, remembering her outburst at the first shoot. He laughed. "I am joking, yes."

"Maybe I should get you in front of the camera. We could see who sells more copies."

"I think you'd win, hands down."

But she wasn't giving up. "I'll be your photographer. I want to boss you around, for once. And I promise you can have as many women in the shots as you like – there, how could you refuse?"

"No, really, I don't want that to happen."

"No? What even with your cherries? They'd get you in the mood, surely?"

"No."

"Are you going shy on me?"

"If you dared, you'd find out. I'd even let you sleep over."

She didn't comment. She knew how quickly he dismissed his women once he was finished with them. Did he mean that?

"Anyway. What were we talking about?" she said.

"Your catalogue."

"Ah, yes."

"Just imagine how many wives and girlfriends will be asked to wear what you're wearing. Did you know sales of blonde hair dye and black shades have gone up?"

"I don't believe my life sometimes…it seems so crazy."

"Well, start believing, and start enjoying it too. Imagine how many kids would love butterfly or pirate queen wallpaper, and duvets, and pillows and curtains?" What a brainwave! How had he not thought of that before?

"I am not a cartoon," she told him firmly, scowling.

"No, but you are larger than life."

"I need some time off."

"Okay. So, I'll offer you a few hours off. Would you come to see my new cars with me?" He was holding his breath to hear her answer, which turned out to be a question: "You're actually asking me?"

"Yes." Her smile of confirmation was all he wanted. "It will be after the summit, so not just yet."

"Wow. Okay."

"How is the summit preparation going?"

"We're almost there. The dancing is quite challenging, and we're rehearsing in costume now – and they're an art form in themselves."

"I expect to be amazed."

"Oh you will be. I hope you've got some other locations in mind for repeat performances."

"I've been thinking about that, yes. When I've seen it we can decide the best use of the show for a wider audience." He paused, watched the smile of surprise at the word 'we'. "How is dear old Harvey? I've not spoken to him since Sunday." He watched her again, searching for clues in her face for any feelings she might have for his friend.

"Fine, as far as I know. I saw him on Monday for a dance lesson. I think I wore him out! I don't suppose there are many women who can claim to have done that whilst being fully dressed."

That was a relief to hear her light-hearted comment, and there was nothing in her tone or look to suggest she was lying.

"I trust he's behaving himself…?"

"I think he knows what would happen if he didn't. Please don't worry about it. I would never have agreed to teach him if I didn't think he could handle himself."

"Good. But I meant what I said on the plane after the White House experience. No one, and that includes my friends, ever get to mistreat you in any way. Whoever they are, I will deal with them, agreed?" He was aware, however, of how those words could be thrown back at him, given how he had treated her…

"I'm not arguing, but you really don't need to worry about Harvey."

"You like him, don't you?" He had a very thin layer of ice to navigate in order to get a few answers, and did not want to appear jealous or in any way mistrusting of their friendship.

"Yes, I do. When he's not being an arrogant chauvinist he's very good company, and he makes me laugh, which I like. I seem to spend far too much time being as serious you at the moment."

"Impossible," he dismissed, making her smile. "Is there anything you need?" he asked.

"What do you mean?"

"You still only have a personal allowance of $500 a week. Is there something you'd like or need that costs a little more?"

"Not that I can think of. I saved up to get a piece of jewellery made."

"What was it?"

"A necklace."

"Are you wearing it?"

"Yes."

"Can I see it?"

She seemed to accept his nosiness and leaned forward and pulled a chain from round her neck, holding it out for him to see. He took it in finger and thumb, feeling the heat in the metal from where it had been resting against her skin. He guessed it was tinted platinum, in a warm golden colour that complimented her skin and hair. Two columns of letters connected as one – 'ec' and 'es' – in a slightly abstract design. It was interesting, and obviously a piece that meant something to her.

"I didn't know you liked Latin?" he said. In his mind he saw 'ecce' and 'esse' – the Latin verbs for 'to behold' and 'to be'.

"It's not Latin," she said softly, not wishing to embarrass him.

"Is it a symbol for something?"

"No."

"Then what?"

"It means alpha and omega, to me anyway."

"That's a rather cryptic answer."

"It's private." Mysty answered firmly, not giving ground. But then, "I'll tell you if you tell me why you didn't marry Rachel."

He rather liked the way she'd played that. "I'll tell you one day."

"Ah, yes, the mythical 'one day' when all will be revealed. Let me know when this might happen and I'll equip myself with a chisel and two blocks of stone and stand on a hilltop somewhere."

He had to smile. "How irreverent."

She smiled back, then frowned, like clouds covering over the sun. "So, when…"

"Yes?"

"Nothing. I was being nosy."

"No, finish your question."

"When did you…find out you'd lost your parents?"

He could see the apology in her eyes for having asked, anticipating him being angry at the intensely personal question. But she was just trying to understand, he could see that.

"They disappeared, on a vacation for their wedding anniversary… on the ocean on their favourite yacht. I was notified within an hour of their disappearance. Everyone in the security surveillance team thought it was a malfunction. It was too bizarre to be real. The search continued – divers, sweeps, radars – until every inch of the ocean for hundreds of miles had been combed. Nothing. Some parts were so deep, but I didn't let anyone give up, I was so sure they'd be found, or my father would have some incredible fail safe somewhere and come home demanding why we'd all been wasting time. But it never happened. Certain people spoke to me and tried to help me realise that…they were gone. It didn't sink in, though, and I still kept thinking my father would come striding through the door, annoyed I was sitting in his chair handling his businesses, as best I could.

"A collection of lawyers came to read the will." He paused at the memory; the day a part of him had died, smothered under the weight of so much. "Everyone wanted the succession from father to son to be as swift and as unproblematic as possible, for the obvious reasons, and my father had anticipated that. So, sooner than expected, I became…the second Mr Blackmoor."

He was surprised at the bitterness in his voice, remembering the sudden, huge responsibility of everything; the media, appointments, meetings, expectations, pressure; the fame, the women, the attention, the loneliness… Almost ten years of his life had gone by, and most of it had felt like one endless business meeting.

He dared look up at her and found her just as she had been, beautiful eyes waiting for his, held captive by his story, by the rare glimpse into the man behind the mask.

"I've never liked calling you that," she said. "I much prefer Daryl."

And there it was, the softness so missing in his life; the comfort of a few simple words, unexpected but so full of meaning.

It was time to leave, and he knew he'd need to wait a while yet to hear the story of the necklace. But he had all the time in the world for her.

"I'm very glad I'm not Satan anymore."

"If you were honest, you'd admit you deserved the horns and the tail at the time."

"Perhaps."

"There's no 'perhaps' about it. I can see you smiling, you know I'm right."

"Your boyfriend is going to have his work cut out with you."

"Well, if he needs any advice I'll send him to you to get a full breakdown on how *not* to behave!"

"And what if he's rubbish in the bedroom? You want me to give him advice on that too?"

"How would I know if he was rubbish?"

Shit. The words were in the air before she'd been able to stop them. A deep blush suffused her cheeks, and in the deafening silence of her own embarrassment she stood up, eyes fixed on the floor, hoping it would open and swallow her up.

"Mysty…"

"I'm going home."

And she was gone, to be replaced by Mac, who looked impressed. "Thirty-five minutes," he observed.

"And she didn't swear at me once."

They took this as some kind of achievement, and strolled to the exit, OG and his charge already en route.

"I look forward to the day you both get into the same car," Mac said as he stepped into his Bentley, feeling more relaxed than he had for a while.

And somewhere, in the wishful thinking, there was a small gleam of confidence that maybe one day they would.

DARYL STROLLED DOWN the stairs and greeted all the familiar faces, some of them old friends of his father's, most of them business associates, the rest part of the elite family that formed the wealthy echelons of his world. Most would be looking forward to Mysty's arrival – although some of the women might be hoping otherwise; or those who disapproved because they didn't quite know what to make of her – and he knew it was because they couldn't resist her beauty or her smile.

"Harvey." Harvey turned instantly, offering his hand, looking relaxed and handsome. Daryl couldn't help thinking that his oldest friend was now a rival, not just a fellow roué. "You're wearing…a coloured shirt?"

"I am. Any objections?"

"No, it's just…unexpected. Any particular reason?" He had to admit the deep-red suited his friend.

"Mysty gave it to me. Apparently, I earned it for having done so well with the tango. 'A shirt with flare' she called it."

Daryl controlled the spark of anger and smiled. "Interesting. You must have really swept her off her feet with your dancing."

"It took some work, but we got there," Harvey commented lightly.

"Maybe she was just being kind. You can't really have learned that much in just three lessons," Guy accused, looking doubtful.

"Was it ballroom-style tango? Because even I know that, and it's not so hard," Robbie threw in, and Harvey glanced at them all. Robbie, Zack and Guy, although they hadn't admitted it, were similarly jealous of her favour towards him.

"So you all think I'm too clumsy to learn real tango! Thanks very much."

"I'll give you thirty grand if you can prove you have," Daryl said smoothly, challenging Harvey with a look that confirmed he meant it.

"I'm in, too," Robbie said.

"And me," Guy added, and looked at Zack.

"It's worth a laugh, at least. I'm in," Zack confirmed.

Harvey laughed. "I'll take you on. All of you. Provided she agrees.

And she and I will split the winnings between us, and I'll take her out for dinner while you mourn your stupidity."

"Where is she, by the way?" Robbie asked.

It was a perfectly timed question as there was a slight stir, and then silence fell across the room.

Daryl cursed himself, and then cursed Harvey when the man made it to the bottom of the stairs before he did. And dammit if she wasn't wearing a dress the same shade of red as his shirt.

"I'm afraid, my dear," he said, as he led her into the room, "this group of strutting charlatans don't believe you taught me to tango, properly. Between them, they have bet $120,000 that you've been easy on me."

"Easy on you? Leaving you breathing harder than a blown horse dripping in sweat with a ripped shirt?" Her eyes met Daryl's, and he was looking far from amused. Great, the mask was back. "Well, it's easily fixed, though I would like to have glass of champagne first," she said. One was instantly brought for her.

"I proposed that we split the money and I will take you out for dinner to celebrate their lack of faith," Harvey dared to add, mighty relieved that she agreed.

"Take off your jacket, Harvey. One of these fops can hold it for you. I'll go and inform the musicians we need something suitable for a tango."

"Daryl, there's a good chap," Harvey said.

He got no reaction from Daryl, who was too infuriated to speak at the sight of his handsome friend looking so toned, and even more good-looking, in the shirt so perfectly tailored to fit, so he hung the jacket over his friend's shoulder, and then walked after her, aware people were looking over, wondering what was about to happen.

The group took up position to watch, and the dancefloor cleared.

Mysty looked at Harvey, and saw his eyes were unsure, his smile unsteady. She saw him glance at the gathered guests.

"Harvey. The musicians are ready."

"Mysty, I don't know if this is such a good idea. Everyone is watching," he whispered, the confidence in his face from only a minute ago now gone.

"Did you not think they would?" Was Harvey backing out?

"A few but…not everyone. I don't think I can do it."

"You're more than capable. I wouldn't have agreed otherwise." She saw his expression go from uncertainty to terror. She was not happy. "It's funny, isn't it? All you men, you're so arrogant and, actually, when it comes to it, you're all spineless. You're only good for one thing, and it's something animals do just as easily. I don't know why I thought you were any better."

She turned away, and was glad when Harvey caught her arm and turned her to face him. Hard. Anyone who wasn't already watching the intriguing clash between the dancers had wandered over to the edge of the dancefloor, where bright stormy indigo moved with dark sapphire-blue.

"Changed your mind?" she challenged, raised eyebrows mocking him, daring him, feeling his body react to her, the tension in his face and muscles exactly what he needed to begin the passion of the dance. Once again, his blood began to run hot and fast. It had been just what he needed.

"I didn't deserve that."

"Roll your sleeves up. You're going to get hot."

He obeyed her, and she prowled round him, arousing the passion further, knowing she had to make him focus on her, not the crowd.

He was ready, his eyes on hers. Perfect. She reached up, pulled a ribbon from her hair and tossed it away. Golden curls fell loose over her shoulders, and she raised her chin, clicked her fingers…and the music began.

Slow, seductive, passionate, the lilting sounds of the violins controlled the rhythm that so suited their mood. They prowled round each other for a few seconds, neither closing the distance, both with arms ready, eyes never leaving the other; and then Harvey took her arm, spun her around, fast, and placed his hand, firm and possessive, against her belly. She lay her head on his shoulder for a single moment, and then they began. The footwork was complex, interwoven with twists and turns so fast and intricate they defied belief. Harvey moved her, pulled her to him, pushed her from him, his hand on her thigh, on her neck, bending her to brush his lips a millimetre from her skin, the harmony of their moves matched only by the intensity of the eye contact, the body contact.

Daryl ground his teeth. Every second of their superb performance was torture.

Harvey couldn't believe how it felt, this rush of…energy, desire, pride, hunger. His eyes went to her lips, wanting them, and then back up to her eyes, knowing she was watching him, their breath laboured, their bodies tight. Her hand felt so right on his cheek, her fingers on his neck, as they held the final move and the music exploded its finale.

Don't kiss me here, not like this, the eyes warned, as the room erupted into applause.

And suddenly they were laughing, bowing, leaving the dancefloor, his hand raising hers in honour of her teaching.

"I'll be damned," Guy muttered. "You really can dance. I insist on being taught next."

She just laughed and shook her head. "I'm not teaching anyone else for a while. Maybe get Harvey to teach you. One of you can pretend to be the lady!"

Harvey unrolled his sleeves and refastened his cufflinks. "Best money I've ever earned," he said, recovering his breath. "I believe you owe me, boys." He turned to Daryl, held his hand out for his jacket, and was silenced by the look that said, *You and me, in private, now.*

Seeing the look, Mysty decided it was time to beat a retreat. "I'm going to find a drink. I'll see you all later," she said, glad to get away from the ferocity in the green eyes.

"You hate me, don't you?" Harvey muttered as he and Daryl left the rest of the group to stand in a quiet corner.

"Very nearly." Daryl growled, doing his best to keep his face neutral and his body language composed, not used to feeling so incandescent with rage for his own best friend.

"Shall I make myself scarce?"

"I think that would be a good idea, for your future health."

But Harvey smiled as he walked away. It was about time his friend had to fight for something he wanted, and a bit of competition never hurt.

MYSTY LEANED ON the balustrade, happy to be watching everyone else for a change. So many dances, and so much talking…

"So, you're hiding up here."

She looked around. His eyes weren't as angry, but neither did they look very friendly, and they stayed fixed on hers.

"You know I don't hide."

"True. Are you alright?"

"Just a little tired. I need more practice at…all of this. I don't know how you do it." She gestured at the ballroom, and the throngs of laughing, dancing people.

"I find not doing the tango usually helps conserve some energy."

"It was one dance, just a bit of fun. I wasn't going to let him be mocked by all of you when he'd put so much effort into getting it right."

"You know Harvey likes you."

His anger had faded, but he needed to say it; dammit, he needed to know how it had felt, how she had felt.

"Harvey likes any woman with a pretty face, Daryl, just like you do."

"I think he likes you a little more than that. He would marry you, if you said yes. He would be quite devoted to you."

She looked at him sharply and narrowed her eyes. "What *do* you men talk about? Has he said something? Or are you stirring? I'm seventeen – a little young for marriage, don't you think? And why would I marry someone like Harvey? For what? A year? Two years of being his favourite plaything and then he has too many drinks one night and ends up in bed with someone else, goes back to the way he is now, living life to the full as a bachelor. I want more than that, Daryl. I deserve more than that."

"I see." It was a huge relief to hear her say that. But was it true?

"Don't say that as if you understand, or care. You're just as bad. Whoever your Mrs Blackmoor ends up being she's going to have to be very understanding of your…affliction."

"Maybe a wife would be the perfect solution, for the affliction. So, despite my affliction, may I ask you to dance? It won't be as racy as a tango, but another waltz perhaps?"

She looked at him, saw the mask had slipped a little again. "It would be rude to refuse such a polite request. Of course you may."

They fell easily into the waltz, but Daryl sensed her nervousness at his touch, and possibly a little uncertainty, too, because he had ignored her all night. He was reminded of Charles's admonition to not ignore the prize filly.

"How about you teach me the tango?" he tried, seeing the alarm in her eyes.

She looked away. "I don't think that's a good idea, do you? Aside from which, you don't have the time. The lessons were hours long, and intensive, and your schedule is made up of ten million different appointments from here until eternity."

"I could make time."

"No."

"Why isn't it a good idea?"

"Because."

"Because what?"

"Because I said so."

She glanced at him. Why was she so hesitant to teach him? Because she didn't know what she would do if he touched her the way Harvey had?

He grinned at her, despite the disappointment of her negative answer. He would persuade her somehow.

"So, if I successfully master the tango under your expert tutelage, one day, when you're ready, will I get a shirt too?"

"Don't think I can't see what you're doing. I'm not agreeing to anything. Why don't you quit harassing me and find your wife and concentrate on making babies? That should keep you distracted for half an hour, at least."

"Are you volunteering?"

"No!"

"But I already know you'd make an excellent mother." He was referring to her love and commitment to the leopards.

"I would make an awful wife!" she growled back, praying no one could hear them.

"I know, but I would overlook that for the sake of the children."

"You hypocritical, arrogant son-of-a… Like your wife wouldn't have to overlook a hundred million things in you, on an *hourly* basis."

He could take so much and then no more. He stopped them in the middle of the dancefloor, and before she could escape used Mac's strategy of lifting her into the air, but in the guise of dancing.

"Daryl!" she hissed, smiling for the people. "Put. Me. Down."

"Not until you apologise." His hold was steady. She wasn't going anywhere.

"What for? Telling the truth?"

He twirled her around. "You're not helping yourself."

"Trust me, neither are you."

"Have you any idea how tempting it is to turn you upside down and shake you?"

She went very still. "That's not a good idea."

"And why not?"

"Because…I'm not wearing any underwear."

It took him a second to register the words, another to put her down, perform a last swirl of waltz, smile to the onlookers, and stroll off the dancefloor, her hand firmly in his.

Pretending nothing was amiss, Daryl got them both another glass of champagne, but Mysty sensed despite the drink the conversation was far from over.

"Are you really not wearing any underwear?" he demanded the moment they faced each other again, and away from prying eyes and ears.

"None of your business."

"I think it is. You can't not wear underwear, Mysty."

"Why not? Who on earth would know?" Of course she was wearing underwear, she had only said it to get him to put her down.

"Hopefully no one. Unless you want someone to find out! Who?"

"Daryl. I was joking. Of course I've got underwear on. What do you take me for? I wanted you to put me down and stop making a spectacle of us out there!"

She had played him. Just like the time in the car, pretending to see blood. This time however, she couldn't just jump out and disappear.

"Fine. Prove it."

"What?"

"Prove it. Show me."

"Please can you hold my champagne, then?" she asked sweetly, reaching down to grab the hem of her dress. Dutifully, he took her glass, leaving him with two glasses and no free hand.

"Mysty, what the hell are you doing?"

There was a defiant gleam in her eye. And before he could react she'd reached for the zip on his trousers with her free hand and pulled it down. She slid two fingers inside, just as he had under the fabric of her dress when they had danced the first time. He had been played. Again. And he was hard, in an instant.

"Oh, very cute – the DB in gold, with gold trim, very tasteful." She smiled brightly, slid the zipper back up, and took her champagne glass back. She then strode away, but turned. "Oh, and Daryl, as you can see, matching." She flicked up the hem of the dark red dress, revealing black lace with a fine gold trim, the curve of her buttock gorgeous. And then she was gone.

"Daryl."

Daryl swung around. "Charles." He forced a composed smile, and prayed the man didn't look down just at that moment.

"So, she and Harvey are getting on well."

"She doesn't feel anything for him, so I'm not worried by their friendship or their dancing," he said, pre-emptively, and the older man eyed him curiously, pausing to choose his next words.

"You set rather a few tongues wagging with your picking her up on the dancefloor like that, and then bringing her out here."

"Let them wag. It has to start sometime and, frankly, I don't really care."

"You're right there."

He needed to change the subject. "Mysty told me about the MJ project, in Harlem."

"Good. I thought she would. She's not one for secrets. She's also agreed to look into the government databases as I have it on good authority – not just yours – that she is rather advanced in her programming skills, etc. She said she's too busy to do it right now, but she will when she has time. We would greatly appreciate it if she found time sooner rather than later." Charles's eyes told Daryl that the 'we' included the president, and no doubt the defence secretary and others in charge of national security.

"Have you agreed a price? I'm not having her do that for free, despite what she might have offered to do. She's far too generous sometimes." Daryl eyed Charles speculatively, but he only smiled.

"No, we haven't agreed anything. When I asked her she said I would have to take it up with her manager." Daryl's look gave way to a wide smile. "I'm hoping you won't put the government in state of poverty."

"I think I can be a little more reasonable than that, Charles. When she has a better idea of what she has to do I will discuss a price with her. I can assure you, though, having had her redesign and upgrade my databases and all the firewalls – which are as yet unbroken and nowhere near being so – what you get will be well worth the money."

"I have no doubt. Nor do I want to overload the poor girl. It is hard to remember sometimes she is only seventeen. She seems so much older and wiser. Not in her face, but… Where does she come from?"

"A long way east. She's had to be a responsible for herself since she was nine – and one might argue even earlier than that. Her story is… not a happy one. Being taken in by Donny Capello was a turning point for her, but she won't talk about much of it, as I believe the memories of losing her family are too traumatic for her."

"So sad. She's such a lovely girl. You'd never think she'd been through all that, would you?"

"No. Mysty always defies the odds, and expectations. No doubt she will do so again at the summit."

"Yes. I can't wait. I know the president is looking forward to seeing her…he wants to make sure there are no hard feelings and all that."

"Despite her temper she doesn't hold grudges, and she is remarkably forgiving when presented with an honest apology."

"Is that so? Sounds like you're speaking from experience?"

Daryl refused to look at him. Why did he talk so willingly about her? He must learn to stop doing that. "Why don't you ask her?"

"I don't think I need to. Thomas and I have a private bet going."

"On what? When the wedding is?"

"No, the first child. Fingers crossed it's a boy, but I'd like to see a few miniature Mystys running around, wouldn't you?"

This time Daryl did look at Charles, and the man gave him a wink – and strolled back into the ballroom, leaving him alone with that tantalising thought whirling through his mind. But not for long.

"Sir?"

"Mac? Anything wrong?"

"No, sir. Just to let you know that Mysty has gone home. It's late, and she said she has an early start tomorrow."

"Make sure O'Grady keeps her away from the studio tomorrow before leaving for Vegas. She needs more rest."

"Will do, sir."

"What are you smiling about?"

"Both of you talk about the other one overworking, yet you're as bad as each other. I could suggest the perfect solution…"

"Trust me, Mac, when the time comes I will explore that solution to the full."

"Shall I get the cars?"

"Yes. I've had enough."

He saw the looks cast his way as he left from women who would happily entertain him for the remainder of the evening. One or two he had sampled, but he felt no inclination to take them up on their silent offers tonight.

He took one last sip of his champagne, and then handed the glass to a passing waiter, intending to head up to the balustrade where Mac was waiting to escort him away.

"Mr Blackmoor?"

"Miss Fleurette. I trust you are well." She was wearing a full-length white gown, her glorious red hair piled in curls on her head.

"Yes, thank you. And yourself?"

"Perfectly fine. I was just leaving. Is there anything the matter?" He hoped his tone had made it clear she was not to waste his time.

"No, not at all. I just wanted to say…" Her eyes fell away. She looked a little thrown, obviously deciding it had been a foolish impulse to speak to this forbidding individual, and who – much to her relief – was now thoroughly disinterested in her. "I just wanted to say how lovely Mysty is. Far lovelier than I imagined she would be." Eyes came back up, and saw a friendlier pair looking down at her. "I hope you will be very happy." With a curtsey she moved away, not giving him a chance to respond, not waiting around to see the surprised lift of his eyebrows.

Daryl nodded a goodbye to Harvey, with whom he could not stay annoyed, and left, already looking forward when he would next see her. However soon it was, it never felt soon enough…

HE EXTRICATED HIMSELF from the dull conversation that had gone on for far too long and wandered off in search of Mysty. Where was she? He'd not been able to travel here with her due to a last-minute conference call, but he hadn't seen her since catching a brief glimpse on arriving – and her look had silently screamed *Get me out of here!*

This party was not like the other. This was a showbiz bash, not just for the rich, but for the rich and famous. There were singers here, and actors and actresses, as well investors in the industry and managers in the industry. He'd wanted to give her a few warnings beforehand, about how to be around these people, but there hadn't been enough time. They were partying on the entire roof of one of the high-rise Manhattan buildings, with a pool and fountains; and drinks flowed as eagerly as the conversation, everyone trying to find out the latest gossip or build bridges with those who could further their career, all dressed in the most ludicrously expensive 'casual' outfits money could buy.

He should be able to find her, despite the crush of people, dressed as she was in gold and purple tiger stripe leggings that showed off her gorgeous legs, a purple satin halter neck top and gold heels.

He patched a call through.

"OG."

"Sir?"

"Do you know where Mysty is?"

"No, sir. But I've received no instruction that she wishes to leave as yet. Is there a problem?"

"Only that I can't find her – anywhere. Try and locate her for me."

"Yes, sir."

Disconnect.

He was glad when he spotted Harvey.

"Daryl."

"Harvey. How are you? No tango tonight?"

Harvey smiled benignly. "No, it's not the done thing to win so much money from one's friends twice in a week."

"You haven't seen Mysty, have you?"

"No. I can't find her either. I…I heard some people talking. I don't think she should be left alone."

Daryl felt the unease seep into his body like poison. "What do you mean?"

"Some of the boys here, they seem to have something going on that I don't like the look of. Lex Huntley seems to be involved–"

Daryl stared at him. "Lex Huntley!"

"Yes. Alexander Huntley. Rachel's brother."

"I know who he is! O'Grady, have you got her yet?"

"The building's structure is making a trace hard. The satellite confirms she's inside the building, but pin-pointing her is taking longer than we hoped. We're switching to a trace-scanner."

"Call Mac. We have reason to believe someone is planning something – Lex Huntley. Start sweeping every room in the building for her. And get his face up on the recognition system." He searched the crowd, hoping for a flash of her hair, the task distracting him from the rising sense of foreboding. Instead of Mysty, he saw Robbie coming towards him. "Robbie, have you've seen Mysty?"

"I saw her talking to that weasel Huntley just a few minutes ago, which surprised me considering what he said to her last week. He was pretending to be friendly from what I could see, and ordered her a cocktail, but his smile was as false as his sister's breasts."

What? How did Robbie know that? He walked over to the bar, trying to appear relaxed, and saw a barely touched cocktail on a mat.

"What is this cocktail?" he asked quietly, the barman going still, watching as his drink became the focus of so much attention.

"Screaming Orgasm, Mr Blackmoor sir. A gentleman requested it for Miss Reverie."

Daryl bent down and sniffed it, instantly suspicious and afraid.

"Harvey. Smell this. Does it smell normal?"

Harvey screwed his face up. "No. I've drunk enough cocktails to know that much." He offered the glass to Robbie for a third opinion, and he concurred.

"Have this taken and tested. Get every bit of information from it you can," Daryl ordered, handing it to one of the suits with finger and thumb. "OG, Mac, have you got anything yet?" he whispered, desperate to avoid attracting attention.

"Nothing. We're working our way down the building."

"We think her drink was spiked. I've sent it for testing."

He heard OG curse. Even someone as able as Mysty would be powerless if she had been drugged.

"We'll help look," Harvey growled into Daryl's ear, perfectly aware of what might happen to her, or what might have happened already.

Daryl nodded and turned, his head low, his mind awash with ideas and the huge gaping question of 'what next?'. It felt ridiculous. So much security, a tracker, and they still couldn't find her! And then he saw it. A snake of broken silver shimmered. Harvey and Robbie watched as he walked a few steps and bent and picked something up off the floor: a small ring; nothing spectacular, yet full of meaning for one particular girl…a girl not known for dropping anything, let alone something so precious. All of his instincts came alive; the adrenaline kicked in and the predator was awake. His girl was in danger and he wanted to find and smash to pieces whosoever it was that had dared touch her.

Turning, he saw a door marked 'Authorised Personnel Only'. He pushed through it, starting down the stairs, Robbie and Harvey charging down behind him. It made sense. Whoever had her would take her where no one would look, and somewhere where they could make a quick getaway. Lex Huntley. Of course. This was revenge for him dumping his sister.

"Mac! OG! I've found her ring. We're heading down the service staircase. Get the sweep on the lower floors. Tell them to look out for any part of her clothing she had on tonight."

There was a chance, a slim one, that Mysty had deliberately taken it off, hoping someone would find it. She might have done the same with her clothes, to leave a trail. Oh God, how he hoped that was the case and not…

All three men continued to storm down the stairs, searching, peering down the stairwell, fast legs unable to move fast enough. Nothing felt enough. Someone had vomited into a corner, and God…a gold shoe another flight down. Hers. Daryl didn't know whether to rejoice or not. At least they were on the right path. Another five floors and they hit the basement, and Robbie pointed: the other shoe, the strap broken. They left it where they found it and went out through the doors, into the underground parking lot, millions of dollars-worth of gleaming cars in rows upon rows.

"If they've taken her in a car…" Harvey gasped, and they ran, looking for an empty space where a car may have recently departed, all three turning left and right. It was like being in a nightmare, a maze…but then eyes found each other, exchanging a split-second of hopelessness. But Daryl refused to entertain failure. No!

"OG! Get the cameras up in the basement. Take them back twenty minutes–"

"Sir, we have her!"

Daryl came to a standstill, and his companions ground to a halt. A door on the far side of the lot was flung open and Mac and OG appeared with a large number of the security detail, OG calling through to Baden. The horrible fear, the dread, rose up to engulf him again; but he moved towards them, needing to know.

"Sir."

OG passed him a handheld, and he forced himself to look at the screen, Harvey and Robbie breathing hard behind him. She was on the floor, knees bent under her, hands just about holding her up. A man he recognised looked down at her, and he was not wearing the charming, easy smile used in polite society.

"Oh God," Harvey whispered.

"Where are they?" Daryl demanded, spinning around to see OG and Mac go to a corner of the parking lot, start scanning and searching what appeared to be a solid steel wall.

He heard a scream and looked back at the screen as Lex crouched down, took a handful of hair and pulled her head back.

"Well, you are even more beautiful in the flesh than you are on screen, and much more beautiful than my sister. Not surprising you caught his eye, is it?"

"Please just let me go."

"Let you go? When we've not even started having fun yet? I don't think so, sweetheart."

Daryl thought she might collapse. He couldn't watch this. Had to watch this. "Do something!" he yelled. "Do something for God's sake!"

She hunched, and vomited, coughing and choking as her body tried desperately to eject more of the poison.

"Oh dear, we can't have that, can we. And after I've gone to such special efforts to meet you." A cloth was wiped over her mouth in an insulting parody of concern, and tossed aside. She was then pulled up and shoved onto a chair.

"O'Grady! Surely you have an override for the door? Why can't you get in?"

"They're in a safe room. It's locked from the inside and they've initialised the panic mode. We need to get in there quietly. We don't want him to–"

"Fucking blow the thing up!" Daryl roared, raw emotion overriding logic.

"Sir, he might kill her…"

"We've got a bet going that two of us can fuck you at the same time. Might even try three of us. Put that pretty mouth to a good use too, hey? Not many virgins get to have such an exciting first time…" Lex started to undo the buttons on her top.

"Who is the 'we'?" Harvey whispered. "Are there others on the way?"

Daryl couldn't even contemplate the answer to that.

"You're more than beautiful, though, do you know that?" Lex continued, voice harsh but full of relish, enjoying his chance to lecture her. "You're a freak, and you're a nuisance. Do you know how many people's singing careers have suffered because of you? America and the world think you're wonderful, don't they? Well, I don't. I hate you. And I hate your manager as well. You know he almost married my sister, don't you?" She nodded, her eyes rolling from the remainder of the drug he had given her, and Lex grabbed her jaw, clawing his fingers into the soft skin as he lifted her face to look at him, trying to force her to focus on his face. "After what he did to her, I don't think I'm going to let him have what he wants from you. And this little concoction is going to make you unrecognisable. I'm doing the world a favour. You're a *freak*. You don't belong at our parties. You need to be put down, before you multiply." He pulled a vial and a syringe from his pocket and waved them in front of her eyes.

"I didn't even want to be famous," she murmured, her eyes tracking the bright pink liquid in the vial.

"Well, too late now, isn't it?"

"Don't. Please don't put that in me!"

"Trust me, sweetheart, when we've finished with you, you'll be glad you're brain damaged. Half of this will be enough for now. The rest will finish the job."

"I'll do what you want, just don't…don't do this!" There was a yelp of panic and she leaned away, fighting him in the only pitiful way she could by raising weak hands that did nothing to stop him.

"We'll get you doing what we want, anyway. Here's to losing your virginity and your marbles, beautiful. It's going to be one wild ride."

Daryl's endurance was up. As if in slow motion he turned in time to see Mac and OG pull out their guns. Time for stealth had run out.

Inside the room, she screamed and struggled harder, managing to push away hard enough to fall out of the chair and away from Lex, creating a brief window of space. It was the whisper of a chance, but the best chance they were going to get.

Eyes shouted the words, and as bullets ripped into the door lock and control panel, Daryl lurched forward to grab and pull. Every muscle in his body felt primed and ready, something primitive awake in his entire being, leaving no room for doubt, for fear. In a curious mixture of slow-motion detail and fast-forward speed, he was through and in, subliminally aware of others by his side.

Caught completely unawares, Lex had no time to react as Daryl grabbed the man from where he was bent over, handfuls of neck and belt strap, and threw him against the wall like a ragdoll. In the next second a fist mashed into Lex's belly, and when the man fought to stand, there was another fist waiting to smack into his face to put him back down on the floor. Winded, bleeding and broken, Lex Huntley was left staring at the shiny footwear of the man he had come to hate with a loathing that went bone-deep.

In the deep silence that followed the storm of righteous violence, both men watched the vial fall from a weakened hand and roll away. Daryl felt himself sag with relief to see that the lid was still on and the lurid liquid still inside. *Thank you, God.*

Approaching from behind, OG reached down, wrapped a handkerchief around it, and picked it up, handing it to a member of his team for safekeeping for what would come next. He went to Mysty, wrapped his jacket around her and held her close.

Another member of the security detail stepped just inside the door.

"We've caught three more arriving to *join* Mr Huntley, sir. We have them detailed and secure outside."

Three. Which would make it four.

All eyes on were on Huntley as the news was delivered. The noiseless, collective sense of disgust becoming so strong it built, pushing against the concrete walls around them, building towards another expression of force, demanding action.

"You bastard Blackmoor!" Lex snarled through broken teeth. "You deserve to lose her, you fucking arrogant shit! I know what you did! You treated my sister like shit, you bastard!"

"What's in it?" Daryl asked, ignoring the accusations, holding up the vial, nodding to Mac, who was happy to take over and put his own rage to good use. While his boss watched on, the ex-military man easily dragged the man up and put a fist into his gut, doubling him up. His mouth opened and closed like a landed fish as the pain stole his breath, but the gleam of hatred still shone in his eyes. As Lex straightened, weakened but not ready to give up the fight, Mac pinned him to the wall with a slam as Daryl asked again, "What's in it?" his eyes as steady and ruthless as a snake with its prey trapped and ready to meet its fate. "You have five seconds."

No mercy, was the message Lex got. He judged it time to give up, not liking his chances against Mac's spade-sized fists.

"It's an enhanced dose. Class A drugs, with some other stuff! I'm not a chemist!"

"No, you're a fool," Daryl said, tempted to inject the contents of the vial into the man. "Mac. Have Mr Huntley charged with everything you can think of – possession, assault, kidnap, attempted murder, attempted rape – and make sure the newspapers know about it by morning. And get some blue lights over here. Make sure the commissioner knows what's going on."

"No! Don't do that! It'll kill my parents! They'll disown me! You have the power not to do this! Think of something else!" A desperate hand reached for Daryl, but he stepped away, wanting to go to her, not spend a single second more of his life in front of this despicable man.

"You do this to her and you expect mercy? Everything you intended for her will be your own fate."

"No! God, no!"

Daryl turned and went to her, knelt down next to her. OG moved away, and he put his arms around her. "It's going to be alright. You'll feel better soon." She vaguely nodded, eyes blinking at him, pupils still dilated. "We'll get you home."

"OG, are the cars ready?"

"Yes, sir."

Daryl stood, and scooped her up as gently as he could, her head lolling against his shoulder.

"Get her back to Lazarus and Lula, and have Baden look her over immediately. I'll see everything finalised here and then I'll be with you."

OG nodded. And took her from him.

Daryl turned to find Robbie and Harvey looking very pale. It could have been a body being loaded into the car. They all knew that.

"Sir. You might want to see this."

Daryl didn't think he did from the look on Mac's face, but he went anyway. His stomach turned over.

"We confiscated it from the three arriving to join Mr Huntley."

From the outside it was an innocuous designer gym bag. On the inside, there were whips, handcuffs, chains, leather straps for restraints, ropes for strangling and equipment for suffocation, a drill, and hooks for the wall – a sick display of pre-planned intent. There was even a box of smelling salts of some kind, to bring her back to some kind of consciousness if she'd found escape through drug-induced oblivion.

She must never know about this.

"Jesus Christ," Harvey muttered. They'd all experimented with some of these items, with consenting other parties, but to use them on an innocent girl. His face was one of utter disgust.

"Get everything catalogued. See what else we can have them charged with," Daryl said.

Mac nodded, understanding perfectly.

"They'll only get light sentences, if at all…" Harvey sighed, sickened even more by the idea of such injustice.

"I'm going to make some calls. Believe me, I'll make sure they suffer." Daryl's eyes told Harvey not to say anything more. "I'll call you both tomorrow and let you know how she is. Until then, if you could give your statements as witnesses, and then stay away from the press that would be appreciated."

He walked away, a light show of blue dancing around him as the NYPD arrived en masse to fill any tarmac space with their boldly striped cars.

Fingers dug deep into his pocket and held the small metal ring. Close. Too close.

FROM HIS OFFICE at home he kept the live update from her apartment running all night. He wasn't going to regret making this decision, but it was the first time he'd had to make such a direct call and it surprised him at how willing he was to make it. Who did they think they were dealing with?

He pressed the button.

"Donny."

"Daryl. Unusual to hear from you at this time. What's the matter?" Donny's face was clouded with concern. "It's about Mysty, isn't it?"

"I'm calling to ask you a favour. You and Sebastian. You'll guess what it is before I finish my recounting of tonight's events."

Daryl saw Donny's face tighten slightly, and knew he had part guessed already. There was only one thing Daryl would need to ask of two mob bosses.

"Just tell me. Don't leave anything out." Blue eyes bored into him, all the more intense for wanting to know what had happened.

Daryl took a breath and began the narrative. And he didn't leave anything out.

"I'm going to crucify him, all of them," Donny snarled, face a mask of fury, knuckles whitening.

"Not all of them."

"Why not?"

"Because it would look suspicious."

"But Lex?"

"Yes. As you will hear in the video file I can send you from security footage, part of his motive was my treatment of his sister. But there is nothing unusual about the fact I broke off the engagement after finding out she cheated. I sent her back to Texas and asked her to never contact me again. My only guess is she lied about how I treated her and he had his reason for revenge."

"Anything else?"

"Fame. Money. Popularity. I don't know precisely how many others were in on it, but apparently people's careers are suffering because of her. He also called her a freak and that he ought to put her down before she multiplied."

"So what exactly do you want?"

"At the moment they've all been arraigned and charged – and no doubt they'll all get bail at some extortionate sum they'll have no problem paying. I want Lex to think he's safe. Wait until the trial starts, which I will make sure is soon, and then everything can be staged to look like suicide, that the shame of disgracing his family was too much to bear. The rest of them? They will stand trial and be sent to a particularly unpleasant institution – I can arrange that too – where they will experience the debasement they planned to exact on her."

"Nothing less than they deserve."

Daryl was glad they were reading off the same page.

"You must realise why I can't do this, but I don't expect it for free... whatever you want–"

"I don't need money. I'll make this happen, and I know Sebastian will agree to help without hesitation. They never met, but he respects Mysty and knows what she is to me. Save your money...for better protection."

Daryl did not miss the loaded tone of that statement. "O'Grady is never more than a few feet from her, so how Lex got her away...it was a party for God's sake...I thought she'd be...I'll send you the file." The remorse was evident.

"You look like shit."

"I'd say that's a pretty accurate description. Donny...how are you?"

There was a long pause. "There is nowhere lower for me to sink than where I am right now."

"Don't say that. I don't like to see you like this. And she would hate to hear you say that."

"Take my misery as a lesson, Daryl, as to what your fate will be if you fuck this up with her." Donny glanced at a computer screen to his right. "Thank you for the file. I'll watch it and make the arrangements."

"Thank you."

"I'm not doing it for you."

"I'm thanking you for doing this for her. You want me to give her a message?"

"What message can you give her that she doesn't already know? Just send me the feed for her apartment so I can see her for a week. I'd like that. I want to know she's okay."

Daryl paused. How did Donny know about the cameras? It was probably an educated guess, but a correct one, and he was in no place to deny it. "Of course."

"One tip, Daryl…don't let her find out they're there because she'll be furious. I had them installed in her apartment in Vegas and she found out. It wasn't good."

"I've no intention of her finding out. It's for her safety and my peace of mind. Nights like tonight worry me."

"I realise. My reasons were the same. How are her nightmares?"

"Not good recently. Any advice?"

"Company. She never has nightmares when…when she sleeps with someone next to her."

It made sense that that was the case. "I'll look after her, Donny, you know I will."

"As much as I want to hate you for it, and I might have had my doubts, I believe you."

"I'll be in touch."

"I'd appreciate that."

Disconnect.

Daryl dragged a hand over his face and looked at the time: 2.30am.

"Mac?"

"Yes, sir?" Mac appeared in an instant.

"I'm going over there."

There was no surprise on Mac's face at this announcement.

HE HEARD BADEN say something to her in German, as he stood in the doorway, and she replied in kind. He smiled, and left her curled up under the bedcovers.

"Well?" he asked as they stepped out into the hallway.

"Fine, except for dehydration and a residual weakness from the type of chemicals used. By some miracle she has escaped any lasting damage, though I'm going to advise that she has trauma counselling. O'Grady, you must make sure that she eats."

"Yes, sir," O'Grady said, and Daryl nodded as the man gathered his coat and left.

He glanced at her. She had been joined by the leopards, both laying as close as possible. "That is the best news we could have hoped for," he sighed, pausing a moment to register his relief. "O'Grady – despite whatever she may argue – she is to rest tomorrow. If she wants to go to the dance studio, that's fine, but not until the afternoon and only for a short time. Clear?"

"Absolutely, sir."

"Please, stay with her tonight."

"Yes, sir."

Daryl started to walk away.

"Daryl?"

He stopped at the sound of her voice. She was standing in the dim hall, her head against the wall.

"Why are you out of bed? How are you feeling?" he asked, going to her, unsure what to do but wanting to hold her so tight. "Please get back into bed."

"Strange. I feel like I'm watching everything, like I'm someone else, still. I couldn't do anything. I had no strength…" Her voice was weak but there were no tears.

"You might be amazing, but you'll still be affected by drugs like the rest of us. None of it was your fault. I should have noticed. I should have got to you sooner…"

"But you did notice. You did find me."

"It shouldn't have happened; I won't let it happen again."

"It's not your fault." She looked at him, trying to reassure him. One of the worst moments of her life and she was still trying to reassure him...

"You are my responsibility." He corrected firmly. "You were still smart enough to leave things for us to find you. I found your ring." He pulled it out of his pocket and reached for her hand. "Edith's ring helped save your life," he said, and slipped it gently back onto the middle finger of her right hand. She watched him, and it was then that her eyes filled with tears, and too many thoughts for a tired mind crowded in. "Go back to bed, please." He gave her her hand back, reluctantly, and she turned and went back into the bedroom and climbed into bed. "I'll come and see you later today."

Daryl, Baden, and OG waited until they saw her settle back in bed, and then closed the door. With heavy hearts they left, a guard stepping up to stand by the door.

IT WAS HARD to believe the day was finally here – the largest gathering of such influential people for a decade – and security was sky-high, to the point of paranoia. The event was due to start at noon, and would continue for another twelve hours, with breaks in between.

He knew her show would be spectacular, but he was concerned for her. The revelations of the attack, and the perpetrator, had triggered a deluge of requests for interviews, but he had made the necessary statements for her, refusing to let her face the cameras herself this time. Thousands had turned out to show their disgust at the men who appeared in court. They'd had death threats and offensive mail, and had needed police protection; whereas her fan mail had soared, and thousands of messages of love and support had appeared on social networks.

Douglas Huntley had tried to persuade him to drop some of the charges against his son, and had hurled accusations at him about Rachel. It transpired the whole family was convinced he'd done a lot more than cast her off after she'd cheated on him – she really was an expert liar, it seemed. Douglas's attitude had changed somewhat when Daryl sent him a recording of what his son had done inside that room, and he retracted all requests for leniency. He had three other children whose positions in society he wanted to protect, and declaring war on a man against whom he could not win for a son who was clearly very much in need of correction wasn't something he was willing to do.

"Daryl?"

Daryl turned quickly. "Charles? Time to go down?"

"Yes. Everything is ready. The president will be arriving in a few minutes."

Daryl nodded and headed to the door, knowing the arrangement was for him and Marshall to lead the gathering into the two-tiered oval auditorium. The seating plan showed no particular favour to anyone, which had been her suggestion. Equality in all things as far as possible. He also did not want to be seen as wholly affiliated with the US government, as he had too many global considerations, and had only requested the specific company of Harvey, who had an honorary invitation in an advisory capacity. The ceiling had recently been heightened, so the acoustics were improved, and it felt like a room of space and light waiting to be filled with debate and discussion – and music and colour, the magic he knew she specialised in.

"How is she?" Charles asked.

"Doing a very good job of keeping it all together. I would like her to talk to someone, as suggested, but it's the one thing she won't do."

"One day she might. Perhaps she's waiting until they're locked up? I can imagine knowing they are still free must be unsettling for her."

They reached the private lift, Daryl flanked by Mac and two grey suits, and Charles with his own security, as silent statues.

"Yes, in a month they should be where they belong." Or dead.

"Thank God you got to her on time…"

"Believe me, Charles, no one is happier than me about that."

The older man saw the remnants of tension in Daryl's face, and a depth to his eyes he had not seen before. They stepped out of the lift, seeing hundreds milling in the auditorium, and he put a hand on Daryl's shoulder. "The question is, Daryl, does she know that?"

The multi-billion dollar question. No, she probably didn't.

Charles gave him a warm smile, however, and they went to greet

Marshall.

But Daryl paused for a moment, not quite ready to join the crush of people, and tapped in a call. "You've checked on her, O'Grady?"

"Yes, sir. She's okay, except she's decided she was mad to have agreed to do this for you."

Daryl smiled instantly. That sounded like her.

"Tell her to get her manager to take it up with me," he said, and Mac grinned.

He saw the Iranian dignitaries as he traversed the wide hall, and made eye contact with the man at their head, who he knew would be sent the moment he had allowed her to handle the call back by the pool all those months ago. The man gave him an imperceptible nod and Daryl returned it with an inclination of his own, and almost a smile. They were there to build bridges; he might as well make the most of that.

And then a large beefy hand was offered, and his elbow clasped at the same time. The president seemed in a very good mood, and he had every reason to be. The stage was set, and he was making history with this event – thanks to Daryl's organisation. Everyone had arrived safely and the twelve-hour event would open a week of discussion and negotiation.

"Daryl."

"Thomas. You're looking well."

"A miracle, considering!" Thomas was always supremely cheerful about his workload and the huge responsibility that came with the job. "You can't complain, either, by the looks of you, despite this latest… debacle."

"I would have used a far stronger word…"

"How is she?"

"Physically, she's fine. The rest, time will take care of."

"And you too, I hope," Thomas said with a small smile that Daryl couldn't resist returning. It felt so good to hear the kindness in the president's voice, wishing him well.

"That's the plan."

"Excellent. Shall we go in?"

Daryl looked over at Mac, who conferred with someone in a low tone and then gave a nod.

The doors were opened from the inside by two figures dressed in livery from about four centuries ago, in rich dark blue, cream and gold, complete with long spears. They stood to attention, eyes to the front, and Daryl enjoyed the murmurs of appreciation around him. All heralded well for the next twelve hours.

WHATEVER THEY HAD been expecting, what he saw was far and away beyond anything he'd ever witnessed, and far too good for there to be a moment of boredom or tiredness. When he'd mingled during the breaks he'd heard only compliments about a show that had dazzled from the opening bars of Handel's 'The Arrival of the Queen of Sheba' to Beethoven's 'Choral Symphony' to close. No country had been left out as the artful choreography blended tribal dancing from Africa, salsa from Spain, and the traditional dances of the Orient, Russia, Indonesia, India, in costumes the colours of which filled the auditorium as dramatically as the music itself. These were interwoven with classic ballroom, sensual Latin and mesmerising ballet. Their eyes had met, just once, when she had risen from a deep curtsey at the end of Elgar's 'Pomp and Circumstance', bedecked as a queen, gems sparkling under the myriad of lights.

Moments from the Olympics, photos or film footage from treaty signings, and times aid had been delivered to countries in need after a natural disaster had been merged with images of previous landmark summits and world events, the moon landing, and some of her own performances – notably the Fortuna jump, which prompted new gasps of amazement. It was a showcase of optimism and pride; of what humankind could achieve when it put its mind to it.

And when it was done, they were gone, like a conjuror's trick. A little bit of Mysty magic to end the show, as if she had signed her signature across the air in gold, as she had before at Celeste. The thousands of airborne lights dimmed and then brightened and gathered to form a spiralling globe, sixty-eight countries highlighted in a different colour for each of the sixty-eight representatives present. 'Summit – 2026' rotated in the centre in gold.

Wow.

Daryl looked around and saw the same feeling mirrored on every face. All had been reminded and encouraged by the glimpses of historical greatness, of the world as one living, breathing thing, and they now had a chance to be a part of history for future generations as the summit unfolded.

He accepted the warm handshakes of those eager to congratulate him, because she wasn't there to take the praise just at that moment, but told each and every one that she had been the architect, the genius, behind every single second of what they had seen.

Finally free, he patched through to O'Grady and was led backstage. He sat down as slowly and gently as he could at the other end of the sofa she was resting on, taking in the resplendent costume, the tumble of curls and the feet tucked up next to her.

"No one ever tell you not to disturb a sleeping tiger?" she said sleepily, her eyes closed but sensing it was him.

"No."

"Well, now you know." She yawned, stretched and opened her eyes to look at him. "So. Did you like it?"

"No." His face serious for all of five seconds, but then he laughed.

"You swine," she said, and used the last vestiges of her energy to whack him with a cushion…that he tossed away. He took her hand. It was trembling.

"I'm joking. It was brilliant, from start to finish. Every minute. When did you last have something to eat – proper food?"

"This morning?" She wasn't sure, if she was honest.

Daryl put a call through, keeping it on speaker.

"O'Grady, make sure there is some tiger food at the apartment ready for her."

She raised her eyebrows at him. *Tiger* food?

"Yes, sir. Any requests, Mysty?"

"You can pick something. You know what I like," she said.

"You got that?" Daryl asked.

"Yes, sir. I'll get the cars out front in ten minutes."

"You are taking tomorrow off. Okay?" He instinctively reached out and rubbed her foot, affectionately, keeping his hand there. It surprised him, the simplicity of the gesture; but it surprised him more that she didn't withdraw it. "If you don't, there's a forfeit."

"Oh really." She didn't sound bothered, and leant her head back on the cushions, eyes closed.

"Nude photoshoot on my desk."

Her face didn't flinch. "That's not so bad. It's big enough to get comfortable, and you're not there this week, so probably the best time to do it."

"I would insist on being there."

"Of course you would."

"So, no working tomorrow, okay?" he persisted, knowing what she was like when it came to overwork, because he was just as bad.

"Yes, boss." She opened her eyes and gave him one of her cheeky salutes. "Have you ever done it on your desk, in your grand office in the sky?" she then asked, her head tilting to one side in the cute way that he loved so much.

Was this a genuine question? If so, it deserved a genuine answer.

"No."

"No? I'd have bet money on you saying yes."

"It wouldn't really work, would it? People are there nearly every hour of the day. Imagine if someone heard something…and then imagine the headline: 'Blackmoor's *Hard* Day at the Office'!"

"But you'd risk having *me* naked on your desk?" Her eyes were merry, and twinkled in the low lights.

"Of course."

"I think I've shocked your staff enough."

"After you brought into question my ability to father children, I don't think there's much left to say or do. Go ahead, shock whoever you like."

"You deserved that."

"Possibly. Maybe."

She laughed as he hedged.

And then they realised they were back to being how they'd been holiday. They could almost be sitting by the pool again, and the mutual, silent realisation kept them quiet for a few moments.

"You're going to be very busy this week, aren't you?" she then asked.

"Yes, very."

"I would like to go back to LA for the week, even just for a few days. I…I want to go home. Would that be okay?"

"I'll get the jet organised for Wednesday. You can soak up some sun. Come back next Monday?" He'd already cancelled Celeste so she could have a proper rest and was pleased he had. He also wanted her out of the city, away from the men who had yet to have justice meted out to them. "Then you can tell me where and how you want to use this show."

"You'll let me do that? Tell you how I'd like to do something?"

"Don't let it go to your head." Green eyes slanted towards her, but her amusement was undimmed.

OG stuck his head around the door. "Cars are here, sir."

"Time to get you home," Daryl said. He stood up and, without asking permission, scooped her up, easily lifting her despite the gown.

"I need my shoes! I'm not meant to take the gown home!"

"You don't need shoes if your feet can't touch the floor, and you can take the gown home."

"You know if you carry me out of here you're going to be on the front of every newspaper tomorrow."

Daryl hadn't planned to pick her up, but it felt so right, and when they emerged into the cool night air, his security cutting a swathe through the tumult of press and cameras, he didn't shy away from the lenses or the flash bulbs, As Charles had said, people would talk, and it would have to start sometime. Why not now?

He felt her grip a little tighter onto his lapel, an unconscious gesture, and he liked it.

Setting her down by the car, she looked like a barefoot queen, and she looked up at him, her eyes bright, curious of his behaviour and the statement he had chosen to make.

"Be good," he said.

"Why? So I can save being bad for when I'm in LA?"

"No. Save that for when you're on my desk."

The tickle of his breath on her cheek as he bent to bid her goodbye, although his lips never actually touched her skin, sent a tingle down her spine nonetheless.

Turning to get into the car, she flashed him a look. "Give your crystal ball a shake, Daryl, it's been lying to you again."

His smile didn't fade as she delivered her retort, with a regal incline of her head, before disappearing into the car. He nodded to the man he trusted to guard over her in his absence. "Take care of her, O'Grady."

He waited patiently for the convoy to move off and for his own transport to arrive, Mac and his men close by.

One day…one day they *would* get into the same car.

SHE AWOKE AT 6am, as she usually did, and the two leopards looked at her expectantly, as they always did. So much for my attempt at a lie in!

"What is this? Grand Central Station?" she asked, when she eventually dragged herself out of bed and into the kitchen and saw the huddle of men.

"Almost. And we have lots of newspapers," Mac said.

"We also have lots of food," OG added.

"Join us?" Daryl asked, his eyes flicking to the paper.

What was he doing there? Shouldn't be on his way to the summit?

She saw the look. "What's wrong?"

"Nothing. It would appear the world thinks everything is…very okay."

She wandered over. Three of the five newspapers had a similar picture of Daryl carrying her out as they'd left last night, he looking handsome and distinguished, she looking beautiful and happy still in her final outfit – a magnificent, purple gown that made her glow brightly under the lights and flashbulbs. The headlines read, 'Who Tamed Who?', 'Beauty Steals the Show,' 'Out of This World…Again', 'Long Live the Queen', and lastly 'A Stellar Double Act.'

"You weren't joking," she said. "Are the news channels just as bad?"

"Just as bad? That's funny!" Mac laughed.

"Tamed? I'm not tamed in the least!" She picked up the bacon sandwich OG put in front of her and took a bite.

"A few presents arrived," OG said, gesturing.

She looked over at the pile of parcels. "Presents? Why?"

"Congratulations and admiration. And you have lots of flowers, including some from the president and Charles. I've put them in the living-room."

She went to the door. "What on earth am I going to do with all of those?"

Daryl laughed, and her eyes went to his. "Looks like you're all ready for a busy day," she said, taking in the immaculate suit and polished shoes.

"Yes. It'll be non-stop, all the way through. You need to rest, though. Agreed, OG?"

"Agreed."

"It's okay, guys. I might go back to bed. Have a Jacuzzi…watch a movie…" Her sideways glance at Daryl told him what she was doing: her pleasantly lazy day was far preferable to the intensity of his.

"Careful, your cruel manager might find some work for you."

"He's not that cruel."

"No?"

"No, he's more like a teddy bear." Mac had to stifle a guffaw, and OG looked away and pretended to cough. "Useless in a bar fight. Can't cut pizza for shit. But good for babysitting leopard cubs."

"How is it, then, if I'm a teddy bear, I don't get any hugs?" He took what he hoped looked like a casual sip of his coffee, and shot a glance at OG and Mac, who left, recognising the silent command.

"Hugs? When have you ever hugged anyone? And haven't you got a summit to go to?" she said, unable to hide her bemused look.

"I think I need a hug before I go."

"Really."

"Yes. In fact, I might just have another coffee while I'm waiting." Pouring himself another cup, he pulled a newspaper towards him, trying to look as relaxed as possible, refusing to meet the eyes that bored into his forehead.

"You'll be late. There are hundreds of people waiting on you!"

"I know."

"You are impossible!"

"I'll accept the promise of a nude photoshoot instead, if you'd rather?"

"When hell freezes over."

"Fine…a hug, then, and a promise to teach me the tango. And maybe I should relax and have a Jacuzzi, too, before I go." He pushed his cup away, and stood and started to undo his tie.

"Daryl!" Her voice halted his progress, and his hands dropped from his tie. He couldn't believe the effort he was going to just for a hug, but he couldn't help himself. "Fine. You win. Nice blackmail." He shrugged, unrepentant. "I hope you display better forms of diplomacy at the summit. I don't think blackmail will go down so well with the powers there."

"Most people are won over by my brilliant rhetoric and amazing charm. It's you who resists."

"With such modesty, I can see why they can't refuse you."

"Sir." Mac poked his head around the corner. "We need to leave." He ducked back out of sight.

"Well. Time for my hug." He slid his hands into his pockets, green eyes expectant.

"You're out of practice. Hands out of pockets, Mr Important."

Laughing, he did as he was told. Yet all the joking, and all the cajoling and hopefulness, hadn't prepared him for the moment she seemed to gather her courage and step closer to him. She reached up, on tiptoes, and put her arms over his shoulders; and, after a moment of hesitation, he slipped his around her, greatly surprised at the easiness of the action.

And it was then that the strangest discovery occurred: she didn't want to let go. It felt so good. She liked the smell of him, and she liked the strength in his arms. It wasn't like a hug from OG, and not like one of Donny's hugs, either – how would she ever forget those? – it was just comforting, and somehow safe. And not in the least bit sexual. Her heart pounded. Was his? How was he feeling? Hugging was something she'd *never* seen him do, let alone request?

She pulled away after a few moments, but he held on. "Any chance of a good luck kiss, for today?" he dared, a cheeky grin spreading across his face, and as she drew breath to chuck a hasty rebuff at him, he rested his fingertip against her lips. "Peace, tiger. When will you realise that sometimes you don't need to fight…?"

He released her, and with a piercing look from the green eyes that always unravelled her, he was on his way.

There were moments with him that felt so, so right… What on earth did that mean?

"YOU KNOW, IF you marry and have children you'll get paternity leave," Mac said when Daryl arrived at the car, the prospect of the long day ahead creasing his brow.

"Then you should start convincing her that's a good idea," Daryl threw back.

"Not in my job description," the big man replied.

"I just added it."

GOD, SHE LOVED being back in LA. So much more space and light – and no press waiting outside the door every minute of every day. She turned on the TV while she ate breakfast.

"*So, Danny, it appears that our talented golden girl has been affected by the attack at the party a weeks ago. Yesterday, for example, she practically ignored the cameras, and there was no real greeting when she flew in. Do you think our daring star has taken a serious blow to her confidence?*"

"*Well, Lisa, it makes me sad to say that I think you may be right. In New York these past few weeks we've barely seen her. She's been very busy, and the security around her has been tightened, as we've all witnessed, but so far I'm not seeing the same open, outspoken girl.*"

"Wow…" Mysty said, her spoonful of cereal suspended in mid-air.

"*We're guessing she's not here for very long, from what we can gather from our press teams. Do you think she's being pressured into returning to New York? Do you think it has anything to do with her relationship with her manager? Things have obviously thawed between them…*" Lisa asked.

"We all know how controlling her manager is. He's also not the type to countenance any disobedience – certainly not from a girl he has worked so hard to bring to the world stage."

"I think it's safe to assume that the tussle – if you like – between them has been won by Mr Blackmoor. But, understandably, Mysty may be traumatised by the experience at the party involving Mr Huntley, who is now awaiting a court date, so is it any surprise she has bowed under pressure? Is it any wonder she has become quite reclusive of late? No one has seen her, and we've been waiting for a while now…"

"Bowed under pressure! Reclusive!"

She looked out of the window, and then marched into the computer room and hacked into the satellite feeds on the vans parked outside the security fence.

Wow…was she going to make their waiting worth it.

She left instructions with Toby and went out onto the balcony. The bright hot sunshine was so welcome, as was the slight breeze. She turned on her shades, tossed her plaited hair over her shoulder and jumped. Seconds later she landed and ran towards the press vans, and heard the shouts as she flipped and landed on the roof of the first van. Slamming the sound box down, she hit the Play button and Green Day's 'American Idiot' blasted into the street… '*Don't want to be an American idiot, one nation controlled by the media…*'

She knew OG would see she was on the move, as her increased heartrate would trigger an alert; and there was no doubt she was going to get into trouble for this, but she ran anyway, pelting down the wide streets of LA's central district, using everything along the way as a prop to her speed – lampposts, mail boxes, car roofs – until she spotted her destination: the huge statue of George Washington, looking distinguished and wise, hands on the lapels of his long jacket. She bounded up the steps, bounced up the thirty feet to his head, and placed a pair of shades on his face, before dropping to the ground and taking off again.

Some of the reporters were on the move behind her, she could hear them, and leapt up onto the railings at the side of the wide highway, swinging across the overhead cables to the station. Balanced on the high wall of the bridge, she waited, and smiled. Man, she was going to give OG a heart attack, and as for what Daryl would say… She heard the train, and jumped, running effortlessly along the roof, carriage after carriage, until the next bridge, where she leapt up, somersaulting twice to land exactly where she needed to be: dead centre between two lines of traffic, braced in a crouch, head up, one hand down.

Hearing the roar of the engines and the growl of tyres of tarmac, she felt the heat and smelt the fumes as she performed one of her favourite moves – using the cars as stepping blocks back across the huge roads. In a perfect arc, she hurtled back to where she had started, flipped back onto the roof of the van and hit Stop just at the tune came to an end.

"Good morning, LA!" she cried and, before anyone could respond, scaled the high security fence once more and strolled back to her building.

She was surrounded in moments, and OG slapped the other half of a set of cuffs onto her wrist.

"Oh come on, OG!" she said, seeing his face and pulling at the cuffs that shackled them together. "I've been a perfect angel for weeks. I was gone less than five minutes!"

But she was whisked through the doors, past the reception desk and into the lift.

"I don't give a fuck!" OG yelled. "Got that, Miss Smarty-pants?"

"Please don't get so upset. They called me a recluse!"

"I don't give a fuck! God knows how many times I've nearly had heart failure in the last year of my life. And God help me get through the next seven!"

"It was just a little run."

"It was not a 'little run'!"

"I knew what I was doing."

"I don't care about your calculations. What I saw was reckless and dangerous. You are grounded!"

"What? Till when?"

"Until lunchtime."

"But I wanted to go to the rink this morning."

"You should have thought about that *before* you decided to do your gazelle-down-a-street impression."

"What if I promise not to do it again?" Mysty held her breath, and saw him think about it.

"And make me dinner tonight?"

"And make you dinner. Whatever you want."

"Fine. We'll leave in an hour, and you'd better be as good as gold otherwise these are going to be featuring once more. I won't stand for it." He lifted their cuffed wrists.

"I promise." She knew the anger was fear speaking, and knew it had been a little reckless to do what she'd done. "I wouldn't have anyone else look after me," she then whispered, which surprised him.

OG sighed, pressing in a call. "Mac."

"OG?"

"Just to warn you, the tiger was on the loose for five minutes. It could very well make it to the news. If he sees it, make sure he knows she's fine and has promised not to do it again."

"On a scale of one to ten, how bad?"

"I'd say a good solid eight."

"Oh, something worth watching then. Don't worry, I'll handle it. She okay?"

"Yeah. She didn't appreciate being called a recluse. How is the boss?"

"Wishing he was in LA."

Disconnect.

"You know one day, when you have kids, and they start doing reckless things and drive you nuts because you worry about them, do me one thing?"

She looked round at him. "What?"

"Remember today and call me and say, 'OG, you were so right.'"

"Sure. Like I'm even having kids."

"Oh, I think you will. At least four. My crystal ball is very accurate."

"At least four? Are you serious? Don't think I want to go through that pain more than once."

"Women forget that pain as soon as they hold their baby in their arms, trust me, otherwise they'd only ever have one. It's also how they put up with asshole husbands so well. They have high endurance levels for stupidity. Without those skills, the population would be declining and the divorce rate would be through the roof."

"But my body is super-sensitive. It's going to hurt like hell."

"Don't tell me the big daring tiger is afraid of pain?" he teased.

"Hell, yes! I am only doing it once, and that's *it*."

He smiled. *You just wait, kiddo. You just wait.*

DARYL CURSED HIMSELF for allowing her to go to LA for a whole week. He'd heard the stories of gate-crashed hotels, car rides wearing only bikinis, pool parties and being photographed with Mark Sorrell – the biggest male heart throb of the moment – in two of LA's swankiest bars, and shooting a *music video* with him? What was she doing? And was this a possible new romance?

But she would be here soon, the highlight of his day. He leaned back in his chair and closed his eyes. He was tired, so tired.

"Mr Blackmoor, I have Mysty and Mr O'Grady here for you."

"Hey Marlene, how are you?" he heard her say. "How did your niece get on with her driving test?"

"Hi, Mysty. She passed, and thank you for asking." Marlene's voice was upbeat – quite a change from the nervous introduction of previous visits. And how did she know about her niece's driving test?

"I'll be coming to her for tips, then, when I take mine – one day! Mac, how are you? You missed me, right?"

He heard Mac laugh and there was a pause, during which he could tell there was an embrace of greeting. "I hear Washington was gifted a pair of shades," the man said.

"He still has them!"

"Marleen, when she's finished hugging everyone else in the building, do send her in."

Daryl smiled, visualising the eye roll, and the door opened.

"Mysty. You remembered me."

"Just about. So much so I brought you a milkshake as a reward for getting through a week of being so serious and grown-up." The now-familiar drink was placed in front of him.

"You mean I really have a natural propensity towards being childish and funny?"

"No, but you played around in the pool on holiday, and watch football with the enthusiasm of a five-year-old, so yes, a bit."

"Don't tell anyone."

"Your double life as a non-suit-wearing loving teddy bear who needs hugs before work is a closely guarded secret."

Exhaling, he sank a little deeper into his chair, the relief at seeing her taking effect. He rubbed his eyes. He should have gone to LA, too, and had a rest.

"Daryl. You look tired. What are you doing tonight?"

He would have liked to have said he was taking her out to dinner, and then home, where he would very much like to… But right then? Just lie down with her by a pool, any pool, and chat like old friends…or even new friends.

"Nothing as yet."

"Well, there's a great jazz show over in the Village. Do you want to go?"

"Sure…"

But the moment's hesitation gave him away. "Do you not like jazz?" she asked.

"I could tonight." Just to be with you.

"No, you really don't like jazz, do you? I've never seen any in your music collection. So why don't you come to my club instead? Invite the boys. Have a night out?"

This was not how he imagined this meeting would go. He needed to brief her, before… "Your club?" he said, suddenly registering the suggestion. "What club?"

"It's in the Village. We have–"

"Since when have you had a club?"

"Since about a…month ago." She looked at him. Was he angry? "Opening night was two weeks ago. We've been packed every night so far. I thought you might have seen the reviews?"

"And what kind of club is it?"

"A dance club – with all kinds of dance. We specialise in cocktails. They're really popular." The pride was obvious. Her eyes were shining.

"And how did you acquire a club in one of the most sought after parts of Manhattan?"

"I kept some money back, from a long time ago," she confessed, and he gritted his teeth. "The rest is in a trust fund, with a trusted executor. It's perfectly legal, and I have no other money hiding anywhere. I also checked and it contravenes nothing of the contract that you made me sign."

"Who is the executor?" He thought about it. "Charles," he said. Trust her to be so efficient.

"Yes."

"You little minx."

"You wouldn't want me any other way. So? Will you come?"

"You want me to come?"

"Yes! I've been to your clubs enough, haven't I? Why not enjoy a night out at my expense?"

"A bit early to be risking your profit margins, isn't it?"

"I'm not doing it to make money. I opened the club to provide opportunities lots of people can only dream about. But it has rules and, so far, everyone has stuck to them. It is a drug-free, drunk-free, harassment-free, violence-free zone."

He had a feeling it would be the sort of place he'd never been to before.

"So, have you thought about what you're doing with your summit performance?" he then asked, taking a pull of milkshake and enjoying the sensation of the cool liquid sliding down his throat.

"Yes. I've sent all the details to you in an email. I've already scoped out the possibilities, so as soon as you say yes I can get started."

"Right. And anything on your debut album yet?"

"I've started it, but other things have taken up my time."

Like Mark Sorrell and opening dance clubs with rules…

"The party incident. How are you feeling?" he ventured. "Have you talked to someone? Even a little?"

"I feel…more like myself. LA really helped. You know, just being with friends. The pool party barbeque was great. I didn't feel afraid. I knew no one was going to spike my drink – how could they with OG standing a few feet away glowering! It helped erase some of the memories."

"Good. Though I'm insulted that I didn't get an invite to the pool party."

"I'll throw another when it gets warmer in New York. You get first invite."

"Thank you. I promise I'll accept," he smiled, but he knew a promise like that could end up being broken because of a meeting or a business emergency.

He glanced at the time. Right on cue.

"Charles."

"Daryl. And Mysty, my dear, how are you?" Charles kissed her cheek.

"I'm peachy. It's him you need to worry about. You've been overworking him!"

"Please, sit down Charles."

"It's good to see you."

Mysty excused herself, giving the secretary of state a conspiratorial look on her way out.

"Where are you going?" Daryl didn't remember their meeting being over. He didn't want her to go so soon.

"I'll be back in a moment."

"So, how are you?" Charles asked. "No wedding date yet?" His eyes twinkled.

"Sadly not."

She returned minutes later. "Marlene has rescheduled your two late meetings, at my request, so you can relax this evening." She looked at him with eyes that told him not to argue. "You're exhausted, I can see that with my eyes shut. And an early night is a rare gift, so take it."

Daryl was too tired to argue, and too stunned to commence a counter argument.

"Well, I never…" Charles didn't know what else to say. He'd never seen such a display of female assertiveness in this revered and hallowed office. He liked it.

"And now I must leave you two to it. I have an album to finish writing!" she declared, smiling widely, and, after kissing Charles on the cheek, left with OG in her wake.

"I'd say that was a sure sign of caring about you," Charles said gently, realising he had witnessed something unusual and significant.

"Maybe, being as busy as she is, she can understand better than most what it's like to be as busy as I am," Daryl said.

"You're right there. You'll get there, with her I mean."

"Not as quickly as I'd like."

"The best things in life can't be rushed, Daryl. She's very young. She's had her heart broken this year, too, and needs time to recover."

"You get on well, don't you? She told me about the club, and the trust fund."

"Good. I'm glad she did. And, yes, we do. She reminds me of my daughter when she was younger, all brightness and generosity. The club is different to any you'll be used to, but I think if you go you'll approve of what she's trying to do. And, frankly, I didn't hesitate to help her. You've been rather high-handed about your control of her finances, as with everything else." He shot Daryl a mildly reproving look. "She's certainly got some business acumen, so maybe trust her a little more?"

"I do. More than she thinks."

Charles smiled, and they left the subject alone to discuss the high points of the summit.

Despite the goodwill everyone had brought to the occasion, the data shared among the delegates was anything but good. The environmental impact of human expansion and industry was proving harder to stop, let alone reverse, than had been hoped. It was getting harder to paint a positive outcome to sell to each other, regardless of the proposals they put forward; and the growing tensions between certain larger nations was creating a new call for worldwide nuclear disarmament. Consequently, far from being able to focus on the economy, they seemed to constantly come back to outstanding issues that previous generations had left in abeyance, or decided were too difficult to confront, hence leaving them to the leaders of the future. But the buck could only get passed so many times. The future had arrived, and it did not make for an appealing proposition.

It was becoming increasingly obvious that the need for action, and drastic change, was becoming more and more pressing. Neither man felt like there was much to smile about by the time they got through their list of discussion points. They were long enough in the tooth to know that change was often the hardest thing for their particular species to accept – so many plates to keep spinning, so many mouths to keep fed, and jobs to secure – so how was it ever going to happen?

"*SO, MARK, HOW was it, making a music video with Mysty? How did it come about? We've not really seen you two together before.*"

Daryl swung around at the mention of her name.

"We met at a party and just got talking. We got on quite well, and I jokingly said I'd love to do a video with her, so she said we should so something, while she was still in LA. It's not like I was going to turn down the chance to work with her!"

"And what is she like to work with? She performs as a solo artiste most of the time, so how was it, the collaboration?"

"I was actually amazed at her skills. I've been on the scene for longer than she has, but she's so creative, and has such a grasp of what she wants and how it'll all work. I'm not going to try and take the credit for any of it. She directed the whole thing. A lot of people probably think that the person they see on TV isn't real, that she doesn't really do what she does, but trust me, she does it all. And she really is as genuine and friendly as she appears to be. I've worked with lots of people, and rarely have I seen people working so well together, and so happy with the result. It's a gift, what she has."

"Wow. That's a real endorsement."

"She worked really hard, every second, not ignoring anything or anyone. There was nothing too small or too big to be dealt with, and the results are there to see. I know she did a cover of '*California Gurls*', but we only had a few days, and she changed it so much. As an artist myself

I wouldn't hesitate to trust my music to her for a revamp in ten years."

"What do you think of the men facing charges for assault, attempted rape and murder?"

"They're sick men. She's a lovely person. Resenting her for her fame is wrong, and whatever motives they had cannot be justified in any way."

"So you'd work with her again?"

"I'd marry her if I thought she'd say yes! So, Mysty, if you're watching, consider this an official proposal! But definitely yes. If the opportunity arose, I'd jump at the chance to work with her." Sorrell smiled, knowing with those few words he was going to get himself a few headlines and send a frenzy of interest and speculation flying around.

"And to the people who criticise the fact she's only done covers so far?"

"I'd say to those people, be patient. She has had a unique rise to fame doing covers, but from her Celeste work, the MJ tour, and the summit performance, it's obvious she has the potential to write some of her own material."

"Did Mysty mention her manager in any way?"

"Not really, except to say he works too hard. I'm not sure what their relationship is, but it's certainly amicable. Beyond that, I have no idea."

"And just because I'm curious…all those people with the relish and melted ice cream…" Sorrell laughed, and Daryl's eyes widened. "Well, it looks real enough, but did you stage those bits?"

"They're real! Mysty went to a couple of hotels and checked with the management first, of course. The cameras were then kept on the people and their reactions. Same with the car going down the street with the girls on the roof. It was brilliant, and we had great fun pulling out the best shots. The two guys falling in the pool was great!"

What?

"And the shot on the plane?"

"I wasn't on the plane when she did that, but she really was on the roof!"

What?

"Wow! She's really determined when she sets her mind on doing something."

"She always wants what she does to be as good as it can be."

"Well it's a philosophy that seems to be working. Congratulations on the huge success of the video, and do let us know if she says yes to the proposal."

"I most definitely will."

You most definitely will not.

"Mac, are the cars ready?"

"Yes, sir."

The door at the back of the hangar opened and she appeared, OG just behind her, and a huddle of suits just behind him.

"Mysty."

"Daryl."

"No hug?" She raised her eyebrows. "Do you like the cars?"

"They are all beautiful. Which ones are yours?"

"Those five."

"Five? Two not enough?"

He got a waft of her scent – what perfume was that?

"I couldn't decide on the colour, and then I remembered someone saying to me once that why be me if I can't do the things I want to do?"

"That someone definitely speaks sense."

"I thought so too. And that someone has a date in front of the camera." He had been looking forward to this particular bit of the afternoon very much.

"I was hoping you'd forget that." She'd not been impressed when he'd mentioned taking some shots of her with the cars.

The door burst open and a number of guys came through, all hurrying and then collecting themselves, eyes half on Daryl, half on Mysty.

"Is this her, Mr Blackmoor sir?"

"Do you know anyone else on the planet as beautiful?"

"Wow! This is amazing. Would she sign something for us, do you think?"

Mysty looked at Daryl, who appeared amused by their childish enthusiasm.

"Mysty, would you sign something for Mr Lucas, the director here? And for some of the others, too."

"I will if they can get their heads around addressing me directly." She turned to them, over six foot in the heels, her beauty and presence clearly intimidating. "Who's got a pen, and what do you want me to write?"

Daryl let her scrawl on t-shirts, hats, caps, photographs, and even bare skin. By the time she was finished, and the elated bunch of males was on its way back to the door, he had his camera ready.

"Right then, princess. Make yourself comfortable on the car, the bronze one."

"Do I really have to?"

"Yes. I'll make it worth your while."

"How?"

"You'll see."

She rolled her eyes and strode towards the bronze open top. "How do you want me?"

"How honest do you want me to be with my answer?"

"Keep it relevant."

"You know the sort of thing…bend over it, legs apart…"

She sighed, and posed. "This is boring."

"You can do better than that."

"I'm doing what you asked me to do."

Daryl approached her, surprising her by moving up close, so close she could feel the fabric of his dark blue chinos against her bare legs. He slid his hand over her hip, and just under the white shirt, the touch gentle yet so intimate, and she felt a quiver inside her, knowing how he liked to bend his women over like this. She felt some part of her respond, and she ached between her thighs, feeling empty, wanting fulfilment. She was glad she was facing away from him. God forbid he should know he could affect her so, even barely touching her.

"I want you to make anyone who sees these pictures want to find you, pull your clothes off and…"

The rich deep tone of his voice was working its magic. "Alright! I get the idea!"

Daryl smiled, and slowly removed his hand, deliberately brushing his fingers along the top of her thigh. He clicked his fingers and music began to play, and she looked around at him, the mane of hair to one side, and arched her back and raised one knee onto the bonnet.

Oh sweet mother of God. Daryl felt muscles tighten, and himself harden. "Crawl onto the bonnet."

"You want me to take my boots off?"

"No!"

"Daryl, it's brand new!"

"Do it. Don't stop now.

"So you don't want any blood left in your head for driving?"

"None."

She crawled up onto the bonnet and lay down on her back, one knee up, the long cream boots reflecting beautifully in the paintwork. She then rolled over, watching him, just as she had at the second underwear shoot. Click-click-click, and he held in a low moan of appreciation as she spread her thighs, knees out to either side, the points of her high heels touching behind her. Her eyes were low, body half-turned, and then she looked up at him, and he knew she was going to give him everything he wanted and more.

It was an hour of blissful seduction as she moved from car to car, the provocative poses coming one after the other, on bonnets and draped over doors and seats, so enticing, legs open, one hand in her hair, eyes brooding, teasing.

Finally, Daryl called a halt. He needed to cool down.

"Sure you don't want to go and splay yourself over a car? I'm sure I could handle the camera for a bit."

"No. But thank you." He took a step towards her. What would happen if he were just to lean in, as if to kiss her? She stepped back. "Now I'm going to take one of them around the track. Without you. So you can experience what it is like to watch and not be allowed to touch…"

The statement was loaded and she knew it, and she instantly felt embarrassed. Why had she felt pressured into doing exactly what he wanted again? Why did he have that effect on her?

He handed his camera to one of his men, who saw it safely stowed in its case and returned to the Bentley. He then nodded at Mac, and they made their way over to the dark blue model S, crouching, begging to be driven.

She watched on the screens, a dark look on her face. OG observed her, and the changing mood.

"He's not really pushing it, is he?"

No one answered. No one would dare voice criticism, except her.

She wandered over to OG, said she was hungry, and he offered to get something from the car.

"Do you have any other cars for test driving?" she asked quietly when he was gone. One of the guys close by looked round at her slowly, a little unsure what to say. Anything he did say might give away his adoration, and then he'd look like an idiot. "Only, I really like cars," she continued, "and I'd really like one or two myself, for the weekends."

"Err…sure," he eventually said. Sell a car to her? Like, that would get him a bonus and a promotion and give him a story to talk about for the rest of the year! "We have these ones here." He led her over to the four parked by the side of the hanger. "Do any of these grab you?"

"I like that one," she said decisively, pointing at the exact same model Daryl was driving but in white.

"Okay…" He held the door open for her to get in. Mysty could have hugged him, but she knew she needed to get onto the track before OG reappeared. "You want me to ride with you, to explain how it works?"

"Is it quite similar to a Ferrari?"

"Quite, yeah."

"Sure, then I'll be fine." She smiled at him, pulled down her shades and started it up. She had closed the door and was gone before he could say another word.

She smiled again when she felt the beast beneath her leap forward towards the track, as if it was hungry to taste the tarmac. This was going to be fun. She played with the car, getting a feel for the power and the handling and the track. Wow, like a bike, but not… It felt great!

"What the…?" Daryl looked in his rear-view mirror, knowing the track was fully reserved for him. Who else was on the track? One more look, and a glint of gold, combined with the speed at which she took the corner, told him exactly who.

"Jesus Christ… Who let her out in that car?" Mac muttered, looking in his side mirror, seeing her dangerously close to them.

"And how come she knows how to drive a car anyway?" Daryl braked for the corner, distracted by her presence, and she bombed past. "Goddammit!"

Furious, he pulled off the track and made his way to the hanger. "How the absolute hell?"

He didn't need to finish the question, punctuating it with the slam of his car door.

"She asked to drive one, apparently. Sweet as a kid asking for candy. I'd gone to get her something to eat from the car. I was gone two minutes." OG's voice was terse, tense arms crossed over his chest, as he watched her lightning-fast progress around the track on the screens.

"She knows about bikes, but cars? And not just any car, a *super car*?"

"We…erm…she asked me to teach her how to drive, in Sicily," OG admitted, rubbing the back of his head, knowing his boss would most likely be tempted to remove it for him.

"In what?" Daryl marched over to the screens and surveyed the data from her car.

"A Porsche. And then a Ferrari. She was really good. She just seems to like things that are…a little fast."

"No shit, O'Grady! Is that why she's now doing 200mph?"

"Call through to the car and tell her to slow down," Mac said as calmly as he could, and the call was placed.

The internal camera view came up on the screen.

"Mysty. What the hell are you doing?"

"I'm driving."

"Why aren't you wearing a seat belt?"

"I don't like wearing them."

"Put it on. Now."

She let go of the steering wheel and used both hands to put her belt on.

"Get your hands back on the wheel!" OG's shout beat Daryl to it.

She careened around the bend, smiling, clearly loving every second. On the straight she finished fastening the belt.

"Please bring the car back to the hanger right now."

"Why? I've got my belt on! Have I broken the track record yet?"

"Mysty–"

"Where is the radio on this thing? There must be one, right? A million dollars must buy you a stereo?"

"Immediately!"

"Immediately?"

"*Yes*!" OG's word of warning came a second too late, as Daryl's emphatic confirmation carried over the sound waves.

"Okay."

She reached down with her right hand and nipped the handbrake on, spun the wheel, hard, and the car followed suit, spirals of smoke rising from the tyres. Collectively, everyone braced, shoulders tensing, expecting the worst; but, in fact, when she was done, saw her sitting calmly in the vehicle, engine still running, facing the opposite way. Her smile, usually beautiful, was now infuriating.

"Does that car have any kind of remote disabling feature?" Daryl asked, clenching his fists and his gut as she hurtled round another bend on her way back.

"No, sir. It's the demo model, and doesn't come with the add-ons."

She'd barely switched the engine off and undone the seatbelt when Daryl was at the door. He reached in and pulled her out. She fought him as he dragged her over to the last of his new cars, in a gleaming turquoise, and deposited her in the passenger seat. Without speaking he pulled the seatbelt across and clipped her in, his green eyes now searing into hers.

"You two, in now!" He pointed and the two leopards ran forward and jumped into the car and sat at her feet. He then threw himself into the driving seat, fired the engine and roared off, heading back towards Manhattan, the atmosphere inside the car as fiery as if laced with gasoline and set to blow at any moment. She barely dared to breathe.

"Will Mac bring your camera?" she asked in a small voice.

"My camera? I don't give a fuck about my camera! I've just watched you careering around a track, in a car you've never driven before, at speeds that would leave nothing but a smear of flesh on the tarmac if it had gone wrong!"

"I didn't..."

"No, you didn't, did you? You never think anything is dangerous, that anything matters, do you? Do you ever think of the consequences *of anything*?

Mysty lowered her head. Her throat closed up. He was so angry, and he was so right, and for the first time in a long time, she felt truly embarrassed.

"I didn't mean to make you this angry. I'm sorry."

He heard the remorse in her voice. But they'd been here too many times before. This needed to be the last.

"What were you thinking? That you'd maybe win an Oscar for your performance out there?"

"No! I just...don't find speed as scary as most people. I don't think of it in the same way."

"Just because you can handle the speed doesn't mean the risks or the consequences are any different!" She swayed as he swerved around a slow-moving line of cars with ruthless proficiency, the throaty engine sounding as angry and determined as the man driving it. "Let me be clear... I am not Franny or Giles, who no doubt indulged you like the prodigal daughter. I am not Donny, either, who I know trusted you, but never put a check on this wild utterly reckless side of you that risks everything for a few seconds or minutes of daredevil behaviour. And I am not Rusty or Slick, who think every time you win a race, however you win, is a good thing!"

The words kept coming. Words no one had ever spoken to her before. It was like he was prising away the sides of the box she kept herself hidden in and was going to expose all her faults and weaknesses.

"When are you going to accept what you are? That you are...you are precious, and stop the childish tantrums every time something doesn't go your way?" he concluded, and finally paused. He could not remember lecturing *anyone* in this scorching fashion before, and wasn't surprised that she didn't answer. He took some slow breaths in an attempt to moderate his tone. "I was perfectly within my rights to ask that you stay with O'Grady rather than come with me to drive the car on the track. I had hoped you would accept the decision in a more mature way, and intended taking you out in this car when I returned. But instead I get another demonstration of Mysty-style defiance, one that would have put your life at risk had something gone wrong out there. This wasn't one of your stunts when something has scared you, but a self-indulgent moment of pure idiocy." He wanted to look at her, but kept his eyes on the road. "I'm disappointed in you."

It was those four words that broke down the last defences, and she felt tears sting her eyes and her throat close up. The inescapable truth was that he was right. This man she had fought against for so long was actually concerned for her? She had let him down. She had pushed him too far, and not because she'd insulted him or hacked into his accounts, but because she'd risked herself. She deserved to hear the anger in his voice, and the disappointment. As much as he had made her feel ashamed, and a part of her wanted to retaliate, another part of her had been paying attention. She'd not been afraid to highlight his failings, many times, when they'd affected her. He'd just done the same, and she had never felt more unconscionably immature beside this smart, hard-working man.

He swung the car off the road and parked on the gravel drive of a large country-style mansion with grand steps leading up to the wide door, and tall columns and archways. The beautiful sign said, 'Highgrove Country Club'. He switched the engine off and looked at her.

"I booked a table for two, but they don't cater for children, so you can stay here." He'd booked the table here because he knew she'd like the gardens, and knew what he'd just said was harsh, wishing he hadn't had cause to say it. "Unless, of course, you can think of an argument to sway me?" he added.

He saw the tiny tremble in her shoulders as she stayed facing out of the window and felt a twinge of tenderness. He didn't want to do this. He hated making her cry. And he didn't really want to leave her in the car.

"Can you please leave the windows down a fraction? Or they'll get too hot," she said, indicating the leopards.

He sighed, desperately wanting to feel the pride of taking her inside with him, but reminded himself that this lesson was important. One day she might understand. One day it might bring them closer. He lowered the windows, enough for the fresh air, but not so low anyone would see her, and got out. Mac was waiting for him with OG, both looking concerned.

"She is taking some time to meditate on her behaviour," was all he said, and strolled up the steps, trying to look carefree and relaxed when he felt anything but. All he wanted to do was go back to her.

She looked out at the beautiful gardens and the grand house, and the row of Bentleys, and never, not since the very beginning, had she felt so unworthy of any of it. She felt small and childish, and wished she could undo what she had done back there. But the damage was done

AN HOUR AND a quarter later, having dropped into an exhausting state of self-recrimination, she swallowed her shame to ask the question she'd been struggling to voice for what felt like an eternity: "Can I go home now, please?"

"No. Not just yet."

Daryl had anticipated she would ask that the moment he returned, but the lesson wasn't over yet. He saw her shoulders sag a little, but took a breath. "I'm going to tell you something now," he said, "about my life."

He started the engine, and pulled back onto the main road back into Manhattan. She didn't say a word, taking comfort from seeing his driving was now calmer, even if his face was still dark and serious.

"When I was sixteen, Harvey and I decided to go out on the town. We both looked old enough to pass as eighteen, and we had the money to do what we liked, and it was not like anyone was going to say no to us, given who I was. We thought it was fantastic. We could have anything we wanted – women, alcohol, drugs, whatever – and we had a very wild night. So wild, in fact, that I was still half drunk and in bed with two women when my father came in. I'd never seen him so furious. That was a morning I'll never forget. And neither will I ever forget the afternoon, when I was taken to our private doctor and treated like the pedigree that had decided to go and hump a few strays. This was followed by a trip to an AIDS ward in the local hospital, and then a ward for drug addicts."

The remembrance of his shame rose up once more, and he cringed as he continued.

"Why do you think my father took me to those places? He took me so that I would see what I stood to lose should I continue to behave in such a way. I know you disapprove of my 'harem', my Cherries…and this may be hard for you to understand, but…" He really hoped she'd grasp the meaning of what he needed to say next. "I have them because they are scrupulously checked. My father taught me that was a safer way to enjoy women. It was part of his lesson to me, to keep me safe, just like I need to keep you safe. I know this is hard, but do you understand?"

"Yes." It was the barest of whispers.

He slowed and pulled the car over. "But he wasn't finished, and the other half of the lesson was the real test. It was a test of character; of learning how to accept lesson and not fight it. And that he did with his words, by making me see my self-worth, and by example. None of this, with us right now, is about me winning. This is about you realising *your* own worth. I've seen you be as smart and grown up as someone ten years older, so wipe your tears, lift your head up and put your shoulders back, and look at me."

She didn't want to look at him and those knowing green eyes. Even if he wasn't angry anymore, the shame still burned bright inside her.

"Don't tell me that you, of all people, are going to disappoint twice in one day. I know you can do this. Look at me."

The quiet sincerity of the words swayed her, and she slowly turned to face him, his eyes intense, the space between them in the car so small. For one crazy second she wished he would lean forward and kiss her, to calm the turmoil and loosen the knot in her stomach. She wanted to feel the strength of his arms around her. Anything would be better than feeling like a small island in an unfriendly sea. She raised her head, took a deep breath and looked at him.

She didn't know quite what to do. She'd never been so ashamed, and yet been given a chance for redemption; never been so chastised by him and yet seen in him a kind of salvation.

He reached over and straightened her shoulders, let his hand rest on her shoulder for a moment. The intensity of the moment kept their eyes on each other, something they would both remember.

"There, I recognise you now. That's the girl I know," he said. "So, where's this club of yours?" He removed his hand, and she felt the heat as if it was still there.

"You still want to go?" she said quietly, in disbelief.

"Yes, I do."

"Now?"

"Yes. Where is it?"

"It's east on Eighth and Fifth, left side of the street facing west."

He nodded. He knew the city well, knew where she meant. He drove over the bridge, and sent a quick destination update to Mac so he knew where they were headed. But then he thought of something he thought she might like to do first, and parked expertly outside a milkshake bar – and all eyes turned to look at the car, clearly wondering who was behind the tinted glass of such a magnificent vehicle.

He handed her a $100 bill. "Let's have a milkshake?" he said.

"No." She gave him the note back.

"No? Mysty, I'm not an ogre…"

"I know. But these are on me."

"You have some money on you?"

She reached inside her clothing and pulled out a fifty. "Two things key to survival: a knife and some emergency money."

"Sweetheart, you don't need to worry about survival anymore. You're never going to want for anything again in your life, don't you see? And you'll never be without OG or Mac or whoever you need to keep you safe." He resisted from mentioning himself, and suddenly realised he'd called her sweetheart. Would she react? He watched carefully as she contemplated his words. When she didn't respond, he said, "You can choose the shakes. I've liked all the others you've chosen. Surprise me."

She nodded, and he touched her hand, and pressed the Unlock button. The way she looked at him as she got out of the car was…what was it? Was he imagining that she seemed to need more than that small touch of reassurance?

He didn't take his eyes off the door of the bar, despite knowing OG and three others were in there with her. People were coming and going, relaxed and smiling. Some clocked the plate on the car – DB 2759 – and he wondered if she would she see the significance of it… Did she remember their first car ride as vividly as he did? That crazy pall mall chase in LA when she asked him for a gun? He had relived the moment a thousand times. The moment he had given her the code to the glove compartment for the weapon, driving the car as she knelt facing the wrong way, calm as anything, and took care of the huge SUV behind them while bullets pinged off metal. That had been one hell of a day. He hoped she would notice it, but couldn't ask if she had.

She reappeared, looking slightly less tense, and reinserted herself into the car while the leopards did their best to welcome her back. "Here you go. Definitely fifty laps in the pool later on, I think."

"What is it called?"

"Campfire Heaven. I just liked the name. But it's melted marshmallow ice cream." He took a sip. "You like it?"

"You can bring me one of these next time you come to my office!" he declared, and she almost laughed with relief. "But I need both hands to drive."

"Shall I hold it?"

"Please."

He handed it to her, and checked his mirror, looking for a gap in the traffic to pull out. Just as he did, there was a deafening screech and a utility truck swerved and ploughed straight into a Mercedes coming in the opposite direction. He braked hard, and instinctively his hand went across her, to protect her. "Are you alright?" he asked instantly.

"Let me out!" She went for the door handle, flicking the lock off that he instantly re-engaged. "It's better you drive alone! My cards are marked!

Please, let me out!"

"No, your cards aren't marked and I'm not driving alone. It's okay. Look at me!"

"Bad things always happen around me, right from when I was a child–"

He immediately understood, and putting his hand on her arm turned her around to face him, putting a halt to the rush of words so he could speak. "That *wasn't* your fault. What happened when you were a child wasn't your fault. Bad things happen, but you don't make them happen. You can't stop people being evil if that's their nature – you're as pure as a snowdrop."

"But it must be my fault! If it weren't for me my family might be alive!" The confession held inside for so long broke out. "It is my fault! It is!"

"How? Why?"

There was no way he could manoeuvre around the carnage of the Mercedes and the truck, so he stayed where he was. Decision made, he focussed completely on her, determined to stay with her through the seconds of pure emotion that seemed to hold them in their own world. Distress sent a tremor through her body so powerful he could feel beneath his hands.

"It happened after my party. My ninth birthday party. One of my school friends was picked up by her father, and my dad saw him talking to my mum and assumed she was having an affair with him. The whole thing happened because of me!"

"No. No it didn't. How could a nine-year-old child be responsible for that?"

He could sense her looking at him; could sense her desperation to believe him, but the fear holding her back. What if she believed him, believed *in* him, and it all went wrong, like with Donny…he let go of her arm and gentle fingers tucked a dangling curl back from her face.

"I know it's not easy for you, and I know how hard it is for you to believe me," he said slowly, not wanting to rush words that were so important, "but I'm asking you to trust me. I really do have your best interests at heart. I know I'm not Donny, but I really do care. I told you, I won't let anything happen to you. Whatever happens, we can deal with it, understand?"

Huge pools of indigo begged him to stop, afraid to believe as much as she wanted to – he could see fear warring with the faith. Seeing the white of her knuckles as she gripped hold of the edge of the seat he knew he needed to ease the tension out of her.

"I'm not taking no for an answer by the way, so you should probably nod soon."

She bit her lip and almost smiled.

"I understand. I do."

Why else would this indomitable man, who had a million other things he could be doing, be taking the time to talk to her, to help her face up to a few long overdue facts about herself, and the beliefs she harboured about her life? To take hold of her fear and draw it out of her like a poison?

"Good. Then you can prove it to me at some point." He lowered his head closer to hers, so that their temples almost touched, the gentleness and intimacy of it as new to him as it was to her. His eyes dipped to her lips, but there was a call buzzing yet again in his ear. "Mac."

"Sir, you two alright?"

"We're okay, thank you. Can you get us a passage out of here? We'd still like to get to Mysty's club."

"Give me a minute."

Disconnect.

"Do you still want to go…?" he then asked her. "We can go home if you prefer?"

"Let's go. I'm okay."

"What's it called, by the way?"

"The Tiger Butterfly."

"Ah, I like it. Very appropriate. What about the one in LA?"

"I've not quite decided, but probably something more Pirate-esque, I think."

"I like that, too."

A few minutes later he spotted the gleaming butterfly over a doorway, wings spread to reveal tiger stripes in gold, black and ivory – a beautiful combination.

"I know it doesn't look much, but–" She got out and pressed some numbers into a panel and it scanned her eyes. A shutter rolled up to reveal an open space. "It's a car lift," she said when she got back in. Staff parking is on the roof. Go on in."

"Wow. Impressive!" he said. "Do you own the whole building?"

"Yep. All eight floors. And a basement. And that one over there." She pointed at another similar building across the road.

"And how did you afford both?" The 'couple of million' that she had siphoned out of her account seemed to have gone a long way.

"This one was pricey, but that one wasn't. It had been on the market for a while, and had no takers. Then it became known – somehow – that planning permission had been granted for this building to be converted into a club, and suddenly the price dropped even lower, so when I put an offer in they jumped at it. I brought some people over from LA, some dancers."

Charles's words came back to him about her 'business acumen'... He'd meant it. She had a natural gift.

"People from LA? From the dance off?"

"Yep. You might recognise some of them." He parked the car and they made their way over to another panel on the wall. "You'll need to be entered into the database or it'll set the alarms off. No unauthorised or unidentified people can use this door."

After various security procedures, his name came up on the panel and it flashed 'Welcome' and the door opened.

He hadn't known what to expect, but what he saw he really liked, from the large ornate mirrors to the chandeliers, from the rich cream walls, with pictures of great dancing moments from her career, including snapshots of dance offs with her friends in LA, to the plush seating.

"Before you think I've grown an ego the size of Manhattan, I didn't put these up. I came in one day and they were there. I guess I kind of like them."

"That is progress, from someone who doesn't even like looking in the mirror," he ventured, trying to sound encouraging without being overbearing.

"Yeah, I guess it is." She threw him a smile, and pushed through a door into a wide corridor. Each of the doors had a name on – 'Bobby', 'Sam' and 'Moses' and they were names he recognised. He noticed there were no job titles, though.

At the end of the corridor she entered some details into another security panel and the door opened. "My office," she said quietly, watching him take in the plain walls and simple desk.

"It's…small."

"Yeah, I know. That's what you're supposed to think…"

He looked at her quizzically as she sat at her desk, and didn't see her press a hidden button. In a matter of seconds the room doubled in size as the computer-generated plain walls dissolved to reveal rich gold and blue brocade walls, along with a large dark wood desk with a complex set of computer panels. There were shelves containing files, and a tall unit with locked boxes inside. A big picture of Lazarus and Lula was on the wall behind her chair, which was to be expected. What he didn't expect was the fish tank that went from floor to ceiling, the water clear and bright in the low light of the room, multi-coloured fish darting in and out of foliage.

"Wow!" he said.

"And watch this!" She pressed a button on the armrest of her chair and it extended sideways, on both sides. "For these two," she said, and the leopards jumped up either side of her. "It saves there being any arguments."

"Brilliant!" She blushed, realising he looked genuinely impressed. "And I'm on the wall?" He pointed at a framed photo of them on holiday, walking back to the clubhouse, the same picture she had put on his bedroom door.

"It was a great moment; I like to be reminded of it," she said, and he had to agree. "What do you think of the fish?" she then asked, going to his side. He liked them, but he was more interested in the way her face lit up watching them. He hadn't expected her to take an interest at all, and it was great to learn something so personal about her. "They seem to live simple lives, but they're very pretty," she laughed, seeing two clown fish skitter over the coral in a chase, with one getting a tail-flap of sand thrown up in its face.

"Ssshhh! They might get upset if they hear you call their lives simple!"

"They'd forget I'd said it in less than three seconds, so it's okay." He was too close. It was doing something to her, having him in her personal office space rather than their usual meeting in his. She watched him lean forward to examine the fish, his profile illuminated by the lights in the tank, the curve of his lips, the beauty of his cheek bones. It was too much. She gestured to the door. "Come on, I'll take you downstairs. This is just the office floor. It's not very exciting."

She led him back out into the corridor, locked the door and then down four flights of stairs. The building was huge, much bigger than it looked from outside. They arrived in a large open space with a balcony running around three sides. There was a large bar, lots of seating, and a dining area. In the centre was a large dancefloor. The dark woods complimented the blue on the walls. Tiger butterfly motifs had been applied to the walls and on the floor. High above them, the same motif looked down from the ceiling. He liked it very much, but could see her scanning his face for any sign of forthcoming criticism, which saddened him. Was he really such a monster?

"Mysty?"

"Moses. How are you?"

Moses – a name he recognised from LA.

"I'm good. You didn't say you were coming? This is so nice."

"An unexpected visit, I know. I wanted Daryl to see the club, just so he knows I'm not up to anything outrageous in here. Daryl, you remember Moses?"

"Of course." Daryl offered his hand.

Moses extended his hand a little nervously now that he knew who the man was who had shown up at the dance-off in LA. "Mr Blackmoor, sir, honoured to meet you. I hope you like what you see."

"So far I have been very impressed. I'm sure it only gets better."

"I leave Moses in charge, as I can't be here all the time, and he does a fantastic job." She turned to Moses. "I have the updated report, thank you. I'll get all that dealt with tonight."

Moses nodded, now looking a little more relaxed.

"Are the boys in the kitchen?"

"Yeah, they're having an experimentation session with the sandwiches."

"Wow! You think they can make me something? Daryl, would you like anything?"

"No, thanks."

"Sure, Mysty. What do you want? You know they'd never say no to you."

"Hamburger, salad, fries. And same again on two plates for these two."

"No problem. You want me to get you some drinks?"

"No, I can get those. I'm sure you were busy doing something. How are the classes going?"

"Really good. We're up to full capacity now, no matter what time of day."

"Excellent. You give me a shout if you need anything."

"Will do." Moses darted off to put her order in.

"So, what would you like to drink?" she asked.

"I'll have a latte, if that's okay. I am driving, after all."

"You'll have to come back another time for a cocktail. We do everything!"

"I'll definitely be coming back to test that statement."

Watching as she calmly and competently fixed his coffee using the espresso machine behind the bar, Daryl let himself relax. This hadn't been how he'd expected the afternoon to go, but it felt good to spend time with her, away from cameras. Questions naturally formed in his mind, and he was ready to ask them when they both heard her name spoken.

Moses reappeared. "So sorry to interrupt," he said. "City Council have called about the health and safety inspection. Can you speak to them?"

"Very curious, considering we had our inspection weeks ago," she muttered, putting the earpiece in. "Just a moment, Daryl."

He nodded, and sipped his latte while she handled the inquiry deftly and quickly, surmising this wasn't an official department phone call, this was a reporter, hoping for a scoop.

"Would you like to tell me your real name, and the news station you work for?" she asked. "Wayne Gibbons. Great, that wasn't so hard, was it. Monday, come and have a night in the club. Get here at seven. I'll tell them to let you in. Bring someone, but no bugs, no cameras, no nothing – and we will check. Understand? Good. No. I have your name. I can find out the rest. Seven sharp. Don't be late."

He was impressed. Again. No pretty dumb fish was she.

The food arrived – presented to her by another fan, Raoul, in his chef's whites and neck scarf. He kissed her cheek and spoke to her in Spanish, before ducking his head in a small bow to the rather impressive-looking man sitting quietly by her side.

"I trust the photos from today aren't going to end up in general circulation?" she asked when Raoul had gone, trying a French fry.

"No. They're for my private collection. But I might put one in the office."

She looked at him; the sheer physicality of him sitting here, next to her in her own club stirring all kinds of feelings. What would it feel like to have his arms around her? To put her arms around him? She put the thought from her mind and concentrated on her food rather than the body she knew was toned and tanned beneath his clothes.

"Daryl?"

"Yes?" He leaned closer.

"I'd really rather you didn't."

His eyes were intense, his lips too close. She felt like someone running too fast down a hill who knew their legs were going to fail them at any moment and they were going to fall and the hill would win.

"Boss?"

"Mac. You found us."

"Everything okay? The roads have been cleared. Unfortunate timing for a blowout," Mac said.

"Yep," she answered a little too quickly, and caught OG's look.

"We'll need to leave for your five o clock appointment soon, sir."

Daryl's heart sank. He'd forgotten about that. How had time flown by so fast?

"Appointment? You don't have to go, do you?" She looked disappointed, and his heart sank further. "You've not seen the whole club yet…"

"I promise I'll come back and see the rest another day," he said, but could see that she didn't really believe him. "We'll leave now. The traffic will be getting worse, and I need to put a suit on."

"Why? You still look smart."

"Mr Hamilton will think he's missed out on some kind of dress down day if he's wearing a suit and I'm not."

"Well, if you are determined to leave, I will walk you out." Abandoning her food, she hopped off the bar stool and headed for the elevators that Daryl had missed first time around, painted to look like doorways. The club was a mixture of overt and subtle, of bold and sleight of hand, a wonderland of possibility. He took one more appreciative look around. It was great what she'd done here, really great. But he knew the real treasure of the place was standing right next to him.

Coming back out into the fresh air on the roof felt strange, so completely had he been immersed in his time with her. OG waited at the door, as she walked out into the fading sun against the backdrop of cityscape.

"Mac, could you sit in the car for a minute while I speak to Daryl?" Keys were tossed over without a word spoken, a stereo could be heard through the window glass, and Daryl stopped his progress towards his beautiful car to give her all his attention. They were far enough away from OG that whatever was said was private.

Sensing she didn't know how to start what she wanted to say, Daryl tried a familiar tease.

"I won't put up any photos from today, if you pose nude on my desk." Her eye roll was almost as deadpan as her face.

"You don't give up do you?"

"At least I'm predictable." He stood contentedly unapologetic, hands in his pockets.

"Most of the time. I wouldn't have predicted a lot of today."

"I owe you a few surprises."

"And I owe you an apology." She countered, finally finding the opening she needed, her chest feeling tight. "I didn't…mean for what happened to happen. And I understand why you were angry. I didn't mean to ruin today." He smiled. And here she was, the girl with the courage to face up to her mistakes and apologise. It was more than he'd been capable of many times, and for that she deserved his respect and acknowledgment.

"It wasn't ruined. It just didn't go to plan."

"No. Now you're just being nice." A sad smile and she bit her lip. "You were right, about a lot of things, and they needed to be said."

"We've always been brutally honest with each other."

"I know, I think that's the best way to be." She took a deep breath. "I meant it when I said I didn't mean for it to happen; but, more importantly, it won't happen again. I promise."

"That's all that matters. Thank you." Daryl didn't want the moment to end, it felt so important, so poignant. "Don't forget what I said today."

"I won't. If you meant it."

"I meant it." How he wished he had the courage to step forward and kiss her cheek, or taste her lips. "I'll see you Tuesday for my tango lesson."

"Yes, you will."

"Be good."

"I will. Don't work too hard."

"I will." She laughed, but rolled her eyes. "So, how do I get out of this place?"

"Take this." She handed him the card she'd used to swipe the security panel on the roof. "The car was loaded into the database, too, so the doors will open for you on the ground floor. The car lift will lock down automatically when you drive out."

He took it and smiled. It was more than just a security card; it was an expression of trust, and for that he was deeply grateful, and humbled.

Getting in the car, he saw that Mac was ready to go, and he drove smoothly into the car lift. He reflected on the fact he'd much preferred his previous driving companion, but feeling pleasantly relaxed, he was content to let Mac drive and share the enjoyment of the new cars.

"So, back there, what did you say to her?"

"Words she needed to hear. Words no one else has dared say to her."

The driving gave them an excuse not to look at each other, Daryl's tone terse, Mac's innocently enquiring. They were nearly back when the conversation sprang up.

"And no tantrum? No tears?"

"She's an intelligent girl, and not too proud to admit she might be wrong sometimes."

"I'm impressed."

"Cheers, Mac. Of course, the only reason I talked to her was for your approval…"

Mac grinned at the sarcastic tone. "Well, it's all rather encouraging considering how she usually reacts to you. It must be love."

"How about you concentrate on your job and leave off being my relationship advisor?"

A warning glance from the green eyes told Mac his good-humoured familiarity on the subject was not appreciated.

"Yes, sir. Of course."

DARYL GOT OUT of the emerald-green Lamborghini and glanced over at Harvey, who had exited the passenger side. It was once again parked on the spotlessly clean roof car park at the one club everyone in New York wanted to go to. Robbie's Ferrari appeared from the car lift with Craig on board and pulled up alongside. They all stood waiting for Zack and Guy to arrive in a similarly eye-catching Aston Martin, imported to the US at huge cost.

As they made their way over to the door, Daryl raised his fingers to his lips, hoping she hadn't spotted them all in the cameras.

"Mysty?"

"Daryl?" She sounded surprised, to say the least, and he was glad there was no noise from the boys in the background.

"Do you think you could come and let us in?"

"Us?"

"The boys and I are on the roof."

Everyone was smiling, but feeling a little embarrassed being stuck on the outside of a door when they were so used to doors being opened for them. It was a novel experience.

"What? All of you?"

"Well, none of them wanted to miss out the chance to come and see your club. We thought we'd surprise you."

"Understatement!" They heard footsteps, and then the door was yanked open, and there she was, knee-high high-heeled patent boots in a rich metallic purple that matched her hot pants, her top tied under her ribcage, silk trailing from her elbows. There was a moment of stunned silence as they took her in, and she surveyed them all: New York's finest and all standing outside her door. "Glory be. Well. Better get you all loaded in. Daryl, you can go through."

She stood aside and let him in, then logged everyone else in, which gave Daryl a chance to watch her, admire the legs and the gorgeousness of her hair. Worn mostly loose, the top had been swirled into a knot of gold with a large butterfly tiger clip to hold it up there. She wore no other jewellery. Didn't need it.

"I see you all came in suitably low-key cars, to just slip in without anyone noticing," she smirked.

"Extra publicity. Can't do any harm," Guy said.

"No, I guess not."

"Though I don't think you need it…the queue was huge when we drove in," Robbie commented, sounding rather impressed.

They looked around at the pictures adorning the walls. Daryl noticed, and rather liked the fact he'd been there before but they were seeing it all for the first time.

"Yes, I know. It's been there since five and we were at full capacity at quarter past seven. I should have bought a bigger building." She rolled her eyes, which made Daryl smile. It always amused him when she underestimated her appeal and her success. In the hall they saw OG and the leopards waiting. She stopped, placed her hand on the wall and waited. "Are you guys coming or do you want to take the stairs?"

Harvey looked at Daryl, who smiled and went to stand next to her, leaving the rest confused. The wall then disintegrated and doors appeared, opening to reveal the plush lift with room enough for all of them. None of them quite knew what to say, but the look on their faces was enough!

Daryl was hoping for a few minutes alone with her, but was content to bide his time, enjoying being near her. He could smell her perfume, but he still hadn't worked out what it was.

"What perfume are you wearing?" he asked simply, rather than spending any more time trying to place it.

The lift came to an almost imperceptible halt on the destination floor.

"I asked someone to make it," she replied, "based on buddleia, the flowering tree that butterflies like. It reminds me of my grandmother's garden." Quiet words.

The next second, she was leading them into the swirl of music, bringing them out onto a walkway a level up from the dancefloor and across from the balcony restaurant to an empty lounge space with low lighting and sumptuous seating. Tables were loaded with snacks; fish tanks sent bubbles around brightly coloured fish.

She settled Lula and Lazarus on a couple of chairs and then led the way to a spiral staircase, tucked away in a corner out of sight. It brought them out onto the lower floor, guarded at the bottom by two security, both in black trousers and t-shirts with a small tiger butterfly motif on the right breast, both built like tanks.

They had been watched the whole way by people in stylish clothing perfect for dancing, people who had stared in wonder as their star moved through their midst – and with such company! No one dared touch her, or come too close, and her male escort was treated to the same deference. She was greeted by Moses, who was in a top hat, coat and tails and holding a cane with the tiger butterfly motif on top. Daryl could see why she'd picked him: he was reliable, and adored being the master of ceremonies; he was the lord of the dance, making sure everyone was welcomed and enjoying themselves. He loved seeing her in this new role as mistress of her domain, at home in the world of music and dance; but he also knew that every other man there did too, and the women, for a different reason. She was sublime; a class apart. Equally, he and his fellow arrivals were getting just as many looks.

The group of girls and guys behind the bar were all in black trousers or leggings and a gold top with the same motif on. It was a tasteful uniform that wasn't too formal, but distinctive, and they all looked happy wearing it.

"So, guys, what are you having?" She sat up on the bar and waved her hand wide.

"What can we have?" Harvey asked…the most obvious question.

"Anything," she smiled, happy to let them choose whatever they wanted.

"Daryl, pick a cocktail, because you had the good sense to invite us to surprise our favourite lady," Harvey invited grandly, gazing around, which made her smile again: this was not the kind of club they were used to.

"Cosmopolitan," Daryl said.

"Excellent. Our speciality. Six of those, then."

The guys behind the bar looked at her intently. "We're one short behind the bar, boss," one of them said.

"Yeah, alright, I'm coming." She swung her legs over, and then they all spread out and started measuring and pouring and spinning bottles behind their backs, completely synchronised. Then the silver shakers were sealed and the juggling started, the shakers flying left and right and front and back; and then a glass slid all the way down from Mysty to the farthest girl, and then another and another until they all had one. Mysty looked at Daryl. He was smiling.

"I told you we specialise in cocktails," she said.

"That was so good! I'm going to order six of everything now, even if no one else wants the same thing!" Harvey laughed, obviously impressed with the show.

"I still prefer the one you made me on the boat," Daryl said quietly as she slipped back over the bar.

"Why? Because I was wearing a bikini?"

"No. Because I didn't have to share you with anyone else while I drank it."

She shot him a look, and then Moses appeared.

"Mysty, sorry to disturb. Mr Blackmoor, sir. Sebastian has arrived. Will you see him upstairs or in your office?"

Daryl scowled at the news. There was only one Sebastian who would be visiting her, and he wasn't happy about it. What did he want? Daryl knew he wouldn't mention the 'arrangement' he had with him about Lex Huntley and the rest, who, with the start of their trial the day after next, were all enjoying their last days of freedom.

"I'll come now, Moses. See what he prefers." She looked around at Daryl, her smile bright. "Stop scowling. It's just a friendly visit. I'll be five minutes. Enjoy yourself." She briefly touched his arm before she walked away, the people parting like the Red Sea once more to let her through. He told himself to relax. Why wouldn't Sebastian come by and say hello when she'd opened an amazing club in his city…besides, she was once Donny's girl.

"Daryl!" Harvey brought his attention back. "Apparently there are all sorts of themed rooms away from this one. Cheryl has offered to show us around…you coming?"

Cheryl was a very pretty brunette whose t-shirt was rather tight and tied under her ribs like Mysty's. But no one could carry the look quite like the girl herself.

Daryl joined the jolly party for a guided tour, and was shown rooms dedicated to music of every genre imaginable. There was a room full of bean bags, hammocks and cushions for people to lie on when they got tired, with a bar never too far away so no one had to wait too long to get served. Photographers were on hand, so guests had a beautiful picture to remember their night by if they wished. There was another room with comfortable sofas and a large glass partitioned wall containing greenery, flowers and butterflies inside. Real butterflies.

A glint of gold caught his eye, and he spotted her with Sebastian, his boys close behind and OG not far behind her. Final words were spoken, and the most feared man in New York lifted her chin with a finger and gave her a gentle smile, and then he was gone. She shook her head, as if in wonderment at her life, and seeing Daryl said, "How did you like my butterflies?"

"They're very pretty, but I prefer the one with two legs."

She laughed and walked with him up the stairs, back towards the main dancefloor. Daryl had been separated from everyone else when he'd paused to watch her with Sebastian, but that suited him just fine. He'd waited four days to see her again, and wanted to check there was no lasting damage from their 'experience' on Thursday; that the intimacy – all be it not of a physical kind – had been real.

She seemed relaxed enough and asked, "Did you bring your dancing shoes?"

"No, I'm saving myself for tomorrow."

"Really? There was me thinking you had more stamina than that. Can't manage two days in a row?"

Her twinkling eyes were beautiful, and he wanted to do far more than answer with words. "I'm interested in your stamina with something other than dancing."

"That's something I don't even know the answer to."

"I volunteer to help you find out…"

Moses appeared as Daryl's words hung unanswered between them, her blush evidence that something was going on behind her eyes.

"Mysty, are you alright to begin soon?" Moses asked.

"Sure. I have an early start tomorrow so I don't want to leave it too late. Tell the guys I'll be there in five."

"Leaving early?" Daryl asked when Moses had gone.

"Rehearsal for opening night for the show that starts on Wednesday. You'll be lucky if I can still stand up let alone teach you the tango."

"Substandard lessons come with a forfeit."

"Oh yes? Let me guess, half an hour nude on your desk?" She rolled her eyes.

"An hour, and another photo shoot."

"And where would that one be?"

"In my jet."

"Oh Lord..."

"Miss Reverie? Sorry to interrupt. Oh, and, erm, Mr Blackmoor, erm, so sorry..." The man's discomfiture increased exponentially when he realised just who she was speaking to. To him, they were the most intimidating pair of people he had ever addressed in his entire professional career.

"Wayne Gibbons, I presume?" Mysty smiled, hoping the smile would put him at ease.

"Yes, ma'am. I just wanted to say thank you for tonight, and apologies again for, erm, the attempt to, erm..."

"Lie your way in to my club."

"Yes. I'm not proud of it and I know you had every right to, erm, not let me come tonight. But I, erm, I don't think you'll be disappointed with my review."

"I hope not, seeing as everyone is having such a good time. You bring someone with you?"

"My girlfriend, yes. She was too shy to, well, come over, but she's having the time of her life. She loves everything you do and she couldn't wait to come here."

"Wow! Well, you have a good night, and if you have any questions ask Moses – the guy with the top hat; I'm sure you've seen him – who manages the club for me in my absence. I trust him to answer for me. If you need a picture or two for your article, again, speak to him, and he can let you view some of the pics our on-hand photographers have taken. Good enough?"

"More than, thank you."

"You do know you're getting an exclusive?"

"I do, yes."

"Good. Then if I ever need an article doing, I'll know who has a willing pen ready?"

"Absolutely. You know where I work."

"Oh yes. Have a good night." She reached towards his ear, and he flinched, but then she revealed a coin with a tiger butterfly print on both sides. "Take this to the bar," she said. "It'll get you and your girlfriend free drinks."

"How did you?"

She smiled. "Magic."

After an awkward sort of bow he backed away, and a woman came straight to his side – his girlfriend, obviously – to find out what her heroine had said.

"You leave an impression on everyone," Daryl remarked.

"If it's a positive one, it can't be a bad thing."

She watched the couple, the way their fingers linked together and how he kissed her temple. She had forgotten what that felt like. "What impression did I have on you?" she asked, looking away.

"I think it's an ongoing thing. Ask me in seven or so years, or fifty…I might extend the contract."

"Don't you have to ask me before doing that?" she said, a little outraged.

"No." His grin was designed to be infuriating.

"Well, excuse me, Mr Manager, I have a crowd to entertain."

"Good luck."

"I don't need luck," she told him firmly, and pulled a tiger butterfly coin from his jacket pocket and put it in his hand, winked and disappeared into the crowd.

He couldn't wait to see what she had planned.

"WELL, GOOD EVENING New York! I hope everyone's happy tonight and having a great time!"

There was the usual deafening cheer.

"That's what I like to hear! Now, as you know, if I'm here they'll always be a little extra going on, and I know we have a lot of our members in tonight, not just the party-people, so we should have some fun. You're welcome to join in all the dances – obviously – though if you don't want to please make some room so the crazy dance people can get hot and sweaty. Without you. We won't take it personally."

A ripple of laughter went around the room. Daryl smiled. He and the guys were in the private lounge above the main floor, with a perfect view of the stage, and he loved watching her work the crowd.

"So, we have five songs tonight, plus one bonus one. And if one more person asks me to do 'California Gurls', which seems to be a very specific request at this particular club following its popularity a while back, I'm going to go exile myself somewhere…so you're getting that anyway."

Daryl felt a pressure on his hand, and reluctantly dragged his eyes away from Mysty to see what it was. Lula was looking up at him, her bright eyes enquiring, her strong, lithe body so much like her owner's. They were such a perfect pair. He reached out a hand and she let him put it on her head to have her ears fondled, and then leant against his leg.

"Daryl, you know, I think you've pulled," Harvey laughed.

It was lovely to have the leopard's trust, but she was not quite the girl he was after… Lazarus then wandered over and sat next to Lula, not within reach but not rejecting his presence either, and watched over the younger female – a stance Daryl could understand.

On stage, Mysty was joined by twelve other dancers, and the music began: 'Evacuate the Dance Floor' by Cascada and, as always, he wasn't disappointed, and, as always, there was a part of him that wished he was down there with the crowd, that wished he knew what it was like to give in completely to the music and just dance.

Maybe after tomorrow's tango lesson he would.

The next was 'Californian Gurls', which he loved but preferred the video, now at two hundred and fifty million downloads. Then came Lady Gaga's 'Just Dance', which she sang; then 'Dance Wiv Me' by Dizzee Rascal, which she danced with a male dancer.

Next was Enrique Iglesias' 'Bailamos' ('We Dance'), and it was beautiful, beginning with the soft strings of a guitar and sung in Spanish. It was exactly the sort of song he wanted to dance to, with her, but had to watch her turn and whirl in the arms of another man, her footwork so intricate, never unsure, despite the heels. 'Tonight we dance, I leave my life in your hands; we take the floor, nothing is forbidden any more... bailamos...we will live this night forever.' He could have sighed with the longing that it was his lips hovering next to her cheek at the end of the dance, her back against her partner's, her hands in his hair, his on her hips.

Tomorrow evening, at 6pm. He was counting the minutes.

The last song, the bonus song, was one Britney's 'Circus', and he was intrigued. What would she do with this? Her magic was unleashed, and everyone stood watching this time, not wanting to miss a moment of her brilliance. 'There are only two types of guys out there: ones that can hang with me and the ones that are scared, so baby I hope that you came prepared. I run a tight ship, so beware. I'm like a ringleader, I call the shots...' Hmm. As always, interesting lyrics... The whip crack was perfectly timed, and gold light poured down to trace her limbs before she launched into the dance, the whip her prop, her plaything, until one last glorious crack as the music faded in a burst of purple fire and light, and then she was gone. Only the whip remained on the floor – to deafening applause.

"Hello, sweetheart."

For one beautiful second, Daryl thought she was talking to him, but turned to see her fussing Lula.

"How come? You were down there...and..." Guy said, and pointed, voicing what everyone was thinking, which made her smile. She sat down with them as the music started up beneath them and the party continued.

"Magic," she said again.

"Fantastic show," Daryl said. One day she would tell him, and he didn't mind employing very pleasurable torture to make her.

Just a snippet of what's to come," she dismissed as Lazarus joined her in the wide chair.

Daryl realised he was tired. "What time is Cinderella leaving the ball to go home and get some sleep?" he asked her quietly. Boy, she looked really tired too. Who was he to complain?

"OG will probably appear any second and glare at me until I let him take me home," she laughed.

"It's gone eleven. It's not early."

"I know. And I have another 5am start. Any chance my manager can work out some way I can get up later when these summit shows are over?"

"If you're nice to him, he does have a few suggestions on how to stay in bed all day…" Five pairs of male eyes looked at him, and then her, with a mixture of astonishment and trepidation. Had he really said that? How would she react? "Just imagine the hours of enjoyment," he added. "And with all the pictures of you looking down from the bedroom walls."

"You have pictures of Mysty in your bedroom…" Harvey said slowly. "And she knows?"

It was great to see the genuine disbelief on Harvey's face. And Harvey couldn't believe the amusement on hers.

"Yes. I already had some up, but she broke in and installed some more while I was out one Sunday."

"Wow. You broke in?" Harvey looked at Mysty, his face incredulous. "And you don't mind that he has pictures of you up on his bedroom wall?"

"I don't mind the ones *I* put up, but I do mind the ones he chose to display."

"No, she doesn't mind at all," Daryl corrected, taking a sip of another cocktail. "I have some great shots from the day we picked up the new cars. Don't I, sweetheart?" All eyes turned to Mysty, who now glared at Daryl. He was clearly relishing the fact he'd called her sweetheart in front of his friends. But again, how would she react? "I'm still deciding where to put the best ones from that shoot," he said, and gazed back impassively, knowing exactly which ones were being mounted up for him.

"Well, I could definitely do with some new artwork for my office," Harvey said smoothly, and there were some nods of agreement.

"No! Daryl don't you dare say yes!"

"What's it worth?"

"I don't know. Just agree with me for once. You said they were for your private collection only. You can't just give them away to anyone!"

"Do some more in the green Lamborghini and I'll agree."

"You are a horrid man. You always resort to blackmail." She crossed her arms.

"Is that a yes? Or shall I give Harvey the pick of the bunch? Because there are some very revealing photos I think he would love to put up in his office, particularly that one when you

"You made me pose for you then, and now you're engineering to make me pose again? Does it ever stop with you?"

"No. Hadn't you realised already?"

She growled, and a cushion came hurtling across the room at him. He ducked. It missed.

"Is that a no?" he asked.

"It's a don't-tempt-me-to-go-and-say-hello-to-your-new-car!"

Zack couldn't help but start laughing, and Robbie then Harvey joined in.

"Why? You want to dangle your thong on the rear view mirror again?"

"That was my joke if you remember and it never happened," she replied with a firm hard edge to her voice.

"I live in hope," Daryl said, playing the wistful look to the full.

"Mysty, kiddo. It's quarter past eleven. You know it's time to go."

"Thank God. Quick, take me home before my manager thinks up something else he wants to photograph me on."

"Or over. Or in," Daryl smiled, and she snatched his cocktail, finished it for him and returned the empty glass.

"Gentlemen…and rogue," she said, looking pointedly at Daryl. "Lovely to see you, enjoy your night. I'm sorry I have to go, but if I don't the Bentley turns into a pumpkin. I'll tell Moses to get you pass keys to the car lift. Enjoy yourselves, but don't drink my bar dry!" And with a defiant shake of her head she was gone. The cats stood, stretched, went to Daryl to have their heads rubbed, and then followed her.

"I'm not sure what I find more surprising," Harvey said. "You and her, or the fact you're now on 'accepted' terms with two leopards." Daryl smiled; it was all of it part of the same phenomenon of knowing her. "I am still your best man, aren't I?" he added.

"Yes, Harvey, you are." It felt so great to indulge in saying the words. It made them almost believable. "Consider yourselves invited to the wedding. Though I swear, one word goes any further than this room and a trashed car will be the least of your worries."

"Super! Hear that boys? More women for the rest of us!" Harvey said, trying to find a silver lining to the knowledge his pursuit of the golden girl would be best aborted. It was obvious who the winner would be, and seeing them together tonight, despite her glares, had been a very convincing demonstration of that. Around Mysty, Daryl came alive, properly, like he occasionally used to when they were younger. She was the perfect antidote to his seriousness and the weight of concerns that rested on his shoulders. And she clearly wasn't intimated by him or who he was, not for a second.

"What pictures have you got of her in your bedroom?" Harvey then asked, most curious.

"You saw the photos from the underwear shoot…so you can imagine. I'll take them down and replace them with a nude, once I've persuaded her."

"Something tells me you still have quite a lot of persuading to do."

"Just a little."

"Well, I wish you the best of luck, and might I suggest 'Harvey' as a most excellent name for one of your children." Harvey toasted his friend, a subtle message that Daryl understood was his way of saying he would be stepping aside, acknowledging his own prior and far more significant attachment to the lady in question.

"We'll bear it in mind."

That answer told Harvey a hell of a lot. It hadn't been, 'I'll bear it in mind' but we. This would be no marriage of convenience – not that anything about them had been convenient so far – but that his friend really was after something very special. It would be marriage in the truest sense. Despite the pictures and the teasing, which was really a bold form of admiration, it was obvious Daryl respected her, and had already started to accept her opinions as important.

"Maybe not the first or second child, maybe the sixth or seventh," Daryl added.

"You will be busy."

"I know."

Daryl's sudden smile said so much, and Harvey threw back his head and laughed; in fact, each one of his friends was delighted to see the happiness and excitement in Daryl's face.

Daryl was content, strangely. It was all to play for.

'AND NOW FOR our entertainments section of the programme… I'm sure there isn't a New Yorker who isn't aware of the new club in Greenwich Village called The Tiger Butterfly, owned and run by our very own Mystery Queen and golden girl. But even more fantastic than the rave reviews and the mile-long queues to get in, is a rather interesting development as regards her manager and some of his friends… Danny, what can you tell us?

Mysty looked up from her breakfast. What now? She really ought to stop putting the TV on in the morning.

'Well, it would seem that after their trip in Mr Blackmoor's new Lamborghini last Thursday – including a milkshake stop in the emerald-green car, where they weren't missed as the licence plate made it rather obvious with the world famous DB initials imprinted on the front – it arrived at the club's rooftop parking last night, along with two other super cars which belong to Mr Blackmoor's friends, one of whom, Harvey Lincoln, Mysty has spent some time with – apparently even teaching him how to tango. That they all turned up at the club together would imply they were confident of a welcome, and reports state that Mysty was seen to be getting along 'very well' with both of the most eligible gentlemen, as well as the others in the group. Aside from putting on – as she always does – a brilliant show for the people last night, she appeared to find nothing amiss with having such company grace her club, despite it not being somewhere they would usually frequent.'

'And what do you think that means? Has the ice finally been broken perhaps? A non-trashed Lamborghini a good sign of something far more?

'It's a bit too early to say but, given the men in question, I'd say their interest and intentions were quite obvious – not that anyone could blame them. Mysty is a girl any man would wish to call their own, and given who she is it's no surprise she has managed to attract the two 'most eligible' of America – or the world in fact. It would end the speculation that there has always been more behind Mr Blackmoor's motives than just money in getting

her to sign a contract, especially as he doesn't need any.'

'But is this a dalliance or something more serious? Blackmoor and Lincoln are both renowned for their taste in beautiful women – and they don't get more beautiful than Mysty – but are we looking at a possible Mrs Blackmoor or Mrs Lincoln? Or just an affair to keep us all guessing?'

'Judging by what we've seen so far, I would put money on it being a Mrs Blackmoor. We've never seen Mr Blackmoor do more than take a woman out to dinner, let alone tolerate one walking out on him and then taking her out in his new car for a milkshake run; and let's not forget there is a whole host of other ways in which the relationship between this unique pair is wholly different to anything that has gone before. Certainly, there hasn't been anything as serious for years now, since the aborted engagement to Miss Huntley.'

'What odds would you give?'

'3-2.'

'And for a Mrs Lincoln?'

'6-1.'

'Wow. So, looks like things are only going to get more exciting. Whichever it ends up being, I think we're assured of the wedding of the century, one way or the other. So, Terry, back to the headlines…'

"Holy fucking hell," she muttered. So they'd gone to her club for a night out, and to satisfy their curiosity about her and Daryl. And as if Daryl or Harvey would consider marrying her? What was that all about? She was only seventeen!

"Kitten?"

"OG?" She swung around. "You just heard all that?"

"Yes. What a compliment…" he said slowly, watching her, trying to judge her reaction.

"Compliment? To be considered as the 'intended' for two of the world's most committed roués? Like they would really even think of me in that way… Are the news people utterly insane?"

"Why wouldn't they think of you like that?"

"Why? Because of who they are? I'm just their performing poodle, OG, and I'm seventeen. I'm nowhere near where they are, in any way;

plus, I'm not even from their 'circle' or whatever they call it. I'm just a novelty. I can't believe you even need me to answer that question." She got down from her stool and flicked the TV off. "Mrs? Me? Good God. Men!" She strode away, with the leopards in her wake to eat in peace in her bedroom.

Mrs Lincoln? Mrs Blackmoor? What the…?

DARYL FOUND HER sitting on a table, leaning on the wall, eyes closed.

"Kitten?" It felt safe enough to say it now without fearing she would throw it back at him.

She opened her eyes. "Daryl. How was today?"

"Dull, but not half as tiring as it looks like yours has been. Are you alright?" He didn't want to give up the lesson, but he didn't like to see her looking so tired. He'd spent most of the day in a state of anxiety, not sure whether to be excited or nervous about the dance lesson: excited that he was finally going to get the chance to dance, something he'd wanted to do for a long time; nervous because of his inability to dance the tango, or any dance, or because he might not be able to control himself. What he really wanted was to see if she gave something away during the lesson that would give him even the tiniest glimpse of how she felt about him. All the banter with the boys was fine, but empty. He wanted her to be a part of his life, but more than even just a part…a driving force equal to his own. He knew from her relationship with Donny she could be, but… with him?

"I'm fine. I was just having a quick snooze." She sat up and stretched and eased herself to the edge of the table, looking him over. "I assume you don't mind if that shirt gets a little sweaty."

"No. You can even rip it off if you like."

"Hmmm. Something tells me I won't need to."

"Why did you rip Harvey's shirt off?"

"Because he wasn't…letting his emotions work for him. He wasn't getting into the mood of it sufficiently, despite having the talent to learn the technical details really well."

"I see. I know you can be a harsh task master, given my experience with the pizza slice."

She laughed. "I am. I do what I have to in order to get results. As a man who frequently resorts to blackmail to get results, I don't think you're in a position to argue."

"I am your willing victim – only don't tell Harvey if I'm appalling bad, he'll never let me forget it."

"I don't think you could be appalling bad. At anything. Least of all the tango. Not if you actually let yourself…let your body speak for you. Put that clever mind somewhere else, like back in your pristine office. You won't need it for the next two hours."

"Kiddo?" OG appeared. "Here you go. Food."

"I told you I'd be okay."

"You haven't had anything since eleven this morning, except water and gels, and I'm not happy seeing your ribs beneath your clothes. Eat the sandwich or I veto the lesson. Your choice."

She had to admit it smelt delicious. "What's in it?"

"Your favourite. Pesto, mozzarella, roast chicken and salsa. Hot."

"Oh alright, you swayed me. Thank you." She reached over and gave her long-suffering bodyguard a hug, and took the plate.

"You make sure she eats that," OG said to Daryl, with a stern look, and left them again.

"You do need to eat," Daryl said.

"I dance better on an empty stomach."

"It's a rehearsal day."

"I know, just…I like things perfect."

"All set for tomorrow?"

She grimaced, clearly not looking forward to the twelve-hour marathon.

"Yes. Everything is fine. I just need an early night and then I'll be all set."

"Then I'll have to save taking you out for dinner to another night…" he said casually, but feeling apprehensive about her answer. He turned and leaned on the table next to her, so she couldn't see his face, his emotions.

"Will this dinner be an improvement on the last one?"

"Absolutely. No caviar. No duck. And no dickhead billionaire."

"Then I'm in."

"Excellent."

"I might even wear a dress."

"I'll have to take you now you've said that."

"Hold this for second." She passed him the rest of the sandwich and hopped off the table and, before he could blink, she'd pulled off her leggings and was rummaging through her bag. Standing there in just her black knickers and short t-shirt she was a sight to behold, and as hard as he tried he couldn't tear his eyes away from her. "What?" she asked. "It's not as if you haven't seen it all before, Daryl, lots of times. Every morning and night, in fact, on your walls." She tied a black wraparound skirt over her hips and pulled a pair of black heels on.

"I've been in my pristine office all day…I'm still adjusting to being around you."

"Ah yes, semi-nakedness and spontaneity…welcome to my world." She nodded at the remainder of the sandwich. "You want to try some?"

"No, you need to eat it."

"You don't know what you're turning down." She sat back on the table to finish it, stretching a piece of mozzarella and licking her fingers.

"That's what I think every time you turn me down."

"Oh dear, you rank down the list from a chicken sandwich, how does that make you feel?" she teased, and before he could reply said, "Now, you've listened to the music I sent you, to give you an idea of what we'll be working with?"

"Yes."

"Good. Okay. Now, first I want you to leave all your ballroom, foxtrot, waltzing stuff somewhere over there. It's all very nice but it won't help you learn the tango." She walked into the middle of the room, gesturing for him to follow. "Remove the jacket. Roll your sleeves up."

He obeyed, silently, and then went to stand opposite her. He could barely concentrate. This was a dream he'd had for so long, and the moment was finally here.

"Alright. So. Starting at the very beginning. As you know, the tango is typified by the passion in the music and that is reflected in the dancing. They are one. People write music to dance to; people dance to music to express themselves, like two halves of the same coin…like you and your handheld."

He smiled, nervously. She started walking around him, and all his senses came alive, not helped by visualising the black knickers under her skirt.

"Now, we both know you're a passionate man; that's why you need five women to wear you out. This is the same emotion you can employ in your dancing, so I won't accept any half-hearted attempts when I know what you're capable of. Now, listen to this music for me." She used the remote control and fifteen seconds of a brilliant piece of music filled the room. It was so stirring it felt wrong not to move. "Tell me, what you hear in that music?" She looked at him straight in the eye. "This isn't a trick question; I just want you to say the first words that come into your head, so you can start engaging with your feelings, because you are allowed to feel things – even you, Mr Important and Sensible."

She was an astute teacher, and he rather worried there would be no rock to hide behind. But did he want to hide?

"Passion, obviously…' he began. "And…frustration. Anger. Aggression. Lust. And beauty." Beauty? Why had he said that? Was he looking at her face too much? Shit. He mustn't panic. "The music is beautiful," he added. "Despite the strong emotions it is a…a wild harmony."

"I like that. Not many people realise that so soon."

"Not many people have watched you dance as much as I have."

For a moment neither spoke, and she watched his face. "Then I'll have to raise my expectations of your performance," she said, and he saw the blush behind the statement.

"What I'm going to do, is go through a range of steps with you," she continued, the blush lingering, "all of which can be expanded upon, linked together and used in any combination to fit the music. There are more, obviously, but there's no point making this overly complicated to start with."

She came to stand alongside him, wondering how the hell she was keeping her cool. Was she really going to teach this man how to tango? It seemed intimate already, with his jacket and tie off, every bit as handsome as he always was, and they hadn't even touched each other yet. Concentrate!

"The first steps are fairly simple, and gentle, so they'll serve as a warmup. Try and relax your muscles…tense muscles aren't good. Keep your muscles engaged, but relaxed. Do you understand?" He nodded, watching her, just three feet away, for the first time his instructor not the instructed.

Mysty swallowed her nervousness, trying to ignore the fact that very soon she would need to touch him, and he her. She couldn't afford to let him know she wanted to…

He followed her guidance, echoing her steps, all the graceful power she knew he was capable of in evidence.

"Right, this last one is a move that can be adapted and used however you need. You can use it to chance direction, pause, all sorts. You will have seen me do it hundreds of times when I'm dancing, but you won't have known what it was for. You have to get me from here, to here…" – she moved away, turned through one rotation with two steps, and stood in front of him with her back to his chest; it was not close enough to touch, but she could have sworn she could feel the heat of him in the air – or was that her nerves? – "using only one hand in mine." She didn't know any more. Her usually reliable senses were letting her down, running amok, not coming back to heel. "Don't worry if you need a few practices to get it right. Most people need to try this a few times."

"Did Harvey?" he asked quietly, sensing some tension beneath her professional, patient exterior.

"Yes. That's why I ripped his shirt and slapped him. He wasn't… tapping into the right emotions to get it right."

Aha. One mystery solved.

She stood waiting, in the original pose, and he enjoyed the moment, every inch of her just there. He looked at her long enough to start his pulse creeping higher, images running through his mind, even from last night as she had been moved swiftly and decisively in her male dancer's arms. Finally, it was into his she would now go, not as his wounded saviour, or as a girl ill or injured and unable to stand, but as a woman, strong, beautiful and irresistible. She didn't break the silence; but she did raise one eyebrow, as if to question the time he was taking. He resisted the urge to smile, and reached out a hand and pulled.

Mysty knew it was her legs that got her there, not her brain. Her heart was beating far too fast, and her body was suddenly aware she was pressed right up against his chest and hips, one hand against her hip, across her body, holding her there. She could smell him, that distinctive aftershave, or whatever he used, and now she really could feel the heat from him, her skin reacting invisibly to the contact. His breath tickled over her temple as he lowered his head a fraction, lips next to her ear. How strong was that arm that held her?

"How was that?" he asked.

Oh God. Why hadn't she moved away yet? Why had she just stood there for a full five seconds, as if she didn't want to move?

"Really good."

She stepped away, so he had to let her go, and walked over to the music system, wishing she had a fan to cool the guilty heat that seeped from her body. Please don't let him see…

"Should we do it again?"

"No, spot on. That was really good."

"You're sure you don't want to rip my shirt?"

He sounded disappointed, and she forced herself to focus on setting up the music…but she couldn't even recollect the name of the piece she wanted just that second; it was like she'd forgotten the alphabet.

"I know you don't like me ruining your clothes, and it's a nice shirt."

"I'm happy to sacrifice it."

She made herself think about that night she'd seen him on his yacht. That was what he did best…using his faultless body to charm women into bed as willing victims to his passion. She was not going to fall for it and, anyway, he should know better given her complete inexperience.

"Maybe I will, later, depending on how you do. Now…" She found the music she wanted, and after a deep breath she turned around…to find him much closer than she'd expected, eyes intense, watching her. What had she been going to say? She walked back to the centre of the room and waited for him to follow.

She got the feeling this was not going to be like dancing with Harvey. There she had been well in control. Now, she felt…well, far from it. When he joined her, she chose to walk around him, escaping the intense green eyes for a few extra seconds.

"As the male lead," she began, "it is always up to you to direct the dance. Hands, eyes, body, simple pressure from fingers will be enough to intimate to your partner – if she's good enough – what you want her to do. It is communication that uses everything except words. That is why it is so hard having a male dancer who has no confidence. If he fails, the dance fails, as the woman can only respond to what she is given. Does that make sense?"

"Perfectly."

"So, initially, while we try something to music, I will say the steps in advance, but you still have to use enough guidance to make the dance happen. It will be a set piece that I know fits the music. Any questions?"

"No."

"Any problems?"

"No."

Damn it. Ask me to stop. Go and check your handheld. Discover an urgent meeting you need to go to.

"So, three things. First, arms. I know you like having your hands in your pockets or scrolling on your handhelds, but right now we want them away from your sides. Second, as I said before, stay engaged but relaxed; it's fluid, it flows; you are an extension of the music now." As she spoke, she had managed to go all the way around him with a minimal number of perfectly balanced steps, demonstrating her point. "Third. No dancer should forget a part of their body or let it drop when it's not being used. Poise is now your favourite word. No hand or arm falls, and the head stays up." Daryl smiled, absorbing every beautiful word. "And don't smile; you're going to hate me in half an hour!"

"I don't think so."

"We'll see."

Please hate me. Get frustrated and walk out.

She started the music and guided his hands to their starting points, the heat of his skin against hers. She was insane to have agreed to this. She could see the hunger in his eyes, just as she had with Harvey, but this was way more powerful and…possessive. Enough to distract. Enough to convince a weak female mind that it was real.

"No." She pulled away after thirty seconds and glared at him, but was only annoyed with herself for the effect he was having on her. "You have to dance like a lover not a toy soldier. Don't pretend you don't know what I'm talking about. Flick your hips with the beat of the music, otherwise it'll be twice as hard for you and look half as good. Stop being Mr Blackmoor. Your name doesn't matter here, or who you are or your money. Just you. Let your body speak for you."

Daryl found it hard not to grin at her seriousness. It would be twice as hard soon, anyway, regardless of his hips. Did she know she was playing with fire? That his body was demanding to pull her closer?

"And how do you know how to dance like a lover?" he asked with a flash of the green eyes.

"Intuition," she snapped. "I guess I'm a natural."

He had no arguments there.

He lost count of the number of times she pulled him up to make him repeat a move, push his arm up, push his shoulders back, or adjust another part of him, making him aware of just how much of his body she was paying attention to, and just how complex the dancing was that she made look effortless.

Eventually satisfied, she started the music from the top, and he had to admit he was surprised at how easily he picked up the sequences. His heart was pounding. He could feel the thrill of knowing he could dance this one dance, just a little, and that it was just the two of them in the room. Beyond that, he simply didn't care. This was it. This was what it felt like!

Her eyes rose up and met his, challenging him, inviting him to surprise her by showing her what he had learned. The music began again, and he reached out and pulled her against him, feeling her muscles tense beneath the skin, her curls against his chest where he'd undone the top buttons. He fought the urge to pick her up and take her over to the table at the side of the room, or pull her down to the floor and finish what his mind had already started…start something in her that he wanted to finish with the attention to detail that she was giving to their dance.

It was heady, glorious movement without words, and she responded to his hands – even though he knew she knew the dance backwards – and didn't move without his direction, making him work every second of the way. But the reward was worth it. Knowing he had that claim on her, that connection. He pulled her round one last time and, without thinking, he turned her an extra turn to land her against his chest, one hand on her back supporting the arch of hers, another guiding her leg over his hips. He looked at her, her beautiful face inches from his, her gorgeous lips just there, and the eyes he could drown in. He could feel the heat of her, and the beat of her heart, fast, like his own.

She didn't move. Didn't struggle. Was this the sign he had been looking for? Could she feel this? He smoothed a hand from her thigh to her backside, under the skirt, and held it there. She still didn't move, and he could hear her fast, soft breaths. Desire broke his control and he leaned in, an inch at a time.

How long had he waited to kiss her? And not the kiss they'd had so long ago, at the Bowl, when it had all been so wrong. He'd wanted it to be right. Was this the right time? It had to be? How would it feel? Never in his life had he wanted to kiss someone so badly; he who never kissed any of his women.

She still hadn't moved, hadn't fought him. So he moved the final inch, and his lips were on hers. Her lips parted for him with gentle but persistent coaxing, and his tongue slipped in to taste her – oh God, the taste of her – his hands tightened in reflex around her, and then it hit him: she wasn't kissing him back.

He pulled away.

He looked at her, desperate to know why.

He slowly released his hold on, eased her upright.

Alarm bells rang; he needed to leave. He let go of her, like she'd burned him. And walked away, rolling down his sleeves and buttoning the cuffs in double-quick time. Self-recrimination flooded through him, and self-doubt. He had been so sure. Why did he always get it wrong with her? He reached for his tie and jacket.

"Daryl. Daryl, don't go."

He hesitated, his jacket in his hand.

"Daryl, it was just a kiss…it happens…when you're dancing like this. I'm not angry."

It wasn't just a kiss to me.

He couldn't bear to turn and look at her, or tell her she was so, so wrong. He'd never felt this way with anyone – the emotion, the longing to be held, the need for tenderness, for intimacy… It hadn't just been a kiss for him.

The silence lasted long painful seconds and then he left, slamming the door behind him.

A moment later Mac was by his side, almost at a jog to keep up with his boss's furious strides.

"Sir?"

"Get the cars."

Mac gave the orders to the drivers, then, "Sir, what's wrong? Something happen in there?"

Goddammit! "Just for once, Mac, do you think you could just do your fucking job and quit with the fucking questions?" He threw himself into the shimmering Bentley sat waiting on the New York street he knew well. A street that he now despised. In a world he despised. "Ride up front."

OG appeared in the doorway, met Mac's look and frowned. Mac shrugged and tapped his earpiece and got into the front: I'll be in contact.

They'd find out one way or the other.

OG went back into the studio. She was on the table again, leaning back, looking sad and confused.

"What happened to make him leave like that?" he asked quietly.

"It was the end of the dance and he…he kissed me. But then he was furious and walked out. I tried telling him it sometimes happens when you're dancing, especially in dances like the tango; and I told him it was just a kiss and I wasn't angry. But he was so angry. Why is he always so angry? It was just a kiss, for God's sake. It was nothing." But then hadn't she wanted him to leave? Willed it almost?

'It was just a kiss…' She knew that wasn't true. But what was she supposed to do with the turmoil of emotions and sensations…his hand stroking her thigh, hold her backside like that, the heat of him, the feel of him…and feel of his kiss, his lips. Oh God…

He stared at her. "You told him it was just a kiss?"

"OG, dancing the tango, it affects guys like that. It's nothing."

Really it was nothing. At all. Please don't let OG see that I'm lying to him. And myself.

OG was finding it hard to shape the words he needed to say to her. Could she really not see just how much her manager wanted far more than a business contract with her?

"Kitten…" Oh God, how can I say this without making her go nuts? "He…can you not see that Daryl has spent the last two years or more trying to tell you, and show you how he feels about… And you told him it was…just a kiss?"

She jumped off the table. "OG, what the fuck are you saying? This is Daryl we're talking about! Daryl who has whole harems of women, who doesn't feel anything? How can I – me, this nobody, this *kid* who insults him and trashes his cars – possibly be so significant to him that one kiss after a dance makes him behave like this?"

"You think anyone else in this world would have got away with that stuff if you didn't mean something to him? You think he flew across America to bust up a guy's face because he thought you'd slept with him for *nothing*?" OG threw back, angry and frustrated that it had all gone so wrong when it had been going so right.

"OG, he only wants me in his bed. He's possessive and jealous, just like most men on the frigging planet! Hasn't he got enough women to choose from?"

Her angry return met silence as OG's face closed up and he reined in his frustration.

"Get your things," he said, "I'm taking you home. Now."

She looked at him. She'd never seen him look so furious. Great. Someone else who was angry with her. Why had Daryl just left? Why couldn't he have stayed and at least talked about… But talked about what? She knew she'd not kissed him back, and she also knew that he knew. But she'd been too stunned that he'd dared to kiss her…and too shocked by her growing urge to wrap herself up in him, around him, and have him hold her. Like a deer staring at a lion, she hadn't been able to move. She'd felt weak, completely captive.

Her irate bodyguard slammed the car door – the first time he'd ever done that – and glared at her.

Oh God, what did it all mean? What did OG mean 'trying to show her and tell her'. Tell her what and show her what? She thought back to them playing around in the pool – and then him leaving. And when he'd stopped her from throwing herself off the top of his penthouse – and then closing up on her again. And them eating pizza and watching the game; and the times they'd really seemed to be talking and…connecting. Oh God, no…and slowly the pieces started to take shape.

"I'll go and speak to him," she said slowly. "I think what I said… well, it came across all wrong."

OG gave her a long stare and his face finally softened. "Alright. Get yourself ready and we'll take you."

"No, I want to ride. And don't say no because I've not been out on one of the bikes for weeks."

She didn't give him a chance to argue. She needed to get in a room with this enigma of a man who she had once hated and now really did not. She needed answers, but how was she going to get him to talk and, more importantly, be absolutely and completely honest about what he had been feeling these last few years?

She pulled her kit on and fired up the Fireblade.

It was time to find out.